T0386115

APOLLONIUS RHODIUS

LCL 1

APOLLONIUS RHODIUS

ARGONAUTICA

EDITED AND TRANSLATED BY

WILLIAM H. RACE

HARVARD UNIVERSITY PRESS

CAMBRIDGE, MASSACHUSETTS
LONDON, ENGLAND
2008

First published 2008

LOEB CLASSICAL LIBRARY® is a registered trademark
of the President and Fellows of Harvard College

ISBN 978-0-674-99630-4

*Composed in ZephGreek and ZephText by
Technologies 'N Typography, Merrimac, Massachusetts.
Printed on acid-free paper and bound by
The Maple-Vail Book Manufacturing Group*

CONTENTS

PREFACE

It is a particular pleasure to offer a text and translation of Apollonius' *Argonautica* at a time of great interest in Hellenistic poetry and culture. The present work is indebted to a line of textual scholars that includes Wellauer, Merkel, Seaton, and, most notably, Vian, whose magisterial Budé edition has set the highest standard in Apollonian scholarship. I have benefited from the immense learning in the commentaries of Mooney, Gillies, Ardizonni, Fränkel, Livrea, Hunter, Campbell, and Cuypers, and from the recent concordance by Papathomopoulos and the lexicon by Pompella.

The text offered here is a fairly conservative one, which does not differ substantially from Vian's edition. I have attempted to produce a text that reflects the main tradition, and where the consensus of MSS makes sense, I have tended to favor that reading. In the sparse apparatus criticus, I have included variants of importance to the sense or ones which have been adopted in other editions. When a variant reading seems especially important, I have glossed it with an alternate translation in italics.

The translation aims at clarity and attempts to follow the word order of the Greek as faithfully as proper English will allow. Although smoother English might often have resulted, I have resisted changing active verbs to passive,

PREFACE

condensing redundant expressions, and rearranging syn-
tactical elements. My goal is always to let the translation
show how I am construing the Greek. But in the interest of
simplicity, I have translated as "Jason" the appellations
"Aesonides" and "son of Aeson," unless the patronymic has
particular importance in its context.

Finally, in gratitude for help closer to home, I wish to
thank graduate students Amanda Mathis, John Henkel,
and Derek Smith, and most especially Professor Andrew
Miller, who improved the translation in more ways than I
can count.

INTRODUCTION

What little information we have about Apollonius Rhodius comes principally from four sources:[1] P. Oxy. 1241 (2nd c.), containing a list of librarians at the Ptolemaic library in Alexandria; two brief lives preserved in the MSS; and a brief entry in the *Suda*. From these scanty and often contradictory reports, we can surmise with some probability that he was originally from Alexandria, that he spent some time in Rhodes, that he was a pupil of Callimachus, and that he was head librarian at the royal library. If the papyrus correctly places his librarianship before that of Eratosthenes, whose appointment began with the reign of Ptolemy III in 247/6, then a likely period of Apollonius' tenure would be c. 270–245 BCE. We have no firm evidence for his date of birth or death.

Anecdotes and Speculation

The explanation for his epithet of "Rhodian" is the subject of anecdotes related by the two lives: when he was young,

---

[1] For a succinct and sensible discussion of Apollonius' life and works upon which I draw, see R. L. Hunter, *Apollonius of Rhodes, Argonautica, Book III* (Cambridge 1989) 1–2.

he recited his *Argonautica*, which was so severely criticized by the public and other poets that he retired in disgrace to Rhodes, where he taught successfully, revised his poem, won critical acclaim, and was honored with the head librarianship at Alexandria. Because in six places the scholia to Book 1 cite lines from a previous edition (προέκδοσις) of the *Argonautica*, many scholars have assumed that these lines represent the failed early version of the poem, but it is also possible that the story of the unsuccessful first version actually arose to explain the circulation of an alternate text.[2]

All four sources state that Apollonius was a student of Callimachus, and one even reports that he was buried beside his teacher. And yet, modern scholars have posited a bitter quarrel between the two. The evidence for this begins with an epigram (A.P. 11.275) lampooning Callimachus, which is ascribed to "Apollonius the Grammarian": "Callimachus: that piece of rubbish, that joke, that blockhead. The cause of this is the author of *The Causes,* Callimachus." In addition, the entry on Callimachus in the *Suda* mentions that Callimachus wrote a poem called *Ibis* that attacked an enemy, who is identified in a parenthesis as Apollonius. With such tenuous leads, scholars have read passages in Callimachus (*Hymn to Apollo* 105–113 and "Prologue" to the *Aetia*) and Apollonius (*Arg.* 3.927–937) as veiled attacks on each other, from which has arisen, in Hunter's words, "a romantic vision of scholarly warfare in which Apollonius was finally driven out of Alexandria by a triumphant Callimachus."[3] But, arguments

---

[2] M. R. Lefkowitz, *The Lives of the Greek Poets* 2nd. ed. (Baltimore 2012) 121–122.

over the historicity of the quarrel aside, the overwhelming trend of recent scholarship has been to emphasize the close relationship between Callimachus and Apollonius in terms of their shared stylistic, poetic, and aesthetic concerns.

Fragmentary Works

Besides the *Argonautica*, Apollonius is credited with writing scholarly prose works on editing Homer ("Against Zenodotus"), on Archilochus, and on problems in Hesiod. His poetic works, besides one tenuously attributed epigram (A.P. 11.275), included *Canobus*, a choliambic poem on Egyptian legends named after Menelaus' helmsman (*frr.* 1–3), and foundation-poems (κτίσεις) on Alexandria (*fr.* 4), Caunus (*fr.* 5), Cnidus (*fr.* 6), Naucratis (*frr.* 7–9), Rhodes (*frr.* 10–11), and Lesbos (*fr.* 12). Of these a mere 33 lines remain. This interest in archaic poetry (especially epic) and the founding of cities is evident as well in the *Argonautica*.

The Argonautica

Three Greek epic poems survive from before the Roman imperial era: Homer's *Iliad* and *Odyssey*, and Apollonius'

---

3 Hunter (above, note 1) 6. The modern scholarly quarrel over the ancient literary one continues in A. Cameron, *Callimachus and His Critics* (Princeton 1995) 214–228, P. Green, *The Argonautika* (Berkeley 1997) 1–3, and M. R. Lefkowitz, "Myth and History in the Biography of Apollonius," in T. D. Papanghelis and A. Rengakos, edd., *A Companion to Apollonius Rhodius* (Leiden 2001) 51–71.

INTRODUCTION

Argonautica. The merit and influence of the first two have never been in question; the third has had a varied reception. In the first century CE, 'Longinus' (33.4) concedes that Apollonius is a careful poet, but far beneath Homer: "Apollonius, for instance, is an impeccable (ἄπτωτος) poet in the *Argonautica* . . . Yet would you not rather be Homer than Apollonius?" In the past two centuries the *Argonautica* was regularly regarded as an inferior, artificial work, typical of the decadent Hellenistic period, characterized by the work of pedantic, bookish ("learned") poets. Indeed, the previous Loeb editor concluded, "He seems to have written the *Argonautica* out of bravado, to show that he *could* write an epic poem."[4] But in the past four decades there has been a renewed interest in Hellenistic poetry and a reevaluation of its merits *on its own terms*, not as a failed attempt to mimic classical poetry. Recent scholars tend to regard the *Argonautica* as a fascinating interface between the past literary tradition and the culture and aesthetic preoccupations of both the Ptolemaic court and the larger Greek world in the third century BCE.

In the wake of Alexander's conquests (334–323 BCE), the Greek-speaking world was confronted with a new political, intellectual, and social situation. The individual poleis, which had previously been the center of social, political, and military concerns from archaic through classical times (c. 750–330 BCE), were swallowed up by large and diverse empires. The center of literary gravity shifted from Athens and mainland Greece to the new, cosmopolitan city of Alexandria in Egypt, center of the Ptolemaic

4 R. C. Seaton, *Apollonius Rhodius: The Argonautica* (Cambridge MA 1912) xi.

kingdom. This fundamental change in location and out-
look engendered a new relationship with the Hellenic lit-
erary past: it became something to be collected, preserved,
and studied. The establishment of the Museum (Shrine of
the Muses) in Alexandria by Ptolemy I was a concrete em-
bodiment of this new attitude toward the past. Faced with
a staggering amount of great literature from the previous
four centuries that included Homer, Archilochus, Pindar,
Aeschylus, Sophocles, and Euripides, the Hellenistic po-
ets found themselves awash with material providing forms,
genres, topics, and issues for treatment. The challenge was
to "make it new."

In the *Argonautica* we see Homer's influence on every
level: indeed, the poem is in many ways "Homer" recrea-
ted for a Hellenistic audience. But at the same time it dif-
fers considerably from the Homeric texts in style, narrative
procedures, and plot construction. We also see Pindar's in-
fluence, not only because his *Pythian* 4 treated Jason's
quest for the fleece, but also in stylistic traits and in the
construction of episodic vignettes, as well as in linking the
myth to the Greek audience of North Africa. Euripides' in-
fluence is especially important, not only because of his fa-
mous *Medea*, but more generally because he helped to
fashion a bridge between the Classical and the Hellenistic
periods. His experimentation with new perspectives of tra-
ditional myths, his emphasis on rhetoric, his interest in de-
picting the psychological state of his characters, and his
transformation of heroic figures into ordinary humans all
appealed to the Hellenistic poets and to Apollonius in par-
ticular.

The *Argonautica* is a compendium of literary forms and
themes. On one level it is a travelogue or *periplous*: the

INTRODUCTION

first two books cover the voyage from Iolcus to Colchis, the
last two the long detour home. It reflects the centuries-old
Greek exploration of the ancient world and the recording
of its geography and ethnography. On the divine level, it
explores new psychological dimensions of individual gods
and local divinities. On the cultural level, it depicts the
spread of Greek civilization and the taming of hostile forces
and people. On the individual level, it treats the matura-
tion of Jason and Medea. In brief, it is a complex cultural
artifact, and its influence on Roman poetry was enormous.
It was translated by Varro of Atax (1st c. BCE) and imitated
by Valerius Flaccus (1st c. CE). It influenced Catullus and
Ovid, and most of all Vergil, whose indebtedness to
Apollonius in his *Aeneid* is immense.[5] The *Argonautica*
provided Vergil with a model of an epic that combined as-
pects of archaic epic, tragedy (Dido), lyric poetry, history
(especially city-founding and ethnography), and religion.

[5] See D. Nelis, *Vergil's Aeneid and the Argonautica of Apollo-
nius Rhodius* (Leeds 2001).

PLOT OUTLINE

PLOT OUTLINE

Book 3

Book 4

BIBLIOGRAPHY

PRINCIPAL EDITIONS

Editio princeps, J. Lascaris, Florence 1496
Editio Aldina, F. Asulanus, Venice 1521
J. Hölzlin, Leiden 1641
R. F. Brunck, Strasbourg 1780
A. Wellauer, Leipzig 1828
R. Merkel, Leipzig 1854
R. C. Seaton, Oxford 1900
H. Fränkel, Oxford 1961
F. Vian, Paris 1974–1981
G. Pompella, Hildesheim 2006

COMMENTARIES

G. W. Mooney, London and Dublin 1912
M. M. Gillies, Book 3, Cambridge 1928
A. Ardizzoni, Book 3, Bari 1958; Book 1, Rome 1967
H. Fränkel, *Noten zu den Argonautika des Apollonios*,
    Munich 1968
E. Livrea, Book 4, Florence 1973
R. L. Hunter, Book 3, Cambridge 1989
M. Campbell, Book 3.1–471 Leiden 1994
M. Cuypers, Book 2.1–310 Leiden 1997
R. Matteo, Book 2, Lecce 2007

BIBLIOGRAPHY

SCHOLIA AND RESOURCES

J. U. Powell, *Collectanea Alexandrina*, Oxford 1925

C. Wendel, ed. *Scholia in Apollonium Rhodium Vetera*, Berlin 1935

M. Campbell, *Index verborum in Apollonium Rhodium*, Hildesheim 1983

G. Lachenaud, *Scholies à Apollonios de Rhodes,* Paris 2010

M. Papathomopoulos, *Apollonii Rhodii Argonauticorum Concordantia*, Hildesheim 1996

G. Pompella, *Apollonii Rhodii Lexicon*, Hildesheim 2002

F. Reich and H. Maehler, *Lexicon in Apollonii Rhodii Argonautica*, Amsterdam 1991–

MANUSCRIPTS

Families of Manuscripts

m	prototype of LA*k*
w	prototype of SG
k	prototype of E
d	consensus of Byzantine manuscripts CDMQR

Principal Extant Manuscripts

L	Laurentianus gr. 32, 9 (960–980)
A	Ambrosianus gr. 120 (beginning of 15th c.)
S	Laurentianus gr. 32, 16 (1280)
G	Guelferbytanus Aug. 4° 10.2 (14th c.)
E	Scorialensis gr. S III 3 (c. 1480)
L^1	revision in L by the original hand
L^2, L^3, L^4	revisions in L by later hands

BIBLIOGRAPHY

Abbreviations

Ω	consensus of most manuscripts
Σ	scholium
Σ^{Ω}	a scholium in most manuscripts
Σ^{LA}	a scholium in L and A
Σ^{Llem}	the lemma of a scholiast in L
L^{2sl}	reading by L^2 *supra lineam*
L^{ac}	reading in L *ante correctionem*
L^{pc}	reading in L *post correctionem*
L^{mg}	reading in L *in margine*
$L^{2\gamma\rho}$	variant reading by L^2
Et. Magn.	*Etymologicum Magnum*
Et. Gen.	*Etymologicum Genuinum*
Flor.	*editio princeps*

Papyri (Cited in This Edition)

Π^1	P. Oxy. 34.2700 (3rd c.)
Π^2	P. Colon. inv. 929 (2nd c.)
Π^3	P.S.I. 15.1478 (1st c. BCE–1st c. CE)
Π^7	P. Mil. 6 et P. Colon. inv. 522 (early 1st c.)
Π^8	P. Amherst 16 (2nd–3rd c.)
Π^9	P. Oxy. 34.2698 (late 2nd c.)
Π^{10}	P. Oxy. 34.2696 (late 2nd c.)
Π^{14}	P. Oxy. 34.2697 (early 3nd c.)
Π^{16}	P. Oxy. 34.2694 (2nd c.)
Π^{18}	P. Berol. 13413 (1st–2nd c.)
Π^{19}	P. Oxy. 34.2699 (2nd c.)
Π^{20}	P. Argentorat. 173 perg. cod. (8th–9th c.)
Π^{21}	P. Oxy. 6.874 (2nd–3rd c.)

BIBLIOGRAPHY

Π[24]	P. Oxy. 34.2693 (early 2nd c.)
Π[25]	P. Oxy. 10.1243 (2nd c.)
Π[29]	P. Oxy. 4.692 (2nd c.)
Π[30]	P. Oxy. 34.2691 (late 1st c. BCE)

For the fragments, I have relied on J. U. Powell, *Collectanea Alexandrina*, Oxford 1925.

The Voyage of the Argo

OCEAN

(Rhine)

RHIPAEAN MTS.

CELTS
Hercynian Peak
Celtic Lakes

SCYTHIA

PLAIN OF
LAURIUM?

(Rhone)

CELTS

Electris?
Eridanus

Ister

SINDI

GRAUCENII

LIGURIANS

Brygean
Islands

Cauliacus

Ister

Stoechades

Aethalia

AUSONIA

Angurum

SEA OF
SARDINIA

Acaea

AUSONIAN
Anthemoessa
SEA

Drepane

THRACE

Iolcus

Thrinacia

LIBYAN SEA

Calliste
(Thera)

Anaphe
Crete

SYRTIS

L. Triton

LIBYA

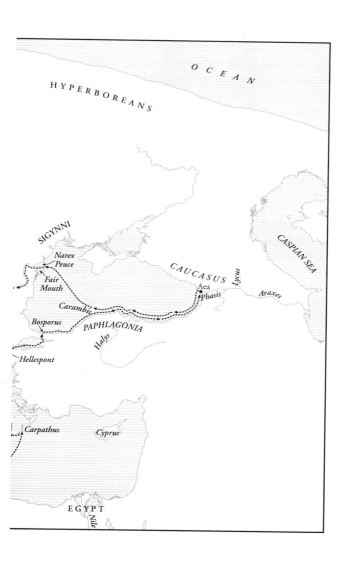

The Mustering, Departure, and Return

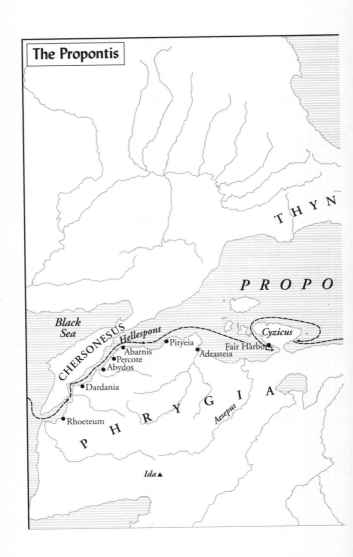

The Propontis

THYN

PROPO

Black
Sea

CHERSONESUS

Hellespont

Abarnis
• Pityeia
• Percote
• Abydos
Adrasteia

Cyzicus

Fair Harbor

• Dardania

PHRYGIA

• Rhoeteum

Aesepus

Ida ▲

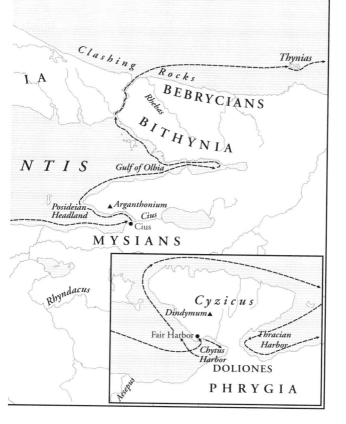

BLACK SEA

Clashing Rocks

Thynias

I A

BEBRYCIANS

Rhebas

BITHYNIA

N T I S

Gulf of Olbia

Posideïan Headland

▲ *Arganthonium*

Cius

• Cius

MYSIANS

Rhyndacus

Cyzicus

Dindymum ▲

Fair Harbor •

Chytus Harbor

Thracian Harbor

DOLIONES

PHRYGIA

Aesepus

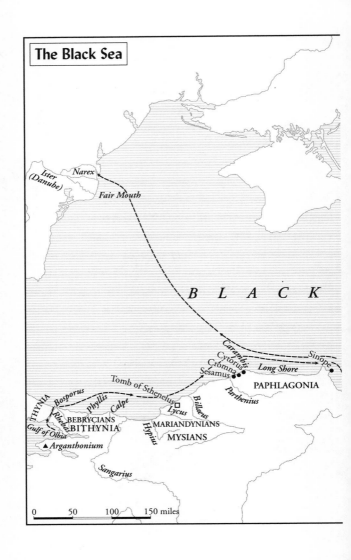

The Black Sea

Ister
(Danube)
Narex
Fair Mouth

BLACK

Carambis
Cytorus
Cromna
Sesamus
Long Shore
Sinope

PAPHLAGONIA

Tomb of Sthenelus

Parthenius

Bosporus
Phyllis
Calpe
Lycus
Billaeus

THYNIA
Rhebas
Gulf of Olbia
BEBRYCIANS
BITHYNIA
Hypius
MARIANDYNIANS
MYSIANS

▲ Arganthonium

Sangarius

0   50   100   150 miles

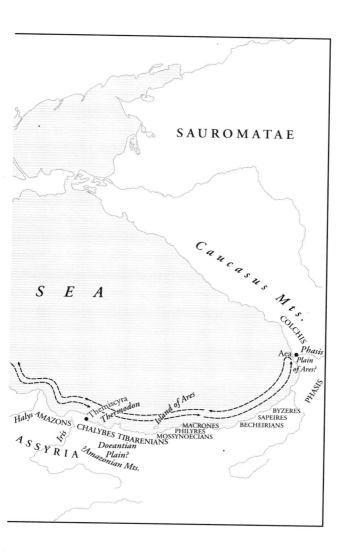

SAUROMATAE

C a u c a s u s   M t s.

COLCHIS

S E A

Aea
Phasis
Plain
of Ares?

PHASIS

Halys AMAZONS
Iris
CHALYBES TIBARENIANS
Themiscyra
Thermodon
Island of Ares
MACRONES
PHILYRES
MOSSYNOECIANS
BYZERES
SAPEIRES
BECHEIRIANS
A S S Y R I A
Doeantian
Plain?
?Amazonian Mts.

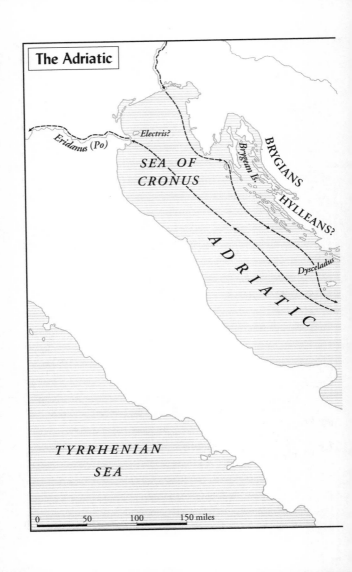

The Adriatic

Eridanus (Po)

Electris?

SEA OF
CRONUS

Brygean Is.

BRYGIANS

HYLLEANS?

Dysceladus

A D R I A T I C

TYRRHENIAN
SEA

| 0 | 50 | 100 | 150 miles |

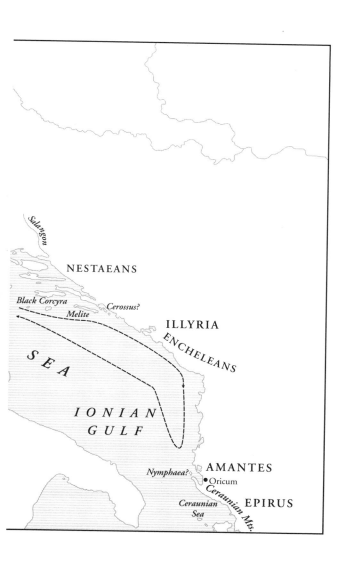

Salargon

NESTAEANS

Black Corcyra   Cerossus?
        Melite

ILLYRIA

ENCHELEANS

S E A

I O N I A N
G U L F

AMANTES

Nymphaea?   ●Oricum

Ceraunian
Sea

Ceraunian Mts.

EPIRUS

Aeolus and Helius

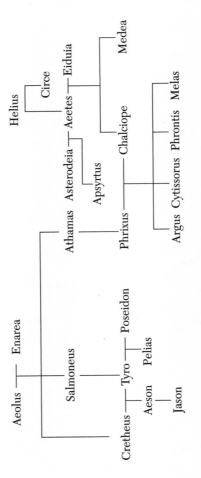

APOLLONIUS RHODIUS

BOOK 1

Ἀρχόμενος σέο, Φοῖβε, παλαιγενέων κλέα φωτῶν
μνήσομαι, οἳ Πόντοιο κατὰ στόμα καὶ διὰ πέτρας
Κυανέας βασιλῆος ἐφημοσύνῃ Πελίαο
χρύσειον μετὰ κῶας ἐύζυγον ἤλασαν Ἀργώ.
5   τοίην γὰρ Πελίης φάτιν ἔκλυεν, ὥς μιν ὀπίσσω
μοῖρα μένει στυγερή, τοῦδ᾽ ἀνέρος, ὅν τιν᾽ ἴδοιτο
δημόθεν οἰοπέδιλον, ὑπ᾽ ἐννεσίῃσι δαμῆναι.
δηρὸν δ᾽ οὐ μετέπειτα τεὴν κατὰ βάξιν Ἰήσων
χειμερίοιο ῥέεθρα κιὼν διὰ ποσσὶν Ἀναύρου
10 ἄλλο μὲν ἐξεσάωσεν ὑπ᾽ ἰλύος, ἄλλο δ᾽ ἔνερθεν
κάλλιπεν αὖθι πέδιλον ἐνισχόμενον προχοῇσιν.
ἵκετο δ᾽ ἐς Πελίην αὐτοσχεδὸν ἀντιβολήσων
εἰλαπίνης, ἣν πατρὶ Ποσειδάωνι καὶ ἄλλοις
ῥέζε θεοῖς, Ἥρης δὲ Πελασγίδος οὐκ ἀλέγιζεν.
15 αἶψα δὲ τόν γ᾽ ἐσιδὼν ἐφράσσατο, καί οἱ ἄεθλον
ἔντυε ναυτιλίης πολυκηδέος, ὄφρ᾽ ἐνὶ πόντῳ
ἠὲ καὶ ἀλλοδαποῖσι μετ᾽ ἀνδράσι νόστον ὀλέσσῃ.

---

1 The Cyanean ("cobalt-blue") rocks, also called the Clashing rocks (Plegades), were located where the Bosporus opens into the Black Sea.

2

BOOK 1

Beginning with you, Phoebus, I shall recall the famous deeds of men born long ago, who, at the command of King Pelias, sailed the well-benched Argo through the mouth of the Black Sea and between the Cyanean rocks[1] to fetch the golden fleece.

For such was the oracle that Pelias heard, that a horrible fate awaited him in the future: to perish through the designs of that man whom he would see coming from the people with only one sandal. And not long afterwards, in accordance with your prophecy, as Jason was crossing the streams of the wintry Anaurus on foot,[2] he rescued one sandal from the mud, but left the other there in the depths, held back by the current. He came right away to Pelias to share in the banquet that the king was offering to his father Poseidon and the rest of the gods, but to Pelasgian Hera he paid no regard.[3] As soon as he saw Jason, he took note, and arranged for him the ordeal of a very arduous voyage, so that either on the sea or else among foreign people he would lose any chance of returning home.

[2] When swollen with winter rains, the Anaurus cascades into the sea near Pagasae, the port of Iolcus.

[3] The Pelasgians were pre-Hellenic inhabitants of Thessaly.

3

νῆα μὲν οὖν οἱ πρόσθεν ἔτι κλείουσιν ἀοιδοὶ
Ἄργον Ἀθηναίης καμέειν ὑποθημοσύνῃσιν.
20 νῦν δ' ἂν ἐγὼ γενεήν τε καὶ οὔνομα μυθησαίμην
ἡρώων, δολιχῆς τε πόρους ἁλός, ὅσσα τ' ἔρεξαν
πλαζόμενοι· Μοῦσαι δ' ὑποφήτορες εἶεν ἀοιδῆς.
    πρῶτά νυν Ὀρφῆος μνησώμεθα, τόν ῥά ποτ'
    αὐτὴ
Καλλιόπη Θρήικι φατίζεται εὐνηθεῖσα
25 Οἰάγρῳ σκοπιῆς Πιμπληίδος ἄγχι τεκέσθαι.
αὐτὰρ τόν γ' ἐνέπουσιν ἀτειρέας οὔρεσι πέτρας
θέλξαι ἀοιδάων ἐνοπῇ ποταμῶν τε ῥέεθρα·
φηγοὶ δ' ἀγριάδες, κείνης ἔτι σήματα μολπῆς,
ἀκτῇ Θρηικίῃ Ζώνης ἔπι τηλεθόωσαι
30 ἑξείης στιχόωσιν ἐπήτριμοι, ἃς ὅ γ' ἐπιπρὸ
θελγομένας φόρμιγγι κατήγαγε Πιερίηθεν.
Ὀρφέα μὲν δὴ τοῖον ἑῶν ἐπαρωγὸν ἀέθλων
Αἰσονίδης Χείρωνος ἐφημοσύνῃσι πιθήσας
δέξατο, Πιερίῃ Βιστωνίδι κοιρανέοντα.
35   ἤλυθε δ' Ἀστερίων αὐτοσχεδόν, ὅν ῥα Κομήτης
γείνατο, δινήεντος ἐφ' ὕδασιν Ἀπιδανοῖο
Πειρεσιὰς ὄρεος Φυλληίου ἀγχόθι ναίων,
ἔνθα μὲν Ἀπιδανός τε μέγας καὶ δῖος Ἐνιπεὺς
ἄμφω συμφορέονται ἀπόπροθεν εἰς ἓν ἰόντες.

18 ἔτι κλείουσιν Ω: ἐπικλείουσιν Brunck

---

4 The rare term ὑποφήτορες most likely means "interpreters"
(cf. A.P. 14.1), but elsewhere Apollonius consistently portrays the

4

As for the ship, the songs of former bards still tell how Argus built it according to Athena's instructions. But now I wish to relate the lineage and names of the heroes, their journeys on the vast sea, and all they did as they wandered; and may the Muses be inspirers[4] of my song.

First then let us mention Orpheus, whom, it is said, Calliope herself once bore near the peak of Pimpleia, after making love to Thracian Oeagrus. And he, they say, charmed the hard boulders on the mountains and the course of rivers with the sound of his songs. And the wild oak trees, signs still to this day of his singing, flourish on the Thracian shore of Zone where they stand in dense, orderly rows, the ones he led forth down from Pieria, charmed by his lyre.[5] Such then was Orpheus, whom Jason, in obedience to Cheiron's behests,[6] welcomed as a helper in his trials, Orpheus, ruler of Bistonian Pieria.

Asterion came immediately, whom Cometes fathered by the waters of the swirling Apidanus, when he dwelt at Peiresiae near the Phylleian mountain, where the mighty Apidanus and glorious Enipeus join their two streams, after coming together from afar.

Muses as the *originators* of his songs (cf. 3.1–5; 4.984 and 1381–1382).

[5] Orpheus is associated with both Thessaly and Thrace. His birthplace, Pimpleia, is located in Thessalian Pieria (also the Muses' birthplace; cf. Hesiod, *Theogony* 53–54). Subsequently, he is said to have ruled at Bistonian (i.e. Thracian) Pieria.

[6] Cheiron was the wise centaur who, according to Pindar (*Pythian* 4.101–115), educated Jason. He is distinct from the un-ruly Centaurs, mentioned below at 42 and 60, who were defeated by the Lapithae.

40   Λάρισαν δ' ἐπὶ τοῖσι λιπὼν Πολύφημος ἵκανεν
Εἰλατίδης, ὃς πρὶν μὲν ἐρισθενέων Λαπιθάων,
ὁππότε Κενταύροις Λαπίθαι ἐπὶ θωρήσσοντο,
ὁπλότερος πολέμιζε· τότ' αὖ βαρύθεσκέ οἱ ἤδη
γυῖα, μένεν δ' ἔτι θυμὸς ἀρήιος ὡς τὸ πάρος περ.

45   οὐδὲ μὲν Ἴφικλος Φυλάκῃ ἔνι δηρὸν ἔλειπτο,
μήτρως Αἰσονίδαο· κασιγνήτην γὰρ ὄπυιεν
Αἴσων Ἀλκιμέδην Φυλακηίδα· τῆς μιν ἀνώγει
πηοσύνη καὶ κῆδος ἐνικρινθῆναι ὁμίλῳ.

     οὐδὲ Φεραῖς Ἄδμητος ἐυρρήνεσσιν ἀνάσσων
50   μίμνεν ὑπὸ σκοπιὴν ὄρεος Χαλκωδονίοιο.

     οὐδ' Ἀλόπῃ μίμνον πολυλήιοι Ἑρμείαο
υἱέες εὖ δεδαῶτε δόλους, Ἔρυτος καὶ Ἐχίων·
τοῖσι δ' ἐπὶ τρίτατος γνωτὸς κίε νισσομένοισιν
Αἰθαλίδης· καὶ τὸν μὲν ἐπ' Ἀμφρυσσοῖο ῥοῇσιν
55   Μυρμιδόνος κούρη Φθιὰς τέκεν Εὐπολέμεια,
τὼ δ' αὖτ' ἐκγεγάτην Μενετηίδος Ἀντιανείρης.

     ἤλυθε δ' ἀφνειὴν προλιπὼν Γυρτῶνα Κόρωνος
Καινεΐδης, ἐσθλὸς μέν, ἑοῦ δ' οὐ πατρὸς ἀμείνων.
Καινέα γὰρ ζῶόν περ ἔτι κλείουσιν ἀοιδοὶ
60   Κενταύροισιν ὀλέσθαι, ὅτε σφέας οἶος ἀπ' ἄλλων
ἤλασ' ἀριστήων· οἱ δ' ἔμπαλιν ὁρμηθέντες
οὔτε μιν ἀγκλῖναι προτέρω σθένον οὔτε δαΐξαι,
ἀλλ' ἄρρηκτος ἄκαμπτος ἐδύσετο νειόθι γαίης,
θεινόμενος στιβαρῇσι καταΐγδην ἐλάτῃσιν.

6

After these, from Larisa came Polyphemus, Eilatus' son, who in former times had fought as a young man among the mighty Lapithae, when the Lapithae armed themselves against the Centaurs. At this point, though, his limbs were already heavy, but his heart still remained as warlike as before.

Nor was Iphiclus left behind for long in Phylace. He was Jason's maternal uncle, for Aeson had married Iphiclus' sister Alcimede, daughter of Phylacus. This kinship with her and connection through marriage prompted him to be included in the crew.

Nor did Admetus, who ruled sheep-rich Pherae, remain beneath the peak of the Chalcodonion mountain.

Nor did Hermes' two sons, Erytus and Echion, possessors of many grain fields and well skilled in trickery, remain at Alope. And third to join them as they set out was their brother Aethalides. It was he whom Eupolemeia of Phthia, Myrmidon's daughter, bore by the streams of Amphryssus, whereas the other two were born to Antianeira, Menetes' daughter.

And from wealthy Gyrton came Caeneus' son, Coronus—a brave man, but no braver than his father. For bards sing of how Caeneus, although still living, perished at the hands of the Centaurs, when, all alone and separated from the other heroes, he routed them. They rallied against him, but were not strong enough to push him back nor to kill him, so instead, unbroken and unbending, he sank beneath the earth, hammered by the downward force of mighty pine trees.[7]

---

[7] They drove him into the underworld like a peg, hence he perished while still alive; cf. Pindar, *fr.* 128f.

65   ἤλυθε δ᾽ αὖ Μόψος Τιταρήσιος, ὃν περὶ πάντων
     Λητοΐδης ἐδίδαξε θεοπροπίας οἰωνῶν·
     ἠδὲ καὶ Εὐρυδάμας Κτιμένου πάις· ἄγχι δὲ λίμνης
     Ξυνιάδος Κτιμένην Δολοπηίδα ναιετάασκεν.
     καὶ μὴν Ἄκτωρ υἷα Μενοίτιον ἐξ Ὀπόεντος
70   ὦρσεν, ἀριστήεσσι σὺν ἀνδράσιν ὄφρα νέοιτο.
     εἵπετο δ᾽ Εὐρυτίων τε καὶ ἀλκήεις Ἐρυβώτης,
     υἷες ὁ μὲν Τελέοντος, ὁ δ᾽ Ἴρου Ἀκτορίδαο·
     ἤτοι ὁ μὲν Τελέοντος ἐυκλειὴς Ἐρυβώτης,
     Ἴρου δ᾽ Εὐρυτίων. σὺν καὶ τρίτος ἦεν Ὀιλεύς,
75   ἔξοχος ἠνορέην καὶ ἐπαῖξαι μετόπισθεν
     εὖ δεδαὼς δήοισιν, ὅτε κλίνωσι φάλαγγας.
     αὐτὰρ ἀπ᾽ Εὐβοίης Κάνθος κίε, τόν ῥα Κάνηθος
     πέμπεν Ἀβαντιάδης λελιημένον· οὐ μὲν ἔμελλε
     νοστήσειν Κήρινθον ὑπότροπος, αἶσα γὰρ ἦν
80   αὐτὸν ὁμῶς Μόψον τε δαήμονα μαντοσυνάων
     πλαγχθέντας Λιβύης ἐνὶ πείρασι δῃωθῆναι.
     ὡς οὐκ ἀνθρώποισι κακὸν μήκιστον ἐπαυρεῖν,
     ὁππότε κἀκείνους Λιβύη ἔνι ταρχύσαντο,
     τόσσον ἑκὰς Κόλχων, ὅσσον τέ περ ἠελίοιο
85   μεσσηγὺς δύσιές τε καὶ ἀντολαὶ εἰσορόωνται.

     67 ἠδὲ Ω: βῆ δὲ Fränkel
     74 ἦεν V²W: ἦεν V: ἦκεν E
     76 κλίνωσι Ω: κλίνειε Σ^L

---

⁸ Apollo.
⁹ The verb must be supplied. Fränkel's emendation of βῆ δὲ is
simple, but has no manuscript authority.

8

Mopsus the Titaresian came as well, whom, beyond all mortals, Leto's son[8] had taught the augury of birds; and Eurydamas, Ctimenus' son, came[9] too; he lived at Dolopian Ctimene near lake Xynias.

Moreover, Actor sent his son Menoetius from Opus to travel with the heroic men.[10]

And Eurytion followed, and valiant Erybotes, one the son of Teleon, the other of Irus, Actor's son. In fact, famous Erybotes was Teleon's son, and Eurytion was Irus'. And third with them came Oïleus, peerless in courage and well skilled at rushing upon the enemy from behind when they broke ranks.[11]

And from Euboea came Canthus, whom Abas' son Canethus sent, all eager to go, but he was not to return home to Cerinthus, for it was fated that he, along with Mopsus the expert at divination, would be killed when wandering within the borders of Libya.[12] Thus no evil is too remote for humans to encounter, seeing that they buried those men in Libya, as far from the Colchians as the distance that is seen between the setting and rising of the sun.[13]

---

[10] Lit. "leading men." Apollonius never calls the crew Argonauts (or even sailors), but "heroes" ($\ἥρωες$) or "leaders" ($\ἀριστῆες$). I have translated both as "heroes."

[11] Or, reading $\kappa\lambda\ίνειε$, *he would break their ranks*. The skill of the Homeric "lesser" Ajax, son of Oïleus, in pursuing a fleeing enemy (*Iliad* 14.520–522) is here transferred to his father.

[12] See 4.1485–1536.

[13] In popular belief, Colchis and Libya were thought to lie in the extreme east and west.

τῷ δ᾽ ἄρ᾽ ἐπὶ Κλυτίος τε καὶ Ἴφιτος ἠγερέθοντο,
Οἰχαλίης ἐπίουροι, ἀπηνέος Εὐρύτου υἷες,
Εὐρύτου, ᾧ πόρε τόξον Ἑκηβόλος· οὐδ᾽ ἀπόνητο
δωτίνης, αὐτῷ γὰρ ἑκὼν ἐρίδηνε δοτῆρι.

90   τοῖσι δ᾽ ἐπ᾽ Αἰακίδαι μετεκίαθον, οὐ μὲν ἅμ᾽
            ἄμφω
οὐδ᾽ ὁμόθεν· νόσφιν γὰρ ἀλευάμενοι κατένασθεν
Αἰγίνης, ὅτε Φῶκον ἀδελφεὸν ἐξενάριξαν
ἀφραδίῃ. Τελαμὼν μὲν ἐν Ἀτθίδι νάσσατο νήσῳ,
Πηλεὺς δὲ Φθίῃ ἔνι δώματα ναῖε λιασθείς.

95   τοῖς δ᾽ ἐπὶ Κεκροπίηθεν ἀρήιος ἤλυθε Βούτης,
παῖς ἀγαθοῦ Τελέοντος, ἐυμμελίης τε Φάληρος.
Ἄλκων μιν προέηκε πατὴρ ἑός· οὐ μὲν ἔτ᾽ ἄλλους
γήραος υἷας ἔχεν βιότοιό τε κηδεμονῆας,
ἀλλά ἑ τηλύγετόν περ ὁμῶς καὶ μοῦνον ἐόντα

100   πέμπεν, ἵνα θρασέεσσι μεταπρέποι ἡρώεσσιν.
Θησέα δ᾽, ὃς περὶ πάντας Ἐρεχθεΐδας ἐκέκαστο,
Ταιναρίην ἀίδηλος ὑπὸ χθόνα δεσμὸς ἔρυκεν,
Πειρίθῳ ἑσπόμενον κεινὴν ὁδόν· ἦ τέ κεν ἄμφω
ῥηίτερον καμάτοιο τέλος πάντεσσιν ἔθεντο.

105   Τῖφυς δ᾽ Ἁγνιάδης Σιφαέα κάλλιπε δῆμον

---

103 κεινὴν AE: κοινὴν SG²ˢˡD

---

14 For Eurytus' disastrous archery contest with Apollo (the Far-Shooter), see *Odyssey* 8.223–228.

15 For the murder of their half-brother Phocus and their exile, see Pindar, *Nemean* 5.9–18. Some scholars argue that ἀφραδίῃ means "unwittingly" and exculpates them to some extent, but A.

10

After him then assembled Clytius and Iphitus, guardians of Oechalia and sons of cruel Eurytus, Eurytus to whom the Far-Shooter gave a bow, but he did not profit from the gift, for he chose to compete with the giver himself.[14]

After them came the sons of Aeacus, but not both together nor from the same place, for they had settled in exile away from Aegina, after they had recklessly killed their brother Phocus.[15] Telamon lived on the Attic island,[16] whereas Peleus had gone off and made his home in Phthia.

After them from Cecropia[17] came the warrior Butes, the son of noble Teleon, and Phalerus of the ashen spear. His father Alcon sent forth the latter; he had no other sons to care for his old age and livelihood, but sent him off, in spite of being his much beloved and only son, to excel among the bold heroes. But as for Theseus, who surpassed all the sons of Erechtheus,[18] an invisible bond was holding him beneath the land of Taenarus, where he had followed Peirithous on a futile journey.[19] Truly that pair would have made the accomplishment of their toil lighter for them all.

And Tiphys, son of Hagnias, left the Thespian district of

elsewhere always uses this word to describe reckless and inconsiderate acts.

[16] Salamis.

[17] Athens. Cecrops was its legendary first king.

[18] Athenians. Erechtheus was a legendary early king of Athens.

[19] Or, reading κοινὴν, *a shared journey*. Theseus and Peirithous went to Hades (an entrance was thought to be at Taenarus on the southernmost tip of the Peloponnesus) to abduct Persephone, but were immobilized by invisible bonds until Heracles eventually freed Theseus.

APOLLONIUS RHODIUS

Θεσπιέων, ἐσθλὸς μὲν ὀρινόμενον προδαῆναι
κῦμ' ἁλὸς εὐρείης, ἐσθλὸς δ' ἀνέμοιο θυέλλας,
καὶ πλόον ἠελίῳ τε καὶ ἀστέρι τεκμήρασθαι.
αὐτή μιν Τριτωνὶς ἀριστήων ἐς ὅμιλον
110 ὦρσεν Ἀθηναίη, μετὰ δ' ἤλυθεν ἐλδομένοισιν.
αὐτὴ γὰρ καὶ νῆα θοὴν κάμε, σὺν δέ οἱ Ἄργος
τεῦξεν Ἀρεστορίδης κείνης ὑποθημοσύνῃσιν·
τῶ καὶ πασάων προφερεστάτη ἔπλετο νηῶν,
ὅσσαι ὑπ' εἰρεσίῃσιν ἐπειρήσαντο θαλάσσης.
115   Φλείας δ' αὖτ' ἐπὶ τοῖσιν Ἀραιθυρέηθεν ἵκανεν,
ἔνθ' ἀφνειὸς ἔναιε, Διωνύσοιο ἕκητι
πατρὸς ἑοῦ, πηγῇσιν ἐφέστιος Ἀσωποῖο.
      Ἀργόθεν αὖ Ταλαὸς καὶ Ἀρήιος, υἷε Βίαντος,
ἤλυθον ἴφθιμός τε Λεώδοκος, οὓς τέκε Πηρὼ
120 Νηληίς· τῆς δ' ἀμφὶ δύην ἐμόγησε βαρεῖαν
Αἰολίδης σταθμοῖσιν ἐν Ἰφίκλοιο Μελάμπους.
      οὐδὲ μὲν οὐδὲ βίην κρατερόφρονος Ἡρακλῆος
πευθόμεθ' Αἰσονίδαο λιλαιομένου ἀθερίξαι.
ἀλλ' ἐπεὶ ἄιε βάξιν ἀγειρομένων ἡρώων,
125 νείον ἀπ' Ἀρκαδίης Λυρκήιον Ἄργος ἀμείψας,
τὴν ὁδόν, ᾗ ζωὸν φέρε κάπριον, ὅς ῥ' ἐνὶ βήσσῃς
φέρβετο Λαμπείης Ἐρυμάνθιον ἂμ μέγα τῖφος,

<hr>

20 Athena is called "Triton-born" by Homer (e.g., *Iliad* 4.515) and Hesiod (*Theogony* 895). She was also associated with rivers named Triton in Boeotia and Thessaly and with lake Triton in Libya. Since Tiphys comes from Boeotia, presumably that river is meant here.

12

Siphae, expert in predicting rising waves on the broad sea, expert too in predicting storm winds and in determining a course by sun or star. Tritonian[20] Athena herself sent him to join the crew of heroes, and he came among men who longed for him. For she herself also fashioned the swift ship, and with her had Argus, son of Arestor, built it according to her instructions. That is why it was the most outstanding of all the ships that have challenged the sea with their oars.

Next in turn came Phleias from Araethyrea, where he lived in wealth thanks to his father Dionysus, in his home near the springs of Asopus.

From Argos in turn came Talaus and Areius, Bias' two sons, and mighty Leodocus,[21] all of whom Pero, Neleus' daughter, bore. It was on her account that the Aeolid Melampus endured grievous hardship in the stalls of Iphiclus.[22]

Nor indeed do we learn that mighty Heracles of steadfast determination disregarded Jason's eager appeals. But rather, when he heard the report that the heroes were gathering, he had just crossed from Arcadia to Lyrceian Argos, on the road by which he was carrying the live boar that fed in the glens of Lampeia throughout the vast Erymanthian marsh.[23] He put it down, bound with ropes,

[21] Leodocus first appears here as Bias' son.

[22] In order to win Pero for his brother Bias, Melampus endured a year's imprisonment in Neleus' cattle stalls.

[23] Heracles' fourth labor was to capture the great boar that ranged in the Erymanthian region of northwest Arcadia. He carried it from mount Lampeia to mount Lyrceion northwest of Argos and left it in Mycenae, where Eurystheus ruled.

τὸν μὲν ἐνὶ πρώτῃσι Μυκηναίων ἀγορῇσιν
δεσμοῖς ἰλλόμενον μεγάλων ἀπεθήκατο νώτων,
130 αὐτὸς δ᾽ ᾗ ἰότητι παρὲκ νόον Εὐρυσθῆος
ὡρμήθη· σὺν καί οἱ Ὕλας κίεν, ἐσθλὸς ὀπάων
πρωθήβης, ἰῶν τε φορεὺς φύλακός τε βιοῖο.

τῷ δ᾽ ἐπὶ δὴ θείοιο κίεν Δαναοῖο γενέθλη,
Ναύπλιος. ἦ γὰρ ἔην Κλυτονήου Ναυβολίδαο,
135 Ναύβολος αὖ Λέρνου· Λέρνον γε μὲν ἴδμεν ἐόντα
Προίτου Ναυπλιάδαο· Ποσειδάωνι δὲ κούρη
πρίν ποτ᾽ Ἀμυμώνη Δαναῒς τέκεν εὐνηθεῖσα
Ναύπλιον, ὃς περὶ πάντας ἐκαίνυτο ναυτιλίῃσιν.

Ἴδμων δ᾽ ὑστάτιος μετεκίαθεν, ὅσσοι ἔναιον
140 Ἄργος, ἐπεὶ δεδαὼς τὸν ἑὸν μόρον οἰωνοῖσιν
ἤιε, μή οἱ δῆμος ἐυκλείης ἀγάσαιτο.
οὐ μὲν ὅ γ᾽ ἦεν Ἄβαντος ἐτήτυμον, ἀλλά μιν αὐτὸς
γείνατο κυδαλίμοις ἐναρίθμιον Αἰολίδῃσιν
Λητοΐδης, αὐτὸς δὲ θεοπροπίας ἐδίδαξεν
145 οἰωνούς τ᾽ ἀλέγειν ἠδ᾽ ἔμπυρα σήματ᾽ ἰδέσθαι.

καὶ μὴν Αἰτωλὶς κρατερὸν Πολυδεύκεα Λήδη
Κάστορά τ᾽ ὠκυπόδων ὦρσεν δεδαημένον ἵππων
Σπάρτηθεν· τοὺς δ᾽ ᾗ γε δόμοις ἔνι Τυνδαρέοιο
τηλυγέτους ὠδῖνι μιῇ τέκεν· οὐδ᾽ ἀπίθησεν
150 λισσομένοις· Ζηνὸς γὰρ ἐπάξια μήδετο λέκτρων.

129 ἀπεθήκατο Ω: ἀπεσείσατο Test.
150 λισσομένοις Meineke: νισσομένοις Ω

14

from his huge back at the edge of the Mycenaeans' assembly place, and set out of his own accord against the will of Eurystheus. And with him went his noble squire Hylas, in the first bloom of youth, to be the bearer of his arrows and guardian of his bow.

And after him then came a descendant of divine Danaus, Nauplius. He was in fact the son of Clytonaeus, son of Naubolus, and Naubolus in turn was Lernus' son. Lernus, we know, was the son of Proteus, son of Nauplius; and once upon a time Danaus' daughter Amymone slept with Poseidon and bore Nauplius,[24] who far surpassed all men in the art of sailing.

And Idmon arrived last of those who lived in Argos, for although he had learned of his own fate through bird omens,[25] he came nonetheless, so that his people would not begrudge him glorious fame. He was not really the son of Abas, but Leto's son himself had fathered him to be numbered among the illustrious Aeolidae, and he himself had taught him the arts of prophecy, to heed bird omens and observe the signs of burnt offerings.

Moreover, Aetolian Leda sent mighty Polydeuces and Castor, skilled with swift-footed horses, from Sparta. These much-beloved sons she bore in one birth in Tyndareus' palace, and she did not oppose their pleas to go, for she had aspirations worthy of Zeus' bed.[26]

---

[24] This ancestor of the Argonaut was credited with founding the port of Nauplion (Pausanias 2.38.2).

[25] Idmon's name means "Knower"; his death is recounted at 2.815–834.

[26] This compressed phrase can mean "worthy of one who shared Zeus' bed" or "worthy of the offspring of Zeus' bed."

οἵ τ᾿ Ἀφαρητιάδαι Λυγκεὺς καὶ ὑπέρβιος Ἴδας
Ἀρήνηθεν ἔβαν, μεγάλῃ περιθαρσέες ἀλκῇ
ἀμφότεροι· Λυγκεὺς δὲ καὶ ὀξυτάτοις ἐκέκαστο
ὄμμασιν, εἰ ἐτεόν γε πέλει κλέος ἀνέρα κεῖνον
155 ῥηιδίως καὶ νέρθε κατὰ χθονὸς αὐγάζεσθαι.

σὺν δὲ Περικλύμενος Νηλήιος ὦρτο νέεσθαι,
πρεσβύτατος παίδων, ὅσσοι Πύλῳ ἐξεγένοντο
Νηλῆος θείοιο· Ποσειδάων δέ οἱ ἀλκὴν
δῶκεν ἀπειρεσίην ἠδ᾿, ὅττι κεν ἀρήσαιτο
160 μαρνάμενος, τὸ πέλεσθαι ἐνὶ ξυνοχῇ πολέμοιο.

καὶ μὴν Ἀμφιδάμας Κηφεύς τ᾿ ἴσαν Ἀρκαδίηθεν,
οἳ Τεγέην καὶ κλῆρον Ἀφειδάντειον ἔναιον,
υἷε δύω Ἀλεοῦ· τρίτατός γε μὲν ἕσπετ᾿ ἰοῦσιν
Ἀγκαῖος· τὸν μέν ῥα πατὴρ Λυκόοργος ἔπεμπεν,
165 τῶν ἄμφω γνωτὸς προγενέστερος. ἀλλ᾿ ὁ μὲν ἤδη
γηράσκοντ᾿ Ἀλεὸν λίπετ᾿ ἂμ πόλιν ὄφρα κομίζοι,
παῖδα δ᾿ ἑὸν σφετέροισι κασιγνήτοισιν ὄπασσεν·
βῆ δ᾿ ὅ γε Μαιναλίης ἄρκτου δέρος, ἀμφίτομόν τε
δεξιτερῇ πάλλων πέλεκυν μέγαν· ἔντεα γάρ οἱ
170 πατροπάτωρ Ἀλεὸς μυχάτῃ ἐνέκρυψε καλιῇ,
αἴ κέν πως ἔτι καὶ τὸν ἐρητύσειε νέεσθαι.

βῆ δὲ καὶ Αὐγείης, ὃν δὴ φάτις Ἠελίοιο
ἔμμεναι· Ἠλείοισι δ᾿ ὅ γ᾿ ἀνδράσιν ἐμβασίλευεν
ὄλβῳ κυδιόων· μέγα δ᾿ ἵετο Κολχίδα γαῖαν
175 αὐτόν τ᾿ Αἰήτην ἰδέειν σημάντορα Κόλχων.

The sons of Aphareus, Lynceus and proud Idas, came from Arene, both very bold in their great might. Lynceus also excelled in having the sharpest eyesight, if indeed the report is true that that man could easily peer even down beneath the earth.

And with them Neleus' son Periclymenus set out to come, the eldest of all the sons who were born in Pylos to divine Neleus. Poseidon had given him boundless might and the ability when fighting to assume any form he prayed to take in the press of battle.[27]

Moreover, from Arcadia came Amphidamas and Cepheus, Aleus' two sons, who dwelt in Tegea and the domain of Apheidas.[28] And third to join them on their way was Ancaeus, whom his father Lycurgus, the older brother of the other two, sent. But Lycurgus was left in the city to care for Aleus, who was already growing old, and sent his own son to accompany his brothers. Ancaeus came wearing the skin of a Maenalian bear and wielding a great double-edged ax in his right hand, because his grandfather Aleus had hidden his armor from him in the back of a granary, hoping that somehow he might still prevent him too from going.

Augeas also came, who in fact was said to be Helius' son. He was king of the Elean people and gloried in his wealth. He was very eager to see the land of Colchis and Aeetes himself, ruler of the Colchians.[29]

---

[27] Poseidon was Neleus' father. For Periclymenus' ability to change into animal forms, cf. Hesiod, *fr.* 33a12–17 M-W.

[28] Legendary king of Tegea, father of Aleus.

[29] Both Augeas ("Bright One") and Aeetes were sons of Helius.

Ἀστέριος δὲ καὶ Ἀμφίων Ὑπερασίου υἷες
Πελλήνης ἀφίκανον Ἀχαιΐδος, ἥν ποτε Πέλλης
πατροπάτωρ ἐπόλισσεν ἐπ' ὀφρύσιν Αἰγιαλοῖο.
   Ταίναρον αὖτ' ἐπὶ τοῖσι λιπὼν Εὔφημος ἵκανεν,
180 τόν ῥα Ποσειδάωνι ποδωκηέστατον ἄλλων
Εὐρώπη Τιτυοῖο μεγασθενέος τέκε κούρη.
κεῖνος ἀνὴρ καὶ πόντου ἐπὶ γλαυκοῖο θέεσκεν
οἴδματος, οὐδὲ θοοὺς βάπτεν πόδας, ἀλλ' ὅσον
   ἄκροις
ἴχνεσι τεγγόμενος διερῇ πεφόρητο κελεύθῳ.
185   καὶ δ' ἄλλω δύο παῖδε Ποσειδάωνος ἵκοντο,
ἤτοι ὁ μὲν πτολίεθρον ἀγαυοῦ Μιλήτοιο
νοσφισθεὶς Ἐργῖνος, ὁ δ' Ἰμβρασίης ἕδος Ἥρης
Παρθενίην Ἀγκαῖος ὑπέρβιος· ἴστορε δ' ἄμφω
ἠμὲν ναυτιλίης ἠδ' ἄρεος εὐχετόωντο.
190   Οἰνεΐδης δ' ἐπὶ τοῖσιν ἀφορμηθεὶς Καλυδῶνος
ἀλκήεις Μελέαγρος ἀνήλυθε, Λαοκόων τε,
Λαοκόων Οἰνῆος ἀδελφεός, οὐ μὲν ἰῆς γε
μητέρος, ἀλλά ἑ θῆσσα γυνὴ τέκε. τὸν μὲν ἄρ'
   Οἰνεὺς
ἤδη γηραλέον κοσμήτορα παιδὸς ἴαλλεν·
195 ὧδ' ἔτι κουρίζων περιθαρσέα δῦνεν ὅμιλον
ἡρώων· τοῦ δ' οὔ τιν' ὑπέρτερον ἄλλον ὀίω
νόσφιν γ' Ἡρακλῆος ἐπελθέμεν, εἴ κ' ἔτι μοῦνον
αὖθι μένων λυκάβαντα μετετράφη Αἰτωλοῖσιν.
καὶ μὴν οἱ μήτρως αὐτὴν ὁδόν, εὖ μὲν ἄκοντι,
200 εὖ δὲ καὶ ἐν σταδίῃ δεδαημένος ἀντιφέρεσθαι,
Θεστιάδης Ἴφικλος ἐφωμάρτησε κιόντι.

18

Asterius and Amphion, Hyperasius' sons, came from
Achaean Pellene, which their grandfather Pelles had once
founded on the slopes of Aegialus.

Next in turn from Taenarus came Euphemus, whom
Europa, daughter of mighty Tityus, bore to Poseidon—the
most fleet-footed of men. That man could run even on the
swell of the gray-green sea without submerging his swift
feet, but barely moistened his toes as he was borne over the
watery way.

And two other sons of Poseidon came. The one, who
left behind the citadel of glorious Miletus, was Erginus,
and the other, who left Parthenia, the seat of Imbrasian[30]
Hera, was proud Ancaeus.[31] Both claimed to be experts at
seamanship and warfare.

After them, from Calydon came Oeneus' son, valiant
Meleager, and Laocoon too, Laocoon, the brother of
Oeneus, though not from the same mother, for a serving-
woman bore him. And Oeneus sent him, already an old
man, as a guide for his son. Thus, while still a boy Meleager
entered the very bold crew of heroes, and I do not believe
that any other man would have come superior to him ex-
cept, to be sure, Heracles, if he had stayed there and been
raised for one more year among the Aetolians. Moreover,
his maternal uncle Iphiclus,[32] Thestius' son, accompanied
him as he went on this journey, an expert with the javelin
and expert too at fighting hand to hand.

[30] Parthenia was another name for the island of Samos; the
Imbrasus flows by Hera's sanctuary there.

[31] Not to be confused with Ancaeus from Arcadia at 164.

[32] Iphiclus was the brother of Meleager's mother, Althaea, to
be distinguished from Jason's uncle (1.45, 1.121).

APOLLONIUS RHODIUS

σὺν δὲ Παλαιμόνιος Λέρνου πάις Ὠλενίοιο,
Λέρνου ἐπίκλησιν, γενεήν γε μὲν Ἡφαίστοιο·
τούνεκ' ἔην πόδε σιφλός· ἀτὰρ δέμας οὔ κέ τις ἔτλη
205 ἠνορέην τ' ὀνόσασθαι, ὃ καὶ μεταρίθμιος ἦεν
πᾶσιν ἀριστήεσσιν Ἰήσονι κῦδος ἀέξων.

ἐκ δ' ἄρα Φωκήων κίεν Ἴφιτος Ὀρνυτίδαο
Ναυβόλου ἐκγεγαώς· ξεῖνος δέ οἱ ἔσκε πάροιθεν,
ἦμος ἔβη Πυθώδε θεοπροπίας ἐρεείνων
210 ναυτιλίης· τόθι γάρ μιν ἑοῖς ὑπέδεκτο δόμοισιν.

Ζήτης αὖ Κάλαΐς τε Βορήιοι υἱες ἵκοντο,
οὕς ποτ' Ἐρεχθηὶς Βορέῃ τέκεν Ὠρείθυια
ἐσχατιῇ Θρήκης δυσχειμέρου· ἔνθ' ἄρα τήν γε
Θρηίκιος Βορέης ἀνερείψατο Κεκροπίηθεν
215 Ἰλισσοῦ προπάροιθε χορῷ ἔνι δινεύουσαν.
καί μιν ἄγων ἕκαθεν, Σαρπηδονίην ὅθι πέτρην
κλείουσιν, ποταμοῖο παρὰ ῥόον Ἐργίνοιο,
λυγαίοις ἐδάμασσε περὶ νεφέεσσι καλύψας.
τὼ μὲν ἐπὶ κροτάφοισι ποδῶν θ' ἑκάτερθεν ἐρεμνὰς
220 σεῖον ἀειρομένω πτέρυγας, μέγα θάμβος ἰδέσθαι,
χρυσείαις φολίδεσσι διαυγέας· ἀμφὶ δὲ νώτοις
κράατος ἐξ ὑπάτοιο καὶ αὐχένος ἔνθα καὶ ἔνθα
κυάνεαι δονέοντο μετὰ πνοιῇσιν ἔθειραι.

οὐδὲ μὲν οὐδ' αὐτοῖο πάις μενέαινεν Ἄκαστος
225 ἰφθίμῳ Πελίαο δόμοις ἔνι πατρὸς ἑοῖο

211 ἵκοντο Ω: ἱκέσθην Et. Magn. et Et. Gen.
219 ἐπὶ κροτάφοισι ποδῶν θ' Kingston ex]οταφοι[ ]ι Π¹:
ἐπ' ἀκροτάτοισι ποδῶν Ω   225 ἑοῖο Π¹ω: ἑῆος mΣ]

20

And with him was Palaemonius, son of Lernus from Olenus. He was called Lernus' son, but really was the off-spring of Hephaestus, which is why he was crippled in both feet, but no one would dare slight his body or his courage, and that is why he was numbered among all the heroes and enhanced Jason's prestige.

Then from the Phocians came Iphitus, offspring of Naubolus, son of Ornytus. He had once hosted Jason when he went to Pytho seeking an oracle concerning his voyage. For it was there that he welcomed him in his palace.

In turn came Zetes and Calaïs, Boreas' sons, whom Oreithyia, Erechtheus' daughter, once bore to Boreas in the furthest reaches of wintry Thrace, to which place Thracian Boreas snatched her away from Cecropia,[33] as she was whirling in the dance near the Ilissus. And carrying her far off to a place they call Sarpedon's rock beside the stream of the Erginus river, he shrouded her in gloomy clouds and subdued her. The two sons were flapping the dark wings on their temples and on both sides of their feet[34] as they soared up—a great wonder to behold—wings gleaming with golden scales. And over their backs, from the top of their heads and necks, their dark hair fluttered here and there in the breeze.

Nor indeed did Acastus, the son of mighty Pelias him-self, desire to remain in the palace of his father, nor did

[33] Attica.

[34] Or, reading ἐπ᾽ ἀκροτάτοισι ποδῶν ἑκάτερθεν, wings *on their ankles on both sides*.

μιμνάζειν, Ἄργος τε θεᾶς ὑποεργὸς Ἀθήνης·
ἀλλ' ἄρα καὶ τὼ μέλλον ἐνικρινθῆναι ὁμίλῳ.

τόσσοι ἄρ' Αἰσονίδῃ συμμήστορες ἠγερέθοντο.
τοὺς μὲν ἀριστῆας Μινύας περιναιετάοντες
230 κίκλησκον μάλα πάντας, ἐπεὶ Μινύαο θυγατρῶν
οἱ πλεῖστοι καὶ ἄριστοι ἀφ' αἵματος εὐχετόωντο
ἔμμεναι· ὡς δὲ καὶ αὐτὸν Ἰήσονα γείνατο μήτηρ
Ἀλκιμέδη Κλυμένης Μινυηίδος ἐκγεγαυῖα.

αὐτὰρ ἐπεὶ δμώεσσιν ἐπαρτέα πάντ' ἐτέτυκτο,
235 ὅσσα περ ἐντύνονται ἐπήρεες ἔνδοθι νῆες,
εὖτ' ἂν ἄγῃ χρέος ἄνδρας ὑπεὶρ ἅλα ναυτίλλεσθαι,
δὴ τότ' ἴσαν μετὰ νῆα δι' ἄστεος, ἔνθα περ ἀκταὶ
κλείονται Παγασαὶ Μαγνήτιδες· ἀμφὶ δὲ λαῶν
πληθὺς ἐπερχομένων ἄμυδις θέεν, οἱ δὲ φαεινοὶ
240 ἀστέρες ὣς νεφέεσσι μετέπρεπον. ὧδε δ' ἕκαστος
ἔννεπεν εἰσορόων σὺν τεύχεσιν ἀίσσοντας·

"Ζεῦ ἄνα, τίς Πελίαο νόος; πόθι τόσσον ὅμιλον
ἡρώων γαίης Παναχαιίδος ἔκτοθι βάλλει;
αὐτῆμάρ κε δόμους ὀλοῷ πυρὶ δηώσειαν
245 Αἰήτεω, ὅτε μή σφιν ἑκὼν δέρος ἐγγυαλίξῃ.
ἀλλ' οὐ φυκτὰ κέλευθα, πόνος δ' ἄπρηκτος ἰοῦσιν."

235 επηρεες Π¹: ἐπαρτέες Ω
239 ἐπερχομένων Ω (πληθὺς): σπερχομένων Meineke
(metri gratia)

---

35 In building the Argo.
36 The extremely rare word συμμήστορες ("fellow advisers")
is often translated as "helpers."

Argus, the goddess Athena's assistant,[35] but it turned out that even these two were to be included in the crew.

Such then is the number of advisers[36] who assembled to aid Jason. The neighboring peoples called all these heroes Minyans, because most of them—and the greatest—claimed to be sprung from the blood of the daughters of Minyas. Likewise Alcimede, the mother who bore Jason himself, was born of Minyas' daughter Clymene.

But when everything had been made ready by the servants, everything that oared ships stock on board when need compels men to voyage over the sea, then the heroes went through the town toward the ship, where the shore is called Magnesian Pagasae.[37] All around them ran a crowd of people gathering together,[38] while the heroes stood out amid them like gleaming stars among the clouds. And thus did each person say upon seeing them hastening with their armor:

"Lord Zeus, what is Pelias' intention? To what place beyond the Panachaean[39] land is he sending so great a crew of heroes? In one day they could destroy Aeetes' palace with deadly fire, if he is unwilling to give them the fleece. But the voyage cannot be avoided, and the task is beyond accomplishment[40] for those who go."

[37] The seaport, about two miles from Iolcus.
[38] Or, reading σπερχομένων, *as they hastened, a crowd of people ran with them.* [39] Panachaean (of all Greece), opposed to Hellas (properly Thessaly in the epic tradition).
[40] This sentence is variously interpreted. Many follow the scholiast's unparalleled gloss of "difficult" for ἄπρηκτος. On my interpretation, the citizens are confident in the heroes' military prowess, but fear that the voyage itself cannot be completed.

APOLLONIUS RHODIUS

ὣς φάσαν ἔνθα καὶ ἔνθα κατὰ πτόλιν· αἱ δὲ
γυναῖκες
πολλὰ μάλ' ἀθανάτοισιν ἐς αἰθέρα χεῖρας ἄειρον,
εὐχόμεναι νόστοιο τέλος θυμηδὲς ὀπάσσαι.
250 ἄλλη δ' εἰς ἑτέρην ὀλοφύρετο δακρυχέουσα·
"δειλὴ Ἀλκιμέδη, καὶ σοὶ κακὸν ὀψέ περ ἔμπης
ἤλυθεν, οὐδ' ἐτέλεσσας ἐπ' ἀγλαΐῃ βιότοιο.
Αἴσων αὖ μέγα δή τι δυσάμμορος· ἦ τέ οἱ ἦεν
βέλτερον, εἰ τὸ πάροιθεν ἐνὶ κτερέεσσιν ἐλυσθεὶς
255 νειόθι γαίης κεῖτο, κακῶν ἔτι νῆις ἀέθλων.
ὣς ὄφελεν καὶ Φρίξον, ὅτ' ὤλετο παρθένος Ἕλλη,
κῦμα μέλαν κριῷ ἅμ' ἐπικλύσαι· ἀλλὰ καὶ αὐδὴν
ἀνδρομέην προέηκε κακὸν τέρας, ὥς κεν ἀνίας
Ἀλκιμέδῃ μετόπισθε καὶ ἄλγεα μυρία θείη."
260 αἱ μὲν ἄρ' ὣς ἀγόρευον ἐπὶ προμολῇσι κιόντων.
ἤδη δὲ δμῶές τε πολεῖς δμωαί τ' ἀγέροντο,
μήτηρ δ' ἀμφ' αὐτὸν βεβολημένη. ὀξὺ δ' ἑκάστην
δῦνεν ἄχος· σὺν δέ σφι πατὴρ ὀλοῷ ὑπὸ γήρᾳ
ἐντυπὰς ἐν λεχέεσσι καλυψάμενος γοάασκεν.
265 αὐτὰρ ὁ τῶν μὲν ἔπειτα κατεπρήυνεν ἀνίας
θαρσύνων, δμώεσσι δ' ἀρήια τεύχε' ἀείρειν
πέφραδεν· οἱ δέ τε σῖγα κατηφέες ἠείροντο.
μήτηρ δ' ὡς τὰ πρῶτ' ἐπεχεύατο πήχεε παιδί,
ὣς ἔχετο κλαίουσ' ἀδινώτερον, ἠύτε κούρη
270 οἰόθεν ἀσπασίως πολιὴν τροφὸν ἀμφιπεσοῦσα

262 δ' Ω: τ' Fränkel
267 δέ τε La Roche: δὲ Ω: δὲ τὰ Merkel

24

Thus they spoke here and there throughout the city, and the women again and again raised their hands skyward to the immortals, beseeching them to grant a heart-cheering return home. And one to another they lamented in tears:

"Poor Alcimede, to you too, late though it is, evil has come, and you have not ended up with splendor in life. Aeson too is unfortunate to a great extent! Truly it would have been better for him, if before this he had been wrapped in a shroud and lay beneath the ground, still unaware of these evil trials. How I wish that when the maiden Helle perished,[41] the dark wave had washed over Phrixus and the ram as well. But that evil monster even emitted a human voice,[42] so as to cause Alcimede pains and countless woes thereafter."

Thus did they speak as the heroes went to the launching place. By now many household servants and serving women had gathered, and Jason's mother, with her arms thrown around him. Sharp grief pierced every woman, and with them groaned his father, tightly wrapped up in bed because of baneful old age. And then Jason sought to assuage their pain with encouraging words, but he told the servants to take up his armaments for war, and they, with downcast looks, silently took them up. But his mother, just as she had thrown her arms around her son from the start, so now she clung to him and wept more profusely, as a girl in her solitude fondly clutches her gray-haired nurse and

---

[41] When Helle and Phrixus fled from their wicked stepmother on the ram, Helle fell off and drowned in the Hellespont, while Phrixus went on to Colchis.

[42] The ram was endowed with speech.

μύρεται, ᾗ οὐκ εἰσιν ἔτ' ἄλλοι κηδεμονῆες,
ἀλλ' ὑπὸ μητρυιῇ βίοτον βαρὺν ἡγηλάζει·
καί ἑ νέον πολέεσσιν ὀνείδεσιν ἐστυφέλιξεν,
τῇ δέ τ' ὀδυρομένῃ δέδεται κέαρ ἔνδοθεν ἄτῃ,
275 οὐδ' ἔχει ἐκφλύξαι τόσσον γόον, ὅσσον ὀρεχθεῖ·
ὣς ἀδινὸν κλαίεσκεν ἑὸν παῖδ' ἀγκὰς ἔχουσα
Ἀλκιμέδη· καὶ τοῖον ἔπος φάτο κηδοσύνῃσιν·
    "αἴθ' ὄφελον κεῖν' ἦμαρ, ὅτ' ἐξειπόντος ἄκουσα
δειλὴ ἐγὼ Πελίαο κακὴν βασιλῆος ἐφετμήν,
280 αὐτίκ' ἀπὸ ψυχὴν μεθέμεν κηδέων τε λαθέσθαι,
ὄφρ' αὐτός με τεῇσι φίλαις ταρχύσαο χερσίν,
τέκνον ἐμόν· τὸ γὰρ οἶον ἔην ἔτι λοιπὸν ἐέλδωρ
ἐκ σέθεν, ἄλλα δὲ πάντα πάλαι θρεπτήρια πέσσω.
νῦν γε μὲν ἡ τὸ πάροιθεν Ἀχαιιάδεσσιν ἀγητὴ
285 δμωὶς ὅπως κενεοῖσι λελείψομαι ἐν μεγάροισιν,
σεῖο πόθῳ μινύθουσα δυσάμμορος, ᾧ ἔπι πολλὴν
ἀγλαΐην καὶ κῦδος ἔχον πάρος, ᾧ ἔπι μούνῳ
μίτρην πρῶτον ἔλυσα καὶ ὕστατον, ἔξοχα γάρ μοι
Εἰλείθυια θεὰ πολέος ἐμέγηρε τόκοιο.
290 ὤ μοι ἐμῆς ἄτης· τὸ μὲν οὐδ' ὅσον οὐδ' ἐν ὀνείρῳ
ὠισάμην, εἰ Φρίξος ἐμοὶ κακὸν ἔσσετ' ἀλύξας."
    ὣς ἥ γε στενάχουσα κινύρετο· ταὶ δὲ γυναῖκες
ἀμφίπολοι γοάασκον ἐπισταδόν· αὐτὰρ ὁ τήν γε
μειλιχίοις ἐπέεσσι παρηγορέων προσέειπεν·
295   "μή μοι λευγαλέας ἐνιβάλλεο, μῆτερ, ἀνίας
ὧδε λίην, ἐπεὶ οὐ μὲν ἐρητύσεις κακότητος
δάκρυσιν, ἀλλ' ἔτι κεν καὶ ἐπ' ἄλγεσιν ἄλγος ἄροιο.

26

sobs, a girl who no longer has others to care for her but leads a wretched life under a stepmother who has just mistreated her with many rebukes, and, as she cries, the heart within her is bound fast with misery, and she cannot sob forth all the groans that well up[43]—so profusely did Alcimede weep, as she held her son in her arms, and spoke these words in her longing:

"How I wish that on that day when I heard to my sorrow King Pelias announce his evil command, I had immediately lost my life and forgotten my cares, so that you could have buried me with your own dear hands, my son. For that was the one hope still remaining for you to fulfill, because I have long enjoyed all the other recompenses due a parent. But now I—once so admired among Achaean women—shall be left in an empty palace like a servant, miserably wasting away out of longing for you, on whose account I enjoyed so much splendor and fame until now, for whom alone, first and last, I loosened my girdle in childbirth, because to me above all others the goddess Eileithyia[44] begrudged many children. What distress is mine! Never once, not even in my dreams, did I imagine that Phrixus' escape would mean woe for me."

Thus she groaned and sobbed, and the serving women wailed in turn,[45] but Jason consoled her with gentle words and said:

"Mother, please do not take upon yourself too many bitter sorrows in this way, for you will not ward off misfortune with tears, but will add yet further grief to your griefs. For

[43] The precise meaning of ὀρεχθέω is difficult to determine; at 2.49 it describes the pounding of a heart.

[44] The goddess of childbirth.   [45] Or *standing by*.

27

APOLLONIUS RHODIUS

πήματα γάρ τ᾽ ἀίδηλα θεοὶ θνητοῖσι νέμουσιν,
τῶν μοῖραν κατὰ θυμὸν ἀνιάζουσά περ ἔμπης
300 τλῆθι φέρειν. θάρσει δὲ συνημοσύνησιν Ἀθήνης
ἠδὲ θεοπροπίησιν, ἐπεὶ μάλα δεξιὰ Φοῖβος
ἔχρη, ἀτὰρ μετέπειτά γ᾽ ἀριστήων ἐπαρωγῇ.
ἀλλὰ σὺ μὲν νῦν αὖθι μετ᾽ ἀμφιπόλοισιν ἔκηλος
μίμνε δόμοις, μηδ᾽ ὄρνις ἀεικελίη πέλε νηί·
305 κεῖσε δ᾽ ὁμαρτήσουσιν ἔται δμῶές τε κιόντι."
      ἦ, καὶ ὁ μὲν προτέρωσε δόμων ἐξῶρτο νέεσθαι.
οἷος δ᾽ ἐκ νηοῖο θυώδεος εἶσιν Ἀπόλλων
Δῆλον ἀν᾽ ἠγαθέην ἠὲ Κλάρον, ἢ ὅ γε Πυθὼ
ἢ Λυκίην εὐρεῖαν ἐπὶ Ξάνθοιο ῥοῇσιν·
310 τοῖος ἀνὰ πληθὺν δήμου κίεν, ὦρτο δ᾽ αὐτὴ
κεκλομένων ἄμυδις. τῷ δὲ ξύμβλητο γεραιὴ
Ἰφιὰς Ἀρτέμιδος πολιηόχου ἀρήτειρα,
καί μιν δεξιτερῆς χειρὸς κύσεν· οὐδέ τι φάσθαι
ἔμπης ἱεμένη δύνατο προθέοντος ὁμίλου,
315 ἀλλ᾽ ἡ μὲν λίπετ᾽ αὖθι παρακλιδόν, οἷα γεραιὴ
ὁπλοτέρων, ὁ δὲ πολλὸν ἀποπλαγχθεὶς ἐλιάσθη.
      αὐτὰρ ἐπεί ῥα πόληος ἐϋδμήτους λίπ᾽ ἀγυιάς,
ἀκτὴν δ᾽ ἵκανεν Παγασηίδα, τῇ μιν ἑταῖροι
δειδέχατ᾽ Ἀργώῃ ἄμυδις παρὰ νηὶ μένοντες.
320 στῆ δ᾽ ἄρ᾽ ἐπὶ προμολῆς· οἱ δ᾽ ἀντίοι ἠγερέθοντο.
ἐς δ᾽ ἐνόησαν Ἄκαστον ὁμῶς Ἄργον τε πόληος
νόσφι καταβλώσκοντας, ἐθάμβησαν δ᾽ ἐσιδόντες
πασσυδίῃ Πελίαο παρὲκ νόον ἰθύοντας.

323 ἰθύοντας Π² Brunck praeeunte: ἰθύνοντας Ω (cf. 2.327)

28

the gods mete out unforeseen woes to mortals, and, although it pains your heart, endure to bear your portion of them. But take courage from the commitments of Athena and from the oracles (for Phoebus has made very favorable prophecies) and, thereafter, from the aid of the heroes. For now, remain calmly here in the house with your maids and do not become an ill omen for the ship: my kinsmen and servants will escort me on my way there."

He spoke and went forth from his home to make his departure. And as Apollo goes from his fragrant temple through holy Delos or Claros, or through Pytho or broad Lycia by the streams of Xanthus, so he went through the crowd of people, and a shout went up as they cheered with one voice. And Iphias met him on his way, an aged priestess of city-protecting Artemis, and kissed him on his right hand, but she was unable to say a word, much as she wished to, because the crowd was rushing forward, but she was left there by the wayside, as an old woman is left behind by the young, and off he went far into the distance.

Now when he had left the well-built streets of the city, he came to the shore of Pagasae, where his comrades, who were waiting together beside the ship Argo, greeted him. He then stood at the launching place, and they assembled in front of him. And they caught sight of Acastus together with Argus coming down from the city and were amazed, one and all,[46] to see them heading towards them against

---

[46] πασσυδίη can mean "one and all" or "at full speed." If taken with ἰθύοντας, it would mean "heading at full speed," but it is doubtful that the sense of speed in this word ever predominates in A.

δέρμα δ' ὁ μὲν ταύροιο ποδηνεκὲς ἀμφέχετ' ὤμους
325 Ἄργος Ἀρεστορίδης λάχνῃ μέλαν, αὐτὰρ ὁ καλὴν
δίπλακα, τήν οἱ ὄπασσε κασιγνήτη Πελόπεια.
ἀλλ' ἔμπης τὼ μέν τε διεξερέεσθαι ἕκαστα
ἔσχετο, τοὺς δ' ἀγορήνδε συνεδριάασθαι ἄνωγεν.
αὐτοῦ δ' ἰλλομένοις ἐπὶ λαίφεσιν ἠδὲ καὶ ἱστῷ
330 κεκλιμένῳ μάλα πάντες ἐπισχερὼ ἑδριόωντο.
τοῖσιν δ' Αἴσονος υἱὸς ἐυφρονέων μετέειπεν·
"ἄλλα μέν, ὅσσα τε νηὶ ἐφοπλίσσασθαι ἔοικεν,
πάντα μάλ' εὖ κατὰ κόσμον ἐπαρτέα κεῖται ἰοῦσιν.
τῶ οὐκ ἂν δηναιὸν ἐχοίμεθα τοῖο ἕκητι
335 ναυτιλίης, ὅτε μοῦνον ἐπιπνεύσουσιν ἀῆται.
ἀλλά, φίλοι, ξυνὸς γὰρ ἐς Ἑλλάδα νόστος ὀπίσσω,
ξυναὶ δ' ἄμμι πέλονται ἐς Αἰήταο κέλευθοι,
τούνεκα νῦν τὸν ἄριστον ἀφειδήσαντες ἕλεσθε
ὄρχαμον ὑμείων, ᾧ κεν τὰ ἕκαστα μέλοιτο,
340 νείκεα συνθεσίας τε μετὰ ξείνοισι βαλέσθαι."
ὣς φάτο· πάπτηναν δὲ νέοι θρασὺν Ἡρακλῆα
ἥμενον ἐν μέσσοισι, μιῇ δέ ἑ πάντες ἀυτῇ
σημαίνειν ἐπέτελλον· ὁ δ' αὐτόθεν, ἔνθα περ ἧστο,
δεξιτερὴν ἀνὰ χεῖρα τανύσσατο, φώνησέν τε·
345 "μή τις ἐμοὶ τόδε κῦδος ὀπαζέτω· οὐ γὰρ ἐγώ γε
πείσομαι, ὥς τε καὶ ἄλλον ἀναστήσεσθαι ἐρύξω.
αὐτός, ὅ τις ξυνάγειρε, καὶ ἀρχεύοι ὁμάδοιο."
ἦ ῥα μέγα φρονέων· ἐπὶ δ' ἤνεον, ὡς ἐκέλευεν

324 ἀμφέχετ' ὤμους Ω: αμπεχετ' ωμοις Π²
333 μάλ' Huet: γὰρ Ω   339 ὑμείων Ω: ἡμείων Ε

the will of Pelias. Argus, Arestor's son, was wearing around his shoulders a shaggy black oxhide that reached to his feet, while the other wore a beautiful, double-folded cloak, which his sister Pelopeia had given him. Nevertheless, Jason refrained from questioning the two of them in detail, and bade all the men sit down in assembly. There, upon the furled sails and the mast that lay on the ground, they all took their seats in order. And Jason addressed them with kind intent:

"All the equipment that a ship should have lies in good order, ready for our departure. Therefore, we shall not for long delay our voyage on that account, if only the breezes will blow. But, my friends, since common to us all is our return again to Hellas, and common to us all is our voyage to Aeetes' land, therefore now without restraint choose the best man as your[47] leader, who will see to each thing, to take on quarrels and agreements with foreigners."

Thus he spoke, and the young men looked around at bold Heracles sitting in their midst and with one voice all kept enjoining him to be in command, but he, from where he was sitting, stretched forth his right hand and said:

"Let no one offer me this honor, for I will not consent, and likewise I shall restrain anyone else from rising. Let the one himself who gathered us together also lead this host."

Thus he spoke high-mindedly,[48] and they approved what

[47] Or, reading ἡμείων with many MSS, *our*. Alternately, *choose the best of you* (or *us*) *to be leader*.

[48] Or *proudly, haughtily*. The same expression is used of haughty Amycus at 2.19 and proud Idas at 3.517.

Ἡρακλέης. ἀνὰ δ' αὐτὸς ἀρήιος ὥρνυτ' Ἰήσων
350 γηθόσυνος, καὶ τοῖα λιλαιομένοις ἀγόρευεν·
"εἰ μὲν δή μοι κῦδος ἐπιτρωπᾶτε μέλεσθαι,
μηκέτ' ἔπειθ', ὡς καὶ πρίν, ἐρητύοιτο κέλευθα.
νῦν γε μὲν ἤδη Φοῖβον ἀρεσσάμενοι θυέεσσιν
δαῖτ' ἐντυνώμεσθα παρασχεδόν. ὄφρα δ' ἴωσιν
355 δμῶες ἐμοὶ σταθμῶν σημάντορες, οἷσι μέμηλεν
δεῦρο βόας ἀγέληθεν ἐὺ κρίναντας ἐλάσσαι,
τόφρα κε νῆ' ἐρύσαιμεν ἔσω ἁλός, ὅπλα τε πάντα
ἐνθέμενοι πεπάλαχθε κατὰ κληῖδας ἐρετμά.
τείως δ' αὖ καὶ βωμὸν ἐπάκτιον Ἐμβασίοιο
360 θείομεν Ἀπόλλωνος, ὅ μοι χρείων ὑπέδεκτο
σημανέειν δείξειν τε πόρους ἁλός, εἴ κε θυηλαῖς
οὗ ἕθεν ἐξάρχωμαι ἀεθλεύων βασιλῆι."
    ἦ ῥα, καὶ εἰς ἔργον πρῶτος τράπεθ'. οἱ δ'
        ἐπανέσταν
πειθόμενοι· ἀπὸ δ' εἵματ' ἐπήτριμα νηήσαντο
365 λείῳ ἐπὶ πλαταμῶνι, τὸν οὐκ ἐπέβαλλε θάλασσα
κύμασι, χειμερίη δὲ πάλαι ἀποέκλυσεν ἅλμη.
νῆα δ' ἐπικρατέως Ἄργου ὑποθημοσύνῃσιν
ἔζωσαν πάμπρωτον ἐυστρεφεῖ ἔνδοθεν ὅπλῳ
τεινάμενοι ἑκάτερθεν, ἵν' ἐὺ ἀραροίατο γόμφοις
370 δούρατα καὶ ῥοθίοιο βίην ἔχοι ἀντιόωσαν.
σκάπτον δ' αἶψα κατ' εὖρος, ὅσον περιβάλλετο
        χῶρος,

354 ἴωσι(ν) AωE: ἴασι(ν) Π3L   371 περιβάλλετο Π3ωd:
περιβάλλεται m | χῶρος Π3Ω: χῶρον G

Heracles was urging. Warlike Jason himself rose joyfully and addressed these words to the eager men:

"If in fact you entrust this honor to my care, then no longer, as before, let the voyage be delayed. Right now, however, let us propitiate Phoebus with sacrifices and immediately prepare a feast. But until the servants arrive, the overseers of my farms who have been charged with carefully selecting cattle from the herd and driving them here, we will haul the ship into the sea, and you can put all the tackle on board and draw lots for the oars along the benches. In the meantime, let us also build an altar on the shore for Apollo Embasius,[49] who in an oracle promised to give me signs and point out the passages of the sea, if with sacrifices in his honor I would begin my task for the king."

He spoke and was the first to turn to the task. The others stood up in obedience and heaped their garments, one on top of another, on a smooth flat stone, which the sea did not beat with its waves, but which the stormy sea-water had long ago washed clean. First of all, on Argus' instructions, they firmly girded the ship with a rope well twisted inside,[50] and pulled it taut on both ends, so that the planks would be joined securely by their pegs and withstand the opposing force of the surge. And immediately they began digging a trench as wide as the space occupied by the ship

---

[49] "Of Embarkation."

[50] The rope presumably goes outside, around the hull, to avoid separation of the planks. ἔνδοθεν ("inside") indicates that the rope was twisted in upon itself (Vian).

ἠδὲ κατὰ πρώειραν ἔσω ἁλός, ὁσσάτιόν περ
ἑλκομένη χείρεσσιν ἐπιδραμέεσθαι ἔμελλεν.
αἰεὶ δὲ προτέρω χθαμαλώτερον ἐξελάχαινον
375 στείρης· ἐν δ᾽ ὁλκῷ ξεστὰς στορέσαντο φάλαγγας·
τὴν δὲ κατάντη κλῖναν ἐπὶ πρώτῃσι φάλαγξιν,
ὥς κεν ὀλισθαίνουσα δι᾽ αὐτάων φορέοιτο.
ὕψι δ᾽ ἄρ᾽ ἔνθα καὶ ἔνθα μεταστρέψαντες ἐρετμὰ
πήχυιον προύχοντα περὶ σκαλμοῖσιν ἔδησαν.
380 τῶν δ᾽ ἐναμοιβαδὶς αὐτοὶ ἐνέσταθεν ἀμφοτέρωθεν,
στέρνα θ᾽ ὁμοῦ καὶ χεῖρας ἐπήλασαν. ἐν δ᾽ ἄρα
    Τῖφυς
βήσαθ᾽, ἵν᾽ ὀτρύνειε νέους κατὰ καιρὸν ἐρύσσαι.
κεκλόμενος δ᾽ ἤϋσε μάλα μέγα· τοὶ δὲ παρᾶσσον
ᾧ κράτεϊ βρίσαντε μιῇ στυφέλιξαν ἐρωῇ
385 νειόθεν ἐξ ἕδρης, ἐπὶ δ᾽ ἐρρώσαντο πόδεσσιν
προπροβιαζόμενοι· ἡ δ᾽ ἕσπετο Πηλιὰς Ἀργὼ
ῥίμφα μάλ᾽, οἱ δ᾽ ἑκάτερθεν ἐπίαχον ἀίσσοντες.
αἱ δ᾽ ἄρ᾽ ὑπὸ τρόπιδι στιβαρῇ στενάχοντο
    φάλαγγες
τριβόμεναι, περὶ δέ σφιν ἀιδνὴ κήκιε λιγνὺς
390 βριθοσύνῃ· κατόλισθε δ᾽ ἔσω ἁλός· οἱ δέ μιν αὖθι
ἂψ ἀνασειράζοντες ἔχον προτέρωσε κιοῦσαν.
σκαλμοῖς δ᾽ ἀμφὶς ἐρετμὰ κατήρτυον, ἐν δέ οἱ ἱστὸν
λαίφεά τ᾽ εὐποίητα καὶ ἁρμαλιὴν ἐβάλοντο.
    αὐτὰρ ἐπεὶ τὰ ἕκαστα περιφραδέως ἀλέγυναν,
395 κληῖδας μὲν πρῶτα πάλῳ διεμοιρήσαντο,

384 βρίσαντε Π³LD: βρίσαντες AωE

34

and as long as the distance from prow to sea that it would travel when pulled by their hands. As they went forward, they dug it ever deeper below the keel. In the trench they laid smooth rollers, and on the first rollers they inclined the ship downwards, so that it would slide along them and be carried forward. Then on both sides they reversed the oars with blades up on deck and handles projecting a cubit, and tied them around the oarlocks. They stationed themselves on either side, one behind each oar, and pushed with their chests and hands. Then Tiphys went on board to urge the youths[51] to pull at the right moment. He shouted a very loud command, and they, immediately applying all their strength, with one thrust dislodged it from its support underneath, and, straining with their feet, forced it forward. The Pelian[52] Argo swiftly followed, and the men on both sides shouted out as they rushed on. And the rollers groaned as they were scraped beneath the sturdy keel, and around them spewed dark smoke because of the weight. It glided down into the sea, and from there[53] they pulled back on the ropes and restrained its forward movement. They attached the oars to the oarlocks on both sides, and loaded on board the mast, well-stitched sails, and provisions.

Now when they had carefully seen to each of these things, they first apportioned the benches by lot, two men

[51] These are presumably the ones who will check the forward motion of the ship once it enters the water.

[52] The Argo's wood came mainly from mount Pelion.

[53] I.e. on land.

ἄνδρ' ἐντυναμένω δοιὼ μίαν· ἐκ δ' ἄρα μέσσην
ᾕρεον Ἡρακλῆι καὶ ἡρώων ἄτερ ἄλλων
Ἀγκαίῳ, Τεγέης ὅς ῥα πτολίεθρον ἔναιεν.
τοῖς μέσσην οἴοισιν ἀπὸ κληῖδα λίποντο
400 αὕτως, οὔ τι πάλῳ· ἐπὶ δ' ἔτρεπον αἰνήσαντες
Τῖφυν ἐυστείρης οἰήια νηὸς ἔρυσθαι.

ἔνθεν δ' αὖ λάιγγας ἁλὸς σχεδὸν ὀχλίζοντες
νήεον αὐτόθι βωμὸν ἐπάκτιον Ἀπόλλωνος
Ἀκτίου Ἐμβασίοιό τ' ἐπώνυμον· ὦκα δὲ τοί γε
405 φιτροὺς ἀζαλέης στόρεσαν καθύπερθεν ἐλαίης.
τείως δ' αὖτ' ἀγέληθεν ἐπιπροέηκαν ἄγοντες
βουκόλοι Αἰσονίδαο δύω βόε. τοὺς δ' ἐρύσαντο
κουρότεροι ἑτάρων βωμοῦ σχεδόν, οἱ δ' ἄρ' ἔπειτα
χέρνιβά τ' οὐλοχύτας τε παρέσχεθον. αὐτὰρ Ἰήσων
410 εὔχετο κεκλόμενος πατρώιον Ἀπόλλωνα·
    "κλῦθι ἄναξ, Παγασάς τε πόλιν τ' Αἰσωνίδα
        ναίων,
ἡμετέροιο τοκῆος ἐπώνυμον, ὅς μοι ὑπέστης
Πυθοῖ χρειομένῳ ἄνυσιν καὶ πείραθ' ὁδοῖο
σημανέειν, αὐτὸς γὰρ ἐπαίτιος ἔπλευ ἀέθλων·
415 αὐτὸς νῦν ἄγε νῆα σὺν ἀρτεμέεσσιν ἑταίροις
κεῖσέ τε καὶ παλίνορσον ἐς Ἑλλάδα· σοὶ δ' ἂν
        ὀπίσσω
τόσσων, ὅσσοι κεν νοστήσομεν, ἀγλαὰ ταύρων
ἱρὰ πάλιν βωμῷ ἐπιθήσομεν· ἄλλα δὲ Πυθοῖ,
ἄλλα δ' ἐς Ὀρτυγίην ἀπερείσια δῶρα κομίσσω.
420 νῦν δ' ἴθι, καὶ τήνδ' ἡμιν, Ἑκηβόλε, δέξο θυηλήν,
ἥν τοι τῆσδ' ἐπίβαθρα χάριν προτεθείμεθα νηὸς

occupying each. But they assigned the middle one to Heracles and, to the exclusion of the other heroes, Ancaeus, who lived in the city of Tegea. For them alone they reserved the middle bench just as it was, without any lot. And by acclamation they entrusted Tiphys with managing the helm of the strong-keeled ship.

Next, they heaved up stones near the sea and raised an altar there on the shore to Apollo in his titles of Actius[54] and Embasius. They quickly laid logs of dried olive wood on top of it. In the meantime, Jason's cowherds had driven before them two bulls from the herd. These the younger comrades dragged near the altar, and the others then brought lustral water and barley meal. But Jason called on Apollo of his fathers and prayed:

"Hear me, lord, you who dwell in Pagasae and the Aesonian city named for my father, you who promised me, when I sought an oracle at Pytho, that you would reveal the accomplishment and ways to conduct my journey, since you yourself were the cause of the enterprise.[55] Now, you yourself guide the ship there and back again to Hellas with my comrades safe and sound, and thereafter in your honor we will again place on this altar glorious sacrifices of as many bulls as the number of us who return, and I shall bring countless other gifts to Pytho and to Ortygia.[56] But for now, Far-Shooter, come and accept this sacrifice of ours, the very first tribute that we offer you for an auspi-

---

[54] "Of the Shore."   [55] Apollo's oracle caused Pelias to send Jason off (1.5–17); Apollo approved of the journey when Jason inquired of his oracle at Delphi and promised to help (cf. 1.359–362); and he even gave him two tripods to take with him (cf. 4.529–532).   [56] Ortygia was the ancient name for Delos.

πρωτίστην· λύσαιμι δ', ἄναξ, ἐπ' ἀπήμονι μοίρῃ
πείσματα σὴν διὰ μῆτιν· ἐπιπνεύσειε δ' ἀήτης
μείλιχος, ᾧ κ' ἐπὶ πόντον ἐλευσόμεθ' εὐδιόωντες."
425 ἦ, καὶ ἅμ' εὐχωλῇ προχύτας βάλε. τὼ δ' ἐπὶ
βουσὶν
ζωσάσθην, Ἀγκαῖος ὑπέρβιος Ἡρακλέης τε.
ἤτοι ὁ μὲν ῥοπάλῳ μέσσον κάρη ἀμφὶ μέτωπα
πλῆξεν, ὁ δ' ἀθρόος αὖθι πεσὼν ἐνερείσατο γαίῃ·
Ἀγκαῖος δ' ἑτέροιο κατὰ πλατὺν αὐχένα κόψας
430 χαλκείῳ πελέκει κρατεροὺς διέκερσε τένοντας·
ἤριπε δ' ἀμφοτέροισι περιρρηδὴς κεράεσσιν.
τοὺς δ' ἕταροι σφάξαν τε θοῶς, δεῖράν τε βοείας,
κόπτον, δαίτρευόν τε, καὶ ἱερὰ μῆρ' ἐτάμοντο,
κὰδ δ' ἄμυδις τά γε πάντα καλύψαντες πύκα δημῷ
435 καῖον ἐπὶ σχίζῃσιν· ὁ δ' ἀκρήτους χέε λοιβὰς
Αἰσονίδης. γήθει δὲ σέλας θηεύμενος Ἴδμων
πάντοσε λαμπόμενον θυέων ἄπο τοῖό τε λιγνὺν
πορφυρέαις ἑλίκεσσιν ἐναίσιμον ἀΐσσουσαν·
αἶψα δ' ἀπηλεγέως νόον ἔκφατο Λητοΐδαο·
440 "ὑμῖν μὲν δὴ μοῖρα θεῶν χρειώ τε περῆσαι
ἐνθάδε κῶας ἄγοντας· ἀπειρέσιοι δ' ἐνὶ μέσσῳ
κεῖσέ τε δεῦρό τ' ἔασιν ἀνερχομένοισιν ἄεθλοι.
αὐτὰρ ἐμοὶ θανέειν στυγερῇ ὑπὸ δαίμονος αἴσῃ
τηλόθι που πέπρωται ἐπ' Ἀσίδος ἠπείροιο.
445 ὧδε κακοῖς δεδαὼς ἔτι καὶ πάρος οἰωνοῖσιν
πότμον ἐμόν, πάτρης ἐξήιον, ὄφρ' ἐπιβαίην
νηός, εὐκλείη δὲ δόμοις ἐπιβάντι λίπηται."
ὣς ἄρ' ἔφη· κοῦροι δὲ θεοπροπίης ἀίοντες

cious embarkation on this ship. May I loose the cables, lord, with a destiny free from harm, relying on your counsel; and may a gentle breeze blow for us, by which we may travel in fair weather over the sea."

He spoke, and as he prayed cast the barley offering. Two comrades, proud Ancaeus and Heracles, girded themselves to slay the bulls. With his club the latter struck his bull in the middle of the head upon its brow; it fell immediately in a heap and lay on the ground. Ancaeus struck the broad neck of the other with his bronze ax and cut through the strong tendons; it fell forward on both horns. The comrades quickly slit their throats and skinned the hides; they dismembered them, cut them up into portions, and removed the sacred thigh bones, and wrapping these all together with a thick coating of fat burned them on the firewood, and Jason poured libations of unmixed wine. Idmon rejoiced to see the flame burning brightly all around from the sacrifice and its smoke rising favorably in dark spirals. At once he forthrightly declared the intention of Leto's son:

"For you men, indeed, the fate of the gods and their oracle ordain that you will return here with the fleece, but countless are the trials in between, both on your way there and returning here. But it is my destiny by the horrible decree of a god to die somewhere far away on the mainland of Asia. Even though I had learned beforehand from unfavorable bird omens that such was my doom, I left my homeland to embark upon the ship, so that, having embarked, glorious fame may be left for me at home."

Thus he spoke, and when the young men heard the

νόστῳ μὲν γήθησαν, ἄχος δ' ἕλεν Ἴδμονος αἴσῃ.
450 ἦμος δ' ἠέλιος σταθερὸν παραμείβεται ἦμαρ,
αἱ δὲ νέον σκοπέλοισιν ὑποσκιόωνται ἄρουραι,
δειελινὸν κλίνοντος ὑπὸ ζόφον ἠελίοιο,
τῆμος ἄρ' ἤδη πάντες ἐπὶ ψαμάθοισι βαθεῖαν
φυλλάδα χευάμενοι πολιοῦ πρόπαρ αἰγιαλοῖο
455 κέκλινθ' ἑξείης· παρὰ δέ σφισι μυρί' ἔκειτο
εἴδατα καὶ μέθυ λαρόν, ἀφυσσαμένων προχοῇσιν
οἰνοχόων. μετέπειτα δ' ἀμοιβαδὶς ἀλλήλοισιν
μυθεῦνθ', οἷά τε πολλὰ νέοι παρὰ δαιτὶ καὶ οἴνῳ
τερπνῶς ἐψιόωνται, ὅτ' ἄατος ὕβρις ἀπείη.
460 ἔνθ' αὖτ' Αἰσονίδης μὲν ἀμήχανος εἰν ἑοῖ αὐτῷ
πορφύρεσκεν ἕκαστα κατηφιόωντι ἐοικώς·
τὸν δ' ἄρ' ὑποφρασθεὶς μεγάλῃ ὀπὶ νείκεσεν Ἴδας·
    "Αἰσονίδη, τίνα τήνδε μετὰ φρεσὶ μῆτιν
        ἑλίσσεις;
    αὔδα ἐνὶ μέσσοισι τεὸν νόον. ἦέ σε δαμνᾷ
465 τάρβος ἐπιπλόμενον, τό τ' ἀνάλκιδας ἄνδρας ἀτύζει;
ἴστω νῦν δόρυ θοῦρον, ὅτῳ περιώσιον ἄλλων
κῦδος ἐνὶ πτολέμοισιν ἀείρομαι, οὐδέ μ' ὀφέλλει
Ζεὺς τόσον, ὁσσάτιόν περ ἐμὸν δόρυ, μή νύ τι πῆμα
λοίγιον ἔσσεσθαι μηδ' ἀκράαντον ἄεθλον
470 Ἴδεω ἑσπομένοιο, καὶ εἰ θεὸς ἀντιόωτο·
τοῖόν μ' Ἀρήνηθεν ἀοσσητῆρα κομίζεις."
    ἦ, καὶ ἐπισχόμενος πλεῖον δέπας ἀμφοτέρῃσιν
πῖνε χαλίκρητον λαρὸν μέθυ, δεύετο δ' οἴνῳ
χείλεα κυάνεαί τε γενειάδες. οἱ δ' ὁμάδησαν
475 πάντες ὁμῶς, Ἴδμων δὲ καὶ ἀμφαδίην ἀγόρευσεν·

prophecy, they rejoiced in their return, but sorrow seized them at Idmon's fate. And at the time when the sun passes midday, and the fields are just filling with shadows from the peaks as the sun inclines beneath the evening darkness, at that time all the men had already spread thick couches of leaves on the sand and were reclining side by side along the gray strand. Beside them lay great quantities of food and sweet wine, which cupbearers had drawn off in jugs. Afterwards, they told stories to one another in turn, of the kind young men often tell as they enjoy themselves pleasantly over a meal and wine, when unbridled rudeness is absent. But at that time, Jason, all helpless, was pondering every concern within himself, like a man in despair. And then Idas spied him and chided him in a loud voice:

"Jason, what is this plan you are turning over in your mind? Declare your thoughts in our midst. Is it fear, the thing that terrifies cowardly men, which assaults and overwhelms you? Let my witness now be this raging spear, with which I win more glory in battles than any other men—nor does Zeus aid me as much as my own spear—that no calamity will be fatal nor any task unaccomplished with Idas on hand, even if a god should stand in the way. Such an ally am I that you are bringing from Arene."

Thus he spoke and, grasping a full cup in both hands, drank the sweet, unmixed wine, and his lips and dark beard were drenched with it. All the men together raised a clamor, but Idmon even spoke out openly:

"δαιμόνιε, φρονέεις ὀλοφώια καὶ πάρος αὐτῷ,
ἦέ τοι εἰς ἄτην ζωρὸν μέθυ θαρσαλέον κῆρ
οἰδάνει ἐν στήθεσσι, θεοὺς δ' ἀνέηκεν ἀτίζειν;
ἄλλοι μῦθοι ἔασι παρήγοροι, οἷσί περ ἀνὴρ
480 θαρσύνοι ἕταρον· σὺ δ' ἀτάσθαλα πάμπαν ἔειπας.
τοῖα φάτις καὶ τοὺς πρὶν ἐπιφλύειν μακάρεσσιν
υἷας Ἀλωιάδας, οἷς οὐδ' ὅσον ἰσοφαρίζεις
ἠνορέην· ἔμπης δὲ θοοῖς ἐδάμησαν ὀιστοῖς
ἄμφω Λητοΐδαο, καὶ ἴφθιμοί περ ἐόντες."
485 ὣς ἔφατ'· ἐκ δ' ἐγέλασσεν ἄδην Ἀφαρήιος Ἴδας,
καί μιν ἐπιλλίζων ἠμείβετο κερτομίοισιν·
"ἄγρει νυν τόδε σῇσι θεοπροπίῃσιν ἐνίσπες,
εἰ καὶ ἐμοὶ τοιόνδε θεοὶ τελέουσιν ὄλεθρον,
οἷον Ἀλωιάδῃσι πατὴρ τεὸς ἐγγυάλιξεν·
490 φράζεο δ' ὅππως χεῖρας ἐμὰς σόος ἐξαλέοιο,
χρειὼ θεσπίζων μεταμώνιον εἴ κεν ἁλώῃς."
χώετ' ἐνιπτάζων· προτέρω δέ κε νεῖκος ἐτύχθη,
εἰ μὴ δηριόωντας ὁμοκλήσαντες ἑταῖροι
αὐτός τ' Αἰσονίδης κατερήτυεν· ἂν δὲ καὶ Ὀρφεὺς
495 λαιῇ ἀνασχόμενος κίθαριν πείραζεν ἀοιδῆς.
ἤειδεν δ' ὡς γαῖα καὶ οὐρανὸς ἠδὲ θάλασσα,
τὸ πρὶν ἐπ' ἀλλήλοισι μιῇ συναρηρότα μορφῇ,
νείκεος ἐξ ὀλοοῖο διέκριθεν ἀμφὶς ἕκαστα·
ἠδ' ὡς ἔμπεδον αἰὲν ἐν αἰθέρι τέκμαρ ἔχουσιν
500 ἄστρα σεληναίη τε καὶ ἠελίοιο κέλευθοι·
οὔρεά θ' ὡς ἀνέτειλε, καὶ ὡς ποταμοὶ κελάδοντες

500 σεληναίη Ω: σεληναίης Flangini

42

"You fool! Have you held self-destructive ideas before this as well, or is the pure wine swelling the impetuous heart in your chest to ruin, and has it impelled you to disrespect the gods? There are other consoling words with which a man could encourage his comrade, but what you have said is utterly outrageous. Such boasts, they say, did the sons of Aloeus[57] too blurt out once against the blessed gods, and you are not in the slightest equal to them in valor. And yet they both were killed by the swift arrows of Leto's son, for all their might."

Thus he spoke, and Idas, son of Aphareus, burst out laughing and, eyeing him askance, answered with cutting words:

"Come on, then, tell me this with your prophetic arts, whether the gods will bring about for me too such a death as the one your father[58] brought upon Aloeus' sons, but take thought for how you may escape from my hands alive, if you should be caught declaring a vain prophecy."

Thus he reviled him in his anger, and the strife would have gone further, had not their comrades and Jason himself rebuked the antagonists and restrained them. Then too Orpheus lifted up his lyre with his left hand and tried out a song.

He sang of how the earth, sky, and sea, at one time combined together in a single form, through deadly strife became separated each from the other; and of how the stars and moon and paths of the sun always keep their fixed place in the sky; and how the mountains arose; and how the

[57] Otus and Ephialtes, who tried to scale heaven by piling mount Ossa upon Olympus and Pelion on them (cf. *Odyssey* 11.307–320).   [58] Apollo.

αὐτῇσιν νύμφῃσι καὶ ἑρπετὰ πάντ᾽ ἐγένοντο.
ἤειδεν δ᾽ ὡς πρῶτον Ὀφίων Εὐρυνόμη τε
Ὠκεανὶς νιφόεντος ἔχον κράτος Οὐλύμποιο·
505 ὥς τε βίῃ καὶ χερσὶν ὁ μὲν Κρόνῳ εἴκαθε τιμῆς,
ἡ δὲ Ῥέῃ, ἔπεσον δ᾽ ἐνὶ κύμασιν Ὠκεανοῖο·
οἱ δὲ τέως μακάρεσσι θεοῖς Τιτῆσιν ἄνασσον,
ὄφρα Ζεὺς ἔτι κοῦρος, ἔτι φρεσὶ νήπια εἰδώς,
Δικταῖον ναίεσκεν ὑπὸ σπέος, οἱ δέ μιν οὔ πω
510 γηγενέες Κύκλωπες ἐκαρτύναντο κεραυνῷ
βροντῇ τε στεροπῇ τε· τὰ γὰρ Διὶ κῦδος ὀπάζει.
ἦ, καὶ ὁ μὲν φόρμιγγα σὺν ἀμβροσίῃ σχέθεν
αὐδῇ·
τοὶ δ᾽ ἄμοτον λήξαντος ἔτι προύχοντο κάρηνα
πάντες ὁμῶς ὀρθοῖσιν ἐπ᾽ οὔασιν ἠρεμέοντες
515 κηληθμῷ· τοῖον σφιν ἐνέλλιπε θελκτὺν ἀοιδῆς.
οὐδ᾽ ἐπὶ δὴν μετέπειτα κερασσάμενοι Διὶ λοιβάς,
ἡ θέμις, ἑστηῶτες ἐπὶ γλώσσῃσι χέοντο
αἰθομέναις, ὕπνου δὲ διὰ κνέφας ἐμνώοντο.
αὐτὰρ ὅτ᾽ αἰγλήεσσα φαεινοῖς ὄμμασιν Ἠὼς
520 Πηλίου αἰπεινὰς ἴδεν ἄκριας, ἐκ δ᾽ ἀνέμοιο
εὔδιοι ἐκλύζοντο τινασσομένης ἁλὸς ἄκραι,
δὴ τότ᾽ ἀνέγρετο Τῖφυς, ἄφαρ δ᾽ ὀρόθυνεν ἑταίρους
βαινέμεναί τ᾽ ἐπὶ νῆα καὶ ἀρτύνασθαι ἐρετμά.
σμερδαλέον δὲ λιμὴν Παγασήιος ἠδὲ καὶ αὐτὴ
525 Πηλιὰς ἴαχεν Ἀργὼ ἐπισπέρχουσα νέεσθαι·
ἐν γάρ οἱ δόρυ θεῖον ἐλήλατο, τό ῥ᾽ ἀνὰ μέσσην

44

echoing rivers with their nymphs and all the land animals came to be. He sang of how, in the beginning, Ophion and Ocean's daughter Eurynome held sway over snowy Olympus, and of how, through force of hand, he ceded rule to Cronus and she to Rhea, and they fell into the waves of the Ocean. These two in the meantime ruled over the blessed Titan gods, while Zeus, still a child and still thinking childish thoughts, dwelt in the Dictaean cave, and the earthborn Cyclopes had not yet armed him with the thunderbolt, thunder, and lightning, for these give Zeus his glory.

Thus he sang, and hushed his lyre along with his divinely beautiful voice. But they, although he had ceased, still leaned their heads forward longingly, one and all, with intent ears, immobile with enchantment—such was the spell of the song that he left within them. Not long thereafter they mixed libations for Zeus, as is right, and stood and poured them on the victims' burning tongues, and turned their thoughts to sleeping through the night.

But when radiant Dawn with shining eyes beheld the steep cliffs of Pelion, and in fair weather the headlands were being washed as the sea was stirred by a breeze, then Tiphys awoke and immediately roused his comrades to board the ship and ready the oars. The harbor of Pagasae let out a terrible shout, and so did the Pelian Argo itself, urging them to depart, for in it was fastened a divine beam

---

515 θεκλτὺν Lobeck: θέλκτυν E: θέλκτην Ω: θέεκλτρον Meineke: θέλξιν Campbell
517 ἑστηῶτες ἐπὶ Mooney: ἐστὶ τέως ἐπί τε Ω

στεῖραν Ἀθηναίη Δωδωνίδος ἥρμοσε φηγοῦ.
οἱ δ᾽ ἀνὰ σέλματα βάντες ἐπισχερὼ ἀλλήλοισιν,
ὡς ἐδάσαντο πάροιθεν ἐρεσσέμεν ᾧ ἐνὶ χώρῳ,
530 εὐκόσμως σφετέροισι παρ᾽ ἔντεσιν ἑδριόωντο.
μέσσῳ δ᾽ Ἀγκαῖος μέγα τε σθένος Ἡρακλῆος
ἵζανον, ἄγχι δέ οἱ ῥόπαλον θέτο· καί οἱ ἔνερθεν
ποσσὶν ὑπεκλύσθη νηὸς τρόπις. εἵλκετο δ᾽ ἤδη
πείσματα, καὶ μέθυ λεῖβον ὕπερθ᾽ ἁλός· αὐτὰρ
        Ἰήσων
535 δακρυόεις γαίης ἀπὸ πατρίδος ὄμματ᾽ ἔνεικεν.
οἱ δ᾽, ὥς τ᾽ ἠίθεοι Φοίβῳ χορὸν ἢ ἐνὶ Πυθοῖ
ἤ που ἐν Ὀρτυγίῃ ἢ ἐφ᾽ ὕδασιν Ἰσμηνοῖο
στησάμενοι, φόρμιγγος ὑπαὶ περὶ βωμὸν ὁμαρτῇ
ἐμμελέως κραιπνοῖσι πέδον ῥήσσωσι πόδεσσιν·
540 ὣς οἱ ὑπ᾽ Ὀρφῆος κιθάρῃ πέπληγον ἐρετμοῖς
πόντου λάβρον ὕδωρ, ἐπὶ δὲ ῥόθια κλύζοντο.
ἀφρῷ δ᾽ ἔνθα καὶ ἔνθα κελαινὴ κήκιεν ἅλμη
δεινὸν μορμύρουσα ἐρισθενέων μένει ἀνδρῶν.
στράπτε δ᾽ ὑπ᾽ ἠελίῳ φλογὶ εἴκελα νηὸς ἰούσης
545 τεύχεα· μακραὶ δ᾽ αἰὲν ἐλευκαίνοντο κέλευθοι,
ἀτραπὸς ὣς χλοεροῖο διειδομένη πεδίοιο.
πάντες δ᾽ οὐρανόθεν λεῦσσον θεοὶ ἤματι κείνῳ
νῆα καὶ ἡμιθέων ἀνδρῶν γένος, οἳ τότ᾽ ἄριστοι
πόντον ἐπιπλώεσκον· ἐπ᾽ ἀκροτάτῃσι δὲ νύμφαι
550 Πηλιάδες κορυφῇσιν ἐθάμβεον εἰσορόωσαι

548 γένος wE: μένος LA

46

that Athena had fashioned from Dodonian oak for the middle of the keel.[59] They went to their benches one behind the other, as they had previously been allotted to row, each in his place, and took their seats in due order next to their weapons. In the middle sat Ancaeus and mighty Heracles; he placed his club next to him, and beneath his feet the ship's keel sank deep. By now the cables were being hauled in, and the men were pouring libations of wine over the sea. But Jason, in tears, turned his eyes away from his fatherland.

And they, as when young men form a chorus to honor Phoebus either in Pytho, or perhaps in Ortygia, or by the waters of Ismenus, and around the altar to the lyre's accompaniment with swift feet they beat the ground all together in rhythm—thus to the accompaniment of Orpheus' lyre did they smite the rushing water of the sea with their oars, and the surge washed over the blades. On this side and that the dark sea water bubbled with foam as it seethed furiously from the strength of the mighty men. Their armor flashed in the sunlight like a flame as the ship proceeded, and their long wake remained ever white, like a path seen across a green plain.

On that day all the gods gazed down from the sky upon the ship and the race of demigods, the best of men who then were sailing over the sea. On the highest peaks, the nymphs of Pelion marveled to see the work of Itonian[60]

[59] Oaks at Dodona, site of Zeus' oracle, were endowed with prophetic speech (cf. *Odyssey* 14.327–328).
[60] Named for Iton in Thessaly, a cult site of Athena.

47

ἔργον Ἀθηναίης Ἰτωνίδος ἠδὲ καὶ αὐτοὺς
ἥρωας χείρεσσιν ἐπικραδάοντας ἐρετμά.
αὐτὰρ ὅ γ᾽ ἐξ ὑπάτου ὄρεος κίεν ἄγχι θαλάσσης
Χείρων Φιλλυρίδης, πολιῇ δ᾽ ἐπὶ κύματος ἀγῇ
555 τέγγε πόδας, καὶ πολλὰ βαρείῃ χειρὶ κελεύων
νόστον ἐπευφήμησεν ἀκηδέα νισσομένοισιν·
σὺν καί οἱ παράκοιτις, ἐπωλένιον φορέουσα
Πηλείδην Ἀχιλῆα, φίλῳ δειδίσκετο πατρί.
      οἱ δ᾽ ὅτε δὴ λιμένος περιηγέα κάλλιπον ἀκτὴν
560 φραδμοσύνῃ μήτι τε δαΐφρονος Ἀγνιάδαο
Τίφυος, ὅς ῥ᾽ ἐνὶ χερσὶν εὔξοα τεχνηέντως
πηδάλι᾽ ἀμφίεπεσκ᾽, ὄφρ᾽ ἔμπεδον ἐξιθύνοι,
δή ῥα τότε μέγαν ἱστὸν ἐνεστήσαντο μεσόδμῃ,
δῆσαν δὲ προτόνοισι τανυσσάμενοι ἑκάτερθεν·
565 κὰδ δ᾽ αὐτοῦ λίνα χεῦαν ἐπ᾽ ἠλακάτην ἐρύσαντες.
ἐν δὲ λιγὺς πέσεν οὖρος· ἐπ᾽ ἰκριόφιν δὲ κάλωας
ξεστῇσιν περόνῃσι διακριδὸν ἀμφιβαλόντες
Τισαίην εὔκηλοι ὑπὲρ δολιχὴν θέον ἄκρην.
τοῖσι δὲ φορμίζων εὐθήμονι μέλπεν ἀοιδῇ
570 Οἰάγροιο πάις Νηοσσόον εὐπατέρειαν
Ἄρτεμιν, ἣ κείνας σκοπιὰς ἁλὸς ἀμφιέπεσκεν
ῥυομένη καὶ γαῖαν Ἰωλκίδα. τοὶ δὲ βαθείης
ἰχθύες ἀίσσοντες ὕπερθ᾽ ἁλός, ἄμμιγα παύροις
ἄπλετοι, ὑγρὰ κέλευθα διασκαίροντες ἕποντο.
575 ὡς δ᾽ ὁπότ᾽ ἀγραύλοιο κατ᾽ ἴχνια σημαντῆρος
μυρία μῆλ᾽ ἐφέπονται ἄδην κεκορημένα ποίης

48

Athena and the heroes themselves plying the oars with their hands. And Cheiron, Philyra's son, came down from the mountaintop to the sea, and, wetting his feet in the gray break of the surf, repeatedly waved encouragement with his mighty hand and wished them a safe return as they set out. And with him his wife,[61] holding Peleus' son Achilles in her arms, showed him to his dear father.

Then, when they had left behind the circular shore of the harbor guided by the instructions and expertise of wise Tiphys, Hagnias' son, who skillfully managed the well-polished tiller in his hands to steer a steady course, they set up the great mast in the mast bed and secured it with forestays which they tightened on both sides. They drew the sail to the top of the mast and let it down from there. A whistling breeze fell upon it, and on the deck they wound the lines[62] separately around the polished cleats and calmly sped past the long Tisaean headland. The son of Oeagrus played his lyre for them and in a well composed song sang of Artemis Ship-Preserver, child of a great father,[63] the goddess who watched over those peaks by the sea and protected the land of Iolcus. And fish darted above the deep sea, great mixed with small, and followed along, leaping through the watery paths. And as when countless sheep follow in the footsteps of a rustic shepherd to the fold after having had

---

[61] Chariclo.

[62] Here probably the sheets attached to the lower corners of the sail; but elsewhere κάλωες are halyards.   [63] Zeus.

---

551 Ἰτωνίδος L³ᵞʳΣΩˡᵉᵐ Et. Magn. et Et. Gen.: Τριτωνίδος LυΕΣˡˡᵉᵐ   556 ἀκηδέα Ω: ἀπηρέα Test.

573 ὕπερθ' Ω: ὑπὲξ Campbell (cf. 4.933)

49

εἰς αὖλιν, ὁ δέ τ' εἶσι πάρος σύριγγι λιγείῃ
καλὰ μελιζόμενος νόμιον μέλος· ὡς ἄρα τοί γε
ὡμάρτευν· τὴν δ' αἰὲν ἐπασσύτερος φέρεν οὖρος.
580   αὐτίκα δ' ἠερίη πολυλήιος αἶα Πελασγῶν
δύετο, Πηλιάδας δὲ παρεξήμειβον ἐρίπνας
αἰὲν ἐπιπροθέοντες, ἔδυνε δὲ Σηπιὰς ἄκρη·
φαίνετο δ' εἰναλίη Σκίαθος, φαίνοντο δ' ἄπωθεν
Πειρεσιαὶ Μάγνησσά θ' ὑπεύδιος ἠπείροιο
585   ἀκτὴ καὶ τύμβος Δολοπήιος· ἔνθ' ἄρα τοί γε
ἑσπέριοι ἀνέμοιο παλιμπνοίῃσιν ἔκελσαν·
καί μιν κυδαίνοντες ὑπὸ κνέφας ἔντομα μήλων
κεῖαν ὀρινομένης ἁλὸς οἴδματι· διπλόα δ' ἀκταῖς
ἤματ' ἐλινύεσκον· ἀτὰρ τριτάτῳ προέηκαν
590   νῆα, τανυσσάμενοι περιώσιον ὑψόθι λαῖφος.
τὴν δ' ἀκτὴν Ἀφέτας Ἀργοῦς ἔτι κικλήσκουσιν.
    ἔνθεν δὲ προτέρωσε παρεξέθεον Μελίβοιαν,
ἀκτήν τ' αἰγιαλόν τε δυσήνεμον εἰσορόωντες·
ἠῶθεν δ' Ὁμόλην αὐτοσχεδὸν εἰσορόωντες
595   πόντῳ κεκλιμένην παρεμέτρεον· οὐδ' ἔτι δηρὸν
μέλλον ὑπὲκ ποταμοῖο βαλεῖν Ἀμύροιο ῥέεθρα.
κεῖθεν δ' Εὐρυμένας τε πολυκλύστους τε φάραγγας
Ὄσσης Οὐλύμποιό τ' ἐσέδρακον· αὐτὰρ ἔπειτα
κλίτεα Παλλήναια Καναστραίην ὑπὲρ ἄκρην
600   ἤνυσαν ἐννύχιοι πνοιῇ ἀνέμοιο θέοντες.

    593 εἰσορόωντες Ω: ἐκνεύσαντες Brunck: ἐκπερόωντες
Meineke

their fill of grass, and he goes in front, beautifully playing a
shepherd's tune on his shrill pipes—thus then did the fish
accompany the ship, and a steady wind bore it ever on-
ward.

Soon the grain-rich land of the Pelasgians sank into the
mist, and, as they sped ever onward, they passed by the
rugged cliffs of Pelion, and the Sepian headland sank from
view. Sciathus appeared in the sea, and far off appeared
Peiresiae and, under a clear sky, the shore of Magnesia on
the mainland and the tomb of Dolops.[64] Here then they
put in at evening because the wind was blowing against
them, and they honored him at nightfall by burning sheep
as victims, while the sea was tossed by the swell. And for
two days they lingered on the shore, but on the third day
they launched the ship and spread on high the large sail.
People still call that shore Aphetae[65] of Argo.

From there they sped onward past Meliboea, seeing[66]
its coast and stormy beach. At daybreak they immediately
saw Homole situated by the sea and skirted it. Soon there-
after they were to pass by the streams of the river
Amyrus.[67] From there they beheld Eurymenae and the
sea-washed ravines of Ossa and Olympus. But then, run-
ning all night with the blowing wind, they passed the cliffs
of Pallene beyond the headland of Canastra. At dawn, as

---

[64] Dolops was a son of Hermes (schol.). The location has not
been identified.   [65] "Launching."   [66] To avoid the
awkward repetition of εἰσορόωντες in the next line, Brunck pro-
posed ἐκνεύσαντες ("avoiding") and Meineke ἐκπερόωντες ("by-
passing"). Wellauer deleted 593; Vian deleted 592–593.

[67] Before reaching the Amyrus (which actually flows into lake
Boebe) they turn east, away from the coast of Thessaly.

ἦρι δὲ νισσομένοισιν Ἄθω ἀνέτελλε κολώνη
Θρηικίη, ἣ τόσσον ἀπόπροθι Λῆμνον ἐοῦσαν,
ὅσσον ἐς ἔνδιόν κεν εὔστολος ὁλκὰς ἀνύσσαι,
ἀκροτάτῃ κορυφῇ σκιάει καὶ ἐσάχρι Μυρίνης.
605 τοῖσιν δ᾽ αὐτῆμαρ μὲν ἄεν καὶ ἐπὶ κνέφας οὖρος
πάγχυ μάλ᾽ ἀκραής, τετάνυστο δὲ λαίφεα νηός.
αὐτὰρ ἅμ᾽ ἠελίοιο βολαῖς ἀνέμοιο λιπόντος
εἰρεσίῃ κραναὴν Σιντηίδα Λῆμνον ἵκοντο.
    ἔνθ᾽ ἄμυδις πᾶς δῆμος ὑπερβασίῃσι γυναικῶν
610 νηλειῶς δέδμητο παροιχομένῳ λυκάβαντι.
δὴ γὰρ κουριδίας μὲν ἀπηνήναντο γυναῖκας
ἀνέρες ἐχθήραντες, ἔχον δ᾽ ἐπὶ ληιάδεσσιν
τρηχὺν ἔρον, ἃς αὐτοὶ ἀγίνεον ἀντιπέρηθεν
Θρηικίην δῃοῦντες· ἐπεὶ χόλος αἰνὸς ὄπαζεν
615 Κύπριδος, οὕνεκά μιν γεράων ἐπὶ δηρὸν ἄτισσαν.
ὦ μέλεαι ζήλοιό τ᾽ ἐπισμυγερῶς ἀκόρητοι·
οὐκ οἶον σὺν τῇσιν ἑοὺς ἔρραισαν ἀκοίτας
ἀμφ᾽ εὐνῇ, πᾶν δ᾽ ἄρσεν ὁμοῦ γένος, ὥς κεν ὀπίσσω
μή τινα λευγαλέοιο φόνου τίσειαν ἀμοιβήν.
620 οἴη δ᾽ ἐκ πασέων γεραροῦ περιφείσατο πατρὸς
Ὑψιπύλεια Θόαντος, ὃ δὴ κατὰ δῆμον ἄνασσεν·
λάρνακι δ᾽ ἐν κοίλῃ μιν ὕπερθ᾽ ἁλὸς ἧκε φέρεσθαι,
αἴ κε φύγῃ. καὶ τὸν μὲν ἐς Οἰνοίην ἐρύσαντο
πρόσθεν, ἀτὰρ Σίκινόν γε μεθύστερον αὐδηθεῖσαν

---

[68] Myrine on southwest Lemnos lies about fifty miles from mount Athos.

they fared on, the Thracian mountain of Athos rose before
them, which with its highest peak casts a shadow over
Lemnos even as far as Myrine, although the island lies as
far away as a well-equipped merchant ship could travel
from dawn to midday.[68] That whole day until dark a very
strong wind was blowing for them, and the ship's sails were
stretched taut. But when the wind died as the sun's rays
disappeared, it was by oar that they reached rocky
Lemnos, the Sintian island.[69]

There, all at once, the whole male population had been
ruthlessly slain by the heinous actions of the women in the
previous year. For the men had come to loathe their legiti-
mate wives and rejected them, whereas they maintained a
violent passion for the captive women whom they them-
selves brought back when pillaging Thrace on the opposite
shore. For the terrible wrath of Cypris[70] was afflicting
them, because they had for a long time deprived her of
honors. O wretched women, sad victims of insatiable jeal-
ousy! Not only did they kill their own husbands along with
the women for making love,[71] but the entire race of men as
well, to avoid paying any retribution later for the atrocious
murder. Alone of all the women, Hypsipyle saved her aged
father Thoas, who in fact was ruling over the people. She
set him to drift on the sea in a hollow chest, in the hope that
he might escape. And fishermen pulled him ashore at what
was formerly the island of Oenoe, but later called Sicinus,

---

[69] The Sintians were early inhabitants of Lemnos.

[70] Aphrodite.   [71] Similarly "for their guilty love"
(Coleridge), "for bedding together" (Green). Others translate,
"on account of their marriage beds" (Seaton) or "in their beds"
(Ardizzoni, Vian), but ἀμφί does not mean "in."

625 νῆσον, ἐπακτῆρες, Σικίνου ἄπο, τόν ῥα Θόαντι
νηιὰς Οἰνοίη νύμφη τέκεν εὐνηθεῖσα.
τῇσι δὲ βουκόλιαί τε βοῶν χάλκειά τε δύνειν
τεύχεα πυροφόρους τε διατμήξασθαι ἀρούρας
ῥηίτερον πάσῃσιν Ἀθηναίης πέλεν ἔργων,
630 οἷς αἰεὶ τὸ πάροιθεν ὁμίλεον. ἀλλὰ γὰρ ἔμπης
ἦ θαμὰ δὴ πάπταινον ἐπὶ πλατὺν ὄμμασι πόντον
δείματι λευγαλέῳ, ὁπότε Θρήικες ἴασιν.
τῶ καὶ ὅτ᾽ ἐγγύθι νήσου ἐρεσσομένην ἴδον Ἀργώ,
αὐτίκα πασσυδίῃ πυλέων ἔκτοσθε Μυρίνης
635 δήια τεύχεα δῦσαι ἐς αἰγιαλὸν προχέοντο,
Θυιάσιν ὠμοβόροις ἴκελαι· φὰν γάρ που ἱκάνειν
Θρήικας· ἡ δ᾽ ἅμα τῇσι Θοαντιὰς Ὑψιπύλεια
δῦν᾽ ἐνὶ τεύχεσι πατρός. ἀμηχανίῃ δ᾽ ἐχέοντο
ἄφθογγοι, τοῖόν σφιν ἐπὶ δέος ᾐωρεῖτο.
640 τείως δ᾽ αὖτ᾽ ἐκ νηὸς ἀριστῆες προέηκαν
Αἰθαλίδην κήρυκα θοόν, τῷ πέρ τε μέλεσθαι
ἀγγελίας καὶ σκῆπτρον ἐπέτρεπον Ἑρμείαο
σφωιτέροιο τοκῆος, ὅς οἱ μνῆστιν πόρε πάντων
ἄφθιτον· οὐδ᾽ ἔτι νῦν περ ἀποιχομένου Ἀχέροντος
645 δίνας ἀπροφάτους ψυχὴν ἐπιδέδρομε λήθη·
ἀλλ᾽ ἥ γ᾽ ἔμπεδον αἰὲν ἀμειβομένη μεμόρηται,
ἄλλοθ᾽ ὑποχθονίοις ἐναρίθμιος, ἄλλοτ᾽ ἐς αὐγὰς
ἠελίου ζωοῖσι μετ᾽ ἀνδράσιν. ἀλλὰ τί μύθους
Αἰθαλίδεω χρειώ με διηνεκέως ἀγορεύειν;
650 ὅς ῥα τόθ᾽ Ὑψιπύλην μειλίξατο δέχθαι ἰόντας

from that Sicinus whom the water nymph Oenoe bore after making love to Thoas. But as for the women, they all found cattle-herding, donning bronze armor, and plowing fields of wheat to be easier than Athena's labors,[72] with which they had always before been occupied. And yet, for all that, often indeed did they scan the broad sea with their eyes in terrible fear for when the Thracians would come. And so, when they saw the Argo being rowed near their island, they immediately, one and all, put on their armor for war and poured forth from the gates of Myrine onto the shore like Thyiades who eat raw flesh,[73] for they undoubtedly thought that the Thracians were coming. And with them Thoas' daughter Hypsipyle put on her father's armor. In helpless distress they streamed forth in silence, such was the fear looming over them.

But in the meantime, the heroes had sent Aethalides forth from the ship, the swift herald to whose care they entrusted their messages and the scepter of Hermes, his father, who had granted him an imperishable remembrance of all things. And not even now, after his departure to the unspeakable[74] eddies of Acheron, has forgetfulness come over his soul, but it is destined to change abodes endlessly, sometimes being numbered among those beneath the earth, at other times in the sunlight among living men. But what need have I to tell at length stories about Aethalides? On that occasion, he persuaded Hypsipyle to receive the

---

[72] I.e. household chores, primarily weaving.

[73] Thyiades (or Thyades) were frenzied female worshipers of Dionysus.

[74] Or *unforeseeable*.

ἤματος ἀνομένοιο διὰ κνέφας· οὐδὲ μὲν ἠοῖ
πείσματα νηὸς ἔλυσαν ἐπὶ πνοιῇ βορέαο.
   Λημνιάδες δὲ γυναῖκες ἀνὰ πτόλιν ἷζον ἰοῦσαι
εἰς ἀγορήν· αὐτὴ γὰρ ἐπέφραδεν Ὑψιπύλεια.

655 καί ῥ' ὅτε δὴ μάλα πᾶσαι ὁμιλαδὸν ἠγερέθοντο,
αὐτίκ' ἄρ' ἥ γ' ἐνὶ τῆσιν ἐποτρύνουσ' ἀγόρευεν·
   "ὦ φίλαι, εἰ δ' ἄγε δὴ μενοεικέα δῶρα πόρωμεν
ἀνδράσιν, οἷά τ' ἔοικεν ἄγειν ἐπὶ νηὸς ἔχοντας,
ἦια καὶ μέθυ λαρόν, ἵν' ἔμπεδον ἔκτοθι πύργων

660 μίμνοιεν, μηδ' ἄμμε κατὰ χρειὼ μεθέποντες
ἀτρεκέως γνώωσι, κακὴ δ' ἐπὶ πολλὸν ἵκηται
βάξις· ἐπεὶ μέγα ἔργον ἐρέξαμεν, οὐδέ τι πάμπαν
θυμηδὲς καὶ τοῖσι τό γ' ἔσσεται, εἴ κε δαεῖεν.
ἡμετέρη μὲν νῦν τοίη παρενήνοθε μῆτις·

665 ὑμέων δ' εἴ τις ἄρειον ἔπος μητίσεται ἄλλη,
ἐγρέσθω· τοῦ γάρ τε καὶ εἵνεκα δεῦρο κάλεσσα."
   ὣς ἄρ' ἔφη, καὶ θῶκον ἐφίζανε πατρὸς ἑοῖο
λάινον. αὐτὰρ ἔπειτα φίλη τροφὸς ὦρτο Πολυξώ,
γήραϊ δὴ ῥικνοῖσιν ἐπισκάζουσα πόδεσσιν,

670 βάκτρῳ ἐρειδομένη, πέρι δὲ μενέαιν' ἀγορεῦσαι·
τῇ καὶ παρθενικαὶ πίσυρες σχεδὸν ἑδριόωντο
ἀδμῆτες λευκῇσιν ἐπιχνοάουσαι ἐθείραις.
στῆ δ' ἄρ' ἐνὶ μέσσῃ ἀγορῇ, ἀνὰ δ' ἔσχεθε δειρὴν
ἦκα μόλις κυφοῖο μεταφρένου, ὧδέ τ' ἔειπεν·

675   "δῶρα μέν, ὡς αὐτῇ περ ἐφανδάνει Ὑψιπυλείῃ,
πέμπωμεν ξείνοισιν, ἐπεὶ καὶ ἄρειον ὀπάσσαι.
ὔμμι γε μὴν τίς μῆτις ἐπαυρέσθαι βιότοιο,
αἴ κεν ἐπιβρίσῃ Θρήιξ στρατὸς ἠέ τις ἄλλος

56

travelers for the night, since the day was waning, but yet at dawn they did not loose the ship's cables because the north wind was blowing.[75]

The Lemnian women came from throughout the city and sat in the assembly, for Hypsipyle herself had given the order. And once they had all gathered in one large group, she immediately spoke in their midst and exhorted them:

"My friends, come, let us give these men gifts to their liking, such things as men ought to take with them on a ship, provisions and sweet wine, so that they might forever remain outside our walls, lest out of need they may come among us and get to know us all too accurately, and an evil report may travel far and wide. For we have done a terrible deed, and it will not be at all heart-cheering to them either, if they were to learn of it. Such, then, is the plan before us now, but if any of you can devise a better proposal, let her rise, because it was also for this reason that I summoned you here."

Thus she spoke and sat down on her father's seat of stone. But then her dear nurse Polyxo rose up, tottering on feet shriveled with age and leaning on a cane, but she was very eager to speak. And near her sat four unwed virgins crowned with white hair. She stood in the middle of the assembly, and with difficulty raised her neck slightly from her stooped back and spoke thus:

"Let us send gifts to the strangers, just as Hypsipyle herself wishes, for it is better to give them. But as for you all, what plan do you have to sustain your livelihood if a Thracian army invades, or some other enemy force, as of-

[75] From Lemnos they needed to sail north toward Samo-thrace.

δυσμενέων, ἅ τε πολλὰ μετ' ἀνθρώποισι πέλονται,
680 ὡς καὶ νῦν ὅδ' ὅμιλος ἀνωίστως ἐφικάνει·
εἰ δὲ τὸ μὲν μακάρων τις ἀποτρέποι, ἄλλα δ'
        ὀπίσσω
μυρία δηιοτῆτος ὑπέρτερα πήματα μίμνει.
εὖτ' ἂν δὴ γεραραὶ μὲν ἀποφθινύθουσι γυναῖκες,
κουρότεραι δ' ἄγονοι στυγερὸν ποτὶ γῆρας ἵκησθε,
685 πῶς τῆμος βώσεσθε, δυσάμμοροι; ἦε βαθείαις
αὐτόματοι βόες ὔμμιν ἐνιζευχθέντες ἀρούραις
γειοτόμον νειοῖο διειρύσσουσιν ἄροτρον,
καὶ πρόκα τελλομένου ἔτεος στάχυν ἀμήσονται;
ἦ μὲν ἐγών, εἰ καί με τὰ νῦν ἔτι πεφρίκασιν
690 Κῆρες, ἐπερχόμενόν που ὀίομαι εἰς ἔτος ἤδη
γαῖαν ἐφέσσεσθαι, κτερέων ἀπὸ μοῖραν ἑλοῦσα
αὔτως, ἧ θέμις ἐστί, πάρος κακότητι πελάσσαι.
ὁπλοτέρῃσι δὲ πάγχυ τάδε φράζεσθαι ἄνωγα·
νῦν γὰρ δὴ παρὰ ποσσὶν ἐπήβολός ἐστ' ἀλεωρή,
695 εἴ κεν ἐπιτρέψητε δόμους καὶ ληίδα πᾶσαν
ὑμετέρην ξείνοισι καὶ ἀγλαὸν ἄστυ μέλεσθαι."

    ὣς ἔφατ'· ἐν δ' ἀγορῇ πλῆτο θρόου, εὔαδε γάρ
        σφιν
μῦθος. ἀτὰρ μετὰ τήν γε παρασχεδὸν αὖτις ἀνῶρτο
Ὑψιπύλη, καὶ τοῖον ὑποβλήδην ἔπος ηὔδα·
700   "εἰ μὲν δὴ πάσῃσιν ἐφανδάνει ἥδε μενοινή,
ἤδη κεν μετὰ νῆα καὶ ἄγγελον ὀτρύναιμι."

    ἦ ῥα, καὶ Ἰφινόην μετεφώνεεν ἆσσον ἐοῦσαν·

    "ὄρσο μοι, Ἰφινόη, τοῦδ' ἀνέρος ἀντιόωσα
ἡμετερόνδε μολεῖν, ὅς τις στόλου ἡγεμονεύει,

ten happens among men, just as now this group has un-
expectedly come? Even if one of the blessed gods were to
avert this threat, countless other woes worse than war re-
main in the future. When in fact the older women die and
you younger ones reach horrible old age without children,
how will you survive then, poor things? Will your oxen yoke
themselves all on their own in the deep fields and pull the
earth-cutting plow through the fallow, and as soon as sum-
mer ends will they harvest the grain? Truly in my case,
even though the Fates of Death have until now shuddered
at the sight of me, I suspect that already within the coming
year I will be clothed in earth and will have received my
due share of burial honors, in the manner that is fitting, be-
fore facing that disaster. But I urge the younger women to
consider this well, for now in fact before your feet lies an
effective means of escape, if you entrust the strangers with
the care of your homes and all your possessions and your
glorious city."

Thus she spoke, and the assembly place was filled with
clamor, for her speech pleased them. Immediately after
her, Hypsipyle rose again and spoke the following words in
reply:

"If then everyone approves of this proposal, at once I
shall even send a messenger to the ship."

She spoke and addressed Iphinoe, who was nearby:

"Please go, Iphinoe, and entreat that man, whoever it is
that leads the expedition, to come to my palace so that I

683 ἀποφθινύθουσι Ω: ἀποφθινύθωσι WO
692 κακότητι SE: κακότητα LAD

APOLLONIUS RHODIUS

705 ὄφρα τί οἱ δήμοιο ἔπος θυμῆρες ἐνίσπω·
καὶ δ' αὐτοὺς γαίης τε καὶ ἄστεος, αἴ κ' ἐθέλωσιν,
κέκλεο θαρσαλέως ἐπιβαινέμεν εὐμενέοντας."
    ἦ, καὶ ἔλυσ' ἀγορήν· μετὰ δ' εἰς ἑὸν ὦρτο
    νέεσθαι.
ὣς δὲ καὶ Ἰφινόη Μινύας ἵκεθ'· οἱ δ' ἐρέεινον
710 χρεῖος ὅ τι φρονέουσα μετήλυθεν· ὦκα δὲ τούς γε
πασσυδίῃ μύθοισι προσέννεπεν ἐξερέοντας·
    "κούρη τοί μ' ἐφέηκε Θοαντιὰς ἐνθάδ' ἰοῦσαν
Ὑψιπύλη καλέειν νηὸς πρόμον, ὅς τις ὄρωρεν,
ὄφρα τί οἱ δήμοιο ἔπος θυμηδὲς ἐνίσπῃ·
715 καὶ δ' αὐτοὺς γαίης τε καὶ ἄστεος, αἴ κ' ἐθέλητε,
κέκλεται αὐτίκα νῦν ἐπιβαινέμεν εὐμενέοντας."
    ὣς ἄρ' ἔφη· πάντεσσι δ' ἐναίσιμος ἥνδανε μῦθος·
Ὑψιπύλην δ' εἴσαντο καταφθιμένοιο Θόαντος
τηλυγέτην γεγαυῖαν ἀνασσέμεν. ὦκα δὲ τόν γε
720 πέμπον ἴμεν, καὶ δ' αὐτοὶ ἐπεντύνοντο νέεσθαι.
    αὐτὰρ ὅ γ' ἀμφ' ὤμοισι, θεᾶς Ἰτωνίδος ἔργον,
δίπλακα πορφυρέην περονήσατο, τήν οἱ ὄπασσεν
Παλλάς, ὅτε πρῶτον δρυόχους ἐπεβάλλετο νηὸς
Ἀργοῦς, καὶ κανόνεσσι δάε ζυγὰ μετρήσασθαι.
725 τῆς μὲν ῥηίτερόν κεν ἐς ἠέλιον ἀνιόντα
ὄσσε βάλοις ἢ κεῖνο μεταβλέψειας ἔρευθος.
δὴ γάρ τοι μέσσῃ μὲν ἐρευθήεσσα τέτυκτο,

705 θυμῆρες Ω: θυμηδὲς Fränkel, Vian
714 θυμηδὲς Π7Ω: θυμῆρες E (cf. 705)

60

may tell him a decision of the people that will please his heart; and as for the men themselves, invite them, if they wish, to enter the land and city confidently as friends."

She spoke and dismissed the assembly, and then proceeded to go home. Likewise, Iphinoe went to the Minyans. They asked what purpose she had in mind in coming to them, and at once she addressed all those who were inquiring with these words:

"Truly it was Thoas' daughter Hypsipyle who dispatched me to come here and summon the commander of the ship, whoever he is, so that she may tell him a decision of the people that will cheer his heart, and she invites you men yourselves, if you wish, to enter the land and city immediately as friends."

Thus she spoke, and her auspicious proposal pleased them all. They supposed that because Thoas had died, Hypsipyle, his only child, was ruling. They quickly sent Jason on his way and readied themselves to go.

And he fastened around his shoulders a double-folded purple cloak, the work of the Itonian goddess, which Pallas[76] had given him when she first began laying the oak props[77] of the ship Argo, and taught him how to measure the cross-beams with a ruler. You could cast your eyes more easily on the rising sun than gaze at that cloak's red color. For indeed its center was red, on its edges it was all

[76] Itonian and Pallas are epithets of Athena.
[77] Or *ribs*.

ἄκρα δὲ πορφυρέη πάντῃ πέλεν· ἐν δ' ἄρ' ἑκάστῳ
τέρματι δαίδαλα πολλὰ διακριδὸν εὖ ἐπέπαστο.
730 ἐν μὲν ἔσαν Κύκλωπες ἐπ' ἀφθίτῳ ἥμενοι ἔργῳ,
Ζηνὶ κεραυνὸν ἄνακτι πονεύμενοι· ὃς τόσον ἤδη
παμφαίνων ἐτέτυκτο, μιῆς δ' ἔτι δεύετο μοῦνον
ἀκτῖνος, τὴν οἵ γε σιδηρείης ἐλάασκον
σφύρῃσιν μαλεροῖο πυρὸς ζείουσαν ἀυτμήν.
735 ἐν δ' ἔσαν Ἀντιόπης Ἀσωπίδος υἱέε δοιώ,
Ἀμφίων καὶ Ζῆθος· ἀπύργωτος δ' ἔτι Θήβη
κεῖτο πέλας, τῆς οἵ γε νέον βάλλοντο δομαίους
ἱέμενοι· Ζῆθος μὲν ἐπωμαδὸν ἠέρταζεν
οὔρεος ἠλιβάτοιο κάρη μογέοντι ἐοικώς·
740 Ἀμφίων δ' ἐπὶ οἷ χρυσέῃ φόρμιγγι λιγαίνων
ἤιε, δὶς τόσση δὲ μετ' ἴχνια νίσσετο πέτρη.
ἑξείης δ' ἤσκητο βαθυπλόκαμος Κυθέρεια
Ἄρεος ὀχμάζουσα θοὸν σάκος· ἐκ δέ οἱ ὤμου
πῆχυν ἔπι σκαιὸν ξυνοχῇ κεχάλαστο χιτῶνος
745 νέρθε παρὲκ μαζοῖο· τὸ δ' ἀντίον ἀτρεκὲς αὕτως
χαλκείῃ δείκηλον ἐν ἀσπίδι φαίνετ' ἰδέσθai.
ἐν δὲ βοῶν ἔσκεν λάσιος νομός· ἀμφὶ δὲ βουσὶν
Τηλεβόαι μάρναντο καὶ υἱέες Ἠλεκτρύωνος,
οἱ μὲν ἀμυνόμενοι, ἀτὰρ οἵ γ' ἐθέλοντες ἀμέρσαι,
750 λῃσταὶ Τάφιοι· τῶν δ' αἵματι δεύετο λειμὼν
ἑρσήεις, πολέες δ' ὀλίγους βιόωντο νομῆας.
ἐν δὲ δύω δίφροι πεπονήατο δηριόωντες.

729 ἐπέπαστο Ruhnken: ἐπέκαστο Ω
745 νέρθε παρὲκ Et. Gen.: νέρθεν ὑπὲρ Ω

purple, and within each border many intricate designs, one after another, were skillfully fashioned.

On it were the Cyclopes, seated at their endless work, toiling over a thunderbolt for Zeus the king. By now it was almost finished in all its brightness, but it still lacked a single ray, which they were beating out with their iron hammers as it spurted a jet of raging fire.

And on it were the twin sons of Antiope, Asopus' daughter, Amphion and Zethus. Nearby was Thebes, still without towers, whose foundation stones they were just now laying with great zeal. Zethus was carrying the top of a high mountain on his shoulders, like a man toiling hard, but after him came Amphion, playing loudly on his golden lyre, and a boulder twice as big followed in his footsteps.

Next in order was fashioned thick-tressed Cytherea,[78] holding up Ares' agile shield. The juncture of her dress had slipped from her shoulder onto her left arm beneath her breast, and her exact reflection could be seen on the bronze shield in front of her.

And on it was a pasture of dense grass for cattle. The Teleboae and the sons of Electryon were fighting over the cattle,[79] the ones defending them, but the others, Taphian plunderers, bent on stealing them. The dewy meadow ran with their blood, and the many attackers were overpowering the few herdsmen.

And on it were wrought two competing chariots. Pelops

[78] Aphrodite.
[79] The Teleboae (Taphians) were notorious pirates; Electryon, Heracles' maternal grandfather, was king of Mycenae.

APOLLONIUS RHODIUS

καὶ τὸν μὲν προπάροιθε Πέλοψ ἴθυνε τινάσσων
ἡνία, σὺν δέ οἱ ἔσκε παραιβάτις Ἱπποδάμεια·
755 τοῦ δὲ μεταδρομάδην ἐπὶ Μυρτίλος ἤλασεν ἵππους,
σὺν τῷ δ' Οἰνόμαος προτενὲς δόρυ χειρὶ μεμαρπὼς
ἄξονος ἐν πλήμνῃσι παρακλιδὸν ἀγνυμένοιο
πῖπτεν, ἐπεσσύμενος Πελοπήια νῶτα δαΐξαι.
    ἐν καὶ Ἀπόλλων Φοῖβος ὀιστεύων ἐτέτυκτο,
760 βούπαις, οὔ πω πολλός, ἑὴν ἐρύοντα καλύπτρης
μητέρα θαρσαλέως Τιτυὸν μέγαν, ὅν ῥ' ἔτεκέν γε
δῖ' Ἐλάρη, θρέψεν δὲ καὶ ἂψ ἐλοχεύσατο Γαῖα.
    ἐν καὶ Φρίξος ἔην Μινύηιος, ὡς ἐτεόν περ
εἰσαΐων κριοῦ, ὁ δ' ἄρ' ἐξενέποντι ἐοικώς.
765 κείνους κ' εἰσορόων ἀκέοις, ψεύδοιό τε θυμόν,
ἐλπόμενος πυκινήν τιν' ἀπὸ σφείων ἐσακοῦσαι
βάξιν, ὃ καὶ δηρόν περ ἐπ' ἐλπίδι θηήσαιο.
    τοῖ' ἄρα δῶρα θεᾶς Ἰτωνίδος ἦεν Ἀθήνης.
δεξιτερῇ δ' ἕλεν ἔγχος ἑκηβόλον, ὅ ῥ' Ἀταλάντη
770 Μαινάλῳ ἔν ποτέ οἱ ξεινήιον ἐγγυάλιξεν,
πρόφρων ἀντομένη· πέρι γὰρ μενέαινεν ἕπεσθαι
τὴν ὁδόν. ἀλλὰ γὰρ αὐτὸς ἑκὼν ἀπερήτυε κούρην,
δεῖσεν δ' ἀργαλέας ἔριδας φιλότητος ἕκητι.

755 τοῦ Maas: τὸν Ω
767 ὃ καὶ δηρόν περ Ω: ὅτευ καὶ δηρὸν West, Fränkel
768 Ἰτωνίδος Hölzlin: Τριτωνίδος Ω

80 Oenomaus, king of Elis, required the suitors of his daughter
Hippodameia to race him. After giving them a head start, he
would catch up and stab them in the back with his spear (cf.

64

steered the one in front as he shook the reins, and riding beside him was Hippodameia. On the other, Myrtilus drove his horses in close pursuit, and with him was Oenomaus, gripping his forward-pointing spear in his hand, but he was falling sideways because the axle had broken in the hub as he was lunging to stab the back of Pelops.[80]

And on it was wrought Phoebus Apollo as a mighty youth, not yet fully grown, shooting at enormous Tityus, who was boldly pulling Apollo's mother by her veil, he whom glorious Elare bore, but whom Earth nursed and gave a second birth.[81]

And on it was Phrixus the Minyan, as if actually listening to the ram, which seemed to be speaking. When looking at them, you would fall silent and be deceived in your heart, expecting to hear some wise pronouncement from them; and so you would gaze for a long time in that expectation.

Such then was the gift of the Itonian goddess Athena. And in his right hand he took up his far-darting spear, which Atalanta once gave him as a guest-gift on mount Maenalus, when she gladly met him, for she was most eager to follow on his voyage. But he himself, of his own accord, kept back the girl because he feared bitter rivalries provoked by love.

Pindar, *Olympian* 1.67–89). In most versions of the story, Pelops bribed Myrtilus to sabotage Oenomaus' chariot with a linchpin of wax.   81 Tityus tried to rape Apollo's mother Leto. There are two versions of the second birth: Zeus hid the pregnant Elare beneath the earth, where she gave birth, or Tityus was so huge that Elare died in childbirth and Earth brought him forth.

APOLLONIUS RHODIUS

βῆ δ᾽ ἴμεναι προτὶ ἄστυ, φαεινῷ ἀστέρι ἶσος,
775 ὅν ῥά τε νηγατέῃσιν ἐεργόμεναι καλύβῃσιν
νύμφαι θηήσαντο δόμων ὕπερ ἀντέλλοντα,
καί σφισι κυανέοιο δι᾽ ἠέρος ὄμματα θέλγει
καλὸν ἐρευθόμενος, γάννυται δέ τε ἠιθέοιο
παρθένος ἱμείρουσα μετ᾽ ἀλλοδαποῖσιν ἐόντος
780 ἀνδράσιν, ᾧ καί μιν μνηστὴν κομέουσι τοκῆες·
τῷ ἴκελος προπόλοιο κατὰ στίβον ἤιεν ἥρως.
καί ῥ᾽ ὅτε δὴ πυλέων τε καὶ ἄστεος ἐντὸς ἔβησαν,
δημότεραι μὲν ὄπισθεν ἐπεκλονέοντο γυναῖκες
γηθόσυναι ξείνῳ· ὁ δ᾽ ἐπὶ χθονὸς ὄμματ᾽ ἐρείσας
785 νίσσετ᾽ ἀπηλεγέως, ὄφρ᾽ ἀγλαὰ δώμαθ᾽ ἵκανεν
Ὑψιπύλης. ἄνεσαν δὲ θύρας προφανέντι θεράπναι
δικλίδας, εὐτύκτοισιν ἀρηρεμένας σανίδεσσιν·
ἔνθα μιν Ἰφινόη κλισμῷ ἔνι παμφανόωντι
ἐσσυμένως καλῆς διὰ παστάδος εἷσεν ἄγουσα
790 ἀντία δεσποίνης. ἡ δ᾽ ἐγκλιδὸν ὄσσε βαλοῦσα
παρθενικὰς ἐρύθηνε παρηίδας· ἔμπα δὲ τόν γε
αἰδομένη μύθοισι προσέννεπεν αἱμυλίοισιν·

"ξεῖνε, τίη μίμνοντες ἐπὶ χρόνον ἔκτοθι πύργων
ἧσθ᾽ αὔτως; ἐπεὶ οὐ μὲν ὑπ᾽ ἀνδράσι ναίεται ἄστυ,
795 ἀλλὰ Θρηικίης ἐπινάστιοι ἠπείροιο
πυροφόρους ἀρόωσι γύας. κακότητα δὲ πᾶσαν
ἐξερέω νημερτές, ἵν᾽ εὖ γνοίητε καὶ αὐτοί.
εὖτε Θόας ἀστοῖσι πατὴρ ἐμὸς ἐμβασίλευεν,

781 προ]πόλοιο κατ[ὰ Π8 Wilamowitz praeeunte: πρὸ
πόληος ἀνὰ Ω   786 θύρα[ς Π8E: πύλας Ω

66

He went on his way toward the city like a shining star,[82] which young brides, confined in newly made quarters, gaze upon as it rises above their houses, and enchants their eyes with its beautiful red luster through the dark sky, and the maiden rejoices as she yearns for the young man who is away among foreign people, for whom her parents are keeping her to be his bride. Like that star the hero followed in the footsteps of the servant.[83] And when they had passed within the gates and the city, the women of the town surged behind them, delighting in the stranger, but he kept his eyes fixed on the ground and went straight on, until he came to the splendid palace of Hypsipyle. When he appeared, the servants opened the folding doors fitted with well-constructed panels. Then Iphinoe led him quickly through a beautiful porch and seated him on a re-splendent chair opposite her mistress, who cast down her eyes, as a blush reddened her virgin cheeks. Nonetheless, in spite of her modesty, she addressed him with cajoling words.

"Stranger, why do you all remain camped as you are so long outside our towers? For the city is not inhabited by men, but they have emigrated and plow the wheat-bearing fields of the Thracian mainland. I shall give a true account of our entire plight, so that you yourselves may also know it well. While my father Thoas ruled the citizens, people

---

[82] Hesperus, the evening star, harbinger of love.

[83] Iphinoe. Or, reading πρὸ πόληος ἀνὰ στίβον, *the hero went along the path in front of the city.*

τηνίκα, Θρηικίην οἵ τ' ἀντία ναιετάουσιν,
800 δήμου ἀπορνύμενοι λαοὶ πέρθεσκον ἐπαύλους
ἐκ νηῶν, αὐτῇσι δ' ἀπείρονα ληίδα κούραις
δεῦρ' ἄγον. οὐλομένης δὲ θεᾶς πορσύνετο μῆτις
Κύπριδος, ἥ τέ σφιν θυμοφθόρον ἔμβαλεν ἄτην·
δὴ γὰρ κουριδίας μὲν ἀπέστυγον, ἔκ τε μελάθρων
805 ᾗ ματίῃ εἴξαντες ἀπεσσεύοντο γυναῖκας,
αὐτὰρ ληιάδεσσι δορικτήταις παρίαυον,
σχέτλιοι. ἦ μὲν δηρὸν ἐτέτλαμεν, εἴ κέ ποτ' αὖτις
ὀψὲ μεταστρέψωσι νόον· τὸ δὲ διπλόον αἰεὶ
πῆμα κακὸν προύβαινεν. ἀτιμάζοντο δὲ τέκνα
810 γνήσι' ἐνὶ μεγάροις, σκοτίη δ' ἀνέτελλε γενέθλη·
αὔτως δ' ἀδμῆτές τε κόραι χῆραί τ' ἐπὶ τῇσιν
μητέρες ἂμ πτολίεθρον ἀτημελέες ἀλάληντο.
οὐδὲ πατὴρ ὀλίγον περ ἑῆς ἀλέγιζε θυγατρός,
εἰ καὶ ἐν ὀφθαλμοῖσι δαϊζομένην ὁρόωτο
815 μητρυιῆς ὑπὸ χερσὶν ἀτασθάλου· οὐδ' ἀπὸ μητρὸς
λώβην ὡς τὸ πάροιθεν ἀεικέα παῖδες ἄμυνον,
οὐδὲ κασιγνήτοισι κασιγνήτη μέλε θυμῷ.
ἀλλ' οἷαι κοῦραι ληίτιδες ἔν τε δόμοισιν
ἔν τε χοροῖς ἀγορῇ τε καὶ εἰλαπίνῃσι μέλοντο,
820 εἰσόκε τις θεὸς ἄμμιν ὑπέρβιον ἔμβαλε θάρσος,
ἂψ ἀνερχομένους Θρηκῶν ἄπο μηκέτι πύργοις
δέχθαι, ἵν' ἢ φρονέοιεν ἅ περ θέμις, ἠέ πῃ ἄλλῃ
αὐταῖς ληιάδεσσιν ἀφορμηθέντες ἵκοιντο.
οἱ δ' ἄρα θεσσάμενοι παίδων γένος, ὅσσον ἔλειπτο

800 ἐπαύλους Π⁹ˢˡ Pierson praeeunte: ἐναύλους Π⁹m

from our land used to go and raid from their ships the dwellings of those who inhabited Thrace opposite us, and they would bring vast amounts of booty here, along with captive girls. But the plan[84] of that destructive goddess Cypris was being fulfilled, for she cast into the men a heart-destroying obsession, for they came to loathe their lawful wives and, giving in to their folly, expelled them from their homes, while they slept with the women captured by their spears, the cruel men! Truly, for a long time we endured it, hoping that at some point they would at last change their minds again, but the evil affliction ever progressed and became twice as bad. Legitimate children were shown no respect in their homes, while a brood of bastards was emerging. Unmarried girls, and widowed mothers too, wandered just as they were, neglected, through the city. Nor did a father have the slightest concern for his daughter, even if he saw her being murdered before his eyes at the hands of her savage stepmother. Nor did sons, as before, protect their mother from disgraceful insults, nor did brothers have any concern in their hearts for a sister. But only the captive girls mattered in their homes, in choruses, in the agora, and in feasts, until some god cast overpowering courage into us, to receive them no longer within the towers when they returned from the Thracians, so that they would either regain a sense of what is right or would depart, captives and all, and go somewhere else. But they then demanded to have all the male

___

84 Or, reading μῆνις, *the wrath.*

___

802 μῆτις ΩΠ⁹: μῆνις Π⁹ˢˡL²ˢˡC
812 ἀτημελέες E: ἀτημελέως Ω

825 ἄρσεν ἀνὰ πτολίεθρον, ἔβαν πάλιν, ἔνθ᾿ ἔτι νῦν περ
Θρηικίης ἄροσιν χιονώδεα ναιετάουσιν.
τῶ ὑμεῖς στρωφᾶσθ᾿ ἐπιδήμιοι· εἰ δέ κεν αὖθι
ναιετάειν ἐθέλοις καί τοι ἄδοι, ἦ τ᾿ ἂν ἔπειτα
πατρὸς ἐμεῖο Θόαντος ἔχοις γέρας· οὐδέ σ᾿ ὀίω
830 γαῖαν ὀνόσσεσθαι· περὶ γὰρ βαθυλήιος ἄλλων
νήσων, Αἰγαίη ὅσσαι εἰν ἁλὶ ναιετάουσιν.
ἀλλ᾿ ἄγε νῦν ἐπὶ νῆα κιὼν ἑτάροισιν ἐνίσπες
μύθους ἡμετέρους, μηδ᾿ ἔκτοθι μίμνε πόληος."
ἴσκεν, ἀμαλδύνουσα φόνου τέλος, οἷον ἐτύχθη
835 ἀνδράσιν· αὐτὰρ ὁ τήν γε παραβλήδην προσέειπεν·
"Ὑψιπύλη, μάλα κεν θυμηδέος ἀντιάσαιμεν
χρησμοσύνης, ἣν ἄμμι σέθεν χατέουσιν ὀπάζεις·
εἶμι δ᾿ ὑπότροπος αὖτις ἀνὰ πτόλιν, εὖτ᾿ ἂν ἕκαστα
ἐξείπω κατὰ κόσμον. ἀνακτορίη δὲ μελέσθω
840 σοί γ᾿ αὐτῇ καὶ νῆσος· ἐγώ γε μὲν οὐκ ἀθερίζων
χάζομαι, ἀλλά με λυγροὶ ἐπισπέρχουσιν ἄεθλοι."
ἦ, καὶ δεξιτερῆς χειρὸς θίγεν· αἶψα δ᾿ ὀπίσσω
βῆ ῥ᾿ ἴμεν· ἀμφὶ δὲ τόν γε νεήνιδες ἄλλοθεν ἄλλαι
μυρίαι εἱλίσσοντο κεχαρμέναι, ὄφρα πυλάων
845 ἐξέμολεν. μετέπειτα δ᾿ ἐυτροχάλοισιν ἀμάξαις
ἀκτὴν εἰσανέβαν ξεινήια πολλὰ φέρουσαι,
μῦθον ὅτ᾿ ἤδη πάντα διηνεκέως ἀγόρευσεν,
τόν ῥα καλεσσαμένη διεπέφραδεν Ὑψιπύλεια·
καὶ δ᾿ αὐτοὺς ξεινοῦσθαι ἐπὶ σφέα δώματ᾿ ἄγεσκον
850 ῥηιδίως· Κύπρις γὰρ ἐπὶ γλυκὺν ἵμερον ὦρσεν
Ἡφαίστοιο χάριν πολυμήτιος, ὄφρα κεν αὖτις

children who remained in the city and went back to the snowy plowland of Thrace, where they dwell to this day. Therefore, all of you stay and reside with us; and if you yourself should wish to live here and would find it agreeable, then truly you would have my father Thoas' position of honor. Nor do I think you will find fault with our land, for it has deeper soil than all the other islands that lie in the Aegean sea. So come now, go to your ship and tell your comrades what I have said and do not continue to remain outside the city."

She spoke, glossing over what act of murder had been carried out against the men; and he said to her in reply:

"Hypsipyle, we shall most gladly accept the heart-cheering assistance that you offer us who are in need of your help, and I shall return again to the city after I report everything in due order. But let sovereignty and the island remain in your own care; yet for my part, I do not refuse out of disdain, but because grievous trials hasten me on."

He spoke and touched her right hand, and immediately set out to go back. And around him from every direction swarmed countless young women full of joy, until he passed outside the gates. Then the women came to the shore in well-wheeled wagons, bringing many guest-gifts, as soon as he had announced from beginning to end the entire proposal Hypsipyle had declared when she summoned him. And the women led the men to their homes to host them—easily, because Cypris had aroused sweet desire in them as a favor to resourceful Hephaestus,[85] so that

[85] Son of Hera and husband of Aphrodite, Hephaestus landed on Lemnos when cast from Olympus by Zeus (*Iliad* 1.590–594) and the island became his province. Homer calls Hephaestus "resourceful" at *Iliad* 21.355.

ναίηται μετόπισθεν ἀκήρατος ἀνδράσι Λῆμνος.
ἔνθ' ὁ μὲν Ὑψιπύλης βασιλήιον ἐς δόμον ὦρτο
Αἰσονίδης· οἱ δ' ἄλλοι ὅπῃ καὶ ἔκυρσαν ἕκαστος,
855 Ἡρακλῆος ἄνευθεν, ὁ γὰρ παρὰ νηὶ λέλειπτο
αὐτὸς ἑκὼν παῦροί τε διακρινθέντες ἑταῖροι.
αὐτίκα δ' ἄστυ χοροῖσι καὶ εἰλαπίνῃσι γεγήθει
καπνῷ κνισήεντι περίπλεον· ἔξοχα δ' ἄλλων
ἀθανάτων Ἥρης υἷα κλυτὸν ἠδὲ καὶ αὐτὴν
860 Κύπριν ἀοιδῇσιν θυέεσσί τε μειλίσσοντο.
ἀμβολίη δ' εἰς ἦμαρ ἀεὶ ἐξ ἤματος ἦεν
ναυτιλίης· δηρὸν δ' ἂν ἐλίννυον αὖθι μένοντες,
εἰ μὴ ἀολλίσσας ἑτάρους ἀπάνευθε γυναικῶν
Ἡρακλέης τοίοισιν ἐνιπτάζων μετέειπεν·
865 "δαιμόνιοι, πάτρης ἐμφύλιον αἷμ' ἀποέργει
ἡμέας; ἦε γάμων ἐπιδευέες ἐνθάδ' ἔβημεν
κεῖθεν, ὀνοσσάμενοι πολιήτιδας; αὖθι δ' ἔαδεν
ναίοντας λιπαρὴν ἄροσιν Λήμνοιο ταμέσθαι;
οὐ μὰν εὐκλειεῖς γε σὺν ὀθνείῃσι γυναιξὶν
870 ἐσσόμεθ' ὧδ' ἐπὶ δηρὸν ἐελμένοι· οὐδέ τι κῶας
αὐτόματον δώσει τις ἑλὼν θεὸς εὐξαμένοισιν.
ἴομεν αὖτις ἕκαστοι ἐπὶ σφέα· τὸν δ' ἐνὶ λέκτροις
Ὑψιπύλης εἰᾶτε πανήμερον, εἰσόκε Λῆμνον
παισὶν ἐπανδρώσῃ, μεγάλη τέ ἑ βάξις ἵκηται."
875 ὣς νείκεσσεν ὅμιλον· ἐναντία δ' οὔ νύ τις ἔτλη
ὄμματ' ἀνασχεθέειν οὐδὲ προτιμυθήσασθαι·

Lemnos would again be populated by males and suffer no harm thereafter.

Then Jason set off for Hypsipyle's royal palace, while the others went wherever each chanced to go, except for Heracles, for he was left behind by the ship of his own accord along with a few chosen comrades. Soon the city was celebrating with dances and feasts, completely filled with the smoke of sacrifices; and beyond all other immortals they propitiated Hera's famous son and Cypris herself with songs and sacrifices.

From one day to the next the voyage was continually postponed, and they would have stayed there and lingered for a long time, had not Heracles gathered his comrades apart from the women and reproached them with these words:

"You fools! Does a kinsman's spilled blood keep us from our homeland?[86] Or did we come here from there in need of wives because we scorn our native women? Have we decided to live here and divide up[87] the rich plowland of Lemnos? We will surely not win fame cooped up like this for a long time with foreign women, nor is there any fleece acting on its own for some god to seize and hand over to us in answer to our prayers. Let each of us return to his own affairs; as for that fellow, let him spend all day long in Hypsipyle's bed until he populates Lemnos with boys and gains a great reputation!"

Thus he upbraided the crew, and no one dared to raise his eyes to meet his or to reply, but they hastened, just as

[86] Punishment for killing a family member was permanent exile.

[87] Or *till*.

ἀλλ᾿ αὔτως ἀγορῆθεν ἐπαρτίζοντο νέεσθαι
σπερχόμενοι. ταὶ δέ σφιν ἐπέδραμον, εὖτ᾿ ἐδάησαν.
ὡς δ᾿ ὅτε λείρια καλὰ περιβρομέουσι μέλισσαι

880 πέτρης ἐκχύμεναι σιμβληΐδος, ἀμφὶ δὲ λειμὼν
ἑρσήεις γάνυται, ταὶ δὲ γλυκὺν ἄλλοτε ἄλλον
καρπὸν ἀμέργουσιν πεποτημέναι· ὣς ἄρα ταί γε
ἐνδυκὲς ἀνέρας ἀμφὶ κινυρόμεναι προχέοντο,
χερσί τε καὶ μύθοισιν ἐδεικανόωντο ἕκαστον,

885 εὐχόμεναι μακάρεσσιν ἀπήμονα νόστον ὀπάσσαι.
ὣς δὲ καὶ Ὑψιπύλη ἠρήσατο χεῖρας ἑλοῦσα
Αἰσονίδεω, τὰ δέ οἱ ῥέε δάκρυα χήτει ἰόντος·

"νίσσεο, καί σε θεοὶ σὺν ἀπηρέσιν αὖτις ἑταίροις
χρύσειον βασιλῆι δέρος κομίσειαν ἄγοντα,

890 αὔτως ὡς ἐθέλεις καί τοι φίλον. ἤδε δὲ νῆσος
σκῆπτρά τε πατρὸς ἐμεῖο παρέσσεται, ἢν καὶ
      ὀπίσσω
δή ποτε νοστήσας ἐθέλῃς ἄψορρον ἱκέσθαι·
ῥηιδίως δ᾿ ἂν ἑοὶ καὶ ἀπείρονα λαὸν ἀγείραις
ἄλλων ἐκ πολίων. ἀλλ᾿ οὐ σύ γε τήνδε μενοινὴν

895 σχήσεις, οὔτ᾿ αὐτὴ προτιόσσομαι ὧδε τελεῖσθαι.
μνώεο μὴν ἀπεών περ ὁμῶς καὶ νόστιμος ἤδη
Ὑψιπύλης· λίπε δ᾿ ἡμῖν ἔπος, τό κεν ἐξανύσαιμι
πρόφρων, ἢν ἄρα δή με θεοὶ δώωσι τεκέσθαι."

τὴν δ᾿ αὖτ᾿ Αἴσονος υἱὸς ἀγαιόμενος προσέειπεν·

900 "Ὑψιπύλη, τὰ μὲν οὕτω ἐναίσιμα πάντα γένοιτο
ἐκ μακάρων· τύνη δ᾿ ἐμέθεν πέρι θυμὸν ἀρείω

74

they were, from the assembly and prepared to depart. The women ran up to them when they learned of it. And as bees buzz about lovely lilies when they pour from their hive in a rock, and all around them the dewy meadow rejoices, and flying from one to another they cull the sweet fruit, thus indeed the women ardently poured forth, all in tears, around the men and greeted each one with hands and words, begging the blessed gods to give them a safe return. Thus too did Hypsipyle pray as she grasped Jason's hands, and her tears flowed out of regret at his departure:

"Go, and may the gods bring you back again with your comrades safe and sound, bearing the golden fleece to your king, just as you wish and desire. This island and my father's scepter will be waiting, if at any time in the future, after returning home, you wish to come back here. You could easily gather for yourself a vast number of people from other cities. But no, you will not come to have this desire, nor do I myself foresee such an outcome. Promise to remember Hypsipyle, both when far away and when already back home. But leave me a word of instruction, which I shall gladly carry out, if in fact the gods grant that I give birth."[88]

In turn, Jason answered her admiringly:

"Hypsipyle, may all those things thus prove propitious with the help of the blessed gods, but concerning me have

[88] In Euripides' *Hypsipyle*, she has two sons by Jason, Thoas and Euneus, the latter king of Lemnos during the Trojan war (cf. *Iliad* 7.467–469).

ἴσχαν᾽, ἐπεὶ πάτρην μοι ἅλις Πελίαο ἕκητι
ναιετάειν· μοῦνόν με θεοὶ λύσειαν ἀέθλων.
εἰ δ᾽ οὔ μοι πέπρωται ἐς Ἑλλάδα γαῖαν ἱκέσθαι
905 τηλοῦ ἀναπλώοντι, σὺ δ᾽ ἄρσενα παῖδα τέκηαι,
πέμπε μιν ἡβήσαντα Πελασγίδος ἔνδον Ἰωλκοῦ
πατρί τ᾽ ἐμῷ καὶ μητρὶ δύης ἄκος, ἢν ἄρα τούς γε
τέτμῃ ἔτι ζώοντας, ἵν᾽ ἄνδιχα τοῖο ἄνακτος
σφοῖσιν πορσύνωνται ἐφέστιοι ἐν μεγάροισιν."
910   ἦ, καὶ ἔβαιν᾽ ἐπὶ νῆα παροίτατος. ὡς δὲ καὶ
          ἄλλοι
βαῖνον ἀριστῆες· λάζοντο δὲ χερσὶν ἐρετμὰ
ἐνσχερὼ ἑζόμενοι· πρυμνήσια δέ σφισιν Ἄργος
λῦσεν ὑπὲκ πέτρης ἁλιμυρέος. ἔνθ᾽ ἄρα τοί γε
κόπτον ὕδωρ δολιχῇσιν ἐπικρατέως ἐλάτῃσιν.
915 ἑσπέριοι δ᾽ Ὀρφῆος ἐφημοσύνῃσιν ἔκελσαν
νῆσον ἐς Ἠλέκτρης Ἀτλαντίδος, ὄφρα δαέντες
ἀρρήτους ἀγανῇσι τελεσφορίῃσι θέμιστας
σωότεροι κρυόεσσαν ὑπὲρ ἅλα ναυτίλλοιντο.
τῶν μὲν ἔτ᾽ οὐ προτέρω μυθήσομαι, ἀλλὰ καὶ αὐτὴ
920 νῆσος ὁμῶς κεχάροιτο καὶ οἳ λάχον ὄργια κεῖνα
δαίμονες ἐνναέται, τὰ μὲν οὐ θέμις ἄμμιν ἀείδειν.
    κεῖθεν δ᾽ εἰρεσίῃ Μέλανος διὰ βένθεα πόντου
ἱέμενοι τῇ μὲν Θρηκῶν χθόνα, τῇ δὲ περαίην

---

89 The precise meaning of this expression is in doubt. I take it
to mean that, whereas a good outcome depends on the gods, he
can assure her of his own intentions. Some interpret him to say,
"have a nobler thought about me," i.e. that Jason is too noble to

greater confidence,[89] for it is sufficient for me to dwell in my homeland by the grace of Pelias—may the gods only deliver me from my trials. But if I am not destined to return to the land of Hellas after my distant voyage, and if you bear a male child, send him when grown to Pelasgian Iolcus to relieve the grief of my father and mother—if at that point he finds them still alive—and to insure that beyond the reach of that king[90] they may be cared for at the hearth of their own home."

He spoke and was the first to board the ship. And likewise the other heroes boarded and took their seats in order and grasped the oars in their hands. Argus loosed for them the stern cables from under the sea-washed rock. Then they began striking the water mightily with their long oars. At evening, on Orpheus' instructions, they put in at the island of Electra,[91] Atlas' daughter, so that by learning secret rites through gentle initiations they might sail more safely over the chilling sea. Of these things, however, I shall speak no further, but bid farewell to the island itself and to the local divinities,[92] to whom belong those mysteries of which I am forbidden to sing.

From there they rowed eagerly across the depths of the Black sea,[93] keeping the land of the Thracians on one side

---

pick up and leave his rightful home in Iolcus, or to take his son away from Hypsipyle.

[90] Pelias, who usurped Aeson's throne.

[91] Samothrace.

[92] The Cabiri, mentioned at Herodotus 2.51, initiation into whose mysteries protected sailors (cf. Diodorus 4.43.1–2).

[93] The Gulf of Saros in the northern Aegean, not our Black Sea.

Ἴμβρον ἔχον καθύπερθε. νέον γε μὲν ἠελίοιο
925 δυομένου Χέρνησον ἐπὶ προύχουσαν ἵκοντο.
ἔνθα σφιν λαιψηρὸς ἄη νότος, ἱστία δ' οὔρῳ
στησάμενοι κούρης Ἀθαμαντίδος αἰπὰ ῥέεθρα
εἰσέβαλον. πέλαγος δὲ τὸ μὲν καθύπερθε λέλειπτο
ἦρι, τὸ δ' ἐννύχιοι Ῥοιτειάδος ἔνδοθεν ἀκτῆς
930 μέτρεον Ἰδαίην ἐπὶ δεξιὰ γαῖαν ἔχοντες.
Δαρδανίην δὲ λιπόντες ἐπιπροσέβαλλον Ἀβύδῳ,
Περκώτην δ' ἐπὶ τῇ καὶ Ἀβαρνίδος ἠμαθόεσσαν
ἠιόνα ζαθέην τε παρήμειβον Πιτύειαν.
καὶ δὴ τοί γ' ἐπὶ νυκτὶ διάνδιχα νηὸς ἰούσης
935 δίνῃ πορφύροντα διήνυσαν Ἑλλήσποντον.

ἔστι δέ τις αἰπεῖα Προποντίδος ἔνδοθι νῆσος
τυτθὸν ἀπὸ Φρυγίης πολυληίου ἠπείροιο
εἰς ἅλα κεκλιμένη, ὅσσον τ' ἐπιμύρεται ἰσθμὸς
χέρσῳ ἔπι πρηνὴς καταειμένος. ἐν δέ οἱ ἀκταὶ
940 ἀμφίδυμοι, κεῖνται δ' ὑπὲρ ὕδατος Αἰσήποιο·
Ἄρκτων μιν καλέουσιν ὄρος περιναιετάοντες·
καὶ τὸ μὲν ὑβρισταί τε καὶ ἄγριοι ἐννάεσκον
Γηγενέες, μέγα θαῦμα περικτιόνεσσιν ἰδέσθαι·
ἐξ γὰρ ἑκάστῳ χεῖρες ὑπέρβιοι ἠερέθοντο,
945 αἱ μὲν ἀπὸ στιβαρῶν ὤμων δύο, ταὶ δ' ὑπένερθεν
τέσσαρες αἰνοτάτῃσιν ἐπὶ πλευρῇς ἀραρυῖαι.
ἰσθμὸν δ' αὖ πεδίον τε Δολίονες ἀμφενέμοντο

939 ἔπι πρηνὴς Hölzlin: ἐπιπρηνής Ω
942 ἐνναίεσκον Merkel: ναιετάουσιν Ω
944 ἠερέθοντο MRQC: ἠερέθονται Ω

and, on the other, the opposing coast of Imbros lying sea-
ward. And just as the sun was setting they reached the tip
of the Chersonesus. There a stiff south wind was blowing
for them, and they raised their sails to the following wind
and entered the choppy currents of Athamas' daughter.[94]
One open sea was left behind at dawn, while during the
night they were traversing another sea inside the headland
of Rhoeteum, as they kept the land of Ida on their right.
After leaving Dardania, they headed for Abydos, after
which they passed Percote, the sandy shore of Abarnis, and
holy Pityeia. And so during that night, as the ship pro-
ceeded by sail and oar,[95] they traversed the length of the
Hellespont, turbulent[96] with eddies.

There is in the Propontis a lofty island,[97] sloping to the
sea, separated from the grain-rich Phrygian mainland by
the short span of an isthmus that descends steeply to the
shore and is washed over by the waves. And on the island
are two shores accessible to ships, and they lie beyond the
Aesepus river. The surrounding people call the island Bear
mountain. On it lived violent and wild Earthborn men, a
great marvel for their neighbors to see, for each bran-
dished six powerful arms, two from their massive shoul-
ders, and four below attached to their fearsome sides. Yet
the Dolionian people inhabited the isthmus and plain, and

[94] Helle; i.e. the Hellespont.

[95] Lit. "as the ship went in two ways." Some interpret this to
mean, "as the ship cut through (the water)."

[96] Or *dark*.

[97] Cyzicus. Because of its low-lying isthmus, the ancients dis-
puted whether it was an island or a peninsula.

ἀνέρες· ἐν δ' ἥρως Αἰνήιος υἱὸς ἄνασσεν
Κύζικος, ὃν κούρη δίου τέκεν Εὐσώροιο
950 Αἰνήτη. τοὺς δ' οὔ τι καὶ ἔκπαγλοί περ ἐόντες
Γηγενέες σίνοντο, Ποσειδάωνος ἀρωγῇ·
τοῦ γὰρ ἔσαν τὰ πρῶτα Δολίονες ἐκγεγαῶτες.
    ἔνθ' Ἀργὼ προύτυψεν ἐπειγομένη ἀνέμοισιν
Θρηικίοις· Καλὸς δὲ λιμὴν ὑπέδεκτο θέουσαν.
955 κεῖσε καὶ εὐναίης ὀλίγον λίθον ἐκλύσαντες
Τίφυος ἐννεσίῃσιν ὑπὸ κρήνῃ ἐλίποντο,
κρήνῃ ὑπ' Ἀρτακίῃ· ἕτερον δ' ἕλον, ὅς τις ἀρήρει,
βριθύν· ἀτὰρ κεῖνόν γε θεοπροπίαις Ἑκάτοιο
Νηλεΐδαι μετόπισθεν Ἰάονες ἱδρύσαντο
960 ἱερόν, ἣ θέμις ἦεν, Ἰησονίης ἐν Ἀθήνης.
    τοὺς δ' ἄμυδις φιλότητι Δολίονες· ἠδὲ καὶ αὐτὸς
Κύζικος ἀντήσαντες, ὅτε στόλον ἠδὲ γενέθλην
ἔκλυον, οἵ τινες εἶεν, εὐξείνως ἀρέσαντο·
καί σφεας εἰρεσίῃ πέπιθον προτέρωσε κιόντας
965 ἄστεος ἐν λιμένι πρυμνήσια νηὸς ἀνάψαι.
ἔνθ' οἵ γ' Ἐκβασίῳ βωμὸν θέσαν Ἀπόλλωνι
εἰσάμενοι παρὰ θῖνα, θυηπολίης τ' ἐμέλοντο.
δῶκεν δ' αὐτὸς ἄναξ λαρὸν μέθυ δευομένοισιν
μῆλά θ' ὁμοῦ· δὴ γάρ οἱ ἔην φάτις, εὖτ' ἂν ἵκωνται
970 ἀνδρῶν ἡρώων θεῖος στόλος, αὐτίκα τόν γε
μείλιχον ἀντιάαν μηδὲ πτολέμοιο μέλεσθαι.
ἶσόν που κἀκείνῳ ἐπισταχύεσκον ἴουλοι,
οὐδέ νύ πω παίδεσσιν ἀγαλλόμενος μεμόρητο,

972 ἶσον Ω: ἁρμοῖ ΣLγρ (cf. Call. fr. 274.1 Pf.)

over them ruled the son of Aeneus, the hero Cyzicus, whom Aenete bore, the daughter of noble Eusorus. To them the Earthborn men, terrifying as they were, did no harm at all, owing to Poseidon's protection, for the Doliones were originally descended from him.

To this place the Argo pressed on, driven by the winds from Thrace, and Fair harbor received the speeding ship. There, too, on Tiphys' instructions they unfastened the small stone serving as an anchor and left it at the base of a spring, the spring of Artacie, and chose a heavier one that suited their needs. But later on, in accordance with the Far-Shooter's oracle, the Ionian sons of Neleus[98] dedicated that first stone as a holy offering, as was proper, in the temple of Athena, Helper of Jason.

In one body the Doliones and Cyzicus himself met them in friendship, and on hearing of their expedition and what their lineage was they welcomed them hospitably, and persuaded them to row further and attach the ship's stern cables in the harbor of the town.[99] Here they built an altar to Apollo Ecbasius,[100] setting it up on the shore, and began preparing sacrifices. The king himself provided sweet wine, which they lacked, along with sheep, for he had received an oracle, that when a god-like expedition of heroic men arrived, he should immediately approach it gently and have no thought of war. As with Jason, the down of his beard was just sprouting, and not yet was it his lot to

[98] These sons of Neleus were sent from Athens to colonize Phrygia (schol.).

[99] They actually move the ship to Chytus harbor the next morning.

[100] "Of Debarkation."

81

ἀλλ' ἔτι οἱ κατὰ δώματ' ἀκήρατος ἦεν ἄκοιτις
975 ὠδίνων, Μέροπος Περκωσίου ἐκγεγαυῖα
Κλείτη ἐυπλόκαμος. τὴν μὲν νέον ἐξέτι πατρὸς
θεσπεσίοις ἕδνοισιν ἀνήγαγεν ἀντιπέρηθεν.
ἀλλὰ καὶ ὡς θάλαμόν τε λιπὼν καὶ δέμνια νύμφης
τοῖς μέτα δαῖτ' ἀλέγυνε, βάλεν δ' ἀπὸ δείματα
        θυμοῦ.
980 ἀλλήλους δ' ἐρέεινον ἀμοιβαδίς· ἤτοι ὁ μέν σφεων
πεύθετο ναυτιλίης ἄνυσιν Πελίαό τ' ἐφετμάς,
οἱ δὲ περικτιόνων πόλιας καὶ κόλπον ἅπαντα
εὐρείης πεύθοντο Προποντίδος· οὐ μὲν ἐπιπρὸ
ἠείδει καταλέξαι ἐελδομένοισι δαῆναι.
985 ἠοῖ δ' εἰσανέβαν μέγα Δίνδυμον, ὄφρα καὶ αὐτοὶ
θηήσαιντο πόρους κείνης ἁλός· ἐν δ' ἄρα τοί γε
νῆα Χυτῷ λιμένι προτέρου ἐξήλασαν ὅρμου·
ἥδε δ' Ἰησονίη πέφαται ὁδός, ἥν περ ἔβησαν.
Γηγενέες δ' ἑτέρωθεν ἀπ' οὔρεος ἀίξαντες
990 φράξαν ἀπειρεσίῃσι Χυτοῦ στόμα νειόθι πέτρης,
πόντιον οἷά τε θῆρα λοχώμενοι ἔνδον ἐόντα.
ἀλλὰ γὰρ αὖθι λέλειπτο σὺν ἀνδράσιν
        ὁπλοτέροισιν
Ἡρακλέης, ὃς δή σφι παλίντονον αἶψα τανύσσας
τόξον ἐπασσυτέρους πέλασε χθονί· τοὶ δὲ καὶ αὐτοὶ
995 πέτρας ἀμφιρρῶγας ἀερτάζοντες ἔβαλλον.
δὴ γάρ που κἀκεῖνα θεὰ τρέφεν αἰνὰ πέλωρα

977 Χυτῷ λιμένι Et. Gen.ᴮ et Et. Magn.: Χυτοῦ λιμένος Ω
990 ἀπειρεσίῃσι Platt: ἀπειρεσίοιο Ω

82

exult in children, but back home his wife Cleite, the fair-haired daughter of Merops of Percote, was still untouched by labor pains. He had just recently brought her, at the cost of marvelous bride gifts, from her father's home on the coast facing the island.[101] But even so he left his bedroom and the bed of his bride to share a feast with them, and banished all fears from his heart. They questioned each other in turn, and he learned from them the purpose of their voyage and about Pelias' commands, while they learned about the cities of his neighbors and the whole gulf of the wide Propontis. But of what lay beyond he did not know enough to give an account, in spite of their desire to learn.

At dawn they climbed lofty Dindymum, to scout for themselves the routes on that sea, while others brought their ship from its former moorage to Chytus harbor.[102] The path they[103] took is called Jason's way. But rushing from the other side of the mountain, the Earthborn men set about blockading the mouth of Chytus from beneath with countless boulders, the way men trap a sea creature lying within. But Heracles, who had been left there[104] with the younger men, immediately drew his backward-bending bow against them and brought them to the ground one after another, while they themselves were lifting and throwing jagged boulders. For no doubt the goddess Hera,

[101] Percote (cf. 1.932) was about 60 miles west of Cyzicus.
[102] Chytus means "blocked."
[103] I.e. the group ascending mount Dindymum.
[104] With the ship to move it to Chytus.

Ἥρη, Ζηνὸς ἄκοιτις, ἀέθλιον Ἡρακλῆι.
σὺν δὲ καὶ ὦλλοι δῆθεν ὑπότροποι ἀντιόωντες,
πρίν περ ἀνελθέμεναι σκοπιήν, ἥπτοντο φόνοιο
1000 Γηγενέων ἥρωες ἀρήιοι, ἠμὲν ὀιστοῖς
ἠδὲ καὶ ἐγχείῃσι δεδεγμένοι, εἰσόκε πάντας
ἀντιβίην ἀσπερχὲς ὀρινομένους ἐδάιξαν.
ὡς δ' ὅτε δούρατα μακρὰ νέον πελέκεσσι τυπέντα
ὑλοτόμοι στοιχηδὸν ἐπὶ ῥηγμῖνι βάλωσιν,
1005 ὄφρα νοτισθέντα κρατεροὺς ἀνεχοίατο γόμφους·
ὡς οἱ ἐνὶ ξυνοχῇ λιμένος πολιοῖο τέταντο
ἑξείης, ἄλλοι μὲν ἐς ἁλμυρὸν ἀθρόοι ὕδωρ
δύπτοντες κεφαλὰς καὶ στήθεα, γυῖα δ' ὕπερθεν
χέρσῳ τεινάμενοι· τοὶ δ' ἔμπαλιν, αἰγιαλοῖο
1010 κράατα μὲν ψαμάθοισι, πόδας δ' εἰς βένθος ἔρειδον,
ἄμφω ἅμ' οἰωνοῖσι καὶ ἰχθύσι κύρμα γενέσθαι.
    ἥρωες δ', ὅτε δή σφιν ἀταρβὴς ἔπλετ' ἄεθλος,
δὴ τότε πείσματα νηὸς ἐπὶ πνοιῇς ἀνέμοιο
λυσάμενοι προτέρωσε διὲξ ἁλὸς οἶδμα νέοντο·
1015 ἡ δ' ἔθεεν λαίφεσσι πανήμερος· οὐ μὲν ἰούσης
νυκτὸς ἔτι ῥιπὴ μένεν ἔμπεδον, ἀλλὰ θύελλαι
ἀντίαι ἁρπάγδην ὀπίσω φέρον, ὄφρ' ἐπέλασσαν
αὖτις ἐυξείνοισι Δολίοσιν. ἐκ δ' ἄρ' ἔβησαν
αὐτονυχί· Ἱερὴ δὲ φατίζεται ἥδ' ἔτι πέτρη,
1020 ᾗ πέρι πείσματα νηὸς ἐπεσσύμενοι ἐβάλοντο.
οὐδέ τις αὐτὴν νῆσον ἐπιφραδέως ἐνόησεν

---

105 This episode is not included in the canonical "Twelve Labors," on which see the note on 1.1318.

Zeus' wife, had been nourishing those terrible monsters too as a labor for Heracles.[105] And then the rest of the warrior heroes joined up with him, having turned back before reaching the peak, and they set about slaying the Earthborn men, meeting their repeated headlong assaults with volleys of arrows and spears until they killed them all. And as when woodcutters throw down long timbers, recently felled by their axes, in a line along the edge of the sea, so that by absorbing moisture they can receive the strong pegs,[106] thus at the narrows of the white-capped harbor they were laid out one after another, some in heaps dipping their heads and chests into the salt water while they stretched their lower limbs out on the land; others, conversely, rested their heads on the sandy shore and their feet in the deep water, both groups to become the prey of birds and fish alike.

Then the heroes, once the trial had ended for them without fear,[107] loosed the ship's cables as the wind came up and headed onward through the sea-swell. The ship sped under sail all day long, but when night came on the rushing wind no longer remained steady, but contrary storm winds seized the ship and carried it back, until they reached once again the hospitable Doliones. That same night they disembarked, and the rock is still called Sacred rock, around which they hastily cast the ship's cables. But no one took care to notice that it was the same island, nor,

---

[106] Moistened timber is recommended for shipbuilding at Theophrastus, *Historia Plantarum* 5.7.4.

[107] Some translate, "when the expedition was safe for them." In either case they avoided having the ship penned in the harbor.

ἔμμεναι· οὐδ' ὑπὸ νυκτὶ Δολίονες ἂψ ἀνιόντας
ἥρωας νημερτὲς ἐπήισαν, ἀλλά που ἀνδρῶν
Μακριέων εἴσαντο Πελασγικὸν ἄρεα κέλσαι.
1025 τῶ καὶ τεύχεα δύντες ἐπὶ σφίσι χεῖρας ἄειραν.
σὺν δ' ἔλασαν μελίας τε καὶ ἀσπίδας
ἀλλήλοισιν
ὀξείῃ ἴκελοι ῥιπῇ πυρός, ἥ τ' ἐνὶ θάμνοις
αὐαλέοισι πεσοῦσα κορύσσεται· ἐν δὲ κυδοιμὸς
δεινός τε ζαμενής τε Δολιονίῳ πέσε δήμῳ.
1030 οὐδ' ὅ γε δηιοτῆτος ὑπὲρ μόρον αὖτις ἔμελλεν
οἴκαδε νυμφιδίους θαλάμους καὶ λέκτρον ἱκέσθαι·
ἀλλά μιν Αἰσονίδης τετραμμένον ἰθὺς ἑοῖο
πλῆξεν ἐπαΐξας στήθος μέσον, ἀμφὶ δὲ δουρὶ
ὀστέον ἐρραίσθη· ὁ δ' ἐνὶ ψαμάθοισιν ἐλυσθεὶς
1035 μοῖραν ἀνέπλησεν. τὴν γὰρ θέμις οὔ ποτ' ἀλύξαι
θνητοῖσιν, πάντῃ δὲ περὶ μέγα πέπταται ἔρκος·
ὣς τὸν ὀιόμενόν που ἀδευκέος ἔκτοθεν ἄτης
εἶναι ἀριστήων αὐτῇ ὑπὸ νυκτὶ πέδησεν
μαρνάμενον κείνοισι. πολεῖς δ' ἐπαρηγόνες ἄλλοι
1040 ἔκταθεν· Ἡρακλέης μὲν ἐνήρατο Τηλεκλῆα
ἠδὲ Μεγαβρόντην· Σφόδριν δ' ἐνάριξεν Ἄκαστος·
Πηλεὺς δὲ Ζέλυν εἷλεν ἀρηίθοόν τε Γέφυρον·
αὐτὰρ ἐυμμελίης Τελαμὼν Βασιλῆα κατέκτα·
Ἴδας δ' αὖ Προμέα, Κλυτίος δ' Ὑάκινθον ἔπεφνεν,
1045 Τυνδαρίδαι δ' ἄμφω Μεγαλοσσάκεα Φλογίον τε·
Οἰνεΐδης δ' ἐπὶ τοῖσιν ἕλε θρασὺν Ἰτυμονῆα
ἠδὲ καὶ Ἀρτακέα, πρόμον ἀνδρῶν· οὓς ἔτι πάντας
ἐνναέται τιμαῖς ἡρωίσι κυδαίνουσιν.

because it was night, did the Doliones clearly recognize that the heroes were returning, but apparently thought a Pelasgian war party of Macrian men[108] had landed, and so they put on their armor and attacked them.

They drove their ashen spears and shields against one another, like a swift rush of fire that falls upon dry brush and rises in a crest; and a tumult both terrible and furious fell upon the Dolionian people. Nor was Cyzicus about to elude his fate and return home from the battle to his bridal chamber and bed, but Jason rushed upon him as he turned to face him, and struck him in the middle of the chest, and the bone shattered around the spear. He crumpled in the sand and fulfilled his destiny. For mortals are never permitted to escape destiny, but its great net is spread all around them. And so, when he doubtless thought he was free of cruel destruction from the heroes, on that very night destiny snared him when he fought against them. And many others helping him were slain. Heracles killed Telecles and Megabrontes; Acastus killed Sphodris; Peleus slew Zelys and the swift warrior Gephyrus; and Telamon of the great ashen spear cut down Basileus; Idas in turn slew Promeus; Clytius killed Hyacinthus; and the two Tyndaridae slew Megalossaces and Phlogius; and, after them, Oeneus' son[109] killed bold Itymoneus and Artaces, leader of men—all of whom to this day the inhabitants glo-

---

[108] These were Greeks from Euboea who settled in the region (schol.).

[109] Meleager, the youngest of the heroes (cf. 1.190–198).

οἱ δ' ἄλλοι εἴξαντες ὑπέτρεσαν, ἠύτε κίρκους
1050 ὠκυπέτας ἀγεληδὸν ὑποτρέσσωσι πέλειαι.
ἐς δὲ πύλας ὁμάδῳ πέσον ἀθρόοι· αἶψα δ' αὐτῆς
πλῆτο πόλις στονόεντος ὑποτροπίῃ πολέμοιο.

ἠῶθεν δ' ὀλοὴν καὶ ἀμήχανον εἰσενόησαν
ἀμπλακίην ἄμφω· στυγερὸν δ' ἄχος εἷλεν ἰδόντας
1055 ἥρωας Μινύας Αἰνήιον υἷα πάροιθεν
Κύζικον ἐν κονίῃσι καὶ αἵματι πεπτηῶτα.
ἤματα δὲ τρία πάντα γόων, τίλλοντό τε χαίτας
αὐτοὶ ὁμῶς λαοί τε Δολίονες. αὐτὰρ ἔπειτα
τρὶς περὶ χαλκείοις σὺν τεύχεσι δινηθέντες
1060 τύμβῳ ἐνεκτερέιξαν, ἐπειρήσαντό τ' ἀέθλων,
ἢ θέμις, ἂμ πεδίον Λειμώνιον· ἔνθ' ἔτι νῦν περ
ἀγκέχυται τόδε σῆμα καὶ ὀψιγόνοισιν ἰδέσθαι.
οὐδὲ μὲν οὐδ' ἄλοχος Κλείτη φθιμένοιο λέλειπτο
οὗ πόσιος μετόπισθε· κακῷ δ' ἐπὶ κύντερον ἄλλο
1065 ἤνυσεν, ἀψαμένη βρόχον αὐχένι. τὴν δὲ καὶ αὐταὶ
νύμφαι ἀποφθιμένην ἀλσηίδες ὠδύραντο·
καί οἱ ἀπὸ βλεφάρων ὅσα δάκρυα χεῦαν ἔραζε,
πάντα τά γε κρήνην τεῦξαν θεαί, ἣν καλέουσιν
Κλείτην, δυστήνοιο περικλεὲς οὔνομα νύμφης.
1070 αἰνότατον δὴ κεῖνο Δολιονίῃσι γυναιξὶν
ἀνδράσι τ' ἐκ Διὸς ἦμαρ ἐπήλυθεν· οὐδὲ γὰρ αὐτῶν
ἔτλη τις πάσσασθαι ἐδητύος, οὐδ' ἐπὶ δηρὸν
ἐξ ἀχέων ἔργοιο μυληφάτου ἐμνώοντο,
ἀλλ' αὔτως ἄφλεκτα διαζώεσκον ἔδοντες.
1075 ἔνθ' ἔτι νῦν, εὖτ' ἄν σφιν ἐτήσια χύτλα χέωνται

rify with heroes' honors. But the rest gave way and fled, as a flock of doves flees before swift-winged hawks. With a din they rushed to the gates in a throng, and the city was immediately filled with loud cries at their retreat from this woeful battle.

At dawn both sides recognized their deadly and irrevocable mistake. Horrible grief seized the Minyan heroes when they saw before them Aeneus' son Cyzicus fallen in dust and blood. For three full days they and the Dolionian people alike lamented and tore their hair. But then, after marching three times around the body in their bronze armor, they laid him in his tomb and competed in games, as is fitting, on the Leimonian plain, where to this day that tomb lies heaped up for later generations to see. Nor indeed did his wife Cleite stay behind after her husband died, but, adding to the woe, she carried out a more horrible deed by fastening a noose around her neck. Even the woodland nymphs themselves lamented her death, and from all the tears they shed for her from their eyes to the ground, the goddesses made a spring, which they call Cleite, the famous[110] name of the unfortunate bride. Indeed, that day was the most dreadful to come from Zeus to the Dolionian women and men. For not one of them could even bear to taste food, and for a long time because of their grief they took no thought of the work of grinding meal, but stayed alive by eating food just as it was, untouched by fire. There to this day, when the Ionians dwelling in Cyzicus pour an-

---

[110] A play on the name Cleite ("Famous").

1059 χαλκείοις σὺν τεύχεσι Ω: χαλκείοισι σὺν ἔντεσι Π[10]

Κύζικον ἐνναίοντες Ἰάονες, ἔμπεδον αἰεὶ
πανδήμοιο μύλης πελανοὺς ἐπαλετρεύουσιν.
    ἐκ δὲ τόθεν τρηχεῖαι ἀνηέρθησαν ἄελλαι
ἤμαθ' ὁμοῦ νύκτας τε δυώδεκα, τοὺς δὲ καταῦθι
1080 ναυτίλλεσθαι ἔρυκον. ἐπιπλομένῃ δ' ἐνὶ νυκτὶ
ὤλλοι μέν ῥα πάρος δεδμημένοι εὐνάζοντο
ὕπνῳ ἀριστῆες πύματον λάχος· αὐτὰρ Ἄκαστος
Μόψος τ' Ἀμπυκίδης ἀδινὰ κνώσσοντας ἔρυντο.
ἡ δ' ἄρ' ὑπὲρ ξανθοῖο καρήατος Αἰσονίδαο
1085 πωτᾶτ' ἀλκυονὶς λιγυρῇ ὀπὶ θεσπίζουσα
λῆξιν ὀρινομένων ἀνέμων· συνέηκε δὲ Μόψος
ἀκταίης ὄρνιθος ἐναίσιμον ὄσσαν ἀκούσας.
καὶ τὴν μὲν θεὸς αὖτις ἀπέτραπεν, ἷζε δ' ὕπερθεν
νηίου ἀφλάστοιο μετήορος ἀίξασα.
1090 τὸν δ' ὅ γε κεκλιμένον μαλακοῖς ἐνὶ κώεσιν οἰῶν
κινήσας ἀνέγειρε παρασχεδόν, ὧδέ τ' ἔειπεν·
    "Αἰσονίδη, χρειώ σε τόδ' ἱερὸν εἰσανιόντα
Δινδύμου ὀκριόεντος ἐύθρονον ἱλάξασθαι
μητέρα συμπάντων μακάρων, λήξουσι δ' ἄελλαι
1095 ζαχρηεῖς· τοίην γὰρ ἐγὼ νέον ὄσσαν ἄκουσα
ἀλκυόνος ἁλίης, ἥ τε κνώσσοντος ὕπερθεν
σεῖο πέριξ τὰ ἕκαστα πιφαυσκομένη πεπότητο.
ἐκ γὰρ τῆς ἄνεμοί τε θάλασσά τε νειόθι τε χθὼν
πᾶσα πεπείρανται νιφόεν θ' ἕδος Οὐλύμποιο·
1100 καί οἱ, ὅτ' ἐξ ὀρέων μέγαν οὐρανὸν εἰσαναβαίνῃ,
Ζεὺς αὐτὸς Κρονίδης ὑποχάζεται, ὡς δὲ καὶ ὦλλοι
ἀθάνατοι μάκαρες δεινὴν θεὸν ἀμφιέπουσιν."

1099 πεπείρανται Köchly: πεπείρηται Ω

nual libations for these dead, they always grind their meal offerings at the public mill.[111]

After this, fierce winds arose for twelve days and nights alike, and kept them there from sailing. But in the following night, while the rest of heroes, long since overcome by sleep, were slumbering during the last watch, Acastus and Mopsus, Ampycus' son, were standing guard over their soundly sleeping comrades. And then above Jason's golden head hovered a halcyon, foretelling with a shrill cry the cessation of the stormy winds. Mopsus understood the auspicious message of the shore bird when he heard it. And then a god[112] turned it away, and it darted up and perched atop the ship's stern ornament. He shook Jason, who was lying in soft woollen fleeces, and woke him at once, and spoke thus:

"Jason, you must go up to that sacred place on rugged Dindymum and propitiate the mother of all the blessed gods on her fine throne,[113] and the furious winds will cease, for such was the message I just heard from the seaborne halcyon, which circled above you while you were sleeping and revealed each of these things. For upon her depend the winds, the sea, the whole earth below, and the snowy seat of Olympus; and when she goes up from the mountains and enters the wide heaven, Zeus himself, Cronus' son, yields place to her, and in the same way the other blessed immortals pay homage to the dread goddess."

[111] As a reminder that the mourners had stopped grinding meal at home.

[112] Probably Rhea, as revealed in Mopsus' speech.

[113] Rhea, the Mother of the gods, associated with Cybele.

ὣς φάτο· τῷ δ᾽ ἀσπαστὸν ἔπος γένετ᾽ εἰσαΐοντι.
ὤρνυτο δ᾽ ἐξ εὐνῆς κεχαρημένος, ὦρσε δ᾽ ἑταίρους
1105 πάντας ἐπισπέρχων, καί τέ σφισιν ἐγρομένοισιν
Ἀμπυκίδεω Μόψοιο θεοπροπίας ἀγόρευσεν.
αἶψα δὲ κουρότεροι μὲν ἀπὸ σταθμῶν ἐλάσαντες
ἔνθεν ἐς αἰπεινὴν ἄναγον βόας οὔρεος ἄκρην·
οἱ δ᾽ ἄρα λυσάμενοι Ἱερῆς ἐκ πείσματα πέτρης
1110 ἤρεσαν ἐς λιμένα Θρηίκιον· ἂν δὲ καὶ αὐτοὶ
βαῖνον, παυροτέρους ἑτάρων ἐν νηὶ λιπόντες.
τοῖσι δὲ Μακριάδες σκοπιαὶ καὶ πᾶσα περαίη
Θρηικίης ἐνὶ χερσὶν ἑαῖς προυφαίνετ᾽ ἰδέσθαι·
φαίνετο δ᾽ ἠερόεν στόμα Βοσπόρου ἠδὲ κολῶναι
1115 Μύσιαι· ἐκ δ᾽ ἑτέρης ποταμοῦ ῥόος Αἰσήποιο
ἄστυ τε καὶ πεδίον Νηπήιον Ἀδρηστείης.
ἔσκε δέ τι στιβαρὸν στύπος ἀμπέλου ἔντροφον
ὕλῃ,
πρόχνυ γεράνδρυον· τὸ μὲν ἔκταμον, ὄφρα πέλοιτο
δαίμονος οὐρείης ἱερὸν βρέτας, ἔξεσε δ᾽ Ἄργος
1120 εὐκόσμως· καὶ δή μιν ἐπ᾽ ὀκριόεντι κολωνῷ
ἵδρυσαν φηγοῖσιν ἐπηρεφὲς ἀκροτάτῃσιν,
αἵ ῥά τε πασάων πανυπέρταται ἐρρίζωνται.
βωμὸν δ᾽ αὖ χέραδος παρενήνεον· ἀμφὶ δὲ φύλλοις
στεψάμενοι δρυΐνοισι θυηπολίης ἐμέλοντο,
1125 Μητέρα Δινδυμίην πολυπότνιαν ἀγκαλέοντες,
ἐνναέτιν Φρυγίης, Τιτίην θ᾽ ἅμα Κύλληνόν τε,
οἳ μοῦνοι πολέων μοιρηγέται ἠδὲ πάρεδροι
Μητέρος Ἰδαίης κεκλῆαται, ὅσσοι ἔασιν

1127 πολέων Ω: πλεόνων Et. Gen.

Thus he spoke, and welcome to Jason were the words he heard. He rose from his bed with joy and hurriedly roused all his comrades; and when they were awake, he told them the prophecies of Ampycus' son Mopsus. Right away the younger men drove oxen from their stalls and led them up from there to the high summit of the mountain. The others loosed the cables from Sacred rock and rowed to the Thracian harbor.[114] They too made the ascent, after leaving only a few comrades on the ship. Before their eyes appeared the Macrian heights and the entire coast of Thrace opposite, as if they held them in their hands. The misty mouth of the Bosporus and the hills of Mysia also appeared, and, on the other side, the stream of the Aesepus river and the city and Nepeian plain of Adrasteia.

There was a sturdy trunk of vine that grew in the forest, very old and dry. They cut this down to make into a sacred image of the mountain goddess,[115] and Argus carved it expertly. And there upon a rugged hilltop they set it up, overshadowed by the tops of oaks, the tallest of all the trees that take root there. Nearby they piled up an altar of stones and, wearing crowns of oak leaves, conducted their sacrifice around it, as they called upon the Dindymian Mother, the much-revered mistress who dwells in Phrygia, along with Titias and Cyllenus, who alone of the many Idaean Dactyls on Crete are called dispensers of destiny and ministers of the Idaean Mother.[116] The nymph Anchiale once

---

[114] For Sacred rock, see 1.1019. The Thracian harbor is on the eastern side of the isthmus.   [115] Rhea/Cybele.

[116] Rhea/Cybele, who is associated with mount Dindymum in central Phrygia and mount Ida on Crete. The Argonauts are now establishing her worship on mount Dindymum near Cyzicus.

Δάκτυλοι Ἰδαῖοι Κρηταιέες, οὕς ποτε νύμφη
1130 Ἀγχιάλη Δικταῖον ἀνὰ σπέος ἀμφοτέρῃσιν
δραξαμένη γαίης Οἰαξίδος ἐβλάστησεν.
πολλὰ δὲ τήν γε λιτῇσιν ἀποστρέψαι ἐριώλας
Αἰσονίδης γουνάζετ' ἐπιλλείβων ἱεροῖσιν
αἰθομένοις· ἄμυδις δὲ νέοι Ὀρφῆος ἀνωγῇ
1135 σκαίροντες βηταρμὸν ἐνόπλιον ὠρχήσαντο,
καὶ σάκεα ξιφέεσσιν ἐπέκτυπον, ὥς κεν ἰωὴ
δύσφημος πλάζοιτο δι' ἠέρος, ἣν ἔτι λαοὶ
κηδείῃ βασιλῆος ἀνέστενον. ἔνθεν ἐσαιεὶ
ῥόμβῳ καὶ τυπάνῳ Ῥείην Φρύγες ἱλάσκονται.
1140 ἡ δέ που εὐαγέεσσιν ἐπὶ φρένα θῆκε θυηλαῖς
ἀνταίη δαίμων, τὰ δ' ἐοικότα σήματ' ἔγεντο.
δένδρεα μὲν καρπὸν χέον ἄσπετον, ἀμφὶ δὲ ποσσὶν
αὐτομάτη φύε γαῖα τερείνης ἄνθεα ποίης·
θῆρες δ' εἰλυούς τε κατὰ ξυλόχους τε λιπόντες
1145 οὐρῇσιν σαίνοντες ἐπήλυθον. ἡ δὲ καὶ ἄλλο
θῆκε τέρας· ἐπεὶ οὔ τι παροίτερον ὕδατι νᾶεν
Δίνδυμον, ἀλλά σφιν τότ' ἀνέβραχε διψάδος αὔτως
ἐκ κορυφῆς ἄλληκτον· Ἰησονίην δ' ἐνέπουσιν
κεῖνο ποτὸν κρήνην περιναιέται ἄνδρες ὀπίσσω.
1150 καὶ τότε μὲν δαῖτ' ἀμφὶ θεᾶς θέσαν οὔρεσιν
Ἄρκτων,
μέλποντες Ῥείην πολυπότνιαν· αὐτὰρ ἐς ἠῶ
ληξάντων ἀνέμων νῆσον λίπον εἰρεσίῃσιν.
ἔνθ' ἔρις ἄνδρα ἕκαστον ἀριστήων ὀρόθυνεν,

1135 ὠρχήσαντο Ω: εἰλίσσοντο Et. Magn. et Et. Gen.

94

bore the Dactyls in the Dictaean cave while clutching the
ground of Oaxus with both hands.[117] Jason supplicated the
goddess with many prayers to turn away the tempest, as he
poured libations on the blazing sacrifices. At the same
time, upon Orpheus' command, the young men leapt as
they danced the dance-in-armor and beat their shields
with their swords, so that any ill-omened cry of grief,
which the people were still sending up in lament for their
king, would be lost in the air. Since then, the Phrygians
have always propitiated Rhea with rhombus and tambou-
rine.[118] The amenable goddess evidently paid heed to their
holy sacrifices, for fitting signs appeared. The trees shed
fruit in abundance, and at their feet the earth spontane-
ously sprouted flowers in the tender grass; wild animals left
their dens and lairs and approached, wagging their tails.
And she performed yet another miracle, for water had
never before flowed on Dindymum, but then, just like that,
it gushed forth for them without cease from the arid peak.
The neighboring peoples have since then called that water
Jason's spring. Then they held a feast in honor of the god-
dess on Bear mountain and hymned Rhea, the much-
revered mistress. But at dawn when the winds had abated,
they rowed away from the island.

Then rivalry spurred on each one of the heroes, to see

[117] Mount Dicte and Oaxus are on Crete. Her ten fingers
(*dactyloi*) represent the ten Dactyls she produced.

[118] The rhombus is a circular piece of metal that makes a roar
when whirled; the typanum (or tympanum) is variously inter-
preted as a tambourine or drum.

ὅς τις ἀπολλήξειε πανύστατος· ἀμφὶ γὰρ αἰθὴρ
1155 νήνεμος ἐστόρεσεν δίνας, κατὰ δ' εὔνασε πόντον.
οἱ δὲ γαληναίῃ πίσυνοι ἐλάασκον ἐπιπρὸ
νῆα βίῃ· τὴν δ' οὔ κε διὲξ ἁλὸς ἀίσσουσαν
οὐδὲ Ποσειδάωνος ἀελλόποδες κίχον ἵπποι.
ἔμπης δ' ἐγρομένοιο σάλου ζαχρηέσιν αὔραις,
1160 αἳ νέον ἐκ ποταμῶν ὑπὸ δείελον ἠερέθονται,
τειρόμενοι καμάτῳ μετελώφεον· αὐτὰρ ὁ τούς γε
πασσυδίῃ μογέοντας ἐφέλκετο κάρτεϊ χειρῶν
Ἡρακλέης, ἐτίνασσε δ' ἀρηρότα δούρατα νηός.
ἀλλ' ὅτε δὴ Μυσῶν λελιημένοι ἠπείροιο
1165 Ῥυνδακίδας προχοὰς μέγα τ' ἠρίον Αἰγαίωνος
τυτθὸν ὑπὲκ Φρυγίης παρεμέτρεον εἰσορόωντες,
δὴ τότ' ἀνοχλίζων τετρηχότος οἴδματος ὁλκοὺς
μεσσόθεν ἆξεν ἐρετμόν· ἀτὰρ τρύφος ἄλλο μὲν
αὐτὸς
ἄμφω χερσὶν ἔχων πέσε δόχμιος, ἄλλο δὲ πόντος
1170 κλύζε παλιρροθίοισι φέρων. ἀνὰ δ' ἕζετο σιγῇ
παπταίνων· χεῖρες γὰρ ἀήθεσον ἠρεμέουσαι.
    ἦμος δ' ἀγρόθεν εἶσι φυτοσκάφος ἤ τις ἀροτρεὺς
ἀσπασίως εἰς αὖλιν ἑὴν δόρποιο χατίζων,
αὐτοῦ δ' ἐν προμολῇ τετρυμένα γούνατ' ἔκαμψεν
1175 αὐσταλέος κονίῃσι, περιτριβέας δέ τε χεῖρας
εἰσορόων κακὰ πολλὰ ἑῇ ἠρήσατο γαστρί·
τῆμος ἄρ' οἵ γ' ἀφίκοντο Κιανίδος ἤθεα γαίης
ἀμφ' Ἀργανθώνειον ὄρος προχοάς τε Κίοιο.

1161 καμάτῳ Et. Magn. et Et. Gen.: καὶ δὴ Ω

96

who would be last to quit, since all around them the still air had smoothed the swirling waters and lulled the sea to sleep. Confident in the calm sea, they propelled the ship forward mightily, and not even Poseidon's storm-footed horses could have overtaken it as it sped through the sea. Nevertheless, when a swell was awakened by the violent winds that arise fresh from rivers toward evening, worn out from their toil, they began to flag. But Heracles kept pulling his weary companions along, one and all, by the strength of his hands, and made the well-joined timbers of the ship quake. But when, in their eagerness to reach the mainland of Mysia, they were passing within sight of the mouth of the Rhyndacus and the great tomb of Aegaeon,[119] a short distance beyond Phrygia, then, as Heracles was heaving up furrows in the rough swell, he broke his oar in the middle. Still grasping a piece of it in his two hands, he fell sideways, while the sea carried the other piece away on its receding wash. He sat up, looking around in silence, for his hands were not used to being idle.

At the hour when a gardener or plowman gladly leaves the field for his hut, longing for dinner, and there on the doorstep, caked with dust, he bends his weary knees and stares at his worn-out hands and heaps curses on his belly, then it was that they reached the homesteads of the Cianian land near the Arganthonian mountain and the mouth of the Cius river. Because they came in friendship,

---

[119] A hundred-handed giant also called Briareus (*Iliad* 1.403).

τοὺς μὲν ἐυξείνως Μυσοὶ φιλότητι κιόντας
1180 δειδέχατ' ἐνναέται κείνης χθονός, ἥιά τέ σφιν
μῆλά τε δευομένοις μέθυ τ' ἄσπετον ἐγγυάλιξαν.
ἔνθα δ' ἔπειθ' οἱ μὲν ξύλα κάγκανα, τοὶ δὲ λεχαίην
φυλλάδα λειμώνων φέρον ἄσπετον ἀμήσαντες
στόρνυσθαι· τοὶ δ' ἀμφὶ πυρήια δινεύεσκον·
1185 οἱ δ' οἶνον κρητῆρσι κέρων, πονέοντό τε δαῖτα,
Ἐκβασίῳ ῥέξαντες ὑπὸ κνέφας Ἀπόλλωνι.
    αὐτὰρ ὁ εὖ δαίνυσθαι ἐοῖς ἑτάροις ἐπιτείλας
βῆ ῥ' ἴμεν εἰς ὕλην υἱὸς Διός, ὥς κεν ἐρετμὸν
οἷ αὐτῷ φθαίη καταχείριον ἐντύνασθαι.
1190 εὖρεν ἔπειτ' ἐλάτην ἀλαλήμενος οὔτε τι πολλοῖς
ἀχθομένην ὄζοις οὐδὲ μέγα τηλεθόωσαν,
ἀλλ' οἷον ταναῆς ἔρνος πέλει αἰγείροιο·
τόσση ὁμῶς μῆκός τε καὶ ἐς πάχος ἦεν ἰδέσθαι.
1195 ῥίμφα δ' οἰστοδόκην μὲν ἐπὶ χθονὶ θῆκε φαρέτρην
αὐτοῖσιν τόξοισιν, ἔδυ δ' ἀπὸ δέρμα λέοντος.
τὴν δ' ὅ γε χαλκοβαρεῖ ῥοπάλῳ δαπέδοιο τινάξας
νειόθεν ἀμφοτέρῃσι περὶ στύπος ἔλλαβε χερσὶν
ἠνορέῃ πίσυνος· ἐν δὲ πλατὺν ὦμον ἔρεισεν
1200 εὖ διαβάς· πεδόθεν δὲ βαθύρριζόν περ ἐοῦσαν
προσφὺς ἐξήειρε σὺν αὐτοῖς ἔχμασι γαίης.
ὡς δ' ὅταν ἀπροφάτως ἱστὸν νεός, εὖτε μάλιστα
χειμερίη ὀλοοῖο δύσις πέλει Ὠρίωνος,
ὑψόθεν ἐμπλήξασα θοὴ ἀνέμοιο κατάιξ
αὐτοῖσι σφήνεσσιν ὑπὲκ προτόνων ἐρύσηται·
1205 ὣς ὅ γε τὴν ἤειρεν. ὁμοῦ δ' ἀνὰ τόξα καὶ ἰοὺς

the Mysians who inhabited that land welcomed them with hospitality and gave them in their need provisions and sheep and abundant wine. Thereupon some of the crew were bringing dry wood, while others were bringing leaves that they had gathered in abundance from the meadows to spread for beds; some were twirling sticks to make fire; and others were mixing wine in bowls and preparing the feast—all after sacrificing at dusk to Apollo Ecbasius.

But the son of Zeus[120] bade his comrades feast well and went off into the woods, so that he could first make himself an oar to fit his hands. In his wanderings he then found a pine tree not burdened with many branches nor sprouting much growth, but one that looked like the shaft of a tall poplar in both height and thickness. He quickly set his arrow-holding quiver along with his bow on the ground and took off his lion skin. With a blow of his bronze-laden club he loosened the tree from the soil below and then wrapped both arms around the trunk, confident in his strength. He braced his broad shoulder against it and planted his feet wide apart. He gripped it tightly and, though its roots were deep, lifted it out of the ground along with the clods of earth that held it. And as when, just as the wintertime setting of baneful Orion occurs,[121] a swift blast of wind from on high unexpectedly strikes a ship's mast and rips it from its stays, wedges and all,[122] so did he lift up the pine tree.

[120] Heracles.
[121] In November, marking the dangerous period for sailing.
[122] The wedges held the mast in place at its base.

1187 ὁ εὖ δαίνυσθαι ἑοῖς ἑτάροις Samuelsson: ὁ δαίνυσθαι ἑτάροις εὖ Ω

99

δέρμα θ᾽ ἑλὼν ῥόπαλόν τε παλίσσυτος ὦρτο
    νέεσθαι.
    τόφρα δ᾽ Ὕλας χαλκέῃ σὺν κάλπιδι νόσφιν
    ὁμίλου
δίζητο κρήνης ἱερὸν ῥόον, ὥς κέ οἱ ὕδωρ
φθαίη ἀφυσσάμενος ποτιδόρπιον, ἄλλα τε πάντα
1210 ὀτραλέως κατὰ κόσμον ἐπαρτίσσειεν ἰόντι.
δὴ γάρ μιν τοίοισιν ἐν ἤθεσιν αὐτὸς ἔφερβεν,
νηπίαχον τὰ πρῶτα δόμων ἐκ πατρὸς ἀπούρας,
δίου Θειοδάμαντος, ὃν ἐν Δρυόπεσσιν ἔπεφνεν
νηλειῶς βοὸς ἀμφὶ γεωμόρου ἀντιόωντα.
1215 ἤτοι ὁ μὲν νειοῖο γύας τέμνεσκεν ἀρότρῳ
Θειοδάμας ἀνίῃ βεβολημένος· αὐτὰρ ὁ τόν γε
βοῦν ἀρότην ἤνωγε παρασχέμεν οὐκ ἐθέλοντα.
ἵετο γὰρ πρόφασιν πολέμου Δρυόπεσσι βαλέσθαι
λευγαλέην, ἐπεὶ οὔ τι δίκης ἀλέγοντες ἔναιον.
1220 ἀλλὰ τὰ μὲν τηλοῦ κεν ἀποπλάγξειεν ἀοιδῆς.
    αἶψα δ᾽ ὅ γε κρήνην μετεκίαθεν, ἣν καλέουσιν
Πηγὰς ἀγχίγυοι περιναιέται. οἱ δέ που ἄρτι
νυμφάων ἵσταντο χοροί· μέλε γάρ σφισι πάσαις,
ὅσσαι κεῖσ᾽ ἐρατὸν νύμφαι ῥίον ἀμφενέμοντο,
1225 Ἄρτεμιν ἐννυχίῃσιν ἀεὶ μέλπεσθαι ἀοιδαῖς.
αἱ μέν, ὅσαι σκοπιὰς ὀρέων λάχον ἢ καὶ ἐναύλους,
αἵ γε μὲν ὑλήωροι ἀπόπροθεν ἐστιχόωντο·
ἡ δὲ νέον κρήνης ἀνεδύετο καλλινάοιο
νύμφη ἐφυδατίη. τὸν δὲ σχεδὸν εἰσενόησεν

Then he picked up his bow and arrows, lion skin, and club, and set out to return.

In the meantime, Hylas went off from the crew with a bronze pitcher in search of a spring's sacred flow, so that he might collect water for the evening meal before Heracles returned and get everything else promptly prepared and in due order for his arrival. For in such habits had Heracles himself raised him, ever since he took him as an infant from the palace of his father, noble Theiodamas, whom he ruthlessly killed among the Dryopians for opposing him over a plowing ox. Now Theiodamas, stricken with pain,[123] was cleaving his fallow fields with a plow, when Heracles ordered him to hand over the plowing ox against his will. For he was eager to create a dire pretext for war against the Dryopians, because they lived there with no concern for justice. But these things would divert me far from my song.

Soon Hylas came to a spring, which the neighboring inhabitants call Pegae.[124] Just about then choruses of nymphs were being formed, for all the nymphs who lived there on the lovely peak[125] made it their concern to hymn Artemis every night with songs. And so all the nymphs who haunted the mountain peaks or rushing streams,[126] and those who were wardens of the woods, were coming in lines from afar; but the water nymph was just rising from the fair-flowing spring. She noticed the boy nearby, glow-

---

[123] The source or meaning of his pain is not known; it may refer to the toil of plowing. The encounter with Theiodamas was also related in Callimachus' *Aetia* (cf. *frr.* 24–25 Pf.).

[124] I.e. Springs.

[125] Of the Arganthonian mountain (cf. 1.1178).

[126] ἐναύλους are variously rendered as "torrents" (Homer), "caves" (schol.), or "dwelling-places" (Hesiod, *Theogony* 129).

1230 κάλλεϊ καὶ γλυκερῇσιν ἐρευθόμενον χαρίτεσσιν·
προς γάρ οἱ διχόμηνις ἀπ᾽ αἰθέρος αὐγάζουσα
βάλλε σεληναίη. τῆς δὲ φρένας ἐπτοίησεν
Κύπρις, ἀμηχανίῃ δὲ μόλις συναγείρατο θυμόν.
αὐτὰρ ὅ γ᾽ ὡς τὰ πρῶτα ῥόῳ ἔνι κάλπιν ἔρεισεν
1235 λέχρις ἐπιχριμφθείς, περὶ δ᾽ ἄσπετον ἔβραχεν ὕδωρ
χαλκὸν ἐς ἠχήεντα φορεύμενον, αὐτίκα δ᾽ ἥ γε
λαιὸν μὲν καθύπερθεν ἐπ᾽ αὐχένος ἄνθετο πῆχυν
κύσσαι ἐπιθύουσα τέρεν στόμα, δεξιτερῇ δὲ
ἀγκῶν᾽ ἔσπασε χειρί· μέσῃ δ᾽ ἐνὶ κάββαλε δίνῃ.
1240   τοῦ δ᾽ ἥρως ἰάχοντος ἐπέκλυεν οἷος ἑταίρων
Εἰλατίδης Πολύφημος, ἰὼν προτέρωσε κελεύθου,
δέκτο γὰρ Ἡρακλῆα πελώριον, ὁππόθ᾽ ἵκοιτο.
βῆ δὲ μεταΐξας Πηγέων σχεδόν, ἠύτε τις θὴρ
ἄγριος, ὅν ῥά τε γῆρυς ἀπόπροθεν ἵκετο μήλων,
1245 λιμῷ δ᾽ αἰθόμενος μετανίσσεται, οὐδ᾽ ἐπέκυρσεν
ποίμνῃσιν· πρὸ γὰρ αὐτοὶ ἐνὶ σταθμοῖσι νομῆες
ἔλσαν· ὁ δὲ στενάχων βρέμει ἄσπετον, ὄφρα
        κάμῃσιν·
ὣς τότ᾽ ἄρ᾽ Εἰλατίδης μεγάλ᾽ ἔστενεν, ἀμφὶ δὲ
        χῶρον
φοίτα κεκληγώς, μελέη δέ οἱ ἔπλετο φωνή.
1250 αἶψα δ᾽ ἐρυσσάμενος μέγα φάσγανον ὦρτο δίεσθαι,
μή πως ἢ θήρεσσιν ἔλωρ πέλοι, ἠέ μιν ἄνδρες
μοῦνον ἐόντ᾽ ἐλόχησαν, ἄγουσι δὲ ληίδ᾽ ἑτοίμην.
ἔνθ᾽ αὐτῷ ξύμβλητο κατὰ στίβον Ἡρακλῆι
γυμνὸν ἐπαΐσσων παλάμῃ ξίφος· εὖ δέ μιν ἔγνω

ing with rosy beauty and sweet charms, for the full moon was casting its rays on him as it gleamed from the sky. Cypris confounded her thoughts, and in her helpless state she could barely collect her spirit.[127] But as soon as he leaned on one side and dipped the pitcher into the stream, and the abundant water gurgled as it poured into the echoing bronze, at once she raised her left arm over his neck in her longing to kiss his tender mouth, while with her right hand she pulled on his elbow and plunged him into the midst of the swirling water.

The only one of the comrades to hear the boy shout was Eilatus' son, the hero Polyphemus, who was heading down the path, for he was expecting massive Heracles to return. He rushed toward the cry and drew near to Pegae, like a wild beast to which comes the bleating of sheep from afar, and, burning with hunger, it goes in pursuit but does not reach the flocks, for beforehand their own shepherds have shut them in their pens, and so he groans and roars vehemently until he tires—so at that time did Eilatus' son groan mightily and wander about the spot calling out, but his shouting was in vain.[128] Immediately he drew his great sword and went off in pursuit, fearing that the boy might be prey to wild animals, or that, all alone as he was, men had ambushed him and were taking away their easy capture. Thereupon, as he was brandishing his bare sword in his hand, he came upon Heracles himself on the path, and

---

[127] θυμός indicates both breath and consciousness. She almost fainted.   [128] Or *became feeble*.

1249 ἔπλετο φωνή Ω: ἔπλετ᾽ αὐτῇ Et. Magn. et Et. Gen.
1250 δίεσθαι Et. Magn.: νέεσθαι Ω

103

1255 σπερχόμενον μετὰ νῆα διὰ κνέφας. αὐτίκα δ᾽ ἄτην
ἔκφατο λευγαλέην βεβαρημένος ἄσθματι θυμόν·
"δαιμόνιε, στυγερόν τοι ἄχος πάμπρωτος ἐνίψω.
οὐ γὰρ Ὕλας κρήνηνδε κιὼν σόος αὖτις ἱκάνει,
ἀλλά ἑ ληιστῆρες ἐνιχρίμψαντες ἄγουσιν,
1260 ἢ θῆρες σίνονται· ἐγὼ δ᾽ ἰάχοντος ἄκουσα."
      ὣς φάτο· τῷ δ᾽ ἀίοντι κατὰ κροτάφων ἅλις ἱδρὼς
κήκιεν, ἐν δὲ κελαινὸν ὑπὸ σπλάγχνοις ζέεν αἷμα.
χωόμενος δ᾽ ἐλάτην χαμάδις βάλεν, ἐς δὲ κέλευθον
τὴν θέεν, ᾗ πόδες αὐτὸν ὑπέκφερον ἀίσσοντα.
1265 ὡς δ᾽ ὅτε τίς τε μύωπι τετυμμένος ἔσσυτο ταῦρος
πίσεά τε προλιπὼν καὶ ἑλεσπίδας, οὐδὲ νομήων
οὐδ᾽ ἀγέλης ὄθεται, πρήσσει δ᾽ ὁδὸν ἄλλοτ᾽
      ἄπαυστος,
ἄλλοτε δ᾽ ἱστάμενος καὶ ἀνὰ πλατὺν αὐχέν᾽ ἀείρων
ἵησιν μύκημα, κακῷ βεβολημένος οἴστρῳ·
1270 ὣς ὅ γε μαιμώων ὀτὲ μὲν θοὰ γούνατ᾽ ἔπαλλεν
συνεχέως, ὀτὲ δ᾽ αὖτε μεταλλήγων καμάτοιο
τῆλε διαπρύσιον μεγάλῃ βοάασκεν ἀυτῇ.
      αὐτίκα δ᾽ ἀκροτάτας ὑπερέσχεθεν ἄκριας ἀστὴρ
ἠῶος, πνοιαὶ δὲ κατήλυθον· ὦκα δὲ Τῖφυς
1275 ἐσβαίνειν ὀρόθυνεν ἐπαυρέσθαι τ᾽ ἀνέμοιο.
οἱ δ᾽ εἴσβαινον ἄφαρ λελιημένοι, ὕψι δὲ νηὸς
εὐναίας ἐρύσαντες ἀνεκρούσαντο κάλωας.
κυρτώθη δ᾽ ἀνέμῳ λίνα μεσσόθι, τῆλε δ᾽ ἀπ᾽ ἀκτῆς
γηθόσυνοι φορέοντο παραὶ Ποσιδήιον ἄκρην.
1280   ἦμος δ᾽ οὐρανόθεν χαροπὴ ὑπολάμπεται ἠὼς
ἐκ περάτης ἀνιοῦσα, διαγλαύσσουσι δ᾽ ἀταρποί,

easily recognized him as he hastened through the darkness to the ship. Immediately he told of the terrible calamity, with a heavy heart and out of breath:

"My poor friend, I shall be the first to tell you of a horrible grief: Hylas went to the spring and has not returned safely, but bandits have attacked him and are taking him away, or beasts are tearing him apart. I heard him shouting."

Thus he spoke. When Heracles heard this, sweat poured forth in abundance down from his temples and the dark blood seethed deep in his gut. In anger he threw the pine tree to the ground, and ran down any path on which his feet carried him headlong. As when, stung by a gadfly, a bull charges forth, leaving the meadows and marshlands, and pays no attention to the herdsmen or the herd, but at times makes his way without stopping, while at other times he stands still and raises his broad neck and lets out a bellow, having been stung by a vicious fly—thus in his frenzy he sometimes moved his swift knees without a break, then sometimes ceased from his labor and shouted piercingly into the distance with a mighty cry.

Soon the morning star rose above the highest peaks, and the breezes swept down. And at once Tiphys urged them to board and take advantage of the wind. In their eagerness they boarded right away, drew the ship's anchors up on deck, and pulled back on the halyards. The sail bulged in the middle from the wind, and far out from the shore they joyfully were being borne past the Posideian headland.

But at the time when bright dawn shines down from the sky, as it rises from the horizon, and the pathways are

APOLLONIUS RHODIUS

καὶ πεδία δροσόεντα φαεινῇ λάμπεται αἴγλῃ,
τῆμος τούς γ' ἐνόησαν ἀιδρείῃσι λιπόντες.
ἐν δέ σφιν κρατερὸν νεῖκος πέσεν, ἐν δὲ κολῳὸς
1285 ἄσπετος, εἰ τὸν ἄριστον ἀποπρολιπόντες ἔβησαν
σφωιτέρων ἑτάρων. ὁ δ' ἀμηχανίῃσιν ἀτυχθεὶς
οὐδέ τι τοῖον ἔπος μετεφώνεεν οὐδέ τι τοῖον
Αἰσονίδης, ἀλλ' ἧστο βαρείῃ νειόθεν ἄτῃ
θυμὸν ἔδων. Τελαμῶνα δ' ἕλεν χόλος, ὧδέ τ' ἔειπεν·
1290   "ἧσ' αὔτως εὔκηλος, ἐπεί νύ τοι ἄρμενον ἦεν
Ἡρακλῆα λιπεῖν· σέο δ' ἔκτοθι μῆτις ὄρωρεν,
ὄφρα τὸ κείνου κῦδος ἀν' Ἑλλάδα μή σε καλύψῃ,
αἴ κε θεοὶ δώωσιν ὑπότροπον οἴκαδε νόστον.
ἀλλὰ τί μύθων ἦδος; ἐπεὶ καὶ νόσφιν ἑταίρων
1295 εἶμι τεῶν, οἳ τόνδε δόλον συνετεκτήναντο."
    ἦ, καὶ ἐς Ἀγνιάδην Τῖφυν θόρε· τὼ δέ οἱ ὄσσε
ὄστλιγγες μαλεροῖο πυρὸς ὣς ἰνδάλλοντο.
καί νύ κεν ἂψ ὀπίσω Μυσῶν ἐπὶ γαῖαν ἵκοντο
λαῖτμα βιησάμενοι ἀνέμου τ' ἄλληκτον ἰωήν,
1300 εἰ μὴ Θρηικίοιο δύω υἷες Βορέαο
Αἰακίδην χαλεποῖσιν ἐρητύεσκον ἔπεσσιν,
σχέτλιοι· ἦ τέ σφιν στυγερὴ τίσις ἔπλετ' ὀπίσσω
χερσὶν ὑφ' Ἡρακλῆος, ὅ μιν δίζεσθαι ἔρυκον.
ἄθλων γὰρ Πελίαο δεδουπότος ἂψ ἀνιόντας
1305 Τήνῳ ἐν ἀμφιρύτῃ πέφνεν, καὶ ἀμήσατο γαῖαν
ἀμφ' αὐτοῖς, στήλας τε δύω καθύπερθεν ἔτευξεν,
ὧν ἑτέρη, θάμβος περιώσιον ἀνδράσι λεύσσειν,
κίνυται ἠχήεντος ὑπὸ πνοιῇ Βορέαο.
καὶ τὰ μὲν ὣς ἤμελλε μετὰ χρόνον ἐκτελέεσθαι.

106

clearly visible, and the dewy plains sparkle in the bright gleam, they realized that they had unwittingly left those men behind. And fierce strife came upon them and a great uproar, to think that they had gone off and abandoned the best man of their comrades. Stunned with helplessness, Jason spoke not a word on one side or the other, but sat there, eating his heart out from deep within at this grievous calamity. And anger took hold of Telamon, and he spoke thus:

"Sit there calmly like that, since it was to your advantage to leave Heracles. It was from you that this plan originated, so that his glory throughout Hellas would not put you in the shade, if the gods grant our return trip home. But what pleasure is there in words? For I will go back, even without the aid of those comrades of yours who helped contrive this treachery."

He spoke and rushed up to Tiphys, Hagnias' son; and his eyes sparkled like flashes of blazing fire. And so they would have gone back again to the land of the Mysians after struggling against the surge and constant blast of the wind, had not the two sons of Thracian Boreas restrained Aeacus' son with harsh words—unfortunate men, for in fact horrible vengeance came upon them later at the hands of Heracles because they had prevented the search for him. For as they were returning from the games held when Pelias died, he killed them in sea-girt Tenos, and heaped earth over them and set two pillars on top, one of which— an extraordinary marvel for men to behold—moves at the gusts of the whistling north wind. And thus were those things to be accomplished in the course of time.

APOLLONIUS RHODIUS

1310 τοῖσιν δὲ Γλαῦκος βρυχίης ἁλὸς ἐξεφαάνθη,
Νηρῆος θείοιο πολυφράδμων ὑποφήτης·
ὕψι δὲ λαχνῆέν τε κάρη καὶ στήθε' ἀείρας
νειόθεν ἐκ λαγόνων στιβαρῇ ἐπορέξατο χειρὶ
νηίου ὁλκαίοιο, καὶ ἴαχεν ἐσσυμένοισιν·
1315 "τίπτε παρὲκ μεγάλοιο Διὸς μενεαίνετε βουλὴν
Αἰήτεω πτολίεθρον ἄγειν θρασὺν Ἡρακλῆα;
Ἄργεΐ οἱ μοῖρ' ἐστὶν ἀτασθάλῳ Εὐρυσθῆι
ἐκπλῆσαι μογέοντα δυώδεκα πάντας ἀέθλους,
ναίειν δ' ἀθανάτοισι συνέστιον, εἴ κ' ἔτι παύρους
1320 ἐξανύσῃ· τῶ μή τι ποθὴ κείνοιο πελέσθω.
αὔτως δ' αὖ Πολύφημον ἐπὶ προχοῇσι Κίοιο
πέπρωται Μυσοῖσι περικλεὲς ἄστυ καμόντα
μοῖραν ἀναπλήσειν Χαλύβων ἐν ἀπείρονι γαίῃ.
αὐτὰρ Ὕλαν φιλότητι θεὰ ποιήσατο νύμφη
1325 ὃν πόσιν, οἷό περ οὕνεκ' ἀποπλαγχθέντες ἔλειφθεν."
ἦ, καὶ κῦμ' ἀλίαστον ἐφέσσατο νειόθι δύψας·
ἀμφὶ δέ οἱ δίνῃσι κυκώμενον ἄφρεεν ὕδωρ
πορφύρεον, κοίλην δὲ διὲξ ἁλὸς ἔκλυσε νῆα.
γήθησαν δ' ἥρωες· ὁ δ' ἐσσυμένως ἐβεβήκει
1330 Αἰακίδης Τελαμὼν ἐς Ἰήσονα, χεῖρα δὲ χειρὶ
ἄκρην ἀμφιβαλὼν προσπτύξατο, φώνησέν τε·
"Αἰσονίδη, μή μοί τι χολώσεαι, ἀφραδίῃσιν
εἴ τί περ ἀασάμην· πέρι γάρ μ' ἄχος ἧκεν ἐνισπεῖν

1333 ἧκεν LωE: εἷλεν L²γρA

108

But to them out of the salty depths appeared Glaucus, the wise interpreter of divine Nereus. Raising up his shaggy head and chest down to his waist, he seized the ship's keel in his mighty hand and shouted to the men in their haste:

"Why, in opposition to the plan of great Zeus, are you determined to take bold Heracles to Aeetes' city? At Argos it is his destiny to toil for arrogant Eurystheus and accomplish twelve labors in all,[129] and to dwell in the home of the immortals if he completes a few more. Therefore, let there be no remorse at all for him. Likewise, it is fated that Polyphemus build a glorious city among the Mysians at the mouth of the Cius and fulfill his destiny in the vast land of the Chalybes. But as for Hylas, a divine nymph has made him her husband out of love; it was for his sake that they wandered off and were left behind."

He spoke and cloaked himself in the restless wave as he plunged below. Around him the dark water foamed as it was stirred in whirlpools and washed the hollow ship on through the sea. The heroes rejoiced, and Aeacus' son Telamon rushed up to Jason, took his hand in his own, embraced him, and said:

"Jason, do not be angry with me, if I foolishly blundered, for excessive grief impelled me to make that arro-

---

[129] The twelve labors of Heracles according to Apollodorus 2.5 (cf. Diodorus Siculus 4.11–26) are: (1) the Nemean lion, (2) the Lernean hydra, (3) the golden-horned doe, (4) the Erymanthian boar, (5) the stables of Augeas, (6) the Stymphalian birds, (7) the Cretan bull, (8) Diomedes' mares, (9) Hippolyte's belt, (10) Geryon's cattle, (11) the golden apples of the Hesperides, (12) bringing Cerberus from Hades.

μῦθον ὑπερφίαλόν τε καὶ ἄσχετον. ἀλλ᾿ ἀνέμοισιν
1335 δώομεν ἀμπλακίην, ὡς καὶ πάρος εὐμενέοντες."
　　τὸν δ᾿ αὖτ᾿ Αἴσονος υἱὸς ἐπιφραδέως προσέειπεν·
　　"ὦ πέπον, ἦ μάλα δή με κακῷ ἐκυδάσσαο μύθῳ,
φὰς ἐνὶ τοῖσιν ἅπασιν ἐνηέος ἀνδρὸς ἀλείτην
ἔμμεναι. ἀλλ᾿ οὔ θήν τοι ἀδευκέα μῆνιν ἀέξω,
1340 πρίν περ ἀνιηθείς· ἐπεὶ οὐ περὶ πώεσι μήλων
οὐδὲ περὶ κτεάτεσσι χαλεψάμενος μενέηνας,
ἀλλ᾿ ἑτάρου περὶ φωτός. ἔολπα δέ τοι σὲ καὶ ἄλλῳ
ἀμφ᾿ ἐμεῦ, εἰ τοιόνδε πέλοι ποτέ, δηρίσασθαι."
　　ἦ ῥα, καὶ ἀρθμηθέντες, ὅπῃ πάρος, ἑδριόωντο.
1345 τὼ δὲ Διὸς βουλῇσιν, ὁ μὲν Μυσοῖσι βαλέσθαι
μέλλεν ἐπώνυμον ἄστυ πολισσάμενος ποταμοῖο
Εἰλατίδης Πολύφημος, ὁ δ᾿ Εὐρυσθῆος ἀέθλους
αὖτις ἰὼν πονέεσθαι. ἐπηπείλησε δὲ γαῖαν
Μυσίδ᾿ ἀναστήσειν αὐτοσχεδόν, ὁππότε μή οἱ
1350 ἢ ζωοῦ εὕροιεν Ὕλα μόρον ἠὲ θανόντος.
τοῖο δὲ ῥύσι᾿ ὄπασσαν ἀποκρίναντες ἀρίστους
υἱέας ἐκ δήμοιο, καὶ ὅρκια ποιήσαντο,
μή ποτε μαστεύοντες ἀπολλήξειν καμάτοιο.
τούνεκεν εἰσέτι νῦν περ Ὕλαν ἐρέουσι Κιανοί,
1355 κοῦρον Θειοδάμαντος, ἐυκτιμένης τε μέλονται
Τρηχῖνος· δὴ γάρ ῥα καταυτόθι νάσσατο παῖδας,
οὕς οἱ ῥύσια κεῖθεν ἐπιπροέηκαν ἄγεσθαι.
　　νηῦν δὲ πανημερίην ἄνεμος φέρε νυκτί τε πάσῃ
λάβρος ἐπιπνείων· ἀτὰρ οὐδ᾿ ἐπὶ τυτθὸν ἄητο

1338 τοῖσιν Ω: τοισίδ᾿ Platt

110

gant and insufferable rebuke. Let us cast that mistake to the winds and be friends as before."

In turn, Jason answered him with due consideration:

"My good friend, you certainly did revile me with a harsh rebuke, claiming in front of them all that I betrayed a man who was kind to me. But I can assure you that I harbor no bitter wrath against you, although before this I was pained, because it was not over flocks of sheep or over possessions that you flared up in anger, but for a man who was your comrade. Indeed, I hope that you would oppose another man as well on my behalf, if a similar situation ever arose."

He spoke, and they sat down, united as before. But as for the two left behind, by Zeus' plan Polyphemus, Eilatus' son, was to found and build a city for the Mysians named for the river,[130] while Heracles was to go back again and perform Eurystheus' labors. He threatened to devastate the Mysian land on the spot, if they did not discover for him the fate of Hylas, whether alive or dead. And as pledges thereof, they chose the noblest boys from the people and handed them over, and swore oaths that they would never cease their efforts in the search. Therefore, to this day the people of Cius ask after Hylas, Theiodamas' son, and keep ties to well-built Trachis, for that is where Heracles settled the boys whom they sent him to take as pledges from their city.

All day long and the entire night a violent wind blew and bore the ship on, but when dawn arose, there was not

[130] Cius.

111

1360   ἠοῦς τελλομένης. οἱ δὲ χθονὸς εἰσανέχουσαν
       ἀκτὴν ἐκ κόλποιο μάλ' εὐρείην ἐσιδέσθαι
       φρασσάμενοι κώπῃσιν ἅμ' ἠελίῳ ἐπέκελσαν.
       [ἠὼς δ' οὐ μετὰ δηρὸν ἐελδομένοισι φαάνθη.]

       1363 versum del. Brunck (= 2.1285)

even the slightest breeze. They observed a projecting stretch of land, which from the gulf[131] looked very broad, and at sunrise they rowed ashore.[132]

[131] The gulf of Olbia at the eastern end of the Propontis, where Nicomedia was later located.

[132] Verse 1363 in all the MSS ("and not long thereafter dawn appeared to their longing eyes") duplicates the final verse of Book 2 and does not make sense here.

BOOK 2

Ἔνθα δ᾽ ἔσαν σταθμοί τε βοῶν αὐλίς τ᾽ Ἀμύκοιο,
Βεβρύκων βασιλῆος ἀγήνορος, ὅν ποτε νύμφη
τίκτε Ποσειδάωνι Γενεθλίῳ εὐνηθεῖσα
Βιθυνὶς Μελίη ὑπεροπληέστατον ἀνδρῶν·
5 ὅς τ᾽ ἐπὶ καὶ ξείνοισιν ἀεικέα θεσμὸν ἔθηκεν,
μή τιν᾽ ἀποστείχειν, πρὶν πειρήσασθαι ἑοῖο
πυγμαχίης· πολέας δὲ περικτιόνων ἐδάιξεν.
καὶ δὲ τότε προτὶ νῆα κιών, χρειὼ μὲν ἐρέσθαι
ναυτιλίης, οἵ τ᾽ εἶεν, ὑπερβασίῃσιν ἄτισσεν,
10 τοῖον δ᾽ ἐν πάντεσσι παρασχεδὸν ἔκφατο μῦθον·
   "κέκλυθ᾽, ἁλίπλαγκτοι, τά περ ἴδμεναι ὕμμιν
      ἔοικεν.
   οὔ τινα θέσμιόν ἐστιν ἀφορμηθέντα νέεσθαι
   ἀνδρῶν ὀθνείων, ὅς κεν Βέβρυξι πελάσσῃ,
   πρὶν χείρεσσιν ἐμῇσιν ἑὰς ἀνὰ χεῖρας ἀεῖραι.
15 τῶ καί μοι τὸν ἄριστον ἀποκριδὸν οἶον ὁμίλου
   πυγμαχίῃ στήσασθε καταυτόθι δηρινθῆναι.
   εἰ δ᾽ ἂν ἀπηλεγέοντες ἐμὰς πατέοιτε θέμιστας,
   ἦ κέν τις στυγερῶς κρατερὴ ἐπιέψετ᾽ ἀνάγκη."
   ἦ ῥα μέγα φρονέων· τοὺς δ᾽ ἄγριος εἰσαΐοντας

114

BOOK 2

Here were located the ox stables and sheepfold of Amycus, the haughty king of the Bebrycians, whom the nymph, Bithynian Melie, having made love to Poseidon Genethlius,[1] once bore—the most arrogant of men, who imposed even on strangers an outrageous law, that no one could depart before making trial of him in boxing; and many were the neighbors he had killed. And on this occasion he went to the ship and insolently scorned to ask the purpose of their voyage or who they were, but immediately made this declaration to all of them:

"Listen, seafaring wanderers, to what it behooves you to know. It is the law that no foreigner who comes to the Bebrycians may depart on his journey before he has raised his hands against my hands. Therefore, select the best man from your crew and put him right here to contend with me in boxing. But if you pay no heed and trample on my laws, assuredly will harsh necessity pursue you with dreadful consequences."

Thus he spoke in his arrogance, and savage anger seized them when they heard this, but the threat struck Poly-

[1] I.e. Poseidon as progenitor of the family.

---

8 χρειὼ μὲν E: χρειὼ μιν Ω

20 εἷλε χόλος· πέρι δ᾽ αὖ Πολυδεύκεα τύψεν ὁμοκλή.
αἶψα δ᾽ ἑῶν ἑτάρων πρόμος ἵστατο, φώνησέν τε·
    "ἴσχεο νῦν, μηδ᾽ ἄμμι κακήν, ὅ τις εὔχεαι εἶναι,
φαῖνε βίην· θεσμοῖς γὰρ ὑπείξομεν, ὡς ἀγορεύεις.
αὐτὸς ἑκὼν ἤδη τοι ὑπίσχομαι ἀντιάασθαι."
25   ὣς φάτ᾽ ἀπηλεγέως. ὁ δ᾽ ἐσέδρακεν ὄμμαθ᾽
        ἑλίξας,
ὥς τε λέων ὑπ᾽ ἄκοντι τετυμμένος, ὅν τ᾽ ἐν ὄρεσσιν
ἀνέρες ἀμφιπένονται· ὁ δ᾽ ἰλλόμενός περ ὁμίλῳ
τῶν μὲν ἔτ᾽ οὐκ ἀλέγει, ἐπὶ δ᾽ ὄσσεται οἰόθεν οἶος
ἄνδρα τόν, ὅς μιν ἔτυψε παροίτατος οὐδ᾽
        ἐδάμασσεν.
30 ἔνθ᾽ αὖ Τυνδαρίδης μὲν ἐύστιπτον θέτο φᾶρος
λεπταλέον, τό ῥά οἷ τις ἐὸν ξεινήιον εἶναι
ὤπασε Λημνιάδων· ὁ δ᾽ ἐρεμνὴν δίπτυχα λώπην
αὐτῇσιν περόνῃσι καλαύροπά τε τρηχεῖαν
κάββαλε, τὴν φορέεσκεν, ὀριτρεφέος κοτίνοιο.
35 αὐτίκα δ᾽ ἐγγύθι χῶρον ἑαδότα παπτήναντες
ἷζον ἑοὺς δίχα πάντας ἐνὶ ψαμάθοισιν ἑταίρους,
οὐ δέμας οὐδὲ φυὴν ἐναλίγκιοι εἰσοράασθαι.
ἀλλ᾽ ὁ μὲν ἢ ὀλοοῖο Τυφωέος ἠὲ καὶ αὐτῆς
Γαίης εἶναι ἔικτο πέλωρ τέκος, οἷα πάροιθεν
40 χωομένη Διὶ τίκτεν· ὁ δ᾽ οὐρανίῳ ἀτάλαντος
ἀστέρι Τυνδαρίδης, οὗ περ κάλλισται ἔασιν
ἑσπερίην διὰ νύκτα φαεινομένου ἀμαρυγαί.
τοῖος ἔην Διὸς υἱός, ἔτι χνοάοντας ἰούλους
ἀντέλλων, ἔτι φαιδρὸς ἐν ὄμμασιν· ἀλλά οἱ ἀλκή
45 καὶ μένος ἠύτε θηρὸς ἀέξετο. πῆλε δὲ χεῖρας

116

deuces most of all. And immediately he stood up as his companions' champion and said:

"Stop now, and make no show of wanton violence against us, whoever you claim to be, for we shall yield to your laws, just as you say. I myself willingly offer right now to face you."

Thus he spoke forthrightly. The other rolled his eyes and glared at him, like a lion wounded by a javelin that men surround in the mountains, and, though hemmed in by the throng, it no longer pays heed to them, but, all alone,[2] eyes that man who first struck but did not kill him.

Then the son of Tyndareus[3] laid aside his closely-woven, delicate robe, which one of the Lemnian women had given him as his guest-present. But the other threw down his double-folded black cloak, clasps and all, and the knotted staff of mountain olive that he was carrying. They quickly spotted a suitable place nearby and seated all their comrades in separate groups on the sand; and neither in form nor stature were the two men alike to behold. The one seemed like the monstrous offspring of deadly Typhoeus or even of Earth herself, like those she had long ago brought forth in anger at Zeus.[4] But Tyndareus' son was like a heavenly star, whose twinkling is most beautiful when it shines through the evening darkness. Such was Zeus' son, still sprouting the first down of a beard, still bright-eyed, but his strength and courage waxed like a wild

---

[2] Or, reading οἶον, *eyes that man alone.*

[3] Polydeuces.   [4] For Typhoeus (called Typhaon at 2.1211), see Hesiod, *Theogony* 820–868.

---

28 οἶος Ω Σ^Ω: οἶον Z^{γρ} Struve

πειράζων, εἴθ' ὡς πρὶν ἐντρόχαλοι φορέονται,
μηδ' ἄμυδις καμάτῳ τε καὶ εἰρεσίη βαρύθοιεν.
οὐ μὰν αὖτ' Ἄμυκος πειρήσατο· σῖγα δ' ἄπωθεν
ἑστηὼς εἰς αὐτὸν ἔχ' ὄμματα, καί οἱ ὀρέχθει
50 θυμὸς ἐελδομένῳ στηθέων ἐξ αἷμα κεδάσσαι.
τοῖσι δὲ μεσσηγὺς θεράπων Ἀμύκοιο Λυκωρεὺς
θῆκε πάροιθε ποδῶν δοιοὺς ἑκάτερθεν ἱμάντας
ὠμούς, ἀζαλέους, πέρι δ' οἵ γ' ἔσαν ἐσκληῶτες.
αὐτὰρ ὁ τόν γ' ἐπέεσσιν ὑπερφιάλοισι μετηύδα·
55 "τῶνδέ τοι ὅν κ' ἐθέλησθα πάλου ἄτερ ἐγγυαλίξω
αὐτὸς ἑκών, ἵνα μή μοι ἀτέμβηαι μετόπισθεν.
ἀλλὰ βάλευ περὶ χειρί· δαεὶς δέ κεν ἄλλῳ ἐνίσποις,
ὅσσον ἐγὼ ῥινούς τε βοῶν περίειμι ταμέσθαι
ἀζαλέας, ἀνδρῶν τε παρηίδας αἵματι φύρσαι."
60 ὣς ἔφατ'· αὐτὰρ ὅ γ' οὔ τι παραβλήδην ἐρίδηνεν·
ἦκα δὲ μειδήσας, οἷ οἱ παρὰ ποσσὶν ἔκειντο,
τοὺς ἕλεν ἀπροφάτως. τοῦ δ' ἀντίος ἤλυθε Κάστωρ
ἠδὲ Βιαντιάδης Ταλαὸς μέγας, ὦκα δ' ἱμάντας
ἀμφέδεον, μάλα πολλὰ παρηγορέοντες ἐς ἀλκήν·
65 τῷ δ' αὖτ' Ἀρητός τε καὶ Ὄρνυτος, οὐδέ τι ᾔδειν,
νήπιοι, ὕστατα κεῖνα κακῇ δήσαντες ἐν αἴσῃ.
οἱ δ' ἐπεὶ οὖν ἐν ἱμᾶσι διασταδὸν ἠρτύναντο,
αὐτίκ' ἀνασχόμενοι ῥεθέων προπάροιθε βαρείας
χεῖρας, ἐπ' ἀλλήλοισι μένος φέρον ἀντιόωντες.
70 ἔνθα δὲ Βεβρύκων μὲν ἄναξ, ἅ τε κῦμα θαλάσσης
τρηχὺ θοὴν ἐπὶ νῆα κορύσσεται, ἡ δ' ὑπὸ τυτθὸν
ἰδρείῃ πυκινοῖο κυβερνητῆρος ἀλύσκει

118

animal's. He swung his arms to test them and see if they moved as nimbly as before and were not heavy from both toil and rowing. But on his side, Amycus did not test himself, but stood back in silence and kept his eyes on him, and his heart was pounding in his eagerness to make blood splatter from the other man's chest. Between them Lycoreus, Amycus' squire, placed before their feet on each side two rawhide thongs, dried ones that were extremely hard. And the king addressed him with haughty words:

"I myself willingly shall let you have whichever of these you wish without casting lots, so that you may not blame me afterwards. Wrap them around your hands, and then you can learn and tell others how I excel at cutting dried ox-hides and spattering men's cheeks with blood."

Thus he spoke. But the other replied with no taunt at all, but smiled softly and took up the thongs that lay at his feet without a word.[5] Castor and mighty Talaus, Bias' son, came to face him and quickly strapped on his thongs, as they proffered many words of encouragement to stand firm.[6] On the king's behalf came Aretus and Ornytus, but little did they know, the fools, that they had tied those thongs for the last time on this ill-fated occasion.

Now when, standing on separate sides, they had equipped themselves with the thongs, they immediately held up their heavy hands before their faces, and, coming together, bore their might against each other. Thereupon the king of the Bebrycians—as when a rough wave of the sea rears up against a swift ship, which barely escapes through the expertise of the wise helmsman as the billow

---

[5] Or *without hesitation*.

[6] Or encouragement *for the fight*.

ἱεμένου φορέεσθαι ἔσω τοίχοιο κλύδωνος·
ὣς ὅ γε Τυνδαρίδην φοβέων ἕπετ', οὐδέ μιν εἴα

75 δηθύνειν. ὁ δ' ἄρ' αἰὲν ἀνούτατος ἦν διὰ μῆτιν
ἀίσσοντ' ἀλέεινεν. ἀπηνέα δ' αἶψα νοήσας
πυγμαχίην, ᾗ κάρτος ἀάατος, ᾗ τε χερείων,
στῆ ῥ' ἄμοτον καὶ χερσὶν ἐναντία χεῖρας ἔμιξεν.
ὡς δ' ὅτε νήια δοῦρα θοοῖς ἀντίξοα γόμφοις

80 ἀνέρες ὑληουργοὶ ἐπιβλήδην ἐλάοντες
θείνωσι σφύρῃσιν, ἐπ' ἄλλῳ δ' ἄλλος ἄηται
δοῦπος ἄδην· ὣς τοῖσι παρήιά τ' ἀμφοτέρωθεν
καὶ γένυες κτύπεον, βρυχὴ δ' ὑπετέλλετ' ὀδόντων
ἄσπετος· οὐδ' ἔλληξαν ἐπισταδὸν οὐτάζοντες,

85 ἔστε περ οὐλοὸν ἆσθμα καὶ ἀμφοτέρους ἐδάμασσεν.
στάντε δὲ βαιὸν ἄπωθεν ἀπωμόρξαντο μετώπων
ἱδρῶ ἅλις, καματηρὸν ἀυτμένα φυσιόωντε.
ἂψ δ' αὖτις συνόρουσαν ἐναντίοι, ἠύτε ταύρω
φορβάδος ἀμφὶ βοὸς κεκοτηότε δηριάασθον.

90 ἔνθα δ' ἔπειτ' Ἄμυκος μὲν ἐπ' ἀκροτάτοισιν ἀερθεὶς
βουτύπος οἷα πόδεσσι τανύσσατο, κὰδ δὲ βαρεῖαν
χεῖρ' ἐπὶ οἷ πελέμιξεν· ὁ δ' ἀίξαντος ὑπέστη
κρᾶτα παρακλίνας, ὤμῳ δ' ἀνεδέξατο πῆχυν
τυτθόν· ὁ δ' ἄγχ' αὐτοῖο παρὲκ γόνυ γουνὸς
        ἀμείβων

95 κόψε μεταΐγδην ὑπὲρ οὔατος, ὀστέα δ' εἴσω
ῥῆξεν· ὁ δ' ἀμφ' ὀδύνῃ γνὺξ ἤριπεν. οἱ δ' ἰάχησαν
ἥρωες Μινύαι· τοῦ δ' ἀθρόος ἔκχυτο θυμός.
    οὐδ' ἄρα Βέβρυκες ἄνδρες ἀφείδησαν βασιλῆος,
ἀλλ' ἄμυδις κορύνας ἀζηχέας ἠδὲ σιγύννους

strives to sweep over its sides—thus did he pursue the son of Tyndareus to frighten him and allowed him no respite. But Polydeuces, ever uninjured, kept evading his onslaught through his skill. But once he had sized up the other's brutal style of boxing—where he was invincible in his strength and where weaker—he stood without wavering and returned blow for blow. And as when carpenters strike ship timbers with their hammers and with repeated blows drive the sharp pegs into the resisting wood, and one after another the thumps unceasingly echo, so cheeks and chins on both sides resounded, and an indescribable clashing of teeth arose, nor did they stop trading blows until dreadful gasping overcame them both. Standing back a little, the two men wiped the copious sweat from their brows, wearily panting for breath. But again they rushed back to face each other, like two enraged bulls fighting over a grazing heifer. Then Amycus, rising up on his toes, extended himself like a slayer of oxen and swung his heavy hand down upon Polydeuces, who withstood his assailant by ducking his head to the side and received the king's forearm just slightly on his shoulder. Keeping close to him, Polydeuces slipped his knee past the other's and with a swift lunge struck him above the ear and shattered the bones within. He sank to his knees in agony. The Minyan heroes cheered, and all at once his life poured out of him.

To be sure, the Bebrycian men did not abandon their king, but all together took up their hardened clubs and

---

76 ἀίσσοντ᾽ Pierson: ἀίσσων Ω

100 ἰθὺς ἀνασχόμενοι Πολυδεύκεος ἀντιάασκον·
τοῦ δὲ πάρος κολεῶν εὐήκεα φάσγαν' ἑταῖροι
ἔσταν ἐρυσσάμενοι. πρῶτός γε μὲν ἀνέρα Κάστωρ
ἤλασ' ἐπεσσύμενον κεφαλῆς ὕπερ· ἡ δ' ἑκάτερθεν
ἔνθα καὶ ἔνθ' ὤμοισιν ἐπ' ἀμφοτέροισι κεάσθη.
105 αὐτὸς δ' Ἰτυμονῆα πελώριον ἠδὲ Μίμαντα,
τὸν μὲν ὑπὸ στέρνοιο θοῷ ποδὶ λὰξ ἐπορούσας
πλῆξε καὶ ἐν κονίῃσι βάλεν· τοῦ δ' ἆσσον ἰόντος
δεξιτερῇ σκαιῆς ὑπὲρ ὀφρύος ἤλασε χειρί,
δρύψε δέ οἱ βλέφαρον, γυμνῇ δ' ὑπελείπετ' ὀπωπή.
110 Ὠρείδης δ' Ἀμύκοιο βίην ὑπέροπλος ὀπάων
οὖτα Βιαντιάδαο κατὰ λαπάρην Ταλαοῖο,
ἀλλά μιν οὐ κατέπεφνεν, ὅσον δ' ἐπὶ δέρματι
    μοῦνον
νηδυίων ἄψαυστος ὑπὸ ζώνην θόρε χαλκός.
αὔτως δ' Ἄρητος μενεδήιον Εὐρύτου υἷα
115 Ἴφιτον ἀζαλέῃ κορύνῃ στυφέλιξεν ἐλάσσας,
οὔ πω κηρὶ κακῇ πεπρωμένον· ἦ τάχ' ἔμελλεν
αὐτὸς δῃώσεσθαι ὑπὸ ξίφεϊ Κλυτίοιο.
    καὶ τότ' ἄρ' Ἀγκαῖος Λυκοόργοιο θρασὺς υἱὸς
αἶψα μάλ' ἀντεταγὼν πέλεκυν μέγαν ἠδὲ κελαινὸν
120 ἄρκτου προσχόμενος σκαιῇ δέρος ἔνθορε μέσσῳ
ἐμμεμαὼς Βέβρυξιν· ὁμοῦ δέ οἱ ἐσσεύοντο
Αἰακίδαι, σὺν δέ σφιν ἀρήιος ὤρνυτ' Ἰήσων.
ὡς δ' ὅτ' ἐνὶ σταθμοῖσιν ἀπείρονα μῆλ' ἐφόβησαν
ἤματι χειμερίῳ πολιοὶ λύκοι ὁρμηθέντες
125 λάθρῃ ἐυρρίνων τε κυνῶν αὐτῶν τε νομήων,

spears and headed straight for Polydeuces, but his comrades drew their sharp-edged swords from their scabbards and stood in front of him. First of all, Castor struck a man rushing at him on the top of his head, which split in two, half upon each of his shoulders. Polydeuces himself faced enormous Itymoneus and Mimas. Leaping forward, he struck the first with a swift kick beneath the chest and hurled him in the dust; and as the other drew near, he hit him with his right hand above the left eyebrow and tore away his eyelid, and his eyeball was left exposed. And Amycus' henchman Oreides, arrogant in his might, wounded Talaus, Bias' son, in the side, but did not kill him, for the bronze sped[7] beneath his belt only as far as the skin without touching his organs. Likewise, Aretus attacked the stalwart soldier Iphitus, Eurytus' son, and struck him with his hard-dried club, but Iphitus was not yet destined for an evil fate—in fact, Aretus himself was soon to be slain by the sword of Clytius.[8]

And then Ancaeus, the bold son of Lycurgus, quickly seized his great ax and, holding his black bearskin before him in his left hand, sprang furiously into the midst of the Bebrycians. And with him charged Aeacus' sons,[9] and with them rushed warlike Jason. And as when gray wolves on a winter day attack countless sheep in their pens and terrify them, having eluded the keen-scented dogs and the shepherds themselves, and they seek out which animal to assail

---

[7] Or, reading τόρε, *pierced*.   [8] Iphitus' brother (cf. 1.86).
[9] Peleus and Telamon.

---

110 Ὠρείδης Ω: Ὠρείτης Et. Gen.
113 θόρε Ω: τόρε Platt

123

μαίονται δ᾽ ὅ τι πρῶτον ἐπαΐξαντες ἕλωσιν,
πόλλ᾽ ἐπιπαμφαλόωντες ὁμοῦ, τὰ δὲ πάντοθεν αὔτως
στείνονται πίπτοντα περὶ σφίσιν· ὡς ἄρα τοί γε
λευγαλέως Βέβρυκας ὑπερφιάλους ἐφόβησαν.

130 ὡς δὲ μελισσάων σμῆνος μέγα μηλοβοτῆρες
ἠὲ μελισσοκόμοι πέτρῃ ἔνι καπνιόωσιν,
αἱ δ᾽ ἤτοι τείως μὲν ἀολλέες ᾧ ἐνὶ σίμβλῳ
βομβηδὸν κλονέονται, ἐπιπρὸ δὲ λιγνυόεντι
καπνῷ τυφόμεναι πέτρης ἑκὰς ἀΐσσουσιν·

135 ὡς οἵ γ᾽ οὐκέτι δὴν μένον ἔμπεδον, ἀλλὰ κέδασθεν
εἴσω Βεβρυκίης, Ἀμύκου μόρον ἀγγελέοντες·
νήπιοι, οὐδ᾽ ἐνόησαν ὃ δή σφισιν ἐγγύθεν ἄλλο
πῆμ᾽ ἀΐδηλον ἔην. πέρθοντο γὰρ ἠμὲν ἀλωαὶ
ἠδ᾽ οἷαι τῆμος δηῷ ὑπὸ δουρὶ Λύκοιο

140 καὶ Μαριανδυνῶν ἀνδρῶν, ἀπεόντος ἄνακτος·
αἰεὶ γὰρ μάρναντο σιδηροφόρου περὶ γαίης.
οἱ δ᾽ ἤδη σταθμούς τε καὶ αὔλια δηιάασκον·
ἤδη δ᾽ ἄσπετα μῆλα περιτροπάδην ἐτάμοντο
ἥρωες· καὶ δή τις ἔπος μετὰ τοῖσιν ἔειπεν·

145 "φράζεσθ᾽ ὅττι κεν ᾗσιν ἀναλκείῃσιν ἔρεξαν,
εἴ πως Ἡρακλῆα θεὸς καὶ δεῦρο κόμισσεν.
ἤτοι μὲν γὰρ ἐγὼ κείνου παρεόντος ἔολπα
οὐδ᾽ ἂν πυγμαχίῃ κρινθήμεναι· ἀλλ᾽ ὅτε θεσμοὺς
ἤλυθεν ἐξερέων, αὐτοῖς ἄφαρ οἷς ἀγόρευεν

150 θεσμοῖσιν ῥοπάλῳ μιν ἀγηνορίης λελαθέσθαι.
ναὶ μὲν ἀκήδεστον γαίῃ ἔνι τόν γε λιπόντες
πόντον ἐπέπλωμεν· μάλα δ᾽ ἡμέων αὐτὸς ἕκαστος
εἴσεται οὐλομένην ἄτην, ἀπάνευθεν ἐόντος."

124

first and carry off, as they survey many at once, while the sheep from all sides merely huddle together as they fall over one another—thus did they grievously terrify the arrogant Bebrycians. And as shepherds or beekeepers smoke a great swarm of bees within a rock, and for a while the flustered bees stay together and buzz in their hive, but when suffocated by the sooty smoke they dart forth far from the rock, likewise the men did not stand firm for much longer, but scattered back into Bebrycia to announce Amycus' death—the fools, for they did not realize that another unforeseen disaster was near at hand for them. For at that time their vineyards and villages were being pillaged by the hostile spear of Lycus and the Mariandynians, while their king was gone. For they were always at war over the iron-bearing territory.[10] And by now they[11] were destroying their stables and sheepfolds; by now the heroes had rounded up and driven off countless sheep. And one of them spoke these words to the others:

"Imagine what they would have done in their cowardice if somehow a god had brought Heracles here too. For I am sure that had he been here, there would have been no boxing match, but as soon as the king came to declare his laws, the club would have made him forget both his haughtiness and those laws he was proclaiming. Yes, we thoughtlessly left him on land when we set out to sea, and full well will every one of us come to know deadly ruin,[12] with him far away."

[10] For the iron-bearing land of the Chalybes, see 2.1000–1008.   [11] The Mariandynians; others understand the Argonauts.   [12] Or *come to recognize our deadly error*.

136 ἀγγελέοντες Ω: αγγελλ[ον]τε[ς Π14

ὣς ἄρ' ἔφη· τὰ δὲ πάντα Διὸς βουλῇσι τέτυκτο.
155 καὶ τότε μὲν μένον αὖθι διὰ κνέφας, ἕλκεά τ'
       ἀνδρῶν
οὐταμένων ἀκέοντο, καὶ ἀθανάτοισι θυηλὰς
ρέξαντες μέγα δόρπον ἐφώπλισαν· οὐδέ τιν' ὕπνος
εἶλε παρὰ κρητῆρι καὶ αἰθομένοις ἱεροῖσιν·
ξανθὰ δ' ἐρεψάμενοι δάφνῃ καθύπερθε μέτωπα
160 ἀγχιάλῳ, τῇ καί τε περὶ πρυμνήσι' ἀνῆπτο,
Ὀρφείῃ φόρμιγγι συνοίμιον ὕμνον ἄειδον
ἐμμελέως· περὶ δέ σφιν ἰαίνετο νήνεμος ἀκτὴ
μελπομένοις· κλεῖον δὲ Θεραπναῖον Διὸς υἷα.
       ἦμος δ' ἥλιος δροσερὰς ἐπέλαμψε κολώνας
165 ἐκ περάτων ἀνιών, ἤγειρε δὲ μηλοβοτῆρας,
δὴ τότε λυσάμενοι νεάτης ἐκ πείσματα δάφνης,
ληίδα τ' εἰσβήσαντες, ὅσην χρεὼ ἦεν ἄγεσθαι,
πνοιῇ δινήεντ' ἀνὰ Βόσπορον ἰθύνοντο.
ἔνθα μὲν ἠλιβάτῳ ἐναλίγκιον οὔρεϊ κῦμα
170 ἀμφέρεται προπάροιθεν ἐπαΐσσοντι ἐοικός,
αἰὲν ὑπὲρ νεφέων ἠερμένον· οὐδέ κε φαίης
φεύξεσθαι κακὸν οἶτον, ἐπεὶ μάλα μεσσόθι νηὸς
λάβρον ἐπικρέμαται καθάπερ νέφος, ἀλλὰ τό γ'
       ἔμπης
στόρνυται, εἴ κ' ἐσθλοῖο κυβερνητῆρος ἐπαύρῃ.
175 τῷ καὶ Τίφυος οἶδε δαημοσύνῃσι νέοντο,

160 τῇ καί τε περὶ Merkel: τῇ καὶ τῇ περὶ Ω: uncis
incluserunt Fränkel, Vian   170 ἐπαΐσσοντι Ω: ἐπαΐξοντι
Vian   173 καθάπερ E: ὑπὲρ Ω: ὥς τε Ardizzoni

126

Thus one of them spoke, but all those things had been accomplished by Zeus' designs. And then they stayed there for the night and tended the injuries of the wounded men. And after sacrificing to the immortals, they prepared a great feast; and sleep overcame no one beside the wine bowl and blazing sacrifices, but they crowned their golden brows with laurel growing by the shore, around which their stern cables had been fastened, and sang a hymn to the accompaniment of Orpheus' lyre in beautiful harmony, and round about them the windless shore was charmed by their singing; and they celebrated Zeus' son[13] from Therapna.

But when the sun, rising from the horizon, lit up the dewy hills and awakened the shepherds, they loosed their cables from the base of the laurel, loaded all the spoils they needed to take, and with a favoring wind began sailing up the swirling Bosporus. Thereupon a wave, ever lifted above the clouds like a lofty mountain, rises[14] up in front, as if rushing upon them. You would not think that they could escape terrible destruction, since it hangs right over the middle of the ship like a violent storm-cloud, but one that nonetheless subsides, if it encounters[15] a good helmsman. Therefore, by means of Tiphys' skills, these men

---

[13] Polydeuces, who with Castor had a cult center at Therapna, a village south of Sparta.

[14] A vivid present tense that may also indicate, as Vian argues, that such a wave at the mouth of the Bosporus was a prevailing condition.

[15] Or, taking ἐπαύρῃ as second-person middle, *if you have the benefit of.*

ἀσκηθεῖς μέν, ἀτὰρ πεφοβημένοι. ἤματι δ᾽ ἄλλῳ
ἀντιπέρην γαίῃ Θυνηίδι πείσματ᾽ ἀνῆψαν.

 ἔνθα δ᾽ ἐπάκτιον οἶκον Ἀγηνορίδης ἔχε Φινεύς,
ὃς περὶ δὴ πάντων ὀλοώτατα πήματ᾽ ἀνέτλη
180 εἵνεκα μαντοσύνης, τήν οἱ πάρος ἐγγυάλιξεν
Λητοΐδης· οὐδ᾽ ὅσσον ὀπίζετο καὶ Διὸς αὐτοῦ
χρείων ἀτρεκέως ἱερὸν νόον ἀνθρώποισιν·
τῶ καί οἱ γῆρας μὲν ἐπὶ δηναιὸν ἴαλλεν,
ἐκ δ᾽ ἕλετ᾽ ὀφθαλμῶν γλυκερὸν φάος· οὐδὲ
   γάνυσθαι
185 εἴα ἀπειρεσίοισιν ὀνείασιν, ὅσσα οἱ αἰεὶ
θέσφατα πευθόμενοι περιναιέται οἴκαδ᾽ ἄγειρον·
ἀλλὰ διὰ νεφέων ἄφνω πέλας ἀίσσουσαι
Ἅρπυιαι στόματος χειρῶν τ᾽ ἀπὸ γαμφηλῇσιν
συνεχέως ἥρπαζον· ἐλείπετο δ᾽ ἄλλοτε φορβῆς
190 οὐδ᾽ ὅσον, ἄλλοτε τυτθόν, ἵνα ζώων ἀκάχοιτο.
καὶ δ᾽ ἐπὶ μυδαλέην ὀδμὴν χέον· οὐδέ τις ἔτλη
μὴ καὶ λευκανίηνδε φορεύμενος, ἀλλ᾽ ἀποτηλοῦ
ἑστηώς· τοῖόν οἱ ἀπέπνεε λείψανα δαιτός.

 αὐτίκα δ᾽ εἰσαΐων ἐνοπὴν καὶ δοῦπον ὁμίλου
195 τούσδ᾽ αὐτοὺς παριόντας ἐπήισεν, ὧν οἱ ἰόντων
θέσφατον ἐκ Διὸς ἦεν ἑῆς ἀπόνασθαι ἐδωδῆς.
ὀρθωθεὶς δ᾽ εὐνῆθεν ἀκήριον ἠύτ᾽ ὄνειρον,
βάκτρῳ σκηπτόμενος ῥικνοῖς ποσὶν ᾖε θύραζε,
τοίχους ἀμφαφόων· τρέμε δ᾽ ἅψεα νισσομένοιο
200 ἀδρανίῃ γήρᾳ τε· πίνῳ δέ οἱ αὐσταλέος χρὼς

177 Θυνηίδι Σ^{Llem}D^{ac} (cf. 460): Βιθυνηίδι (Βιθυνίδι G) Ω

128

sailed on unharmed, although terrified. On the next day they fastened their cables to the Thynian land on the opposite coast.[16]

There Agenor's son Phineus had his home on the shore. He suffered the most terrible woes of all men because of the prophetic art that Leto's son[17] had given him long before. For he showed not the slightest reverence even for Zeus himself by accurately prophesying his sacred intentions to men. Therefore Zeus sent upon him a prolonged old age, and took sweet light from his eyes, and did not allow him to enjoy all the lavish gifts of food that the neighboring people gathered for him in his house whenever they asked for oracles. But swooping suddenly through the clouds to his side, the Harpies continually snatched the food from his mouth and hands with their beaks. Sometimes not even a morsel of food was left, at other times just enough for him to stay alive and suffer. Furthermore, they would shed a putrid stench upon it: no one could bear even to stand at a distance, let alone bring it up to his mouth—so terribly did the remains of his meal reek.

As soon as he heard the voices and footsteps of the crew, he recognized that those passing by were the very men, upon whose arrival an oracle from Zeus had foretold to him that he would take pleasure in his food. Rising from his bed like a lifeless dream and propping himself up on a stick, he went on his withered feet to the door, feeling his way along the walls. His limbs trembled from weakness and old age as he moved. His body was dry and caked with

---

[16] The Thynian coast on the European side of the Bosporus, opposite the Bebrycians in Bithynia.

[17] Apollo.

APOLLONIUS RHODIUS

ἐσκλήκει, ῥινοὶ δὲ σὺν ὀστέα μοῦνον ἔεργον.
ἐκ δ' ἐλθὼν μεγάροιο καθέζετο γοῦνα βαρυνθεὶς
οὐδοῦ ἐπ' αὐλείοιο· κάρος δέ μιν ἀμφεκάλυψεν
πορφύρεος, γαῖαν δὲ πέριξ ἐδόκησε φέρεσθαι
205 νειόθεν, ἀβληχρῷ δ' ἐπὶ κώματι κέκλιτ' ἄναυδος.
οἱ δέ μιν ὡς εἴδοντο, περισταδὸν ἠγερέθοντο
καὶ τάφον. αὐτὰρ ὁ τοῖσι μάλα μόλις ἐξ ὑπάτοιο
στήθεος ἀμπνεύσας μετεφώνεε μαντοσύνῃσιν·
      "κλῦτε, Πανελλήνων προφερέστατοι, εἰ ἐτεὸν δὴ
210 οἴδ' ὑμεῖς, οὓς δὴ κρυερῇ βασιλῆος ἐφετμῇ
Ἀργῴης ἐπὶ νηὸς ἄγει μετὰ κῶας Ἰήσων—
ὑμεῖς ἀτρεκέως· ἔτι μοι νόος οἶδεν ἕκαστα
ᾗσι θεοπροπίῃσι· χάριν νύ τοι, ὦ ἄνα Λητοῦς
υἷε, καὶ ἀργαλέοισιν ἀνάπτομαι ἐν καμάτοισιν.
215 Ἱκεσίου πρὸς Ζηνός, ὅ τις ῥίγιστος ἀλιτροῖς
ἀνδράσι, Φοίβου τ' ἀμφὶ καὶ αὐτῆς εἵνεκεν Ἥρης
λίσσομαι, ᾗ περίαλλα θεῶν μέμβλεσθε κιόντες,
χραίσμετέ μοι, ῥύσασθε δυσάμμορον ἀνέρα λύμης,
μηδέ μ' ἀκηδείῃσιν ἀφορμήθητε λιπόντες
220 αὔτως. οὐ γὰρ μοῦνον ἐπ' ὀφθαλμοῖσιν Ἐρινὺς
λὰξ ἐπέβη, καὶ γῆρας ἀμήρυτον ἐς τέλος ἕλκω·
πρὸς δ' ἔτι πικρότατον κρέμαται κακὸν ἄλλο
      κακοῖσιν·
Ἅρπυιαι στόματός μοι ἀφαρπάζουσιν ἐδωδὴν
ἔκποθεν ἀφράστοιο καταΐσσουσαι ὀλέθρου.
225 ἴσχω δ' οὔ τινα μῆτιν ἐπίρροθον· ἀλλά κε ῥεῖα
αὐτὸς ἐὸν λελάθοιμι νόον δόρποιο μεμηλὼς
ἢ κείνας, ὧδ' αἶψα διηέριαι ποτέονται.

130

filth, and his skin was all that held his bones together. Once he left the house, he sat down, knees exhausted, on the threshold of the courtyard; dark stupor came over him, and the ground beneath him seemed to spin, and he slumped into feeble unconsciousness, unable to speak. When they saw him, they gathered round and stood in wonder. And with great effort he drew a breath from depths[18] of his chest and spoke to them in words of prophecy:

"Hear me, greatest of all the Hellenes, if truly you are the ones whom Jason, at the dire command of his king, is leading on the ship Argo to fetch the fleece—and you clearly are they, since my mind still knows everything with its prophetic powers; I give you thanks, O son of Leto, my lord, even in the midst of terrible suffering. In the name of Zeus, Protector of Suppliants, who is most terrifying to sinful men, and for Phoebus' sake, and for the sake of Hera herself, whom of all the gods your travels most concern, I beseech you, help me! Rescue an unfortunate man from outrageous treatment; do not thoughtlessly go off and leave me in this state. For not only has a Fury trampled on my eyes with her foot, and I drag out to its end an interminable old age, but in addition to these evils yet another of the most painful sort hangs over me: the Harpies swoop down from some unseen place of destruction and snatch the food from my mouth. I have no strategy to help me. But when I long for a meal, I could more easily escape my own thought than I could escape them, so swiftly do they

---

[18] Others interpret this to mean that he drew a shallow breath from the top of his chest.

---

222 δ᾽ ἔτι E: δ᾽ ἐπὶ Hölzlin: δέ τι Ω

τυτθὸν δ᾽ ἦν ἄρα δή ποτ᾽ ἐδητύος ἄμμι λίπωσιν,
πνεῖ τόδε μυδαλέον τε καὶ οὐ τλητὸν μένος ὀδμῆς.
230 οὔ κέ τις οὐδὲ μίνυνθα βροτῶν ἄνσχοιτο πελάσσας,
οὐδ᾽ εἴ οἱ ἀδάμαντος ἐληλάμενον κέαρ εἴη.
ἀλλά με πικρὴ δῆτα καὶ ἄατος ἴσχει ἀνάγκη
μίμνειν καὶ μίμνοντα κακῇ ἐν γαστέρι θέσθαι.
τὰς μὲν θέσφατόν ἐστιν ἐρητῦσαι Βορέαο
235 υἱέας· οὐδ᾽ ὀθνεῖοι ἀλαλκήσουσιν ἐόντες,
εἰ δὴ ἐγὼν ὁ πρίν ποτ᾽ ἐπικλυτὸς ἀνδράσι Φινεὺς
ὄλβῳ μαντοσύνῃ τε, πατὴρ δέ με γείνατ᾽ Ἀγήνωρ,
τῶν δὲ κασιγνήτην, ὅτ᾽ ἐνὶ Θρήκεσσιν ἄνασσον,
Κλειοπάτρην ἕδνοισιν ἐμὸν δόμον ἦγον ἄκοιτιν."
240 ἴσκεν Ἀγηνορίδης· ἀδινὸν δ᾽ ἔλε κῆδος ἕκαστον
ἡρώων, πέρι δ᾽ αὖτε δύω υἷας Βορέαο.
δάκρυ δ᾽ ὀμορξαμένω σχεδὸν ἤλυθον, ὧδέ τ᾽ ἔειπεν
Ζήτης ἀσχαλόωντος ἑλὼν χερὶ χεῖρα γέροντος·
"ἆ δείλ᾽, οὔ τινά φημι σέθεν σμυγερώτερον
                                                    ἄλλον
245 ἔμμεναι ἀνθρώπων. τί νύ τοι τόσα κήδε᾽ ἀνῆπται;
ἦ ῥα θεοὺς ὀλοῇσι παρήλιτες ἀφραδίῃσιν
μαντοσύνας δεδαώς· τῶ τοι μέγα μηνίωσιν;
ἄμμι γε μὴν νόος ἔνδον ἀτύζεται ἱεμένοισιν
χραισμεῖν, εἰ δὴ πρόχνυ γέρας τόδε πάρθετο
                                                    δαίμων
250 νῶιν· ἀρίζηλοι γὰρ ἐπιχθονίοισιν ἐνιπαὶ
ἀθανάτων· οὐδ᾽ ἂν πρὶν ἐρητύσαιμεν ἰούσας
Ἁρπυίας, μάλα περ λελιημένοι, ἔστ᾽ ἂν ὀμόσσῃς,
μὴ μὲν τοῖό γ᾽ ἕκητι θεοῖς ἀπὸ θυμοῦ ἔσεσθαι."

fly through the air. And if they ever do leave me a morsel of food, it gives off a powerful stench that is putrid and intolerable. No mortal could bear to come near it even for a moment, not even if his heart were forged of adamant. But a truly painful and unending necessity compels me to stay there and, staying, to put it in my cursed stomach. There is an oracle that the sons of Boreas will restrain them, nor will those who drive them away be strangers, if truly I am Phineus, who was once famed among men for wealth and prophecy, and if the father who begot me was Agenor, and if, when I ruled among the Thracians, it was their sister Cleopatra whom I brought to my home with bride-gifts as my wife."

Thus spoke Agenor's son, and deep compassion seized each of the heroes, but especially the two sons of Boreas. Wiping away their tears, they went up to him, and thus spoke Zetes, taking the hand of the suffering old man in his own:

"Oh, poor man! No other mortal, I think, is more wretched than you. Why then have so many ills been laid upon you? Surely you sinned against the gods out of baneful recklessness through your knowledge of prophecy, and that is why they feel great wrath against you. As for us, however, our minds are troubled within us, though we long to help, as to whether a god has truly proffered this honor to the two of us. For rebukes from the immortals are obvious to earthly men, and we shall not fend off the Harpies when they come, in spite of our great desire, until you have sworn that we will not lose the gods' favor for that reason."

APOLLONIUS RHODIUS

ὣς φάτο· τοῦ δ' ἰθὺς κενεὰς ὁ γεραιὸς ἀνέσχεν
255 γλήνας ἀμπετάσας, καὶ ἀμείψατο τοῖσδ' ἐπέεσσιν·
"σίγα· μή μοι ταῦτα νόῳ ἐνιβάλλεο, τέκνον.
ἴστω Λητοῦς υἱός, ὅ με πρόφρων ἐδίδαξεν
μαντοσύνας· ἴστω δὲ δυσώνυμος, ἥ μ' ἔλαχεν, Κήρ,
καὶ τόδ' ἐπ' ὀφθαλμῶν ἀλαὸν νέφος, οἵ θ' ὑπένερθεν
260 δαίμονες, οἳ μηδ' οἶδε θανόντι περ εὐμενέοιεν,
ὡς οὔ τις θεόθεν χόλος ἔσσεται εἵνεκ' ἀρωγῆς."
τὼ μὲν ἔπειθ' ὅρκοισιν ἀλαλκέμεναι μενέαινον.
αἶψα δὲ κουρότεροι πεπονήατο δαῖτα γέροντι,
λοίσθιον Ἁρπυίῃσιν ἑλώριον· ἐγγύθι δ' ἄμφω
265 στῆσαν, ἵνα ξιφέεσσιν ἐπεσσυμένας ἐλάσειαν.
καὶ δὴ τὰ πρώτισθ' ὁ γέρων ἔψαυεν ἐδωδῆς,
αἱ δ' ἄφαρ, ἠύτ' ἄελλαι ἀδευκέες ἢ στεροπαὶ ὥς,
ἀπρόφατοι νεφέων ἐξάλμεναι ἐσσεύοντο
κλαγγῇ μαιμώωσαι ἐδητύος. οἱ δ' ἐσιδόντες
270 ἥρωες μεσσηγὺς ἀνίαχον· αἱ δ' ἅμ' αὐτῇ
πάντα καταβρώξασαι ὑπὲρ πόντοιο φέροντο
τῆλε παρέξ· ὀδμὴ δὲ δυσάνσχετος αὖθι λέλειπτο.
τάων δ' αὖ κατόπισθε δύω υἷες Βορέαο
φάσγαν' ἐπισχόμενοι ὀπίσω θέον. ἐν γὰρ ἔηκεν
275 Ζεὺς μένος ἀκάματόν σφιν· ἀτὰρ Διὸς οὔ κεν ἐπέσθην
νόσφιν, ἐπεὶ ζεφύροιο παραΐσσεσκον ἀέλλας
αἰέν, ὅτ' ἐς Φινῆα καὶ ἐκ Φινῆος ἴοιεν.
ὡς δ' ὅτ' ἐνὶ κνημοῖσι κύνες δεδαημένοι ἄγρης

260 οἶδε Ω: ὧδε Ε

134

Thus he spoke. The old man opened his blank eyes and directed them straight up at him, and answered with these words:

"Hush! Please do not put such thoughts in your head, my son. Let my witness be Leto's son, who with good will taught me prophecy; let my witnesses be the accursed Fate that was allotted to me, this cloud of blindness upon my eyes, and the gods of the underworld—may even these not look kindly upon me when I am dead[19]—that there will be no anger from the gods because of your help."

Then, because of his oath, the two of them were eager to drive the pests away. Quickly the younger men prepared a feast for the old man, the final plunder for the Harpies. The two brothers stood nearby to strike them with their swords when they swooped down. And at the very instant the old man touched the food, suddenly the Harpies, like harsh[20] storm-winds or lightning flashes, without warning sprang from the clouds and swooped down with a shriek in their lust for the food. When they saw them in mid-flight, the heroes cried out, but as they shouted, the Harpies gulped down everything and flew over the sea far away, and an unbearable stench was left there. But behind them raced the two sons of Boreas in pursuit, holding up their swords. For Zeus had put tireless strength into them, and without Zeus' help they could not have kept up, because the Harpies always outstripped the blasts of the west wind[21] whenever they came to Phineus or left him. And as when upon mountainsides dogs skilled at hunting run on

---

[19] If, that is, he is forsworn.   [20] Or *sudden*.

[21] The west wind (Zephyr) was considered the fastest of the winds (cf. *Iliad* 19.415–416).

ἢ αἶγας κεραοὺς ἠὲ πρόκας ἰχνεύοντες
280 θείωσιν, τυτθὸν δὲ τιταινόμενοι μετόπισθεν
ἄκρης ἐν γενύεσσι μάτην ἀράβησαν ὀδόντας·
ὡς Ζήτης Κάλαΐς τε μάλα σχεδὸν ἀίσσοντες
τάων ἀκροτάτῃσιν ἐπέχραον ἤλιθα χερσίν.
καί νύ κε δή σφ' ἀέκητι θεῶν διεδηλήσαντο
285 πολλὸν ἑκὰς νήσοισιν ἔπι Πλωτῇσι κιχόντες,
εἰ μὴ ἄρ' ὠκέα Ἶρις ἴδεν, κατὰ δ' αἰθέρος ἆλτο
οὐρανόθεν, καὶ τοῖα παραιφαμένη κατέρυκεν·
    "οὐ θέμις, ὦ υἱεῖς Βορέω, ξιφέεσσιν ἐλάσσαι
Ἁρπυίας, μεγάλοιο Διὸς κύνας· ὅρκια δ' αὐτὴ
290 δώσω ἐγών, ὡς οὔ οἱ ἔτι χρίμψουσιν ἰοῦσαι."
    ὣς φαμένη λοιβὴν Στυγὸς ὤμοσεν, ἥ τε θεοῖσιν
ῥιγίστη πάντεσσιν ὀπιδνοτάτη τε τέτυκται,
μὴ μὲν Ἀγηνορίδαο δόμοις ἔτι τάσδε πελάσσαι
εἰσαῦτις Φινῆος, ἐπεὶ καὶ μόρσιμον ἦεν.
295 οἱ δ' ὅρκῳ εἴξαντες ὑπέστρεφον ἂψ ἐπὶ νῆα
σώεσθαι· Στροφάδας δὲ μετακλείουσ' ἄνθρωποι
νήσους τοῖό γ' ἕκητι, πάρος Πλωτὰς καλέοντες.
Ἅρπυιαι τ' Ἶρίς τε διέτμαγον· αἱ μὲν ἔδυσαν
κευθμῶνα Κρήτης Μινωίδος, ἡ δ' ἀνόρουσεν
300 Οὔλυμπόνδε θοῇσι μεταχρονίη πτερύγεσσιν.
    τόφρα δ' ἀριστῆες πινόεν περὶ δέρμα γέροντος
πάντῃ φοιβήσαντες ἐπικριδὸν ἱρεύσαντο
μῆλα, τά τ' ἐξ Ἀμύκοιο λεηλασίης ἐκόμισαν.
αὐτὰρ ἐπεὶ μέγα δόρπον ἐνὶ μεγάροισιν ἔθεντο,
305 δαίνυνθ' ἑζόμενοι· σὺν δέ σφισι δαίνυτο Φινεὺς
ἁρπαλέως, οἷόν τ' ἐν ὀνείρασι θυμὸν ἰαίνων.

the track of horned goats or deer, and at full stretch a little behind them snap the front teeth in their jaws in vain, so Zetes and Calaïs rushed very near, just grazing them in vain with their fingertips. And they would surely have torn them to pieces against the will of the gods when they caught up with them far away at the Floating islands, had not swift Iris seen them and leapt down through the air from heaven and restrained them with these words of persuasion:

"It is not permitted, O sons of Boreas, to strike the Harpies, great Zeus' hounds, with your swords. And I myself will swear an oath that they will never again go near him."

Thus she spoke and swore by a libation from the Styx, which for all the gods is most terrifying and awesome, that never again thereafter would those Harpies go near the house of Agenor's son Phineus, for this was also fate's decree. They yielded to her oath and turned around to hasten back to the ship. For that reason, men call those islands by the new name of Turning islands,[22] though previously calling them the Floating islands. The Harpies and Iris parted: they entered a cavern on Minoan Crete, while she rose high in the air to Olympus on her swift wings.

In the meantime, the heroes cleansed the old man's filthy body all over and sacrificed choice sheep, which they had gotten from their plundering of Amycus. And when they had set out a great dinner in the hall, they sat down and dined, and Phineus feasted with them greedily, gratifying his heart as in a dream. Then, when they had taken

---

[22] Two small islands about thirty miles south of Zacynthus.

297 τοῖό γ' Ω: τοῖο Wellauer

ἔνθα δ᾽, ἐπεὶ δόρποιο κορέσσαντ᾽ ἠδὲ ποτῆτος,
παννύχιοι Βορέω μένον υἱέας ἐγρήσσοντες·
αὐτὸς δ᾽ ἐν μέσσοισι παρ᾽ ἐσχάρῃ ἧσθ᾽ ὁ γεραιὸς
310 πείρατα ναυτιλίης ἐνέπων ἄνυσίν τε κελεύθου·
   "κλῦτέ νυν· οὐ μὲν πάντα πέλει θέμις ὕμμι
      δαῆναι
ἀτρεκές· ὅσσα δ᾽ ὄρωρε θεοῖς φίλον, οὐκ ἐπικεύσω·
ἀασάμην καὶ πρόσθε Διὸς νόον ἀφραδίῃσιν
χρείων ἑξείης τε καὶ ἐς τέλος· ὧδε γὰρ αὐτὸς
315 βούλεται ἀνθρώποις ἐπιδευέα θέσφατα φαίνειν
μαντοσύνης, ἵνα καί τι θεῶν χατέωσι νόοιο.
   "πέτρας μὲν πάμπρωτον ἀφορμηθέντες ἐμεῖο
Κυανέας ὄψεσθε δύω ἁλὸς ἐν ξυνοχῇσιν.
τάων οὔ τινά φημι διαμπερὲς ἐξαλέασθαι·
320 οὐ γάρ τε ῥίζῃσιν ἐρήρεινται νεάτῃσιν,
ἀλλὰ θαμὰ ξυνίασιν ἐναντίαι ἀλλήλῃσιν
εἰς ἕν, ὕπερθε δὲ πολλὸν ἁλὸς κορθύεται ὕδωρ
βρασσόμενον, στρηνὲς δὲ περὶ στυφελῇ βρέμει
      ἀκτή.
τῶ νῦν ἡμετέρῃσι παραιφασίῃσι πίθεσθε,
325 εἰ ἐτεὸν πυκινῷ τε νόῳ μακάρων τ᾽ ἀλέγοντες
πείρετε, μηδ᾽ αὕτως αὐτάγρετον οἶτον ὀλέσθαι
ἀφραδέως ἰθύετ᾽ ἐπισπόμενοι νεότητι.
οἰωνῷ δὴ πρόσθε πελειάδι πειρήσασθαι
νηὸς ἄπο προμεθέντες ἐφιέμεν. ἢν δὲ δι᾽ αὐτῶν

323 στυφελῇ . . . ἀκτή E et Et. Magn.: στυφελῇ . . . ἀκτῇ Ω
326 ὀλέσθαι Hölzlin: ὄλησθε Ω

their fill of dinner and drink, they stayed awake all night waiting for Boreas' sons. The old man himself sat in their midst by the hearth and told how to conduct their voyage and complete their journey.

"Listen then. It is not permitted for you to know everything exactly, but however much is pleasing to the gods I shall not hide from you. I made a mistake before by recklessly prophesying Zeus' intentions in every detail and to the end. For thus does Zeus himself wish to reveal incomplete oracles to men through divination, so that they may lack some portion of the gods' intentions.

"After you leave me, you will first of all see the twin Cyanean rocks where the sea narrows. No one, I assure you, has escaped through them, for they are not firmly fixed with deep roots, but constantly come together and collide with each other, and above them rises a great mass of seething sea water, and all around them the rocky shore resounds with a harsh roar. Therefore, heed my instructions now, if truly you make your voyage with a prudent mind and have due respect for the blessed gods—and do not vainly rush in to die a self-chosen death by thoughtlessly yielding to youth. First, let a dove test them as an omen by sending it forth from the ship.[23] If it passes safely

---

[23] Or, reading ἀποπρὸ μεθέντας ἐφίεμαι, *I bid you first send a dove far from the ship.*

---

327 ἰθύετ' Pierson: ἰθύνετ' Ω: ἢ θύνετ' E: εἰ θύνετ' Wilamowitz

328 πειρήσασθαι L: πειρήσεσθε D: πειρήσασθε Ω

329 ἄπο προ- (ἀποπρὸ, ἀπὸ πρὸ) μεθέντες ἐφίεμεν Ω: μεθέντας ἐφίεμαι Madvig, Vian

330 πετράων Πόντονδε σόη πτερύγεσσι δίηται,
μηκέτι δὴν μηδ᾽ αὐτοὶ ἐρητύεσθε κελεύθου,
ἀλλ᾽ εὖ καρτύναντες ἑαῖς ἐνὶ χερσὶν ἐρετμὰ
τέμνεθ᾽ ἁλὸς στεινωπόν, ἐπεὶ φάος οὔ νύ τι τόσσον
ἔσσετ᾽ ἐν εὐχωλῇσιν, ὅσον τ᾽ ἐνὶ κάρτεϊ χειρῶν.
335 τῶ καὶ τἆλλα μεθέντες ὀνήιστον πονέεσθαι
θαρσαλέως· πρὶν δ᾽ οὔ τι θεοὺς λίσσεσθαι ἐρύκω.
εἰ δέ κεν ἀντικρὺ πταμένη μεσσηγὺς ὄληται,
ἄψορροι στέλλεσθαι, ἐπεὶ πολὺ βέλτερον εἶξαι
ἀθανάτοις· οὐ γάρ κε κακὸν μόρον ἐξαλέαισθε
340 πετράων, οὐδ᾽ εἴ κε σιδηρείη πέλοι Ἀργώ.
ὦ μέλεοι, μὴ τλῆτε παρὲξ ἐμὰ θέσφατα βῆναι,
εἰ καί με τρὶς τόσσον ὀίεσθ᾽ Οὐρανίδῃσιν,
ὅσσον ἀνάρσιός εἰμι, καὶ εἰ πλείον στυγέεσθαι·
μὴ τλῆτ᾽ οἰωνοῖο πάρεξ ἔτι νηὶ περῆσαι.
345   "καὶ τὰ μὲν ὥς κε πέλῃ, τὼς ἔσσεται. ἢν δὲ
          φύγητε
σύνδρομα πετράων ἀσκηθέες ἔνδοθι Πόντου,
αὐτίκα Βιθυνῶν ἐπὶ δεξιὰ γαῖαν ἔχοντες
πλώετε ῥηγμῖνας πεφυλαγμένοι, εἰσόκεν αὖτε
Ῥήβαν ὠκυρόην ποταμὸν ἀκτήν τε Μέλαιναν
350 γνάμψαντες νήσου Θυνηίδος ὅρμον ἵκησθε.
κεῖθεν δ᾽ οὐ μάλα πουλὺ διὲξ ἁλὸς ἀντιπέραιαν
γῆν Μαριανδυνῶν ἐπικέλσετε νοστήσαντες.
ἔνθα μὲν εἰς Ἀίδαο καταιβάτις ἐστὶ κέλευθος,
ἀκτή τε προβλὴς Ἀχερουσιὰς ὑψόθι τείνει,
355 δινήεις τ᾽ Ἀχέρων αὐτὴν διὰ νειόθι τέμνων
ἄκρην ἐκ μεγάλης προχοὰς ἵησι φάραγγος.

on its wings through these rocks to the Black Sea, then you yourselves must no longer hold back from your course, but gripping the oars tightly in your hands plow your way through the sea's narrows, for deliverance will not depend nearly as much on prayers as on the strength of your hands. Therefore, disregarding everything else, strain to your utmost with courage, though before that time I do not at all forbid praying to the gods. But if it flies forth and is killed midway, head back, for it is much better to yield to the immortals, since you could not escape a terrible death from the rocks, not even if the Argo were made of iron. O hapless men, do not dare to go against my prophecies, even if you think me three times as hateful to the sons of Heaven as I am, or even more. Do not dare to travel any further in your ship against the omen.

"But those things will turn out as they will. If you do escape the clashing of the rocks and enter the Black Sea unscathed, immediately sail on, keeping the land of the Bithynians on your right and watching out for reefs, until in turn you round the swift-flowing Rhebas river and the Black promontory and reach the harbor of the island of Thynias. Proceeding from there a short distance over the sea, you must put in at the land of the Mariandynians on the opposite shore. Here is a path that descends to the abode of Hades, and the jutting Acherusian headland extends high up, and swirling Acheron, cutting its way below through the headland itself, sends forth its waters from a

---

349 ἀκτήν Ω: ἄκρην Chrestien (ex 651)

ἀγχίμολον δ᾽ ἐπὶ τῇ πολέας παρανεῖσθε κολωνοὺς
Παφλαγόνων, τοῖσίν τ᾽ Ἐνετήιος ἐμβασίλευσεν
πρῶτα Πέλοψ, τοῦ καί περ ἀφ᾽ αἵματος
εὐχετόωνται.

360   "ἔστι δέ τις ἄκρη Ἑλίκης κατεναντίον Ἄρκτου,
πάντοθεν ἠλίβατος, καί μιν καλέουσι Κάραμβιν,
τῆς καὶ ὑπὲρ βορέαο περισχίζονται ἄελλαι·
ὧδε μάλ᾽ ἂμ πέλαγος τετραμμένη αἰθέρι κύρει.
τήνδε περιγνάμψαντι Πολὺς παρακέκλιται ἤδη
365 αἰγιαλός. Πολέος δ᾽ ἐπὶ πείρασιν αἰγιαλοῖο
ἀκτῇ ἐπὶ προβλῆτι ῥοαὶ Ἅλυος ποταμοῖο
δεινὸν ἐρεύγονται· μετὰ τόνδ᾽ ἀγχίρροος Ἶρις
μειότερος λευκῇσιν ἑλίσσεται εἰς ἅλα δίναις.
κεῖθεν δὲ προτέρωσε μέγας καὶ ὑπείροχος ἀγκὼν
370 ἐξανέχει γαίης· ἐπὶ δὲ στόμα Θερμώδοντος
κόλπῳ ἐν εὐδιόωντι Θεμισκύρειον ὑπ᾽ ἄκρην
μύρεται, εὐρείης διαειμένος ἠπείροιο.
ἔνθα δὲ Δοίαντος πεδίον, σχεδόθεν δὲ πόληες
τρισσαὶ Ἀμαζονίδων, μετά τε σμυγερώτατοι ἀνδρῶν
375 τρηχείην Χάλυβες καὶ ἀτειρέα γαῖαν ἔχοντες,
ἐργατίναι· τοὶ δ᾽ ἀμφὶ σιδήρεα ἔργα μέλονται.
ἄγχι δὲ ναιετάουσι πολύρρηνες Τιβαρηνοὶ
Ζηνὸς Εὐξείνοιο Γενηταίην ὑπὲρ ἄκρην.
τοῖς δ᾽ ἐπὶ Μοσσύνοικοι ὁμούριοι ὑλήεσσαν
380 ἐξείης ἤπειρον ὑπωρείας τε νέμονται,
δουρατέοις πύργοισιν ἐν οἰκία τεκτήναντες

   379: τοῖς E: τῇ LAS

deep chasm. Not far from it you will sail past many hills of the Paphlagonians, whose first king was Enetean Pelops,[24] of whose blood they claim to be.

"There is a headland opposite Helice the Bear[25] that is steep on all sides; they call it Carambis, and above it the blasts of the north wind are split in two, so high does it rise to the upper air as it faces the open sea. As soon as one rounds it, the Long shore stretches alongside. At the end of the Long shore, beyond a jutting promontory, the waters of the Halys river gush forth with a terrible roar. Not far beyond it flows the Iris, a smaller river, that rolls into the sea with white-capped eddies. Further on from there a large and prominent headland juts out from the shore, and next comes the mouth of the Thermodon, which flows into a placid bay at the base of the Themiscyreian promontory after winding through the broad mainland. Here is the plain of Doeas, and nearby are the Amazons' three cities; next are the Chalybes, most wretched of men, who possess a rugged and unyielding land, laborers who are engaged in ironworking. Nearby, past the Genetaean headland belonging to Zeus Euxenius,[26] live the Tibarenians, rich in sheep. Next in order and sharing a border with them, the Mossynoecians inhabit the wooded plain and lower mountain slopes, having built their wooden homes within towers

[24] The Enetians inhabited Paphlagonia (cf. *Iliad* 2.851–852); other authors locate Pelops in Lydia or Phrygia.
[25] The Big Dipper; hence the headland faces north.
[26] "Of Hospitality."

143

381a κάλινα καὶ πύργους εὐπηγέας, οὓς καλέουσιν
381b μόσσυνας, καὶ δ' αὐτοὶ ἐπώνυμοι ἔνθεν ἔασιν.
      "τοὺς παραμειβόμενοι λισσῇ ἐπικέλσετε νήσῳ,
      μήτι παντοίῃ μέγ' ἀναιδέας ἐξελάσαντες
      οἰωνούς, οἳ δῆθεν ἀπειρέσιοι ἐφέπουσιν
385   νῆσον ἐρημαίην· τῇ μέν τ' ἐνὶ νηὸν Ἄρηος
      λάινεον ποίησαν Ἀμαζονίδων βασίλειαι
      Ὀτρηρή τε καὶ Ἀντιόπη, ὁπότε στρατόωντο.
      ἔνθα γὰρ ὔμμιν ὄνειαρ ἀδευκέος ἐξ ἁλὸς εἶσιν
      ἄρρητον· τῶ καί τε φίλα φρονέων ἀγορεύω
390   ἰσχέμεν. ἀλλὰ τίη με πάλιν χρειὼ ἀλιτέσθαι
      μαντοσύνῃ τὰ ἕκαστα διηνεκὲς ἐξενέποντα;
      "νήσου δὲ προτέρωσε καὶ ἠπείροιο περαίης
      φέρβονται Φίλυρες· Φιλύρων δ' ἐφύπερθεν ἔασιν
      Μάκρωνες, μετὰ δ' αὖ περιώσια φῦλα Βεχείρων·
395   ἐξείης δὲ Σάπειρες ἐπὶ σφίσι ναιετάουσιν,
      Βύζηρες δ' ἐπὶ τοῖσιν ὁμώλακες, ὧν ὕπερ ἤδη
      αὐτοὶ Κόλχοι ἔχονται ἀρήιοι. ἀλλ' ἐνὶ νηὶ
      πείρεθ', ἕως μυχάτη κεν ἐνιχρίμψητε θαλάσσῃ.
      ἔνθα δ' ἐπ' ἠπείροιο Κυταιίδος ἠδ' Ἀμαραντῶν
400   τηλόθεν ἐξ ὀρέων πεδίοιό τε Κιρκαίοιο
      Φᾶσις δινήεις εὐρὺν ῥόον εἰς ἅλα βάλλει.
      κείνου νῆ' ἐλάοντες ἐπὶ προχοὰς ποταμοῖο,
      πύργους εἰσόψεσθε Κυταιέος Αἰήταο,
      ἄλσος τε σκιόεν Ἄρεος, τόθι κῶας ἐπ' ἄκρης
405   πεπτάμενον φηγοῖο δράκων, τέρας αἰνὸν ἰδέσθαι,

381a–381b om. Brunck

made of timber, along with sturdy towers they call 'mossynes,' and from these the people themselves take their name.[27]

"Once you pass by those people, you must put in at a smooth[28] island, after using every kind of ploy to drive away the very vicious birds that inhabit the deserted island in countless numbers. On it Otrere and Antiope, queens of the Amazons, built a stone temple to Ares, when they were on campaign. For there help will come to you from the harsh sea, unspoken though it must remain. Therefore it is with good will that I tell you to stop there. But what need have I to sin again through my art of prophecy by revealing every detail to the end?

"Beyond the island and the mainland across from it live the Philyres, and past the Philyres are the Macrones, and after them in turn the countless tribes of Becheirians. Next in order after them dwell the Sapeires, then the Byzeres with lands adjoining theirs, beyond whom at last dwell the warlike Colchians themselves. But continue by ship until you reach the innermost recess of the sea. Here on the Cytaean[29] mainland, coming from the Amarantian mountains far away and from the plain of Circe, the swirling Phasis sends its broad stream into the sea. As you guide your ship into the mouth of that river, you will see the towers of Cytaean Aeetes and the shady grove of Ares, where a snake—a dreadful monster to behold—glares all around, keeping watch over the fleece that is spread out on the top

---

[27] Although verses 381ab (deleted by Brunck) are somewhat awkward and repetitious, they do provide some worthwhile information.   [28] Or *rugged* (schol.).   [29] I.e. Colchian, named from the town Cytaea or Cyte on the Phasis river.

ἀμφὶς ὀπιπεύει δεδοκημένος· οὐδέ οἱ ἦμαρ,
οὐ κνέφας ἥδυμος ὕπνος ἀναιδέα δάμναται ὄσσε."
     ὣς ἄρ' ἔφη· τοὺς δ' εἶθαρ ἕλεν δέος εἰσαΐοντας.
δὴν δ' ἔσαν ἀμφασίῃ βεβολημένοι· ὀψὲ δ' ἔειπεν
410 ἥρως Αἴσονος υἱὸς ἀμηχανέων κακότητι·
     "ὦ γέρον, ἤδη μέν τε διίκεο πείρατ' ἀέθλων
ναυτιλίης καὶ τέκμαρ, ὅτῳ στυγερὰς διὰ πέτρας
πειθόμενοι Πόντονδε περήσομεν· εἰ δέ κεν αὖτις
τάσδ' ἡμῖν προφυγοῦσιν ἐς Ἑλλάδα νόστος ὀπίσσω
415 ἔσσεται, ἀσπαστῶς κε παρὰ σέο καὶ τὸ δαείην.
πῶς ἔρδω, πῶς αὖτε τόσην ἁλὸς εἶμι κέλευθον,
νῆις ἐὼν ἑτάροις ἅμα νήισιν; Αἶα δὲ Κολχὶς
Πόντου καὶ γαίης ἐπικέκλιται ἐσχατιῇσιν."
     ὣς φάτο· τὸν δ' ὁ γεραιὸς ἀμειβόμενος
          προσέειπεν·
420   "ὦ τέκος, εὖτ' ἂν πρῶτα φύγῃς ὀλοὰς διὰ
          πέτρας,
θάρσει· ἐπεὶ δαίμων ἕτερον πλόον ἡγεμονεύσει
ἐξ Αἴης, μετὰ δ' Αἶαν ἅλις πομπῆες ἔσονται.
ἀλλά, φίλοι, φράζεσθε θεᾶς δολόεσσαν ἀρωγὴν
Κύπριδος· ἐν γὰρ τῇ κλυτὰ πείρατα κεῖται ἀέθλων·
425 καὶ δέ με μηκέτι τῶνδε περαιτέρω ἐξερέεσθε."
     ὣς φάτ' Ἀγηνορίδης· ἐπὶ δὲ σχεδὸν υἱέε δοιὼ
Θρηικίου Βορέαο κατ' αἰθέρος ἀίξαντε
οὐδῷ ἔπι κραιπνοὺς ἔβαλον πόδας· οἱ δ' ἀνόρουσαν
ἐξ ἑδέων ἥρωες, ὅπως παρεόντας ἴδοντο.
430 Ζήτης δ' ἱεμένοισιν, ἔτ' ἄσπετον ἐκ καμάτοιο
ἆσθμ' ἀναφυσιόων, μετεφώνεεν, ὅσσον ἄπωθεν

of an oak tree. Neither by day or night does sweet sleep overcome his restless eyes."

Thus he spoke, and fear immediately seized them as they heard this. For a long time they were struck speechless, but at last the hero Jason, feeling helpless in the face of the danger, spoke:

"O old man, so far you have gone through the ways to accomplish our tasks on the voyage and the sign which we must obey to pass through the horrible rocks to the Black Sea, but I would gladly learn from you as well whether, once we escape them, we shall accomplish a return back again to Hellas afterwards. How can I do it, how shall I make such a long journey over the sea a second time, inexperienced as I am, with inexperienced comrades? Colchian Aea lies at the end of the Black Sea and of the world."

Thus he spoke, and the old man said to him in reply:

"O my child, as soon as you escape through the deadly rocks, be confident, for a god will lead you by a different route from Aea, while on the way to Aea you will have guides enough. But, my friends, be mindful of the wily assistance of the goddess Cypris, for with her lies the glorious accomplishment of your tasks. Yet do not question me any further about these matters."

Thus spoke Agenor's son, and right away Thracian Boreas' two sons sprang down through the air and set their swift feet on the threshold. The heroes rose from their seats when they saw them in their presence. Still panting heavily from his toil, Zetes told his eager listeners how far

---

424 ἐν γὰρ τῇ Σ ad 3.946: ἐκ γὰρ τῆς Ω

ἤλασαν, ἠδ᾽ ὡς Ἶρις ἐρύκακε τάσδε δαΐξαι,
ὅρκιά τ᾽ εὐμενέουσα θεὰ πόρεν, αἱ δ᾽ ὑπέδυσαν
δείματι Δικταίης περιώσιον ἄντρον ἐρίπνης.
435 γηθόσυνοι δῆπειτα δόμοις ἔνι πάντες ἑταῖροι
αὐτός τ᾽ ἀγγελίῃ Φινεὺς πέλεν. ὦκα δὲ τόν γε
Αἰσονίδης περιπολλὸν ἐυφρονέων προσέειπεν·
    "ἦ ἄρα δή τις ἔην, Φινεῦ, θεός, ὃς σέθεν ἄτης
κήδετο λευγαλέης, καὶ δ᾽ ἡμέας αὖθι πέλασσεν
440 τηλόθεν, ὄφρα τοι υἷες ἀμύνειαν Βορέαο·
εἰ δὲ καὶ ὀφθαλμοῖσι φόως πόροι, ἦ τ᾽ ἂν ὀίω
γηθήσειν, ὅσον εἴ περ ὑπότροπος οἴκαδ᾽ ἱκοίμην."
    ὣς ἔφατ᾽· αὐτὰρ ὁ τόν γε κατηφήσας προσέειπεν·
    "Αἰσονίδη, τὸ μὲν οὐ παλινάγρετον, οὐδέ τι
        μῆχος
445 ἔστ᾽ ὀπίσω· κεναὶ γὰρ ὑποσμύχονται ὀπωπαί.
ἀντὶ δὲ τοῦ θάνατόν μοι ἄφαρ θεὸς ἐγγυαλίξαι,
καί τε θανὼν πάσῃσι μετέσσομαι ἀγλαΐησιν."
    ὣς τώ γ᾽ ἀλλήλοισι παραβλήδην ἀγόρευον.
αὐτίκα δ᾽ οὐ μετὰ δηρὸν ἀμειβομένων ἐφαάνθη
450 Ἠριγενής. τὸν δ᾽ ἀμφὶ περικτίται ἠγερέθοντο
ἀνέρες, οἳ καὶ πρόσθεν ἐπ᾽ ἤματι κεῖσε θάμιζον
αἰὲν ὁμῶς φορέοντες ἑῆς ἀπὸ μοῖραν ἐδωδῆς·
τοῖς ὁ γέρων πάντεσσιν, ὅ τις καὶ ἀφαυρὸς ἵκοιτο,
ἔχραεν ἐνδυκέως, πολέων δ᾽ ἀπὸ πήματ᾽ ἔλυσεν
455 μαντοσύνῃ· τῷ καί μιν ἐποιχόμενοι κομέεσκον.
σὺν τοῖσιν δ᾽ ἵκανε Παραίβιος, ὅς ῥά οἱ ἦεν
φίλτατος· ἀσπάσιος δὲ δόμοις ἔνι τούς γ᾽ ἐνόησεν·

away they had driven the Harpies, how Iris had stopped them from killing them, and how the kindly goddess had sworn oaths, and how the Harpies had descended out of fear into a huge cavern on the Dictaean crag. Thereupon all the comrades in the hall—and Phineus himself—were delighted at the news. Immediately Jason, brimming with good will, said to him:

"Truly, after all, Phineus, there was a god who cared about your sad calamity and brought us here from far away, so that Boreas' sons might help you. And if he would also bring light to your eyes, truly I think that I would rejoice as much as if I were to come back home."

Thus he spoke, but the other became downcast and answered him:

"Jason, that cannot be undone, and there is no remedy hereafter, for my empty eyes are wasting away. Instead of that, I wish the god would give me death straightway, and once I die I shall be in full splendor."[30]

Thus the two men spoke and answered each other. And soon thereafter, while they were still conversing, Dawn appeared. Around the old man gathered the neighbors who, before this as well, came there day after day, without fail bringing a portion of their food. And to everyone who came, even the poorest, the old man would prophesy with kind intent, and he freed many of them from their afflictions through his prophecy; that is why they would come and care for him. And with them came Paraebius, who was his dearest friend. He was delighted to see those men in

---

[30] "Splendor" is regularly a metaphor for success and fame.

πρὶν γὰρ δή νύ ποτ' αὐτὸς ἀριστήων στόλον
   ἀνδρῶν
Ἑλλάδος ἐξανιόντα μετὰ πτόλιν Αἰήταο
460 πείσματ' ἀνάψασθαι μυθήσατο Θυνίδι γαίῃ,
οἵ τέ οἱ Ἁρπυίας Διόθεν σχήσουσιν ἰούσας.
τοὺς μὲν ἔπειτ' ἐπέεσσιν ἀρεσσάμενος πυκινοῖσιν
πέμφ' ὁ γέρων, οἷον δὲ Παραίβιον αὐτόθι μίμνειν
κέκλετ' ἀριστήεσσι σὺν ἀνδράσιν. αἶψα δὲ τόν γε
465 σφωιτέρων ὀίων ὅ τις ἔξοχος εἰς ἓ κομίσσαι
ἧκεν ἐποτρύνας· τοῦ δ' ἐκ μεγάροιο κιόντος
μειλιχίως ἐρέτῃσιν ὁμηγερέεσσι μετηύδα·
   "ὦ φίλοι, οὐκ ἄρα πάντες ὑπέρβιοι ἄνδρες ἔασιν
οὐδ' εὐεργεσίης ἀμνήμονες· ὡς καὶ ὅδ' ἀνὴρ
470 τοῖος ἐὼν δεῦρ' ἦλθεν, ἑὸν μόρον ὄφρα δαείη.
εὖτε γὰρ οὖν ὡς πλεῖστα κάμοι καὶ πλεῖστα
   μογήσαι,
δὴ τότε μιν περιπολλὸν ἐπασσυτέρη βιότοιο
χρησμοσύνη τρύχεσκεν· ἐπ' ἤματι δ' ἦμαρ ὀρώρει
κύντερον, οὐδέ τις ἦν ἀνάπευσις μογέοντι.
475 ἀλλ' ὅ γε πατρὸς ἑοῖο κακὴν τίνεσκεν ἀμοιβὴν
ἀμπλακίης. ὁ γὰρ οἶος ἐν οὔρεσι δένδρεα τέμνων
δή ποθ' ἁμαδρυάδος νύμφης ἀθέριξε λιτάων,
ἥ μιν ὀδυρομένη ἀδινῷ μειλίσσετο μύθῳ,
μὴ ταμέειν πρέμνον δρυὸς ἥλικος, ᾗ ἔπι πουλὺν
480 αἰῶνα τρίβεσκε διηνεκές· αὐτὰρ ὁ τήν γε
ἀφραδέως ἔτμηξεν ἀγηνορίῃ νεότητος.
τῷ δ' ἄρα νηκερδῆ νύμφη πόρεν οἶτον ὀπίσσω
αὐτῷ καὶ τεκέεσσιν. ἐγώ γε μέν, εὖτ' ἀφίκανεν,

the house, because long before this the seer himself had
declared that an expedition of heroes on their way from
Hellas to Aeetes' city would fasten their cables to the
Thynian land, and would, with Zeus' help, stop the Harpies
from coming to him. Then the old man, after satisfying the
visitors with wise advice, dismissed them, but bade
Paraebius alone remain there with the heroes. He imme-
diately dispatched him with instructions to bring him the
best of his own sheep. And when he had left the hall,
Phineus spoke gently to the gathering of oarsmen:

"O my friends, not all men, after all, are arrogant or for-
getful of kindness done them. So did this man, being such
as he is, come here to learn about his fate. For whenever he
worked at his utmost and toiled at his utmost, the ever-in-
creasing neediness of his life would wear him down. Day
after day it grew worse, and he had no respite from his toil.
In fact, he was paying the cruel penalty for his father's mis-
take. For once upon a time, when he was all alone cutting
trees in the mountains, his father disregarded the prayers of
a Hamadryad nymph, who tearfully begged him with a
fervent appeal not to cut the trunk of an oak tree that was
as old as she, in which she had continually lived her long
life. But he, in the haughtiness of youth, recklessly cut it
down. And so the nymph bestowed a profitless doom
thereafter upon the man himself and his children. For my
part, when he came to see me, I recognized the offense

---

471 μογῆσαι Merkel: μογῆσοι ASE

APOLLONIUS RHODIUS

ἀμπλακίην ἔγνων· βωμὸν δ' ἐκέλευσα καμόντα
485 Θυνιάδος νύμφης λωφήια ῥέξαι ἐπ' αὐτῷ
ἱερά, πατρῴην αἰτεύμενον αἶσαν ἀλύξαι.
ἔνθ' ἐπεὶ ἔκφυγε κῆρα θεήλατον, οὔ ποτ' ἐμεῖο
ἐκλάθετ', οὐδ' ἀθέρισσε· μόλις δ' ἀέκοντα θύραζε
πέμπω, ἐπεὶ μέμονέν γε παρέμμεναι ἀσχαλόωντι."
490 ὣς φάτ' Ἀγηνορίδης· ὁ δ' ἐπισχεδὸν αὐτίκα δοιὼ
ἤλυθ' ἄγων ποίμηθεν ὄις. ἀνὰ δ' ἵστατ' Ἰήσων,
ἂν δὲ Βορήιοι υἷες ἐφημοσύνῃσι γέροντος.
ὦκα δὲ κεκλόμενοι Μαντήιον Ἀπόλλωνα
ῥέζον ἐπ' ἐσχαρόφιν νέον ἤματος ἀνομένοιο.
495 κουρότεροι δ' ἑτάρων μενοεικέα δαῖτ' ἀλέγυνον.
ἔνθ' εὖ δαισάμενοι, τοὶ μὲν παρὰ πείσματα νηός,
τοὶ δ' αὐτοῦ κατὰ δώματ' ἀολλέες εὐνάζοντο.

ἦρι δ' ἐτήσιοι αὖραι ἐπέχραον, αἵ τ' ἀνὰ πᾶσαν
γαῖαν ὁμῶς τοιῇδε Διὸς πνείουσιν ἀρωγῇ.
500 Κυρήνη πέφαταί τις ἕλος πάρα Πηνειοῖο
μῆλα νέμειν προτέροισι παρ' ἀνδράσιν· εὔαδε γάρ
οἱ
παρθενίη καὶ λέκτρον ἀκήρατον. αὐτὰρ Ἀπόλλων
τήν γ' ἀνερειψάμενος ποταμῷ ἔπι ποιμαίνουσαν
τηλόθεν Αἱμονίης χθονίης παρακάτθετο νύμφαις,
505 αἳ Λιβύην ἐνέμοντο παραὶ Μυρτώσιον αἶπος.

499 ἀρωγῇ Ω: ἀνωγῇ MRQ

---

31 "Of Prophecy."
32 The Etesian ("Annual") winds blow from the northwest.

152

and ordered him to build an altar to the Thynian nymph and to make sacrifices of atonement upon it, begging to be free of the fate inherited from his father. Then, ever since he escaped the heaven-sent doom, he has never forgotten or disregarded me, and only with difficulty and against his will can I send him out of the house, so determined is he to stay by me in my affliction."

Thus spoke Agenor's son, and right away Paraebius returned, bringing two sheep from the flock. Jason stood up, as did Boreas' sons, at the old man's bidding. Without delay they called upon Apollo Manteius[31] and began sacrificing on the hearth just as the day was waning. The younger comrades prepared a heart-cheering feast. Then, after feasting well, they went to bed, some by the ship's cables, others there in groups throughout the house.

At dawn the Etesian winds were gusting,[32] the ones that blow equally over all the earth owing to Zeus' assistance[33] of the following sort. A certain Cyrene is said to have been pasturing sheep near the marsh of the Peneus among men of former times, for she cherished her virginity and chaste bed.[34] But while she was tending her sheep by the river, Apollo snatched her far away from Haemonia[35] and placed her among the indigenous nymphs who inhabited Libya near the hill of Myrtles.[36] There she bore Phoe-

[33] Or, reading ἀνωγῇ, command.

[34] Shepherding was a male occupation; for Cyrene's dislike of female tasks (and another version of the story), see Pindar, *Pythian* 9.1–70.

[35] Thessaly.

[36] Probably a hill west of Cyrene (cf. Callimachus, *Hymn* 2.91).

ἔνθα δ᾽ Ἀρισταῖον Φοίβῳ τέκεν, ὃν καλέουσιν
Ἀγρέα καὶ Νόμιον πολυλήιοι Αἱμονιῆες.
τὴν μὲν γὰρ φιλότητι θεὸς ποιήσατο νύμφην
αὐτοῦ μακραίωνα καὶ ἀγρότιν· υἷα δ᾽ ἔνεικεν
510 νηπίαχον Χείρωνος ὑπ᾽ ἄντροισιν κομέεσθαι.
τῷ καὶ ἀεξηθέντι θεαὶ γάμον ἐμνήστευσαν
Μοῦσαι, ἀκεστορίην τε θεοπροπίας τ᾽ ἐδίδαξαν·
καί μιν ἑῶν μήλων θέσαν ἤρανον, ὅσσ᾽ ἐνέμοντο
ἂμ πεδίον Φθίης Ἀθαμάντιον ἀμφί τ᾽ ἐρυμνὴν
515 Ὄθρυν καὶ ποταμοῦ ἱερὸν ῥόον Ἀπιδανοῖο.
ἦμος δ᾽ οὐρανόθεν Μινωίδας ἔφλεγε νήσους
Σείριος, οὐδ᾽ ἐπὶ δηρὸν ἔην ἄκος ἐνναέτῃσιν,
τῆμος τόν γ᾽ ἐκάλεσσαν ἐφημοσύνῃς Ἑκάτοιο
λοιμοῦ ἀλεξητῆρα. λίπεν δ᾽ ὅ γε πατρὸς ἐφετμῇ
520 Φθίην, ἐν δὲ Κέῳ κατενάσσατο, λαὸν ἀγείρας
Παρράσιον, τοὶ πέρ τε Λυκάονός εἰσι γενέθλης·
καὶ βωμὸν ποίησε μέγαν Διὸς Ἰκμαίοιο,
ἱερά τ᾽ εὖ ἔρρεξεν ἐν οὔρεσιν ἀστέρι κείνῳ
Σειρίῳ αὐτῷ τε Κρονίδῃ Διί. τοῖο δ᾽ ἕκητι
525 γαῖαν ἐπιψύχουσιν ἐτήσιοι ἐκ Διὸς αὖραι
ἤματα τεσσαράκοντα, Κέῳ δ᾽ ἔτι νῦν ἱερῆες
ἀντολέων προπάροιθε Κυνὸς ῥέζουσι θυηλάς.

καὶ τὰ μὲν ὣς ὑδέονται· ἀριστῆες δὲ καταῦθι
μίμνον ἐρυκόμενοι· ξεινήια δ᾽ ἄσπετα Θυνοὶ

---

37 "Hunter and Shepherd."
38 Libya.

154

bus' son, Aristaeus, whom the Haemonians, rich in wheat fields, call Agreus and Nomius.[37] For in his love for her the god made her a long-lived nymph in that land[38] and a huntress, whereas he took their infant son to be raised in Cheiron's cave. And when he grew up, the divine Muses arranged his marriage[39] and taught him healing and prophecy, and they made him keeper of all their sheep that grazed on the Athamantian plain of Phthia and around steep Othrys and the sacred stream of the Apidanus river. But when from the sky Sirius was scorching the Minoan islands,[40] and for a long time the inhabitants had no relief, then they summoned him on the instructions of the Far-Shooter[41] to ward off the pestilence. And he left Phthia at the command of his father[42] and settled in Ceos, having gathered the Parrhasian people who are of the lineage of Lycaon.[43] And he built a great altar to Zeus Icmaeus[44] and duly performed sacrifices on the mountains to that star Sirius and to Zeus himself, son of Cronus. And for this reason the Etesian winds sent by Zeus cool the land for forty days, and still today in Ceos priests make sacrifices before the Dog Star rises.

And thus the story is told. But the heroes were held back and remained there,[45] while the Thynians sent them

---

[39] To Autonoe, daughter of Cadmus; their son was Actaeon (cf. Hesiod, *Theogony* 976–977).

[40] The Cyclades, over which Minos ruled.

[41] Apollo.   [42] Apollo.

[43] Lycaon was an early king of the Arcadians (Parrhasians).

[44] "Of Rain."

[45] The winds impeded their journey north through the Bosporus.

530 πᾶν ἦμαρ Φινῆι χαριζόμενοί προΐαλλον.
ἐκ δὲ τόθεν μακάρεσσι δυώδεκα δωμήσαντες
βωμὸν ἁλὸς ῥηγμῖνι πέρην καὶ ἐφ᾿ ἱερὰ θέντες,
νῆα θοὴν εἴσβαινον ἐρεσσέμεν· οὐδὲ πελείης
τρήρωνος λήθοντο μετὰ σφίσιν, ἀλλ᾿ ἄρα τήν γε
535 δείματι πεπτηυῖαν ἑῇ φέρε χειρὶ μεμαρπὼς
Εὔφημος· γαίης δ᾿ ἀπὸ διπλόα πείσματ᾿ ἔλυσαν.

οὐδ᾿ ἄρ᾿ Ἀθηναίην προτέρω λάθον ὁρμηθέντες·
αὐτίκα δ᾿ ἐσσυμένως νεφέλης ἐπιβᾶσα πόδεσσιν
κούφης, ἥ κε φέροι μιν ἄφαρ βριαρήν περ ἐοῦσαν,
540 σεύατ᾿ ἴμεν Πόντονδε, φίλα φρονέουσ᾿ ἐρέτῃσιν.
ὡς δ᾿ ὅτε τις πάτρηθεν ἀλώμενος—οἷά τε πολλὰ
πλαζόμεθ᾿ ἄνθρωποι τετληότες—οὐδέ τις αἶα
τηλουρός, πᾶσαι δὲ κατόψιοί εἰσι κέλευθοι,
σφωιτέρους δ᾿ ἐνόησε δόμους, ἄμυδις δὲ κέλευθος
545 ὑγρή τε τραφερή τ᾿ ἰνδάλλεται, ἄλλοτε δ᾿ ἄλλῃ
ὀξέα πορφύρων ἐπιμαίεται ὀφθαλμοῖσιν·
ὡς ἄρα καρπαλίμως κούρη Διὸς ἀίξασα
θῆκεν ἐπ᾿ ἀξείνοιο πόδας Θυνηίδος ἀκτῆς.

οἱ δ᾿ ὅτε δὴ σκολιοῖο πόρου στεινωπὸν ἵκοντο
550 τρηχείῃς σπιλάδεσσιν ἐεργμένον ἀμφοτέρωθεν,
δινήεις δ᾿ ὑπένερθεν ἀνακλύζεσκεν ἰοῦσαν
νῆα ῥόος, πολλὸν δὲ φόβῳ προτέρωσε νέοντο,
ἤδη δέ σφισι δοῦπος ἀρασσομένων πετράων
νωλεμὲς οὔατ᾿ ἔβαλλε, βόων δ᾿ ἁλιμυρέες ἀκταί·
555 δὴ τότ᾿ ἔπειθ᾿ ὁ μὲν ὦρτο πελειάδα χειρὶ μεμαρπὼς

countless guest-gifts every day out of gratitude to Phineus. And afterwards they built an altar to the twelve blessed gods on the opposite seashore, placed offerings upon it, and boarded their swift ship to row. Nor did they forget to take a timorous dove with them, but indeed Euphemus brought one, quivering with fear, that he grasped in his hand. And from the land they loosed the two cables.

Nor was their going forth unnoticed by Athena. She immediately rushed to set foot on a light cloud, which would carry her quickly, mighty though she was, and she hastened to the Black Sea with friendly intentions towards the oarsmen. And as when a man roams from his homeland—as we suffering humans often must wander—and no land is distant but all routes are visible,[46] and he thinks of his own home, and pictures at once the way by sea and land, and in his swift thoughts seeks now one place, now another with his eyes—so quickly did Zeus' daughter spring down and plant her feet on the inhospitable[47] Thynian shore.

Now when they reached the narrow portion of the winding passage, which was hemmed in on both sides by jagged rocks, and when a swirling current surged up from below against the ship as it advanced, they proceeded very fearfully, for already the thudding of the crashing rocks constantly struck their ears, and the sea-washed headlands resounded. At that point Euphemus, grasping the dove in

[46] I.e. to the mind's eye. One who wanders from his home to distant lands can instantaneously traverse in his thoughts the intervening routes from one place to another. This complex simile is based on *Iliad* 15.80–83 (applying to Hera).

[47] Some edd. capitalize, "on the Thynian shore of the Inhospitable sea (i.e. Black Sea)."

APOLLONIUS RHODIUS

Εὔφημος πρῴρης ἐπιβήμεναι, οἱ δ᾽ ὑπ᾽ ἀνωγῇ
Τίφυος Ἀγνιάδαο θελήμονα ποιήσαντο
εἰρεσίην, ἵν᾽ ἔπειτα διὲκ πέτρας ἐλάσειαν
κάρτεϊ ᾧ πίσυνοι. τὰς δ᾽ αὐτίκα λοίσθιον ἄλλων
560 οἰγομένας ἀγκῶνα περιγνάμψαντες ἴδοντο·
σὺν δέ σφιν χύτο θυμός. ὁ δ᾽ ἀίξαι πτερύγεσσιν
Εὔφημος προέηκε πελειάδα, τοὶ δ᾽ ἅμα πάντες
ἤειραν κεφαλὰς ἐσορώμενοι· ἡ δὲ δι᾽ αὐτῶν
ἔπτατο· ταὶ δ᾽ ἄμυδις πάλιν ἀντίαι ἀλλήλῃσιν
565 ἄμφω ὁμοῦ ξυνιοῦσαι ἐπέκτυπον. ὦρτο δὲ πολλὴ
ἅλμη ἀναβρασθεῖσα νέφος ὥς· αὖε δὲ πόντος
σμερδαλέον· πάντῃ δὲ περὶ μέγας ἔβρεμεν αἰθήρ.
κοῖλαι δὲ σπήλυγγες ὑπὸ σπιλάδας τρηχείας
κλυζούσης ἁλὸς ἔνδον ἐβόμβεον, ὑψόθι δ᾽ ὄχθης
570 λευκὴ καχλάζοντος ἀνέπτυε κύματος ἄχνη.
νῆα δ᾽ ἔπειτα πέριξ εἴλει ῥόος. ἄκρα δ᾽ ἔκοψαν
οὐραῖα πτερὰ ταί γε πελειάδος· ἡ δ᾽ ἀπόρουσεν
ἀσκηθής. ἐρέται δὲ μέγ᾽ ἴαχον· ἔβραχε δ᾽ αὐτὸς
Τῖφυς ἐρεσσέμεναι κρατερῶς· οἴγοντο γὰρ αὖτις
575 ἄνδιχα. τοὺς δ᾽ ἐλάοντας ἔχεν τρόμος, ὄφρα μιν
αὐτὴ
πλημυρὶς παλίνορσος ἀνερχομένη κατένεικεν
εἴσω πετράων. τότε δ᾽ αἰνότατον δέος εἷλεν
πάντας· ὑπὲρ κεφαλῆς γὰρ ἀμήχανος ἦεν ὄλεθρος.
ἤδη δ᾽ ἔνθα καὶ ἔνθα διὰ πλατὺς εἴδετο Πόντος,
580 καί σφισιν ἀπροφάτως ἀνέδυ μέγα κῦμα πάροιθεν
κυρτόν, ἀποτμῆγι σκοπιῇ ἴσον· οἱ δ᾽ ἐσιδόντες
ἤμυσαν λοξοῖσι καρήασιν, εἴσατο γάρ ῥα

158

his hand, rose to mount the prow, while the crew, at the command of Hagnias' son Tiphys, rowed at ease, so that later they could count on their strength to propel the ship through the rocks. And as soon as they rounded the last bend of all, they saw the rocks opening apart,[48] and their hearts melted. And Euphemus sent forth the dove to dart forward on its wings, while all the crew together raised their heads to watch. She flew between them, and the two rocks came back together again with a crash. A mass of seething spray shot up like a cloud, and the sea roared terrifyingly, and the vast sky rumbled all around. The hollow caverns at the base of the jagged rocks boomed as the sea surged within, while the white foam of the crashing wave spurted high above the cliff. Then the current began spinning the ship around. The rocks cut off the tips of the dove's tail feathers, but she flew away unharmed. The oarsmen gave a great cheer, and Tiphys himself shouted for them to row with all their might, for the rocks were opening apart again. Trembling gripped them as they rowed, until that very surge with its returning wash carried them back between the rocks—then the most awful terror seized them all, for above their heads hung inescapable destruction. By now, on their left and right, the broad Black Sea was visible through the rocks, but without warning an enormous wave rose up in front, arching over them like a sheer cliff. When they saw it, they turned aside their heads and ducked, for it seemed about to crash down over the

[48] Some edd. follow the scholium and translate, "And as they rounded a bend they saw the rocks opening for the last time of all" (Seaton).

νηὸς ὑπὲρ πάσης κατεπάλμενον ἀμφικαλύψειν.
ἀλλά μιν ἔφθη Τῖφυς ὑπ' εἰρεσίῃ βαρύθουσαν
585 ἀγχαλάσας· τὸ δὲ πολλὸν ὑπὸ τρόπιν ἐξεκυλίσθη,
ἐκ δ' αὐτὴν πρύμνηθεν ἀνείρυσε τηλόθι νῆα
πετράων, ὑψοῦ δὲ μεταχρονίη πεφόρητο.
Εὔφημος δ' ἀνὰ πάντας ἰὼν βοάασκεν ἑταίρους
ἐμβαλέειν κώπῃσιν ὅσον σθένος· οἱ δ' ἀλαλητῷ
590 κόπτον ὕδωρ. ὅσσον δ' ἂν ὑπείκαθε νηῦς ἐρέτῃσιν,
δὶς τόσον ἂψ ἀπόρουσεν· ἐπεγνάμπτοντο δὲ κῶπαι
ἠΰτε καμπύλα τόξα βιαζομένων ἡρώων.
     ἔνθεν δ' αὐτίκ' ἔπειτα καταρρεπὲς ἔσσυτο κῦμα,
ἡ δ' ἄφαρ ὥς τε κύλινδρος ἐπέτρεχε κύματι λάβρῳ
595 προπροκαταΐγδην κοίλης ἁλός. ἐν δ' ἄρα μέσσαις
Πληγάσι δινήεις εἶχεν ῥόος· αἱ δ' ἑκάτερθεν
σειόμεναι βρόμεον, πεπέδητο δὲ νήια δοῦρα.
καὶ τότ' Ἀθηναίη στιβαρῆς ἀντέσπασε πέτρης
σκαιῇ, δεξιτερῇ δὲ διαμπερὲς ὧσε φέρεσθαι.
600 ἡ δ' ἰκέλη πτερόεντι μετήορος ἔσσυτ' ὀϊστῷ·
ἔμπης δ' ἀφλάστοιο παρέθρισαν ἄκρα κόρυμβα
νωλεμὲς ἐμπλήξασαι ἐναντίαι. αὐτὰρ Ἀθήνη
Οὔλυμπόνδ' ἀνόρουσεν, ὅτ' ἀσκηθεῖς ὑπάλυξαν.
πέτραι δ' εἰς ἕνα χῶρον ἐπισχεδὸν ἀλλήλῃσιν
605 νωλεμὲς ἐρρίζωθεν· ὃ δὴ καὶ μόρσιμον ἦεν
ἐκ μακάρων, εὖτ' ἄν τις ἰδὼν διὰ νηὶ περάσσῃ.

593 καταρρεπὲς Et. Gen. et Anecd. Par. 4.55, 67 (= ἑτε-
ρορρεπής, Heschy.): κατηρεφὲς Ω

entire ship and overwhelm it. But before it could, Tiphys eased up on the ship that was laboring under the rowing, and the mass of the wave rolled away beneath the keel; and it pulled the ship itself by the stern far back from the rocks, as it was borne high up in the air. And Euphemus, going up and down among all his comrades, shouted at them to put all their strength into their oars, and with a loud cry they kept striking the water. But whatever progress the ship might have made in obedience to its rowers, it shot back twice as far, and the oars bent back like curved bows as the heroes strained at them.

Then immediately thereafter a wave from the opposite direction[49] rushed upon them, and at once the ship began riding the violent wave like a roller, plunging forward through the hollow sea. Then the swirling current held it right in the middle of the Clashing rocks, and they were shaking and rumbling on both sides, while the ship's timbers were held fast there. Then Athena braced her left hand against a mighty rock and with her right pushed the ship on its way through. Like a feathered arrow it sped through the air, but all the same the rocks sheared off the very tip of the stern ornament when they dashed firmly together. But Athena sprang back to Olympus when they had escaped unharmed. The rocks became rooted firmly together in one place, as had been fated by the blessed gods, once someone beheld them[50] and passed between them in his ship.

---

[49] Or, reading the MSS' κατηρεφὲς, *a vaulted wave.*

[50] For τις ἰδών, cf. 2.318–319 (ὄψεσθε... οὔ τινα). After seeing the danger the rocks pose, one must have the courage to sail between them.

οἱ δέ που ὀκρυόεντος ἀνέπνεον ἄρτι φόβοιο
ἠέρα παπταίνοντες ὁμοῦ πέλαγός τε θαλάσσης
τηλ' ἀναπεπτάμενον· δὴ γὰρ φάσαν ἐξ Ἀίδαο
610 σώεσθαι. Τῖφυς δὲ παροίτατος ἤρχετο μύθων·
"ἔλπομαι αὐτῇ νηὶ τό γ' ἔμπεδον ἐξαλέασθαι
ἡμέας· οὐδέ τις ἄλλος ἐπαίτιος, ὅσσον Ἀθήνη,
ἥ οἱ ἐνέπνευσεν θεῖον μένος, εὖτέ μιν Ἄργος
γόμφοισιν συνάρασσε· θέμις δ' οὐκ ἔστιν ἀλῶναι.
615 Αἰσονίδη, τύνη δὲ τεοῦ βασιλῆος ἐφετμήν,
εὖτε διὲκ πέτρας φυγέειν θεὸς ἧμιν ὄπασσεν,
μηκέτι δείδιθι τοῖον, ἐπεὶ μετόπισθεν ἀέθλους
εὐπαλέας τελέεσθαι Ἀγηνορίδης φάτο Φινεύς."
ἦ ῥ' ἅμα καὶ προτέρωσε παραὶ Βιθυνίδα γαῖαν
620 νῆα διὲκ πέλαγος σεῦεν μέσον. αὐτὰρ ὁ τόν γε
μειλιχίοις ἐπέεσσι παραβλήδην προσέειπεν·
"Τῖφυ, τίη μοι ταῦτα παρηγορέεις ἀχέοντι;
ἤμβροτον ἀασάμην τε κακὴν καὶ ἀμήχανον ἄτην.
χρῆν γὰρ ἐφιεμένοιο καταντικρὺ Πελίαο
625 αὐτίκ' ἀνήνασθαι τόνδε στόλον, εἰ καὶ ἔμελλον
νηλειῶς μελεϊστὶ κεδαιόμενος θανέεσθαι.
νῦν δὲ περισσὸν δεῖμα καὶ ἀτλήτους μελεδῶνας
ἄγκειμαι, στυγέων μὲν ἁλὸς κρυόεντα κέλευθα
νηὶ διαπλώειν, στυγέων δ' ὅτ' ἐπ' ἠπείροιο
630 βαίνωμεν· πάντῃ γὰρ ἀνάρσιοι ἄνδρες ἔασιν.
αἰεὶ δὲ στονόεσσαν ἐπ' ἤματι νύκτα φυλάσσω,
ἐξότε τὸ πρώτιστον ἐμὴν χάριν ἠγερέθεσθε,
φραζόμενος τὰ ἕκαστα. σὺ δ' εὐμαρέως ἀγορεύεις,

No doubt they caught their breath again after their chilling terror, as they surveyed both the sky and the expanse of sea stretching into the distance, for indeed they thought they had been saved from Hades. Tiphys was the first to begin speaking:

"I believe that it is thanks to the ship itself that we safely made this escape, but no one is as responsible as Athena, who breathed divine strength into it when Argus fastened it with pegs; and it is not right for it to be destroyed. Jason, for your part, no longer be so fearful of your king's command, now that a god has allowed us to escape through the rocks, since Agenor's son Phineus said that afterwards our tasks would be easily accomplished."[51]

He said this as he was speeding the ship forward along the Bithynian coast through the open water. But Jason addressed him with gentle words in reply:

"Tiphys, why are you saying these consoling words to me in my distress? I made a mistake and committed a terrible and irreversible error. For when Pelias gave his order, I should have immediately refused this expedition outright, even if I was bound to die, cruelly torn limb from limb. But now I am given over to[52] excessive fear and unbearable worries, dreading to sail over the chilling paths of the sea in a ship, and dreading the time when we set foot on land, for everywhere are hostile men. And always, day after day, ever since you first gathered together for my sake, I spend the dreary night thinking about every detail. You

---

[51] Phineus' words are at 2.420–422.

[52] The precise meaning of ἄγκειμαι is in doubt. Other translations are "I am wrapped in" (Seaton) and "I have laid on me as a burden" (Mooney).

οἶον ἑῆς ψυχῆς ἀλέγων ὕπερ· αὐτὰρ ἐγώ γε
635 εἶο μὲν οὐδ' ἠβαιὸν ἀτύζομαι· ἀμφὶ δὲ τοῖο
καὶ τοῦ, ὁμῶς καὶ σεῖο καὶ ἄλλων δείδι' ἑταίρων,
εἰ μὴ ἐς Ἑλλάδα γαῖαν ἀπήμονας ὕμμε κομίσσω."
    ὣς φάτ' ἀριστήων πειρώμενος· οἱ δ' ὁμάδησαν
θαρσαλέοις ἐπέεσσιν. ὁ δὲ φρένας ἔνδον ἰάνθη
640 κεκλομένων, καί ῥ' αὖτις ἐπιρρήδην μετέειπεν·
    "ὦ φίλοι, ὑμετέρῃ ἀρετῇ ἔνι θάρσος ἀέξω.
τούνεκα νῦν οὐδ' εἴ κε διὲξ Ἀίδαο βερέθρων
στελλοίμην, ἔτι τάρβος ἀνάψομαι, εὖτε πέλεσθε
ἔμπεδοι ἀργαλέοις ἐνὶ δείμασιν. ἀλλ' ὅτε πέτρας
645 Πληγάδας ἐξέπλωμεν, ὀίομαι οὐκ ἔτ' ὀπίσσω
ἔσσεσθαι τοιόνδ' ἕτερον φόβον, εἰ ἐτεόν γε
φραδμοσύνῃ Φινῆος ἐπισπόμενοι νεόμεσθα."
    ὣς φάτο· καὶ τοίων μὲν ἐλώφεον αὐτίκα μύθων,
εἰρεσίῃ δ' ἀλίαστον ἔχον πόνον. αἶψα δὲ τοί γε
650 Ῥήβαν ὠκυρόην ποταμὸν σκόπελόν τε Κολώνης,
ἄκρην δ' οὐ μετὰ δηθὰ παρεξενέοντο Μέλαιναν,
τῇ δ' ἄρ' ἐπὶ προχοὰς Φυλληίδας, ἔνθα πάροιθεν
Διψακὸς υἷ' Ἀθάμαντος ἑοῖς ὑπέδεκτο δόμοισιν,
ὁππόθ' ἅμα κριῷ φεῦγεν πόλιν Ὀρχομενοῖο·
655 τίκτε δέ μιν νύμφη λειμωνιάς· οὐδέ οἱ ὕβρις
ἥνδανεν, ἀλλ' ἐθελημὸς ἐφ' ὕδασι πατρὸς ἑοῖο
μητέρι συνναίεσκεν ἐπάκτια πώεα φέρβων.
τοῦ μέν θ' ἱερὸν αἶψα, καὶ εὐρείας ποταμοῖο
ἠιόνας πεδίον τε, βαθυρρείοντά τε Κάλπην
660 δερκόμενοι παράμειβον. ὁμῶς δ' ἐπὶ ἤματι νύκτα

164

speak easily, since you are concerned with your own life alone, whereas I am not in the slightest distraught about mine, but fear for this man and that man, and equally for you and the other comrades, if I do not bring you back safe and sound to the land of Hellas."

Thus he spoke to test the heroes. But they shouted back with words full of courage. His mind within was cheered at their outcry, and this time he addressed them straightforwardly:

"O my friends, thanks to your valor my courage grows. Now, therefore, not even if I should voyage through the chasms of Hades shall I any longer let fear fasten upon me, since you are steadfast in terrible dangers. No, since we have sailed through the Clashing rocks, I believe that there will never be another such terror in the future, if indeed we follow Phineus' advice on our journey."

Thus he spoke, and they immediately ceased from such talk and devoted unabating toil to rowing. Soon they passed by the swift-flowing Rhebas river and the peak of Colone, and not long thereafter passed by the Black cape,[53] and after it the mouth of the Phyllis river, where Dipsacus had in the past welcomed Athamas' son[54] into his home, when he was fleeing with the ram from the city of Orchomenus. A meadow nymph bore Dipsacus, who had no fondness for violence, but was content to live with his mother by the waters of his father,[55] pasturing his flocks on the shore. They soon sighted and passed by his temple, the broad banks of the river, the plain, and the deep-flowing Calpe river. And at the close of day they likewise spent the

---

[53] Called Black promontory at 2.349.
[54] Phrixus.   [55] The river god, Phyllis.

νήνεμον ἀκαμάτῃσιν ἐπερρώοντ᾽ ἐλάτῃσιν.
οἷον δὲ πλαδόωσαν ἐπισχίζοντες ἄρουραν
ἐργατίναι μογέουσι βόες, πέρι δ᾽ ἄσπετος ἱδρὼς
εἴβεται ἐκ λαγόνων τε καὶ αὐχένος, ὄμματα δέ σφιν
665 λοξὰ παραστρωφῶνται ὑπὸ ζυγοῦ, αὐτὰρ ἀυτμὴ
αὐαλέη στομάτων ἄμοτον βρέμει· οἱ δ᾽ ἐνὶ γαίῃ
χηλὰς σκηρίπτοντε πανημέριοι πονέονται·
τοῖς ἴκελοι ἥρωες ὑπὲξ ἁλὸς εἷλκον ἐρετμά.
ἦμος δ᾽ οὔτ᾽ ἄρ πω φάος ἄμβροτον, οὔτ᾽ ἔτι λίην
670 ὀρφναίη πέλεται, λεπτὸν δ᾽ ἐπιδέδρομε νυκτὶ
φέγγος, ὅτ᾽ ἀμφιλύκην μιν ἀνεγρόμενοι καλέουσιν,
τῆμος ἐρημαίης νήσου λιμέν᾽ εἰσελάσαντες
Θυνιάδος καμάτῳ πολυπήμονι βαῖνον ἔραζε.
τοῖσι δὲ Λητοῦς υἱός, ἀνερχόμενος Λυκίηθεν
675 τῆλ᾽ ἐπ᾽ ἀπείρονα δῆμον Ὑπερβορέων ἀνθρώπων,
ἐξεφάνη· χρύσεοι δὲ παρειάων ἑκάτερθεν
πλοχμοὶ βοτρυόεντες ἐπερρώοντο κιόντι·
λαιῇ δ᾽ ἀργύρεον νώμα βιόν, ἀμφὶ δὲ νώτοις
ἰοδόκη τετάνυστο κατωμαδόν· ἡ δ᾽ ὑπὸ ποσσὶν
680 σείετο νῆσος ὅλη, κλύζεν δ᾽ ἐπὶ κύματα χέρσῳ.
τοὺς δ᾽ ἕλε θάμβος ἰδόντας ἀμήχανον, οὐδέ τις
          ἔτλη
ἀντίον αὐγάσσασθαι ἐς ὄμματα καλὰ θεοῖο.
στὰν δὲ κάτω νεύσαντες ἐπὶ χθονός· αὐτὰρ ὁ τηλοῦ
βῆ ῥ᾽ ἴμεναι πόντονδε δι᾽ ἠέρος. ὀψὲ δὲ τοῖον
685 Ὀρφεὺς ἔκφατο μῦθον ἀριστήεσσι πιφαύσκων·
"εἰ δ᾽ ἄγε δὴ νῆσον μὲν Ἑῴου Ἀπόλλωνος
τήνδ᾽ ἱερὴν κλείωμεν, ἐπεὶ πάντεσσι φαάνθη

windless night exerting their strength in tireless rowing.
And as when plowing oxen labor at cleaving a waterlogged
field, and untold sweat pours from their sides and necks,
while their eyes roll sideways under the yoke, and parched
breath incessantly thunders from their mouths, and all day
long they toil as they plant their hooves in the ground—like
them the heroes kept pulling their oars up out of the sea.

At the time when the divine light has not yet come, nor
is it still completely dark, but a faint glimmer comes upon
the night, when men awake and call it morning twilight,
then they rowed into the harbor of the deserted island of
Thynias and, after their exhausting toil, stepped ashore. To
them the son of Leto, on his way up from Lycia far off to
the countless folk[56] of the Hyperborean people, appeared.
His golden locks flowed in clusters over both cheeks as he
went; in his left hand he held his silver bow, and his quiver
was slung over his back from his shoulder. Beneath his feet
the whole island shook, and waves washed over the dry
land. Helpless wonder seized them when they saw him,
and no one dared to look directly into the beautiful eyes of
the god. They stood with heads bowed to the ground, but
he proceeded far out to sea through the air. At last Or-
pheus made this declaration to the heroes:

"Come, let us name this the sacred island of Apollo
Heoïus,[57] because he appeared at dawn to us all as he passed

[56] Or *to the vast territory*. Apollo spent winters in Lycia, sum-
mers with the Hyperboreans ("those beyond the north wind").
[57] "Of the Dawn."

ἠῶος μετιών· τὰ δὲ ῥέξομεν οἷα πάρεστιν,
βωμὸν ἀναστήσαντες ἐπάκτιον. εἰ δ' ἂν ὀπίσσω
690 γαῖαν ἐς Αἱμονίην ἀσκηθέα νόστον ὀπάσσῃ,
δὴ τότε οἱ κεραῶν ἐπὶ μηρία θήσομεν αἰγῶν·
νῦν δ' αὔτως κνίσῃ λοιβῇσί τε μειλίξασθαι
κέκλομαι. ἀλλ' ἵληθι, ἄναξ, ἵληθι φαανθείς."

ὣς ἄρ' ἔφη· καὶ τοὶ μὲν ἄφαρ βωμὸν τετύκοντο
695 χερμάσιν· οἱ δ' ἀνὰ νῆσον ἐδίνεον, ἐξερέοντες
εἴ κέ τιν' ἢ κεμάδων ἢ ἀγροτέρων ἐσίδοιεν
αἰγῶν, οἷά τε πολλὰ βαθείῃ βόσκεται ὕλῃ.
τοῖσι δὲ Λητοΐδης ἄγρην πόρεν· ἐκ δέ νυ πάντων
εὐαγέως ἱερῷ ἀνὰ διπλόα μηρία βωμῷ
700 καῖον, ἐπικλείοντες Ἑώιον Ἀπόλλωνα.
ἀμφὶ δὲ δαιομένοις εὐρὺν χορὸν ἐστήσαντο,
καλὸν Ἰηπαιήον' Ἰηπαιήονα Φοῖβον
μελπόμενοι· σὺν δέ σφιν ἐὺς πάις Οἰάγροιο
Βιστονίῃ φόρμιγγι λιγείης ἦρχεν ἀοιδῆς·
705 ὥς ποτε πετραίῃ ὑπὸ δειράδι Παρνησσοῖο
Δελφύνην τόξοισι πελώριον ἐξενάριξεν,
κοῦρος ἐὼν ἔτι γυμνός, ἔτι πλοκάμοισι γεγηθώς—
ἱλήκοις· αἰεί τοι, ἄναξ, ἄτμητοι ἔθειραι,
αἰὲν ἀδήλητοι· τὼς γὰρ θέμις. οἰόθι δ' αὐτὴ
710 Λητὼ Κοιογένεια φίλαις ἐνὶ χερσὶν ἀφάσσει—
πολλὰ δὲ Κωρύκιαι νύμφαι, Πλειστοῖο θύγατρες,

---

58 "Hail to the Healing God, hail to the Healing God Phoe-
bus." For the chant, cf. the *Homeric Hymn to Apollo* 517.

by, and let us set up an altar on the shore and sacrifice whatever is at hand. And if hereafter he grants us a safe return to the Haemonian land, then indeed we shall place on his altar the thighs of horned goats. But for now, I bid you propitiate him as best we can with the savor of meat and libations. Be gracious, lord, be gracious, you who appeared to us."

Thus he spoke, and some of the men immediately constructed an altar of stones, while others went about the island, seeing if they could spot some fawn or wild goat, animals that often forage in deep woods. Leto's son provided them quarry, and so from each of them they piously burned two thighs on the holy altar, as they invoked Apollo Heoïus. Around the burning offerings they formed a broad choral dance and chanted the beautiful "Iêpaiêon, Phoebus Iêpaiêon."[58] And among them the noble son of Oeagrus led off a clear song on his Bistonian lyre, telling how once upon a time beneath Parnassus' rocky ridge the god killed monstrous Delphynes[59] with his arrows, when he was still a naked[60] boy, still delighting in his long locks—be gracious,[61] lord, may your hair always remain unshorn, always unharmed, for such is right; and only Leto herself, Coeus' daughter, strokes it with her dear hands—and often

---

Callimachus (cf. *Hymn* 2.97–104) adopts the etymology: ἵει, παῖ, ἰόν "Shoot, boy, an arrow." For an ancient discussion of the chant's origin, see Athenaeus 15.701ce.

[59] The snake (usually called Python) that guarded Delphi, here masculine, elsewhere feminine (Delphinê).

[60] Some translate "beardless."

[61] The narrator inserts his own request (708–710).

APOLLONIUS RHODIUS

θαρσύνεσκον ἔπεσσιν, Ἰήιε κεκληγυῖαι·
ἔνθεν δὴ τόδε καλὸν ἐφύμνιον ἔπλετο Φοίβῳ.
αὐτὰρ ἐπειδὴ τόν γε χορείῃ μέλψαν ἀοιδῇ,
715 λοιβαῖς εὐαγέεσσιν ἐπώμοσαν, ἦ μὲν ἀρήξειν
ἀλλήλοις εἰσαιὲν ὁμοφροσύνῃσι νόοιο,
ἁπτόμενοι θυέων· καί τ' εἰσέτι νῦν γε τέτυκται
κεῖσ' Ὁμονοίης ἱρὸν εὔφρονος, ὅ ῥ' ἐκάμοντο
αὐτοὶ κυδίστην τότε δαίμονα πορσαίνοντες.
720   ἦμος δὲ τρίτατον φάος ἤλυθε, δὴ τότ' ἔπειτα
ἀκραεῖ ζεφύρῳ νῆσον λίπον αἰπήεσσαν.
ἔνθεν δ' ἀντιπέρην ποταμοῦ στόμα Σαγγαρίοιο
καὶ Μαριανδυνῶν ἀνδρῶν ἐριθηλέα γαῖαν
ἠδὲ Λύκοιο ῥέεθρα καὶ Ἀνθεμοεισίδα λίμνην
725 δερκόμενοι παράμειβον· ὑπὸ πνοιῇ δὲ κάλωες
ὅπλα τε νήια πάντα τινάσσετο νισσομένοισιν.
ἠῶθεν δ', ἀνέμοιο διὰ κνέφας εὐνηθέντος,
ἀσπασίως ἄκρης Ἀχερουσίδος ὅρμον ἵκοντο.
ἡ μέν τε κρημνοῖσιν ἀνίσχεται ἠλιβάτοισιν,
730 εἰς ἅλα δερκομένη Βιθυνίδα· τῇ δ' ὑπὸ πέτραι
λισσάδες ἐρρίζωνται ἁλίβροχοι, ἀμφὶ δὲ τῇσιν
κῦμα κυλινδόμενον μεγάλα βρέμει· αὐτὰρ ὕπερθεν
ἀμφιλαφεῖς πλατάνιστοι ἐπ' ἀκροτάτῃ πεφύασιν.
ἐκ δ' αὐτῆς εἴσω κατακέκλιται ἤπειρόνδε
735 κοίλη ὕπαιθα νάπη, ἵνα τε σπέος ἔστ' Ἀίδαο
ὕλῃ καὶ πέτρῃσιν ἐπηρεφές, ἔνθεν αὐτμὴ
πηγυλίς, ὀκρυόεντος ἀναπνείουσα μυχοῖο
συνεχές, ἀργινόεσσαν ἀεὶ περιτέτροφε πάχνην,

712 ἰήιε Ω: ἴη ἴε Fränkel

170

did the Corycian nymphs, the daughters of Pleistus,[62] encourage him with their words, as they shouted Iêie.[63] From there arose this beautiful refrain for Phoebus.

But when they had celebrated him with their choral song, they swore an oath with holy libations as they laid hands upon the sacrifice, that they would forever aid one another in singleness of mind. And still to this day a shrine stands there to kindly Concord, which they themselves built at that time to honor the most glorious goddess.

When the third morning's light came, they left the steep island with a strong west wind. Then on the coast opposite them they sighted and passed by the mouth of the Sangarius river, the fertile land of the Mariandynian people, the streams of the Lycus, and lake Anthemoeisis. Under the force of the wind the halyards and all the ship's tackle shook as they proceeded. At dawn, after the wind had died down during the night, they were glad to reach the harbor of the Acherusian headland. It rises in steep cliffs, facing the Bithynian sea. At its base, rocks washed smooth by the sea are rooted in place, and around them the waves roll with a mighty roar, but above, spreading plane trees grow on the highest peak. Down from it towards the interior slopes a hollow valley, where the cave of Hades lies, covered over with woods and rocks, from which an ice-cold vapor, blowing up continuously from its chill

---

[62] The Corycian cave was on mount Parnassus, the Pleistus a nearby river.

[63] The MSS' ἰήιε is the common invocation of Apollo expressing the ritual shout "iê, iê." Fränkel's emendation (ἴη ἴε) would emphasize its supposed etymology: "shoot, shoot."

ἤ τε μεσημβριόωντος ἰαίνεται ἠελίοιο.
740 σιγῇ δ' οὔ ποτε τήν γε κατὰ βλοσυρὴν ἔχει ἄκρην,
ἀλλ' ἄμυδις πόντοιό θ' ὕπο στένει ἠχήεντος
φύλλων τε πνοιῇσι τινασσομένων μυχίῃσιν.
ἔνθα δὲ καὶ προχοαὶ ποταμοῦ Ἀχέροντος ἔασιν,
ὅς τε διὲξ ἄκρης ἀνερεύγεται εἰς ἅλα βάλλων
745 ἠοίην, κοίλη δὲ φάραγξ κατάγει μιν ἄνωθεν.
τὸν μὲν ἐν ὀψιγόνοισι Σοωναύτην ὀνόμηναν
Νισαῖοι Μεγαρῆες, ὅτε νάσσεσθαι ἔμελλον
γῆν Μαριανδυνῶν· δὴ γάρ σφεας ἐξεσάωσεν
αὐτῇσιν νήεσσι κακῇ χρίμψαντας ἀέλλῃ.
750 τῇ ῥ' οἵ γ' αὐτίκα νηὶ διὲξ Ἀχερουσίδος ἄκρης
εἴσωποὶ ἀνέμοιο νέον λήγοντος ἔκελσαν.

     οὐδ' ἄρα δηθὰ Λύκον, κείνης πρόμον ἠπείροιο,
καὶ Μαριανδυνοὺς λάθον ἀνέρας ὁρμισθέντες
αὐθένται Ἀμύκοιο κατὰ κλέος, ὃ πρὶν ἄκουον·
755 ἀλλὰ καὶ ἀρθμὸν ἔθεντο μετὰ σφίσι τοῖο ἔκητι,
αὐτὸν δ' ὥς τε θεὸν Πολυδεύκεα δεξιόωντο
πάντοθεν ἀγρόμενοι· ἐπεὶ ἦ μάλα τοί γ' ἐπὶ δηρὸν
ἀντιβίην Βέβρυξιν ὑπερφιάλοις πολέμιζον.
καὶ δὴ πασσυδίῃ μεγάρων ἔντοσθε Λύκοιο
760 κεῖν' ἦμαρ φιλότητι, μετὰ πτολίεθρον ἰόντες,
δαίτην ἀμφίεπον, τέρποντό τε θυμὸν ἔπεσσιν.
Αἰσονίδης μέν οἱ γενεὴν καὶ οὔνομ' ἑκάστου
σφωιτέρων μυθεῖθ' ἑτάρων, Πελίαό τ' ἐφετμάς,

depth, ever forms a glistening frost which melts in the mid-day sun. Silence never envelops that grim headland, but moaning arises from both the echoing sea and the leaves rustled by the breezes from the depths. Here too is the mouth of the Acheron river, which gushes through the headland and issues into the eastern sea,[64] for a hollow ravine carries it down from above. In later generations, Nisaean Megarians named it the Soönautes river,[65] when they were on their way to settle the land of the Mari-andynians, for it saved them along with their ships when they encountered a violent storm. Here the heroes imme-diately came with their ship through the Acherusian head-land and, since the wind had just ceased, moored within.[66]

Not for long were Lycus, lord of that mainland, and the Mariandynian people unaware that those who had an-chored were the killers of Amycus, according to the report they had previously heard. But for that reason they even made a pact of friendship with them and, gathering from all around, welcomed Polydeuces himself as if he were a god, since he had been warring for a very long time against the arrogant Bebrycians. And so they went all to-gether to the city, and that day in Lycus' palace they par-took of a feast in friendship and delighted their hearts in conversation. Jason told him the lineage and name of each of his comrades, and told of Pelias' commands, and how

[64] I.e. the Black Sea.

[65] Nisaea is the port city of Megara; Soönautes means "Sailor-saving."

[66] Presumably they sailed through the headland by means of the Acheron river, in which they moored.

ἠδ᾽ ὡς Λημνιάδεσσιν ἐπεξεινοῦντο γυναιξίν,
765 ὅσσα τε Κύζικον ἀμφὶ Δολιονίην ἐτέλεσσαν·
Μυσίδα θ᾽ ὡς ἀφίκοντο Κίον θ᾽, ὅθι κάλλιπον ἥρω
Ἡρακλέην ἀέκοντι νόῳ, Γλαύκοιό τε βάξιν
πέφραδε, καὶ Βέβρυκας ὅπως Ἄμυκόν τ᾽ ἐδάιξαν·
καὶ Φινῆος ἔειπε θεοπροπίας τε δύην τε,
770 ἠδ᾽ ὡς Κυανέας πέτρας φύγον, ὥς τ᾽ ἀβόλησαν
Λητοΐδῃ κατὰ νῆσον. ὁ δ᾽ ἐξείης ἐνέποντος
θέλγετ᾽ ἀκουῇ θυμόν· ἄχος δ᾽ ἕλεν Ἡρακλῆι
λειπομένῳ, καὶ τοῖον ἔπος πάντεσσι μετηύδα·
    "ὦ φίλοι, οἵου φωτὸς ἀποπλαγχθέντες ἀρωγῆς
775 πείρετ᾽ ἐς Αἰήτην τόσσον πλόον. εὖ γὰρ ἐγώ μιν
Δασκύλου ἐν μεγάροισι καταυτόθι πατρὸς ἐμεῖο
οἶδ᾽ ἐσιδών, ὅτε δεῦρο δι᾽ Ἀσίδος ἠπείροιο
πεζὸς ἔβη ζωστῆρα φιλοπτολέμοιο κομίζων
Ἱππολύτης· ἐμὲ δ᾽ εὗρε νέον χνοάοντα ἰούλους.
780 ἔνθα δ᾽ ἐπὶ Πριόλαο κασιγνήτοιο θανόντος
ἡμετέρου Μυσοῖσιν ὑπ᾽ ἀνδράσιν, ὅν τινα λαὸς
οἰκτίστοις ἐλέγοισιν ὀδύρεται ἐξέτι κείνου,
ἀθλεύων Τιτίην ἀπεκαίνυτο πυγμαχέοντα
καρτερόν, ὃς πάντεσσι μετέπρεπεν ἠιθέοισιν
785 εἶδός τ᾽ ἠδὲ βίην, χαμάδις δέ οἱ ἤλασ᾽ ὀδόντας.
αὐτὰρ ὁμοῦ Μυσοῖσιν ἐμῷ ὑπὸ πατρὶ δάμασσεν
Μύγδονας, οἳ ναίουσιν ὁμώλακας ἧμιν ἀρούρας,

765 Δολιονίην m: Δολιονίην τ᾽ w
779 χνοάοντα(s) ἰούλους Ω: χνοάοντα παρειάς Et. Magn.
787 Μύγδονας Σ: καὶ Φρύγας Ω

174

they were hosted by the Lemnian women, all they did around Dolionian Cyzicus,[67] and how they came to Mysia and Cius, where they unintentionally left the hero Heracles; and he recounted Glaucus' oracle and how they slew the Bebrycians and Amycus. He also told about Phineus' prophecies and his affliction, how they escaped the Cyanean rocks, and how they met Leto's son at the island. Lycus was enchanted in his heart at hearing him relate this succession of events, but grief seized him at the abandonment of Heracles, and he spoke these words to all of them:

"O my friends, what a man it was whose help you have lost as you undertake such a long a voyage to Aeetes! For I know him well, having seen him right here in the palace of my father Dascylus, when he came here on foot across the mainland of Asia on his quest for the belt of war-loving Hippolyte.[68] He met me when the down of my beard was just growing.[69] Then he, competing in the games held when my brother Priolas was killed by the Mysians, whom the people have mourned ever since with most sorrowful dirges, defeated in boxing mighty Titias, who surpassed all the young men in beauty and strength, and knocked his teeth to the ground. And besides the Mysians, he subdued to my father's rule the Mygdones, who inhabit the lands

[67] The city. Other editors retain the τ' of some MSS: "concerning Cyzicus (the king) and in the Dolionian (land)."
[68] Heracles' ninth labor was to acquire the belt of the Amazon queen Hippolyte; cf. 2.966–969.
[69] Or, reading παρειάς, *on my cheeks.*

φῦλά τε Βιθυνῶν αὐτῇ κτεατίσσατο γαίῃ,
ἔστ' ἐπὶ Ῥηβαίου προχοὰς σκόπελόν τε Κολώνης·
790 Παφλαγόνες τ' ἐπὶ τοῖς Πελοπήιοι εὔκαθον αὔτως,
ὅσσους Βιλλαίοιο μέλαν περιάγνυται ὕδωρ.
ἀλλά με νῦν Βέβρυκες ὑπερβασίῃ τ' Ἀμύκοιο
τηλόθι ναιετάοντος ἐνόσφισαν Ἡρακλῆος,
δὴν ἀποτεμνόμενοι γαίης ἅλις, ὄφρ' ἐβάλοντο
795 οὖρα βαθυρρείοντος ὑφ' εἰαμεναῖς Ὑπίοιο.
ἔμπης δ' ἐξ ὑμέων ἔδοσαν τίσιν· οὐδέ ἕ φημι
ἤματι τῷδ' ἀέκητι θεῶν ἐπελάσσαι ἄρηα,
Τυνδαρίδην Βέβρυξιν, ὅτ' ἀνέρα κεῖνον ἔπεφνεν.
τῶ νῦν ἤν τιν' ἐγὼ τῖσαι χάριν ἄρκιός εἰμι,
800 τίσω προφρονέως· ἡ γὰρ θέμις ἠπεδανοῖσιν
ἀνδράσιν, εὖτ' ἄρξωσιν ἀρείονες ἄλλοι ὀφέλλειν.
ξυνῇ μὲν πάντεσσιν ὁμόστολον ὕμμιν ἔπεσθαι
Δάσκυλον ὀτρυνέω, ἐμὸν υἱέα· τοῖο δ' ἰόντος,
ἦ τ' ἂν ἐυξείνοισι διὲξ ἁλὸς ἀντιάοιτε
805 ἀνδράσιν, ὄφρ' αὐτοῖο ποτὶ στόμα Θερμώδοντος.
νόσφι δὲ Τυνδαρίδαις Ἀχερουσίδος ὑψόθεν ἀκτῆς
εἴσομαι ἱερὸν αἰπύ, τὸ μὲν μάλα τηλόθι πάντες
ναυτίλοι ἂμ πέλαγος θηεύμενοι ἱλάξονται·
καί κέ σφιν μετέπειτα πρὸ ἄστεος, οἷα θεοῖσιν,
810 πίονας εὐαρότοιο γύας πεδίοιο ταμοίμην."

798 Τυνδαρ(ε)ίδην Ω: Τυνδαρ(ε)ίδη B² Flor. Σ (ὦ Πολύ-
δευκες) | ἔπεφνεν wE: ἔπεφνες LA

176

adjoining ours, and conquered the tribes of Bithynians, land and all, as far as the mouth of the Rhebas and the peak of Colone. In addition to these, the Pelopeian Paphlagonians[70] yielded without a fight, all the ones around whom breaks the dark water of the Billaeus. But now, with Heracles living far away, the Bebrycians and the arrogance of Amycus have robbed me, and for a long time they have been cutting off large portions of my land, to the point that they have established their boundaries at the meadows of the deep-flowing Hypius. Nevertheless, they have paid the penalty at your hands, and I do not believe it was without divine favor that the son of Tyndareus brought war on the Bebrycians on that day he slew that man.[71] Therefore, now whatever recompense I have means enough to pay, I shall pay gladly, since it is right for weaker men to do so when others who are stronger help them first. To accompany all of you and share your voyage, I am sending Dascylus, my own son. If he goes along, truly you will meet hospitable men on your way through the sea as far as the mouth of the Thermodon itself. And besides that, for the sons of Tyndareus I shall build a lofty temple on the top of the Acherusian headland, which all sailors on the sea will behold from very far away and seek their[72] favor; and after that I shall set apart for them, as for gods, rich fields of well-tilled plain in front of the city."

[70] For Pelops as the progenitor of the Paphlagonians, see 2.357–359.

[71] Or, reading Τυνδαρίδη ... ἔπεφνες, *I do not believe it was without divine favor that I made war against the Bebrycians, son of Tyndareus, on that day you killed that man.*

[72] Castor and Polydeuces would become protectors of sailors.

ὡς τότε μὲν δαῖτ᾽ ἀμφὶ πανήμεροι ἐψιόωντο.
ἠρί γε μὴν ἐπὶ νῆα κατήισαν ἐγκονέοντες·
καὶ δ᾽ αὐτὸς σὺν τοῖσι Λύκος κίε, μυρί᾽ ὀπάσσας
δῶρα φέρειν· ἅμα δ᾽ υἷα δόμων ἔκπεμπε νέεσθαι.

815　　ἔνθα δ᾽ Ἀβαντιάδην πεπρωμένη ἤλασε μοῖρα
Ἴδμονα, μαντοσύνῃσι κεκασμένον· ἀλλά μιν οὔ τι
μαντοσύναι ἐσάωσαν, ἐπεὶ χρεὼ ἦγε δαμῆναι.
κεῖτο γὰρ εἰαμενῇ δονακώδεος ἐν ποταμοῖο
ψυχόμενος λαγόνας τε καὶ ἄσπετον ἰλύι νηδὺν

820　　κάπριος ἀργιόδων, ὀλοὸν τέρας, ὅν ῥα καὶ αὐταὶ
νύμφαι ἑλειονόμοι ὑπεδείδισαν· οὐδέ τις ἀνδρῶν
ἠείδει, οἶος δὲ κατὰ πλατὺ βόσκετο τῖφος.
αὐτὰρ ὅ γ᾽ ἰλυόεντος ἀνὰ θρωσμοὺς ποταμοῖο
νίσσετ᾽ Ἀβαντιάδης· ὁ δ᾽ ἄρ᾽ ἔκποθεν ἀφράστοιο

825　　ὕψι μάλ᾽ ἐκ δονάκων ἀναπάλμενος ἤλασε μηρὸν
αἴγδην, μέσσας δὲ σὺν ὀστέῳ ἶνας ἔκερσεν.
ὀξὺ δ᾽ ὅ γε κλάγξας οὔδει πέσεν· οἱ δὲ τυπέντος
ἀθρόοι ἀντιάχησαν. ὀρέξατο δ᾽ αἶψ᾽ ὀλοοῖο
Πηλεὺς αἰγανέην φύγαδ᾽ εἰς ἕλος ὁρμηθέντος

830　　καπρίου· ἔσσυτο δ᾽ αὖτις ἐναντίος· ἀλλά μιν Ἴδας
οὔτασε, βεβρυχὼς δὲ θοῷ περικάππεσε δουρί.
καὶ τὸν μὲν χαμάδις λίπον αὐτόθι πεπτηῶτα·
τὸν δ᾽ ἕταροι ἐπὶ νῆα φέρον ψυχορραγέοντα
ἀχνύμενοι, χείρεσσι δ᾽ ἑῶν ἐνικάτθαν᾽ ἑταίρων.

835　　ἔνθα δὲ ναυτιλίης μὲν ἐρητύοντο μέλεσθαι,
ἀμφὶ δὲ κηδείῃ νέκυος μένον ἀσχαλόωντες.
ἤματα δὲ τρία πάντα γόων· ἑτέρῳ δέ μιν ἤδη
τάρχυον μεγαλωστί· συνεκτερέιζε δὲ λαὸς

In this fashion then they took pleasure all day long in the feast. But at dawn they hastened down to the ship, and Lycus himself went with them, after giving them countless gifts to take along. And he sent his son from home to go with them.

And there his fated destiny struck Abas' son Idmon, who excelled at prophecy. But his prophecy did nothing to save him, since necessity was leading him on to be killed. For in the meadow of a reed-filled river, cooling its sides and huge belly in the mud, lay a white-tusked boar, a deadly monster that even the marshland nymphs themselves dreaded. No man knew it was there, for it was feeding all by itself in the broad marsh.[73] But Abas' son was walking along the raised banks of the muddy river, when from some hidden lair it sprang high up from the reeds and gashed his thigh as it charged, and sliced the sinews and bone in half. He let out a piercing scream and fell to the ground, and all the others, when he was struck, shouted back to him. Peleus immediately threw his hunting spear at the murderous boar, which had rushed in flight into the swamp; then it turned back and charged him, but Idas struck it, and with a squeal it fell impaled on the sharp spear. They left it there on the ground where it had fallen, but his sorrowing comrades carried Idmon, breathing his last, to the ship, and it was in the arms of his comrades that he died.

Then they stopped caring about sailing and stayed there in grief for the burial of the corpse. For three full days they mourned. On the next day they finally buried him with full honors. The people joined in the funeral rites

[73] Or, *no man knew it existed, for it fed all by itself.*

αὐτῷ ὁμοῦ βασιλῆι Λύκῳ· παρὰ δ' ἄσπετα μῆλα,
840 ἦ θέμις οἰχομένοισι, ταφήια λαιμοτόμησαν.
καὶ δή τοι κέχυται τοῦδ' ἀνέρος ἐν χθονὶ κείνῃ
τύμβος· σῆμα δ' ἔπεστι καὶ ὀψιγόνοισιν ἰδέσθαι,
νηίου ἐκ κοτίνοιο φάλαγξ· θαλέθει δέ τε φύλλοις
ἄκρης τυτθὸν ἔνερθ' Ἀχερουσίδος. εἰ δέ με καὶ τὸ
845 χρειὼ ἀπηλεγέως Μουσέων ὕπο γηρύσασθαι,
τόνδε πολισσοῦχον διεπέφραδε Βοιωτοῖσιν
Νισαίοισί τε Φοῖβος ἐπιρρήδην ἱλάεσθαι,
ἀμφὶ δὲ τήν γε φάλαγγα παλαιγενέος κοτίνοιο
ἄστυ βαλεῖν, οἱ δ' ἀντὶ θεουδέος Αἰολίδαο
850 Ἴδμονος εἰσέτι νῦν Ἀγαμήστορα κυδαίνουσιν.
    τίς γὰρ δὴ θάνεν ἄλλος; ἐπεὶ καὶ ἔτ' αὖτις
        ἔχευαν
ἥρωες τότε τύμβον ἀποφθιμένου ἑτάροιο·
δοιὰ γὰρ οὖν κείνων ἔτι σήματα φαίνεται ἀνδρῶν.
Ἀγνιάδην Τῖφυν θανέειν φάτις· οὐδέ οἱ ἦεν
855 μοῖρ' ἔτι ναυτίλλεσθαι ἑκαστέρω. ἀλλά νυ καὶ τὸν
αὖθι μινυνθαδίη πάτρης ἑκὰς εὔνασε νοῦσος,
εἰσότ' Ἀβαντιάδαο νέκυν κτερέιξεν ὅμιλος.
ἄτλητον δ' ὀλοῷ ἐπὶ πήματι κῆδος ἕλοντο·
δὴ γὰρ ἐπεὶ καὶ τόνδε παρασχεδὸν ἐκτερέιξαν,
860 αὐτοῦ ἀμηχανίῃσιν ἁλὸς προπάροιθε πεσόντες,
ἐντυπὰς εὐκήλως εἰλυμένοι οὔτε τι σίτου
μνώοντ' οὔτε ποτοῖο· κατήμυσαν δ' ἀχέεσσιν
θυμόν, ἐπεὶ μάλα πολλὸν ἀπ' ἐλπίδος ἔπλετο
    νόστος.

180

along with king Lycus himself, and by his grave, as is
proper for those who have departed, they slaughtered
countless sheep as funeral offerings. And so this man's
burial mound was raised in that land, and upon it stands a
marker for future generations to see, a trunk of wild olive
used for shipbuilding. It flourishes with leaves, a little be-
low the Acherusian headland. And if I must, at the Muses'
insistence, forthrightly declare this fact as well, Phoebus
explicitly directed the Boeotians and Nisaeans to worship
this man as "city guardian" and to establish a town around
the trunk of ancient wild olive, but instead of the god-fear-
ing Aeolid Idmon, to this day they honor Agamestor.[74]

Who else then died? For the heroes heaped up yet an-
other burial mound at that time for a departed comrade,
since two grave-markers of those men can still be seen. It is
reported that Hagnias' son Tiphys died; nor was it his fate
to sail any further. Rather, a brief illness laid him as well to
rest there, far from his homeland, just after the crew had
buried the corpse of Abas' son. Unbearable was the grief
they suffered at this dreadful calamity, for as soon as they
had buried him too, they collapsed in helplessness there by
the sea, and, wrapping themselves up tightly in their cloaks
without stirring, took no thought of food or drink. Their
hearts were downcast in distress, since very far from their
hopes was a successful return home. And they would have

[74] When the Boeotians from Tanagra and Nisaeans from
Megara (cf. 2.746–748) settled the region in the 6th century, they
founded the city of Heraclea and worshipped the local hero
Agamestor. Cf. Pausanias 5.26.7.

843 νηίου Ω: νήιος M et Merkel   848 τήν γε Ω: τήνδε Σ

καί νύ κ' ἔτι προτέρω τετιημένοι ἰσχανόωντο,
865 εἰ μὴ ἄρ' Ἀγκαίῳ περιώσιον ἔμβαλεν Ἥρη
θάρσος, ὃν Ἰμβρασίοισι παρ' ὕδασιν Ἀστυπάλαια
τίκτε Ποσειδάωνι· περιπρὸ γὰρ εὖ ἐκέκαστο
ἰθύνειν· Πηλῆα δ' ἐπεσσύμενος προσέειπεν·

"Αἰακίδη, πῶς καλὸν ἀφειδήσαντας ἀέθλων
870 γαίη ἐν ἀλλοδαπῇ δὴν ἔμμεναι; οὐ μὲν ἄρηος
ἴδριν ἐόντα με τόσσον ἄγει μετὰ κῶας Ἰήσων
Παρθενίης ἀπάνευθεν, ὅσον τ' ἐπίστορα νηῶν.
τῶ μή τοι τυτθόν γε δέος περὶ νηὶ πελέσθω.
ὣς δὲ καὶ ἄλλοι δεῦρο δαήμονες ἄνδρες ἔασιν,
875 τῶν ὅ τινα πρύμνης ἐπιβήσομεν, οὔ τις ἰάψει
ναυτιλίην. ἀλλ' ὦκα παραιφάμενος τάδε πάντα
θαρσαλέως ὀρόθυνον ἐπιμνήσασθαι ἀέθλου."

ὣς φάτο· τοῖο δὲ θυμὸς ἀέξετο γηθοσύνῃσιν.
αὐτίκα δ' οὐ μετὰ δηρὸν ἐνὶ μέσσοις ἀγόρευσεν·

880 "δαιμόνιοι, τί νυ πένθος ἐτώσιον ἴσχομεν αὔτως;
οἱ μὲν γάρ ποθι τοῦτον, ὃν ἔλλαχον, οἶτον ὄλοντο·
ἡμῖν μὲν γὰρ ἔασι κυβερνητῆρες ὁμίλῳ
καὶ πολέες. τῶ μή τι διατριβώμεθα πείρης·
ἀλλ' ἔγρεσθ' εἰς ἔργον ἀπορρίψαντες ἀνίας."

885 τὸν δ' αὖτ' Αἴσονος υἱὸς ἀμηχανέων προσέειπεν·
"Αἰακίδη, πῇ δ' οἶδε κυβερνητῆρες ἔασιν;
οὓς μὲν γὰρ τὸ πάροιθε δαήμονας εὐχόμεθ' εἶναι,
οἵδε κατηφήσαντες ἐμεῦ πλέον ἀσχαλόωσιν.

873 τοι LAE: μοι L²ˢˡω: τι EᵃᶜD   878 ἀέξετο ω: ὀρέξετο
LA: ὀρέξατο E   882 μὲν Ω: δ' ἐν Merkel

stayed there grieving even longer, had not Hera put extraordinary courage into Ancaeus, whom Astypalaea bore to Poseidon by the waters of the Imbrasus,[75] for he was exceptionally skilled at steering. He ran up to Peleus and said:

"Son of Aeacus, how can it be noble for us to neglect our tasks and linger for a long time in a foreign land? Certainly it is not so much for my skill in war that Jason is leading me far from Parthenia to fetch the fleece as it is for my knowledge of ships. Therefore, do not have the slightest fear for the ship.[76] Likewise, there are other skilled men here, none of whom will do any harm to our sailing if we place him at the helm. But quickly encourage them with all this and confidently urge them to remember their task."

Thus he spoke. Peleus' heart swelled[77] with joy, and immediately, without delay, he spoke in their midst:

"Poor souls, why ever do we cling to fruitless grief like this? Those men, I think, died the death they were allotted, but we have steersmen in our crew, indeed many. Therefore let us not at all put off our attempt. Come, cast away your sorrows and rouse yourselves to work."

But Jason, feeling helpless, replied to him in turn:

"Son of Aeacus, where are these helmsmen of yours? For the ones we once considered experts are these men, who are more despondent and distressed than I am.

[75] The Imbrasus river on the island of Samos connects Ancaeus with Imbrasian Hera (cf. 1.186–189).

[76] Or, reading μοι, *please let there be not the slightest fear for the ship.*

[77] Or, reading ὀρέξατο, *bounded.*

τῷ καὶ ὁμοῦ φθιμένοισι κακὴν προτιόσσομαι ἄτην,
890 εἰ δὴ μήτ' ὀλοοῖο μετὰ πτόλιν Αἰήταο
ἔσσεται ἠὲ καὶ αὖτις ἐς Ἑλλάδα γαῖαν ἱκέσθαι
πετράων ἔκτοσθε· καταυτόθι δ' ἄμμε καλύψει
ἀκλειῶς κακὸς οἶτος ἐτώσια γηράσκοντας."

    ὣς ἔφατ'· Ἀγκαῖος δὲ μάλ' ἐσσυμένως ὑπέδεκτο
895 νῆα θοὴν ἄξειν· δὴ γὰρ θεοῦ ἐτράπεθ' ὁρμῇ.
τὸν δὲ μετ' Ἐργῖνος καὶ Ναύπλιος Εὔφημός τε
ὤρνυντ' ἰθύνειν λελιημένοι. ἀλλ' ἄρα τούς γε
ἔσχεθον, Ἀγκαίῳ δὲ πολεῖς ᾔνησαν ἑταίρων.

    ἠῷοι δήπειτα δυωδεκάτῳ ἐπέβαινον
900 ἤματι· δὴ γάρ σφιν ζεφύρου μέγας οὖρος ἄητο.
καρπαλίμως δ' Ἀχέροντα διεξεπέρησαν ἐρετμοῖς,
ἐκ δ' ἔχεαν πίσυνοι ἀνέμῳ λίνα, πουλὺ δ' ἐπιπρὸ
λαιφέων πεπταμένων τέμνον πλόον εὐδιόωντες.
ὦκα δὲ Καλλιχόροιο παρὰ προχοὰς ποταμοῖο
905 ἤλυθον, ἔνθ' ἐνέπουσι Διὸς Νυσήιον υἷα,
Ἰνδῶν ἡνίκα φῦλα λιπὼν κατενάσσατο Θήβας,
ὀργιάσαι στῆσαί τε χοροὺς ἄντροιο πάροιθεν,
ᾧ ἐν ἀμειδήτους ἁγίας ηὐλίζετο νύκτας,
ἐξ οὗ Καλλίχορον ποταμὸν περιναιετάοντες
910 ἠδὲ καὶ Αὔλιον ἄντρον ἐπωνυμίην καλέουσιν.

    ἔνθεν δὲ Σθενέλου τάφον ἔδρακον Ἀκτορίδαο,
ὅς ῥά τ' Ἀμαζονίδων πολυθαρσέος ἐκ πολέμοιο
ἂψ ἀνιών—δὴ γὰρ συνανήλυθεν Ἡρακλῆι—
βλήμενος ἰῷ κεῖθεν ἐπ' ἀγχιάλου θάνεν ἀκτῆς.

Therefore, I foresee for us an evil demise along with our dead comrades, if we shall neither reach the city of murderous Aeetes nor pass again beyond the rocks to the land of Hellas, but an evil fate will bury us here without fame as we grow old in vain."

Thus he spoke, and Ancaeus very readily offered to steer the swift ship, for he had been impelled by a god's prompting. And after him rose Erginus, Nauplius, and Euphemus, all eager to steer. But the others held them back, since many of their comrades preferred Ancaeus.

And so at dawn on the twelfth day they embarked, because a strong west wind was blowing for them. Quickly they rowed out through the Acheron river and, relying on the wind, let out their canvas, and with sails spread wide were plowing their way far forward in the fair weather. Soon they passed the mouth of the Callichorus river, where, they say, Zeus' Nysean son,[78] after leaving the tribes of Indians and settling at Thebes, celebrated his rites and instituted choruses in front of the cave in which he had spent grim nights of rituals,[79] and since then, the local inhabitants have called the river by the name of Callichorus and the cave Aulion.[80]

Next they saw the tomb of Actor's son Sthenelus, who had returned from a courageous war against the Amazons (for he had gone there with Heracles) and, wounded by an arrow there, died on the shore by the sea. But indeed they

---

[78] Dionysus; mount Nysa is variously located in Thrace, Libya, India, and elsewhere.

[79] The Bacchic mysteries were frightening (schol.).

[80] Callichorus means "with lovely choruses"; Aulion, "resting-place" (punning on ηὐλίζετο, "spent the night").

915 οὐ μέν θην προτέρω ἔτ᾽ ἐμέτρεον· ἧκε γὰρ αὐτὴ
Φερσεφόνη ψυχὴν πολυδάκρυον Ἀκτορίδαο
λισσομένην τυτθόν περ ὀμήθεας ἄνδρας ἰδέσθαι.
τύμβου δὲ στεφάνης ἐπιβὰς σκοπιάζετο νῆα,
τοῖος ἐών, οἷος πόλεμόνδ᾽ ἴεν, ἀμφὶ δὲ καλὴ
920 τετράφαλος φοίνικι λόφῳ ἐπελάμπετο πήληξ.
καί ῥ᾽ ὁ μὲν αὖτις ἔδυ μέλανα ζόφον· οἱ δ᾽
ἐσιδόντες
θάμβησαν. τοὺς δ᾽ ὦρσε θεοπροπέων ἐπικέλσαι
Ἀμπυκίδης Μόψος λοιβῇσί τε μειλίξασθαι.
οἱ δ᾽ ἀνὰ μὲν κραιπνῶς λαῖφος σπάσαν, ἐκ δὲ
βαλόντες
925 πείσματ᾽ ἐν αἰγιαλῷ Σθενέλου τάφον ἀμφεπένοντο,
χύτλα τέ οἱ χεύαντο καὶ ἥγνισαν ἔντομα μήλων.
ἄνδιχα δ᾽ αὖ χύτλων Νηοσσόῳ Ἀπόλλωνι
βωμὸν δειμάμενοι μῆρ᾽ ἔφλεγον· ἂν δὲ καὶ Ὀρφεὺς
θῆκε λύρην· ἐκ τοῦ δὲ Λύρη πέλει οὔνομα χώρῳ.
930   αὐτίκα δ᾽ οἵ γ᾽ ἀνέμοιο κατασπέρχοντος ἔβησαν
νῆ᾽ ἔπι, κὰδ δ᾽ ἄρα λαῖφος ἐρυσσάμενοι τανύοντο
ἐς πόδας ἀμφοτέρους. ἡ δ᾽ ἐς πέλαγος πεφόρητο
ἐντενές, ἠΰτε τίς τε δι᾽ ἠέρος ὑψόθι κίρκος
ταρσὸν ἐφεὶς πνοιῇ φέρεται ταχύς, οὐδὲ τινάσσει
935 ῥιπὴν εὐκήλοισιν ἐνευδιόων πτερύγεσσιν.
καὶ δὴ Παρθενίοιο ῥοὰς ἁλιμυρήεντος,
πρηϋτάτου ποταμοῦ, παρεμέτρεον, ᾧ ἔνι κούρη
Λητωΐς, ἄγρηθεν ὅτ᾽ οὐρανὸν εἰσαναβαίνῃ,

920 ἐπελάμπετο Ω: απ[ελάμπετο Π16

186

proceeded no further, for Persephone herself sent forth Sthenelus' tearful soul, begging to behold even for a moment men of his own kind. He mounted the crown of his tomb and gazed upon the ship, appearing as he did when he went to war, and about his head gleamed a beautiful four-peaked helmet with a red crest. And then he went down again into the dark gloom, and they were amazed at the sight. Ampycus' son Mopsus, interpreting the divine will, urged them to land and propitiate him with libations. They quickly drew up the sail[81] and cast the cables onto the beach and paid homage to Sthenelus' tomb; and they poured drink offerings to him and consecrated sheep as victims. Then, apart from the libations, they built an altar for Apollo Ship-Preserver and burned thigh pieces on it. Orpheus also dedicated his lyre, and for that reason Lyra is the name of the place.

And soon, as the wind was urging them on, they boarded the ship and drew down the sail and stretched it tight by both sheets. The ship was borne to deep water at full stretch, as when a hawk on high spreads its wings to the wind and is borne swiftly through the air and does not alter its flight as it glides in a clear sky on steady wings. And so they passed by the streams of Parthenius that flows into the sea, a most gentle river, in which Leto's daughter,[82] when from the hunt she goes up to heaven, cools her body with

---

[81] Sails were hauled up to the yard for storage and let down for sailing.

[82] Artemis, the virgin goddess (hence the name Parthenius).

---

921 ἔδυ] μελανα Π16 Bywater praeeunte: ἔδυνε μέλαν Ω
928 μῆρ' Brunck: μῆλ' Ω

ὃν δέμας ἱμερτοῖσιν ἀναψύχει ὑδάτεσσιν.

940 νυκτὶ δ' ἔπειτ' ἄλληκτον ἐπιπροτέρωσε θέοντες
Σήσαμον αἰπεινούς τε παρεξενέοντ' Ἐρυθίνους,
Κρωβίαλον Κρωμνάν τε καὶ ὑλήεντα Κύτωρον.
ἔνθεν δ' αὖτε Κάραμβιν ἅμ' ἠελίοιο βολῇσιν
γνάμψαντες παρὰ Πουλὺν ἔπειτ' ἤλαυνον ἐρετμοῖς

945 αἰγιαλὸν πρόπαν ἦμαρ ὁμῶς καὶ ἐπ' ἤματι νύκτα.
    αὐτίκα δ' Ἀσσυρίης ἐπέβαν χθονός, ἔνθα
        Σινώπην
θυγατέρ' Ἀσωποῖο καθίσσατο, καί οἱ ὄπασσεν
παρθενίην Ζεὺς αὐτὸς ὑποσχεσίῃσι δολωθείς.
δὴ γὰρ ὁ μὲν φιλότητος ἐέλδετο, νεῦσε δ' ὅ γ' αὐτῇ

950 δωσέμεναι, ὅ κεν ᾖσι μετὰ φρεσὶν ἰθύσειεν·
ἡ δέ ἑ παρθενίην ᾐτήσατο κερδοσύνῃσιν.
ὣς δὲ καὶ Ἀπόλλωνα παρήπαφεν εὐνηθῆναι
ἱέμενον, ποταμόν τ' ἐπὶ τοῖς Ἅλυν· οὐδὲ μὲν ἀνδρῶν
τήν γέ τις ἱμερτῇσιν ἐν ἀγκοίνῃσι δάμασσεν.

955 ἔνθα δὲ Τρικκαίοιο ἀγαυοῦ Δηιμάχοιο
υἷες, Δηιλέων τε καὶ Αὐτόλυκος Φλογίος τε,
τῆμος ἔθ' Ἡρακλῆος ἀποπλαγχθέντες ἔναιον·
οἵ ῥα τόθ', ὡς ἐνόησαν ἀριστήων στόλον ἀνδρῶν,
σφᾶς αὐτοὺς νημερτὲς ἐπέφραδον ἀντιάσαντες·

960 οὐδ' ἔτι μιμνάζειν θέλον ἔμπεδον, ἀλλ' ἐνὶ νηὶ
ἀργέσταο παρᾶσσον ἐπιπνείοντος ἔβησαν.
    τοῖσι δ' ὁμοῦ μετέπειτα θοῇ πεφορημένοι αὔρῃ
λεῖπον Ἅλυν ποταμόν, λεῖπον δ' ἀγχίρροον Ἶριν
ἠδὲ καὶ Ἀσσυρίης πρόχυσιν χθονός. ἤματι δ' αὐτῷ

965 γνάμψαν Ἀμαζονίδων ἕκαθεν λιμενήοχον ἄκρην·

188

its pleasing waters. Then during the night they sped onward without stopping and sailed by Sesamus, steep Erythini, Crobialus, Cromna, and wooded Cytorus. Next, they rounded Carambis as the sun's first rays appeared, and then coasted along the Long shore by rowing all day and the following night.

And soon they went ashore on the Assyrian land, where Zeus himself had settled Sinope, Asopus' daughter, and had granted her perpetual virginity, having been tricked by his own promises. For he wanted to make love to her, but consented to give her whatever she desired in her own mind, so she slyly asked him for her virginity. In the same way she fooled Apollo when he longed to sleep with her, and besides these the Halys river, and no man ever subdued her in his loving embraces. In that place still lived the sons of noble Deimachus of Tricca[83]—Deileon, Autolycus, and Phlogius—ever since they became separated from Heracles.[84] Then, when they spotted the expedition of heroic men, they went to meet them and told them truly about themselves; and they no longer wished to remain there forever, but as soon as the northwest wind began blowing, they boarded the ship.

Then, accompanied by these men, they were borne by the swift breeze and left behind the Halys river, left behind the Iris that flows nearby, as well as the river delta of the Assyrian land.[85] On the same day they rounded from a distance the headland of the Amazons that encloses their

---

[83] A city in Thessaly (*Iliad* 2.729).
[84] During his expedition against the Amazons.
[85] The alluvial deposits of these two rivers flowing into the Black Sea in Cappadocia.

ἔνθα ποτὲ προμολοῦσαν Ἀρητιάδα Μελανίππην
ἥρως Ἡρακλέης ἐλοχήσατο, καί οἱ ἄποινα
Ἱππολύτη ζωστῆρα παναίολον ἐγγυάλιξεν
ἀμφὶ κασιγνήτης, ὁ δ᾽ ἀπήμονα πέμψεν ὀπίσσω.
970 τῆς οἵ γ᾽ ἐν κόλπῳ προχοαῖς ἔπι Θερμώδοντος
κέλσαν, ἐπεὶ καὶ πόντος ὀρίνετο νισσομένοισιν.
τῷ δ᾽ οὔ τις ποταμῶν ἐναλίγκιος, οὐδὲ ῥέεθρα
τόσσ᾽ ἐπὶ γαῖαν ἵησι παρὲξ ἕθεν ἄνδιχα βάλλων·
τετράκις εἰς ἑκατὸν δεύοιτό κεν, εἴ τις ἕκαστα
975 πεμπάζοι. μία δ᾽ οἴη ἐτήτυμος ἔπλετο πηγή·
ἥ μέν τ᾽ ἐξ ὀρέων κατανίσσεται ἠπειρόνδε
ὑψηλῶν, ἅ τέ φασιν Ἀμαζόνια κλείεσθαι·
ἔνθεν δ᾽ αἰπυτέρην ἐπικίδναται ἔνδοθι γαῖαν
ἀντικρύ· τῶ καί οἱ ἐπίστροφοί εἰσι κέλευθοι·
980 αἰεὶ δ᾽ ἄλλυδις ἄλλη, ὅπῃ κύρσειε μάλιστα
ἠπείρου χθαμαλῆς, εἱλίσσεται, ἡ μὲν ἄπωθεν,
ἡ δὲ πέλας· πολέες δὲ πόροι νώνυμνοι ἔασιν,
ὅππῃ ὑπεξαφύονται· ὁ δ᾽ ἀμφαδὸν ἄμμιγα παύροις
πόντον ἐς Ἄξεινον κυρτὴν ὑπερεύγεται ἄκρην.
985 καί νύ κε δηθύνοντες Ἀμαζονίδεσσιν ἔμιξαν
ὑσμίνην, καὶ δ᾽ οὔ κεν ἀναιμωτί γ᾽ ἐρίδηναν—
οὐ γὰρ Ἀμαζονίδες μάλ᾽ ἐπητέες οὐδὲ θέμιστας
τίουσαι πεδίον Δοιάντιον ἀμφενέμοντο,
ἀλλ᾽ ὕβρις στονόεσσα καὶ Ἄρεος ἔργα μεμήλει·
990 δὴ γὰρ καὶ γενεὴν ἔσαν Ἄρεος Ἁρμονίης τε
νύμφης, ἥ τ᾽ Ἀρηῒ φιλοπτολέμους τέκε κούρας,
ἄλσεος Ἀκμονίοιο κατὰ πτύχας εὐνηθεῖσα—
εἰ μὴ ἄρ᾽ ἐκ Διόθεν πνοιαὶ πάλιν ἀργέσταο

harbor.[86] Here the hero Heracles had once ambushed Melanippe, Ares' daughter, when she came forth; and Hippolyte gave him her glistening belt as ransom for her sister, and he sent her back unharmed. They moored in the bay of that headland near the mouth of the Thermodon, since the sea was becoming rough for traveling. No river is like that one, nor does any send forth from itself over the land so many separate streams. If anyone were to count each one, he would be four short of one hundred. But only one true source exists, and this flows down to the plain from high mountains, which, they say, are called the Amazonian mountains. From there it spreads straight into higher ground, and that is why its courses are meandering: one constantly winds this way, another that way, wherever each most readily finds low-lying land—one far away, another close by. Many of the branches have no names where they are drained off, but the river, joined by a few streams, empties in full view into the Inhospitable sea[87] beneath the curved headland. And they would have lingered there and engaged the Amazons in battle, and not without bloodshed would they have fought—for the Amazons who lived on the plain of Doeas were by no means gentle or respectful of justice, but devoted to grievous violence and the works of Ares, for indeed they were descended from Ares and the nymph Harmonia, who bore war-loving daughters to Ares after sleeping with him in the glens of the Acmonian grove—had not the northwest breezes sent by Zeus re-

---

[86] Traditionally called the cape of Heracles; its harbor was Themiscyra (cf. 2.371).

[87] The non-euphemistic name for the Black Sea.

APOLLONIUS RHODIUS

ἤλυθον· οἱ δ' ἀνέμῳ περιηγέα κάλλιπον ἄκρην,
995 ἔνθα Θεμισκύρειαι Ἀμαζόνες ὡπλίζοντο.
οὐ γὰρ ὁμηγερέες μίαν ἂμ πόλιν, ἀλλ' ἀνὰ γαῖαν
κεκριμέναι κατὰ φῦλα διάτριχα ναιετάασκον·
νόσφι μὲν αἵδ' αὐταί, τῇσιν τότε κοιρανέεσκεν
Ἱππολύτη, νόσφιν δὲ Λυκάστιαι ἀμφενέμοντο,
1000 νόσφι δ' ἀκοντοβόλοι Χαδήσιαι. ἤματι δ' ἄλλῳ
νυκτί τ' ἐπιπλομένη Χαλύβων παρὰ γαῖαν ἵκοντο.
τοῖσι μὲν οὔτε βοῶν ἄροτος μέλει οὔτε τις ἄλλη
φυταλιὴ καρποῖο μελίφρονος, οὐδὲ μὲν οἵ γε
ποίμνας ἐρσήεντι νομῷ ἔνι ποιμαίνουσιν·
1005 ἀλλὰ σιδηροφόρον στυφελὴν χθόνα γατομέοντες
ὦνον ἀμείβονται βιοτήσιον· οὐδέ ποτέ σφιν
ἠὼς ἀντέλλει καμάτων ἄτερ, ἀλλὰ κελαινῇ
λιγνύι καὶ καπνῷ κάματον βαρὺν ὀτλεύουσιν.
τοὺς δὲ μετ' αὐτίκ' ἔπειτα Γενηταίου Διὸς ἄκρην
1010 γνάμψαντες σώοντο παρὲξ Τιβαρηνίδα γαῖαν·
ἔνθ' ἐπεὶ ἄρ κε τέκωνται ὑπ' ἀνδράσι τέκνα
γυναῖκες,
αὐτοὶ μὲν στενάχουσιν ἐνὶ λεχέεσσι πεσόντες,
κράατα δησάμενοι· ταὶ δ' εὖ κομέουσιν ἐδωδῇ
ἀνέρας ἠδὲ λοετρὰ λεχώια τοῖσι πένονται.
1015 ἱερὸν αὖτ' ἐπὶ τοῖσιν ὄρος καὶ γαῖαν ἄμειβον,
ᾗ ἔνι Μοσσύνοικοι ἀν' οὔρεα ναιετάουσιν
μόσσυνας, καὶ δ' αὐτοὶ ἐπώνυμοι ἔνθεν ἔασιν.
ἀλλοίη δὲ δίκη καὶ θέσμια τοῖσι τέτυκται.
ὅσσα μὲν ἀμφαδίη ῥέζειν θέμις ἢ ἐνὶ δήμῳ

192

turned. And thanks to the wind they left behind the rounded headland, where the Themiscyreian Amazons were arming themselves. For the Amazons were not gathered together in one city, but lived throughout the land divided into three tribes. In one part lived the Themiscyreians themselves, over whom Hippolyte then ruled, in another the Lycastians, and in another the spear-throwing Chadesians. During the next day and following night they coasted along the land of the Chalybes.

These people care nothing for plowing with oxen or for planting any honey-sweet fruit, nor do they pasture sheep in a dewy meadow, but they dig the hard, iron-bearing earth and barter it for life-sustaining goods. A dawn without labors never rises for them, but amid black sooty flames and smoke they endure heavy labor.

Then, beyond those people, they immediately rounded the headland of Zeus Genetaeus[88] and sped past the land of the Tibarenians. There, when wives bear children to their husbands, the men fall on the beds and groan with their heads bound up, while the women keep the men well fed and prepare childbirth baths for them.

Then, after those people, they passed a sacred mountain and the land where the Mossynoecians dwell in the mountains in "mossynes,"[89] and they take their own name from these. They have strange laws and customs. Everything that is right for us to do openly, either in public or in

[88] Named for the Genes (or Genetes) river (Strabo 12.3.17).
[89] "Towers," hence Mossynoecians, "Tower-dwellers"; cf. 2.381b.

1017 del. Platt (= 381b)

APOLLONIUS RHODIUS

1020 ἢ ἀγορῇ, τάδε πάντα δόμοις ἔνι μηχανόωνται·
ὅσσα δ' ἐνὶ μεγάροις πεπονήμεθα, κεῖνα θύραζε
ἀψεγέως μέσσῃσιν ἐνὶ ῥέζουσιν ἀγυιαῖς.
οὐδ' εὐνῆς αἰδὼς ἐπιδήμιος, ἀλλὰ σύες ὣς
φορβάδες, οὐδ' ἡβαιὸν ἀτυζόμενοι παρεόντας,
1025 μίσγονται χαμάδις ξυνῇ φιλότητι γυναικῶν.
αὐτὰρ ἐν ὑψίστῳ βασιλεὺς μόσσυνι θαάσσων
ἰθείας πολέεσσι δίκας λαοῖσι δικάζει,
σχέτλιος· ἢν γάρ πού τι θεμιστεύων ἀλίτηται,
λιμῷ μιν κεῖν' ἦμαρ ἐνικλείσαντες ἔχουσιν.
1030   τοὺς παρανισσόμενοι καὶ δὴ σχεδὸν ἀντιπέρηθεν
νήσου Ἀρητιάδος τέμνον πλόον εἰρεσίῃσιν
ἡμάτιοι· λιαρὴ γὰρ ὑπὸ κνέφας ἔλλιπεν αὔρη.
ἤδη καί τιν' ὕπερθεν Ἀρήιον ἀίσσοντα
ἐννάετην νήσοιο δι' ἠέρος ὄρνιν ἴδοντο,
1035 ὅς ῥα τιναξάμενος πτέρυγας κατὰ νῆα θέουσαν
ἧκ' ἐπὶ οἷ πτερὸν ὀξύ· τὸ δ' ἐν λαιῷ πέσεν ὤμῳ
δίου Ὀιληος· μεθέηκε δὲ χερσὶν ἐρετμὸν
βλήμενος· οἱ δὲ τάφον πτερόεν βέλος εἰσορόωντες.
καὶ τὸ μὲν ἐξείρυσσε παρεδριόων Ἐρυβώτης,
1040 ἕλκος δὲ ξυνέδησεν, ἀπὸ σφετέρου κολεοῖο
λυσάμενος τελαμῶνα κατήορον. ἐκ δ' ἐφαάνθη
ἄλλος ἐπὶ προτέρῳ πεποτημένος· ἀλλά μιν ἥρως
Εὐρυτίδης Κλυτίος—πρὸ γὰρ ἀγκύλα τείνατο τόξα,
ἧκε δ' ἐπ' οἰωνὸν ταχινὸν βέλος—αὐτὰρ ἔπειτα
1045 πλῆξεν· δινηθεὶς δὲ θοῆς πέσεν ἀγχόθι νηός.
τοῖσιν δ' Ἀμφιδάμας μυθήσατο παῖς Ἀλεοῖο·
"νῆσος μὲν πέλας ἧμιν Ἀρητιάς· ἴστε καὶ αὐτοὶ

194

the market place, they carry out at home. Everything we
perform indoors, they do outdoors, without censure, in the
middle of the streets. There is no public shame in love-
making, but like pigs that feed in herds, they are not in the
slightest abashed with others present and have promiscu-
ous intercourse with women right on the ground. But the
king sits in the highest tower and renders straight judg-
ments to the multitude, the poor man, for if he happens to
make some mistake in his adjudication, they keep him
locked up without food for that day.

They passed by those people and were now plowing
their way near the island of Ares lying in front of them, by
rowing all day long, for the gentle breeze had left them at
night's end. At this point they saw one of Ares' birds that
inhabited the island darting through the air overhead. It
shook its wings down upon the speeding ship and shot a
sharp feather at it, which landed on the left shoulder of
noble Oïleus. He dropped the oar from his hands when he
was struck, and the others were astonished to see the
feathered dart. His bench-mate Erybotes pulled it out and
bound up the wound, having taken off the strap from
which his own sword sheath was suspended. Another bird
flew into view after the first, but the hero Clytius, Eurytus'
son—for he had strung his curved bow beforehand and
shot a speeding arrow at the bird—hit it, and it spun
around and fell near the swift ship.

Amphidamas, Aleus' son, then spoke to them:

"The island of Ares is near us, as you yourselves know

τούσδ' ὄρνιθας ἰδόντες. ἐγὼ δ' οὐκ ἔλπομαι ἰοὺς
τόσσον ἐπαρκέσσειν εἰς ἔκβασιν· ἀλλά τιν' ἄλλην
1050 μῆτιν πορσύνωμεν ἐπίρροθον, εἴ κ' ἐπικέλσαι
μέλλετε Φινῆος μεμνημένοι, ὡς ἐπέτελλεν.
οὐδὲ γὰρ Ἡρακλέης, ὁπότ' ἤλυθεν Ἀρκαδίηνδε,
πλωάδας ὄρνιθας Στυμφαλίδος ἔσθενε λίμνης
ὤσασθαι τόξοισι—τὸ μέν τ' ἐγὼ αὐτὸς ὄπωπα—
1055 ἀλλ' ὅ γε χαλκείην πλαταγὴν ἐνὶ χερσὶ τινάσσων
δούπει ἐπὶ σκοπιῆς περιμήκεος, αἱ δ' ἐφέβοντο
τηλοῦ ἀτυζηλῷ ὑπὸ δείματι κεκληγυῖαι.
τῶ καὶ νῦν τοίην τιν' ἐπιφραζώμεθα μῆτιν·
αὐτὸς δ' ἂν τὸ πάροιθεν ἐπιφρασθεὶς ἐνέποιμι.
1060 ἀνθέμενοι κεφαλῇσιν ἀερσιλόφους τρυφαλείας,
ἡμίσεες μὲν ἐρέσσετ' ἀμοιβαδίς, ἡμίσεες δὲ
δούρασί τε ξυστοῖσι καὶ ἀσπίσιν ἄρσετε νῆα.
αὐτὰρ πασσυδίῃ περιώσιον ὄρνυτ' ἀυτὴν
ἀθρόοι, ὄφρα κολῳὸν ἀηθείῃ φοβέωνται
1065 νεύοντάς τε λόφους καὶ ἐπήορα δούραθ' ὕπερθεν.
εἰ δέ κεν αὐτὴν νῆσον ἱκώμεθα, δὴ τότ' ἔπειτα
σὺν κελάδῳ σακέεσσι πελώριον ὄρσετε δοῦπον."
    ὣς ἄρ' ἔφη· πάντεσσι δ' ἐπίρροθος ἥνδανε μῆτις.
ἀμφὶ δὲ χαλκείας κόρυθας κεφαλῇσιν ἔθεντο
1070 δεινὸν λαμπομένας, ἐπὶ δὲ λόφοι ἐσσείοντο
φοινίκεοι. καὶ τοὶ μὲν ἀμοιβήδην ἐλάασκον·
τοὶ δ' αὖτ' ἐγχείῃσι καὶ ἀσπίσι νῆ' ἐκάλυψαν.
ὡς δ' ὅτε τις κεράμῳ κατερέψεται ἔρκιον ἀνήρ,
δώματος ἀγλαΐην τε καὶ ὑετοῦ ἔμμεναι ἄλκαρ,
1075 ἄλλῳ δ' ἔμπεδον ἄλλος ὁμῶς ἐπαμοιβὸς ἄρηρεν·

from seeing these birds. But I do not think that arrows will provide sufficient help for going ashore. Let us arrange some other strategy to aid us, if you intend to make land-fall, mindful of what Phineus instructed.[90] For not even Heracles, when he traveled to Arcadia, was strong enough to drive off the birds floating on the Stymphalian lake with his bow—I saw it myself—but he made a racket by shaking a bronze rattle in his hands as he stood on a high peak, and they fled far away, screeching in bewildered panic. There-fore, now as well let us devise some such strategy, and I will tell you what I myself have already devised. Having set your high-crested helmets on your heads, half of you take turns rowing, half of you barricade the ship with your pol-ished spears and shields. Then all together make a prodi-gious clamor, so that because of the unfamiliarity they will flee the noise, the bobbing crests, and the upward-point-ing spears. And if we land on the island itself, at that point raise an enormous din with your shields and shouting."

Thus he spoke, and his helpful strategy pleased them all. They put on their heads their bronze helmets, shining frightfully, on which waved plumes of red. Half of the men took turns rowing, while the rest covered the ship with their spears and shields. And as when a man roofs his dwelling with tiles to be an adornment for the house and protection from rain, and every tile fits snugly against the

90 Cf. 2.382–390.

1050 κ' Ω: γ' Brunck

ὣς οἵ γ' ἀσπίσι νῆα συναρτύναντες ἔρεψαν.
οἵη δὲ κλαγγὴ δήου πέλει ἐξ ὁμάδοιο
ἀνδρῶν κινυμένων, ὁπότε ξυνίωσι φάλαγγες·
τοίη ἄρ' ὑψόθι νηὸς ἐς ἠέρα κίδνατ' ἀυτή.
1080 οὐδέ τιν' οἰωνῶν ἔτ' ἐσέδρακον, ἀλλ' ὅτε νήσῳ
χρίμψαντες σακέεσσιν ἐπέκτυπον, αὐτίκ' ἄρ' οἵ γε
μυρίοι ἔνθα καὶ ἔνθα πεφυζότες ἠερέθοντο.
ὣς δ' ὁπότε Κρονίδης πυκινὴν ἐφέηκε χάλαζαν
ἐκ νεφέων ἀνά τ' ἄστυ καὶ οἰκία, τοὶ δ' ὑπὸ τοῖσιν
1085 ἐνναέται κόναβον τεγέων ὕπερ εἰσαΐοντες
ἧνται ἀκήν, ἐπεὶ οὔ σφε κατέλλαβε χείματος ὥρη
ἀπροφάτως, ἀλλὰ πρὶν ἐκαρτύναντο μέλαθρον·
ὣς πυκινὰ πτερὰ τοῖσιν ἐφίεσαν ἀίσσοντες
ὕψι μάλ' ἂμ πέλαγος περάτης εἰς οὔρεα γαίης.
1090 τίς γὰρ δὴ Φινῆος ἔην νόος, ἐνθάδε κέλσαι
ἀνδρῶν ἡρώων θεῖον στόλον; ἢ καὶ ἔπειτα
ποῖον ὄνειαρ ἔμελλεν ἐελδομένοισιν ἱκέσθαι;
    υἱῆες Φρίξοιο μετὰ πτόλιν Ὀρχομενοῖο
ἐξ Αἴης ἐνέοντο παρ' Αἰήταο Κυταίου,
1095 Κολχίδα νῆ' ἐπιβάντες, ἵν' ἄσπετον ὄλβον ἄρωνται
πατρός· ὁ γὰρ θνῄσκων ἐπετείλατο τήνδε κέλευθον.
καὶ δὴ ἔσαν νήσοιο μάλα σχεδὸν ἤματι κείνῳ,
Ζεὺς δ' ἀνέμου βορέαο μένος κίνησεν ἀῆναι,
ὕδατι σημαίνων διερὴν ὁδὸν Ἀρκτούροιο.
1100 αὐτὰρ ὅ γ' ἠμάτιος μὲν ἐν οὔρεσι φύλλ' ἐτίνασσεν
τυτθὸν ἐπ' ἀκροτάτοισιν ἀήσυρος ἀκρεμόνεσσιν·
νυκτὶ δ' ἔβη πόντονδε πελώριος, ὦρσε δὲ κῦμα
κεκληγὼς πνοιῇσι· κελαινὴ δ' οὐρανὸν ἀχλὺς

next one, thus did they roof over the ship with their shields by locking them together. And like the screaming that arises from a warring host of charging men when their formations collide, such was the shout that spread high above the ship into the air. They no longer saw a single bird, but when they neared the island and beat their shields, suddenly, by the thousands, they took flight in panic this way and that. And as when the son of Cronus casts a dense hailstorm from the clouds onto a town and its houses, and the inhabitants within them listen to the din above their roofs as they sit quietly, for the season of storms has not come upon them unexpectedly, but they have strengthened their roofs beforehand—thus did the birds cast a shower of feathered darts upon them as they sped off high over the sea to the mountains at the end of the earth.

What then was Phineus' purpose in having the god-like expedition of heroic men land here? And what sort of help was thereafter to come to them as they hoped it would?

The sons of Phrixus were sailing toward the city of Orchomenus from Aea, away from Cytaean Aeetes, aboard a Colchian ship, to obtain the boundless wealth of their father, for as he was dying he had ordered this voyage. And so on that day they were very close to the island, and Zeus roused the might of the north wind to blow, as he marked with rain the wet path of Arcturus.[91] And all day long the gentle wind barely shook the leaves in the mountains on the highest branches, but at night it came with gigantic force upon the sea and stirred up the waves with its shrieking blasts. A dark mist veiled the sky, and nowhere were

---

[91] The heliacal rising of Arcturus occurs in mid-September, beginning the rainy season.

ἄμπεχεν, οὐδέ πῃ ἄστρα διαυγέα φαίνετ᾽ ἰδέσθαι
1105 ἐκ νεφέων, σκοτόεις δὲ περὶ ζόφος ἠρήρειστο.
οἱ δ᾽ ἄρα μυδαλέοι, στυγερὸν τρομέοντες ὄλεθρον,
υἱῆες Φρίξοιο φέρονθ᾽ ὑπὸ κύμασιν αὔτως.
ἱστία δ᾽ ἐξήρπαξ᾽ ἀνέμου μένος, ἠδὲ καὶ αὐτὴν
νῆα διάνδιχ᾽ ἔαξε τινασσομένην ῥοθίοισιν.
1110 ἔνθα δ᾽ ὑπ᾽ ἐννεσίῃσι θεῶν πίσυρές περ ἐόντες
δούρατος ὠρέξαντο πελωρίου, οἷά τε πολλὰ
ῥαισθείσης κεκέδαστο θοοῖς συναρηρότα γόμφοις.
καὶ τοὺς μὲν νῆσόνδε, παρὲξ ὀλίγον θανάτοιο,
κύματα καὶ ῥιπαὶ ἀνέμου φέρον ἀσχαλόωντας·
1115 αὐτίκα δ᾽ ἐρράγη ὄμβρος ἀθέσφατος, ὗε δὲ πόντον
καὶ νῆσον καὶ πᾶσαν ὅσην κατεναντία νήσου
χώρην Μοσσύνοικοι ὑπέρβιοι ἀμφενέμοντο.
τοὺς δ᾽ ἄμυδις κρατερῷ σὺν δούρατι κύματος ὁρμὴ
υἱῆας Φρίξοιο μετ᾽ ἠιόνας βάλε νήσου
1120 νύχθ᾽ ὕπο λυγαίην. τὸ δὲ μυρίον ἐκ Διὸς ὕδωρ
λῆξεν ἅμ᾽ ἠελίῳ· τάχα δ᾽ ἐγγύθεν ἀντεβόλησαν
ἀλλήλοις· Ἄργος δὲ παροίτατος ἔκφατο μῦθον·

"ἀντόμεθα πρὸς Ζηνὸς Ἐποψίου, οἵ τινές ἐστε
ἀνδρῶν, εὐμενέειν τε καὶ ἀρκέσσαι χατέουσιν.
1125 πόντῳ γὰρ τρηχεῖαι ἐπιβρίσασαι ἄελλαι
νηὸς ἀεικελίης διὰ δούρατα πάντ᾽ ἐκέδασσαν,
ᾗ ἔνι πείρομεν οἶδμα κατὰ χρέος ἐμβεβαῶτες.
τούνεκα νῦν ὑμέας γουναζόμεθ᾽, αἴ κε πίθησθε,
δοῦναι ὅσον τ᾽ εἴλυμα περὶ χροός, ἠδὲ κομίσσαι
1130 ἀνέρας οἰκτείραντες ὁμήλικας ἐν κακότητι.

the bright stars to be seen shining through the clouds, but all around a murky darkness had settled in. Drenched and dreading a horrible death, the sons of Phrixus were being carried along at the whim of the waves. The force of the wind tore away their sails and broke the ship itself in two as it was tossed on the breakers. Then, by the designs of the gods those four grabbed onto a huge beam, one of many such held together by sharp pegs that had been scattered when the ship broke apart. The waves and blasts of the wind were carrying them toward the island, in distress and on the brink of death, when suddenly a tremendous rainstorm burst forth and began pouring upon the sea, the island, and all the land opposite the island, where the insolent Mossynoecians lived. The force of the waves hurled Phrixus' sons, together with the strong beam, onto the shores of the island in the dark of night. The deluge of water from Zeus ceased at sunrise, and before long the two groups came near and met one another. Argus was the first to speak out:

"In the name of Zeus the Watcher, we beg you, whoever you are of men, to be kind and help us in our need. For fierce tempests bore down upon the sea and scattered all the timbers of the wretched ship in which we were crossing the waves, having embarked of necessity.[92] Therefore, we now beseech you, in the hope that you will agree, to give us a mere covering to wrap around our bodies and to help, out of pity, men your own age in distress. Have re-

[92] Or, reading ἐπὶ χρέος, *on business.*

1127 πείρομεν οἶδμα Π[18lem]: τειρόμενοι ἄμ' Ω | κατὰ Köchly: ἐπὶ Ω   1130 οἰκτείραντες S: οἰκτείραντας Ω

ἀλλ᾿ ἱκέτας ξείνους Διὸς εἵνεκεν αἰδέσσασθε
Ξεινίου Ἱκεσίου τε· Διὸς δ᾿ ἄμφω ἱκέται τε
καὶ ξεῖνοι· ὁ δέ που καὶ ἐπόψιος ἄμμι τέτυκται."
   τὸν δ᾿ αὖτ᾿ Αἴσονος υἱὸς ἐπιφραδέως ἐρέεινεν,
1135 μαντοσύνας Φινῆος ὀισσάμενος τελέεσθαι·
   "ταῦτα μὲν αὐτίκα πάντα παρέξομεν εὐμενέοντες·
ἀλλ᾿ ἄγε μοι κατάλεξον ἐτήτυμον, ὁππόθι γαίης
ναίετε, καὶ χρέος, οἷον ὑπεὶρ ἅλα νεῖσθαι ἀνώγει,
αὐτῶν θ᾿ ὑμείων ὄνομα κλυτὸν ἠδὲ γενέθλην."
1140   τὸν δ᾿ Ἄργος προσέειπεν ἀμηχανέων κακότητι·
   "Αἰολίδην Φρίξον τιν᾿ ἀφ᾿ Ἑλλάδος Αἶαν
     ἱκέσθαι
ἀτρεκέως δοκέω που ἀκούετε καὶ πάρος αὐτοί,
Φρίξον, ὅ τις πτολίεθρον ἀνήλυθεν Αἰήταο
κριοῦ ἐπαμβεβαώς, τόν ῥα χρύσειον ἔθηκεν
1145 Ἑρμείας—κῶας δὲ καὶ εἰσέτι νῦν κεν ἴδοισθε
1145a πεπτάμενον λασίοισιν ἐπὶ δρυὸς ἀκρεμόνεσσιν—
τὸν μὲν ἔπειτ᾿ ἔρρεξεν ἑῆς ὑποθημοσύνῃσιν
Φυξίῳ ἐκ πάντων Κρονίδῃ Διί· καί μιν ἔδεκτο
Αἰήτης μεγάρῳ, κούρην τέ οἱ ἐγγυάλιξεν
Χαλκιόπην ἀνάεδνον εὐφροσύνῃσι νόοιο·
1150 τῶν ἐξ ἀμφοτέρων εἰμὲν γένος. ἀλλ᾿ ὁ μὲν ἤδη
γηραιὸς θάνε Φρίξος ἐν Αἰήταο δόμοισιν·
ἡμεῖς δ᾿ αὐτίκα πατρὸς ἐφετμάων ἀλέγοντες
νεύμεθ᾿ ἐς Ὀρχομενὸν κτεάνων Ἀθάμαντος ἕκητι.

1145a del. Brunck (= 2.1270)

spect for suppliant strangers for the sake of Zeus, God of
Strangers and Suppliants—for both suppliants and strang-
ers belong to Zeus—and he, I think, is a watcher over us
too."

In turn, Jason judiciously questioned him, surmising
that Phineus' prophecies were being fulfilled.

"We will provide all those things right away out of kind-
ness. But come, tell me truthfully in what country you live,
what sort of necessity compels you to travel on the sea, and
what famous names and lineage are your own?"

And Argus, feeling helpless in his distress, responded:

"That a certain Aeolid named Phrixus came from Hel-
las to Aea you yourselves, I think, have accurately heard
before this; Phrixus, that is, who went to the city of Aeetes,
riding on a ram that Hermes had turned to gold; and you
may still today see its fleece spread out on the leafy
branches of an oak tree.[93] That ram, by its own instruc-
tions,[94] he afterwards sacrificed to Cronus' son Zeus, the
God of Fugitives, above all other gods. And Aeetes re-
ceived him into his home and betrothed his daughter
Chalciope to him without any bride price in the gladness of
his spirit. We are the children of those two. But Phrixus, al-
ready an old man, died in Aeetes' palace, and right away in
obedience to our father's commands we are traveling to
Orchomenus to secure the possessions of Athamas.[95] And

---

[93] Brunck deleted line 1145a, "spread out on the leafy
branches of an oak tree," because it duplicates 1270.

[94] The ram could speak (cf. 1.257–258, 763–764).

[95] Phrixus' father, formerly king of Orchomenus.

APOLLONIUS RHODIUS

εἰ δὲ καὶ οὔνομα δῆθεν ἐπιθύεις δεδαῆσθαι,
1155 τῷδε Κυτίσσωρος πέλει οὔνομα, τῷδέ τε Φρόντις,
τῷ δὲ Μέλας· ἐμὲ δ' αὐτὸν ἐπικλείοιτέ κεν Ἄργον."
ὣς φάτ'· ἀριστῆες δὲ συνηβολίῃ κεχάροντο,
καί σφεας ἀμφίεπον περιθαμβέες. αὐτὰρ Ἰήσων
ἐξαῦτις κατὰ μοῖραν ἀμείψατο τοῖσδ' ἐπέεσσιν·
1160 "ἦ ἄρα δὴ γνωτοὶ πατρώιοι ἄμμιν ἐόντες
λίσσεσθ' εὐμενέοντας ἐπαρκέσσαι κακότητα.
Κρηθεὺς γὰρ ῥ' Ἀθάμας τε κασίγνητοι γεγάασιν,
Κρηθῆος δ' υἱωνὸς ἐγὼ σὺν τοισίδ' ἑταίροις
Ἑλλάδος ἐξ αὐτῆς νέομ' ἐς πόλιν Αἰήταο.
1165 ἀλλὰ τὰ μὲν καὶ ἐσαῦτις ἐνίψομεν ἀλλήλοισιν.
νῦν δ' ἔσσασθε πάροιθεν. ὑπ' ἐννεσίῃσι δ' ὀίω
ἀθανάτων ἐς χεῖρας ἐμὰς χατέοντας ἱκέσθαι."
ἦ ῥα, καὶ ἐκ νηὸς δῶκέ σφισιν εἵματα δῦναι.
πασσυδίῃ δήπειτα κίον μετὰ νηὸν Ἄρηος,
1170 μῆλ' ἱερευσόμενοι· περὶ δ' ἐσχάρῃ ἐστήσαντο
ἐσσυμένως, ἥ τ' ἐκτὸς ἀνηρεφέος πέλε νηοῦ
στιάων· εἴσω δὲ μέλας λίθος ἠρήρειστο
ἱερός, ᾧ ποτε πᾶσαι Ἀμαζόνες εὐχετόωντο·
οὐδέ σφιν θέμις ἦεν, ὅτ' ἀντιπέρηθεν ἵκοιντο,
1175 μήλων τ' ἠδὲ βοῶν τῇδ' ἐσχάρῃ ἱερὰ καίειν·
ἀλλ' ἵππους δαίτρευον ἐπηετανὸν κομέουσαι.
αὐτὰρ ἐπεὶ ῥέξαντες ἐπαρτέα δαῖτα πάσαντο,
δὴ τότ' ἄρ' Αἰσονίδης μετεφώνεεν, ἦρχέ τε μύθων·

1160 ἐόντες IˢˡZ Flor.: ἰόντες Ω

204

if indeed you desire to learn our names as well, this one's name is Cytissorus, that one's is Phrontis, and this one's is Melas. You may call me Argus."

Thus he spoke, and the heroes rejoiced at the encounter and in great wonderment attended to them. And Jason in turn responded fittingly with these words:

"Truly, then, it is as our relatives on my father's side that you beg[96] us to be kind and alleviate your misfortune. For Cretheus and Athamas were brothers, and I, Cretheus' grandson, am traveling with these comrades from that very Hellas to the city of Aeetes. But we will speak with one other about that at a later time. But now, first put on some clothing. I believe that it was by the designs of the immortals that you have come to my hands in need."

He spoke and gave them clothing from the ship to put on. Then they all went together to the temple of Ares to sacrifice sheep. They quickly took their places around the altar, which was made of pebbles, outside the roofless temple. Inside, a black stone stood fixed, a sacred one, to which all the Amazons once prayed; and whenever they came across from the mainland, it was forbidden for them to burn sacrifices of sheep or bulls on that altar, but they butchered horses that they fattened for a year. But when the heroes had performed the sacrifice and eaten the feast they had prepared, then Jason spoke among them and began with these words:

[96] Or, reading ἰόντες, *Truly, then, you come as our relatives on my father's side and beg.*

"Ζεὺς αὐτὸς τὰ ἕκαστ᾽ ἐπιδέρκεται, οὐδέ μιν
   ἄνδρες
1180 λήθομεν ἔμπεδον, οἵ τε θεουδέες οὐδὲ δίκαιοι.
ὡς μὲν γὰρ πατέρ᾽ ὑμὸν ὑπεξείρυτο φόνοιο
μητρυιῆς, καὶ νόσφιν ἀπειρέσιον πόρεν ὄλβον·
ὡς δὲ καὶ ὑμέας αὖτις ἀπήμονας ἐξεσάωσεν
χείματος οὐλομένοιο. πάρεστι δὲ τῆσδ᾽ ἐπὶ νηὸς
1185 ἔνθα καὶ ἔνθα νέεσθαι, ὅπη φίλον, εἴτε μετ᾽ Αἶαν,
εἴτε μετ᾽ ἀφνειὴν θείου πόλιν Ὀρχομενοῖο.
τὴν γὰρ Ἀθηναίη τεχνήσατο, καὶ τάμε χαλκῷ
δούρατα Πηλιάδος κορυφῆς πάρα, σὺν δέ οἱ Ἄργος
τεῦξεν· ἀτὰρ κείνην γε κακὸν διὰ κῦμ᾽ ἐκέδασσεν,
1190 πρὶν καὶ πετράων σχεδὸν ἐλθεῖν, αἵ τ᾽ ἐνὶ Πόντῳ
στεινωπῷ συνίασι πανήμεροι ἀλλήλῃσιν.
ἀλλ᾽ ἄγεθ᾽ ὧδε καὶ αὐτοὶ ἐς Ἑλλάδα μαιομένοισιν
κῶας ἄγειν χρύσειον ἐπίρροθοι ἄμμι πέλεσθε
καὶ πλόου ἡγεμόνης, ἐπεὶ Φρίξοιο θυηλὰς
1195 στέλλομαι ἀμπλήσων, Ζηνὸς χόλον Αἰολίδῃσιν."
   ἴσκε παρηγορέων· οἱ δ᾽ ἔστυγον εἰσαΐοντες·
οὐ γὰρ ἔφαν τεύξεσθαι ἐνηέος Αἰήταο
κῶας ἄγειν κριοῖο μεμαότας· ὧδε δ᾽ ἔειπεν
Ἄργος, ἀτεμβόμενος τοῖον στόλον ἀμφιπένεσθαι·
1200   "ὦ φίλοι, ἡμέτερον μὲν ὅσον σθένος οὔ ποτ᾽
   ἀρωγῆς
σχήσεται οὐδ᾽ ἠβαιόν, ὅτε χρειώ τις ἵκηται.
ἀλλ᾽ αἰνῶς ὀλοῇσιν ἀπηνείῃσιν ἄρηρεν

1179 αὐτὸς SE: αἰτεῖ LG: ἔτι A: ἐτεὸν Meineke

206

"Zeus himself[97] beholds everything, nor do we men ever elude his view, whether we are god-fearing or unjust. For just as he rescued your father from murder at the hands of his step-mother[98] and gave him boundless wealth besides,[99] so he saved you as well, unharmed, from the deadly storm. On this ship of ours one can travel here or there, wherever he pleases, whether to Aea or to the wealthy city of divine Orchomenus. For Athena designed it and with a bronze ax cut its timbers from[100] the peak of Pelion, and with her help Argus constructed it. But a vicious wave shattered that ship of yours before it came near the rocks that clash together all day long in the straits of the Black Sea.[101] But come now, you yourselves be our helpers, for we desire to take the golden fleece to Hellas, and be guides for our voyage, since I am on my way to atone for the sacrifice of Phrixus, the cause of Zeus' anger against the Aeolids."

Thus he spoke to win them over, but they were horrified to hear it, because they did not think that the heroes would find Aeetes friendly if they desired to take the ram's fleece. Argus spoke as follows, reproaching them for undertaking such an expedition:

"O my friends, all the strength we possess to aid you will never be lacking, not the slightest bit, when any need arises. But Aeetes is terrifyingly armed with murderous

---

[97] Or, reading ἐτεὸν, *truly*.   [98] Ino.

[99] Some translate νόσφι as "far away" (i.e. in Colchis).

[100] Or, reading πέρι, *around*.   [101] Jason is apparently unaware that the rocks are now stationary.

1180 οὐδὲ Ω: ἠδὲ Stephanus   1188 πάρα E: πέρι Ω

Αἰήτης· τῷ καὶ πέρι δείδια ναυτίλλεσθαι.
στεῦται δ' Ἡελίου γόνος ἔμμεναι, ἀμφὶ δὲ Κόλχων
1205 ἔθνεα ναιετάουσιν ἀπείρονα· καὶ δέ κεν Ἄρει
σμερδαλέην ἐνοπὴν μέγα τε σθένος ἰσοφαρίζοι.
οὐ μὰν οὐδ' ἀπάνευθεν ἑλεῖν δέρος Αἰήταο
ῥηίδιον· τοῖός μιν ὄφις περί τ' ἀμφί τ' ἔρυται
ἀθάνατος καὶ ἄυπνος, ὃν αὐτὴ Γαῖ' ἀνέφυσεν
1210 Καυκάσου ἐν κνημοῖσι, Τυφαονίη ὅθι πέτρη,
ἔνθα Τυφάονά φασι Διὸς Κρονίδαο κεραυνῷ
βλήμενον, ὁππότε οἱ στιβαρὰς ἐπορέξατο χεῖρας,
θερμὸν ἀπὸ κρατὸς στάξαι φόνον· ἵκετο δ' αὔτως
οὔρεα καὶ πεδίον Νυσήιον, ἔνθ' ἔτι νῦν περ
1215 κεῖται ὑποβρύχιος Σερβωνίδος ὕδασι λίμνης."

     ὣς ἄρ' ἔφη· πολέεσσι δ' ἐπὶ χλόος εἷλε παρειὰς
αὐτίκα, τοῖον ἄεθλον ὅτ' ἔκλυον· αἶψα δὲ Πηλεὺς
θαρσαλέως ἐπέεσσιν ἀμείψατο, φώνησέν τε·
     "μὴ δ' οὕτως, ἠθεῖε, λίην δειδίσσεο μύθῳ·
1220 οὔτε γὰρ ὧδ' ἀλκὴν ἐπιδευόμεθ', ὥς τε χερείους
ἔμμεναι Αἰήταο σὺν ἔντεσι πειρηθῆναι·
ἀλλὰ καὶ ἡμέας οἴω ἐπισταμένους πολέμοιο
κεῖσε μολεῖν μακάρων σχεδὸν αἵματος ἐκγεγαῶτας.
τῷ εἰ μὴ φιλότητι δέρος χρύσειον ὀπάσσει,
1225 οὔ οἱ χραισμήσειν ἐπιέλπομαι ἔθνεα Κόλχων."

1218 θαρσαλέως Ω: θαρσαλέοις Köchly
1219 μύθῳ LEγρSAγρ: θύμῳ L²γρAωE

cruelty, and for that reason I fear very much to make the voyage. He claims to be the son of Helius, and all around dwell countless tribes of Colchians. Even for Ares he would be a match with his terrifying war-cry and mighty strength. No, not even taking the fleece without Aeetes' knowledge is easy, for such is the snake that keeps guard all around it, one that is immortal and sleepless, which Earth herself produced on the slopes of the Caucasus, by the rock of Typhaon, where they say Typhaon dripped warm blood from his head when he was blasted by the thunderbolt of Zeus, Cronus' son, when he raised his mighty hands against the god. He went in that condition to the mountains and plain of Nysa, where to this day he lies submerged beneath the waters of lake Serbonis."[102]

Thus he spoke, and at once pallor spread over the cheeks of many of them, when they heard tell of such a task. But right away Peleus replied courageously with these words and said:

"Do not, my good friend, seek to frighten us so much with your talk.[103] We are not so lacking in valor as to be inferior to Aeetes in a trial of arms, but rather I think that we go there with knowledge of war ourselves, being closely related by blood to the blessed gods. Therefore, if he will not hand over the golden fleece out of friendship, I do not expect that the tribes of Colchians will be of help to him."

---

[102] Located between Syria and Egypt. Other accounts place Typhaon (or Typhoeus) in Tartarus (cf. Hesiod, *Theogony* 820–868), Cilicia (cf. *Iliad* 2.782–783), or under mount Aetna (cf. Pindar, *Pythian* 1.13–28).

[103] Or, reading θύμῳ, *do not be so afraid in your heart*.

ὣς οἵ γ᾽ ἀλλήλοισιν ἀμοιβαδὸν ἠγορόωντο,
μέσφ᾽ αὖτις δόρποιο κορεσσάμενοι κατέδαρθεν.
ἦρι δ᾽ ἀνεγρομένοισιν εὐκραὴς ἄεν οὖρος·
ἱστία δ᾽ ἤειραν, τὰ δ᾽ ὑπαὶ ῥιπῆς ἀνέμοιο
1230 τείνετο· ῥίμφα δὲ νῆσον ἀποπροέλειπον Ἄρηος.
νυκτὶ δ᾽ ἐπιπλομένη Φιλυρηίδα νῆσον ἄμειβον·
ἔνθα μὲν Οὐρανίδης Φιλύρῃ Κρόνος, εὖτ᾽ ἐν
    Ὀλύμπῳ
Τιτήνων ἤνασσεν, ὁ δὲ Κρηταῖον ὑπ᾽ ἄντρον
Ζεὺς ἔτι Κουρήτεσσι μετετρέφετ᾽ Ἰδαίοισιν,
1235 Ῥείην ἐξαπαφὼν παρελέξατο· τοὺς δ᾽ ἐνὶ λέκτροις
τέτμε θεὰ μεσσηγύς· ὁ δ᾽ ἐξ εὐνῆς ἀνορούσας
ἔσσυτο χαιτήεντι φυὴν ἐναλίγκιος ἵππῳ·
ἡ δ᾽ αἰδοῖ χῶρόν τε καὶ ἤθεα κεῖνα λιποῦσα
Ὠκεανὶς Φιλύρη εἰς οὔρεα μακρὰ Πελασγῶν
1240 ἦλθ᾽, ἵνα δὴ Χείρωνα πελώριον, ἄλλα μὲν ἵππῳ,
ἄλλα θεῷ ἀτάλαντον, ἀμοιβαίῃ τέκεν εὐνή.
    κεῖθεν δ᾽ αὖ Μάκρωνας ἀπειρεσίην τε Βεχείρων
γαῖαν ὑπερφιάλους τε παρεξενέοντο Σάπειρας,
Βύζηράς τ᾽ ἐπὶ τοῖσιν· ἐπιπρὸ γὰρ αἰὲν ἔτεμνον
1245 ἐσσυμένως λιαροῖο φορεύμενοι ἐξ ἀνέμοιο.
καὶ δὴ νισσομένοισι μυχὸς διεφαίνετο Πόντου,
καὶ δὴ Καυκασίων ὀρέων ἀνέτελλον ἐρίπναι
ἠλίβατοι, τόθι γυῖα περὶ στυφελοῖσι πάγοισιν
ἰλλόμενος χαλκέῃσιν ἀλυκτοπέδῃσι Προμηθεὺς
1250 αἰετὸν ἥπατι φέρβε παλιμπετὲς ἀίσσοντα.
τὸν μὲν ἐπ᾽ ἀκροτάτης ἴδον ἕσπερον ὀξέι ῥοίζῳ
νηὸς ὑπερπτάμενον νεφέων σχεδόν· ἀλλὰ καὶ ἔμπης

Thus they addressed one another in turn until, once again replenished by a meal, they went to sleep.

And when they arose at dawn, a fresh breeze was blowing. They hoisted the sail, which stretched taut under the rush of the wind, and they soon left behind the island of Ares. The following night they passed the island of Philyra. It was there that Uranus' son Cronus—when he ruled over the Titans on Olympus and Zeus was still being raised in the Cretan cave by the Idaean Curetes—deceived Rhea and lay with Philyra. When the goddess surprised them in the midst of their lovemaking, he leapt out of bed and ran off in the form of a long-maned horse. Out of shame, Philyra, Ocean's daughter, left that region and its dwellings and came to the high mountains of the Pelasgians,[104] where she bore prodigious Cheiron, partly like a horse and partly like a god, because of the alteration during intercourse.

From there they sailed past the Macrones, the vast land of the Becheirians, the savage Sapeires, and, beyond them, the Byzeres, for they were ever plowing their way rapidly, borne on by a gentle wind. And then, as they proceeded, the end of the Black Sea came into view, and then, rising above the horizon were the steep cliffs of the Caucasus mountains, where Prometheus, his limbs bound fast to the hard cliffs by unbreakable bronze bonds, fed his liver to an eagle ever flying back to him. They saw it at dusk flying with a loud whirr above the top of the ship near the clouds,

[104] In particular mount Pelion in Thessaly.

λαίφεα πάντ' ἐτίναξε παραιθύξας πτερύγεσσιν·
οὐ γὰρ ὅ γ' αἰθερίοιο φυὴν ἔχεν οἰωνοῖο,
1255 ἶσα δ' ἐυξέστοις ὠκύπτερα πάλλεν ἐρετμοῖς.
δηρὸν δ' οὐ μετέπειτα πολύστονον ἄιον αὐδὴν
ἧπαρ ἀνελκομένοιο Προμηθέος· ἔκτυπε δ' αἰθὴρ
οἰμωγῇ, μέσφ' αὖτις ἀπ' οὔρεος ἀίσσοντα
αἰετὸν ὠμηστὴν αὐτὴν ὁδὸν εἰσενόησαν.
1260 ἐννύχιοι δ' Ἄργοιο δαημοσύνησιν ἵκοντο
Φᾶσίν τ' εὐρὺ ῥέοντα καὶ ἔσχατα πείρατα Πόντου.
αὐτίκα δ' ἱστία μὲν καὶ ἐπίκριον ἔνδοθι κοίλης
ἱστοδόκης στείλαντες ἐκόσμεον· ἐν δὲ καὶ αὐτὸν
ἱστὸν ἄφαρ χαλάσαντο παρακλιδόν· ὦκα δ'
ἐρετμοῖς
1265 εἰσέλασαν ποταμοῖο μέγαν ῥόον· αὐτὰρ ὁ πάντη
καχλάζων ὑπόεικεν. ἔχον δ' ἐπ' ἀριστερὰ χειρῶν
Καύκασον αἰπήεντα Κυταιίδα τε πτόλιν Αἴης,
ἔνθεν δ' αὖ πεδίον τὸ Ἀρήιον ἱερά τ' ἄλση
τοῖο θεοῦ, τόθι κῶας ὄφις εἴρυτο δοκεύων
1270 πεπτάμενον λασίοισιν ἐπὶ δρυὸς ἀκρεμόνεσσιν.
αὐτὸς δ' Αἰσονίδης χρυσέῳ ποταμόνδε κυπέλλῳ
οἴνου ἀκηρασίοιο μελισταγέας χέε λοιβὰς
Γαίῃ τ' ἐνναέταις τε θεοῖς ψυχαῖς τε καμόντων
ἡρώων· γουνοῦτο δ' ἀπήμονας εἶναι ἀρωγοὺς
1275 εὐμενέως, καὶ νηὸς ἐναίσιμα πείσματα δέχθαι.
αὐτίκα δ' Ἀγκαῖος τοῖον μετὰ μῦθον ἔειπεν·
  "Κολχίδα μὲν δὴ γαῖαν ἱκάνομεν ἠδὲ ῥέεθρα
Φάσιδος· ὥρη δ' ἧμιν ἐνὶ σφίσι μητιάασθαι

but nonetheless it made all the sails flap as it darted past on its wings, for it did not have the form of a bird of the air but plied its long wing-feathers like well-polished oars. Not long thereafter, they heard the tormented cry of Prometheus as his liver was being torn out. The air resounded with his shrieking until they saw the flesh-eating eagle flying back from the mountain by the same route.

During the night, relying on Argus' expertise, they reached the wide-flowing Phasis and the furthest reaches of the Black Sea. At once they took down the sail and yard and stowed them in the hollow mast-holder, and right away lowered the mast itself alongside. They quickly rowed into the mighty current of the river, and, seething all around, it gave way before them. They kept the high Caucasus and the Cytaean city of Aea on their left hand and, on the other, the plain of Ares and that god's sacred grove, where the watchful snake was guarding the fleece, spread out on the leafy branches of an oak tree. Jason himself from a golden goblet poured libations of sweet honey and unmixed wine into the river in honor of Earth, the indigenous gods, and the souls of the dead heroes. He besought them to be kindly helpers out of good will and to receive the ship's cables auspiciously. Immediately Ancaeus spoke these words to them:

"We have now come to the land of Colchis and the stream of the Phasis. It is time for us to plan among our-

εἴτ᾽ οὖν μειλιχίῃ πειρησόμεθ᾽ Αἰήταο,
1280 εἴτε καὶ ἀλλοίη τις ἐπήβολος ἔσσεται ὁρμή."

ὣς ἔφατ᾽· Ἄργου δ᾽ αὖτε παρηγορίῃσιν Ἰήσων
ὑψόθι νῆ᾽ ἐκέλευσεν ἐπ᾽ εὐναίῃσιν ἐρύσσαι,
δάσκιον εἰσελάσαντας ἕλος· τὸ δ᾽ ἐπισχεδὸν ἦεν
νισσομένων. ἔνθ᾽ οἵ γε διὰ κνέφας ηὐλίζοντο·
1285 ἠὼς δ᾽ οὐ μετὰ δηρὸν ἐελδομένοισι φαάνθη.

214

selves whether we shall test Aeetes with courtesy, or whether some other approach will be effective."

Thus he spoke, but on the advice of Argus, Jason ordered them to hold the ship afloat with anchors after rowing it into an overgrown backwater, and one was near where they came in. There they spent the night, and not long thereafter dawn appeared to their longing eyes.

BOOK 3

Εἰ δ' ἄγε νῦν, Ἐρατώ, παρά θ' ἵστασο καί μοι
    ἔνισπε,
ἔνθεν ὅπως ἐς Ἰωλκὸν ἀνήγαγε κῶας Ἰήσων
Μηδείης ὑπ' ἔρωτι· σὺ γὰρ καὶ Κύπριδος αἶσαν
ἔμμορες, ἀδμήτας δὲ τεοῖς μελεδήμασι θέλγεις
5 παρθενικάς· τῶ καί τοι ἐπήρατον οὔνομ' ἀνῆπται.
    ὣς οἱ μὲν πυκινοῖσιν ἀνώιστως δονάκεσσιν
μίμνον ἀριστῆες λελοχημένοι· αἱ δ' ἐνόησαν
Ἥρη Ἀθηναίη τε, Διὸς δ' αὐτοῖο καὶ ἄλλων
ἀθανάτων ἀπονόσφι θεῶν θάλαμόνδε κιοῦσαι
10 βούλευον. πείραζε δ' Ἀθηναίην πάρος Ἥρη·
    "αὐτὴ νῦν προτέρη, θύγατερ Διός, ἄρχεο βουλῆς.
τί χρέος; ἦε δόλον τινὰ μήσεαι, ᾧ κεν ἑλόντες
χρύσεον Αἰήταο μεθ' Ἑλλάδα κῶας ἄγοιντο;
οὐκ ἄρ τόν γ' ἐπέεσσι παραιφάμενοι πεπίθοιεν
15 μειλιχίοις· ἤτοι μὲν ὑπερφίαλος πέλει αἰνῶς,
ἔμπης δ' οὔ τινα πεῖραν ἀποτρωπᾶσθαι ἔοικεν."
    ὣς φάτο· τὴν δὲ παράσσον Ἀθηναίη προσέειπεν·
    "καὶ δ' αὐτὴν ἐμὲ τοῖα μετὰ φρεσὶν ὁρμαίνουσαν,

14 ου]κ αρ Π[19]: ἢ καὶ Ω
15 ἤτοι μεν Π[19]: ἢ γὰρ ὁ μὲν Ω: ἢ γὰρ ὅδ᾽ Ε

BOOK 3

Come now, Erato,[1] stand by my side and tell me how from here Jason brought the fleece back to Iolcus with the aid of Medea's love, for you have a share also of Cypris' power and enchant unwed girls with your anxieties; and that is why your lovely name has been attached to you.

In this way[2] the heroes were waiting out of sight in ambush within the dense reeds, but Hera and Athena took note of them and went to a room away from Zeus himself and the other immortal gods and began making plans. Hera opened by testing Athena:

"You yourself be first now, daughter of Zeus, to initiate a plan. What must we do? Will you contrive some trick whereby they might seize Aeetes' golden fleece and take it to Hellas? After all, he is not one they could win over and persuade with gentle words. Indeed he is terribly arrogant, but nonetheless one should not turn away from any attempt."

Thus she spoke, and Athena answered her at once:

"I too, Hera, have been pondering in my mind those

---

[1] One of the nine Muses (Hesiod, *Theogony* 78), invoked to assist in the story of love (*eros*) dominating this half of the epic.
[2] As they were at the end of Book 2.

᾿Ήρη, ἀπηλεγέως ἐξείρεαι. ἀλλά τοι οὔ πω
20 φράσσασθαι νοέω τοῦτον δόλον, ὅς τις ὀνήσει
θυμὸν ἀριστήων· πολέας δ᾽ ἐπεδοίασα βουλάς.”
ἦ, καὶ ἐπ᾽ οὔδεος αἵ γε ποδῶν πάρος ὄμματ᾽
ἔπηξαν,
ἄνδιχα πορφύρουσαι ἐνὶ σφίσιν· αὐτίκα δ᾽ ᾿Ήρη
τοῖον μητιόωσα παροιτέρη ἔκφατο μῦθον·
25 “δεῦρ᾽ ἴομεν μετὰ Κύπριν· ἐπιπλόμεναι δέ μιν
ἄμφω
παιδὶ ἑῷ εἰπεῖν ὀτρύνομεν, αἴ κε πίθηται
κούρην Αἰήτεω πολυφάρμακον οἷσι βέλεσσιν
θέλξαι ὀιστεύσας ἐπ᾽ Ἰήσονι. τὸν δ᾽ ἂν ὀίω
κείνης ἐννεσίῃσιν ἐς Ἑλλάδα κῶας ἀνάξειν.”
30 ὣς ἄρ᾽ ἔφη· πυκινὴ δὲ συνεύαδε μῆτις Ἀθήνῃ,
καί μιν ἔπειτ᾽ ἐξαῦτις ἀμείβετο μειλιχίοισιν·
“῎Ήρη, νήιδα μέν με πατὴρ τέκε τοῖο βολάων,
οὐδέ τινα χρειὼ θελκτήριον οἶδα πόθοιο·
εἰ δέ σοι αὐτῇ μῦθος ἐφανδάνει, ἦ τ᾽ ἂν ἐγώ γε
35 ἑσποίμην, σὺ δέ κεν φαίης ἔπος ἀντιόωσα.”
ἦ, καὶ ἀναΐξασαι ἐπὶ μέγα δῶμα νέοντο
Κύπριδος, ὅ ῥά τέ οἱ δεῖμεν πόσις ἀμφιγυήεις,
ὁππότε μιν τὰ πρῶτα παραὶ Διὸς ἦγεν ἄκοιτιν.
ἔρκεα δ᾽ εἰσελθοῦσαι ὑπ᾽ αἰθούσῃ θαλάμοιο
40 ἔσταν, ἵν᾽ ἐντύνεσκε θεὰ λέχος Ἡφαίστοιο.
ἀλλ᾽ ὁ μὲν ἐς χαλκεῶνα καὶ ἄκμονας ἦρι βεβήκει,

things you openly ask about, but so far I cannot think of any such trick to tell you that will bolster the heroes' courage, although I have mulled over many plans."

She spoke, and they fixed their eyes on the ground in front of their feet, separately brooding within themselves. Presently, Hera was first to have an idea and to make this proposal:

"Come, let us go visit Cypris and together approach her and urge her to speak to her son, in hopes that he will be persuaded to shoot Aeetes' daughter, expert in magic drugs, with his arrows and enchant her with love for Jason, for I think that with her counsels he will take the fleece back to Hellas."

Thus she spoke, and her shrewd idea also pleased Athena, and once again she answered her with gentle words:

"Hera, my father bore me without knowledge of his arrows,[3] nor do I know of any enchantment to induce desire. But if you yourself approve of the plan, truly I would follow along, but please do the speaking when making the request."[4]

She spoke, and they sprang up and went to the great house of Cypris, which her lame husband had built for her when he first took her as his wife from Zeus. They entered the courtyard and stood within the portico of the room where the goddess shared the bed of Hephaestus. But he had gone off at daybreak to the anvils of his forge in a vast

---

[3] As a virgin goddess not even conceived by sexual intercourse, Athena has no familiarity with Eros' weapons.

[4] ἀντιόωσα can also mean *when meeting her.*

νήσοιο Πλαγκτῆς εὐρὺν μυχόν, ᾧ ἔνι πάντα
δαίδαλα χάλκευεν ῥιπῇ πυρός· ἡ δ' ἄρα μούνη
ἧστο δόμῳ δινωτὸν ἀνὰ θρόνον ἄντα θυράων.
45 λευκοῖσιν δ' ἑκάτερθε κόμας ἐπιειμένη ὤμοις
κόσμει χρυσείῃ διὰ κερκίδι, μέλλε δὲ μακροὺς
πλέξασθαι πλοκάμους· τὰς δὲ προπάροιθεν ἰδοῦσα
ἔσχεθεν, εἴσω τέ σφ' ἐκάλει, καὶ ἀπὸ θρόνου ὦρτο,
εἷσέ τ' ἐνὶ κλισμοῖσιν· ἀτὰρ μετέπειτα καὶ αὐτὴ
50 ἵζανεν, ἀψήκτους δὲ χεροῖν ἀνεδήσατο χαίτας.
τοῖα δὲ μειδιόωσα προσέννεπεν αἱμυλίοισιν·
 "ἠθεῖαι, τίς δεῦρο νόος χρειώ τε κομίζει
δηναιὰς αὔτως; τί δ' ἱκάνετον, οὔ τι πάρος γε
λίην φοιτίζουσαι, ἐπεὶ περίεστε θεάων;"
55 τὴν δ' Ἥρη τοίοισιν ἀμειβομένη προσέειπεν·
 "κερτομέεις, νῶιν δὲ κέαρ συνορίνεται ἄτῃ.
ἤδη γὰρ ποταμῷ ἐνὶ Φάσιδι νῆα κατίσχει
Αἰσονίδης ἠδ' ἄλλοι, ὅσοι μετὰ κῶας ἕπονται·
τῶν ἤτοι πάντων μέν, ἐπεὶ πέλας ἔργον ὄρωρεν,
60 δείδιμεν ἐκπάγλως, περὶ δ' Αἰσονίδαο μάλιστα.
τὸν μὲν ἐγών, εἰ καί περ ἐς Ἅιδα ναυτίλληται
λυσόμενος χαλκέων Ἰξίονα νειόθι δεσμῶν,
ῥύσομαι, ὅσσον ἐμοῖσιν ἐνὶ σθένος ἔπλετο γυίοις,
ὄφρα μὴ ἐγγελάσῃ Πελίης κακὸν οἶτον ἀλύξας,
65 ὅς μ' ὑπερηνορέῃ θυέων ἀγέραστον ἔθηκεν.
καὶ δ' ἄλλως ἔτι καὶ πρὶν ἐμοὶ μέγα φίλατ' Ἰήσων,
ἐξότ' ἐπὶ προχοῇσιν ἅλις πλήθοντος Ἀναύρου

cavern in the Wandering island,[5] where he forged all his ingenious works by the blast of fire. She, then, sat all alone at home on an inlaid seat facing the door. Having let down her hair over her white shoulders on either side, she was parting it with a golden comb and was about to braid the long curls. But when she saw the goddesses before her, she stopped and called them inside, rose from her seat, and had them sit in chairs. And then she herself sat down and tied up her uncombed hair with her hands. With a smile she addressed them thus with wheedling words:

"Dear ladies, what purpose or need brings you here like this after so long? Why have you both come, being infrequent visitors in the past because you are most important goddesses?"

Hera, in answer, addressed her with these words:

"You can be sarcastic, but our hearts are being shaken by disaster, for already Jason is mooring his ship in the Phasis river with all the others who are following him in quest of the fleece. To be sure, we are extremely worried for all of them, since their task looms near, but especially for Jason. I would safeguard him, even if he voyaged to Hades to free Ixion from his bronze fetters down there,[6] with all the strength that is in my body, to insure that Pelias not make a mockery of me by escaping his evil doom, he who haughtily deprived me of honor in his sacrifices. Furthermore, even before that, Jason became greatly beloved by me, ever since he met me by the streams of the flooding

---

[5] Apollonius locates his workshop on one of the "Wandering" (Lipari) islands off the northeast coast of Sicily, whereas Homer had located it on Olympus.

[6] Ixion had tried to rape Hera and was bound to a wheel.

ἀνδρῶν εὐνομίης πειρωμένη ἀντεβόλησεν
θήρης ἐξανιών· νιφετῷ δ' ἐπαλύνετο πάντα
70 οὔρεα καὶ σκοπιαὶ περιμήκεες, οἱ δὲ κατ' αὐτῶν
χείμαρροι καναχηδὰ κυλινδόμενοι φορέοντο.
γρηὶ δέ μ' εἰσαμένην ὀλοφύρατο, καί μ' ἀναείρας
αὐτὸς ἑοῖς ὤμοισι διὲκ προαλὲς φέρεν ὕδωρ.
τῶ νύ μοι ἄλληκτον περιτίεται· οὐδέ κε λώβην
75 τίσειεν Πελίης, εἰ μὴ σύ γε νόστον ὀπάσσεις."
    ὣς ηὔδα. Κύπριν δ' ἐνεοστασίη λάβε μύθων.
ἅζετο δ' ἀντομένην Ἥρην ἕθεν εἰσορόωσα,
καί μιν ἔπειτ' ἀγανοῖσι προσέννεπεν ἥ γ' ἐπέεσσιν·
    "πότνα θεά, μή τοί τι κακώτερον ἄλλο πέλοιτο
80 Κύπριδος, εἰ δὴ σεῖο λιλαιομένης ἀθερίζω
ἢ ἔπος ἠέ τι ἔργον, ὅ κεν χέρες αἵδε κάμοιεν
ἠπεδαναί· καὶ μή τις ἀμοιβαίη χάρις ἔστω."
    ὣς ἔφαθ'· Ἥρη δ' αὖτις ἐπιφραδέως ἀγόρευσεν·
    "οὔ τι βίης χατέουσαι ἱκάνομεν οὐδέ τι χειρῶν,
85 ἀλλ' αὔτως ἀκέουσα τεῷ ἐπικέκλεο παιδὶ
παρθένον Αἰήτεω θέλξαι πόθῳ Αἰσονίδαο.
εἰ γάρ οἱ κείνη συμφράσσεται εὐμενέουσα,
ῥηιδίως μιν ἑλόντα δέρος χρύσειον ὀίω
νοστήσειν ἐς Ἰωλκόν, ἐπεὶ δολόεσσα τέτυκται."
90   ὣς ἄρ' ἔφη. Κύπρις δὲ μετ' ἀμφοτέρῃσιν ἔειπεν·
    "Ἥρη Ἀθηναίη τε, πίθοιτό κεν ὔμμι μάλιστα
ἢ ἐμοί. ὑμείων γὰρ ἀναιδήτῳ περ ἐόντι
τυτθή γ' αἰδὼς ἔσσετ' ἐν ὄμμασιν· αὐτὰρ ἐμεῖο
οὐκ ὄθεται, μάλα δ' αἰὲν ἐριδμαίνων ἀθερίζει.
95 καὶ δή οἱ μενέηνα, περισχομένη κακότητι,

Anaurus, when I was testing men's righteousness, and he was returning from the hunt. All the mountains and high peaks were being sprinkled with snow, and down from them torrents were tumbling in crashing cascades. And in my disguise as an old woman he took pity on me and lifting me onto his own shoulders proceeded to carry me through the rushing water. That is why he is ceaselessly held in highest honor by me—nor will Pelias pay for his outrage, unless you grant his return home."

Thus she spoke, and speechless amazement seized Cypris. She was awestruck to see Hera beseeching her, and then she addressed her with gentle words:

"Mighty goddess, may nothing be more vile to you than Cypris, if indeed, when you desire something, I slight you, either in word or in any deed which these hands might perform, weak as they are; and let there be no favor in return."

Thus she spoke, and again Hera judiciously replied:

"We have not come in need of force or strength of hands. No, just calmly call upon your son to enchant Aeetes' daughter with desire for Jason, for if she will give him kindly advice, I believe that he will readily seize the golden fleece and return to Iolcus, because she is very cunning."

Thus she spoke, and Cypris said to both of them:

"Hera and Athena, he would obey you much more than me, for impudent as he is, he will have at least a little respect in his eyes for you, whereas he pays no attention to me and incessantly picks a quarrel and belittles me. Moreover, vexed by his bad behavior, I became angry with him

---

81 αἴδε D: αἴ γε Ω

αὐτοῖσιν τόξοισι δυσηχέας ἆξαι ὀιστοὺς
ἀμφαδίην. τοῖον γὰρ ἐπηπείλησε χαλεφθείς·
εἰ μὴ τηλόθι χεῖρας, ἕως ἔτι θυμὸν ἐρύκει,
ἔξω ἐμάς, μετέπειτά γ' ἀτεμβοίμην ἑοὶ αὐτῇ."
100   ὣς φάτο· μείδησαν δὲ θεαὶ καὶ ἐσέδρακον ἄντην
ἀλλήλαις. ἡ δ' αὖτις ἀκηχεμένη προσέειπεν·
"ἄλλοις ἄλγεα τἀμὰ γέλως πέλει, οὐδέ τί με χρὴ
μυθεῖσθαι πάντεσσιν· ἅλις εἰδυῖα καὶ αὐτή.
νῦν δ' ἐπεὶ ὔμμι φίλον τόδε δὴ πέλει ἀμφοτέρῃσιν,
105   πειρήσω καί μιν μειλίξομαι, οὐδ' ἀπιθήσει."
ὣς φάτο· τὴν δ' Ἥρη ῥαδινῆς ἐπεμάσσατο
      χειρός,
ἦκα δὲ μειδιόωσα παραβλήδην προσέειπεν·
"οὕτω νῦν, Κυθέρεια, τόδε χρέος, ὡς ἀγορεύεις,
ἔρξον ἄφαρ· καὶ μή τι χαλέπτεο μηδ' ἐρίδαινε
110   χωομένη σῷ παιδί· μεταλλήξει γὰρ ὀπίσσω."
ἦ ῥα, καὶ ἔλλιπε θῶκον· ἐφωμάρτησε δ' Ἀθήνη·
ἐκ δ' ἴσαν ἄμφω ταί γε παλίσσυτοι. ἡ δὲ καὶ αὐτὴ
βῆ ῥ' ἴμεν Οὐλύμποιο κατὰ πτύχας, εἴ μιν ἐφεύροι.
εὗρε δὲ τόν γ' ἀπάνευθε Διὸς θαλερῇ ἐν ἀλωῇ,
115   οὐκ οἶον, μετὰ καὶ Γανυμήδεα, τόν ῥά ποτε Ζεὺς
οὐρανῷ ἐγκατένασσεν ἐφέστιον ἀθανάτοισιν,
κάλλεος ἱμερθείς. ἀμφ' ἀστραγάλοισι δὲ τώ γε
χρυσείοις, ἅ τε κοῦροι ὁμήθεες, ἑψιόωντο.
καί ῥ' ὁ μὲν ἤδη πάμπαν ἐνίπλεον ᾧ ὑπὸ μαζῷ
120   μάργος Ἔρως λαιῆς ὑπίσχανε χειρὸς ἀγοστόν,
ὀρθὸς ἐφεστηώς, γλυκερὸν δέ οἱ ἀμφὶ παρειὰς

and was determined to break his evil-sounding arrows, bow and all, before his very eyes, for in a tantrum he threatened that if I did not keep my hands off him while he still controlled his temper, I would thereafter have only myself to blame."

Thus she spoke, and the goddesses smiled and looked at each another. But in exasperation she spoke again:

"My troubles are a joke to others and I ought not tell them to everyone, for it is enough that I know them myself. But now, since this is pleasing to both of you, I will make an attempt and coax him, and he will not disobey."

Thus she spoke, and Hera took her slender hand and with a gentle smile said in reply:

"Now, Cytherea, do this task right away just as you propose, and do not be at all cross or quarrelsome with your son out of anger, for he will stop this in the future."

She spoke and left her seat. Athena accompanied her, and the two of them set out to go back. But Cypris herself went down the glens of Olympus to find her son. And she found him off in Zeus' fertile orchard, not alone, but with Ganymede, whom Zeus had once settled in heaven to live with the immortals, smitten with longing for his beauty. The two of them were playing for golden knucklebones, as boys who are playmates do. And by this time greedy Eros was holding the palm of his left hand completely full of them up under his breast, standing upright, and the sweet

χροιῆς θάλλεν ἔρευθος· ὁ δ' ἐγγύθεν ὀκλαδὸν ἧστο
σῖγα κατηφιόων· δοιὼ δ' ἔχεν, ἄλλον ἔτ' αὔτως
ἄλλῳ ἐπιπροϊείς, κεχόλωτο δὲ καγχαλόωντι.
125 καὶ μὴν τούς γε παρᾶσσον ἐπὶ προτέροισιν
            ὀλέσσας
βῆ κενεαῖς σὺν χερσὶν ἀμήχανος, οὐδ' ἐνόησεν
Κύπριν ἐπιπλομένην. ἡ δ' ἀντίη ἵστατο παιδός,
καί μιν ἄφαρ γναθμοῖο κατασχομένη προσέειπεν·
"τίπτ' ἐπιμειδιάᾳς, ἄφατον κακόν; ἦέ μιν αὔτως
130 ἤπαφες, οὐδὲ δίκῃ περιέπλεο νῆιν ἐόντα;
εἰ δ' ἄγε μοι πρόφρων τέλεσον χρέος, ὅττι κεν εἴπω,
καί κέν τοι ὀπάσαιμι Διὸς περικαλλὲς ἄθυρμα
κεῖνο, τό οἱ ποίησε φίλη τροφὸς Ἀδρήστεια
ἄντρῳ ἐν Ἰδαίῳ ἔτι νήπια κουρίζοντι,
135 σφαῖραν εὐτρόχαλον, τῆς οὐ σύ γε μείλιον ἄλλο
χειρῶν Ἡφαίστοιο κατακτεατίσσῃ ἄρειον.
χρύσεα μέν οἱ κύκλα τετεύχαται, ἀμφὶ δ' ἑκάστῳ
διπλόαι ἁψῖδες περιηγέες εἰλίσσονται·
κρυπταὶ δὲ ῥαφαί εἰσιν, ἕλιξ δ' ἐπιδέδρομε πάσαις
140 κυανέη· ἀτὰρ εἴ μιν ἑαῖς ἐνὶ χερσὶ βάλοιο,
ἀστὴρ ὣς φλεγέθοντα δι' ἠέρος ὁλκὸν ἵησιν.
τήν τοι ἐγὼν ὀπάσω· σὺ δὲ παρθένον Αἰήταο
θέλξον ὀιστεύσας ἐπ' Ἰήσονι· μηδέ τις ἔστω
ἀμβολίη, δὴ γάρ κεν ἀφαυροτέρη χάρις εἴη."
145   ὣς φάτο· τῷ δ' ἀσπαστὸν ἔπος γένετ' εἰσαΐοντι.
μείλια δ' ἔκβαλε πάντα, καὶ ἀμφοτέρῃσι χιτῶνος
νωλεμὲς ἔνθα καὶ ἔνθα θεᾶς ἔχεν ἀμφιμεμαρπώς·
λίσσετο δ' αἶψα πορεῖν αὐτοσχεδόν. ἡ δ' ἀγανοῖσιν

blush of his complexion bloomed on his cheeks. But the other boy sat crouched nearby, downcast in silence. He had two knucklebones left, which he threw one after the other still in vain, and was infuriated as the other laughed out loud. And then, after immediately losing these in addition to the others, he went away empty-handed and helpless, nor did he notice that Cypris had approached. She stood in front of her son and at once took hold of his chin and said:

"Why are you gloating, you unspeakable rascal? Is it because you cheated him as usual and unfairly triumphed over that naive child? Come, be kind to me and do the task I tell you and I will give you Zeus' gorgeous plaything, that one his dear nurse Adresteia made him when he was still a babbling infant in the Idaean cave—a perfectly round ball; no better toy will you get from the hands of Hephaestus. Its segments are made of gold and around each of them wind two circular bands; the seams are hidden, for a dark-blue spiral runs over them all. And if you toss it in your hands, it throws off a flaming trail through the air like a star. I will give it to you, but you must shoot Aeetes' daughter and enchant her with love for Jason. Let there be no delay, for then my gratitude would be less."

Thus she spoke, and welcome to him were the words he heard. He dropped all his playthings and with both hands grabbed hold of the goddess' tunic on both sides and clung tightly. He begged her to hand it over right away, then and

---

122 χροιῆς E: χροιῇ Ω
147 θεᾶς Ω: θεὰν Fränkel

ἀντομένη μύθοισιν ἐπειρύσσασα παρειὰς
150 κύσσε ποτισχομένη, καὶ ἀμείβετο μειδιόωσα·
    "ἴστω νῦν τόδε σεῖο φίλον κάρη ἠδ' ἐμὸν αὐτῆς·
ἦ μέν τοι δῶρόν γε παρέξομαι οὐδ' ἀπατήσω,
εἴ κεν ἐνισκίμψῃς κούρῃ βέλος Αἰήταο."

    φῆ· ὁ δ' ἄρ' ἀστραγάλους συναμήσατο, κὰδ δὲ
        φαεινῷ
155 μητρὸς ἑῆς εὖ πάντας ἀριθμήσας βάλε κόλπῳ.
αὐτίκα δ' ἰοδόκην χρυσέη περικάτθετο μίτρῃ
πρέμνῳ κεκλιμένην, ἀνὰ δ' ἀγκύλον εἵλετο τόξον.
βῆ δὲ διὲκ μεγάλοιο Διὸς πάγκαρπον ἀλωήν,
αὐτὰρ ἔπειτα πύλας ἐξήλυθεν Οὐλύμποιο
160 αἰθερίας. ἔνθεν δὲ καταιβάτις ἐστὶ κέλευθος
οὐρανίη· δοιὼ δὲ πόλον ἀνέχουσι κάρηνα
οὐρέων ἠλιβάτων, κορυφαὶ χθονός, ἧχί τ' ἀερθεὶς
ἠέλιος πρώτῃσιν ἐρεύθεται ἀκτίνεσσιν.
νειόθι δ' ἄλλοτε γαῖα φερέσβιος ἄστεά τ' ἀνδρῶν
165 φαίνετο καὶ ποταμῶν ἱεροὶ ῥόοι, ἄλλοτε δ' αὖτε
ἄκριες, ἀμφὶ δὲ πόντος ἀν' αἰθέρα πολλὸν ἰόντι.

    ἥρωες δ' ἀπάνευθεν ἑῆς ἐπὶ σέλμασι νηὸς
ἐν ποταμῷ καθ' ἕλος λελοχημένοι ἠγορόωντο.
αὐτὸς δ' Αἰσονίδης μετεφώνεεν· οἱ δ' ὑπάκουον
170 ἠρέμα ᾗ ἐνὶ χώρῃ ἐπισχερὼ ἑδριόωντες·

    "ὦ φίλοι, ἤτοι ἐγὼ μὲν ὅ μοι ἐπιανδάνει αὐτῷ
ἐξερέω, τοῦ δ' ὕμμι τέλος κρηῆναι ἔοικεν.

---

158 μεγάλοιο Gerhard, Fränkel e Π[20] μεγαλοιο θ[: μεγά-
ροιο Ω

there, but she entreated him with gentle words, drew his cheeks to her, held him tight and kissed him, and replied with a smile:

"Let my witness now be this dear head of yours and my very own, that I will truly give you that gift and not cheat you, if you will strike Aeetes' daughter with your arrow."

She spoke, and he gathered up his dice and, after carefully counting all of them, tossed them into his mother's radiant lap. At once he slung on by its golden strap his quiver that had been leaning against a tree-trunk and took up his curved bow. He traversed the fruit-filled orchard of mighty Zeus and then passed through the ethereal gates of Olympus. From there a path descends from heaven; and two peaks of lofty mountains uphold the sky, the highest points on earth, where the risen sun grows red with its first rays. And beneath him at times appeared life-sustaining earth and cities of men and divine streams of rivers, and then at other times mountain peaks, while all around was the sea as he traveled through the vast sky.

But the heroes,[7] remaining apart in ambush on the benches of their ship within the backwater of the river, were holding an assembly. Jason himself was speaking, while they listened in silence, each sitting in place row upon row:

"My friends, I will state what I myself favor, but it befits you to accomplish its end. For in common is our need, and

[7] This returns to the situation at 3.6–7.

161 πόλον Platt: πόλοι Ω
166 αἰθέρα E²: αἰθέρι Ω

ξυνὴ γὰρ χρειώ, ξυνοὶ δέ τε μῦθοι ἔασιν
πᾶσιν ὁμῶς· ὁ δὲ σῖγα νόον βουλήν τ' ἀπερύκων
175 ἴστω καὶ νόστου τόνδε στόλον οἶος ἀπούρας.
ὦλλοι μὲν κατὰ νῆα σὺν ἔντεσι μίμνεθ' ἔκηλοι·
αὐτὰρ ἐγὼν ἐς δώματ' ἐλεύσομαι Αἰήταο,
υἷας ἑλὼν Φρίξοιο δύο τ' ἐπὶ τοῖσιν ἑταίρους.
πειρήσω δ' ἐπέεσσι παροίτερον ἀντιβολήσας,
180 εἴ κ' ἐθέλοι φιλότητι δέρος χρύσειον ὀπάσσαι,
ἦε καὶ οὔ, πίσυνος δὲ βίῃ μετιόντας ἀτίσσει.
ὧδε γὰρ ἐξ αὐτοῖο πάρος κακότητα δαέντες
φρασσόμεθ' εἴτ' ἄρηι συνοισόμεθ' εἴτε τις ἄλλη
μῆτις ἐπίρροθος ἔσται ἐεργομένοισιν αὐτῆς.
185 μηδ' αὔτως ἀλκῇ, πρὶν ἔπεσσί γε πειρηθῆναι,
τόνδ' ἀπαμείρωμεν σφέτερον κτέρας· ἀλλὰ πάροιθεν
λωίτερον μύθῳ μιν ἀρέσσασθαι μετιόντας.
πολλάκι τοι ῥέα μῦθος, ὅ κεν μόλις ἐξανύσειεν
ἠνορέη, τόδ' ἔρεξε κατὰ χρέος, ᾗ περ ἐῴκει
190 πρηΰνας. ὁ δὲ καί ποτ' ἀμύμονα Φρίξον ἔδεκτο
μητρυιῆς φεύγοντα δόλον πατρός τε θυηλάς,
πάντες ἐπεὶ πάντῃ, καὶ ὅ τις μάλα κύντατος
ἀνδρῶν,
Ξεινίου αἰδεῖται Ζηνὸς θέμιν ἠδ' ἀλεγίζει."
ὣς φάτ'· ἐπήνησαν δὲ νέοι ἔπος Αἰσονίδαο
195 πασσυδίῃ, οὐδ' ἔσκε παρὲξ ὅ τις ἄλλο κελεύοι.
καὶ τότ' ἄρ' υἷας Φρίξου Τελαμῶνά θ' ἕπεσθαι

178 τ' SpcG: δ' mSac

common to all alike is the right of speech. And if anyone withholds his thoughts and counsel in silence, let him know that he, and he alone, deprives this expedition of its return home. The rest of you, then, remain quietly with your weapons on the ship, but I shall go to the palace of Aeetes, taking along Phrixus' sons[8] and two comrades as well. Upon meeting him I will first test him with words to see if he might be willing to hand over the golden fleece out of friendship, or else not, but trusting in his power will treat our coming lightly. For in that way, having first learned his wickedness[9] from himself, we will consider whether to engage him in battle or whether some other plan will aid us if we refrain from fighting. Let us not merely by force, before at least testing him with words, deprive him of his own possession. No, first it is better to meet with him and seek his favor with speech. Often, you know, that which prowess could scarcely accomplish, speech easily brings to a proper conclusion, when it is appropriately soothing. And once before he took in blameless Phrixus, who was fleeing his stepmother's treachery and his father's sacrifices,[10] since all men everywhere— even the most shameless of men—respect the rule of Zeus Xenius and heed it."

Thus he spoke, and the young men approved Jason's words with one voice, nor was there anyone who urged something different. Thereupon he summoned Phrixus'

---

[8] Argus, Cytissorus, Phrontis, and Melas (see 2.1155–1156).

[9] Some edd. prefer *our distress*.

[10] His wicked stepmother Ino bribed the envoys to the Delphic oracle to declare that Athamas should sacrifice Phrixus to relieve a famine (Apollodorus, *Bibliotheca* 1.9.1).

ὦρσε καὶ Αὐγείην· αὐτὸς δ' ἕλεν Ἑρμείαο
σκῆπτρον. ἄφαρ δ' ἄρα νηὸς ὑπὲρ δόνακάς τε καὶ
   ὕδωρ
χέρσονδ' ἐξαπέβησαν ἐπὶ θρωσμοῦ πεδίοιο.
200 Κίρκαιον τόδε που κικλήσκεται· ἔνθα δὲ πολλαὶ
ἑξείης πρόμαλοί τε καὶ ἰτέαι ἐκπεφύασιν,
τῶν καὶ ἐπ' ἀκροτάτων νέκυες σειρῇσι κρέμανται
δέσμιοι. εἰσέτι νῦν γὰρ ἄγος Κόλχοισιν ὄρωρεν
ἀνέρας οἰχομένους πυρὶ καιέμεν· οὐδ' ἐνὶ γαίῃ
205 ἔστι θέμις στείλαντας ὕπερθ' ἐπὶ σῆμα χέεσθαι,
ἀλλ' ἐν ἀδεψήτοισι κατειλύσαντε βοείαις
δενδρέων ἐξάπτειν ἑκὰς ἄστεος. ἠέρι δ' ἴσην
καὶ χθὼν ἔμμορεν αἶσαν, ἐπεὶ χθονὶ ταρχύουσιν
θηλυτέρας· ἡ γάρ τε δίκη θεσμοῖο τέτυκται.
210   τοῖσι δὲ νισσομένοις Ἥρη φίλα μητιόωσα
ἠέρα πουλὺν ἐφῆκε δι' ἄστεος, ὄφρα λάθοιεν
Κόλχων μυρίον ἔθνος ἐς Αἰήταο κιόντες.
ὦκα δ' ὅτ' ἐκ πεδίοιο πόλιν καὶ δώμαθ' ἵκοντο
Αἰήτεω, τότε δ' αὖτις ἀπεσκέδασεν νέφος Ἥρη.
215 ἔσταν δ' ἐν προμολῇσι τεθηπότες ἕρκε' ἄνακτος
εὐρείας τε πύλας καὶ κίονας, οἳ περὶ τοίχους
ἑξείης ἄνεχον· θριγκὸς δ' ἐφύπερθε δόμοιο
λαΐνεος χαλκέῃσιν ἐπὶ γλυφίδεσσιν ἀρήρει.
εὔκηλοι δ' ὑπὲρ οὐδὸν ἔπειτ' ἔβαν. ἄγχι δὲ τοῖο
220 ἡμερίδες χλοεροῖσι καταστεφέες πετάλοισιν
ὑψοῦ ἀειρόμεναι μέγ' ἐθήλεον, αἱ δ' ὑπὸ τῇσιν
ἀέναοι κρῆναι πίσυρες ῥέον, ἃς ἐλάχηνεν
Ἥφαιστος· καί ῥ' ἡ μὲν ἀναβλύεσκε γάλακτι,

232

sons, along with Telamon and Augeas, to accompany him, and he himself took Hermes' scepter. Then at once they passed from the ship to dry land, beyond the reeds and water, onto the rising ground of the plain. This plain is, I believe,[11] called Circe's, where many tamarisks and willows grow in rows, on whose topmost branches hang dead bodies bound with cords. For to this day it is a sacrilege for Colchians to cremate men who have passed on, nor is it permitted to bury them in the ground and raise a mound over them, but rather to wrap them in untanned oxhides and suspend them from trees far from the city. And the earth shares an equal portion with the air, since they bury their women in the ground. For that is the manner of their custom.

As they proceeded, Hera with friendly devising placed a thick mist throughout the city, so they might elude the numberless race of Colchians as they went to Aeetes' palace. But as soon as they came from the plain to the city and to the palace of Aeetes, Hera then again dispersed the cloud. They stood in the vestibule, amazed at the king's courtyard and at the wide gates and columns that rose up in rows around the walls; and up above the house a stone entablature rested upon bronze capitals. Then they calmly crossed the threshold. Near it, vines covered with green leaves rose high up in full bloom, and beneath them ran four ever-flowing springs, which Hephaestus had dug. One

---

[11] Or, reading τό γε δή, *This plain is in fact*.

---

198 ἄρα E: ἀνὰ Ω   200 τόδε που Ω: τό γε δή (vel τότε δή) Et. Magn. et Et. Gen.   209 τε Brunck: κε Ω

ἡ δ᾽ οἴνῳ, τριτάτη δὲ θυώδεϊ νᾶεν ἀλοιφῇ·
225 ἡ δ᾽ ἄρ᾽ ὕδωρ προρέεσκε, τὸ μέν ποθι δυομένῃσιν
θέρμετο Πληιάδεσσιν, ἀμοιβηδὶς δ᾽ ἀνιούσαις
κρυστάλλῳ ἴκελον κοίλης ἀνεκήκιε πέτρης.
τοῖ᾽ ἄρ᾽ ἐνὶ μεγάροισι Κυταιέος Αἰήταο
τεχνήεις Ἥφαιστος ἐμήσατο θέσκελα ἔργα.
230 καί οἱ χαλκόποδας ταύρους κάμε, χάλκεα δέ σφεων
ἦν στόματ᾽, ἐκ δὲ πυρὸς δεινὸν σέλας ἀμπνείεσκον·
πρὸς δὲ καὶ αὐτόγυον στιβαροῦ ἀδάμαντος ἄροτρον
ἤλασεν, Ἡελίῳ τίνων χάριν, ὅς ῥά μιν ἵπποις
δέξατο Φλεγραίῃ κεκμηότα δηιοτῆτι.
235 ἔνθα δὲ καὶ μέσσαυλος ἐλήλατο, τῇ δ᾽ ἐπὶ πολλαὶ
δικλίδες εὐπηγεῖς θάλαμοί τ᾽ ἔσαν ἔνθα καὶ ἔνθα·
δαιδαλέη δ᾽ αἴθουσα παρὲξ ἑκάτερθε τέτυκτο.
λέχρις δ᾽ αἰπύτεροι δόμοι ἕστασαν ἀμφοτέρωθεν·
τῶν ἤτοι ἄλλον μέν, ὅ τις καὶ ὑπείροχος ἦεν,
240 κρείων Αἰήτης σὺν ἑῇ ναίεσκε δάμαρτι,
ἄλλον δ᾽ Ἄψυρτος ναῖεν πάις Αἰήταο.
τὸν μὲν Καυκασίη νύμφη τέκεν Ἀστερόδεια,
πρίν περ κουριδίην θέσθαι Εἰδυῖαν ἄκοιτιν,
Τηθύος Ὠκεανοῦ τε πανοπλοτάτην γεγαυῖαν·
245 καί μιν Κόλχων υἷες ἐπωνυμίην Φαέθοντα
ἔκλεον, οὕνεκα πᾶσι μετέπρεπεν ἠιθέοισιν.
τοὺς δ᾽ ἔχον ἀμφίπολοί τε καὶ Αἰήταο θύγατρες
ἄμφω, Χαλκιόπη Μήδειά τε. τῇ μὲν ἄρ᾽ οἵ γε

239 ἄλλον SE: ἄλλων LAGD: ἄλλῳ WB²O
241 ἄλλον wD: ἄλλῳ m
248 post hunc versum lacunam statuit Madvig

234

gushed with milk, another with wine, the third flowed with fragrant oil, while the last poured forth water, which, it is said, grew warm when the Pleiades set,[12] but in turn at their rising bubbled forth like ice from the hollow rock. Such, then, were the wondrous works in Cytaean[13] Aeetes' palace that Hephaestus the craftsman had contrived. And he fashioned for him bronze-hooved bulls, and bronze were their mouths, through which they breathed a fierce blast of fire. He also forged a plow, all of one piece, made of strong adamant, repaying a favor to Helius, who had taken him in his chariot when he was exhausted from the fighting at Phlegra.[14] And here a central door was forged,[15] and next to it were many well-built double doors and rooms in both directions, while an ornate colonnade ran all along both sides. At angles on either side stood taller buildings. In the loftiest one lived King Aeetes with his wife, while in the other lived Aeetes' son Apsyrtus, whom the Caucasian nymph Asterodeia bore before Aeetes had made Eidyia, the youngest daughter of Tethys and Ocean, his wedded wife. And the sons of the Colchians called him by the name Phaethon,[16] because he outshone all the young men. But in the rooms lived the servants and Aeetes' two daughters, Chalciope and Medea. It was the latter whom they [en-

[12] The Pleiades set in November and rise in May.

[13] I.e. Colchian.

[14] In the Gigantomachy. Helius was Aeetes' father.

[15] This metal door led from the courtyard to the main hall (*megaron*). On each side of the door were rooms within the portico.

[16] Apsyrtus is called Phaethon ("Shining One"), appropriately for a descendant of Helius; cf. also Pasiphae, ("Shining to All").

* * *

ἐκ θαλάμου θάλαμόνδε κασιγνήτην μετιοῦσαν.
250 Ἥρη γάρ μιν ἔρυκε δόμῳ· πρὶν δ' οὔ τι θάμιζεν
ἐν μεγάροις, Ἑκάτης δὲ πανήμερος ἀμφεπονεῖτο
νηόν, ἐπεί ῥα θεῆς αὐτὴ πέλεν ἀρήτειρα.
καί σφεας ὡς ἴδεν ἆσσον, ἀνίαχεν. ὀξὺ δ' ἄκουσεν
Χαλκιόπη· δμωαὶ δὲ ποδῶν προπάροιθε βαλοῦσαι
255 νήματα καὶ κλωστῆρας ἀολλέες ἔκτοθι πᾶσαι
ἔδραμον· ἡ δ' ἅμα τῇσιν ἑοὺς υἱῆας ἰδοῦσα
ὑψοῦ χάρματι χεῖρας ἀνέσχεθεν· ὡς δὲ καὶ αὐτοὶ
μητέρα δεξιόωντο καὶ ἀμφαγάπαζον ἰδόντες
γηθόσυνοι· τοῖον δὲ κινυρομένη φάτο μῦθον·
260 "ἔμπης οὐκ ἄρ' ἐμέλλετ' ἀκηδείῃ με λιπόντες
τηλόθι πλάγξασθαι, μετὰ δ' ὑμέας ἔτραπεν αἶσα.
δειλὴ ἐγώ, οἷον πόθον Ἑλλάδος ἔκποθεν ἄτης
λευγαλέης Φρίξοιο ἐφημοσύνῃσιν ἕλεσθε
πατρός. ὁ μὲν θνῄσκων στυγερὰς ἐπετέλλετ' ἀνίας
265 ἡμετέρῃ κραδίῃ· τί δέ κεν πόλιν Ὀρχομενοῖο,
ὅς τις ὅδ' Ὀρχομενός, κτεάνων Ἀθάμαντος ἕκητι
μητέρ' ἐὴν ἀχέουσαν ἀποπρολιπόντες ἵκοισθε;"
       ὣς ἔφατ'· Αἰήτης δὲ πανύστατος ὦρτο θύραζε,
ἐκ δ' αὐτὴ Εἴδυια δάμαρ κίεν Αἰήταο,
270 Χαλκιόπης ἀίουσα. τὸ δ' αὐτίκα πᾶν ὁμάδοιο
ἕρκος ἐπεπλήθει· τοὶ μὲν μέγαν ἀμφεπένοντο

256 τῇσιν Ω: τοῖσιν AD   263 ἐφημοσύνῃσιν ἕλεσθε
Huet: ἐφημοσύνῃσι νέεσθαι mG: ἐφημοσύνῃσι νέεσθε SD:
ἐφημοσύνῃσιν ἕθεσθε Fränkel ex Π21 -ῃ[σι]ν̣ε̣ν̣εσ̣[θε

countered]¹⁷ going from one room to another to visit her sister. For Hera had detained her at home, though before that she was not often in the palace, but spent all day tending Hecate's temple, since she herself was the priestess of the goddess. And when she saw them approaching, she screamed. Chalciope heard it clearly, and the maids threw their yarn and spindles at their feet and all ran out in a throng. And Chalciope, in their midst,¹⁸ saw her sons and threw high her hands in joy; and likewise, when they saw their mother, they held out their arms and embraced her joyfully. And she sobbed as she said this:

"So after all then, you were not going to abandon me in your thoughtlessness and wander far away, but fate has turned you back. Poor me! What a longing for Hellas you conceived from some dreadful delusion on the orders of your father Phrixus! As he was dying, he gave commands that brought terrible pains to my heart. Why should you go to the city of Orchomenus, whoever that Orchomenus is, to get Athamas' possessions, and leave your mother in grief?"

Thus she spoke. And last of all Aeetes came forth, and Eidyia herself, Aeetes' wife, came out when she heard Chalciope. Immediately the whole courtyard was filled with noise. Of the many servants, some were busy prepar-

---

¹⁷ A line has apparently dropped out here.
¹⁸ Or, reading τοῖσιν, *And Chalciope saw her sons among them* (the Argonauts).

---

264 ἐπετέλλετ' Π²¹RQ: ἐπετείλατ' Ω

ταῦρον ἅλις δμῶες, τοὶ δὲ ξύλα κάγκανα χαλκῷ
κόπτον, τοὶ δὲ λοετρὰ πυρὶ ζέον· οὐδέ τις ἦεν,
ὃς καμάτου μεθίεσκεν ὑποδρήσσων βασιλῆι.

275　　τόφρα δ᾽ Ἔρως πολιοῖο δι᾽ ἠέρος ἷξεν ἄφαντος,
τετρηχώς, οἷόν τε νέαις ἐπὶ φορβάσιν οἶστρος
τέλλεται, ὅν τε μύωπα βοῶν κλείουσι νομῆες.
ὦκα δ᾽ ὑπὸ φλιὴν προδόμῳ ἔνι τόξα τανύσσας
ἰοδόκης ἀβλῆτα πολύστονον ἐξέλετ᾽ ἰόν.

280　　ἐκ δ᾽ ὅ γε καρπαλίμοισι λαθὼν ποσὶν οὐδὸν ἄμειψεν
ὀξέα δενδίλλων· αὐτῷ δ᾽ ὑπὸ βαιὸς ἐλυσθεὶς
Αἰσονίδῃ γλυφίδας μέσσῃ ἐνικάτθετο νευρῇ,
ἰθὺς δ᾽ ἀμφοτέρῃσι διασχόμενος παλάμῃσιν
ἧκ᾽ ἐπὶ Μηδείῃ· τὴν δ᾽ ἀμφασίη λάβε θυμόν.

285　　αὐτὸς δ᾽ ὑψορόφοιο παλιμπετὲς ἐκ μεγάροιο
καγχαλόων ἤιξε· βέλος δ᾽ ἐνεδαίετο κούρῃ
νέρθεν ὑπὸ κραδίῃ φλογὶ εἴκελον. ἀντία δ᾽ αἰεὶ
βάλλεν ἐπ᾽ Αἰσονίδην ἀμαρύγματα, καί οἱ ἄηντο
στηθέων ἐκ πυκιναὶ καμάτῳ φρένες· οὐδέ τιν᾽ ἄλλην

290　　μνῆστιν ἔχεν, γλυκερῇ δὲ κατείβετο θυμὸν ἀνίῃ.
ὡς δὲ γυνὴ μαλερῷ περὶ κάρφεα χεύετο δαλῷ
χερνῆτις, τῇ περ ταλασήια ἔργα μέμηλεν,
ὥς κεν ὑπωρόφιον νύκτωρ σέλας ἐντύναιτο
ἄγχι μάλ᾽ ἐζομένη· τὸ δ᾽ ἀθέσφατον ἐξ ὀλίγοιο

295　　δαλοῦ ἀνεγρόμενον σὺν κάρφεα πάντ᾽ ἀμαθύνει·
τοῖος ὑπὸ κραδίῃ εἰλυμένος αἴθετο λάθρῃ

288 ἐπ᾽ wD: ὑπ᾽ m
294 ἐζομένη Hemsterhuis: ἐγρομένη Ω

238

ing a great bull, others were chopping dry kindling with bronze axes, and others were boiling bath water on a fire. And there was no one who was slacking from toil in serving the king.

In the meantime, Eros arrived unseen through the bright air, full of turmoil,[19] as when a stinging fly attacks grazing young heifers—the one cowherds call the gadfly. And quickly, at the base of the doorpost in the vestibule, he strung his bow and from his quiver took an arrow never shot before, bringer of much sorrow. From there, with swift steps he crossed the threshold unobserved, as he looked keenly around. He crouched down small at the feet of Jason himself, placed the arrow's notches in the center of the bowstring, pulled it straight apart with both hands, and shot at Medea; and speechless amazement seized her heart. He darted back out of the high-roofed hall, laughing out loud, and the arrow burned deep down in the girl's heart like a flame. She continually cast bright glances straight at Jason, and wise thoughts fluttered from her breast in her distress. She could remember nothing else, for her heart was flooding with sweet pain. And as when a woman piles twigs around a flaming brand, a working woman whose task is wool-spinning, so as to furnish light under her roof at night as she sits close by,[20] and the flame rises prodigiously from the small brand and consumes all the twigs together—such was the destructive love that

[19] Some consider τετρηχώς transitive, *causing turmoil*.
[20] Or, reading ἐγρομένη, *when she awakes very early*.

οὖλος ἔρως· ἀπαλὰς δὲ μετετρωπᾶτο παρειὰς
ἐς χλόον, ἄλλοτ᾽ ἔρευθος, ἀκηδείῃσι νόοιο.

δμῶες δ᾽ ὁππότε δή σφιν ἐπαρτέα θῆκαν ἐδωδήν,
300 αὐτοί τε λιαροῖσιν ἐφαιδρύναντο λοετροῖς,
ἀσπασίως δόρπῳ τε ποτῆτί τε θυμὸν ἄρεσσαν.
ἐκ δὲ τοῦ Αἰήτης σφετέρης ἐρέεινε θυγατρὸς
υἷας τοίοισι παρηγορέων ἐπέεσσιν·

"παιδὸς ἐμῆς κοῦροι Φρίξοιό τε, τὸν περὶ πάντων
305 ξείνων ἡμετέροισιν ἐνὶ μεγάροισιν ἔτισα,
πῶς Αἶάνδε νέεσθε παλίσσυτοι; ἦέ τις ἄτη
σωομένοις μεσσηγὺς ἐνέκλασεν; οὐ μὲν ἐμεῖο
πείθεσθε προφέροντος ἀπείρονα μέτρα κελεύθου.
ᾔδειν γάρ ποτε πατρὸς ἐν ἅρμασιν Ἠελίοιο
310 δινεύσας, ὅτ᾽ ἐμεῖο κασιγνήτην ἐκόμιζεν
Κίρκην ἑσπερίης εἴσω χθονός, ἐκ δ᾽ ἱκόμεσθα
ἀκτὴν ἠπείρου Τυρσηνίδος, ἔνθ᾽ ἔτι νῦν περ
ναιετάει, μάλα πολλὸν ἀπόπροθι Κολχίδος αἴης.
ἀλλὰ τί μύθων ἦδος; ἃ δ᾽ ἐν ποσὶν ὑμῖν ὄρωρεν,
315 εἴπατ᾽ ἀριφραδέως, ἠδ᾽ οἵ τινες οἵδ᾽ ἐφέπονται
ἀνέρες, ὅππῃ τε γλαφυρῆς ἐκ νηὸς ἔβητε."

τοῖά μιν ἐξερέοντα κασιγνήτων προπάροιθεν
Ἄργος, ὑποδδείσας ἀμφὶ στόλῳ Αἰσονίδαο,
μειλιχίως προσέειπεν, ἐπεὶ προγενέστερος ἦεν·
320 "Αἰήτη, κείνην μὲν ἄφαρ διέχευαν ἄελλαι
ζαχρηεῖς, αὐτοὺς δ᾽ ὑπὸ δούρασι πεπτηῶτας
νήσου Ἐνναλίοιο ποτὶ ξερὸν ἔκβαλε κῦμα
λυγαίῃ ὑπὸ νυκτί· θεὸς δέ τις ἄμμ᾽ ἐσάωσεν·
οὐδὲ γὰρ αἳ τὸ πάροιθεν ἐρημαίην κατὰ νῆσον

curled beneath her heart and burned in secret. And her tender cheeks turned now pale, now red, in the distraction of her mind.

Now when the servants had set out the feast prepared for them and they had refreshed themselves with warm baths, they gladly satisfied their hearts with food and drink. Thereafter Aeetes questioned his daughter's sons, encouraging them with these words:

"Sons of my daughter and of Phrixus, whom I honored above all other guests in my palace, how is it that you have come back to Aea? Did some disaster thwart you as you were hastening on your way? Indeed, you would not believe me when I told of the immense distance of the trip. For I noted it once after taking a ride in my father Helius' chariot, when he was taking my sister Circe to the western land and we came to the coast of the Tyrrhenian mainland,[21] where she dwells to this day, very far from the Colchian land.[22] But what pleasure is there in words? Tell me plainly what things got in your way, and who these men are that accompany you, and where you came ashore from your hollow ship."

Such were his questions, and Argus, fearing for the expedition of Jason, answered him gently, ahead of his brothers, for he was the eldest.

"Aeetes, furious storms soon broke that ship apart, and as we huddled on timbers a wave cast us forth onto the dry land of Enyalius'[23] island in the dark of night. And some god saved us, for even those birds of Ares that formerly

---

[21] On the west coast of Italy.
[22] Or *Colchian Aea.*
[23] A title of Ares.

325 ηὐλίζοντ' ὄρνιθες Ἀρήιαι, οὐδ' ἔτι κείνας
εὕρομεν, ἀλλ' οἵ γ' ἄνδρες ἀπήλασαν, ἐξαποβάντες
νηὸς ἑῆς προτέρῳ ἐνὶ ἤματι· καί σφ' ἀπέρυκεν
ἡμέας οἰκτείρων Ζηνὸς νόος ἠέ τις αἶσα·
αὐτίκ' ἐπεὶ καὶ βρῶσιν ἅλις καὶ εἵματ' ἔδωκαν,
330 οὔνομά τε Φρίξοιο περικλεὲς εἰσαΐοντες
ἠδ' αὐτοῖο σέθεν· μετὰ γὰρ τεὸν ἄστυ νέονται.
χρειὼ δ' ἢν ἐθέλῃς ἐξίδμεναι, οὔ σ' ἐπικεύσω.
τόνδε τις ἱέμενος πάτρης ἀπάνευθεν ἐλάσσαι
καὶ κτεάνων βασιλεύς, περιώσιον οὕνεκεν ἀλκῇ
335 σφωιτέρῃ πάντεσσι μετέπρεπεν Αἰολίδῃσιν,
πέμπει δεῦρο νέεσθαι, ἀμήχανον· οὐδ' ὑπαλύξειν
στεῦται ἀμειλίκτοιο Διὸς θυμαλγέα μῆνιν
καὶ χόλον οὐδ' ἄτλητον ἄγος Φρίξοιό τε ποινὰς
Αἰολιδέων γενεήν, πρὶν ἐς Ἑλλάδα κῶας ἱκέσθαι.
340 νῆα δ' Ἀθηναίη Παλλὰς κάμεν, οὐ μάλα τοίην,
οἷαί περ Κόλχοισι μετ' ἀνδράσι νῆες ἔασιν,
τάων αἰνοτάτης ἐπεκύρσαμεν· ἤλιθα γάρ μιν
λάβρον ὕδωρ πνοιή τε διέτμαγεν. ἡ δ' ἐνὶ γόμφοις
ἴσχεται, ἢν καὶ πᾶσαι ἐπιβρίσωσιν ἄελλαι·
345 ἶσον δ' ἐξ ἀνέμοιο θέει καὶ ὅτ' ἀνέρες αὐτοὶ
νωλεμέως χείρεσσιν ἐπισπέρχωσιν ἐρετμοῖς.
τῇ δ' ἐναγειράμενος Παναχαΐδος εἴ τι φέριστον
ἡρώων, τεὸν ἄστυ μετήλυθε, πόλλ' ἐπαληθεὶς

---

24 Some edd. take περιώσιον with ἱέμενος in the preceding
clause, *exceedingly eager.*
25 The thematic word ἀμήχανον can be masculine (referring

242

nested on the deserted island we found no longer there, but these men had driven them off, having disembarked from their ship the previous day. And the will of Zeus, taking pity on us, or some fate, detained them there, for they immediately gave us both food and clothing in abundance upon hearing the famous name of Phrixus—and yours as well, for they are on their way to your city. And if you want to know their mission, I shall not conceal it from you. A certain king, eager to drive this man far away from his homeland and possessions because he surpassed by far[24] all the Aeolidae with his prowess, sends him to voyage here, all helpless.[25] And the king asserts that the race of the Aeolidae will not escape from the heart-grieving wrath and anger of implacable Zeus nor the unbearable pollution and retribution stemming from Phrixus,[26] until the fleece comes to Hellas. But Pallas Athena built their ship, one not at all like the ships found among the Colchian people—the worst one of which we happened to have, for the violent sea and wind completely demolished it. But theirs holds firm in its wooden pegs, even when all the storm-winds bear down on it, and it runs equally well by wind as when the men themselves propel it unceasingly by rowing with their hands. Having gathered on it the best of the heroes from all of Achaea, he has come to your city, after wander-

---

to τόνδε, this man, Jason), "him, being helpless (either to refuse or to accomplish such a mission)" or neuter (referring to the mission), "it, being impossible."

[26] For Jason's mission to atone for the attempted sacrifice of Phrixus, see 2.1194–1195.

ἄστεα καὶ πελάγη στυγερῆς ἁλός, εἴ οἱ ὀπάσσαις.
350 αὐτῷ δ' ὥς κεν ἅδῃ, τὼς ἔσσεται· οὐ γὰρ ἱκάνει
χερσὶ βιησόμενος, μέμονεν δέ τοι ἄξια τίσειν
δωτίνης, ἀίων ἐμέθεν μέγα δυσμενέοντας
Σαυρομάτας, τοὺς σοῖσιν ὑπὸ σκήπτροισι
     δαμάσσει.
εἰ δὲ καὶ οὔνομα δῆθεν ἐπιθύεις γενεήν τε
355 ἴδμεναι, οἵ τινές εἰσιν, ἕκαστά γε μυθησαίμην.
τόνδε μέν, οἷό περ οὕνεκ' ἀφ' Ἑλλάδος ὧλλοι
     ἄγερθεν,
κλείουσ' Αἴσονος υἱὸν Ἰήσονα Κρηθεΐδαο·
εἰ δ' αὐτοῦ Κρηθῆος ἐτήτυμόν ἐστι γενέθλης,
οὕτω κεν γνωτὸς πατρώιος ἄμμι πέλοιτο·
360 ἄμφω γὰρ Κρηθεὺς Ἀθάμας τ' ἔσαν Αἰόλου υἷες,
Φρίξος δ' αὖτ' Ἀθάμαντος ἔην πάις Αἰολίδαο.
τόνδε δ' ἄρ', Ἡλίου γόνον ἔμμεναι εἴ τιν' ἀκούεις,
δέρκεαι Αὐγείην· Τελαμὼν δ' ὅ γε, κυδίστοιο
Αἰακοῦ ἐκγεγαώς, Ζεὺς δ' Αἰακὸν αὐτὸς ἔτικτεν.
365 ὣς δὲ καὶ ὧλλοι πάντες, ὅσοι συνέπονται ἑταῖροι,
ἀθανάτων υἷές τε καὶ υἱωνοὶ γεγάασιν."
     τοῖα παρέννεπεν Ἄργος· ἄναξ δ' ἐπεχώσατο
        μύθοις
εἰσαΐων, ὑψοῦ δὲ χόλῳ φρένες ἠερέθοντο.
φῆ δ' ἐπαλαστήσας· μενέαινε δὲ παισὶ μάλιστα
370 Χαλκιόπης, τῶν γάρ σφε μετελθέμεν οὕνεκ' ἐώλπει·
ἐκ δέ οἱ ὄμματ' ἔλαμψεν ὑπ' ὀφρύσιν ἱεμένοιο·
     "οὐκ ἄφαρ ὀφθαλμῶν μοι ἀπόπροθι, λωβητῆρες,
νεῖσθ' αὐτοῖσι δόλοισι παλίσσυτοι ἔκτοθι γαίης,

ing to many cities and on the depths of the loathsome sea, in hopes that you will give it to him. And as you yourself prefer, so shall it be, for he does not come to use force of arms, but is eager to give you worthy recompense for the gift—having heard from me that the Sauromatae are bitter enemies of yours, he will subdue them beneath your scepter. And if indeed you also desire to know the names and lineage of these men, I will tell you everything. This man on whose behalf the others gathered from Hellas, they call Jason, son of Aeson who was Cretheus' son. And if he truly is from the race of Cretheus himself, then he would be our kinsman on our father's side, for Cretheus and Athamas were both sons of Aeolus, and Phrixus in turn was the son of Athamas who was Aeolus' son. And this man you see here, if you have heard tell of a son of Helius, is Augeas, and this is Telamon, son of most glorious Aeacus, and Zeus himself fathered Aeacus. And likewise all the other comrades who follow him are sons or grandsons of immortals."

Saying such things, Argus sought to win him over, but the king became furious at the words he was hearing and his mind rose high in anger. He spoke full of wrath and was especially vexed at Chalciope's sons, because he thought it was on their behalf that the strangers had come. His eyes flashed out beneath his eyebrows in his rage:

"Won't you get out of my sight at once, you scoundrels, and go back, deceptions and all, from this land before one

πρίν τινα λευγαλέον τε δέρος καὶ Φρίξον ἰδέσθαι;
375 αὐτίχ᾽ ὁμαρτήσαντες ἀφ᾽ Ἑλλάδος, οὐδ᾽ ἐπὶ κῶας,
σκῆπτρα δὲ καὶ τιμὴν βασιληίδα δεῦρο νέεσθε.
εἰ δέ κε μὴ προπάροιθεν ἐμῆς ἥψασθε τραπέζης,
ἦ τ᾽ ἂν ἀπὸ γλώσσας τε ταμὼν καὶ χεῖρε κεάσσας
ἀμφοτέρας οἴοισιν ἐπιπροέηκα πόδεσσιν,
380 ὥς κεν ἐρητύοισθε καὶ ὕστερον ὁρμηθῆναι·
οἷα δὲ καὶ μακάρεσσιν ἐπεψεύσασθε θεοῖσιν."

φῆ ῥα χαλεψάμενος· μέγα δὲ φρένες Αἰακίδαο
νειόθεν οἰδαίνεσκον, ἐέλδετο δ᾽ ἔνδοθι θυμὸς
ἀντιβίην ὀλοὸν φάσθαι ἔπος· ἀλλ᾽ ἀπέρυκεν
385 Αἰσονίδης, πρὸ γὰρ αὐτὸς ἀμείψατο μειλιχίοισιν·

"Αἰήτη, σχέο μοι τῷδε στόλῳ. οὔ τι γὰρ αὔτως
ἄστυ τεὸν καὶ δώμαθ᾽ ἱκάνομεν, ὥς που ἔολπας,
οὐδὲ μὲν ἱέμενοι. τίς δ᾽ ἂν τόσον οἶδμα περῆσαι
τλαίη ἑκὼν ὀθνεῖον ἐπὶ κτέρας; ἀλλά με δαίμων
390 καὶ κρυερὴ βασιλῆος ἀτασθάλου ὦρσεν ἐφετμή.
δὸς χάριν ἀντομένοισι· σέθεν δ᾽ ἐγὼ Ἑλλάδι πάσῃ
θεσπεσίην οἴσω κληηδόνα. καὶ δέ τοι ἤδη
πρόφρονές εἰμεν ἄρηι θοὴν ἀποτῖσαι ἀμοιβήν,
εἴτ᾽ οὖν Σαυρομάτας γε λιλαίεαι εἴτε τιν᾽ ἄλλον
395 δῆμον σφωιτέροισιν ὑπὸ σκήπτροισι δαμάσσαι."

ἴσκεν ὑποσσαίνων ἀγανῇ ὀπί· τοῖο δὲ θυμὸς

---

27 In his anger, Aeetes refers to Phrixus as if still alive. Others interpret this as hendiadys, "Phrixus' fleece."

28 Aeetes presumably refers to Argus' claim that the gods and fate brought the groups together on Ares' island (3.323–328),

of you, to his regret, sets eyes on the fleece and on Phrixus?[27] You banded together immediately and came here from Hellas, not for the fleece, but for my scepter and royal throne. If you had not first touched my table, I can assure you that I would have cut out your tongues, chopped off both hands, and sent you forth with only your feet, so that you might be prevented from setting out a second time, and because you have attributed such lies even to the blessed gods!"[28]

Thus he spoke in anger, and mightily from deep down swelled the mind of Aeacus' son,[29] and his heart within longed to utter a deadly threat in defiance, but Jason checked him, for he himself first answered with gentle words:

"Aeetes, please show restraint concerning this expedition. For we do not at all come to your city and palace for the reason you apparently think, nor yet because we are eager to do so. Who would willingly dare to cross so great a sea for someone else's possession? No, a god[30] and the dire command of an insolent king urged me. Grant a favor to your suppliants, and I shall bear to all Hellas your marvelous reputation. Furthermore, we are ready right now to make you a swift repayment in war, whether it be those Sauromatae or any other people you desire to subdue beneath your scepter."

Thus he spoke, reassuring him with a gentle voice, but

whereas he believes that they had conspired in Hellas to usurp his throne.

[29] Telamon.

[30] Presumably Apollo, whose oracle encouraged Jason (cf. 1.411–416).

διχθαδίην πόρφυρεν ἐνὶ στήθεσσι μενοινήν,
ἤ σφεας ὁρμηθεὶς αὐτοσχεδὸν ἐξεναρίζοι,
ἦ ὅ γε πειρήσαιτο βίης. τό οἱ εἴσατ' ἄρειον
400 φραζομένῳ, καὶ δή μιν ὑποβλήδην προσέειπεν·
    "ξεῖνε, τί κεν τὰ ἕκαστα διηνεκέως ἀγορεύοις;
εἰ γὰρ ἐτήτυμόν ἐστε θεῶν γένος, ἠὲ καὶ ἄλλως
οὐδὲν ἐμεῖο χέρηες ἐπ' ὀθνείοισιν ἔβητε,
δώσω τοι χρύσειον ἄγειν δέρος, ἤν κ' ἐθέλησθα,
405 πειρηθείς· ἐσθλοῖς γὰρ ἐπ' ἀνδράσιν οὔ τι μεγαίρω,
ὡς αὐτοὶ μυθεῖσθε τὸν Ἑλλάδι κοιρανέοντα.
πεῖρα δέ τοι μενεός τε καὶ ἀλκῆς ἔσσετ' ἄεθλος,
τόν ῥ' αὐτὸς περίειμι χεροῖν ὀλοόν περ ἐόντα.
δοιώ μοι πεδίον τὸ Ἀρήιον ἀμφινέμονται
410 ταύρω χαλκόποδε στόματι φλόγα φυσιόωντες·
τοὺς ἐλάω ζεύξας στυφελὴν κατὰ νειὸν Ἄρηος
τετράγυον, τὴν αἶψα ταμὼν ἐπὶ τέλσον ἀρότρῳ
οὐ σπόρον ὁλκοῖσιν Δηοῦς ἐνιβάλλομαι ἀκτῇ,
ἀλλ' ὄφιος δεινοῖο μεταλδήσκοντας ὀδόντας
415 ἀνδράσι τευχηστῇσι δέμας· τοὺς δ' αὖθι δαΐζων
κείρω ἐμῷ ὑπὸ δουρὶ περισταδὸν ἀντιόωντας.
ἠέριος ζεύγνυμι βόας καὶ δείελον ὥρην
παύομαι ἀμήτοιο. σὺ δ', εἰ τάδε τοῖα τελέσσεις,
αὐτῆμαρ τόδε κῶας ἀποίσεαι εἰς βασιλῆος·
420 πρὶν δέ κεν οὐ δοίην, μηδ' ἔλπεο· δὴ γὰρ ἀεικὲς
ἄνδρ' ἀγαθὸν γεγαῶτα κακωτέρῳ ἀνέρι εἶξαι."

    413 ἀκτῇ Ω: ἀκτήν E

248

the other's heart within his breast was pondering two different courses, whether he should attack and slay them on the spot, or should make a test of strength. The latter seemed better to him on consideration, and he said to him in reply:

"My guest-friend, why should you tell me all these details from beginning to end? For if truly you and your men are descendants of gods or have come in other respects not a bit inferior to me to gain the possessions of another, I shall give you the golden fleece to take, if you wish, after you have undergone a test, for when it comes to noble men, I do not begrudge anything, as does that ruler in Hellas[31] you yourselves tell of. And yours shall be a test of mettle and strength, one which I myself can accomplish with my hands, even though it is deadly. I have two bronze-hooved oxen that graze in the plain of Ares, breathing fire from their mouths. I yoke and drive them over Ares' hard fallow field of four acres, which I quickly cleave with a plow as far as the headland and cast in the furrows not seed that produces Demeter's grain but the teeth of a dread serpent that grow into the form of armed men. These I slay on the spot, cutting them down with my spear as they come at me from all sides. In the morning I yoke the oxen and at the hour of dusk I stop my harvesting. And for your part, if you accomplish such deeds as these, then on that very day you shall take that fleece back to your king's abode, but until then I will not surrender it, and do not expect me to do so, for indeed it is unseemly for a man of noble birth to yield to an inferior man."

[31] Pelias.

ὣς ἄρ' ἔφη· ὁ δὲ σῖγα ποδῶν πάρος ὄμματα
    πήξας
ἧστ' αὔτως ἄφθογγος, ἀμηχανέων κακότητι.
βουλὴν δ' ἀμφὶ πολὺν στρώφα χρόνον, οὐδέ πη
    εἶχεν
425 θαρσαλέως ὑποδέχθαι, ἐπεὶ μέγα φαίνετο ἔργον.
ὀψὲ δ' ἀμειβόμενος προσελέξατο κερδαλέοισιν·
    "Αἰήτη, μάλα τοί με δίκη περιπολλὸν ἐέργεις.
τῶ καὶ ἐγὼ τὸν ἄεθλον ὑπερφίαλόν περ ἐόντα
τλήσομαι, εἰ καί μοι θανέειν μόρος. οὐ γὰρ ἔτ'
    ἄλλο
430 ῥίγιον ἀνθρώποισι κακῆς ἐπικείσετ' ἀνάγκης,
ἥ με καὶ ἐνθάδε νεῖσθαι ἐπέχραεν ἐκ βασιλῆος."
    ὣς φάτ' ἀμηχανίῃ βεβολημένος· αὐτὰρ ὁ τόν γε
σμερδαλέοις ἐπέεσσι προσέννεπεν ἀσχαλόωντα·
    "ἔρχεο νῦν μεθ' ὅμιλον, ἐπεὶ μέμονάς γε πόνοιο·
435 εἰ δὲ σύ γε ζυγὰ βουσὶν ὑποδδείσαις ἐπαεῖραι,
ἠὲ καὶ οὐλομένου μεταχάσσεαι ἀμήτοιο,
αὐτῷ κεν τὰ ἕκαστα μέλοιτό μοι, ὄφρα καὶ ἄλλος
ἀνὴρ ἐρρίγῃσιν ἀρείονα φῶτα μετελθεῖν."
    ἴσκεν ἀπηλεγέως· ὁ δ' ἀπὸ θρόνου ὤρνυτ'
    Ἰήσων,
440 Αὐγείης Τελαμών τε παρασχεδόν· εἵπετο δ' Ἄργος
οἶος, ἐπεὶ μεσσηγὺς ἔτ' αὐτόθι νεῦσε λιπέσθαι
αὐτοκασιγνήτοις. οἱ δ' ἤισαν ἐκ μεγάροιο·
θεσπέσιον δ' ἐν πᾶσι μετέπρεπεν Αἴσονος υἱὸς
κάλλεϊ καὶ χαρίτεσσιν· ἐπ' αὐτῷ δ' ὄμματα κούρη
445 λοξὰ παρὰ λιπαρὴν σχομένη θηεῖτο καλύπτρην,

Thus he spoke, and in silence Jason fixed his eyes in front of his feet and sat like that, speechless and helpless in his distress. For a long time he turned over and over a plan of action, but could find no way to accept the challenge with confidence, for the task seemed enormous. But at last he answered and addressed him with astute[32] words:

"Aeetes, truly it is with justice that you constrain me so very much. Therefore, I too shall endure that contest, although it is overwhelming, even if it is my fate to die. For nothing else more horrible will befall men than evil necessity, which compelled me to come here at a king's command."

Thus he spoke, stricken with helplessness, and with terrifying words the king addressed him in his distress:

"Go now to join your crew, since you are so eager for toil. But if you should be afraid to put the yoke on the oxen or else shrink from the deadly harvest, then I myself shall see to all the details,[33] so that another man as well may shudder to approach[34] a superior man."

Thus he spoke in blunt terms. Jason rose from his seat, as at once did Augeas and Telamon, but only Argus followed, for in the meantime he had nodded to his brothers to remain there longer. They proceeded from the hall, and marvelously among them all did Jason stand out for his beauty and grace, and the girl, fixing her eyes upon him at an angle, gazed from beside her shining veil, smoldering

---

[32] Lit. "profitable."   [33] I.e. of his threat at 3.378–380.
[34] μετελθεῖν is nicely ambiguous, meaning "approach, visit, petition, or attack."

---

442 ἤισαν Rzach (cf. 3.1331): ἤεσαν vel ἤεσαν Ω

κῆρ ἄχεϊ σμύχουσα, νόος δέ οἱ ἠΰτ' ὄνειρος
ἑρπύζων πεπότητο μετ' ἴχνια νισσομένοιο.
καί ῥ' οἱ μέν ῥα δόμων ἐξήλυθον ἀσχαλόωντες·
Χαλκιόπη δὲ χόλον πεφυλαγμένη Αἰήταο
450 καρπαλίμως θαλαμόνδε σὺν υἱάσιν οἷσι βεβήκει.
αὔτως δ' αὖ Μήδεια μετέστιχε· πολλὰ δὲ θυμῷ
ὥρμαιν', ὅσσα τ' Ἔρωτες ἐποτρύνουσι μέλεσθαι·
προπρὸ δ' ἄρ' ὀφθαλμῶν ἔτι οἱ ἰνδάλλετο πάντα,
αὐτός θ' οἷος ἔην, οἵοισί τε φάρεσιν ἧστο,
455 οἷά τ' ἔειφ', ὥς θ' ἕζετ' ἐπὶ θρόνου, ὥς τε θύραζε
ἤιεν· οὐδέ τιν' ἄλλον ὀίσσατο πορφύρουσα
ἔμμεναι ἀνέρα τοῖον· ἐν οὔασι δ' αἰὲν ὀρώρει
αὐδή τε μῦθοί τε μελίφρονες, οὓς ἀγόρευσεν.
τάρβει δ' ἀμφ' αὐτῷ, μή μιν βόες ἠὲ καὶ αὐτὸς
460 Αἰήτης φθίσειεν· ὀδύρετο δ' ἠΰτε πάμπαν
ἤδη τεθνειῶτα· τέρεν δέ οἱ ἀμφὶ παρειὰς
δάκρυον αἰνοτάτῳ ἐλέῳ ῥέε κηδοσύνῃσιν.
ἦκα δὲ μυρομένη λιγέως ἀνενείκατο μῦθον·
    "τίπτε με δειλαίην τόδ' ἔχει ἄχος; εἴθ' ὅ γε
        πάντων
465 φθίσεται ἡρώων προφερέστατος εἴτε χερείων,
ἑρρέτω—ἦ μὲν ὄφελλεν ἀκήριος ἐξαλέασθαι—
ναὶ δὴ τοῦτό γε, πότνα θεὰ Περσηί, πέλοιτο,
οἴκαδε νοστήσειε φυγῶν μόρον· εἰ δέ μιν αἶσα
δμηθῆναι ὑπὸ βουσί, τόδε προπάροιθε δαείη,
470 οὕνεκεν οὔ οἱ ἐγώ γε κακῇ ἐπαγαίομαι ἄτῃ."
    ἡ μὲν ἄρ' ὣς ἐόλητο νόον μελεδήμασι κούρη.
    οἱ δ' ἐπεὶ οὖν δήμου τε καὶ ἄστεος ἐκτὸς ἔβησαν

with grief in her heart, while her mind, creeping like a dream, fluttered after his footsteps as he went. And so they left the palace in distress, while Chalciope, guarding against Aeetes' anger, swiftly retired to her room with her sons. And Medea likewise left after her, and in her heart mulled over and over all the concerns that the Loves[35] stir up, and right before her eyes everything was still visible to her—what he himself was like, what clothes he was wearing, what he said, how he sat on his chair, and how he walked to the door. As she pondered, she did not think that any other man was like him, and ever in her ears rang his voice and the honey-sweet words he had spoken. She was afraid for him, lest the oxen or else Aeetes himself would kill him, and she lamented as if he were already dead and gone, and in her grief tender tears of most profound pity ran down her cheeks. Softly sobbing, she uttered plaintive words:

"Why is this sorrow gripping poor me? Whether he goes to his death as the best of all the heroes or the worst, let him go—yet I truly wish that he had escaped unharmed—yes, mighty goddess, daughter of Perses,[36] grant this at least, that he escape death and return home. But if it is his fate to be killed by the oxen, let him learn ahead of time that I for one take no delight in his evil demise."

In this way then was the girl's mind beset with anxieties.

But when the heroes had left the people and the town

---

[35] It is often impossible to distinguish between lower-case love(s) and upper-case Love(s).

[36] Hecate was the daughter of the Titan Perses (Hesiod, *Theogony* 409–411).

τὴν ὁδόν, ἣν τὸ πάροιθεν ἀνήλυθον ἐκ πεδίοιο,
δὴ τότ᾽ Ἰήσονα τοῖσδε προσέννεπεν Ἄργος
ἔπεσσιν·

475 "Αἰσονίδη, μῆτιν μὲν ὀνόσσεαι, ἥν τιν᾽ ἐνίψω·
πείρης δ᾽ οὐ μάλ᾽ ἔοικε μεθιέμεν ἐν κακότητι.
κούρην δή τινα πρόσθεν ἐπέκλυες αὐτὸς ἐμεῖο
φαρμάσσειν Ἑκάτης Περσηίδος ἐννεσίῃσιν.
τὴν εἴ κεν πεπίθοιμεν, ὀίομαι, οὐκέτι τάρβος
480 ἔσσετ᾽ ἀεθλεύοντι δαμήμεναι· ἀλλὰ μάλ᾽ αἰνῶς
δείδω, μή πως οὔ μοι ὑποσταίη τό γε μήτηρ.
ἔμπης δ᾽ ἐξαῦτις μετελεύσομαι ἀντιβολήσων,
ξυνὸς ἐπεὶ πάντεσσιν ἐπικρέμαθ᾽ ἡμῖν ὄλεθρος."

ἴσκεν εὐφρονέων· ὁ δ᾽ ἀμείβετο τοῖσδ᾽ ἐπέεσσιν·
485 "ὦ πέπον, εἴ νύ τοι αὐτῷ ἐφανδάνει, οὔ τι
    μεγαίρω·
βάσκ᾽ ἴθι καὶ πυκινοῖσι τεὴν παρὰ μητέρα μύθοις
ὄρνυθι λισσόμενος. μελέη γε μὲν ἡμῖν ὄρωρεν
ἐλπωρή, ὅτε νόστον ἐπετραπόμεσθα γυναιξίν."

ὣς ἔφατ᾽· ὦκα δ᾽ ἕλος μετεκίαθον. αὐτὰρ ἑταῖροι
490 γηθόσυνοι ἐρέεινον, ὅπως παρεόντας ἴδοντο·
τοῖσιν δ᾽ Αἰσονίδης τετιημένος ἔκφατο μῦθον·

"ὦ φίλοι, Αἰήταο ἀπηνέος ἄμμι φίλον κῆρ
ἀντικρὺ κεχόλωται· ἕκαστα γὰρ οὔ νύ τι τέκμωρ
οὔτ᾽ ἐμοὶ οὔτε κεν ὕμμι διειρομένοισι πέλοιτο·
495 φῆ δὲ δύω πεδίον τὸ Ἀρήιον ἀμφινέμεσθαι
ταύρω χαλκόποδε στόματι φλόγα φυσιόωντας·
τετράγυον δ᾽ ὑπὸ τοῖσιν ἐφίετο νειὸν ἀρόσσαι·

497 ὑπὸ Samuelsson: ἐπὶ Ω
254

by the same road on which they had previously come up from the plain, then Argus addressed Jason with these words:

"Jason, you will not think much of the plan I am going to propose, but we really must not forgo an attempt in our distress. You yourself have previously heard me tell of a certain girl who concocts drugs with the guidance of Hecate, daughter of Perses. If we could persuade her, I think there will no longer be any fear of your being defeated in the contest. But I am terribly afraid that my mother will not undertake this for me. Nevertheless, I shall go back again to beg her, for a common destruction hangs over us all."

Thus he spoke with kind intent, and Jason answered with these words:

"Dear friend, if you yourself approve, I do not begrudge it. Go off to your mother and urge her to action by pleading with wise words. But desperate indeed is our hope, when we have entrusted our return to women."

Thus he spoke, and soon they reached the backwater. And their companions joyfully questioned them when they saw them in their presence, but in sorrow Jason spoke out these words to them:

"My friends, cruel Aeetes' dear[37] heart is thoroughly angry at us—but as to the details, it would serve no purpose for me to tell or for you to ask about them—and he said that two bronze-hooved oxen graze in the plain of Ares, breathing fire from their mouths. He ordered me to plow four acres of fallow land with them and said he would

---

[37] The Homeric phrase φίλον κῆρ occurs only here and with obvious irony.

δώσειν δ' ἐξ ὄφιος γενύων σπόρον, ὅς ῥ' ἀνίησιν
γηγενέας χαλκέοις σὺν τεύχεσιν· ἤματι δ' αὐτῷ
500 χρειὼ τούς γε δαΐξαι. ὁ δή νύ οἱ—οὔ τι γὰρ ἄλλο
βέλτερον ἦν φράσσασθαι—ἀπηλεγέως ὑπέστην."
    ὣς ἄρ' ἔφη· πάντεσσι δ' ἀνήνυτος εἴσατ' ἄεθλος·
δὴν δ' ἄνεῳ καὶ ἄναυδοι ἐς ἀλλήλους ὁρόωντο,
ἄτῃ ἀμηχανίῃ τε κατηφέες. ὀψὲ δὲ Πηλεὺς
505 θαρσαλέως μετὰ πᾶσιν ἀριστήεσσιν ἔειπεν·
    "ὥρη μητιάασθαι ὅ κ' ἔρξομεν. οὐ μὲν ἔολπα
βουλῆς εἶναι ὄνειαρ, ὅσον τ' ἐπὶ κάρτεϊ χειρῶν.
εἰ μέν νυν τύνη ζεῦξαι βόας Αἰήταο,
ἥρως Αἰσονίδη, φρονέεις, μέμονάς τε πόνοιο,
510 ἦ τ' ἂν ὑποσχεσίην πεφυλαγμένος ἐντύναιο·
εἰ δ' οὔ τοι μάλα θυμὸς ἑῇ ἐπὶ πάγχυ πέποιθεν
ἠνορέῃ, μήτ' αὐτὸς ἐπείγεο μήτε τιν' ἄλλον
τῶνδ' ἀνδρῶν πάπταινε παρήμενος· οὐ γὰρ ἐγώ γε
σχήσομ', ἐπεὶ θάνατός γε τὸ κύντατον ἔσσεται
515   ἄλγος."
    ὣς ἔφατ' Αἰακίδης· Τελαμῶνι δὲ θυμὸς ὀρίνθη,
σπερχόμενος δ' ἀνόρουσε θοῶς· ἐπὶ δὲ τρίτος Ἴδας
ὦρτο μέγα φρονέων, ἐπὶ δ' υἱέε Τυνδαρέοιο·
σὺν δὲ καὶ Οἰνεΐδης ἐναρίθμιος αἰζηοῖσιν
ἀνδράσιν, οὐδέ περ ὅσσον ἐπανθιόωντας ἰούλους
520 ἀντέλλων· τοίῳ οἱ ἀείρετο κάρτεϊ θυμός.
οἱ δ' ἄλλοι εἴξαντες ἀκὴν ἔχον. αὐτίκα δ' Ἄργος
τοῖον ἔπος μετέειπεν ἐελδομένοισιν ἀέθλου·

517 υἱέε Merkel: υἷες Ω

give me seed from a serpent's jaws that would sprout earthborn men in bronze armor, and that on the same day I would have to slay them. And so, since I could think of nothing better, I accepted that task of his unconditionally."

Thus he spoke. The contest seemed impossible to everyone, and for a long time in speechless silence they looked at one another, dispirited by the calamity and their helplessness. But at last Peleus spoke bravely to all the heroes:

"It is time to devise what we shall do. Yet I do not expect as much help to come from counsel as resides in the strength of our hands. So if you, heroic son of Aeson, intend to yoke Aeetes' oxen and are eager for the task, then truly you should keep your promise and get yourself ready. But if your heart is not completely confident in its[38] prowess, neither act in haste nor sit by and look around for any other of these men, because I for one will not hold back, since the worst pain will be but death."

So spoke the son of Aeacus, and Telamon's heart was stirred, and he eagerly rose up at once, and third thereafter rose Idas proudly, and thereafter the twin sons of Tyndareus, as well as Oeneus' son,[39] who was numbered among the men in their prime, although sprouting not even a little downy growth—with such strength was his heart lifted up. The rest yielded and kept silent. And right away Argus spoke these words to those who were eager for the contest:

[38] Or *your*.
[39] Meleager.

"ὦ φίλοι, ἤτοι μὲν τόδε λοίσθιον· ἀλλά τιν᾽ οἴω
μητρὸς ἐμῆς ἔσσεσθαι ἐναίσιμον ὕμμιν ἀρωγήν.
525 τῶ καί περ μεμαῶτες ἐρητύοισθ᾽ ἐνὶ νηὶ
τυτθὸν ἔθ᾽ ὡς τὸ πάροιθεν, ἐπεὶ καὶ ἐπισχέμεν
ἔμπης
λώιον ἢ κακὸν οἶτον ἀφειδήσαντας ἑλέσθαι.
κούρη τις μεγάροισιν ἐνιτρέφετ᾽ Αἰήταο,
τὴν Ἑκάτη περίαλλα θεὰ δάε τεχνήσασθαι
530 φάρμαχ᾽, ὅσ᾽ ἤπειρός τε φύει καὶ νήχυτον ὕδωρ·
τοῖσι καὶ ἀκαμάτοιο πυρὸς μειλίσσετ᾽ ἀυτμή,
καὶ ποταμοὺς ἵστησιν ἄφαρ κελαδεινὰ ῥέοντας,
ἄστρα τε καὶ μήνης ἱερῆς ἐπέδησε κελεύθους.
τῆς μὲν ἀπὸ μεγάροιο κατὰ στίβον ἐνθάδ᾽ ἰόντες
535 μνησάμεθ᾽, εἴ κε δύναιτο, κασιγνήτη γεγαυῖα,
μήτηρ ἡμετέρη πεπιθεῖν ἐπαρῆξαι ἀέθλῳ.
εἰ δὲ καὶ αὐτοῖσιν τόδ᾽ ἐφανδάνει, ἦ τ᾽ ἂν ἱκοίμην
ἤματι τῷδ᾽ αὐτῷ πάλιν εἰς δόμον Αἰήταο
πειρήσων· τάχα δ᾽ ἂν σὺν δαίμονι πειρηθείην."
540 ὣς φάτο· τοῖσι δὲ σῆμα θεοὶ δόσαν εὐμενέοντες.
τρήρων μὲν φεύγουσα βίην κίρκοιο πελειὰς
ὑψόθεν Αἰσονίδεω πεφοβημένη ἔμπεσε κόλποις,
κίρκος δ᾽ ἀφλάστῳ περικάππεσεν. ὦκα δὲ Μόψος
τοῖον ἔπος μετὰ πᾶσι θεοπροπέων ἀγόρευσεν·
545 "ὕμμι, φίλοι, τόδε σῆμα θεῶν ἰότητι τέτυκται·
οὐδέ πῃ ἄλλως ἐστὶν ὑποκρίνασθαι ἄρειον,

531 ἀυτμή Ω: ἀυτμήν E
533 ἱερῆς Ω: ἱερὰς Wifstrand

"My friends, truly that is the last resort.[40] But I think that from my mother you shall have some opportune help. Therefore, although you are eager, remain in the ship a little while longer as before, since it is nonetheless better to hold back than recklessly to choose[41] an evil fate. There is a certain girl being raised in Aeetes' palace, whom the goddess Hecate has taught to employ with exceeding skill all the drugs that the land and full-flowing waters produce. With these even the blast of unwearying fire is softened,[42] and she can suddenly halt the flow of roaring rivers and arrest the stars and the paths of the sacred moon. We thought of her as we were coming here on the path from the palace, wondering if my mother, who is her sister, might be able to persuade her to aid in the contest. And if you yourselves approve of it, truly I would go this very day back to Aeetes' palace to attempt it, and perhaps I may make the attempt with divine help."

Thus he spoke, and the gods gave them a sign out of good will: a timid dove fleeing from a mighty hawk fell panic-stricken from on high into Jason's lap, while the hawk impaled itself on the stern-ornament. And at once Mopsus spoke in prophecy and addressed these words to them all:

"It was for you, my friends, that this sign occurred by the will of the gods, and there is no better way to interpret

---

[40] I.e. to face certain death.
[41] Or *suffer*.
[42] Or, reading ἀντμήν, *she softens the blast.*

παρθενικὴν δ' ἐπέεσσι μετελθέμεν ἀμφιέποντας
μήτι παντοίῃ. δοκέω δέ μιν οὐκ ἀθερίζειν,
εἰ ἐτεὸν Φινεύς γε θεῇ ἐνὶ Κύπριδι νόστον
550 πέφραδεν ἔσσεσθαι. κείνης δ' ὅ γε μείλιχος ὄρνις
πότμον ὑπεξήλυξε. κέαρ δέ μοι ὡς ἐνὶ θυμῷ
τόνδε κατ' οἰωνὸν προτιόσσεται, ὡς δὲ πέλοιτο.
ἀλλά, φίλοι, Κυθέρειαν ἐπικλείοντες ἀμύνειν,
ἤδη νῦν Ἄργοιο παραιφασίῃσι πίθεσθε."
555 ἴσκεν· ἐπήνησαν δὲ νέοι Φινῆος ἐφετμὰς
μνησάμενοι. μοῦνος δ' Ἀφαρήιος ἄνθορεν Ἴδας
δείν' ἐπαλαστήσας μεγάλῃ ὀπί, φώνησέν τε·
"ὦ πόποι, ἦ ῥα γυναιξὶν ὁμόστολοι ἐνθάδ'
ἔβημεν,
οἳ Κύπριν καλέουσιν ἐπίρροθον ἄμμι πέλεσθαι,
560 οὐκέτ' Ἐνυαλίοιο μέγα σθένος· ἐς δὲ πελείας
καὶ κίρκους λεύσσοντες ἐρητύεσθε ἀέθλων.
ἔρρετε, μηδ' ὕμμιν πολεμήια ἔργα μέλοιτο,
παρθενικὰς δὲ λιτῇσιν ἀνάλκιδας ἠπεροπεύειν."
ὣς ηὔδα μεμαώς· πολέες δ' ὁμάδησαν ἑταῖροι
565 ἦκα μάλ', οὐδ' ἄρα τίς οἱ ἐναντίον ἔκφατο μῦθον.
χωόμενος δ' ὅ γ' ἔπειτα καθέζετο· τοῖσι δ' Ἰήσων
αὐτίκ' ἐποτρύνων τὸν ἑὸν νόον ὧδ' ἀγόρευεν·
"Ἄργος μὲν παρὰ νηός, ἐπεὶ τόδε πᾶσιν ἔαδεν,
στελλέσθω· ἀτὰρ αὐτοὶ ἐπὶ χθονὸς ἐκ ποταμοῖο
570 ἀμφαδὸν ἤδη πείσματ' ἀνάψομεν· ἦ γὰρ ἔοικεν
μηκέτι δὴν κρύπτεσθαι ὑποπτήσσοντας αὐτήν."

571 ὑποπτήσσοντας Pierson (metri gratia): πτήσσοντας Ω:
‹ἅ τε› πτήσσοντας Fränkel

260

it than this: for us to approach the maiden with entreaties, making use of every sort of stratagem. And I do not think she will refuse, if in fact Phineus declared that our return would lie with the goddess Cypris,[43] since hers was the gentle bird that escaped its doom. And as the heart within my breast foretells in accordance with this bird-omen, just so may it turn out. Come, my friends, call on Cytherea[44] to defend us and without delay heed the counsels of Argus."

He spoke, and the young men approved when they recalled the commands of Phineus. But Idas alone, Aphareus' son, leapt up, venting his terrible anger in a loud voice, and said:

"For shame! We have surely come here as shipmates of women, those who call on Cypris to be our helper, no longer on the great strength of Enyalius. But you look to doves and hawks and shrink from contests.[45] Away with you: let not deeds of war concern you but seducing defenseless girls with entreaties!"

Thus he spoke vehemently, and many of the companions murmured softly,[46] but in fact no one spoke a word against him. Still angry, he then sat down. Presently, Jason roused them to action and stated his own thoughts thus:

"Let Argus go forth from the ship, since everyone approves of that, and let us now leave the river[47] and openly fasten the stern cables to land, for we should no longer remain hidden and cowering[48] from battle."

[43] Phineus' words are at 2.423–424.   [44] Aphrodite.

[45] Some edd. punctuate differently: "those who call on Cypris to be our helper. No longer looking to the great strength of Enyalius but to doves and hawks, you shrink from contests."

[46] Their murmur indicates disapproval of Idas.

[47] Where they were at anchor in the backwater.

[48] Or, reading Fränkel's ⟨ἅ τε⟩ πτήσσοντας, *as if cowering.*

ὡς ἄρ' ἔφη· καὶ τὸν μὲν ἄφαρ προΐαλλε νέεσθαι
καρπαλίμως ἐξαῦτις ἀνὰ πτόλιν, οἱ δ' ἐπὶ νηὸς
εὐναίας ἐρύσαντες ἐφετμαῖς Αἰσονίδαο
575 τυτθὸν ὑπὲξ ἔλεος χέρσῳ ἐπέκελσαν ἐρετμοῖς.
αὐτίκα δ' Αἰήτης ἀγορὴν ποιήσατο Κόλχων
νόσφιν ἑοῖο δόμου, τόθι περ καὶ πρόσθε κάθιζον,
ἀτλήτους Μινύαισι δόλους καὶ κήδεα τεύχων.
στεῦτο δ', ἐπεί κεν πρῶτα βόες διαδηλήσονται
580 ἄνδρα τόν, ὅς ῥ' ὑπέδεκτο βαρὺν καμέεσθαι ἄεθλον,
δρυμὸν ἀναρρήξας λασίης καθύπερθε κολώνης
αὔτανδρον φλέξειν δόρυ νήιον, ὄφρ' ἀλεγεινὴν
ὕβριν ἀποφλύξωσιν ὑπέρβια μηχανόωντες.
οὐδὲ γὰρ Αἰολίδην Φρίξον μάλα περ χατέοντα
585 δέχθαι ἐνὶ μεγάροισιν ἐφέστιον, ὃς περὶ πάντων
ξείνων μειλιχίῃ τε θεουδείῃ τ' ἐκέκαστο,
εἰ μή οἱ Ζεὺς αὐτὸς ἀπ' οὐρανοῦ ἄγγελον ἧκεν
Ἑρμείαν, ὥς κεν προσκηδέος ἀντιάσειεν·
μὴ καὶ λῃστῆρας ἑὴν ἐς γαῖαν ἰόντας
590 ἔσσεσθαι δηναιὸν ἀπήμονας, οἷσι μέμηλεν
ὀθνείοις ἐπὶ χεῖρα ἑὴν κτεάτεσσιν ἀείρειν,
κρυπταδίους τε δόλους τεκταινέμεν, ἠδὲ βοτήρων
αὔλια δυσκελάδοισιν ἐπιδρομίῃσι δαΐξαι.
νόσφι δὲ οἷ αὐτῷ φάτ' ἐοικότα μείλια τίσειν
595 υἷας Φρίξοιο, κακορρέκτῃσιν ὀπηδοὺς
ἀνδράσι νοστήσαντας ὁμιλαδόν, ὄφρα ἑ τιμῆς

Thus he spoke and at once dispatched Argus to return at full speed to the city, while they, on Jason's orders, raised the anchors on board and rowed the ship ashore not far from the backwater.

Aeetes immediately[49] held an assembly of the Colchians away from his palace, in a place where they used to convene before this, while he devised intolerable treachery and woes for the Minyans.[50] He declared that once the oxen had torn apart that man who had agreed to endure the grievous contest, he would cut down the grove atop the wooded hill and burn the ship's timbers along with its crew, so that those contriving wanton acts would splutter out their baneful insolence. For he said that he would not have received the Aeolid Phrixus as a guest in his palace in spite of his great need—he who surpassed all strangers in gentleness and fear of the gods—had not Zeus himself sent his messenger Hermes to him from heaven, so that he[51] might find an affectionate host; much less that bandits coming to his land would remain unpunished for very long, those whose concern it is to lay their hands on other people's possessions, hatch secret plots, and plunder shepherds' folds in horrid-sounding raids. And apart from them, he said[52] that the sons of Phrixus would pay him personally a fitting recompense for returning in company with a gang of evildoing men, in order to expel him callously from his honor

---

[49] I.e. right after Jason and his men had left at 3.442.

[50] I.e. the Argonauts (cf. 1.228–233).

[51] Phrixus.

[52] Some interpret νόσφι δὲ οἷ αὐτῷ φάτ' to mean "he thought apart to himself," and did not share this information with the people.

καὶ σκήπτρων ἐλάσειαν ἀκηδέες, ὥς ποτε βάξιν
λευγαλέην οὗ πατρὸς ἐπέκλυεν Ἠελίοιο,
χρειώ μιν πυκινόν τε δόλον βουλάς τε γενέθλης
600   σφωιτέρης ἄτην τε πολύτροπον ἐξαλέασθαι·
τῶ καὶ ἐελδομένους πέμπεν ἐς Ἀχαιίδα γαῖαν
πατρὸς ἐφημοσύνῃ δολιχὴν ὁδόν· οὐδὲ θυγατρῶν
εἶναί οἱ τυτθόν γε δέος, μή πού τινα μῆτιν
φράσσωνται στυγερήν, οὐδ' υἱέος Ἀψύρτοιο,
605   ἀλλ' ἐνὶ Χαλκιόπης γενεῇ τάδε λυγρὰ τετύχθαι.
καὶ ῥ' ὁ μὲν ἄσχετα ἔργα πιφαύσκετο δημοτέροισιν
χωόμενος, μέγα δέ σφιν ἀπείλεε νῆά τ' ἐρύσθαι
ἠδ' αὐτούς, ἵνα μή τις ὑπὲκ κακότητος ἀλύξῃ.
τόφρα δὲ μητέρ' ἑήν, μετιὼν δόμον Αἰήταο,
610   Ἄργος παντοίοισι παρηγορέεσκεν ἔπεσσιν,
Μήδειαν λίσσεσθαι ἀμυνέμεν· ἡ δὲ καὶ αὐτὴ
πρόσθεν μητιάασκε· δέος δέ μιν ἴσχανε θυμόν,
μή πως ἠὲ παρ' αἶσαν ἐτώσια μειλίσσοιτο
πατρὸς ἀτυζομένην ὀλοὸν χόλον, ἠὲ λιτῇσιν
615   ἑσπομένης ἀρίδηλα καὶ ἀμφαδὰ ἔργα πέλοιτο.
κούρην δ' ἐξ ἀχέων ἀδινὸς κατελώφεεν ὕπνος
λέκτρῳ ἀνακλινθεῖσαν. ἄφαρ δέ μιν ἠπεροπῆες,
οἷά τ' ἀκηχεμένην, ὀλοοὶ ἐρέθεσκον ὄνειροι·
τὸν ξεῖνον δ' ἐδόκησεν ὑφεστάμεναι τὸν ἄεθλον,
620   οὔ τι μάλ' ὁρμαίνοντα δέρος κριοῖο κομίσσαι,
οὐδέ τι τοῖο ἕκητι μετὰ πτόλιν Αἰήταο
ἐλθέμεν, ὄφρα δέ μιν σφέτερον δόμον εἰσαγάγοιτο

601 πέμπεν Ω: πέμπειν V² Stephanus

264

and his throne—as he had once heard in a dread oracle from his father Helius, that he needed to avoid the shrewd treachery and plots of his own family and their wily destruction. And that is why he sent them off, as they wished, to the land of Achaea on a long journey at their father's urging.[53] And he said he had not the slightest fear of his daughters, lest they somehow contrive some hateful scheme, nor of his son Apsyrtus, but that these dreadful things had come to be in Chalciope's offspring. And so he angrily proclaimed these horrible deeds to his townsmen and with strong threats ordered them to keep watch on the ship and its crew, so that no one might escape an evil end.

In the meantime, Argus had returned to the palace of Aeetes and with every sort of argument was pleading with his mother to beg Medea to help. And Chalciope herself had been considering it before this, but fear gripped her heart, lest perhaps her entreaties would be inappropriate and ineffective because her sister dreaded their father's deadly anger, or if she did yield to her prayers, that her deeds would come to light and be exposed.

As for the girl, deep sleep was furnishing relief from her troubles as she lay in bed. But soon deceptive, baleful dreams began to disturb her, as they do when a girl is in distress. She imagined that the stranger had accepted the contest, not at all because he desired to take back the ram's fleece, nor was it for that reason he had come to Aeetes' city, but to take her to his own home as his wedded wife.

---

[53] If the finite verb πέμπεν is correct, this sentence is evidently an explanation by the author/narrator. Their father Phrixus ordered them to return to Orchomenus to take possession of his inheritance (cf. 2.1093–1096 and 3.262–267).

APOLLONIUS RHODIUS

κουριδίην παράκοιτιν. ὀίετο δ' ἀμφὶ βόεσσιν
αὐτὴ ἀεθλεύουσα μάλ' εὐμαρέως πονέεσθαι·
625 σφωιτέρους δὲ τοκῆας ὑποσχεσίης ἀθερίζειν,
οὕνεκεν οὐ κούρη ζεῦξαι βόας, ἀλλά οἱ αὐτῷ
προύθεσαν· ἐκ δ' ἄρα τοῦ νεῖκος πέλεν ἀμφήριστον
πατρί τε καὶ ξείνοις· αὐτῇ δ' ἐπιέτρεπον ἄμφω
τὼς ἔμεν, ὥς κεν ἑῇσι μετὰ φρεσὶν ἰθύσειεν·
630 ἡ δ' ἄφνω τὸν ξεῖνον, ἀφειδήσασα τοκήων,
εἵλετο· τοὺς δ' ἀμέγαρτον ἄχος λάβεν, ἐκ δ'
            ἐβόησαν
χωόμενοι· τὴν δ' ὕπνος ἅμα κλαγγῇ μεθέηκεν.
παλλομένη δ' ἀνόρουσε φόβῳ, περί τ' ἀμφί τε
            τοίχους
πάπτηνεν θαλάμοιο· μόλις δ' ἐσαγείρατο θυμὸν
635 ὡς πάρος ἐν στέρνοις, ἀδινὴν δ' ἀνενείκατο φωνήν·
    "δειλὴ ἐγών, οἷόν με βαρεῖς ἐφόβησαν ὄνειροι.
δείδια, μὴ μέγα δή τι φέρῃ κακὸν ἥδε κέλευθος
ἡρώων· περί μοι ξείνῳ φρένες ἠερέθονται.
μνάσθω ἑὸν κατὰ δῆμον Ἀχαιίδα τηλόθι κούρην,
640 ἄμμι δὲ παρθενίη τε μέλοι καὶ δῶμα τοκήων.
ἔμπα γε μήν, θεμένη κύνεον κέαρ, οὐκέτ' ἄνευθεν
αὐτοκασιγνήτης πειρήσομαι, εἴ κέ μ' ἀέθλῳ
χραισμεῖν ἀντιάσῃσιν, ἐπὶ σφετέροις ἀχέουσα
παισί· τό κέν μοι λυγρὸν ἐνὶ κραδίῃ σβέσαι
            ἄλγος."
645 ἦ ῥα, καὶ ὀρθωθεῖσα θύρας ὤιξε δόμοιο
νήλιπος οἰέανος· καὶ δὴ λελίητο νέεσθαι

She dreamed that she herself competed against the oxen and very easily performed the task, but that her parents took back their promise, because they had not set the task for their daughter to yoke the oxen, but for him alone. Thereupon a contentious disagreement arose between her father and the strangers, and both sides turned the decision over to her to be as she desired in her own mind. And she immediately chose the stranger with no regard for her parents. Measureless grief seized them, and they shouted out in anger, and at their cry sleep released her. Shaking with fear, she bolted up and stared around and about at the walls of her room. With difficulty she collected her spirit back in her breast as before and brought forth a sorrowful voice:

"Poor me! How these dire dreams have frightened me! I fear that this expedition of heroes will indeed bring some great harm—my mind is all aflutter about the stranger. Let him woo an Achaean girl far away among his own people, and let my care be for virginity and the home of my parents. Yet nevertheless, I will make my heart shameless and, no longer remaining aloof, will test my sister, to see if she will entreat me to aid in the contest because she is distressed for her sons—that would quench the terrible pain in my heart."

She spoke and rose up and opened the doors of her chamber, barefoot in a single gown.[54] And she truly desired

---

[54] An outer garment would normally be worn outside one's room.

---

644 σβέσαι Madvig: σβέσοι Ω

αὐτοκασιγνήτηνδε καὶ ἕρκεος οὐδὸν ἄμειψεν·
δὴν δὲ καταυτόθι μίμνεν ἐνὶ προδόμῳ θαλάμοιο
αἰδοῖ ἐεργομένη· μετὰ δ' ἐτράπετ' αὖτις ὀπίσσω
650 στρεφθεῖσ'· ἐκ δὲ πάλιν κίεν ἔνδοθεν, ἄψ τ' ἀλέεινεν
εἴσω· τηΰσιοι δὲ πόδες φέρον ἔνθα καὶ ἔνθα·
ἤτοι ὅτ' ἰθύσειεν, ἔρυκέ μιν ἔνδοθεν αἰδώς·
αἰδοῖ δ' ἐργομένην θρασὺς ἵμερος ὀτρύνεσκεν.
τρὶς μὲν ἐπειρήθη, τρὶς δ' ἔσχετο· τέτρατον αὖτις
655 λέκτροισιν πρηνὴς ἐνικάππεσεν εἱλιχθεῖσα.
ὡς δ' ὅτε τις νύμφη θαλερὸν πόσιν ἐν θαλάμοισιν
μύρεται, ᾧ μιν ὄπασσαν ἀδελφεοὶ ἠδὲ τοκῆες,
οὐδέ τί πω πάσαις ἐπιμίσγεται ἀμφιπόλοισιν
αἰδοῖ ἐπιφροσύνῃ τε, μυχῷ δ' ἀχέουσα θαάσσει,
660 τὸν δέ τις ὤλεσε μοῖρα, πάρος ταρπήμεναι ἄμφω
δήνεσιν ἀλλήλων· ἡ δ' ἔνδοθι δαιομένη περ
σῖγα μάλα κλαίει χῆρον λέχος εἰσορόωσα,
μή μιν κερτομέουσαι ἐπιστοβέωσι γυναῖκες·
τῇ ἰκέλη Μήδεια κινύρετο. τὴν δέ τις ἄφνω
665 μυρομένην μεσσηγὺς ἐπιπρομολοῦσ' ἐνόησεν
δμωάων, ἥ οἱ ἐπέτις πέλε κουρίζουσα·
Χαλκιόπῃ δ' ἤγγειλε παρασχεδόν· ἡ δ' ἐνὶ παισὶν
ἧστ' ἐπιμητιόωσα κασιγνήτην ἀρέσασθαι.
ἀλλ' οὐδ' ὣς ἀπίθησεν, ὅτ' ἔκλυεν ἀμφιπόλοιο
670 μῦθον ἀνώιστον· διὰ δ' ἔσσυτο θαμβήσασα
ἐκ θαλάμου θαλαμόνδε διαμπερές, ᾧ ἔνι κούρη
κέκλιτ' ἀκηχεμένη, δρύψεν δ' ἑκάτερθε παρειάς.
ὡς δ' ἴδε δάκρυσιν ὄσσε πεφυρμένα, φώνησέν μιν·

647 ἄμειψεν Ω: ἀμεῖψαι Fränkel

to visit her sister and crossed the threshold to the court-
yard, but for a long time she remained there in the vesti-
bule of her room, held back by shame. She turned around
and went back again, but once more came forth from
within,[55] and again shrank back inside. Her feet carried
her back and forth in vain: whenever she started forth,
shame held her back inside, but while restrained by
shame, bold desire kept urging her on. Three times she
tried, three times she halted. The fourth time she whirled
back around and fell face down on her bed. And as when a
bride in her bedroom weeps for her youthful husband, to
whom her brothers and parents have given her, and she
does not yet associate with all the servants out of shame
and discretion, but sits in a corner grieving—a husband
some doom had slain before the two of them could enjoy
each other's counsels—and, although burning inside as she
beholds her widowed bed, she wails in silence, lest the
women criticize and scoff at her; like her did Medea la-
ment. But suddenly in the midst of her weeping one of the
servants approached and noticed her, a young girl who was
her attendant. She immediately told Chalciope, who was
sitting with her sons, pondering how to win over her sister.
But nonetheless,[56] she did not disobey when she heard the
servant's unexpected report, but rushed in amazement out
through her room straight to the room where the girl lay
grieving and had scratched both of her cheeks. When she
saw her eyes dimmed with tears, she said to her:

[55] Into the vestibule.
[56] I.e. although absorbed in her planning.

657 ἠδὲ Ω: ἠὲ Brunck

"ὤ μοι ἐγώ, Μήδεια, τί δὴ τάδε δάκρυα λείβεις;
675 τίπτ' ἔπαθες; τί τοι αἰνὸν ὑπὸ φρένας ἵκετο πένθος;
ἤ νύ σε θευμορίη περιδέδρομεν ἅψεα νοῦσος,
ἠέ τιν' οὐλομένην ἐδάης ἐκ πατρὸς ἐνιπὴν
ἀμφί τ' ἐμοὶ καὶ παισίν; ὄφελλέ με μήτε τοκήων
δῶμα τόδ' εἰσοράαν μηδὲ πτόλιν, ἀλλ' ἐπὶ γαίης
680 πείρασι ναιετάειν, ἵνα μηδέ περ οὔνομα Κόλχων."
ὣς φάτο· τῆς δ' ἐρύθηνε παρήια· δὴν δέ μιν
αἰδὼς
παρθενίη κατέρυκεν ἀμείψασθαι μεμαυῖαν.
μῦθος δ' ἄλλοτε μέν οἱ ἐπ' ἀκροτάτης ἀνέτελλεν
γλώσσης, ἄλλοτ' ἔνερθε κατὰ στῆθος πεπότητο·
685 πολλάκι δ' ἱμερόεν μὲν ἀνὰ στόμα θυῖεν ἐνισπεῖν,
φθογγῇ δ' οὐ προύβαινε παροιτέρω. ὀψὲ δ' ἔειπεν
τοῖα δόλῳ· θρασέες γὰρ ἐπεκλονέεσκον Ἔρωτες·
"Χαλκιόπη, περί μοι παίδων σέο θυμὸς ἄηται,
μή σφε πατὴρ ξείνοισι σὺν ἀνδράσιν αὐτίκ'
ὀλέσσῃ·
690 τοῖα κατακνώσσουσα μινυνθαδίῳ νέον ὕπνῳ
λεύσσω ὀνείρατα λυγρά—τά τις θεὸς ἀκράαντα
θείη, μηδ' ἀλεγεινὸν ἐφ' υἱάσι κῆδος ἕλοιο."
φῆ ῥα κασιγνήτης πειρωμένη, εἴ κέ μιν αὐτὴ
ἀντιάσειε πάροιθεν ἑοῖς τεκέεσσιν ἀμύνειν.
695 τὴν δ' αἰνῶς ἄτλητος ἐπέκλυσε θυμὸν ἀνίη
δείματι, τοῖ' ἐσάκουσεν· ἀμείβετο δ' ὧδ' ἐπέεσσιν·
"καὶ δ' αὐτὴ τάδε πάντα μετήλυθον ὁρμαίνουσα,
εἴ τινα συμφράσσαιο καὶ ἀρτύνειας ἀρωγήν.
ἀλλ' ὄμοσον Γαῖάν τε καὶ Οὐρανόν, ὅττι τοι εἴπω

"Woe is me, Medea, why ever are you shedding these tears? What has happened to you? What terrible sorrow has come upon your mind? Has some heaven-sent sickness encompassed your body, or have you learned of some deadly threat from our father concerning me and my sons? I wish I did not behold this house of our parents or even this city, but lived at the ends of the earth, where not even the name of Colchians is known."

Thus she spoke. The girl's cheeks blushed, and for a long time her virgin shame restrained her, although she longed to reply. At one moment her words rose up to the tip of her tongue, but at another fluttered deep down in her breast. Often they rushed up to her lovely lips for utterance, but went no further to become speech. At last she spoke these words deceitfully, for the bold Loves were urging her on:

"Chalciope, my heart is trembling for your sons, in fear that our father will slay them immediately along with the strangers. Such dreadful dreams have I been seeing just now while slumbering in a brief sleep—may a god make them unfulfilled, and may you never suffer painful sorrow on account of your sons!"

She spoke, testing her sister, to see if Chalciope herself would take the lead in begging her to defend her sons. Utterly unbearable pain flooded Chalciope's heart in fear of what she heard, and she answered with these words:

"I too have been pondering all these things and came here myself, to see if you would take counsel with me and provide some help. Come, swear by Earth and Heaven

700 σχήσειν ἐν θυμῷ σύν τε δρήστειρα πέλεσθαι.
λίσσομ᾽ ὑπὲρ μακάρων σέο τ᾽ αὐτῆς ἠδὲ τοκήων,
μή σφε κακῇ ὑπὸ κηρὶ διαρραισθέντας ἰδέσθαι
λευγαλέως· ἢ σοί γε φίλοις σὺν παισὶ θανοῦσα
εἴην ἐξ Ἀίδεω στυγερὴ μετόπισθεν Ἐρινύς."
705 ὣς ἄρ᾽ ἔφη· τὸ δὲ πολλὸν ὑπεξέχυτ᾽ αὐτίκα
    δάκρυ,
νειόθι δ᾽ ἀμφοτέρῃσι περίσχετο γούνατα χερσίν,
σὺν δὲ κάρη κόλποις περικάββαλεν. ἔνθ᾽ ἐλεεινὸν
ἄμφω ἐπ᾽ ἀλλήλῃσι θέσαν γόον· ὦρτο δ᾽ ἰωὴ
λεπταλέη διὰ δώματ᾽ ὀδυρομένων ἀχέεσσιν.
710 τὴν δὲ πάρος Μήδεια προσέννεπεν ἀσχαλόωσα·
    "δαιμονίη, τί νύ τοι ῥέξω ἄκος, οἷ᾽ ἀγορεύεις,
ἀράς τε στυγερὰς καὶ Ἐρινύας; αἲ γὰρ ὄφελλεν
ἔμπεδον εἶναι ἐπ᾽ ἄμμι τεοὺς υἷας ἔρυσθαι.
ἴστω Κόλχων ὅρκος ὑπέρβιος, ὅν τιν᾽ ὀμόσσαι
715 αὐτὴ ἐποτρύνεις, μέγας Οὐρανὸς ἠδ᾽ ὑπένερθεν
Γαῖα, θεῶν μήτηρ, ὅσσον σθένος ἐστὶν ἐμεῖο,
μή σ᾽ ἐπιδευήσεσθαι ἀνυστά περ ἀντιόωσαν."
    φῆ ἄρα· Χαλκιόπη δ᾽ ἠμείβετο τοῖσδ᾽ ἐπέεσσιν·
    "οὐκ ἂν δὴ ξείνῳ τλαίης χατέοντι καὶ αὐτῷ
720 ἢ δόλον ἤ τινα μῆτιν ἐπιφράσσασθαι ἀέθλου,
παίδων εἴνεκ᾽ ἐμεῖο; καὶ ἐκ κείνοιο δ᾽ ἱκάνει
Ἄργος ἐποτρύνων με τεῆς πειρῆσαι ἀρωγῆς·
μεσσηγὺς μὲν τόν γε δόμῳ λίπον ἐνθάδ᾽ ἰοῦσα."

707 περικάββαλεν wE: περικάββαλον LA
710 ἀσχαλόωσα Ω: ἀσχαλόωσαν Fränkel

that you will keep what I tell you in your heart and be my helpmate. I implore you by the blessed gods, yourself, and our parents, not to look on while they are piteously destroyed by an evil death. Otherwise, may I die with my dear sons and hereafter be a horrible Fury from Hades for you."

Thus she spoke, and immediately a torrent of tears burst forth, and from below she embraced Medea's knees with both hands and at the same time let her head fall onto Medea's lap.[57] Then, next to one another, they both made a pitiful lament, and the wailing sound rose through the house as they wept in anguish. Full of grief, Medea addressed her sister first:

"My poor sister, what remedy can I provide you, when you speak of such things as horrible curses and Furies? If only it were firmly in my power to save your sons. Let my witness be the mighty oath of the Colchians, which you yourself are urging me to swear, and great Heaven and Earth below, mother of the gods, that with all the strength in my possession, you shall not lack help, if what you request can indeed be accomplished."

She spoke, and Chalciope answered with these words:

"Could you not then dare to contrive on behalf of the stranger, since he himself is in need as well, a trick or some plan with regard to the contest for my sons' sake? Indeed it is from him[58] that Argus has come, urging me to try to gain your help. While he was asking, I left him in my room to come here."

---

[57] Or, reading περικάββαλον, *they let their heads fall onto their own breasts.*   [58] Jason (the stranger).

---

723 τόν γε LA: τόνδε wE | δόμῳ H: δόμων SEˢˡ: δόμον rell.

ὣς φάτο· τῇ δ' ἔντοσθεν ἀνέπτατο χάρματι
θυμός·
725 φοινίχθη δ' ἄμυδις καλὸν χρόα, κὰδ δέ μιν ἀχλὺς
εἷλεν ἰαινομένην. τοῖον δ' ἐπὶ μῦθον ἔειπεν·
"Χαλκιόπη, ὡς ὔμμι φίλον τερπνόν τε τέτυκται,
ὣς ἔρξω. μὴ γάρ μοι ἐν ὀφθαλμοῖσι φαείνοι
ἠὼς μηδέ με δηρὸν ἔτι ζώουσαν ἴδοιο,
730 εἴ κέ τι σῆς ψυχῆς προφερέστερον ἠέ τι παίδων
σῶν θείην, οἳ δή μοι ἀδελφειοὶ γεγάασιν,
κηδεμόνες τε φίλοι καὶ ὁμήλικες· ὣς δὲ καὶ αὐτὴν
φημὶ κασιγνήτην τε σέθεν κούρην τε πέλεσθαι,
ἶσον ἐπεὶ κείνοις με τεῷ ἐπαείραο μαζῷ
735 νηπυτίην, ὡς αἰὲν ἐγώ ποτε μητρὸς ἄκουον.
ἀλλ' ἴθι, κεῦθε δ' ἐμὴν σιγῇ χάριν, ὄφρα τοκῆας
λήσομαι ἐντύνουσα ὑπόσχεσιν· ἦρι δὲ νηὸν
εἴσομαι εἰς Ἑκάτης θελκτήρια φάρμακα ταύρων
οἰσομένη ξείνῳ, ὑπὲρ οὗ τόδε νεῖκος ὄρωρεν."
740 ὣς ἥ γ' ἐκ θαλάμοιο πάλιν κίε, παισί τ' ἀρωγὴν
αὐτοκασιγνήτης διεπέφραδε. τήν γε μὲν αὖτις
αἰδώς τε στυγερόν τε δέος λάβε μουνωθεῖσαν,
τοῖα παρὲξ οὗ πατρὸς ἐπ' ἀνέρι μητιάασθαι.
νὺξ μὲν ἔπειτ' ἐπὶ γαῖαν ἄγεν κνέφας· οἱ δ' ἐνὶ
πόντῳ

730 εἴ κέ τι Wellauer: εἴ γέ τι Huet: εἰ ἔτι (vel ἢ ἔτι) Ω
732 αὐτὴν m: αὐτὴ w
733 κασιγνήτην Π⁴m: κασιγνήτη w | κούρην m: κούρη w
738 εἴσομαι L²ˢ¹Eᵃᶜ: οἴσομαι LAwE²d

Thus she spoke, and Medea's heart within her leapt for joy. At the same time her lovely skin turned red, and a mist covered her eyes as she warmed with pleasure. She replied with these words:

"Chalciope, whatever you and your sons find welcome and pleasing, I shall do. May the dawn not shine in my eyes, nor may you see me alive much longer, if I hold anything of more importance than your life or that of your sons, who are my brothers, beloved guardians, and childhood companions. Likewise, I declare myself to be your sister and daughter, for you nursed me at your breast equally with them when I was a baby,[59] as I always heard from our mother in the past. But come, hide my kindness in silence, so that I can fulfill my promise without our parents' knowledge. At dawn I shall go to the temple of Hecate, in order to take the drugs for charming the oxen to the stranger on whose account this strife arose."

Thus Chalciope went back from the room and informed her sons of her sister's aid. But shame and terrible dread again seized Medea when she was left alone, to be devising such things for a man without her father's knowledge.

Then night was drawing darkness over the earth, and

[59] By Vian's calculations, Medea and Phrixus' sons are between sixteen and twenty, Chalciope around thirty-five, Apsyrtus (by a previous marriage) around forty, and Aeetes in his sixties.

---

739 hic versus deest in codd. et pap., legitur in ΣLA
741 τήν γε μὲν αὖτις Platt: τὴν δὲ μεταῦτις Köchly: τὴν δέ μιν αὖθις Ω

APOLLONIUS RHODIUS

745 ναυτίλοι εἰς Ἑλίκην τε καὶ ἀστέρας Ὠρίωνος
ἔδρακον ἐκ νηῶν, ὕπνοιο δὲ καί τις ὁδίτης
ἤδη καὶ πυλαωρὸς ἐέλδετο, καί τινα παίδων
μητέρα τεθνεώτων ἀδινὸν περὶ κῶμ' ἐκάλυπτεν·
οὐδὲ κυνῶν ὑλακὴ ἔτ' ἀνὰ πτόλιν, οὐ θρόος ἦεν
750 ἠχήεις· σιγῇ δὲ μελαινομένην ἔχεν ὄρφνην.
ἀλλὰ μάλ' οὐ Μήδειαν ἐπὶ γλυκερὸς λάβεν ὕπνος·
πολλὰ γὰρ Αἰσονίδαο πόθῳ μελεδήματ' ἔγειρεν
δειδυῖαν ταύρων κρατερὸν μένος, οἷσιν ἔμελλεν
φθίσθαι ἀεικελίῃ μοίρῃ κατὰ νειὸν Ἄρηος.
755 πυκνὰ δέ οἱ κραδίη στηθέων ἔντοσθεν ἔθυιεν,
ἠελίου ὥς τίς τε δόμοις ἐνιπάλλεται αἴγλη
ὕδατος ἐξανιοῦσα, τὸ δὴ νέον ἠὲ λέβητι
ἠέ που ἐν γαυλῷ κέχυται, ἡ δ' ἔνθα καὶ ἔνθα
ὠκείῃ στροφάλιγγι τινάσσεται ἀίσσουσα·
760 ὣς δὲ καὶ ἐν στήθεσσι κέαρ ἐλελίζετο κούρης.
δάκρυ δ' ἀπ' ὀφθαλμῶν ἐλέῳ ῥέεν· ἔνδοθι δ' αἰεὶ
τεῖρ' ὀδύνη σμύχουσα διὰ χροὸς ἀμφί τ' ἀραιὰς
ἶνας καὶ κεφαλῆς ὑπὸ νείατον ἰνίον ἄχρις,
ἔνθ' ἀλεγεινότατον δύνει ἄχος, ὁππότ' ἀνίας
765 ἀκάματοι πραπίδεσσιν ἐνισκίμψωσιν Ἔρωτες.
φῆ δέ οἱ ἄλλοτε μὲν θελκτήρια φάρμακα ταύρων
δωσέμεν· ἄλλοτε δ' οὔ τι, καταφθίσθαι δὲ καὶ αὐτή·
αὐτίκα δ' οὔτ' αὐτὴ θανέειν, οὐ φάρμακα δώσειν,
ἀλλ' αὔτως εὔκηλος ἐὴν ὀτλησέμεν ἄτην.
770 ἑζομένη δἤπειτα δοάσσατο, φώνησέν τε·

276

the sailors on the sea looked towards Helice and the stars of Orion from their ships,[60] and by now the traveler and gate-keeper were longing for sleep, and deep slumber was enfolding the mother whose children had died; and no longer was there barking of dogs through the city nor echoing sounds, but silence gripped the darkening night. But by no means had sweet sleep overtaken Medea, because in her longing for Jason many anxieties kept her awake, as she dreaded the great strength of the oxen that were going to make him die a horrid death in the field of Ares. Over and over the heart within her breast fluttered wildly, as when a ray of sunlight bounds inside a house as it leaps from water freshly poured into a cauldron or perhaps into a bucket, and quivers and darts here and there from the rapid swirling—thus did the girl's heart tremble in her breast. Tears of pity poured from her eyes, and deep within a pain tortured her constantly as it smoldered through her body and along the delicate nerves and deep down beneath the nape of the neck,[61] where the sharpest anguish penetrates whenever the tireless Loves inflict pains upon the spirit.[62] At one moment she was determined to give him the drugs for charming the oxen; at another by no means to give them but to perish herself as well; then immediately neither to die herself nor to give the drugs, but to endure her calamity in silence just as she was doing. Then she sat there in doubt and said:

---

[60] Aratus (*Phaenomena* 37–41) says that Greek sailors steered by Helice (Ursa Major), which appears large and bright at the beginning of night, and calculated time by the constellation Orion (*Phaenomena* 730–731).   [61] The occiput.   [62] A. uses the obsolete term πραπίδεσσιν (mind, spirit) only here.

"δειλὴ ἐγώ, νῦν ἔνθα κακῶν ἢ ἔνθα γένωμαι;
πάντη μοι φρένες εἰσὶν ἀμήχανοι, οὐδέ τις ἀλκὴ
πήματος, ἀλλ' αὔτως φλέγει ἔμπεδον. ὡς ὄφελόν γε
Ἀρτέμιδος κραιπνοῖσι πάρος βελέεσσι δαμῆναι,
775 πρὶν τόν γ' εἰσιδέειν, πρὶν Ἀχαιίδα γαῖαν ἱκέσθαι
Χαλκιόπης υἷας· τοὺς μὲν θεὸς ἤ τις Ἐρινὺς
ἄμμι πολυκλαύτους δεῦρ' ἤγαγε κεῖθεν ἀνίας.
φθίσθω ἀεθλεύων, εἴ οἱ κατὰ νειὸν ὀλέσθαι
μοῖρα πέλει· πῶς γάρ κεν ἐμοὺς λελάθοιμι τοκῆας
780 φάρμακα μησαμένη; ποῖον δ' ἐπὶ μῦθον ἐνίψω;
τίς δὲ δόλος, τίς μῆτις ἐπίκλοπος ἔσσετ' ἀρωγῆς;
ἦ μιν ἄνευθ' ἑτάρων προσπτύξομαι οἶον ἰδοῦσα;
δύσμορος· οὐ μὲν ἔολπα καταφθιμένοιό περ ἔμπης
λωφήσειν ἀχέων· τότε δ' ἂν κακὸν ἄμμι πέλοιτο
785 κεῖνος, ὅτε ζωῆς ἀπαμείρεται. ἐρρέτω αἰδώς,
ἐρρέτω ἀγλαΐη· ὁ δ' ἐμῇ ἰότητι σαωθεὶς
ἀσκηθής, ἵνα οἱ θυμῷ φίλον, ἔνθα νέοιτο·
αὐτὰρ ἐγὼν αὐτῆμαρ, ὅτ' ἐξανύσειεν ἄεθλον,
τεθναίην, ἢ λαιμὸν ἀναρτήσασα μελάθρῳ
790 ἢ καὶ πασσαμένη ῥαιστήρια φάρμακα θυμοῦ.
ἀλλὰ καὶ ὣς φθιμένη μοι ἐπιλλίξουσιν ὀπίσσω
κερτομίας· τηλοῦ δὲ πόλις περὶ πᾶσα βοήσει
πότμον ἐμόν· καί κέν με διὰ στόματος φορέουσαι
Κολχίδες ἄλλυδις ἄλλαι ἀεικέα μωμήσονται·
795 'ἥ τις κηδομένη τόσον ἀνέρος ἀλλοδαποῖο
κάτθανεν, ἥ τις δῶμα καὶ οὓς ᾔσχυνε τοκῆας
μαργοσύνῃ εἴξασα.' τί δ' οὐκ ἐμὸν ἔσσεται αἶσχος;
ὤ μοι ἐμῆς ἄτης. ἦ τ' ἂν πολὺ κέρδιον εἴη

"O poor me! Must I now be in misery wherever I turn?
In every direction my mind is helpless, and there is no help
for the pain, but it burns steadily just like this. If only I had
been killed by Artemis' swift arrows before I laid eyes
on him, before Chalciope's sons had reached the land of
Achaea.[63] A god or some Fury led them here from that
place to cause me pains full of lamentation. Let him perish
in the contest, if it is his destiny to die in the field, for how
without my parents' knowledge could I prepare the drugs?
And then, what story can I tell? What trick, what scheme
will conceal my help?[64] If I catch sight of him alone with-
out his comrades, shall I greet him? Unhappy me! Even if
he perishes, I do not hope to find relief from anguish, for
then he would cause me misery when he is deprived of life.
Away with shame, away with glory! Once he is saved thanks
to me, let him go unharmed wherever his heart desires. Yet
for my part, on that very day when he completes his task,
may I die, either by attaching my neck to a roof-beam or
else by swallowing life-destroying drugs. But nonetheless,
even though I am dead, people will hereafter look askance
and reproach me, and far and wide the entire city will
shout out my fate and the Colchian women will savagely
revile me as they bear my story on their lips hither and yon:
'She cared so much for a foreign man that she died; she dis-
graced her home and her parents by yielding to lust.' What
disgrace will not be mine? What distress is mine! Truly, it

---

[63] Medea, like her father (cf. 3.375), believes that they actually
got to Greece.

[64] Or *what deceptive scheme will be of help.*

τῇδ' αὐτῇ ἐν νυκτὶ λιπεῖν βίον ἐν θαλάμοισιν,
800 πότμῳ ἀνωίστῳ κάκ' ἐλέγχεα πάντα φυγοῦσαν,
πρὶν τάδε λωβήεντα καὶ οὐκ ὀνομαστὰ τελέσσαι."
    ἦ, καὶ φωριαμὸν μετεκίαθεν, ᾗ ἔνι πολλὰ
φάρμακά οἱ, τὰ μὲν ἐσθλά, τὰ δὲ ῥαιστήρι', ἔκειτο.
ἐνθεμένη δ' ἐπὶ γούνατ' ὀδύρετο, δεῦε δὲ κόλπους
805 ἄλληκτον δακρύοισι, τὰ δ' ἔρρεεν ἀσταγὲς αὔτως,
αἴν' ὀλοφυρομένης τὸν ἑὸν μόρον. ἵετο δ' ἥ γε
φάρμακα λέξασθαι θυμοφθόρα, τόφρα πάσαιτο·
ἤδη καὶ δεσμοὺς ἀνελύετο φωριαμοῖο
ἐξελέειν μεμαυῖα, δυσάμμορος· ἀλλά οἱ ἄφνω
810 δεῖμ' ὀλοὸν στυγεροῖο κατὰ φρένας ἦλθ' Ἀίδαο.
ἔσχετο δ' ἀμφασίῃ δηρὸν χρόνον. ἀμφὶ δὲ πᾶσαι
θυμηδεῖς βιότοιο μεληδόνες ἰνδάλλοντο·
μνήσατο μὲν τερπνῶν, ὅσ' ἐνὶ ζωοῖσι πέλονται,
μνήσαθ' ὁμηλικίης περιγηθέος, οἷά τε κούρη·
815 καί τέ οἱ ἠέλιος γλυκίων γένετ' εἰσοράασθαι
ἢ πάρος, εἰ ἐτεόν γε νόῳ ἐπεμαίεθ' ἕκαστα.
καὶ τὴν μέν ῥα πάλιν σφετέρων ἀποκάτθετο
                                        γούνων,
Ἥρης ἐννεσίῃσι μετάτροπος, οὐδ' ἔτι βουλὰς
ἄλλῃ δοιάζεσκεν· ἐέλδετο δ' αἶψα φανῆναι
820 ἠῶ τελλομένην, ἵνα οἱ θελκτήρια δοίη
φάρμακα συνθεσίῃσι καὶ ἀντήσειεν ἐς ὠπήν.
πυκνὰ δ' ἀνὰ κληῖδας ἑῶν λύεσκε θυράων,
αἴγλην σκεπτομένη· τῇ δ' ἀσπάσιον βάλε φέγγος
Ἠριγενής, κίνυντο δ' ἀνὰ πτολίεθρον ἕκαστοι.
825   ἔνθα κασιγνήτους μὲν ἔτ' αὐτόθι μεῖναι ἀνώγει

280

would be much better for me to quit life this very night in my room and by a mysterious death flee all evil reproaches before carrying out these shameful and unnamable deeds."

She spoke and fetched a chest in which lay her many drugs, some good, some harmful. And placing it on her knees, she wept and soaked her lap with incessant tears that flowed in streams as she sat there, bitterly lamenting her own fate. She longed to choose lethal drugs to swallow and was already loosening the fastenings of the chest in her eagerness to take them out, unfortunate girl! But suddenly a dread fear of hateful Hades entered her mind, and for a long time she held back in dumbfounded silence. Around her appeared all of life's heart-warming concerns: she remembered all the pleasures that exist among the living and recalled, as a girl would, her joyful age-mates, and the sun became sweeter for her to behold than ever before, as she truly grasped each of these with her mind. Then she put the chest back down off her knees, having changed her mind at the prompting of Hera; and no longer was she in doubt as to different plans, but longed for the rising dawn to appear quickly, so that she could give him the spell-casting drugs as she had promised, and meet him face to face. Again and again she loosened the bolts on her doors, peering for a gleam. And welcome to her was the light that Dawn cast, and people began stirring throughout the city.

Then Argus told his brothers to remain there longer to

Ἄργος, ἵνα φράζοιντο νόον καὶ μήδεα κούρης·
αὐτὸς δ᾽ αὖτ᾽ ἐπὶ νῆα κίεν προπάροιθε λιασθείς.
   ἡ δ᾽ ἐπεὶ οὖν τὰ πρῶτα φαεινομένην ἴδεν ἠῶ
παρθενική, ξανθὰς μὲν ἀνήψατο χερσὶν ἐθείρας,
830 αἵ οἱ ἀτημελίῃ καταειμέναι ἠερέθοντο,
αὐσταλέας δ᾽ ἔψησε παρηίδας, αὐτὰρ ἀλοιφῇ
νεκταρέῃ φαιδρύνετ᾽ ἔπι χρόα· δῦνε δὲ πέπλον
καλόν, εὐγνάμπτοισιν ἀρηρέμενον περόνῃσιν,
ἀμβροσίῳ δ᾽ ἐφύπερθε καρήατι βάλλε καλύπτρην
835 ἀργυφέην. αὐτοῦ δὲ δόμοις ἔνι δινεύουσα
στεῖβε πέδον λήθῃ ἀχέων, τά οἱ ἐν ποσὶν ἦεν
θεσπέσι᾽, ἄλλα τ᾽ ἔμελλεν ἀεξήσεσθαι ὀπίσσω.
κέκλετο δ᾽ ἀμφιπόλοισιν, αἵ οἱ δυοκαίδεκα πᾶσαι
ἐν προδόμῳ θαλάμοιο θυώδεος ηὐλίζοντο
840 ἥλικες, οὔ πω λέκτρα σὺν ἀνδράσι πορσύνουσαι,
ἐσσυμένως οὐρῆας ὑποζεύξασθαι ἀπήνῃ,
οἵ κέ μιν εἰς Ἑκάτης περικαλλέα νηὸν ἄγοιεν.
ἔνθ᾽ αὖτ᾽ ἀμφίπολοι μὲν ἐφοπλίζεσκον ἀπήνην·
ἡ δὲ τέως γλαφυρῆς ἐξείλετο φωριαμοῖο
845 φάρμακον, ὅ ῥά τέ φασι Προμήθειον καλέεσθαι.
τῷ εἴ κ᾽ ἐννυχίοισιν ἀρεσσάμενος θυέεσσιν
Δαῖραν μουνογένειαν ἑὸν δέμας ἰκμαίνοιτο,
ἦ τ᾽ ἂν ὅ γ᾽ οὔτε ῥηκτὸς ἔοι χαλκοῖο τυπῇσιν,
οὔτε κεν αἰθομένῳ πυρὶ εἰκάθοι, ἀλλὰ καὶ ἀλκῇ
850 λωίτερος κεῖν᾽ ἦμαρ ὁμῶς κάρτει τε πέλοιτο.
πρωτοφυὲς τό γ᾽ ἀνέσχε καταστάξαντος ἔραζε
αἰετοῦ ὠμηστέω κνημοῖς ἔνι Καυκασίοισιν
αἱματόεντ᾽ ἰχῶρα Προμηθῆος μογεροῖο.

ascertain the girl's state of mind and plans, while he himself left and returned in advance of them to the ship.

Now as soon as the maiden saw dawn appearing, with her hands she bound up her golden hair, which through her neglect hung down loose. She wiped[65] her tear-stained cheeks and freshened her skin with oil fragrant as nectar. She donned a beautiful robe fitted with elegantly curved pins, and upon her divinely beautiful head she cast a silver-white veil. And as she roamed there in the house, she trod the floor oblivious of the griefs—prodigious ones close at hand for her, and others destined to multiply thereafter. She called for her handmaids, twelve in all, who slept in the vestibule of her fragrant room, the same age as she and not yet sharing beds with husbands, and ordered them to yoke mules swiftly to the wagon, so they could draw her to the splendid temple of Hecate. Thereupon the handmaids set about preparing the wagon. She, meanwhile, took from the hollow chest a drug which they say is called Promethean. If, after appeasing the only-begotten Daira[66] with nocturnal sacrifices, a man should anoint his body with this drug, he would truly be impervious to strokes of bronze and not yield to blazing fire, but for that day would be superior both in valor and might. It first sprouted when the flesh-eating eagle dripped the bloody ichor of tortured Prometheus to the ground on the cliffs of Caucasus. From

[65] Or, reading ἔψηχε, *she rubbed*.
[66] Here a cultic name of Hecate, otherwise a chthonic deity associated with Eleusis and Persephone.

831 ἔψησε Ω: ἔψηχε Et. Gen. (cf. 4.164)
847 Δαῖραν *w*: κούρην *m*

τοῦ δ᾽ ἤτοι ἄνθος μὲν ὅσον πήχυιον ὕπερθεν
855 χροιῇ Κωρυκίῳ ἴκελον κρόκῳ ἐξεφαάνθη,
καυλοῖσιν διδύμοισιν ἐπήορον· ἡ δ᾽ ἐνὶ γαίῃ
σαρκὶ νεοτμήτῳ ἐναλιγκίη ἔπλετο ῥίζα.
τῆς οἵην τ᾽ ἐν ὄρεσσι κελαινὴν ἰκμάδα φηγοῦ
Κασπίῃ ἐν κόχλῳ ἀμήσατο φαρμάσσεσθαι,
860 ἑπτὰ μὲν ἀενάοισι λοεσσαμένη ὑδάτεσσιν,
ἑπτάκι δὲ Βριμὼ κουροτρόφον ἀγκαλέσασα,
Βριμὼ νυκτιπόλον, χθονίην, ἐνέροισιν ἄνασσαν,
λυγαίῃ ἐνὶ νυκτὶ σὺν ὀρφναίοις φαρέεσσιν.
μυκηθμῷ δ᾽ ὑπένερθεν ἐρεμνὴ σείετο γαῖα,
865 ῥίζης τεμνομένης Τιτηνίδος· ἔστενε δ᾽ αὐτὸς
Ἰαπετοῖο πάις ὀδύνῃ πέρι θυμὸν ἀλύων.
τό ῥ᾽ ἥ γ᾽ ἐξανελοῦσα θυώδεϊ κάτθετο μίτρῃ,
ἥ τέ οἱ ἀμβροσίοισι περὶ στήθεσσιν ἔερτο.
ἐκ δὲ θύραζε κιοῦσα θοῆς ἐπεβήσατ᾽ ἀπήνης,
870 σὺν δέ οἱ ἀμφίπολοι δοιαὶ ἑκάτερθεν ἔβησαν.
αὐτὴ δ᾽ ἡνί᾽ ἔδεκτο καὶ εὐποίητον ἱμάσθλην
δεξιτερῇ, ἔλαεν δὲ δι᾽ ἄστεος· αἱ δὲ δὴ ἄλλαι
ἀμφίπολοι, πείρινθος ἐφαπτόμεναι μετόπισθεν,
τρώχων εὐρεῖαν κατ᾽ ἀμαξιτόν, ἂν δὲ χιτῶνας
875 λεπταλέους λευκῆς ἐπιγουνίδος ἄχρις ἄειρον.
οἵη δὲ λιαροῖσιν ἐφ᾽ ὕδασι Παρθενίοιο,
ἠὲ καὶ Ἀμνισοῖο λοεσσαμένη ποταμοῖο
χρυσείοις Λητωὶς ἐφ᾽ ἅρμασιν ἑστηυῖα
ὠκείαις κεμάδεσσι διεξελάῃσι κολώνας,
880 τηλόθεν ἀντιόωσα πολυκνίσου ἑκατόμβης·

it emerged a flower a cubit high above ground in color like
a Corycian crocus,[67] supported by two stalks, but in the
earth its root was like freshly cut flesh. Its sap, like the
black juice of a mountain oak, she had collected in a Cas-
pian shell to prepare the drug, after bathing herself seven
times in ever-flowing streams,[68] and calling seven times on
Brimo[69] the youth-nourisher, Brimo the night-wanderer,
the infernal goddess, queen of the nether dead—all in the
gloom of night, clad in dark garments. And with a bellow
the black earth beneath shook when the Titanian[70] root
was cut, and the son of Iapetus himself groaned, distressed
at heart with pain. This drug she then took out and placed
in the fragrant band that was fastened around her divinely
beautiful breasts. She went outside and mounted the swift
wagon, and two maidservants mounted with her, one on ei-
ther side.[71] She herself took the reins and a well-wrought
whip in her right hand and drove through the city. The rest
of the handmaids, holding on to the wicker basket of the
wagon from behind, ran along the broad road and lifted
their delicate robes up to their white thighs. And as when
by the warm waters of Parthenius, or after bathing in the
Amnisus river, Leto's daughter[72] stands in her golden char-
iot drawn by swift deer and drives through the hills, com-
ing from afar to partake of a savory hecatomb, and with her

[67] Corycus in Cilicia was famous for its saffron.
[68] Or *in seven ever-flowing streams* (schol.).
[69] "The Roarer," a title of Hecate.
[70] Prometheus' father was the Titan Iapetus.
[71] Or *two on each side*.
[72] Artemis.

285

τῇ δ' ἅμα νύμφαι ἔπονται ἀμορβάδες, αἱ μὲν ἀπ'
   αὐτῆς
ἀγρόμεναι πηγῆς Ἀμνισίδος, αἱ δὲ λιποῦσαι
ἄλσεα καὶ σκοπιὰς πολυπίδακας· ἀμφὶ δὲ θῆρες
κνυζηθμῷ σαίνουσιν ὑποτρομέοντες ἰοῦσαν·
885 ὣς αἵ γ' ἐσσεύοντο δι' ἄστεος, ἀμφὶ δὲ λαοὶ
εἶκον ἀλευάμενοι βασιληίδος ὄμματα κούρης.
αὐτὰρ ἐπεὶ πόλιος μὲν ἐυδμήτους λίπ' ἀγυιάς,
νηὸν δ' εἰσαφίκανε διὲκ πεδίων ἐλάουσα,
δὴ τότ' ἐυτροχάλοιο κατ' αὐτόθι βήσατ' ἀπήνης
890 ἱεμένη, καὶ τοῖα μετὰ δμωῇσιν ἔειπεν·
   "ὦ φίλαι, ἦ μέγα δή τι παρήλιτον, οὐδ' ἐνόησα
μὴ ἴμεν ἀλλοδαποῖσι μετ' ἀνδράσιν, οἵ τ' ἐπὶ γαῖαν
ἡμετέρην στρωφῶσιν· ἀμηχανίη βεβόληται
πᾶσα πόλις· τὸ καὶ οὔ τις ἀνήλυθε δεῦρο γυναικῶν
895 τάων, αἳ τὸ πάροιθεν ἐπημάτιαι ἀγέρονται.
ἀλλ' ἐπεὶ οὖν ἱκόμεσθα καὶ οὔ νύ τις ἄλλος ἔπεισιν,
εἰ δ' ἄγε μολπῇ θυμὸν ἀφειδείως κορέσωμεν
μειλιχίῃ, τὰ δὲ καλὰ τερείνης ἄνθεα ποίης
λεξάμεναι τότ' ἔπειτ' αὐτὴν ἀπονισσόμεθ' ὥρην.
900 καὶ δέ κε σὺν πολέεσσιν ὀνείασιν οἴκαδ' ἵκοισθε
ἤματι τῷδ', εἴ μοι συναρέσσετε τήνδε μενοινήν.
Ἄργος γάρ μ' ἐπέεσσι παρατρέπει, ὡς δὲ καὶ αὐτὴ
Χαλκιόπη—τὰ δὲ σῖγα νόῳ ἔχετ' εἰσαΐουσαι
ἐξ ἐμέθεν, μὴ πατρὸς ἐς οὔατα μῦθος ἵκηται—
905 τὸν ξεῖνόν με κέλονται, ὅ τις περὶ βουσὶν ὑπέστη,

follow nymphs in attendance—some gathering from the very source of the Amnisus, others having left groves and peaks with many springs—and all around wild animals fawn on her, cowering with whimpers as she makes her way; thus did they hasten through the city, and all around them the people gave way as they avoided the eyes of the royal maiden. But after she had left the well-built streets of the city and, having crossed the plain, arrived at the temple, then at once she stepped down from her well-wheeled wagon, all eager, and said the following to her handmaids:

"My friends, I truly made a great mistake, and I did not realize that I should not go out among the foreign men who roam about our country, for the whole city is stricken with helpless dismay, and therefore none of the women who formerly gathered every day has come here. But since in fact we have arrived and no one else will come here, let us without restraint satisfy our hearts with gentle play,[73] and then, after plucking those beautiful flowers from the tender grass, we shall return at the same hour as usual. Furthermore, you might go back home with many presents today, if you will grant this desire of mine. For Argus tries to win me over with entreaties, as does Chalciope herself (but what you hear from me keep silently in your minds, so that word does not reach my father's ears): with regard to that stranger who agreed to compete with the oxen, they

---

[73] The word μολπή indicates that singing and dancing are a major component of their amusement. The scene is modeled on the play of Nausicaa and her handmaids at *Odyssey* 6.101.

881 ἀπ' Fränkel: ἐπ' Ω   882 λιποῦσαι Struve: δὴ ἄλλαι Ω (ex 872)   901 τῷδ' Platt: τῷ Ω

δῶρ' ἀποδεξαμένην ὀλοῶν ῥύσασθαι ἀέθλων.
αὐτὰρ ἐγὼ τὸν μῦθον ἐπήνεον ἠδὲ καὶ αὐτὸν
κέκλομαι εἰς ὠπὴν ἑτάρων ἄπο μοῦνον ἱκέσθαι,
ὄφρα τὰ μὲν δασόμεσθα μετὰ σφίσιν, εἴ κεν
              ὀπάσσῃ
910 δῶρα φέρων, τῷ δ' αὖτε κακώτερον ἄλλο πόρωμεν
φάρμακον. ἀλλ' ἀπονόσφι πέλεσθέ μοι, εὖτ' ἂν
              ἵκηται."
       ὣς ηὔδα· πάσῃσι δ' ἐπίκλοπος ἥνδανε μῆτις.
       αὐτίκα δ' Αἰσονίδην ἑτάρων ἄπο μοῦνον ἐρύσσας
Ἄργος, ὅτ' ἤδη τήνδε κασιγνήτων ἐσάκουσεν,
915 ἠερίην Ἑκάτης ἱερὸν μετὰ νηὸν ἰοῦσαν,
ἦγε διὲκ πεδίου· ἅμα δέ σφισιν εἵπετο Μόψος
Ἀμπυκίδης, ἐσθλὸς μὲν ἐπιπροφανέντας ἐνισπεῖν
οἰωνούς, ἐσθλὸς δὲ σὺν εὖ φράσσασθαι ἰοῦσιν.
       ἔνθ' οὔ πώ τις τοῖος ἐπὶ προτέρων γένετ' ἀνδρῶν,
920 οὔθ' ὅσοι ἐξ αὐτοῖο Διὸς γένος, οὔθ' ὅσοι ἄλλων
ἀθανάτων ἥρωες ἀφ' αἵματος ἐβλάστησαν,
οἷον Ἰήσονα θῆκε Διὸς δάμαρ ἤματι κείνῳ
ἠμὲν ἐσάντα ἰδεῖν ἠδὲ προτιμυθήσασθαι·
τὸν καὶ παπταίνοντες ἐθάμβεον αὐτοὶ ἑταῖροι
925 λαμπόμενον χαρίτεσσιν· ἐγήθησεν δὲ κελεύθῳ
Ἀμπυκίδης, ἤδη που ὀισσάμενος τὰ ἕκαστα.
       ἔστι δέ τις πεδίοιο κατὰ στίβον ἐγγύθι νηοῦ
αἴγειρος φύλλοισιν ἀπειρεσίοις κομόωσα·
τῇ θαμὰ δὴ λακέρυζαι ἐπηυλίζοντο κορῶναι,

914: τήνδε Ω: τήν γε S

288

are asking me to accept his gifts and save him from the deadly contest. And I assented to their request and am asking him to come alone, apart from his comrades, to meet face to face, so that we can divide among ourselves any gifts he brings to give to us, and in return we can give him some other thing more baneful,[74] a drug. But please stay back when he comes."

Thus she spoke, and the deceptive scheme pleased them all.

Argus immediately drew Jason alone, apart from his comrades, as soon as he had heard from his brothers that she had gone at daybreak to Hecate's holy temple, and began leading him across the plain. With them followed Mopsus, son of Ampycus, expert at interpreting birds that appeared before him, and expert at giving good advice to fellow travelers.[75]

Never before had there been such a man in earlier generations, neither among all the descendants of Zeus himself nor among all the heroes sprung from the blood of the other immortals, as on that day Zeus' wife had made Jason, both to behold and to converse with. Even his very comrades marveled as they gazed upon him, radiant with graces; and Ampycus' son rejoiced in their journey, no doubt already foreseeing each thing.

There stands a poplar by the path in the plain near the temple, crowned with countless leaves. In it chattering crows often roosted, one of which, as they passed, batted

[74] I.e. than the gifts he is supposedly bringing.
[75] Mopsus used both skills at 1.1086–1097 and 3.543–548.

APOLLONIUS RHODIUS

930 τάων τις μεσσηγὺς ἀνὰ πτερὰ κινήσασα
ὑψοῦ ἐπ' ἀκρεμόνων Ἥρης ἠνίπαπε βουλαῖς·
    "ἀκλειὴς ὅδε μάντις, ὃς οὐδ' ὅσα παῖδες ἴσασιν
οἶδε νόῳ φράσσασθαι, ὁθούνεκεν οὔτε τι λαρὸν
οὔτ' ἐρατὸν κούρη κεν ἔπος προτιμυθήσαιτο
935 ἠιθέῳ, εὖτ' ἄν σφιν ἐπήλυδες ἄλλοι ἔπωνται.
ἔρροις, ὦ κακόμαντι, κακοφραδές· οὐδέ σε Κύπρις
οὔτ' ἀγανοὶ φιλέοντες ἐπιπνείουσιν Ἔρωτες."
    ἴσκεν ἀτεμβομένη· μείδησε δὲ Μόψος ἀκούσας
ὀμφὴν οἰωνοῖο θεήλατον, ὧδέ τ' ἔειπεν·
940 "τύνη μὲν νηόνδε θεᾶς ἴθι, τῷ ἔνι κούρην   ·
δήεις, Αἰσονίδη· μάλα δ' ἠπίη ἀντιβολήσεις
Κύπριδος ἐννεσίῃς, ἥ τοι συνέριθος ἀέθλων
ἔσσεται, ὡς δὴ καὶ πρὶν Ἀγηνορίδης φάτο Φινεύς.
νῶι δ', ἐγὼν Ἄργος τε, δεδεγμένοι εὖτ' ἂν ἵκηαι,
945 τῷδ' αὐτῷ ἐνὶ χώρῳ ἀπεσσόμεθ'· οἰόθι δ' αὐτὸς
λίσσεό μιν πυκινοῖσι παρατροπέων ἐπέεσσιν."
    ἦ ῥα περιφραδέως, ἐπὶ δὲ σχεδὸν ἤνεον ἄμφω.
    οὐδ' ἄρα Μηδείης θυμὸς τράπετ' ἄλλα νοῆσαι
μελπομένης περ ὅμως· πᾶσαι δέ οἱ, ἤν τιν' ἀθύροι
950 μολπήν, οὐκ ἐπὶ δηρὸν ἐφήνδανεν ἐψιάασθαι,
ἀλλὰ μεταλλήγεσκεν ἀμήχανος· οὐδέ ποτ' ὄσσε
ἀμφιπόλων μεθ' ὅμιλον ἔχ' ἀτρέμας, ἐς δὲ
        κελεύθους
τηλόσε παπταίνεσκε παρακλίνουσα παρειάς.

931 βουλαῖς Chrestien: βουλάς Ω
944 εὖτ' Ω: ἔστ' Π24

its wings high up in the branches and at Hera's devising scolded:[76]

"No fame has the seer who has not the sense to conceive in his mind even as much as children know, that no girl would speak any sweet or loving word to a young man when strangers accompany him.[77] Off with you, incompetent seer, incompetent advisor; neither Cypris nor the gentle Loves inspire you with their favor."

Thus it spoke in reproach, but Mopsus smiled when he heard the divinely inspired voice of the bird, and spoke thus:

"Jason, you go to the goddess' temple, wherein you will meet the girl. And you will find her very kindly disposed through the prompting of Cypris, who will be your helper in the contest, just as Phineus, Agenor's son, foretold.[78] But the two of us, Argus and I, will stay back in this very spot and wait until you return; all on your own you must make your plea and win her over with wise words."

Thus he spoke very advisedly, and the other two approved at once.

Nor indeed could Medea's heart be turned to pay attention to other things,[79] in spite of her play, for of all the games she played, none pleased her to enjoy for long, but she kept breaking off, helplessly distracted. She could never keep her eyes steadily on the throng of handmaids, but kept turning her face toward the roadways as she

[76] Or, reading the MSS' βουλάς, *declared the counsels of Hera*.
[77] Or *them*.
[78] At 2.423–424.
[79] I.e. than Jason's arrival (cf. 3.911, "when he comes").

ἦ θαμὰ δὴ στηθέων ἐάγη κέαρ, ὁππότε δοῦπον
955 ἢ ποδὸς ἢ ἀνέμοιο παραθρέξαντα δοάσσαι.
αὐτὰρ ὅ γ᾽ οὐ μετὰ δηρὸν ἐελδομένῃ ἐφαάνθη,
ὑψόσ᾽ ἀναθρῴσκων ἅ τε Σείριος Ὠκεανοῖο,
ὃς δ᾽ ἤτοι καλὸς μὲν ἀρίζηλός τ᾽ ἐσιδέσθαι
ἀντέλλει, μήλοισι δ᾽ ἐν ἄσπετον ἧκεν ὀιζύν·
960 ὣς ἄρα τῇ καλὸς μὲν ἐπήλυθεν εἰσοράασθαι
Αἰσονίδης, κάματον δὲ δυσίμερον ὦρσε φαανθείς.
ἐκ δ᾽ ἄρα οἱ κραδίη στηθέων πέσεν, ὄμματα δ᾽
    αὔτως
ἤχλυσαν, θερμὸν δὲ παρηίδας εἷλεν ἔρευθος·
γούνατα δ᾽ οὔτ᾽ ὀπίσω οὔτε προπάροιθεν ἀεῖραι
965 ἔσθενεν, ἀλλ᾽ ὑπένερθε πάγη πόδας. αἱ δ᾽ ἄρα τείως
ἀμφίπολοι μάλα πᾶσαι ἀπὸ σφείων ἐλίασθεν.
τὼ δ᾽ ἄνεῳ καὶ ἄναυδοι ἐφέστασαν ἀλλήλοισιν,
ἢ δρυσὶν ἢ μακρῇσιν ἐειδόμενοι ἐλάτῃσιν,
αἵ τε παρᾶσσον ἕκηλοι ἐν οὔρεσιν ἐρρίζωνται
970 νηνεμίῃ, μετὰ δ᾽ αὖτις ὑπὸ ῥιπῆς ἀνέμοιο
κινύμεναι ὁμάδησαν ἀπείριτον· ὣς ἄρα τώ γε
μέλλον ἅλις φθέγξασθαι ὑπὸ πνοιῇσιν Ἔρωτος.
γνῶ δέ μιν Αἰσονίδης ἄτῃ ἐνιπεπτηυῖαν
θευμορίῃ, καὶ τοῖον ὑποσσαίνων φάτο μῦθον·
975   "τίπτε με, παρθενική, τόσον ἅζεαι οἷον ἐόντα;
οὔ τοι ἐγών, οἷοί τε δυσαυχέες ἄλλοι ἔασιν
ἀνέρες, οὐδ᾽, ὅτε περ πάτρῃ ἔνι ναιετάασκον,
ἦα πάρος. τῶ μή με λίην ὑπεραίδεο, κούρη,
ἤ τι παρεξερέεσθαι ὅ τοι φίλον ἠέ τι φάσθαι.
980 ἀλλ᾽ ἐπεὶ ἀλλήλοισιν ἱκάνομεν εὐμενέοντες

292

peered far in the distance. Again and again her heart broke in her breast, whenever she was unsure whether the sound that passed by was that of a footstep or of the wind. But before long he appeared to her longing eyes, striding on high like Sirius[80] from the Ocean, which rises beautiful and bright to behold, but casts unspeakable grief on the flocks. So did Jason come to her, beautiful to behold, but by appearing he aroused lovesick distress. Then her heart dropped out of her breast, her eyes darkened with mist of their own accord, and a hot blush seized hold of her cheeks. She had no strength to raise her knees and go backwards or forwards, but her feet were stuck fast beneath her. In the meantime, all her handmaids had withdrawn from them. The two stood facing each other in speechless silence, like oaks or lofty pines that stand rooted quietly side by side in the mountains when there is no wind, but then, when shaken by a gust of wind, they rustle ceaselessly—thus were these two about to speak a great deal under the force of Love's breezes. Jason recognized that the distress into which she had plunged was heaven-sent, and to reassure her spoke these words:

"Why, maiden, are you so afraid of me, when I am all alone? I assure you, I am not an insolent braggart as other men are, nor was I before, when I lived in my own country. So, young woman, do not be too much in awe of me either to ask for anything that pleases you or to say anything. But since we have come with good will for each other into this

---

[80] Sirius, the Dog Star, rises at the end of July, marking the season of heat and pestilence (cf. 2.516–517).

---

958 δ᾿ ἤτοι Hermann: δή τοι Ω

χώρῳ ἐν ἠγαθέῳ, ἵνα τ᾽ οὐ θέμις ἔστ᾽ ἀλιτέσθαι,
ἀμφαδίην ἀγόρευε καὶ εἴρεο· μηδέ με τερπνοῖς
φηλώσῃς ἐπέεσσιν, ἐπεὶ τὸ πρῶτον ὑπέστης
αὐτοκασιγνήτῃ μενοεικέα φάρμακα δώσειν.
985 πρός σ᾽ αὐτῆς Ἑκάτης μειλίσσομαι ἠδὲ τοκήων
καὶ Διός, ὃς ξείνοις ἱκέτῃσί τε χεῖρ᾽ ὑπερίσχει·
ἀμφότερον δ᾽ ἱκέτης ξεῖνός τέ τοι ἐνθάδ᾽ ἱκάνω,
χρειοῖ ἀναγκαίῃ γουνούμενος· οὐ γὰρ ἄνευθεν
ὑμείων στονόεντος ὑπέρτερος ἔσσομ᾽ ἀέθλου.
990 σοὶ δ᾽ ἂν ἐγὼ τίσαιμι χάριν μετόπισθεν ἀρωγῆς,
ἣ θέμις, ὡς ἐπέοικε διάνδιχα ναιετάοντας,
οὔνομα καὶ καλὸν τεύχων κλέος· ὣς δὲ καὶ ὧλλοι
ἥρωες κλήσουσιν ἐς Ἑλλάδα νοστήσαντες
ἡρώων τ᾽ ἄλοχοι καὶ μητέρες, αἵ νύ που ἤδη
995 ἡμέας ἠιόνεσσιν ἐφεζόμεναι γοάουσιν·
τάων ἀργαλέας κεν ἀποσκεδάσειας ἀνίας.
δή ποτε καὶ Θησῆα κακῶν ὑπελύσατ᾽ ἀέθλων
παρθενικὴ Μινωὶς ἐυφρονέουσ᾽ Ἀριάδνη,
ἣν ῥά τε Πασιφάη κούρη τέκεν Ἠελίοιο.
1000 ἀλλ᾽ ἡ μὲν καὶ νηός, ἐπεὶ χόλον εὔνασε Μίνως,
σὺν τῷ ἐφεζομένη πάτρην λίπε· τὴν δὲ καὶ αὐτοὶ
ἀθάνατοι φίλαντο, μέσῳ δέ οἱ αἰθέρι τέκμωρ
ἀστερόεις στέφανος, τόν τε κλείουσ᾽ Ἀριάδνης,
πάννυχος οὐρανίοισιν ἑλίσσεται εἰδώλοισιν.
1005 ὣς καὶ σοὶ θεόθεν χάρις ἔσσεται, εἴ κε σαώσεις
τόσσον ἀριστήων ἀνδρῶν στόλον. ἦ γὰρ ἔοικας
ἐκ μορφῆς ἀγανῇσιν ἐπητείῃσι κεκάσθαι."

81 Cf. 3.737–739.

holy place where it is forbidden to do wrong, speak openly and ask questions. And do not deceive me with sweet words, now that you have promised your sister to give me heart-cheering drugs.[81] I implore you by Hecate herself, by your parents, and by Zeus, who holds his protective hand over guests and suppliants—for I have come to you here as both suppliant and guest, at your knees because of compelling need—for without your[82] aid I will not prevail in the dire contest. And thereafter, as is right, I would repay you with gratitude for your help, as befits those who dwell far apart, by making glorious your name and fame. And likewise the other heroes will celebrate you when they return to Hellas, and so will the heroes' wives and mothers—who, I think, at this moment are sitting on the shore mourning for us—since you would dispel their grievous pains. Once upon a time Ariadne, Minos' maiden daughter, rescued Theseus as well from terrible trials through her kindness, she whom Helius' daughter Pasiphae bore.[83] But she, once Minos had calmed his anger, even boarded his ship with him and left her country; and even the immortals themselves loved her, and in the midst of the sky her sign, a crown of stars they call Ariadne's,[84] turns all night among the heavenly constellations. Likewise, you too will have gratitude from the gods, if you save so great an expedition of heroic men. For truly, to judge from your lovely form, you seem to excel in gentle civility."

---

[82] The plural diffuses the responsibility, "you and your sister" (Seaton) or "you and the gods" (Mooney).   [83] Pasiphae is thus Aeetes' half-sister.   [84] The bridal crown Dionysus gave Ariadne became the *Corona borealis* (Aratus, *Phaenomena* 71–72). Jason tactfully leaves out Theseus' abandonment of Ariadne on Naxos before Dionysus rescued her.

ὣς φάτο κυδαίνων· ἡ δ' ἐγκλιδὸν ὄσσε βαλοῦσα
νεκτάρεον μείδησε· χύθη δέ οἱ ἔνδοθι θυμὸς
1010 αἴνῳ ἀειρομένης, καὶ ἀνέδρακεν ὄμμασιν ἄντην·
οὐδ' ἔχεν ὅττι πάροιθεν ἔπος προτιμυθήσαιτο,
ἀλλ' ἄμυδις μενέαινεν ἀολλέα πάντ' ἀγορεῦσαι.
προπρὸ δ' ἀφειδήσασα θυώδεος ἔξελε μίτρης
φάρμακον· αὐτὰρ ὅ γ' αἶψα χεροῖν ὑπέδεκτο
γεγηθώς.
1015 καί νύ κέ οἱ καὶ πᾶσαν ἀπὸ στηθέων ἀρύσασα
ψυχὴν ἐγγυάλιξεν ἀγαιομένη χατέοντι·
τοῖος ἀπὸ ξανθοῖο καρήατος Αἰσονίδαο
στράπτεν ἔρως ἡδεῖαν ἀπὸ φλόγα, τῆς δ' ἀμαρυγὰς
ὀφθαλμῶν ἥρπαζεν· ἰαίνετο δὲ φρένας εἴσω
1020 τηκομένη, οἷόν τε περὶ ῥοδέεσσιν ἐέρση
τήκεται ἠῴοισιν ἰαινομένη φαέεσσιν.
ἄμφω δ' ἄλλοτε μέν τε κατ' οὔδεος ὄμματ' ἔρειδον
αἰδόμενοι, ὁτὲ δ' αὖτις ἐπὶ σφίσι βάλλον ὀπωπάς,
ἱμερόεν φαιδρῆσιν ὑπ' ὀφρύσι μειδιόωντες.
1025 ὀψὲ δὲ δὴ τοίοισι μόλις προσπτύξατο κούρη·
"φράζεο νῦν, ὥς κέν τοι ἐγὼ μητίσομ' ἀρωγήν.
εὖτ' ἂν δὴ μετιόντι πατὴρ ἐμὸς ἐγγυαλίξῃ
ἐξ ὄφιος γεννῶν ὀλοοὺς σπείρασθαι ὀδόντας,
δὴ τότε μέσσην νύκτα διαμμοιρηδὰ φυλάξας,
1030 ἀκαμάτοιο ῥοῇσι λοεσσάμενος ποταμοῖο,
οἶος ἄνευθ' ἄλλων ἐνὶ φάρεσι κυανέοισιν
βόθρον ὀρύξασθαι περιηγέα· τῷ δ' ἔνι θῆλυν
ἀρνειὸν σφάζειν καὶ ἀδαίετον ὠμοθετῆσαι
αὐτῷ πυρκαϊὴν εὖ νηήσας ἐπὶ βόθρῳ·

Thus he spoke, honoring her, and she cast her eyes down and smiled with divine sweetness. Her heart melted within her as she was uplifted by his praise, and she raised her eyes and looked into his face; yet she did not know what word to utter first, but was bursting to say everything all at once. Casting off all restraint, she took the drug from her fragrant sash, and he received it at once into his hands with joy. And then she would even have drawn out her whole soul from her breast and given it to him, exulting in his need for her[85]—such was the love[86] flashing its sweet flame from Jason's golden head and captivating the bright sparkles of her eyes; and her mind within her warmed as she melted like the dew on roses that melts when warmed by the rays of the dawn. Sometimes they both fixed their eyes on the ground bashfully, but then again they cast glances at each other with loving smiles beneath radiant brows. And then at last the girl managed to address these words to him:

"Listen carefully now, so that I can devise help for you. After you go to meet my father and he gives you the deadly teeth from the snake's jaws to sow, then watch for the time when the night is divided in the middle and bathe in the streams of a tireless river; and, alone, apart from all others, clad in dark garments, dig a round pit. Slay a female sheep in it and place the unbutchered carcass on a pyre which you have carefully erected over the pit itself. Appease

---

[85] Or *exultingly, if he had needed it.*

[86] Many edd. capitalize Eros here and see the god's continuing work.

APOLLONIUS RHODIUS

1035 μουνογενῇ δ᾿ Ἑκάτην Περσηίδα μειλίσσοιο,
λείβων ἐκ δέπαος σιμβλήια ἔργα μελισσέων.
ἔνθα δ᾿ ἐπεί κε θεὰν μεμνημένος ἱλάσσηαι,
ἂψ ἀπὸ πυρκαϊῆς ἀναχάζεο· μηδέ σε δοῦπος
ἠὲ ποδῶν ὄρσῃσι μεταστρεφθῆναι ὀπίσσω
1040 ἠὲ κυνῶν ὑλακή, μή πως τὰ ἕκαστα κολούσας
οὐδ᾿ αὐτὸς κατὰ κόσμον ἑοῖς ἑτάροισι πελάσσῃς.
ἦρι δὲ μυδήνας τόδε φάρμακον, ἠύτ᾿ ἀλοιφῇ
γυμνωθεὶς φαίδρυνε τεὸν δέμας· ἐν δέ οἱ ἀλκὴ
ἔσσετ᾿ ἀπειρεσίη μέγα τε σθένος, οὐδέ κε φαίης
1045 ἀνδράσιν, ἀλλὰ θεοῖσιν ἰσαζέμεν ἀθανάτοισιν·
πρὸς δὲ καὶ αὐτῷ δουρὶ σάκος πεπαλαγμένον ἔστω
καὶ ξίφος. ἔνθ᾿ οὐκ ἄν σε διατμήξειαν ἀκωκαὶ
γηγενέων ἀνδρῶν οὐδ᾿ ἄσχετος ἀίσσουσα
φλὸξ ὀλοῶν ταύρων. τοῖός γε μὲν οὐκ ἐπὶ δηρὸν
1050 ἔσσεαι, ἀλλ᾿ αὐτῆμαρ· ὅμως σύ γε μή ποτ᾿ ἀέθλου
χάζεο. καὶ δέ τοι ἄλλο παρὲξ ὑποθήσομ᾿ ὄνειαρ·
αὐτίκ᾿ ἐπὴν κρατεροὺς ζεύξῃς βόας, ὦκα δὲ πᾶσαν
χερσὶ καὶ ἠνορέῃ στυφελὴν διὰ νειὸν ἀρόσσῃς,
οἱ δ᾿ ἤδη κατὰ ὦλκας ἀνασταχύωσι γίγαντες
1055 σπειρομένων ὄφιος δνοφερὴν ἐπὶ βῶλον ὀδόντων,
αἴ κεν ὀρινομένους πολέας νειοῖο δοκεύσῃς,
λάθρῃ λᾶαν ἄφες στιβαρώτερον· οἱ δ᾿ ἂν ἐπ᾿ αὐτῷ,
καρχαλέοι κύνες ὥς τε περὶ βρώμης, ὀλέκοιεν
ἀλλήλους· καὶ δ᾿ αὐτὸς ἐπείγεο δηιοτῆτος
1060 ἰθῦσαι. τὸ δὲ κῶας ἐς Ἑλλάδα τοῖό γ᾿ ἕκητι
οἴσεαι ἐξ Αἴης τηλοῦ ποθί· νίσσεο δ᾿ ἔμπης,
ᾗ φίλον, ἤ τοι ἕαδεν ἀφορμηθέντι νέεσθαι."

298

Hecate, the only child of Perses, as you pour from a goblet libations of the hive-held labors of bees. Then, after you propitiate the goddess with due heed,[87] withdraw from the pyre and let neither the sound of footsteps make you turn back around, nor the barking of dogs, lest you invalidate all these rites and you yourself fail to return in good order to your comrades. At dawn moisten this drug, strip, and anoint your body as with oil; and in it there will be unbounded valor and great strength, and you would think it equal not to men's bodies but to those of the immortal gods. Moreover, along with your spear let your shield and sword be sprinkled. Then the earthborn men's spear points will not penetrate you nor the unbearable flame shooting from the deadly oxen. Not for long, however, will you remain in this state, but for that day only. Nonetheless, you must never shrink from the contest. And I shall give you yet another piece of helpful advice. As soon as you yoke the mighty bulls and swiftly plow through all the hard field with might and main, and once those giants are sprouting up along the furrows when the snake's teeth are sown on the darkened soil, if you spot many of them arising from the field, without being seen cast a mighty stone, and over it, like ravenous dogs over food, they will kill one another; and you yourself hasten to rush into the fray. And as far as the contest is concerned, you shall bear the fleece to Hellas—somewhere far away from Aea. All the same, go where you wish or it pleases you to travel once you have departed."

[87] I.e. both to Medea's instructions and to what the goddess requires.

1062 ἤ τοι Π²⁵m: ἦ τοι E²: εἴ τι w

ὣς ἄρ' ἔφη, καὶ σῖγα ποδῶν πάρος ὄσσε
  βαλοῦσα
θεσπέσιον λιαροῖσι παρηίδα δάκρυσι δεῦεν
1065 μυρομένη, ὅ τ' ἔμελλεν ἀπόπροθι πολλὸν ἑοῖο
πόντον ἐπιπλάγξεσθαι. ἀνιηρῷ δέ μιν ἄντην
ἐξαῦτις μύθῳ προσεφώνεεν, εἷλέ τε χειρὸς
δεξιτερῆς· δὴ γάρ οἱ ἀπ' ὀφθαλμοὺς λίπεν αἰδώς·
  "μνώεο δ', ἢν ἄρα δή ποθ' ὑπότροπος οἴκαδ'
    ἵκηαι,
1070 οὔνομα Μηδείης· ὣς δ' αὖτ' ἐγὼ ἀμφὶς ἐόντος
μνήσομαι. εἰπὲ δέ μοι πρόφρων τόδε· πῇ τοι ἔασιν
δώματα; πῇ νῦν ἔνθεν ὑπεὶρ ἅλα νηὶ περήσεις;
ἦ νύ που ἀφνειοῦ σχεδὸν ἵξεαι Ὀρχομενοῖο
ἦε καὶ Αἰαίης νήσου πέλας; εἰπὲ δὲ κούρην,
1075 ἥν τινα τήνδ' ὀνόμηνας ἀριγνώτην γεγαυῖαν
Πασιφάης, ἣ πατρὸς ὁμόγνιός ἐστιν ἐμεῖο."
  ὣς φάτο· τὸν δὲ καὶ αὐτὸν ὑπήιε δάκρυσι κούρης
οὖλος ἔρως, τοῖον δὲ παραβλήδην ἔπος ηὔδα·
  "καὶ λίην οὐ νύκτας ὀίομαι οὐδέ ποτ' ἦμαρ
1080 σεῦ ἐπιλήσεσθαι, προφυγὼν μόρον, εἰ ἐτεόν γε
φεύξομαι ἀσκηθὴς ἐς Ἀχαιίδα, μηδέ τιν' ἄλλον
Αἰήτης προβάλῃσι κακώτερον ἄμμιν ἄεθλον.
εἰ δέ τοι ἡμετέρην ἐξίδμεναι εὔαδε πάτρην,
ἐξερέω· μάλα γάρ με καὶ αὐτὸν θυμὸς ἀνώγει.
1085 ἔστι τις αἰπεινοῖσι περίδρομος οὔρεσι γαῖα,
πάμπαν εὔρρηνός τε καὶ εὔβοτος, ἔνθα Προμηθεὺς
Ἰαπετιονίδης ἀγαθὸν τέκε Δευκαλίωνα,
ὃς πρῶτος ποίησε πόλεις καὶ ἐδείματο νηοὺς

Thus she spoke, and casting her eyes in silence before her feet, wet her divinely beautiful cheeks with hot tears, lamenting because he was about to wander on the sea very far from her. And again she addressed him to his face with these pained words and took his right hand, for indeed shame had left her eyes:

"And remember, if in fact you ever return home, the name of Medea, and likewise I shall remember you, although you are far away. And kindly tell me this. Where is your home? Where then from here will you voyage by ship over the sea? Will you perhaps go near prosperous Orchomenus or near the island of Aeaea?[88] And tell me about that girl, whoever she is that you named, the famous daughter of that Pasiphae who is related to my father."[89]

Thus she spoke, and over him as well, at the girl's tears, was stealing destructive love, and he answered in these words:

"Truly I do not think I shall ever, night or day, forget you, provided I avoid death—if I really do escape unharmed to Achaea, and if Aeetes does not set some worse trial before us. But if it pleases you to know about my country, I shall speak out, for greatly does my own heart also bid me. There is a land ringed by steep mountains, abounding in sheep and pastures, where Prometheus, son of Iapetus, fathered good Deucalion, who was the first to found cities

[88] The two western locations Medea has heard of: Orchomenus, home of Phrixus, and Aeaea, home of Circe.
[89] Cf. 3.999.

ἀθανάτοις, πρῶτος δὲ καὶ ἀνθρώπων βασίλευσεν·
1090 Αἱμονίην δὴ τήν γε περικτίονες καλέουσιν.
ἐν δ' αὐτῇ Ἰαωλκός, ἐμὴ πόλις, ἐν δὲ καὶ ἄλλαι
πολλαὶ ναιετάουσιν, ἵν' οὐδέ περ οὔνομ' ἀκοῦσαι
Αἰαίης νήσου· Μινύην γε μὲν ὁρμηθέντα,
Αἰολίδην Μινύην, ἔνθεν φάτις Ὀρχομενοῖο
1095 δή ποτε Καδμείοισιν ὁμούριον ἄστυ πολίσσαι.
ἀλλὰ τίη τάδε τοι μεταμώνια πάντ' ἀγορεύω,
ἡμετέρους τε δόμους τηλεκλείτην τ' Ἀριάδνην,
κούρην Μίνωος, τό περ ἀγλαὸν οὔνομα κείνην
παρθενικὴν καλέεσκον ἐπήρατον, ἥν μ' ἐρεείνεις;
1100 αἴθε γάρ, ὡς Θησῆι τότε ξυναρέσσατο Μίνως
ἀμφ' αὐτῆς, ὡς ἄμμι πατὴρ τεὸς ἄρθμιος εἴη."
    ὣς φάτο μειλιχίοισι καταψήχων ὀάροισιν·
τῆς δ' ἀλεγεινόταται κραδίην ἐρέθεσκον ἀνίαι,
καί μιν ἀκηχεμένη ἀδινῷ προσπτύξατο μύθῳ·
1105 "Ἑλλάδι που τάδε καλά, συνημοσύνας ἀλεγύνειν·
Αἰήτης δ' οὐ τοῖος ἐν ἀνδράσιν, οἷον ἔειπας
Μίνω Πασιφάης πόσιν ἔμμεναι, οὐδ' Ἀριάδνῃ
ἰσοῦμαι. τῶ μή τι φιλοξενίην ἀγόρευε.
ἀλλ' οἷον τύνη μὲν ἐμεῦ, ὅτ' Ἰωλκὸν ἵκηαι,
1110 μνώεο, σεῖο δ' ἐγὼ καὶ ἐμῶν ἀέκητι τοκήων
μνήσομαι. ἔλθοι δ' ἡμῖν ἀπόπροθεν ἠέ τις ὄσσα
ἠέ τις ἄγγελος ὄρνις, ὅτ' ἐκλελάθοιο ἐμεῖο·
ἢ αὐτήν με ταχεῖαι ὑπὲρ πόντοιο φέροιεν
ἐνθένδ' εἰς Ἰαωλκὸν ἀναρπάξασαι ἄελλαι,
1115 ὄφρα σ' ἐν ὀφθαλμοῖσιν ἐλεγχείας προφέρουσα

and build temples to the immortals, and first also to rule over men. The neighboring people call this land Haemonia. And in it lies Iolcus itself, my city, and in it lie many others besides, where not even the name of the island of Aeaea is heard. Yet there is a story that once upon a time Minyas set out from there,[90] Minyas son of Aeolus, and founded the city of Orchomenus[91] on the border with the Cadmeians. But why am I telling you all these pointless things about my home and Minos' daughter, far-famed Ariadne, by which splendid name they called that lovely maiden, whom you are asking me about? Would that, just as Minos back then came to an agreement with Theseus over her, so might your father be on our side."

So he spoke, soothing her with gentle talk, but most bitter pains were troubling her heart, and in her sorrow she addressed him with fervent words:

"In Hellas perhaps it is noble to abide by agreements, but Aeetes is not such among men as you said was Pasiphae's husband Minos, nor do I liken myself to Ariadne. Therefore, do not speak of any guest-friendship, but simply remember me when you reach Iolcus, and I shall remember you even in spite of my parents. But from far away may some rumor or messenger-bird come to us when you have forgotten me, or may swift storm-winds sweep me up and carry me in person over the sea from here to Iolcus, so that I may reproach you to your face and remind you that it

[90] I.e. Haemonia (Thessaly).
[91] Named for Minyas' son. Minyas' father, Aeolus, was the son of Deucalion.

μνήσω ἐμῇ ἰότητι πεφυγμένον· αἴθε γὰρ εἴην
ἀπροφάτως τότε σοῖσιν ἐφέστιος ἐν μεγάροισιν."
　　ὣς ἄρ' ἔφη, ἐλεεινὰ καταπροχέουσα παρειῶν
δάκρυα· τὴν δ' ὅ γε δῆθεν ὑποβλήδην προσέειπεν·
1120　"δαιμονίη, κενεὰς μὲν ἔα πλάζεσθαι ἀέλλας,
ὣς δὲ καὶ ἄγγελον ὄρνιν, ἐπεὶ μεταμώνια βάζεις.
εἰ δέ κεν ἤθεα κεῖνα καὶ Ἑλλάδα γαῖαν ἵκηαι,
τιμήεσσα γυναιξὶ καὶ ἀνδράσιν αἰδοίη τε
ἔσσεαι· οἱ δέ σε πάγχυ θεὸν ὣς πορσανέουσιν,
1125　οὕνεκα τῶν μὲν παῖδες ὑπότροποι οἴκαδ' ἵκοντο
σῇ βουλῇ, τῶν δ' αὖτε κασίγνητοί τε ἔται τε
καὶ θαλεροὶ κακότητος ἄδην ἐσάωθεν ἀκοῖται.
ἡμέτερον δὲ λέχος θαλάμοις ἔνι κουριδίοισιν
πορσανέεις· οὐδ' ἄμμε διακρινέει φιλότητος
1130　ἄλλο, πάρος θάνατόν γε μεμορμένον ἀμφικαλύψαι."
　　ὣς φάτο· τῇ δ' ἔντοσθε κατείβετο θυμὸς ἀκουῇ,
ἔμπης δ' ἔργ' ἀίδηλα κατερρίγησεν ἰδέσθαι.
σχετλίη, οὐ μὲν δηρὸν ἀπαρνήσεσθαι ἔμελλεν
Ἑλλάδα ναιετάειν· ὣς γὰρ τόδε μήδετο Ἥρη,
1135　ὄφρα κακὸν Πελίῃ ἱερὴν ἐς Ἰωλκὸν ἵκηται
Αἰαίη Μήδεια λιποῦσ' ἄ<πο> πατρίδα γαῖαν.
　　ἤδη δ' ἀμφίπολοι μὲν ὀπιπεύουσαι ἄπωθεν
σιγῇ ἀνιάζεσκον· ἐδεύετο δ' ἤματος ὥρη
ἂψ οἰκόνδε νέεσθαι ἑὴν μετὰ μητέρα κούρην.
1140　ἡ δ' οὔ πω κομιδῆς μιμνήσκετο, τέρπετο γάρ οἱ

1135 ἵκηται Ω: ἵκοιτο Brunck
1136 λιποῦσ' ἄ<πο> Köchly: λιποῦσα Ω

304

was through my help that you escaped—then may I appear unexpectedly at the hearth in your palace."

Thus she spoke, letting pitiful tears stream down her cheeks, and he then said to her in reply:

"Poor girl, let those storm-winds wander aimlessly, and that messenger-bird as well, for you are talking nonsense. If you come to those places and the land of Hellas, you will be held in honor and respect by women and men, and they will venerate you like a goddess, some because their sons returned home thanks to your counsel, but others because their brothers, kinsmen, and vigorous husbands were saved from so much harm. And in our wedding chamber you shall share our bed, and nothing shall come between us and our love, until fated death enshrouds us."

Thus he spoke, and her heart within her melted at hearing this, but nonetheless she shuddered to behold her destructive deeds.[92] The poor girl! Not for long was she going to refuse to live in Hellas, for Hera had so contrived it that Aeaean Medea would come to holy Iolcus as Pelias' bane after forsaking her native land.

By now the handmaids, keeping watch from a distance in silence, were becoming distressed because the time of day was running out for the girl to return home to her mother. But not yet would she have thought of returning,

---

[92] Or *her unforeseen deeds*. The sense depends upon whether Medea is disturbed by the things she is doing (cf. 3.1161–1162) or is afraid of what the future might bring (cf. 3.1132–1136).

θυμὸς ὁμῶς μορφῇ τε καὶ αἰμυλίοισι λόγοισιν,
εἰ μὴ ἄρ᾽ Αἰσονίδης πεφυλαγμένος ὀψέ περ ηὔδα·
    "ὥρη ἀποβλώσκειν, μὴ πρὶν φάος ἠελίοιο
δύῃ ὑποφθάμενον καί τις τὰ ἕκαστα νοήσῃ
1145 ὀθνείων· αὖτις δ᾽ ἀβολήσομεν ἐνθάδ᾽ ἰόντες."
    ὣς τώ γ᾽ ἀλλήλων ἀγανοῖς ἐπὶ τόσσον ἔπεσσιν.
πείρηθεν· μετὰ δ᾽ αὖτε διέτμαγον. ἤτοι Ἰήσων
εἰς ἑτάρους καὶ νῆα κεχαρμένος ὦρτο νέεσθαι,
ἡ δὲ μετ᾽ ἀμφιπόλους· αἱ δὲ σχεδὸν ἀντεβόλησαν
1150 πᾶσαι ὁμοῦ, τὰς δ᾽ οὔ τι περιπλομένας ἐνόησεν·
ψυχὴ γὰρ νεφέεσσι μεταχρονίη πεπότητο.
αὐτομάτοις δὲ πόδεσσι θοῆς ἐπεβήσατ᾽ ἀπήνης,
καί ῥ᾽ ἑτέρῃ μὲν χειρὶ λάβ᾽ ἡνία, τῇ δ᾽ ἄρ᾽
            ἱμάσθλην
δαιδαλέην οὐρῆας ἐλαυνέμεν· οἱ δὲ πόλινδε
1155 θῦνον ἐπειγόμενοι ποτὶ δώματα. τὴν δ᾽ ἄρ᾽ ἰοῦσαν
Χαλκιόπη περὶ παισὶν ἀκηχεμένη ἐρέεινεν·
ἡ δὲ παλιντροπίῃσιν ἀμήχανος οὔτε τι μύθων
ἔκλυεν, οὔτ᾽ αὐδῆσαι ἀνειρομένη λελίητο.
ἷζε δ᾽ ἐπὶ χθαμαλῷ σφέλαϊ κλιντῆρος ἔνερθεν
1160 λέχρις ἐρεισαμένη λαιῇ ἐπὶ χειρὶ παρειήν·
ὑγρὰ δ᾽ ἐνὶ βλεφάροις ἔχεν ὄμματα, πορφύρουσα
οἷον ἑῇ κακὸν ἔργον ἐπιξυνώσατο βουλῇ.
    Αἰσονίδης δ᾽ ὅτε δὴ ἑτάροις ἐξαῦτις ἔμικτο
ἐν χώρῃ, ὅθι τούς γε καταπρολιπὼν ἐλιάσθη,
1165 ὦρτ᾽ ἰέναι σὺν τοῖσι, πιφαυσκόμενος τὰ ἕκαστα,

1155 ἄρ᾽ ἰοῦσαν Ω: ἀνιοῦσαν D

306

for her heart was delighting both in his beauty and in his beguiling words, had not Jason watched the time and at last said:

"It is time to depart, lest the light of the sun go down before we get back, and some stranger becomes aware of everything. But we shall come here again to meet."

Thus they tested each other to this extent with gentle words and thereafter separated. For his part, Jason set out joyously to return to his comrades and the ship, and she to join her handmaids, who all in a group drew near to greet her, but she took no notice whatsoever of them as they gathered around her, for her soul had flown high up in the clouds. With feet that moved of their own accord she mounted the swift wagon; she took the reins in one hand and the cunningly made whip in the other to drive the mules, which rushed in haste to the city and the palace. When she arrived, Chalciope, distraught for her sons, began questioning her, but she, helpless in the face of her changing thoughts, did not hear a word or have any desire to answer her questions. She sat on a low stool at the foot of her bed, resting her cheek at an angle on her left hand. Her eyes remained languid within her eyelids,[93] as she pondered what a wicked deed she had taken part in through her own counsel.

Now when Jason rejoined his companions[94] in the place where he had left them when he went on, he set out with them to join the band of heroes, relating everything on the

[93] Perhaps depicting the blank stare familiar from funerary monuments.

[94] Argus and Mopsus, who remained at the poplar tree (3.945–946).

ἡρώων ἐς ὅμιλον· ὁμοῦ δ' ἐπὶ νῆα πέλασσαν.
οἱ δέ μιν ἀμφαγάπαζον, ὅπως ἴδον, ἔκ τ' ἐρέοντο·
αὐτὰρ ὁ τοῖς πάντεσσι μετέννεπε δήνεα κούρης,
δεῖξέ τε φάρμακον αἰνόν. ὁ δ' οἰόθεν οἶος ἑταίρων
1170 Ἴδας ἧστ' ἀπάνευθε δακὼν χόλον· οἱ δὲ δὴ ἄλλοι
γηθόσυνοι, τῆμος μέν, ἐπεὶ κνέφας ἔργαθε νυκτός,
εὔκηλοι ἐμέλοντο περὶ σφίσιν· αὐτὰρ ἅμ' ἠοῖ
πέμπον ἐς Αἰήτην ἰέναι σπόρον αἰτήσοντας
ἄνδρε δύω, πρὸ μὲν αὐτὸν ἀρηίφιλον Τελαμῶνα,
1175 σὺν δὲ καὶ Αἰθαλίδην, υἷα κλυτὸν Ἑρμείαο.
βὰν δ' ἴμεν, οὐδ' ἁλίωσαν ὁδόν· πόρε δέ σφιν
    ἰοῦσιν
κρείων Αἰήτης χαλεποὺς ἐς ἄεθλον ὀδόντας
Ἀονίοιο δράκοντος, ὃν Ὠγυγίῃ ἐνὶ Θήβῃ
Κάδμος, ὅτ' Εὐρώπην διζήμενος εἰσαφίκανεν,
1180 πέφνεν Ἀρητιάδι κρήνῃ ἐπίουρον ἐόντα·
ἔνθα καὶ ἐννάσθη πομπῇ βοός, ἥν οἱ Ἀπόλλων
ὤπασε μαντοσύνῃσι προηγήτειραν ὁδοῖο.
τοὺς δὲ θεὰ Τριτωνὶς ὑπὲκ γενύων ἐλάσασα
Αἰήτῃ πόρε δῶρον ὁμῶς αὐτῷ τε φονῆι.
1185 καὶ ῥ' ὁ μὲν Ἀονίοισιν ἐνισπείρας πεδίοισιν
Κάδμος Ἀγηνορίδης γαιηγενῆ εἴσατο λαόν,
Ἄρεος ἀμώοντος ὅσοι ὑπὸ δουρὶ λίποντο·

---

95 I.e. Boeotian. The Aones, descended from Poseidon's son
Aon, were the pre-Cadmeian inhabitants.
96 Ogygus was the first king of Boeotia, before the Aonians.
The name came to mean "primeval."

way; and in a group they approached the ship. When the comrades saw him, they welcomed him and questioned him, and to all of them he told the girl's instructions and showed them the dread drug. Idas alone of the comrades sat apart, biting back his anger, but the rest were full of joy, and for the time being, since the dark of night restrained them, they calmly went about their own affairs. But at daybreak they sent two men to go to Aeetes and ask for the seed: foremost, Telamon himself, beloved of Ares, and with him Aethalides, Hermes' famous son. They set out and went on no vain journey, for when they arrived King Aeetes gave them the deadly teeth for the contest, the ones from the Aonian[95] snake, the guardian of the spring of Ares, which Cadmus slew in Ogygian[96] Thebes when he came there in search of Europa.[97] It was there he settled, guided by the heifer that Apollo had provided for him with his oracles to lead him on his journey. The Tritonian goddess[98] knocked the teeth from its jaws and gave them in equal portions as a gift to Aeetes and to the slayer himself. Cadmus, son of Agenor, sowed his in the Aonian plain and founded the earthborn people from all those left when Ares was reaping them with his spear.[99] But Aeetes then

---

[97] Europa, Cadmus' sister, was abducted by Zeus disguised as a bull. Cadmus was told by Apollo to follow a cow until it lay down to rest, at which place he was to sacrifice the animal and found a city (Thebes). In order to draw water at Ares' spring for the sacrifice, he had to kill the guardian serpent.   [98] Athena.

[99] Cadmus got the men who emerged from the teeth to fight among themselves by throwing stones in their midst. The five remaining Spartoi ("Sown Men") became the ancestors of the Thebans. For Ares as the sower of the teeth, see Euripides, *Heracles* 252–253.

τοὺς δὲ τότ᾽ Αἰήτης ἔπορεν μετὰ νῆα φέρεσθαι
προφρονέως, ἐπεὶ οὔ μιν ὀίσσατο πείρατ᾽ ἀέθλου
1190 ἐξανύσειν, εἰ καί περ ἐπὶ ζυγὰ βουσὶ βάλοιτο.
  Ἥλιος μὲν ἄπωθεν ἐρεμνὴν δύετο γαῖαν
ἑσπέριος, νεάτας ὑπὲρ ἄκριας Αἰθιοπήων·
Νὺξ δ᾽ ἵπποισιν ἔβαλλεν ἔπι ζυγά· τοὶ δὲ χαμεύνας
ἔντυον ἥρωες παρὰ πείσμασιν. αὐτὰρ Ἰήσων,
1195 αὐτίκ᾽ ἐπεί ῥ᾽ Ἑλίκης εὐφεγγέος ἀστέρες Ἄρκτου
ἔκλιθεν, οὐρανόθεν δὲ πανεύκηλος γένετ᾽ αἰθήρ,
βῆ ῥ᾽ ἐς ἐρημαίην, κλωπήιος ἠύτε τις φώρ,
σὺν πᾶσιν χρήεσσι· πρὸ γάρ τ᾽ ἀλέγυνεν ἕκαστα
ἠμάτιος· θῆλυν μὲν ὄιν γάλα τ᾽ ἔκτοθι ποίμνης
1200 Ἄργος ἰὼν ἤνεικε, τὰ δ᾽ ἐξ αὐτῆς ἕλε νηός.
ἀλλ᾽ ὅτε δὴ ἴδε χῶρον, ὅ τις πάτου ἔκτοθεν ἦεν
ἀνθρώπων, καθαρῇσιν ὑπεύδιος εἰαμενῇσιν,
ἔνθ᾽ ἤτοι πάμπρωτα λοέσσατο μὲν ποταμοῖο
εὐαγέως θείοιο τέρεν δέμας, ἀμφὶ δὲ φᾶρος
1205 ἕσσατο κυάνεον, τὸ μέν οἱ πάρος ἐγγυάλιξεν
Λημνιὰς Ὑψιπύλη, ἀδινῆς μνημήιον εὐνῆς.
πήχυιον δ᾽ ἄρ᾽ ἔπειτα πέδῳ ἔνι βόθρον ὀρύξας
νήησεν σχίζας, ἐπὶ δ᾽ ἀρνειοῦ τάμε λαιμόν,
αὐτόν τ᾽ εὖ καθύπερθε τανύσσατο· δαῖε δὲ φιτροὺς
1210 πῦρ ὑπένερθεν ἱείς, ἐπὶ δὲ μιγάδας χέε λοιβάς,
Βριμὼ κικλήσκων Ἑκάτην ἐπαρωγὸν ἀέθλων.
καί ῥ᾽ ὁ μὲν ἀγκαλέσας πάλιν ἔστιχεν· ἡ δ᾽ ἀίουσα
κευθμῶν ἐξ ὑπάτων δεινὴ θεὸς ἀντεβόλησεν

1192 ἑσπέριος Ω: ἑσπερίων Fränkel

310

gave his teeth to be carried back to the ship, and gladly so, because he did not think Jason would complete the requirements of the task, even if he should put the yoke on the oxen.

Helius was sinking far away beneath the dark earth in the west, beyond the furthest peaks of the Ethiopians,[100] and Night was putting the yoke on her horses; and the heroes were preparing their beds beside the ship's cables. But Jason, as soon as the stars of Helice, the bright-shining Bear, had set, and the air under heaven had become completely still, went to a deserted place, like some stealthy thief, with all the things he needed, for he had prepared everything ahead of time during the day: Argus had gone and fetched a ewe and milk from the flock, while he had taken the rest from the ship itself. But when he saw a place that was far from the beaten track of men in clear meadows under an open sky, there he first of all washed his tender body piously in the divine river and donned a dark robe, which Lemnian Hypsipyle had previously given him as a memento of their fervent[101] lovemaking. Next he dug a pit in the ground a cubit long, stacked firewood, slit the sheep's throat over it, and duly laid out the carcass on top. He kindled the woodpile by placing fire beneath it and poured mixed libations[102] on top, as he invoked Hecate Brimo to be a helper in the contest. And after calling on her, he withdrew, and the dread goddess heard him and came from the deepest depths to receive Jason's sacrifice.

[100] The Ethiopians were thought to inhabit the extreme eastern and western ends of the world (*Odyssey* 1.23–24).
[101] Or *frequent*.
[102] Presumably of honey (3.1036) and sheep's milk (3.1199).

ἱροῖς Αἰσονίδαο· πέριξ δέ μιν ἐστεφάνωντο
1215 σμερδαλέοι δρυΐνοισι μετὰ πτόρθοισι δράκοντες,
στράπτε δ' ἀπειρέσιον δαΐδων σέλας· ἀμφὶ δὲ
τήν γε
ὀξείη ὑλακῇ χθόνιοι κύνες ἐφθέγγοντο.
πίσεα δ' ἔτρεμε πάντα κατὰ στίβον· αἱ δ' ὀλόλυξαν
νύμφαι ἑλειονόμοι ποταμηίδες, αἳ περὶ κείνην
1220 Φάσιδος εἰαμενὴν Ἀμαραντίου εἱλίσσονται.
Αἰσονίδην δ' ἤτοι μὲν ἕλεν δέος, ἀλλά μιν οὐδ' ὣς
ἐντροπαλιζόμενον πόδες ἔκφερον, ὄφρ' ἑτάροισιν
μίκτο κιών. ἤδη δὲ φόως νιφόεντος ὕπερθεν
Καυκάσου ἠριγενὴς Ἠὼς βάλεν ἀντέλλουσα.
1225   καὶ τότ' ἄρ' Αἰήτης περὶ μὲν στήθεσσιν ἕεστο
θώρηκα στάδιον, τόν οἱ πόρεν ἐξεναρίξας
σφωιτέρης Φλεγραῖον Ἄρης ὑπὸ χερσὶ Μίμαντα·
χρυσείην δ' ἐπὶ κρατὶ κόρυν θέτο τετραφάληρον
λαμπομένην, οἷόν τε περίτροχον ἔπλετο φέγγος
1230 ἠελίου, ὅτε πρῶτον ἀνέρχεται Ὠκεανοῖο.
ἂν δὲ πολύρρινον νώμα σάκος, ἂν δὲ καὶ ἔγχος
δεινόν, ἀμαιμάκετον· τὸ μὲν οὔ κέ τις ἄλλος ὑπέστη
ἀνδρῶν ἡρώων, ὅτε κάλλιπον Ἡρακλῆα
τῆλε παρέξ, ὅ κεν οἶος ἐναντίβιον πτολέμιξεν.
1235 τῷ δὲ καὶ ὠκυπόδων ἵππων εὐπηγέα δίφρον
ἔσχε πέλας Φαέθων ἐπιβήμεναι· ἂν δὲ καὶ αὐτὸς
βήσατο, ῥυτῆρας δὲ χεροῖν ἕλεν. ἐκ δὲ πόληος
ἤλασεν εὐρεῖαν κατ' ἀμαξιτόν, ὥς κεν ἀέθλῳ
παρσταίη· σὺν δέ σφιν ἀπείριτος ἔσσυτο λαός.
1240 οἷος δ' Ἴσθμιον εἶσι Ποσειδάων ἐς ἀγῶνα

312

Encircling her head were horrifying snakes among sprigs of oak, while the boundless radiance of torches flashed, and hellhounds bayed shrilly around her. All the watery meadows shook at her footstep, and the marsh-dwelling river nymphs wailed, those who dance around that marshy meadow of Amarantian Phasis.[103] Fear indeed gripped Jason, but even so he did not turn around as his feet carried him away, until he came back and joined his comrades. By then early-rising Dawn had come up and cast her light above snowy Caucasus.

At that time Aeetes put around his chest a rigid breastplate that Ares had given him after slaying Phlegraean Mimas with his own hands.[104] Upon his head he placed a golden, four-crested helmet, shining like the round light of the sun when it first rises from Ocean. And he took up and wielded his shield of many hides as well as his terrible, overpowering spear, which none of the heroes could have withstood, once they had left Heracles far behind, who alone could have faced it in combat. Phaethon had brought his well-built chariot with swift-footed horses near at hand for him to mount; and he got in and took the reins in his hands. He drove from the city on the wide highway to attend the contest, and with him hurried a multitude of people. Like Poseidon, when he goes to the Isthmian games

---

[103] The Phasis river rose in the Amarantian mountains (cf. 2.399–401).

[104] Ares, Zeus, and Hephaestus are variously credited with slaying the Giant Mimas in the Phlegraean fields, located in the Chalcidice.

1237: ἕλεν Brunck: ἔχεν Ω

ἅρμασιν ἐμβεβαώς, ἢ Ταίναρον ἢ ὅ γε Λέρνης
ὕδωρ ἠὲ καὶ ἄλσος Ὑαντίου Ὀγχηστοῖο,
καί τε Καλαύρειαν μετὰ δὴ θαμὰ νίσσεται ἵπποις,
Πέτρην θ' Αἱμονίην ἢ δενδρήεντα Γεραιστόν·
1245 τοῖος ἄρ' Αἰήτης Κόλχων ἀγὸς ἦεν ἰδέσθαι.

    τόφρα δὲ Μηδείης ὑποθημοσύνῃσιν Ἰήσων
φάρμακα μυδήνας ἠμὲν σάκος ἀμφεπάλυννεν
ἠδὲ δόρυ βριαρόν, περὶ δὲ ξίφος. ἀμφὶ δ' ἑταῖροι
πείρησαν τευχέων βεβιημένοι, οὐδ' ἐδύναντο
1250 κεῖνο δόρυ γνάμψαι τυτθόν γέ περ, ἀλλὰ μάλ'
      αὔτως
ἀαγὲς κρατερῇσιν ἐνεσκλήκει παλάμῃσιν.
αὐτὰρ ὁ τοῖς ἄμοτον κοτέων Ἀφαρήιος Ἴδας
κόψε παρ' οὐρίαχον μεγάλῳ ξίφει· ἆλτο δ' ἀκωκὴ
ῥαιστὴρ ἄκμονος ὥς τε παλιντυπές, οἱ δ' ὁμάδησαν
1255 γηθόσυνοι ἥρωες ἐπ' ἐλπωρῇσιν ἀέθλου.
καὶ δ' αὐτὸς μετέπειτα παλύνετο· δῦ δέ μιν ἀλκὴ
σμερδαλέη ἄφατός τε καὶ ἄτρομος, αἱ δ' ἑκάτερθεν
χεῖρες ἐπερρώσαντο περὶ σθένεϊ σφριγόωσαι.
ὡς δ' ὅτ' ἀρήιος ἵππος ἐελδόμενος πολέμοιο
1260 σκαρθμῷ ἐπιχρεμέθων κρούει πέδον, αὐτὰρ ὕπερθεν
κυδιόων ὀρθοῖσιν ἐπ' οὔασιν αὐχέν' ἀείρει·
τοῖος ἄρ' Αἰσονίδης ἐπαγαίετο κάρτεϊ γυίων·
πολλὰ δ' ἄρ' ἔνθα καὶ ἔνθα μετάρσιον ἴχνος
    ἔπαλλεν,
ἀσπίδα χαλκείην μελίην τ' ἐν χερσὶ τινάσσων.

    1243 δὴ θαμὰ D: δῆθ' ἅμα Ω

314

mounted in his chariot, or to Taenarus or Lerna's waters or to his precinct at Hyantian Onchestus, and often[105] travels with his horses to Calaurea and Haemonian Petra or forested Geraestus[106]—such was Aeetes, leader of the Colchians, to behold.

In the meantime, following Medea's instructions, Jason moistened the drug and sprinkled it on his shield and mighty spear, and all over his sword. Around him his comrades tested his weapons by using all their strength, but they were unable to bend that spear even a little, for it remained unbroken and firm as ever in their powerful hands. But nursing his implacable grudge against them,[107] Apharian Idas struck near the butt-end of the spear with his great sword, but the edge rebounded like a hammer from an anvil, and the heroes cheered for joy with high hopes for the contest. Then Jason sprinkled himself, and into him entered terrifying prowess, inexpressible and unflinching, and on either side his hands moved nimbly, swelling mightily with power. And as when a war horse, eager for battle, whinnies and beats the ground as it prances, and proudly lifts high its neck with ears erect—so did Jason exult in the strength of his limbs, and often would he leap in the air here and there, brandishing his bronze shield and ashen spear in his hands. You would think that wintry light-

---

[105] Or, reading δῆθ᾽ ἅμα, *thereafter*.

[106] All are cultic centers of Poseidon: the Isthmus (at Corinth), Taenarus (southern tip of the Peloponnesus), Lerna (in the Argolid), Onchestus (in Boeotia), Celaurea (island off the eastern tip of the Argolid), Petra (in Thessaly), and Geraestus (in Euboea).

[107] Cf. 3.556–566 and 3.1169–1170.

1265 φαίης κεν ζοφεροῖο κατ' αἰθέρος ἀίσσουσαν
χειμερίην στεροπὴν θαμινὸν μεταπαιφάσσεσθαι
ἐκ νεφέων, ὅτε πέρ τε μελάντατον ὄμβρον ἄγωνται.
καὶ τότ' ἔπειτ' οὐ δηρὸν ἔτι σχήσεσθαι ἀέθλων
μέλλον· ἀτὰρ κληῖσιν ἐπισχερὼ ἱδρυθέντες
1270 ῥίμφα μάλ' ἐς πεδίον τὸ Ἀρήιον ἠπείγοντο.
τόσσον δὲ προτέρω πέλεν ἄστεος ἀντιπέρηθεν,
ὅσσον τ' ἐκ βαλβῖδος ἐπήβολος ἅρματι νύσσα
γίγνεται, ὁππότ' ἄεθλα καταφθιμένοιο ἄνακτος
κηδεμόνες πεζοῖσι καὶ ἱππήεσσι τίθενται.
1275 τέτμον δ' Αἰήτην τε καὶ ἄλλων ἔθνεα Κόλχων,
τοὺς μὲν Καυκασίοισιν ἐφεσταότας σκοπέλοισιν,
τὸν δ' αὐτοῦ παρὰ χεῖλος ἑλισσόμενον ποταμοῖο.
       Αἰσονίδης δ', ὅτε δὴ πρυμνήσια δῆσαν ἑταῖροι,
δή ῥα τότε ξὺν δουρὶ καὶ ἀσπίδι βαῖν' ἐς ἄεθλον,
1280 νηὸς ἀποπροθορών· ἄμυδις δ' ἕλε παμφανόωσαν
χαλκείην πήληκα θοῶν ἔμπλειον ὀδόντων
καὶ ξίφος ἀμφ' ὤμοις, γυμνὸς δέμας, ἄλλα μὲν
       Ἄρει
εἴκελος, ἄλλα δέ που χρυσαόρῳ Ἀπόλλωνι.
παπτήνας δ' ἀνὰ νειὸν ἴδε ζυγὰ χάλκεα ταύρων
1285 αὐτόγυόν τ' ἐπὶ τοῖς στιβαροῦ ἀδάμαντος ἄροτρον.
χρίμψε δ' ἔπειτα κιών, παρὰ δ' ὄβριμον ἔγχος
       ἔπηξεν

1267 ὅτε πέρ τε Ziegler: ὅτ' ἔπειτα Ω

316

ning springing from a black sky was constantly flashing forth from the clouds when they bring their darkest rainstorm. Then, not for long thereafter were they to hold back from their trials, but sitting in rows on their benches they quickly sped to the plain of Ares. It lay further on,[108] across from the city as far as is the finishing-post to be reached by a chariot from the starting-point, when at a king's death his kinsmen hold games for runners and horsemen. When they came upon Aeetes and the hosts of the Colchians besides, the latter were seated on the Caucasian heights, while he was there driving back and forth along the edge of the river.[109]

And then Jason, as soon as his comrades had fastened the stern cables, went striding with his spear and shield to the contest, after leaping forth from the ship. At the same time he took the shining bronze helmet full of the sharp teeth and his sword slung on his shoulders, his body naked, in some ways like Ares, but in other ways perhaps like Apollo of the golden sword.[110] He surveyed the field and saw the oxen's bronze yoke and beside it the plow, all one piece, of hard adamant. Then he came up next to it, fixed his mighty spear upright on its end, and set aside his hel-

[108] Up the river from where they moored at 3.573–575.

[109] The Colchians are seated on the higher ground of the north bank of the river; the king is impatiently driving along the bank. Some take ἑλισσόμενον with χεῖλος, "by the winding edge of the river."

[110] With his hoplite shield and spear he resembles Ares; with his sword on his shoulders he resembles Apollo. His nakedness is variously explained as depicting a figure in heroic art or a farmer stripped to plow and sow (cf. Hesiod, *Works and Days* 391).

ὀρθὸν ἐπ᾽ οὐριάχῳ, κυνέην δ᾽ ἀποκάτθετ᾽ ἐρείσας.
βῆ δ᾽ αὐτῇ προτέρωσε σὺν ἀσπίδι νήριτα ταύρων
ἴχνια μαστεύων. οἱ δ᾽ ἔκποθεν ἀφράστοιο
1290 κευθμῶνος χθονίου, ἵνα τέ σφισιν ἔσκε βόαυλα
καρτερὰ λιγνυόεντι πέριξ εἰλυμένα καπνῷ,
ἄμφω ὁμοῦ προγένοντο πυρὸς σέλας ἀμπνείοντες.
ἔδδεισαν δ᾽ ἥρωες, ὅπως ἴδον· αὐτὰρ ὁ τούς γε,
εὖ διαβάς, ἐπιόντας, ἅ τε σπιλὰς εἰν ἁλὶ πέτρη
1295 μίμνει ἀπειρεσίῃσι δονεύμενα κύματ᾽ ἀέλλαις.
πρόσθε δέ οἱ σάκος ἔσχεν ἐναντίον· οἱ δέ μιν ἄμφω
μυκηθμῷ κρατεροῖσιν ἐνέπληξαν κεράεσσιν,
οὐδ᾽ ἄρα μιν τυτθόν περ ἀνώχλισαν ἀντιόωντες.
ὡς δ᾽ ὅτ᾽ ἐνὶ τρητοῖσιν ἐΰρρινοι χοάνοισιν
1300 φῦσαι χαλκήων ὁτὲ μέν τ᾽ ἀναμαρμαίρουσιν
πῦρ ὀλοὸν πιμπρᾶσαι, ὅτ᾽ αὖ λήγουσιν ἀϋτμῆς,
δεινὸς δ᾽ ἐξ αὐτοῦ πέλεται βρόμος, ὁππότ᾽ ἀΐξῃ
νειόθεν· ὣς ἄρα τώ γε θοὴν φλόγα φυσιόωντες
ἐκ στομάτων ὁμάδευν, τὸν δ᾽ ἄμφεπε δήιον αἶθος
1305 βάλλον ἅ τε στεροπή· κούρης δέ ἑ φάρμακ᾽ ἔρυτο.
καί ῥ᾽ ὅ γε δεξιτεροῖο βοὸς κέρας ἄκρον
ἐρύσσας
εἷλκεν ἐπικρατέως παντὶ σθένει, ὄφρα πελάσσῃ
ζεύγλῃ χαλκείῃ· τὸν δ᾽ ἐν χθονὶ κάββαλεν ὀκλάξ,
ῥίμφα ποδὶ κρούσας πόδα χάλκεον· ὣς δὲ καὶ
ἄλλον
1310 σφῆλε γνὺξ ἐπιόντα, μιῇ βεβολημένον ὁρμῇ.
εὐρὺ δ᾽ ἀποπροβαλὼν χαμάδις σάκος, ἔνθα καὶ
ἔνθα,

met by leaning it against the spear. He marched forward with only his shield to examine the countless tracks of the oxen. From some unseen hollow in the earth, where they had their strong stalls that were enveloped all around in sooty smoke, the two emerged together, breathing a blast of fire. The heroes took fright when they saw them, but Jason planted his feet firmly apart and awaited their onset, as a jutting rock in the sea awaits the waves propelled by countless storm-winds. He held his shield in front of him to oppose them, and with a bellow they both struck it with their strong horns, but did not heave it up even a little with their onrush. And as when through the holes of a furnace strong leather bellows of bronze-smiths at times cause ravening fire to burn and blaze up, but then, when they cease their blowing, a terrible roar arises from the fire when it springs up from below—thus indeed the two oxen roared as they breathed forth the darting flame from their mouths, and the searing heat enveloped him, striking like lightning, but the girl's drugs protected him.

Then, pulling on the tip of the right ox's horn, he dragged it mightily with all his strength, until he brought it to the bronze yoke. He threw it down to the ground on its knees by swiftly kicking its bronze hoof with his foot. Likewise, he brought the other to its knees as it charged,[111] when it was struck with a single blow. He flung his broad shield away from him to the ground and, with his feet

---

[111] Or, reading ἐριπόντα, *he brought the other down, having fallen on its knees.*

1304 ἄμφεπε Merkel: ἀμφί τε Ω   1305 βάλλον Wellauer, Merkel: βάλλεν Ω   1310 ἐπιόντα Ω: ἐριπόντα LᵃᶜD

τῇ καὶ τῇ βεβαώς, ἄμφω ἔχε πεπτηῶτας
γούνασιν ἐν προτέροισι, διὰ φλογὸς εἶθαρ ἐλυσθείς.
θαύμασε δ' Αἰήτης σθένος ἀνέρος. οἱ δ' ἄρα τείως
1315 Τυνδαρίδαι (δὴ γάρ σφι πάλαι προπεφραδμένον
      ἦεν)
ἀγχίμολον ζυγά οἱ πεδόθεν δόσαν ἀμφιβαλέσθαι.
αὐτὰρ ὁ εὖ ἐνέδησε λόφοις· μεσσηγὺ δ' ἀείρας
χάλκεον ἱστοβοῆα θοῇ συνάρασσε κορώνῃ
ζεύγληθεν. καὶ τὼ μὲν ὑπὲκ πυρὸς ἂψ ἐπὶ νῆα
1320 χαζέσθην· ὁ δ' ἄρ' αὖτις ἑλὼν σάκος ἔνθετο νώτῳ
ἐξόπιθεν, καὶ γέντο θοῶν ἔμπλειον ὀδόντων
πήληκα βριαρὴν δόρυ τ' ἄσχετον, ᾧ ῥ' ὑπὸ μέσσας
ἐργατίνης ὥς τίς τε Πελασγίδι νύσσεν ἀκαίνῃ
οὐτάζων λαγόνας· μάλα δ' ἔμπεδον εὖ ἀραρυῖαν
1325 τυκτὴν ἐξ ἀδάμαντος ἐπιθύνεσκεν ἐχέτλην.
      οἱ δ' εἵως μὲν δὴ περιώσια θυμαίνεσκον,
λάβρον ἐπιπνείοντε πυρὸς σέλας· ὦρτο δ' ἀυτμὴ
ἠύτε βυκτάων ἀνέμων βρόμος, οὕς τε μάλιστα
δειδιότες μέγα λαῖφος ἁλίπλοοι ἐστείλαντο.
1330 δηρὸν δ' οὐ μετέπειτα κελευόμενοι ὑπὸ δουρὶ
ἤισαν. ὀκριόεσσα δ' ἐρείκετο νειὸς ὀπίσσω,
σχιζομένη ταύρων τε βίῃ κρατερῷ τ' ἀροτῆρι·
δεινὸν δ' ἐσμαράγευν ἄμυδις κατὰ ὦλκας ἀρότρου
βώλακες ἀγνύμεναι ἀνδραχθέες. εἵπετο δ' αὐτὸς
1335 λαιὸν ἐπὶ στιβαρῷ πιέσας ποδί· τῆλε δ' ἑοῖο
βάλλεν ἀρηρομένην αἰεὶ κατὰ βῶλον ὀδόντας

planted apart, held on either side of him the two oxen that had fallen on their forelegs, as he was immediately[112] enveloped in flames. Aeetes was astonished at the man's strength. Meanwhile, the sons of Tyndareus (as they had been instructed from the start) drew near and handed him the yoke from the ground to put on the oxen. He fastened it securely on their necks; and lifting up the bronze yoke-pole between them, he fastened it by its sharp tip to the yoke-loop. His two companions withdrew from the fire back to the ship, and again he took up his shield and slung it behind his back. He grasped the strong helmet filled with the sharp teeth and his resistless spear, with which he prodded them, like a farmer with a Pelasgian goad, jabbing the middle of their flanks, and very steadily guided the well-constructed plow handle made of adamant.

For a while the oxen raged furiously, breathing forth a fierce blaze of fire, and their breath arose like the roar of blustering winds that mariners dread the most and thus furl their mainsail. But not long thereafter, when urged on by the spear, they moved forward. Behind them the rugged field was broken up, split open by the force of the oxen and the mighty plowman, and all the while clods of earth, of the size that a man could carry, made a terrible din along the plow's furrows as they were broken apart. He followed behind, pressing down the plowshare with a firm foot, and far from him cast the teeth along whatever furrow had been

---

[112] After discarding his shield.

1317 λόφοις E: λόφους Ω
1326 δ᾽ εἴως μὲν δὴ Merkel: δήτοι εἴως[vel εἴως] μὲν δὴ LAG: δὴ τείως μὲν SE

ἐντροπαλιζόμενος, μή οἱ πάρος ἀντιάσειεν.
γηγενέων ἀνδρῶν ὀλοὸς στάχυς· οἱ δ' ἄρ' ἐπιπρὸ
χαλκείῃς χηλῇσιν ἐρειδόμενοι πονέοντο.

1340 ἦμος δὲ τρίτατον λάχος ἤματος ἀνομένοιο
λείπεται ἐξ ἠοῦς, καλέουσι δὲ κεκμηῶτες
ἐργατίναι γλυκερόν σφιν ἄφαρ βουλυτὸν ἱκέσθαι,
τῆμος ἀρήροτο νειὸς ὑπ' ἀκαμάτῳ ἀροτῆρι,
τετράγυός περ ἐοῦσα, βοῶν τ' ἀπελύετ' ἄροτρα.

1345 καὶ τοὺς μὲν πεδίονδε διεπτοίησε φέβεσθαι·
αὐτὰρ ὁ ἂψ ἐπὶ νῆα πάλιν κίεν, ὄφρ' ἔτι κεινὰς
γηγενέων ἀνδρῶν ἴδεν αὔλακας· ἀμφὶ δ' ἑταῖροι
θάρσυνον μύθοισιν. ὁ δ' ἐκ ποταμοῖο ῥοάων
αὐτῇ ἀφυσσάμενος κυνέῃ σβέσεν ὕδατι δίψαν·

1350 γνάμψε δὲ γούνατ' ἐλαφρά, μέγαν δ' ἐμπλήσατο
          θυμὸν
ἀλκῆς μαιμώων συῒ εἴκελος, ὅς ῥά τ' ὀδόντας
θήγει θηρευτῇσιν ἐπ' ἀνδράσιν, ἀμφὶ δὲ πολλὸς
ἀφρὸς ἀπὸ στόματος χαμάδις ῥέε χωομένοιο.

οἱ δ' ἤδη κατὰ πᾶσαν ἀνασταχύεσκον ἄρουραν
1355 γηγενέες· φρίξεν δὲ περὶ στιβαροῖς σακέεσσιν
δούρασί τ' ἀμφιγύοις κορύθεσσί τε λαμπομένῃσιν
Ἄρηος τέμενος φθισιμβρότου· ἵκετο δ' αἴγλη
νειόθεν Οὐλυμπόνδε δι' ἠέρος ἀστράπτουσα.
ὡς δ' ὁπότ' ἐς γαῖαν πολέος νιφετοῖο πεσόντος

1360 ἂψ ἀπὸ χειμερίας νεφέλας ἐκέδασσαν ἄελλαι
λυγαίῃ ὑπὸ νυκτί, τὰ δ' ἀθρόα πάντα φαάνθη
τείρεα λαμπετόωντα διὰ κνέφας· ὡς ἄρα τοί γε
λάμπον ἀναλδήσκοντες ὑπὲρ χθονός. αὐτὰρ Ἰήσων

plowed, ever turning around to make sure no deadly crop of earthborn men overtook him first. The oxen toiled forward, treading with their bronze hooves.

But at the time when a third of the day remains as it draws to a close from dawn, and tired farmers call for the sweet unyoking to come for them at once, then was the field plowed by the tireless plowman, although it was four acres, and he loosed the plow from the oxen. He shooed them off in flight toward the plain and went back again to the ship, so long as he saw that the furrows were still empty of earthborn men. And around him his comrades encouraged him with their words. He quenched his thirst with water he had drawn with his own helmet from the streams of the river. He flexed his knees to make them nimble and filled his great heart with prowess, raging like a boar that whets its tusks for use against hunters, and all around froth spills to the ground in abundance from its angry mouth.

By now the earthborn men were sprouting up over all the field, and the precinct of man-destroying Ares bristled all around with stout shields, two-edged spears, and shining helmets, and the gleam went up from below, flashing through the air to Olympus. And as when, after a great snow has fallen on the earth, storm-winds scatter back again[113] the wintry clouds in the dark of night, and all the stars come out together and shine through the darkness— thus indeed did they shine as they emerged above ground.

[113] Or, reading αἶψ', *suddenly scatter*.

1353 ῥέε Ω: ῥεῖ Samuelsson
1360 ἂψ Ω: αἶψ' L^{ac}.

μνήσατο Μηδείης πολυκερδέος ἐννεσιάων,
1365 λάζετο δ' ἐκ πεδίοιο μέγαν περιηγέα πέτρον,
δεινὸν Ἐνυαλίου σόλον Ἄρεος· οὔ κέ μιν ἄνδρες
αἰζηοὶ πίσυρες γαίης ἄπο τυτθὸν ἄειραν·
τόν ῥ' ἀνὰ χεῖρα λαβὼν μάλα τηλόθεν ἔμβαλε
    μέσσοις
ἀΐξας· αὐτὸς δ' ὑφ' ἑὸν σάκος ἕζετο λάθρῃ
1370 θαρσαλέως· Κόλχοι δὲ μέγ' ἴαχον, ὡς ὅτε πόντος
ἴαχεν ὀξείῃσιν ἐπιβρομέων σπιλάδεσσιν·
τὸν δ' ἕλεν ἀμφασίη ῥιπῇ στιβαροῖο σόλοιο
Αἰήτην. οἱ δ' ὥς τε θοοὶ κύνες ἀμφιθορόντες
ἀλλήλους βρυχηδὸν ἐδήιον· οἱ δ' ἐπὶ γαῖαν
1375 μητέρα πῖπτον ἑοῖς ὑπὸ δούρασιν, ἠΰτε πεῦκαι
ἢ δρύες, ἅς τ' ἀνέμοιο κατάικες δονέουσιν.
οἷος δ' οὐρανόθεν πυρόεις ἀναπάλλεται ἀστὴρ
ὁλκὸν ὑπαυγάζων, τέρας ἀνδράσιν, οἵ μιν ἴδωνται
μαρμαρυγῇ σκοτίοιο δι' ἠέρος ἀΐξαντα·
1380 τοῖος ἄρ' Αἴσονος υἱὸς ἐπέσσυτο γηγενέεσσιν·
γυμνὸν δ' ἐκ κολεοῖο φέρεν ξίφος, οὖτα δὲ μίγδην
ἀμώων, πολέας μὲν ἔτ' ἐς νηδὺν λαγόνας τε

* * *

ἡμίσεας δ' ἀνέχοντας ἐς ἠέρα, τοὺς δὲ καὶ ἄχρις
γούνων τελλομένους, τοὺς δὲ νέον ἑστηῶτας,
1385 τοὺς δ' ἤδη καὶ ποσσὶν ἐπειγομένους ἐς ἄρηα.
ὡς δ' ὁπότ' ἀγχούροισιν ἐγειρομένου πολέμοιο

1368 χεῖρα Ω: χειρὶ Richards: ῥεῖα Fränkel
1382 post hunc versum lacunam statuit Fränkel

But Jason recalled the instructions of shrewd Medea and seized a great round boulder from the plain, a fearsome throwing-stone of Ares Enyalius—not even four men in their prime could have lifted it even a little from the ground. He picked it up in his hand,[114] darted forward, and from far away threw it into their midst, while he himself crouched out of sight beneath his shield in full confidence. The Colchians roared loudly, as when the sea roars as it crashes against jutting rocks, but speechlessness seized Aeetes at the cast of the stout stone. The earthborn men rushed like fierce dogs around it and with a clamor went about killing one another. They fell upon mother earth beneath their own spears, like pines or oaks that wind-storms drive down. And as when a fiery star springs forth from heaven bearing a trail of light, an omen for men who see it darting with a gleam through the dark sky—such indeed was Jason as he rushed upon the earthborn men. He wielded his bare sword drawn from its sheath and, reaping indiscriminately, struck many [who were half-buried in the earth][115] up to their bellies and flanks . . . some half-risen into the air, some grown as far as their knees, some just beginning to stand, and others already hastening on foot to battle. And as when a war breaks out between neighboring

---

[114] Although ἀνὰ χεῖρα is unusual, neither Richards' facile χειρὶ (*with his hand*) or Fränkel's ῥεῖα (*easily*) is convincing.

[115] A verse has apparently dropped out.

1384 γούνων Struve: ὤμων Ω | δὲ Ω: δ᾽ αὖ Z
1386 ἀγχούροισιν w: ἀμφ᾽ ούροισιν m

δείσας γειομόρος, μή οἱ προτάμωνται ἀρούρας,
ἅρπην εὐκαμπῆ νεοθηγέα χερσὶ μεμαρπὼς
ὠμὸν ἐπισπεύδων κείρει στάχυν, οὐδὲ βολῆσιν
1390 μίμνει ἐς ὡραίην τερσήμεναι ἠελίοιο·
ὣς τότε γηγενέων κεῖρεν στάχυν· αἵματι δ' ὁλκοὶ
ἠΰτε κρηναῖαι ἀμάραι πλήθοντο ῥοῇσιν.
πῖπτον δ', οἱ μὲν ὀδὰξ τετρηχότα βῶλον ὀδοῦσιν
λαζόμενοι πρηνεῖς, οἱ δ' ἔμπαλιν, οἱ δ' ἐπ' ἀγοστῷ
1395 καὶ πλευροῖς, κήτεσσι δομὴν ἀτάλαντοι ἰδέσθαι·
πολλοὶ δ', οὐτάμενοι πρὶν ὑπὸ χθονὸς ἴχνος ἀεῖραι,
ὅσσον ἄνω προύτυψαν ἐς ἠέρα, τόσσον ἔραζε
βριθόμενοι πλαδαροῖσι καρήασιν ἠρήρειντο.
ἔρνεά που τοίως, Διὸς ἄσπετον ὀμβρήσαντος,
1400 φυταλιῇ νεόθρεπτα κατημύουσιν ἔραζε
κλασθέντα ῥίζηθεν, ἀλωήων πόνος ἀνδρῶν,
τὸν δὲ κατηφείη τε καὶ οὐλοὸν ἄλγος ἱκάνει
κλήρου σημαντῆρα φυτοτρόφον· ὣς τότ' ἄνακτος
Αἰήταο βαρεῖαι ὑπὸ φρένας ἦλθον ἀνῖαι.
1405 ἤιε δ' ἐς πτολίεθρον ὑπότροπος ἄμμιγα Κόλχοις,
πορφύρων, ᾗ κέ σφι θοώτερον ἀντιόῳτο.
ἦμαρ ἔδυ, καὶ τῷ τετελεσμένος ἦεν ἄεθλος.

peoples[116] and a farmer, fearing that they will harvest his fields before he does, takes in his hands a curved, freshly sharpened sickle and hastily cuts the unripe crop without waiting for the season when it has dried in the sun's rays— so did he then cut down the crop of earthborn men, and the furrows were filled with blood like the channels of a spring with flowing waters. They fell, some on their faces, biting the plowed-up clod with their teeth, others on their backs, others on their palms and sides, with bodies like those of sea-monsters to behold. And many, struck before raising their feet from under the ground, leaned over to the earth as far as they had sprung up into the air, weighed down by their limp heads. In such a manner, I suppose, after Zeus has rained incessantly, newly planted shoots in an orchard, the work of gardeners, nod to earth when broken off at the root, and discouragement and deadly sorrow come to the owner of the land who was growing them—so at that time did grave pains come upon the mind of King Aeetes. He turned and went back to the city along with the Colchians, pondering how he might more expeditiously thwart the heroes. The day set, and Jason's contest was at an end.

[116] Or, reading ἀμφ' οὔροισιν, *breaks out over boundaries.*

BOOK 4

Αὐτὴ νῦν κάματόν γε, θεά, καὶ δήνεα κούρης
Κολχίδος ἔννεπε, Μοῦσα, Διὸς τέκος· ἦ γὰρ ἐμοί γε
ἀμφασίη νόος ἔνδον ἑλίσσεται ὁρμαίνοντι,
ἠέ μιν ἄτης πῆμα δυσίμερον ἦ τό γ' ἐνίσπω
5 φύζαν ἀεικελίην, ᾗ κάλλιπεν ἔθνεα Κόλχων.

ἤτοι ὁ μὲν δήμοιο μετ' ἀνδράσιν, ὅσσοι ἄριστοι,
παννύχιος δόλον αἰπὺν ἐπὶ σφίσι μητιάασκεν
οἷσιν ἐνὶ μεγάροις, στυγερῷ ἐπὶ θυμὸν ἀέθλῳ
Αἰήτης ἄμοτον κεχολωμένος, οὐδ' ὅ γε πάμπαν
10 θυγατέρων τάδε νόσφιν ἑῶν τελέεσθαι ἐώλπει.

τῇ δ' ἀλεγεινότατον κραδίῃ φόβον ἔμβαλεν Ἥρη·
τρέσσεν δ' ἠύτε τις κούφη κεμάς, ἥν τε βαθείης
τάρφεσιν ἐν ξυλόχοιο κυνῶν ἐφόβησεν ὁμοκλή·
αὐτίκα γὰρ νημερτὲς ὀίσσατο, μή μιν ἀρωγὴν
15 ληθέμεν, αἶψα δὲ πᾶσαν ἀναπλήσειν κακότητα.
τάρβει δ' ἀμφιπόλους ἐπιίστορας· ἐν δέ οἱ ὄσσε
πλῆτο πυρός, δεινὸν δὲ περιβρομέεσκον ἀκουαί·
πυκνὰ δὲ λαυκανίης ἐπεμάσσετο, πυκνὰ δὲ κουρὶξ
ἑλκομένη πλοκάμους γοερῇ βρυχήσατ' ἀνίῃ.
20 καί νύ κεν αὐτοῦ τῆμος ὑπὲρ μόρον ὤλετο κούρη

BOOK 4

Now, goddess,[1] you yourself tell of the distress and thoughts[2] of the Colchian girl, O Muse, daughter of Zeus, for truly the mind within me whirls in speechless stupor, as I ponder whether to call it the lovesick affliction of obsession or shameful panic, which made her leave the Colchian people.

Aeetes spent the entire night in his palace with the leading men of his people, plotting an inescapable trap for the heroes, violently angry in his heart at the appalling contest, for he did not think for a moment that it was accomplished without the involvement of his daughters. But into Medea's heart Hera cast excruciating fear, and she bolted like a nimble fawn which the baying of dogs frightens in the thickets of a dense wood, for she at once correctly surmised that her assistance was no secret to her father and that she would soon suffer the full extent of misery. She was in dread of the servants who knew of it; her eyes filled with fire and her ears roared terribly. Again and again she clutched her throat; again and again she pulled on the locks of her hair and moaned in woeful pain. Then and there the girl would have died before her appointed

---

[1] Either Erato, invoked at 3.1, or another, unnamed, Muse.
[2] Or *counsels, plans, wiles.*

φάρμακα πασσαμένη, Ἥρης δ' ἁλίωσε μενοινάς,
εἰ μή μιν Φρίξοιο θεὰ σὺν παισὶ φέβεσθαι
ὦρσεν ἀτυζομένην. πτερόεις δέ οἱ ἐν φρεσὶ θυμὸς
ἰάνθη, μετὰ δ' ἥ γε παλίσσυτος ἀθρόα κόλπῳ
25 φάρμακα πάντ' ἄμυδις κατεχεύατο φωριαμοῖο.
κύσσε δ' ἑόν τε λέχος καὶ δικλίδας ἀμφοτέρωθεν
σταθμοὺς καὶ τοίχων ἐπαφήσατο· χερσί τε μακρὸν
ῥηξαμένη πλόκαμον, θαλάμῳ μνημήια μητρὶ
κάλλιπε παρθενίης, ἀδινῇ δ' ὀλοφύρατο φωνῇ·
30   "τόνδε τοι ἀντ' ἐμέθεν ταναὸν πλόκον εἶμι
          λιποῦσα,
μῆτερ ἐμή· χαίροις δὲ καὶ ἄνδιχα πολλὸν ἰούσῃ·
χαίροις Χαλκιόπη καὶ πᾶς δόμος. αἴθε σε πόντος,
ξεῖνε, διέρραισεν, πρὶν Κολχίδα γαῖαν ἱκέσθαι."
   ὣς ἄρ' ἔφη· βλεφάρων δὲ κατ' ἀθρόα δάκρυα
       χεῦεν.
35 οἵη δ' ἀφνειοῖο διειλυσθεῖσα δόμοιο
ληιάς, ἥν τε νέον πάτρης ἀπενόσφισεν αἶσα,
οὐδέ νύ πω μογεροῖο πεπείρηται καμάτοιο,
ἀλλ' ἔτ' ἀηθέσσουσα δύην καὶ δούλια ἔργα
εἶσιν ἀτυζομένη χαλεπὰς ὑπὸ χεῖρας ἀνάσσης·
40 τοίη ἄρ' ἱμερόεσσα δόμων ἐξέσσυτο κούρη.
τῇ δὲ καὶ αὐτόματοι θυρέων ὑπόειξαν ὀχῆες
ὠκείαις ἄψορροι ἀναθρῴσκοντες ἀοιδαῖς.
γυμνοῖσιν δὲ πόδεσσιν ἀνὰ στεινὰς θέεν οἴμους,
λαιῇ μὲν χερὶ πέπλον ἐπ' ὀφρύσιν ἀμφὶ μέτωπα

24 κόλπῳ Platt: κόλπων Ω

time by swallowing poison and would have thwarted Hera's designs, had not the goddess driven her to flee in panic with Phrixus' sons. Her fluttering heart relaxed[3] in her breast, and then, with a change of mind, she poured together all the drugs from the chest into her lap.[4] She kissed her bed and the doorjambs on either side of the double-doors and stroked the walls. She tore off a long lock of hair with her hands and left it behind for her mother as a memento of her maidenhood, and lamented in a plaintive voice:

"I go, leaving you this long tress in my stead, my mother. I wish you well, although I am going far away. I wish you well, Chalciope and the entire house. Would that the sea had torn you to pieces, stranger, before you had come to the Colchian land!"

Thus she spoke, and a flood of tears poured down from under her eyelids. And like a captive woman slinking[5] through her wealthy home, one whom fate has recently deprived of her homeland, and who has not yet experienced hard labor, but still unaccustomed to misery and the toils of slavery goes in terror under the brutal hands of a mistress—thus did the lovely girl rush from her home. And all on their own the bolts of the doors yielded for her, springing back at her swiftly working incantations. She ran barefoot down narrow paths, holding her robe with her left

---

[3] Or *her heart took wing and relaxed* (schol.).

[4] Or, reading the MSS' κόλπων, *she took the drugs from her lap and poured them all together into the chest.*

[5] Or, reading διελκυσθεῖσα, *having been dragged.*

---

35 διειλυσθεῖσα Ω: διελκυσθεῖσα Ardizzoni
38 δύην Huet: δύης Ω

331

45 στειλαμένη καὶ καλὰ παρήια, δεξιτερῇ δὲ
ἄκρην ὑψόθι πέζαν ἀερτάζουσα χιτῶνος.
καρπαλίμως δ' ἀίδηλον ἀνὰ στίβον ἔκτοθι πύργων
ἄστεος εὐρυχόροιο φόβῳ ἵκετ', οὐδέ τις ἔγνω
τήνδε φυλακτήρων, λάθε δέ σφεας ὁρμηθεῖσα.
50 ἔνθεν ἴμεν νηόνδε μάλ' ἐφράσατ'· οὐ γὰρ ἀίδρις
ἦεν ὁδῶν, θαμὰ καὶ πρὶν ἀλωμένη ἀμφί τε νεκροὺς
ἀμφί τε δυσπαλέας ῥίζας χθονός, οἷα γυναῖκες
φαρμακίδες· τρομερῷ δ' ὑπὸ δείματι πάλλετο θυμός.
τὴν δὲ νέον Τιτηνὶς ἀνερχομένη περάτηθεν
55 φοιταλέην ἐσιδοῦσα θεὰ ἐπεχήρατο Μήνη
ἁρπαλέως, καὶ τοῖα μετὰ φρεσὶν ᾗσιν ἔειπεν·
    "οὐκ ἄρ' ἐγὼ μούνη μετὰ Λάτμιον ἄντρον
    ἀλύσκω,
οὐδ' οἴη καλῷ περιδαίομαι Ἐνδυμίωνι.
ἦ θαμὰ δὴ καὶ σεῖο, κύον, δολίῃσιν ἀοιδαῖς
60 μνησαμένη φιλότητος, ἵνα σκοτίῃ ἐνὶ νυκτὶ
φαρμάσσῃς εὔκηλος, ἅ τοι φίλα ἔργα τέτυκται.
νῦν δὲ καὶ αὐτὴ δῆθεν ὁμοίης ἔμμορες ἄτης,
δῶκε δ' ἀνιηρόν τοι Ἰήσονα πῆμα γενέσθαι
δαίμων ἀλγινόεις. ἀλλ' ἔρχεο, τέτλαθι δ' ἔμπης,
65 καὶ πινυτή περ ἐοῦσα, πολύστονον ἄλγος ἀείρειν."

50 ἔνθεν ἴμεν Hartung: ἔνθ' ἐνὶ μὲν Ω
59 κύον Ω: κύων E: κίον B²ᵞʳ: κύθον Fränkel

___

6 The Moon was the daughter of the Titans Theia and
Hyperion (Hesiod, *Theogony* 371–374).

332

hand above her eyebrows to cover her forehead and beautiful cheeks, while with her right she lifted up the hem of her garment. Quickly, down a hidden footpath, she arrived in fear outside the ramparts of the spacious city, nor did any of the guards recognize her, but she sped by them unseen. From there she carefully considered how to get to the temple, for she was not ignorant of the ways, having often in the past wandered in search of corpses and noxious roots from the earth, as sorceresses do, but her heart was throbbing with trembling dread. And when the Titanian goddess,[6] the Moon, newly rising above the horizon, saw her wandering in distress, she exulted gleefully over her and spoke these thoughts to herself:

"So I am not the only one, after all, to flee to the Latmian cave, nor alone in burning for handsome Endymion.[7] How often indeed did your crafty incantations, shameless one, remind me of my love,[8] so that in the dark of night you could calmly work the spells that are dear to you. But now it appears that you too have been allotted a similar obsession, for a cruel god has given you Jason as a grievous affliction. Go on, and in spite of your cleverness bring yourself to endure pain full of tears."

[7] The Moon visited the shepherd Endymion as he slept in a cave on mount Latmos in Caria.

[8] This passage is notoriously difficult. I have followed Vian's text and interpretation. Since there is no main verb, some editors have emended κύον ("shameless one") to κίον ("I went"), with the sense, "How often, because of your crafty incantations, did I go when mindful of love." Sorceresses were thought to "draw down" the moon to earth to work their spells in complete darkness. The girl who callously manipulated the goddess for her own ends is now ironically (δῆθεν, 62) stealing off to her own lover.

ὣς ἄρ' ἔφη· τὴν δ' αἶψα πόδες φέρον
ἐγκονέουσαν.
ἀσπασίως δ' ὄχθῃσιν ἐπηέρθη ποταμοῖο
ἀντιπέρην λεύσσουσα πυρὸς σέλας, ὅ ῥά τ' ἀέθλου
παννύχιοι ἥρωες ἐυφροσύνῃσιν ἔδαιον.
70 ὀξείῃ δήπειτα διὰ κνέφας ὄρθια φωνῇ
ὁπλότατον Φρίξοιο περαιόθεν ἧπυε παίδων,
Φρόντιν. ὁ δὲ ξὺν ἑοῖσι κασιγνήτοις ὄπα κούρης
αὐτῷ τ' Αἰσονίδῃ τεκμαίρετο· σῖγα δ' ἑταῖροι
θάμβεον, εὖτ' ἐνόησαν ὃ δὴ καὶ ἐτήτυμον ἦεν.
75 τρὶς μὲν ἀνήυσεν, τρὶς δ' ὀτρύνοντος ὁμίλου
Φρόντις ἀμοιβήδην ἀντίαχεν· οἱ δ' ἄρα τείως
ἥρωες μετὰ τήν γε θοοῖς ἐλάασκον ἐρετμοῖς.
οὔ πω πείσματα νηὸς ἐπ' ἠπείροιο περαίης
βάλλον, ὁ δὲ κραιπνοὺς χέρσῳ πόδας ἧκεν Ἰήσων
80 ὑψοῦ ἀπ' ἰκριόφιν· μετὰ δὲ Φρόντις τε καὶ Ἄργος,
υἷε δύω Φρίξου, χαμάδις θόρον. ἡ δ' ἄρα τούς γε
γούνων ἀμφοτέρῃσι περισχομένη προσέειπεν·
    "ἔκ με, φίλοι, ῥύσασθε δυσάμμορον, ὡς δὲ καὶ
αὐτοὺς
ὑμέας, Αἰήταο· πρὸ γάρ τ' ἀναφανδὰ τέτυκται
85 πάντα μάλ', οὐδέ τι μῆχος ἱκάνεται. ἀλλ' ἐπὶ νηὶ
φεύγωμεν, πρὶν τόν γε θοῶν ἐπιβήμεναι ἵππων.
δώσω δὲ χρύσειον ἐγὼ δέρος εὐνήσασα
φρουρὸν ὄφιν· τύνη δὲ θεοὺς ἐνὶ σοῖσιν ἑταίροις,
ξεῖνε, τεῶν μύθων ἐπιίστορας, οὕς μοι ὑπέστης,
90 ποίησαι, μηδ' ἔνθεν ἑκαστέρω ὁρμηθεῖσαν
χήτεϊ κηδεμόνων ὀνοτὴν καὶ ἀεικέα θείης."

Thus she spoke, and the girl's feet carried her swiftly as she hastened on. She climbed the bank of the river and gladly saw on the opposite side the light of a fire, which the heroes were burning all night long to celebrate the contest. Then, in a clear voice through the darkness, she cried aloud from the further bank to Phrontis, the youngest of Phrixus' sons, and he, along with his brothers and Jason himself, recognized the girl's voice. The comrades marvelled in silence, when they realized what was in fact occurring. Three times she called out, and three times at the crew's bidding Phrontis shouted back in reply. Meanwhile, the heroes were swiftly rowing to meet her. Before they could cast the ship's cables onto the opposite shore, Jason leapt with swift feet to land from high on the deck, and behind him Phrontis and Argus, Phrixus' two sons, jumped ashore. She clasped their knees with both hands and said to them:

"Rescue poor me, my friends, and yourselves as well, from Aeetes, for absolutely everything has come to light, and no remedy is at hand. Come, let us escape by ship before he mounts his swift chariot. I will get you the golden fleece by putting the guardian snake to sleep. For your part, stranger, in the presence of your comrades take the gods as witnesses to the pledges you made me,[9] and do not render me, once I have traveled far from here, despised and dishonored through lack of guardians."

[9] Cf. 3.1122–1130.

---

86 τόνγ[ε Π[29] et Brunck: τόνδε *w*E: τῶνδε LA

ἴσκεν ἀκηχεμένη· μέγα δὲ φρένες Αἰσονίδαο
γήθεον. αἶψα δέ μιν περὶ γούνασι πεπτηυῖαν
ἦκ' ἀναειρόμενος προσπτύξατο, θάρσυνέν τε·
95   "δαιμονίη, Ζεὺς αὐτὸς Ὀλύμπιος ὅρκιος ἔστω
Ἥρη τε Ζυγίη, Διὸς εὐνέτις, ἦ μὲν ἐμοῖσιν
κουριδίην σε δόμοισιν ἐνιστήσεσθαι ἄκοιτιν,
εὖτ' ἂν ἐς Ἑλλάδα γαῖαν ἱκώμεθα νοστήσαντες."
     ὣς ηὔδα, καὶ χεῖρα παρασχεδὸν ἤραρε χειρὶ
100 δεξιτερήν. ἡ δέ σφιν ἐς ἱερὸν ἄλσος ἀνώγει
νῆα θοὴν ἐλάαν αὐτοσχεδόν, ὄφρ' ἔτι νύκτωρ
κῶας ἑλόντες ἄγοιντο παρὲκ νόον Αἰήταο.
ἔνθ' ἔπος ἠδὲ καὶ ἔργον ὁμοῦ πέλεν ἐσσυμένοισιν·
εἰς γάρ μιν βήσαντες ἀπὸ χθονὸς αὐτίκ' ἔωσαν
105 νῆα· πολὺς δ' ὀρυμαγδὸς ἐπειγομένων ἐλάτῃσιν
ἦεν ἀριστήων. ἡ δ' ἔμπαλιν ἀίσσουσα
γαίῃ χεῖρας ἔτεινεν ἀμήχανος· αὐτὰρ Ἰήσων
θάρσυνέν τ' ἐπέεσσι καὶ ἴσχανεν ἀσχαλόωσαν.
     ἦμος δ' ἀνέρες ὕπνον ἀπ' ὀφθαλμῶν ἐβάλοντο
110 ἀγρόται, οἵ τε κύνεσσι πεποιθότες οὔ ποτε νύκτα
ἄγχαυρον κνώσσουσιν, ἀλευάμενοι φάος ἠοῦς,
μὴ πρὶν ἀμαλδύνῃ θηρῶν στίβον ἠδὲ καὶ ὀδμὴν
θηρείην λευκῇσιν ἐνισκίμψασα βολῇσιν·
τῆμος ἄρ' Αἰσονίδης κούρη τ' ἀπὸ νηὸς ἔβησαν
115 ποιήεντ' ἀνὰ χῶρον, ἵνα Κριοῦ καλέονται
Εὐναί, ὅθι πρῶτον κεκμηότα γούνατ' ἔκαμψεν,
νώτοισιν φορέων Μινυήιον υἷ' Ἀθάμαντος.
ἐγγύθι δ' αἰθαλόεντα πέλεν βωμοῖο θέμεθλα,
ὅν ῥά ποτ' Αἰολίδης Διὶ Φυξίῳ εἴσατο Φρίξος,

She spoke in anguish, but Jason's mind rejoiced greatly. At once he lifted her gently from where she had fallen about his knees and spoke kindly and reassured her:

"Poor girl! Let Olympian Zeus himself be witness to my oath and Hera too, goddess of marriage and sharer of Zeus' bed, that I shall truly establish you in my home as my lawfully wedded wife when we reach the land of Hellas on our return."

Thus he spoke, and immediately grasped her right hand in his. She ordered them to steer the swift ship to the hallowed grove at once, so that while it was still dark they could get the fleece and take it away against the will of Aeetes. Then word and deed became one, so great was their haste: they brought her on board and immediately pushed the ship off from land, and loud was the splashing as the heroes bore down on the oars. But she rushed to the stern and stretched out her hands helplessly towards land, while Jason reassured her with words and held her back in her distress.

And at the time when hunters cast sleep from their eyes, who, relying on their hounds, never slumber during the last portion of night, to avoid the light of dawn before it effaces the trail of game and smell of quarry when it strikes with its white rays—at that time Jason and the girl disembarked onto a grassy spot called Ram's rest, where the ram first bent its knees in exhaustion from carrying the Minyan son of Athamas[10] on its back. Nearby was the sooty base of the altar that the Aeolid Phrixus[11] had once erected for Zeus, Protector of Fugitives, when he sacrificed that all-

---

[10] Phrixus.
[11] Phrixus was Aeolus' grandson.

120 ῥέζων κεῖνο τέρας παγχρύσεον, ὥς οἱ ἔειπεν
Ἑρμείας πρόφρων ξυμβλήμενος. ἔνθ᾽ ἄρα τούς γε
Ἄργου φραδμοσύνῃσιν ἀριστῆες μεθέηκαν.

τὼ δὲ δι᾽ ἀτραπιτοῖο μεθ᾽ ἱερὸν ἄλσος ἵκοντο,
φηγὸν ἀπειρεσίην διζημένω, ᾗ ἔπι κῶας
125 βέβλητο, νεφέλῃ ἐναλίγκιον, ἥ τ᾽ ἀνιόντος
ἠελίου φλογερῇσιν ἐρεύθεται ἀκτίνεσσιν.
αὐτὰρ ὁ ἀντικρὺ περιμήκεα τείνετο δειρὴν
ὀξὺς ἀύπνοισιν προϊδὼν ὄφις ὀφθαλμοῖσιν
νισσομένους, ῥοίζει δὲ πελώριον· ἀμφὶ δὲ μακραὶ
130 ἠιόνες ποταμοῖο καὶ ἄσπετον ἴαχεν ἄλσος.
ἔκλυον οἳ καὶ πολλὸν ἑκὰς Τιτηνίδος Αἴης
Κολχίδα γῆν ἐνέμοντο παρὰ προχοῇσι Λύκοιο,
ὅς τ᾽ ἀποκιδνάμενος ποταμοῦ κελάδοντος Ἀράξεω
Φάσιδι συμφέρεται ἱερὸν ῥόον, οἱ δὲ συνάμφω
135 Καυκασίην ἅλαδ᾽ εἰς ἓν ἐλαυνόμενοι προχέουσιν·
δείματι δ᾽ ἐξέγροντο λεχωίδες, ἀμφὶ δὲ παισὶν
νηπιάχοις, οἵ τέ σφιν ὑπ᾽ ἀγκαλίδεσσιν ἴαυον,
ῥοίζῳ παλλομένοις χεῖρας βάλον ἀσχαλόωσαι.
ὡς δ᾽ ὅτε τυφομένης ὕλης ὕπερ αἰθαλόεσσαι
140 καπνοῖο στροφάλιγγες ἀπείριτοι εἰλίσσονται,
ἄλλη δ᾽ αἶψ᾽ ἑτέρῃ ἐπιτέλλεται αἰὲν ἐπιπρὸ
νειόθεν εἰλίγγοισιν ἐπήορος ἐξανιοῦσα·
ὣς τότε κεῖνο πέλωρον ἀπειρεσίας ἐλέλιξεν
ῥυμβόνας ἀζαλέῃσιν ἐπηρεφέας φολίδεσσιν.
145 τοῖο δ᾽ ἑλισσομένοιο κατόμματον εἴσατο κούρη,

145 κατόμματον Ω: κατ᾽ ὄμματα Bigot, Merkel | εἴσατο
G²ˢˡE: εἴσετο Ω: νίσσετο Merkel

338

golden marvel, as Hermes had told him to do when the god graciously happened upon him.[12] It was there that the heroes, following Argus' instructions, put them ashore.

The two of them went along a pathway toward the hallowed grove, in search of the huge oak tree on which the fleece had been hung, like a cloud that glows red from the fiery beams of the rising sun. But right in front of them the snake stretched out its enormous neck, having alertly seen them approaching with its sleepless eyes, and hissed monstrously. All around, the long banks of the river and the boundless grove echoed; even those heard it who lived far away from Titanian[13] Aea in the Colchian land by the waters of the Lycus, which branches from the roaring Araxes river and joins its sacred stream with the Phasis, and the two of them, flowing in one stream, pour into the Caucasian sea.[14] Young mothers awoke in fear and anxiously clasped their newborn babies, who, asleep in their arms, were trembling at the hissing. And as when countless swirls of sooty smoke spiral above a smoldering forest, and one follows another in quick succession, ever lifted on the swirls from below, so did that huge beast then roll his countless coils covered with dry scales. But as it was coiling, the girl rushed to look it in the eye,[15] and in a

---

[12] Hermes frequently happens upon people to give them helpful advice, as in the case of Priam (*Iliad* 24.330–467) and Odysseus (*Odyssey* 10.274–309).

[13] Aeetes' grandfather was the Titan Hyperion.

[14] I.e. the Black Sea.

[15] I follow Vian (and the schol.) in taking εἴσατο as the Homeric aorist of ἵεμαι, "rush."

APOLLONIUS RHODIUS

Ὕπνον ἀοσσητῆρα, θεῶν ὕπατον, καλέουσα
ἡδείῃ ἐνοπῇ θέλξαι τέρας· αὖε δ' ἄνασσαν
νυκτιπόλον, χθονίην, εὐαντέα δοῦναι ἐφορμήν.
εἵπετο δ' Αἰσονίδης πεφοβημένος· αὐτὰρ ὅ γ' ἤδη
150 οἴμῃ θελγόμενος δολιχὴν ἀνελύετ' ἄκανθαν
γηγενέος σπείρης, μήκυνε δὲ μυρία κύκλα,
οἷον ὅτε βληχροῖσι κυλινδόμενον πελάγεσσιν
κῦμα μέλαν κωφόν τε καὶ ἄβρομον· ἀλλὰ καὶ ἔμπης
ὑψοῦ σμερδαλέην κεφαλὴν μενέαινεν ἀείρας
155 ἀμφοτέρους ὀλοῇσι περιπτύξαι γενύεσσιν.
ἡ δέ μιν ἀρκεύθοιο νέον τετμηότι θαλλῷ
βάπτουσ' ἐκ κυκεῶνος ἀκήρατα φάρμακ' ἀοιδαῖς
ῥαῖνε κατ' ὀφθαλμῶν, περί τ' ἀμφί τε νήριτος ὀδμὴ
φαρμάκου ὕπνον ἔβαλλε· γένυν δ' αὐτῇ ἐνὶ χώρῃ
160 θῆκεν ἐρεισάμενος, τὰ δ' ἀπείρονα πολλὸν ὀπίσσω
κύκλα πολυπρέμνοιο διὲξ ὕλης τετάνυστο.

ἔνθα δ' ὁ μὲν χρύσειον ἀπὸ δρυὸς αἴνυτο κῶας,
κούρης κεκλομένης, ἡ δ' ἔμπεδον ἑστηυῖα
φαρμάκῳ ἔψηχεν θηρὸς κάρη, εἰσόκε δή μιν
165 αὐτὸς ἑὴν ἐπὶ νῆα παλιντροπάασθαι Ἰήσων
ἤνωγεν· λεῖπεν δὲ πολύσκιον ἄλσος Ἄρηος.
ὡς δὲ σεληναίης διχομήνιδα παρθένος αἴγλην
ὑψόθεν ἐξανέχουσαν ὑπωροφίου θαλάμοιο
λεπταλέῳ ἑανῷ ὑποΐσχεται, ἐν δέ οἱ ἦτορ
170 χαίρει δερκομένης καλὸν σέλας· ὣς τότ' Ἰήσων

166 λεῖπεν Sd: λίπεν mG: λεῖπον Naber
167 σεληναίης Et. Gen.: σεληναίην Ω

340

sweet voice called to her aid Sleep, highest of the gods, to enchant the monster, and invoked the queen of the underworld,[16] the night-wanderer, to grant a favorable venture.[17] Jason followed in fear, but the snake, already enchanted by her song, was relaxing the long spine of its earthborn[18] coils and stretching out its myriad spirals, like a dark wave when it rolls mute and soundless on a sluggish sea. But all the same, it raised up its horrific head, eager to clasp them both in its deadly jaws. But she dipped a freshly cut sprig of juniper into a potion and sprinkled powerful drugs in its eyes as she sang incantations, and all around the pervasive scent of the drug was casting sleep. It laid its jaw to rest on that very spot, and those countless spirals lay stretched out far behind through the dense woods.

Then, at the girl's command, he took the golden fleece from the oak tree, while she stood fast and kept rubbing the head of the beast with the drug, until Jason himself told her to turn back toward their ship, and she left[19] the shade-filled grove of Ares. And as a young girl catches on her delicate gown the beam of a full moon as it shines forth high above her upper room, and her heart within her rejoices as she beholds the beautiful gleam, so joyfully then did Jason

---

[16] Hecate.

[17] Or, taking εὐαντέα as an epithet of the goddess (Vian), *to be gracious and grant an approach.*

[18] For its birth from Earth see 2.1208–1210.

[19] Or, reading λεῖπον, *they left.*

---

168 ὑπωροφίου Bigot: ὑπωρόφιον Ω

APOLLONIUS RHODIUS

γηθόσυνος μέγα κῶας ἑαῖς ἀναείρετο χερσίν,
καί οἱ ἐπὶ ξανθῇσι παρηίσιν ἠδὲ μετώπῳ
μαρμαρυγῇ ληνέων φλογὶ εἴκελον ἷζεν ἔρευθος.
ὅσση δὲ ῥινὸς βοὸς ἤνιος ἢ ἐλάφοιο
175 γίγνεται, ἥν τ᾽ ἀγρῶσται ἀχαινέην καλέουσιν,
τόσσον ἔην, πάντῃ χρύσεον, ἐφύπερθε δ᾽ ἄωτον
βεβρίθει λήνεσσιν ἐπηρεφές· ἤλιθα δὲ χθὼν
αἰὲν ὑποπρὸ ποδῶν ἀμαρύσσετο νισσομένοιο.
ἤιε δ᾽ ἄλλοτε μὲν λαιῷ ἐπιειμένος ὤμῳ
180 αὐχένος ἐξ ὑπάτοιο ποδηνεκές, ἄλλοτε δ᾽ αὖτε
εἴλει ἀφασσόμενος· περὶ γὰρ δίεν, ὄφρα ἑ μή τις
ἀνδρῶν ἠὲ θεῶν νοσφίσσεται ἀντιβολήσας.
      Ἠὼς μέν ῥ᾽ ἐπὶ γαῖαν ἐκίδνατο, τοὶ δ᾽ ἐς ὅμιλον
ἷξον. θάμβησαν δὲ νέοι μέγα κῶας ἰδόντες
185 λαμπόμενον στεροπῇ ἴκελον Διός, ὦρτο δ᾽ ἕκαστος
ψαῦσαι ἐελδόμενος δέχθαι τ᾽ ἐνὶ χερσὶν ἑῇσιν·
Αἰσονίδης δ᾽ ἄλλους μὲν ἐρήτυε, τῷ δ᾽ ἐπὶ φᾶρος
κάββαλε νηγάτεον. πρύμνῃ δ᾽ ἐνεείσατο κούρην
ἀνθέμενος, καὶ τοῖον ἔπος μετὰ πᾶσιν ἔειπεν·
190   "μηκέτι νῦν χάζεσθε, φίλοι, πάτρηνδε νέεσθαι·
ἤδη γὰρ χρειώ, τῆς εἵνεκα τήνδ᾽ ἀλεγεινὴν
ναυτιλίην ἔτλημεν ὀιζύι μοχθίζοντες,
εὐπαλέως κούρης ὑπὸ δήνεσι κεκράανται.
τὴν μὲν ἐγὼν ἐθέλουσαν ἀνάξομαι οἴκαδ᾽ ἄκοιτιν
195 κουριδίην· ἀτὰρ ὕμμες, Ἀχαιίδος οἷά τε πάσης
αὐτῶν θ᾽ ὑμείων ἐσθλὴν ἐπαρωγὸν ἐοῦσαν,

171 ἀναείρετο w: ἐναείρατο m

342

lift up the great fleece in his hands, and upon his golden cheeks and forehead there settled a red glow like a flame from the shimmering of the wool. As large as the hide of a yearling ox or of the deer which hunters call the *achaiines*,[20] so great it was, all golden, and its fleecy covering was heavy with wool. The ground at his feet sparkled brightly with every step he took. Sometimes he went draping it over his left shoulder from the top of his neck to his foot, but at other times he rolled it up and stroked it, for he greatly feared that some man or god would come and take it from him.

Dawn was spreading over the earth when they joined the crew. The young men marveled when they saw the great fleece shining like a thunderbolt of Zeus, and each one leapt up, eager to touch it and take it in his hands, but Jason restrained them all and covered it with a newly woven robe. He lifted the girl and seated her in the stern, and spoke the following to them all:

"My friends, no longer now refrain from returning to your homeland, because now the purpose for which we toiled in misery and endured this arduous journey has been easily accomplished through the girl's counsels. With her consent I shall take her home to be my lawfully wedded wife, and for your part, inasmuch as she is the noble savior of all Achaea and of yourselves, you must protect

[20] Such deer are mentioned by Aristotle, *Historia Animalium* 506a24 and 611b18, and Oppian, *Cynegetica* 2.426, but little is known of them.

---

176 ἐφύπερθε δ᾽ Merkel: ἐφύπερθεν Ω

APOLLONIUS RHODIUS

σώετε· δὴ γάρ που μάλ', ὀίομαι, εἶσιν ἐρύξων
Αἰήτης ὁμάδῳ πόντονδ' ἴμεν ἐκ ποταμοῖο.
ἀλλ' οἱ μὲν διὰ νηὸς ἀμοιβαδὶς ἀνέρος ἀνὴρ
200 ἑζόμενος πηδοῖσιν ἐρέσσετε, τοὶ δὲ βοείας
ἀσπίδας ἡμίσεες δήων θοὸν ἔχμα βολάων
προσχόμενοι νόστῳ ἐπαμύνετε. νῦν δ' ἐνὶ χερσὶν
παῖδας ἑοὺς πάτρην τε φίλην γεραρούς τε τοκῆας
ἴσχομεν, ἡμετέρῃ δ' ἐπερείδεται Ἑλλὰς ἐφορμῇ
205 ἠὲ κατηφείην ἢ καὶ μέγα κῦδος ἀρέσθαι."
    ὣς φάτο· δῦνε δὲ τεύχε' ἀρήια· τοὶ δ' ἰάχησαν
θεσπέσιον μεμαῶτες. ὁ δὲ ξίφος ἐκ κολεοῖο
σπασσάμενος πρυμναῖα νεὼς ἀπὸ πείσματ' ἔκοψεν·
ἄγχι δὲ παρθενικῆς κεκορυθμένος ἰθυντῆρι
210 Ἀγκαίῳ παρέβασκεν· ἐπείγετο δ' εἰρεσίῃ νηῦς
σπερχομένων ἄμοτον ποταμοῦ ἄφαρ ἐκτὸς ἐλάσσαι.
    ἤδη δ' Αἰήτῃ ὑπερήνορι πᾶσί τε Κόλχοις
Μηδείης περίπυστος ἔρως καὶ ἔργ' ἐτέτυκτο.
ἐς δ' ἀγορὴν ἀγέροντ' ἐνὶ τεύχεσιν, ὅσσα τε πόντου
215 κύματα χειμερίοιο κορύσσεται ἐξ ἀνέμοιο,
ἢ ὅσα φύλλα χαμᾶζε περικλαδέος πέσεν ὕλης
φυλλοχόῳ ἐνὶ μηνί—τίς ἂν τάδε τεκμήραιτο;—
ὣς οἱ ἀπειρέσιοι ποταμοῦ παρεμέτρεον ὄχθας,
κλαγγῇ μαιμώοντες. ὁ δ' εὐτύκτῳ ἐνὶ δίφρῳ
220 Αἰήτης ἵπποισι μετέπρεπεν, οὕς οἱ ὄπασσεν
Ἥλιος πνοιῇσιν ἐειδομένους ἀνέμοιο,
σκαιῇ μέν ῥ' ἐνὶ χειρὶ σάκος δινωτὸν ἀείρων,
τῇ δ' ἑτέρῃ πεύκην περιμήκεα, πὰρ δέ οἱ ἔγχος
ἀντικρὺ τετάνυστο πελώριον· ἡνία δ' ἵππων

344

her, for I reckon that Aeetes will doubtless come with his host to prevent us from going from the river into the sea. So let every second one of you throughout the ship sit and ply the oars, and let the other half secure our return by holding their oxhide shields in front of them as a ready defense against enemy missiles. And now in our hands we hold our children, our dear homeland, and our aged parents; and on our venture depends whether Hellas wins dejection or else great fame."

Thus he spoke and donned his battle armor, and they shouted with prodigious enthusiasm. He drew his sword from its sheath and chopped off the ship's stern cables. Close by the girl, he took his stand fully armed at the side of the helmsman, Ancaeus. The ship sped on with their rowing, as they strained unceasingly to propel it clear of the river as quickly as possible.

By this time Medea's love and deeds had become widely known to haughty Aeetes and all the Colchians. They thronged to the assembly in their armor, as numerous as waves of the sea that arise from a stormy wind,[21] or as the leaves that fall to the ground from a forest thick with branches in the month when leaves are shed—who could count them?—thus, beyond number they poured along the banks of the river, shouting eagerly. In his well-built chariot, Aeetes was conspicuous for his horses, swift as blasts of wind, which Helius had given him. In his left hand he held up his round shield, in the other an enormous pine torch,[22] while at his side his gigantic spear pointed for-

---

[21] Or *as waves of the stormy sea that arise from the wind.*
[22] He had intended to burn the Argo (3.581–582).

225 γέντο χεροῖν Ἄψυρτος. ὑπεκπρὸ δὲ πόντον ἔταμνεν
νηῦς ἤδη κρατεροῖσιν ἐπειγομένη ἐρέτῃσιν
καὶ μεγάλου ποταμοῖο καταβλώσκοντι ῥεέθρῳ.
αὐτὰρ ἄναξ ἄτῃ πολυπήμονι χεῖρας ἀείρας
Ἥλιον καὶ Ζῆνα κακῶν ἐπιμάρτυρας ἔργων
230 κέκλετο, δεινὰ δὲ παντὶ παρασχεδὸν ἤπυε λαῷ·
εἰ μή οἱ κούρην αὐτάγρετον ἢ ἀνὰ γαῖαν
ἢ πλωτῆς εὑρόντες ἔτ᾽ εἰν ἁλὸς οἴδματι νῆα
ἄξουσιν καὶ θυμὸν ἐνιπλήσει μενεαίνων
τίσασθαι τάδε πάντα, δαήσονται κεφαλῇσιν
235 πάντα χόλον καὶ πᾶσαν ἑὴν ὑποδέγμενοι ἄτην.
      ὣς ἔφατ᾽ Αἰήτης· αὐτῷ δ᾽ ἐνὶ ἤματι Κόλχοι
νῆάς τ᾽ εἰρύσσαντο καὶ ἄρμενα νηυσὶ βάλοντο,
αὐτῷ δ᾽ ἤματι πόντον ἀνήιον· οὐδέ κε φαίης
τόσσον νηίτην στόλον ἔμμεναι, ἀλλ᾽ οἰωνῶν
240 ἰλαδὸν ἄσπετον ἔθνος ἐπιβρομέειν πελάγεσσιν.
      οἱ δ᾽, ἀνέμου λαιψηρὰ θεῆς βουλῇσιν ἀέντος
Ἥρης, ὄφρ᾽ ὤκιστα κακὸν Πελίαο δόμοισιν
Αἰαίη Μήδεια Πελασγίδα γαῖαν ἵκηται,
ἠοῖ ἐνὶ τριτάτῃ πρυμνήσια νηὸς ἔδησαν
245 Παφλαγόνων ἀκτῇσι πάροιθ᾽ Ἅλυος ποταμοῖο·
ἡ γάρ σφ᾽ ἐξαποβάντας ἀρέσσασθαι θυέεσσιν
ἠνώγει Ἑκάτην. καὶ δὴ τὰ μέν, ὅσσα θυηλὴν
κούρη πορσανέουσα τιτύσκετο—μήτε τις ἴστωρ
εἴη μήτ᾽ ἐμὲ θυμὸς ἐποτρύνειεν ἀείδειν—
250 ἅζομαι αὐδῆσαι· τό γε μὴν ἔδος ἐξέτι κείνου,
ὅ ῥα θεᾷ ἥρωες ἐπὶ ῥηγμῖσιν ἔδειμαν,
ἀνδράσιν ὀψιγόνοισι μένει καὶ τῆμος ἰδέσθαι.

346

ward. Apsyrtus grasped the horses' reins in both hands. But by now the ship was on ahead cleaving the open sea, sped by the mighty oarsmen and the great river's downward flood. And the king in grievous distress raised his hands and invoked Helius and Zeus as witnesses of their wicked deeds, and straightway pronounced dire consequences for all his people: that if they did not bring him his daughter, seized by their own hands, either on land or finding the ship still on the swell of the open sea, so that he might satisfy his anger in his eagerness to punish all these deeds, that they would learn with their lives what it was to receive the full measure of his wrath and all the distress that he felt.

Thus spoke Aeetes. On that very day the Colchians hauled their ships to water and loaded the tackle on the ships, and that very day they put out to sea. You would not think so great a host was a fleet of ships, but that a countless multitude of birds in flocks was clamoring over the waves.

As for the heroes, with a wind blowing swiftly by the designs of the goddess Hera, so that Aeaean Medea might reach the Pelasgian land as quickly as possible to be a bane to the house of Pelias, on the third morning they secured their ship's cables to the shore of the Paphlagonians at the mouth of the Halys river, because Medea ordered them to disembark and propitiate Hecate with sacrifices. Now all the things that the girl prepared in order to carry out the sacrifice—may no man know them, nor may my heart urge me to sing of them—I dread to tell, and yet from that time the sanctuary which the heroes built on the shore for the goddess remains even to this day for later generations to

αὐτίκα δ᾽ Αἰσονίδης ἐμνήσατο, σὺν δὲ καὶ ὧλλοι
ἥρωες, Φινῆος, ὃ δὴ πλόον ἄλλον ἔειπεν
255 ἐξ Αἴης ἔσσεσθαι· ἀνώιστος δ᾽ ἐτέτυκτο
πᾶσιν ὁμῶς. Ἄργος δὲ λιλαιομένοις ἀγόρευσεν·
"νεύμεθ᾽ ἐς Ὀρχομενόν, τὴν ἔχραεν ὕμμι
περῆσαι
νημερτὴς ὅδε μάντις, ὅτῳ ξυνέβητε πάροιθεν.
ἔστιν γὰρ πλόος ἄλλος, ὃν ἀθανάτων ἱερῆες
260 πέφραδον, οἳ Θήβης Τριτωνίδος ἐκγεγάασιν.
οὔ πω τείρεα πάντα, τά τ᾽ οὐρανῷ εἰλίσσονται,
οὐδέ τί πω Δαναῶν ἱερὸν γένος ἦεν ἀκοῦσαι
πευθομένοις· οἷοι δ᾽ ἔσαν Ἀρκάδες Ἀπιδανῆες,
Ἀρκάδες, οἳ καὶ πρόσθε σεληναίης ὑδέονται
265 ζώειν φηγὸν ἔδοντες ἐν οὔρεσιν· οὐδὲ Πελασγὶς
χθὼν τότε κυδαλίμοισιν ἀνάσσετο Δευκαλίδῃσιν,
ἦμος ὅτ᾽ Ἠερίη πολυλήιος ἐκλήιστο
μήτηρ Αἴγυπτος προτερηγενέων αἰζηῶν,
καὶ ποταμὸς Τρίτων εὐρύρροος, ᾧ ὕπο πᾶσα
270 ἄρδεται Ἠερίη, Διόθεν δέ μιν οὔ ποτε δεύει
ὄμβρος· ἅλις προχοῇσι δ᾽ ἀνασταχύουσιν ἄρουραι.
ἔνθεν δή τινά φασι πέριξ διὰ πᾶσαν ὁδεῦσαι

257 νεύμεθ᾽ ἐς PE: ν(ε)ισόμεθ᾽ SG: νεισόμεθ᾽ ἐς LA
269 εὐρύρροος Meineke: εὔρροος Ω

23 Cf. 2.421–422.
24 Vian convincingly argues that νεύμεθ᾽ is an imperfect and
refers to the voyage of Argus and his brothers to Orchomenus be-
fore they were shipwrecked and met Jason.

see. Immediately thereafter, Jason, along with the rest of the heroes, recalled that Phineus had said that the route from Aea would be different,[23] but it remained a mystery to all alike. They eagerly listened when Argus spoke to them:

"We were traveling[24] to Orchomenus by the course which that unerring seer directed you to travel, the seer you encountered before meeting us. For there exists another sea route, which the priests of the immortals who were offspring of Triton's daughter Thebe[25] revealed. Not yet did all the stars that revolve in the sky exist, nor yet was there a sacred race of the Danaans for explorers to hear of. Only Apidanian[26] Arcadians existed, Arcadians who are said to have lived in the mountains eating acorns even before the moon existed;[27] nor at that time was the Pelasgian land ruled by the glorious sons of Deucalion,[28] in the days when Egypt, the mother of men of long ago, was called grain-rich Eërie[29] and the wide-flowing river was called Triton, by which all of Eërie is watered, for Zeus' rain never wets it, but thanks to its streams the fields bear bountiful crops.[30] From here, they say, a man traveled all

[25] The eponymous nymph of Egyptian Thebes; Triton here designates the Nile (cf. 269).   [26] I.e. Peloponnesian.

[27] The Arcadians were widely believed to have been the oldest Hellenes and to have lived on acorns (cf. Herodotus 1.66).

[28] He and Pyrrha produced the race of Greeks after a great flood (cf. Pindar, *Olympian* 9.43–53).

[29] As a description of Egypt, the word probably means hazy (cf. Aeschylus, *Suppliants* 75).

[30] Or, taking ἅλις with the first clause (Vian), *never wets it in abundance, but thanks to its streams the fields bear crops.*

Εὐρώπην Ἀσίην τε βίῃ καὶ κάρτεϊ λαῶν
σφωιτέρων θάρσει τε πεποιθότα· μυρία δ' ἄστη
275 νάσσατ' ἐποιχόμενος, τὰ μὲν ἦ ποθι ναιετάουσιν
ἠὲ καὶ οὔ· πουλὺς γὰρ ἄδην ἐπενήνοθεν αἰών.
Αἶά γε μὴν ἔτι νῦν μένει ἔμπεδον υἱωνοί τε
τῶνδ' ἀνδρῶν, οὓς ὅς γε καθίσσατο ναιέμεν Αἶαν·
οἳ δή τοι γραπτῦς πατέρων ἔθεν εἰρύονται,
280 κύρβιας, οἷς ἔνι πᾶσαι ὁδοὶ καὶ πείρατ' ἔασιν
ὑγρῆς τε τραφερῆς τε πέριξ ἐπινισσομένοισιν.
ἔστι δέ τις ποταμός, ὕπατον κέρας Ὠκεανοῖο,
εὐρύς τε προβαθής τε καὶ ὁλκάδι νηὶ περῆσαι·
Ἴστρον μιν καλέοντες ἑκὰς διετεκμήραντο·
285 ὃς δ' ἤτοι τείως μὲν ἀπείρονα τέμνετ' ἄρουραν
εἷς οἷος, πηγαὶ γὰρ ὑπὲρ πνοιῆς βορέαο
Ῥιπαίοις ἐν ὄρεσσιν ἀπόπροθι μορμύρουσιν·
ἀλλ' ὁπόταν Θρηκῶν Σκυθέων τ' ἐπιβήσεται οὔρους,
ἔνθα διχῇ, τὸ μὲν ἔνθα μετ' ἠοίην ἅλα βάλλει
290 τῇδ' ὕδωρ, τὸ δ' ὄπισθε βαθὺν διὰ κόλπον ἵησιν
σχιζόμενος πόντου Τρινακρίου εἰσανέχοντα,
γαίῃ ὃς ὑμετέρῃ παρακέκλιται, εἰ ἐτεὸν δὴ
ὑμετέρης γαίης Ἀχελώιος ἐξανίησιν."
ὣς ἄρ' ἔφη· τοῖσιν δὲ θεὰ τέρας ἐγγυάλιξεν
295 αἴσιον, ᾧ καὶ πάντες ἐπευφήμησαν ἰδόντες
στέλλεσθαι τήνδ' οἶμον· ἐπιπρὸ γὰρ ὁλκὸς ἐτύχθη
οὐρανίης ἀκτῖνος, ὅπῃ καὶ ἀμεύσιμον ἦεν.

285 δ' ἤτοι Hermann: δή τοι Ω   288 ἐπιβήσεται E: ἐν-
ιβήσεται Ω   289 ἠοίην Guyet, Vian: ἰονίην Ω

350

around Europe and Asia,[31] relying on the strength, might, and courage of his soldiers. He founded countless cities on his way, some of which are perhaps still inhabited, others not, for a great stretch of time has since passed. Aea, at least, has continued to exist to this day, along with the descendants of those men whom that king settled to dwell in Aea. They, in fact, preserve their forefathers' writings, pillars on which are found all the routes and boundaries of the sea and land for those who travel around them. There is a river, the northernmost branch of Ocean, wide and quite deep enough even for a barge to navigate; they call it the Ister and have traced its far reaches. For some time it cuts through endless fields in a single stream, for its sources seethe and roar beyond the blast of the north wind far away in the Rhipaean mountains. But once it enters the borders of the Thracians and Scythians, it divides in two and pours part of its water here into the eastern sea,[32] but sends the opposite part through the deep gulf jutting out from the Trinacrian sea,[33] which borders on your land, if in fact the Achelous river flows forth from your land."

Thus he spoke, and to them the goddess[34] gave a favorable omen, at the sight of which they all shouted their approval of traveling by this route. For in front of them appeared the trail of a heavenly ray,[35] showing where they

[31] Sesostris, a legendary king of Egypt. See Herodotus 2.102–106, who claims the Colchians were descended from the Egyptians settled there by Sesostris.   [32] I.e. the Black Sea.

[33] The Trinacrian (Sicilian) sea is at the south end of the Adriatic. The Achelous flows into it from the Pindus mountains.

[34] Hera.

[35] Presumably a shooting star or meteor.

γηθόσυνοι δὲ Λύκοιο καταυτόθι παῖδα λιπόντες
λαίφεσι πεπταμένοισιν ὑπεὶρ ἄλα ναυτίλλοντο
300 οὔρεα Παφλαγόνων θηεύμενοι· οὐδὲ Κάραμβιν
γνάμψαν, ἐπεὶ πνοιαί τε καὶ οὐρανίου πυρὸς αἴγλη
μίμνεν, ἕως Ἴστροιο μέγαν ῥόον εἰσαφίκοντο.

Κόλχοι δ' αὖτ', ἄλλοι μὲν ἐτώσια μαστεύοντες
Κυανέας Πόντοιο διὲκ πέτρας ἐπέρησαν,
305 ἄλλοι δ' αὖ ποταμὸν μετεκίαθον, οἷσιν ἄνασσεν
Ἄψυρτος, Καλὸν δὲ διὰ στόμα πεῖρε λιασθείς·
τῷ καὶ ὑπέφθη τούς γε βαλὼν ὕπερ αὐχένα γαίης
κόλπον ἔσω πόντοιο πανέσχατον Ἰονίοιο.
Ἴστρῳ γάρ τις νῆσος ἐέργεται οὔνομα Πεύκη
310 τριγλώχιν, εὖρος μὲν ἐς αἰγιαλοὺς ἀνέχουσα,
στεινὸν δ' αὖτ' ἀγκῶνα ποτὶ ῥόον, ἀμφὶ δὲ δοιαὶ
σχίζονται προχοαί· τὴν μὲν καλέουσι Νάρηκος,
τὴν δ' ὑπὸ τῇ νεάτῃ Καλὸν στόμα· τῇδε διαπρὸ
Ἄψυρτος Κόλχοι τε θοώτερον ὡρμήθησαν,
315 οἱ δ' ὑψοῦ νήσοιο κατ' ἀκροτάτης ἐνέοντο
τηλόθεν. εἰαμενῇσι δ' ἐν ἄσπετα πώεα λεῖπον
ποιμένες ἄγραυλοι νηῶν φόβῳ, οἷά τε θῆρας
ὀσσόμενοι πόντου μεγακήτεος ἐξανιόντας.
οὐ γάρ πω ἁλίας γε πάρος ποθὶ νῆας ἴδοντο,
320 οὔτ' οὖν Θρήιξιν μιγάδες Σκύθαι οὐδὲ Σίγυννοι,

313 τῇδε SᵖᶜWIF: τῇ δὲ Ω

could find passage. Full of joy, they left Lycus' son[36] there and set out on the sea with sails spread wide, keeping in view the mountains of the Paphlagonians. But they did not round Carambis[37] because the winds and gleam of heavenly fire stayed with them until they reached the Ister's mighty stream.

But as for the Colchians, one contingent sailed out of the Black Sea through the Cyanean rocks in a vain search,[38] whereas the rest made for the river under the command of Apsyrtus, who took a separate course and entered the river by Fair mouth, thereby crossing the neck of land ahead of the heroes to enter the furthest gulf of the Ionian sea.[39] For a certain three-cornered island named Peuce is enclosed by the Ister, with its wide side projecting out to the coast and its narrow end toward the river, around which the outflow splits in two. They call the one entrance Narex, the other, on the southern end, Fair mouth. It was through the latter that Apsyrtus and the Colchians sped more quickly, whereas the heroes sailed far north to the top of the island. In the marshlands, rural shepherds abandoned their vast flocks in fear of the ships, believing them to be creatures emerging from the monster-harboring sea. For they had never before seen any sea-going ships—neither the Scythians who mingle with the Thracians, nor

---

[36] Dascylus had joined them at 2.814.   [37] Instead of following the southern coast, they headed north across the Black Sea.   [38] This fleet will later appear at Phaeacia.

[39] I.e. the northern end of the Adriatic. The "neck of land" designates the long stretch of territory (the present-day Balkans) between the Black Sea and the Adriatic. After projecting their arrival in the Adriatic, the narrator backtracks to fill in the details.

οὔτ᾽ οὖν Γραυκένιοι, οὔθ᾽ οἱ περὶ Λαύριον ἤδη
Σίνδοι ἐρημαῖον πεδίον μέγα ναιετάοντες.
　　αὐτὰρ ἐπεί τ᾽ Ἄγγουρον ὄρος καὶ ἄπωθεν ἐόντα
Ἀγγούρου ὄρεος σκόπελον παρὰ Καυλιακοῖο,
325　ᾧ πέρι δὴ σχίζων Ἴστρος ῥόον ἔνθα καὶ ἔνθα
βάλλει ἁλός, πεδίον τε τὸ Λαύριον ἠμείψαντο,
δή ῥα τότε Κρονίην Κόλχοι ἅλαδ᾽ ἐκπρομολόντες,
πάντη, μή σφε λάθοιεν, ὑπετμήξαντο κελεύθους.
οἱ δ᾽ ὄπιθεν ποταμοῖο κατήλυθον, ἐκ δ᾽ ἐπέρησαν
330　δοιὰς Ἀρτέμιδος Βρυγηίδας ἀγχόθι νήσους.
τῶν δ᾽ ἤτοι ἑτέρῃ μὲν ἐν ἱερὸν ἔσκεν ἔδεθλον·
ἐν δ᾽ ἑτέρῃ, πληθὺν πεφυλαγμένοι Ἀψύρτοιο,
βαῖνον· ἐπεὶ κείνας πολέων λίπον ἔνδοθι νήσους
αὔτως ἁζόμενοι κούρην Διός, αἱ δὲ δὴ ἄλλαι
335　στεινόμεναι Κόλχοισι πόρους εἴρυντο θαλάσσης.
ὣς δὲ καὶ εἰς ἀκτὰς πληθὺν λίπεν ἀγχόθι νήσων
μέσφα Σαλαγγῶνος ποταμοῦ καὶ Νέστιδος αἴης.
　　ἔνθα κε λευγαλέῃ Μινύαι τότε δηιοτῆτι
παυρότεροι πλεόνεσσιν ὑπείκαθον, ἀλλὰ πάροιθεν
340　συνθεσίην, μέγα νεῖκος ἀλευάμενοι, ἐτάμοντο·
κῶας μὲν χρύσειον, ἐπεί σφισιν αὐτὸς ὑπέστη
Αἰήτης, εἰ κεῖνοι ἀναπλήσειαν ἀέθλους,
ἔμπεδον εὐδικίῃ σφέας ἐξέμεν, εἴτε δόλοισιν
εἴτε καὶ ἀμφαδίην αὔτως ἀέκοντος ἀπηύρων·
345　αὐτὰρ Μήδειάν γε—τὸ γὰρ πέλεν ἀμφήριστον—

321 Γραυκένιοι Π¹⁶Ω: Τραυκένιοι Kassel
336 ἀκτὰς Lᵖᶜ: ἄλλας Ω | νήσων WᵐᵍV²ˢˡ: νήσους Ω

the Sigynni, nor yet the Graucenii, nor the Sindi, who by then inhabited the great desert plain of Laurium.

But when they had passed mount Angurum and, far from mount Angurum, passed the cliff of Cauliacus, around which the Ister divides and pours its water into the seas on either side,[40] and passed the plain of Laurium, the Colchians then sailed forth into the sea of Cronus[41] and cut off the passages in all directions, so that their foes could not elude them. And the heroes came down the river behind them and arrived at the two nearby Brygean islands belonging to Artemis. On one of them was her sacred shrine, but they landed on the other, thereby avoiding Apsyrtus' forces. For they had left those islands, amongst so many others, just as they were, out of reverence for Zeus' daughter,[42] whereas the others teemed with Colchians and blocked access to the sea. Similarly, Apsyrtus had left numerous troops on the shores near the islands as far as the Salangon river and the Nestian land.

Then and there the outnumbered Minyans would have succumbed in a dreadful battle, but before that they made an agreement and avoided a great quarrel. It stipulated that they would rightfully retain the golden fleece for good, since Aeetes himself had promised it to them if they completed the contests—whether they acquired it by deception or just took it openly without permission—but that they would entrust Medea, since her case was in dispute,

[40] Into the Black Sea in the east and the Adriatic in the west.
[41] The Adriatic, also called the gulf of Rhea (Cronus' wife).
[42] Artemis.

---

340 συνθεσίην Schneider: συνθεσίη Ω: συνθεσίας E

παρθέσθαι κούρῃ Λητωίδι νόσφιν ὁμίλου,
εἰσόκε τις δικάσῃσι θεμιστούχων βασιλήων
εἴτε μιν εἰς πατρὸς χρειὼ δόμον αὖτις ἱκάνειν
εἴτε μεθ᾽ Ἑλλάδα γαῖαν ἀριστήεσσιν ἔπεσθαι.

350   ἔνθα δ᾽ ἐπεὶ τὰ ἕκαστα νόῳ πεμπάσσατο κούρη,
δή ῥά μιν ὀξεῖαι κραδίην ἐλέλιξαν ἀνῖαι
νωλεμές. αἶψα δὲ νόσφιν Ἰήσονα μοῦνον ἑταίρων
ἐκπροκαλεσσαμένη ἄγεν ἄλλυδις, ὄφρ᾽ ἐλίασθεν
πολλὸν ἑκάς, στονόεντα δ᾽ ἐνωπαδὶς ἔκφατο μῦθον·

355   "Αἰσονίδη, τίνα τήνδε συναρτύνασθε μενοινὴν
ἀμφ᾽ ἐμοί; ἦέ σε πάγχυ λαθιφροσύναις ἐνέηκαν
ἀγλαΐαι, τῶν δ᾽ οὔ τι μετατρέπῃ, ὅσσ᾽ ἀγόρευες
χρειοῖ ἐνισχόμενος; ποῦ τοι Διὸς Ἱκεσίοιο
ὅρκια, ποῦ δὲ μελιχραὶ ὑποσχεσίαι βεβάασιν;

360 ἧς ἐγὼ οὐ κατὰ κόσμον ἀναιδήτῳ ἰότητι
πάτρην τε κλέα τε μεγάρων αὐτούς τε τοκῆας
νοσφισάμην, τά μοι ἦεν ὑπέρτατα, τηλόθι δ᾽ οἴη
λυγρῇσιν κατὰ πόντον ἅμ᾽ ἀλκυόνεσσι φορεῦμαι,
σῶν ἕνεκεν καμάτων, ἵνα μοι σόος ἀμφί τε βουσὶν

365 ἀμφί τε γηγενέεσσιν ἀναπλήσειας ἀέθλους·
ὕστατον αὖ καὶ κῶας, ἐπεί τ᾽ ἐπάιστον ἐτύχθη,
εἷλες ἐμῇ ματίῃ, κατὰ δ᾽ οὐλοὸν αἶσχος ἔχευα
θηλυτέραις· τῷ φημι τεὴ κούρη τε δάμαρ τε

    348 post 348 legitur in codd. hic versus (= 2.1186) εἴτε μετ᾽
ἀφνειὴν θείου πόλιν Ὀρχομενοῖο: del. Ruhnken
    366 ἐπεί τ᾽ ἐπάιστον ἐτύχθη Mooney: ἐπεί τε παιστὸν
ἐτύχθη LA: ἐπεί τ᾽ ἐπάιστος ἐτύχθην w: ἐφ᾽ ᾧ πλόος ὕμμιν
ἐτύχθη E

to Leto's daughter,[43] away from the crew, until some one of the kings with legal authority could judge whether she had to return to her father's home or accompany the heroes to the land of Hellas.[44]

Now when the girl took stock of all this in her mind, intense pains shook her heart without cease.[45] She immediately summoned Jason alone, apart from his comrades, and led him elsewhere until they were far away, and spoke sorrowful words to his face:

"Jason, what is this pact that you all have devised concerning me? Have your successes driven you to complete forgetfulness? Do you care nothing about all you said when you were constrained by need? Where have your oaths to Zeus, Protector of Suppliants, gone? Where your honey-sweet promises? It was because of these that, contrary to decency and with shameless resolve, I abandoned my country, the glory of my home, and my very parents, the things which were dearest to me, and am borne far away, all alone on the sea with the mournful kingfishers, all because of your troubles, so that through me you could safely complete the contests with the oxen and earthborn men. And then finally, once that became known, it was by my folly that you also got the fleece, while I brought terrible disgrace upon womankind. Therefore, I declare that it is as your daughter, wife, and sister that I am following you

---

[43] Artemis.   [44] After 348 all MSS include the verse εἴτε μετ' ἀφνειὴν θείου πόλιν Ὀρχομενοῖο (= 2.1186): "or to the wealthy city of divine Orchomenus," which would allow Medea to follow her brothers. The scholia do not mention it, it is not referred to again in the text, and Ruhnken deleted it. Vian, however, defends it.   [45] Or *violently*.

APOLLONIUS RHODIUS

αὐτοκασιγνήτη τε μεθ᾽ Ἑλλάδα γαῖαν ἕπεσθαι.
370 πάντῃ νῦν πρόφρων ὑπερίστασο, μηδέ με μούνην
σεῖο λίπῃς ἀπάνευθεν, ἐποιχόμενος βασιλῆας,
ἀλλ᾽ αὔτως εἴρυσο· δίκη δέ τοι ἔμπεδος ἔστω
καὶ θέμις, ἣν ἄμφω συναρέσσαμεν· ἢ σύ γ᾽ ἔπειτα
φασγάνῳ αὐτίκα τόνδε μέσον διὰ λαιμὸν ἀμῆσαι,
375 ὄφρ᾽ ἐπίηρα φέρωμαι ἐοικότα μαργοσύνῃσιν.
σχέτλιε, εἰ ⟨γάρ⟩ κέν με κασιγνήτοιο δικάσσῃ
ἔμμεναι οὗτος ἄναξ, τῷ ἐπίσχετε τάσδ᾽ ἀλεγεινὰς
ἄμφω συνθεσίας, πῶς ἵξομαι ὄμματα πατρός;
ἦ μάλ᾽ ἐυκλειής. τίνα δ᾽ οὐ τίσιν ἠὲ βαρεῖαν
380 ἄτην οὐ σμυγερῶς δεινῶν ὕπερ, οἷα ἔοργα,
ὀτλήσω, σὺ δέ κεν θυμηδέα νόστον ἕλοιο;
μὴ τό γε παμβασίλεια Διὸς τελέσειεν ἄκοιτις,
ᾗ ἔπι κυδιάεις. μνήσαιο δὲ καί ποτ᾽ ἐμεῖο
στρευγόμενος καμάτοισι, δέρος δέ τοι ἶσον ὀνείρῳ
385 οἴχοιτ᾽ εἰς ἔρεβος μεταμώνιον· ἐκ δέ σε πάτρης
αὐτίκ᾽ ἐμαί σ᾽ ἐλάσειαν Ἐρινύες, οἷα καὶ αὐτὴ
σῇ πάθον ἀτροπίῃ. τὰ μὲν οὐ θέμις ἀκράαντα
ἐν γαίῃ πεσέειν, μάλα γὰρ μέγαν ἤλιτες ὅρκον,
νηλεές· ἀλλ᾽ οὔ θήν μοι ἐπιλλίζοντες ὀπίσσω
390 δὴν ἔσσεσθ᾽ εὔκηλοι ἕκητί γε συνθεσιάων."
    ὣς φάτ᾽ ἀναζείουσα βαρὺν χόλον· ἵετο δ᾽ ἥ γε
νῆα καταφλέξαι διά τ᾽ ἔμπεδα πάντα κεάσσαι,

376 ⟨γάρ⟩ κέν με Wilamowitz: κέν με LA: κεν δή με E
384 ὀνείρῳ Miller: ὀνείροις Ω
390 ἔσσεσθ᾽ Wifstrand: ἔσ(σ)εσθε vel ἔσ(σ)εσθαι Ω

358

to the land of Hellas. Be willing, then, to protect me in every way. Do not leave me all alone and far from you when you go off to the kings, but defend me no matter what. Hold fast to justice and that moral right to which we both consented. Otherwise, go on and at once run your sword straight through my throat, so that I may receive a fitting reward for my acts of lust. You heartless thing! For if that king to whom the two of you entrust this cruel agreement judges that I belong to my brother, how can I go face my father? A very fine reputation I shall have! What punishment or grievous torment shall I not endure in agony for the terrible things I have done, while you would win your longed-for homecoming? May Zeus' wife, the all-ruling queen in whom you glory, never accomplish that! May you remember me some day when you are wracked by troubles, and may the fleece vanish like a dream into the lower darkness all for naught, and may my Furies immediately drive you from your homeland, given how I myself have suffered by your heartlessness. Moral right will not permit these curses to fall to the ground unfulfilled, for you have forsworn a great oath, pitiless one. But I can assure you that not for long hereafter will you all sit at ease and mock me— for all your agreements."

Thus she spoke, seething with bitter rage. She longed to burn up the ship, to destroy everything completely,[46]

---

[46] Or, reading ἀμφαδὰ, *to destroy everything before their eyes.*

---

391 ἀναζείουσα Ruhnken: ἀνιάζουσα Ω
392 ἔμπεδα Ω: ἀμφαδὰ Campbell

ἐν δὲ πεσεῖν αὐτῇ μαλερῷ πυρί. τοῖα δ᾽ Ἰήσων
μειλιχίοις ἐπέεσσιν ὑποδδείσας προσέειπεν·

395   "ἴσχεο, δαιμονίη· τὰ μὲν ἀνδάνει οὐδ᾽ ἐμοὶ αὐτῷ,
ἀλλά τιν᾽ ἀμβολίην διζήμεθα δηιοτῆτος,
ὅσσον δυσμενέων ἀνδρῶν νέφος ἀμφιδέδηεν
εἵνεκα σεῦ. πάντες γάρ, ὅσοι χθόνα τήνδε νέμονται,
Ἀψύρτῳ μεμάασιν ἀμυνέμεν, ὄφρα σε πατρί,

400   οἷά τε ληισθεῖσαν, ὑπότροπον οἴκαδ᾽ ἄγοιντο·
αὐτοὶ δὲ στυγερῷ κεν ὀλοίμεθα πάντες ὀλέθρῳ,
μείξαντες δαῒ χεῖρας· ὅ τοι καὶ ῥίγιον ἄλγος
ἔσσεται, εἴ σε θανόντες ἕλωρ κείνοισι λίποιμεν.
ἥδε δὲ συνθεσίη κρανέει δόλον, ᾧ μιν ἐς ἄτην

405   βήσομεν· οὐδ᾽ ἂν ὁμῶς περιναιέται ἀντιόωσιν
Κόλχοις ἦρα φέροντες ὑπὲρ σέο, νόσφιν ἄνακτος,
ὅς τοι ἀοσσητήρ τε κασίγνητός τε τέτυκται·
οὐδ᾽ ἂν ἐγὼ Κόλχοισιν ὑπείξω μὴ πτολεμίζειν
ἀντιβίην, ὅτε μή με διὲξ εἴωσι νέεσθαι."

410   ἴσκεν ὑποσσαίνων· ἡ δ᾽ οὐλοὸν ἔκφατο μῦθον·
"φράζεο νῦν· χρειὼ γὰρ ἀεικελίοισιν ἐπ᾽ ἔργοις
καὶ τόδε μητίσασθαι, ἐπεὶ τὸ πρῶτον ἀάσθην
ἀμπλακίῃ, θεόθεν δὲ κακὰς ἤνυσσα μενοινάς.
τύνη μὲν κατὰ μῶλον ἀλέξεο δούρατα Κόλχων·

415   αὐτὰρ ἐγὼ κεῖνόν γε τεὰς ἐς χεῖρας ἱκέσθαι
μειλίξω· σὺ δέ μιν φαιδροῖς ἀγαπάζεο δώροις,
εἴ κέν πως κήρυκας ἀπερχομένους πεπίθοιμι
οἰόθεν οἶον ἐμοῖσι συναρθμῆσαι ἐπέεσσιν.
ἔνθ᾽ εἴ τοι τόδε ἔργον ἐφανδάνει, οὔ τι μεγαίρω,

420   κτεῖνέ τε καὶ Κόλχοισιν ἀείρεο δηιοτῆτα."

and to throw herself into the raging fire. Jason became alarmed and said to her with gentle words:

"Calm yourself, poor girl! These terms do not please me either, but we are seeking some way to postpone a battle, when so great a cloud of enemy men blazes around us because of you. For all the inhabitants of this land are eager to help Apsyrtus and his men take you back home to your father, in the belief that you were kidnapped. And we ourselves would all die a terrible death if we fought them hand-to-hand—which will be an even bitterer pain for you, should we be killed and leave you as their prey. This agreement, however, will set a trap whereby we can lure him to his demise. For the indigenous people will not be so disposed to side with the Colchians in opposing us for your sake in the absence of the commander who is your guardian and brother. Nor will I hesitate to fight man-to-man with the Colchians, if they do not allow me to sail past them."

Thus he spoke to reassure her, and she responded with deadly words:

"Listen to me now, for I am compelled, given my shameful deeds, to contrive this one as well, since first I went astray by mistake and under divine influence carried out wicked designs. For your part, fend off the spears of the Colchians in battle; and I will induce him to come into your hands. But you must entice him with splendid gifts, in hopes that I may persuade the heralds going to him to make him come all alone to listen to my words. Then, if this deed has your approval—and I will not oppose it—kill him and do battle with the Colchians."

APOLLONIUS RHODIUS

ὣς τώ γε ξυμβάντε μέγαν δόλον ἠρτύναντο
Ἀψύρτῳ, καὶ πολλὰ πόρον ξεινήια δῶρα,
οἷς μέτα καὶ πέπλον δόσαν ἱερὸν Ὑψιπυλείης
πορφύρεον. τὸν μέν ῥα Διωνύσῳ κάμον αὐταὶ
425 Δίῃ ἐν ἀμφιάλῳ Χάριτες θεαί, αὐτὰρ ὁ παιδὶ
δῶκε Θόαντι μεταῦτις, ὁ δ᾽ αὖ λίπεν Ὑψιπυλείῃ,
ἡ δ᾽ ἔπορ᾽ Αἰσονίδῃ πολέσιν μετὰ καὶ τὸ φέρεσθαι
γλήνεσιν εὐεργὲς ξεινήιον. οὔ μιν ἀφάσσων
οὔτε κεν εἰσορόων γλυκὺν ἵμερον ἐμπλήσειας·
430 τοῦ δὲ καὶ ἀμβροσίη ὀδμὴ πέλεν ἐξέτι κείνου,
ἐξ οὗ ἄναξ αὐτὸς Νυσήιος ἐγκατέλεκτο
ἀκροχάλιξ οἴνῳ καὶ νέκταρι, καλὰ μεμαρπὼς
στήθεα παρθενικῆς Μινωίδος, ἥν ποτε Θησεὺς
Κνωσσόθεν ἑσπομένην Δίῃ ἔνι κάλλιπε νήσῳ.
435 ἡ δ᾽ ὅτε κηρύκεσσιν ἐπεξυνώσατο μύθους,
θελγέμεν, εὖτ᾽ ἂν πρῶτα θεᾶς μετὰ νηὸν ἵκηται
συνθεσίῃ νυκτός τε μέλαν κνέφας ἀμφιβάλῃσιν,
ἐλθέμεν, ὄφρα δόλον συμφράσσεται, ᾧ κεν ἑλοῦσα
χρύσειον μέγα κῶας ὑπότροπος αὖτις ὀπίσσω
440 βαίη ἐς Αἰήταο δόμους· πέρι γάρ μιν ἀνάγκη
υἱῆες Φρίξοιο δόσαν ξείνοισιν ἄγεσθαι·
τοῖα παραιφαμένη θελκτήρια φάρμακ᾽ ἔπασσεν
αἰθέρι καὶ πνοιῇσι, τά κεν καὶ ἄπωθεν ἐόντα
ἄγριον ἠλιβάτοιο κατ᾽ οὔρεος ἤγαγε θῆρα.

430 πέλεν Ω: μένεν Π16 Vian
436 μετ]ὰ Π16 Brunck praeeunte: περὶ Ω: παρὰ NC
438 ὦ]ι Π16 Brunck praeeunte: ὥς Ω

362

Thus the two agreed and prepared great treachery against Apsyrtus, and they sent him many gifts of hospitality, among which they provided a sacred robe of Hypsipyle, a purple one, which the divine Graces themselves had made for Dionysus on sea-girt Dia. He gave it to his son Thoas thereafter, who in turn left it to Hypsipyle, who gave it among many other treasures to Jason to take away as a well-wrought gift of hospitality. Neither by stroking it or gazing upon it could you satisfy your sweet longing, and it had an ambrosial fragrance, lasting from the time when the Nysean king[47] himself lay down in it, tipsy with wine and nectar, as he clasped the beautiful breasts of Minos' maiden daughter,[48] whom Theseus had previously abandoned on the island of Dia, after she had followed him from Cnossus. For her part, after she conveyed her message to the heralds—they were to persuade him[49] to come as soon as she had reached the goddess' temple according to the agreement, when the deep darkness of night would envelop them, so that she could devise a plot with him, whereby she would take the great golden fleece and go back again to the home of Aeetes, because, she said, the sons of Phrixus had forcibly handed her over to the strangers to take away—saying such deceitful things, she released into the air and the breezes enchanting drugs, which could have lured a wild beast, even one far away, down from a steep mountain.

[47] Dionysus; cf. 2.905.
[48] Ariadne.
[49] Apsyrtus.

445   σχέτλι᾽ Ἔρως, μέγα πῆμα, μέγα στύγος
      ἀνθρώποισιν,
ἐκ σέθεν οὐλόμεναί τ᾽ ἔριδες στοναχαί τε γόοι τε,
ἄλγεά τ᾽ ἄλλ᾽ ἐπὶ τοῖσιν ἀπείρονα τετρήχασιν.
δυσμενέων ἐπὶ παισὶ κορύσσεο, δαῖμον, ἀερθείς,
οἷος Μηδείῃ στυγερὴν φρεσὶν ἔμβαλες ἄτην.
450   πῶς γὰρ δὴ μετιόντα κακῷ ἐδάμασσεν ὀλέθρῳ
      Ἄψυρτον; τὸ γὰρ ἧμιν ἐπισχερὼ ἦεν ἀοιδῆς.

      ἧμος ὅτ᾽ Ἀρτέμιδος νήσῳ ἔνι τήν γ᾽ ἐλίποντο
συνθεσίῃ, τοὶ μέν ῥα διάνδιχα νηυσὶν ἔκελσαν
σφωιτέραις κρινθέντες· ὁ δ᾽ ἐς λόχον ἦεν Ἰήσων
455   δέγμενος Ἄψυρτόν τε καὶ οὓς ἐξαῦτις ἑταίρους.
αὐτὰρ ὅ γ᾽ αἰνοτάτῃσιν ὑποσχεσίῃσι δολωθεὶς
καρπαλίμως ᾗ νηὶ διὲξ ἁλὸς οἶδμα περήσας,
νύχθ᾽ ὕπο λυγαίην ἱερῆς ἐπεβήσετο νήσου·
οἰόθι δ᾽ ἀντικρὺ μετιὼν πειρήσατο μύθοις
460   εἷο κασιγνήτης, ἀταλὸς πάις οἷα χαράδρης
χειμερίης, ἣν οὐδὲ δι᾽ αἰζηοὶ περόωσιν,
εἴ κε δόλον ξείνοισιν ἐπ᾽ ἀνδράσι τεχνήσαιτο.
καὶ τὼ μὲν τὰ ἕκαστα συνῄνεον ἀλλήλοισιν·
αὐτίκα δ᾽ Αἰσονίδης πυκινοῦ ἔκπαλτο λόχοιο
465   γυμνὸν ἀνασχόμενος παλάμῃ ξίφος. αἶψα δὲ κούρη
ἔμπαλιν ὄμματ᾽ ἔνεικε, καλυψαμένη ὀθόνῃσιν,
μὴ φόνον ἀθρήσειε κασιγνήτοιο τυπέντος.
τὸν δ᾽ ὅ γε, βουτύπος ὥς τε μέγαν κερεαλκέα
      ταῦρον,
πλῆξεν ὀπιπεύσας νηοῦ σχεδόν, ὅν ποτ᾽ ἔδειμαν
470   Ἀρτέμιδι Βρυγοὶ περιναιέται ἀντιπέρηθεν.

Cruel Love, great affliction, great abomination for humans; from you come deadly quarrels and groans and laments,[50] and countless other pains besides these are stirred up. May it be against my enemies' children, O god, that you rise up and arm yourself, being such as when you cast abominable madness[51] into the mind of Medea. How, then, did she slay Apsyrtus by wicked murder when he came to meet her? For that must come next in our song.

After the heroes had left her on the island of Artemis according to the agreement, the two parties separated and landed their ships on their respective sides, whereas Jason went into ambush to wait for Apsyrtus and thereafter for his own comrades. But Apsyrtus, fooled by her horrendous promises, quickly crossed the swell of the sea in his ship and in the dark of night set foot on the holy island. He went all alone directly to meet her and tested his own sister with words—as a little boy tests a winter torrent that not even grown men can cross—to see if she would contrive a plot against the foreigners. The two were agreeing with each other on every detail, when suddenly Jason leapt from his dense[52] ambush, holding high his naked sword in his hand. The girl immediately averted her eyes and covered them with her veil, so as not to see the blood of her brother when he was hit. And Jason struck him, as a butcher strikes a great strong-horned bull, having kept watch near the temple which the Brygians, who lived on the mainland oppo-

---

[50] Or, reading πόνοι, *toils*.   [51] *Atê*, which in A. has a wide range of meanings: "madness, obsession, error, distress, disaster, demise."   [52] Or *cunning*.

---

446 γόοι Ω: πόνοι Π[16]

τοῦ ὅ γ᾽ ἐνὶ προδόμῳ γνὺξ ἤριπε· λοίσθια δ᾽ ἥρως
θυμὸν ἀναπνείων χερσὶν μέλαν ἀμφοτέρῃσιν
αἷμα κατ᾽ ὠτειλὴν ὑποΐσχετο· τῆς δὲ καλύπτρην
ἀργυφέην καὶ πέπλον ἀλευομένης ἐρύθηνεν.

475   ὀξὺ δὲ πανδαμάτωρ λοξῷ ἴδεν οἷον ἔρεξαν
ὄμματι νηλειὴς ὀλοφώιον ἔργον Ἐρινύς.
ἥρως δ᾽ Αἰσονίδης ἐξάργματα τάμνε θανόντος,
τρὶς δ᾽ ἀπέλειξε φόνου, τρὶς δ᾽ ἐξ ἄγος ἔπτυσ᾽
        ὀδόντων,
ἣ θέμις αὐθέντῃσι δολοκτασίας ἱλάεσθαι.

480   ὑγρὸν δ᾽ ἐν γαίῃ κρύψεν νέκυν, ἔνθ᾽ ἔτι νῦν περ
κείαται ὀστέα κεῖνα μετ᾽ ἀνδράσιν Ἀψυρτεῦσιν.

        οἱ δ᾽ ἄμυδις πυρσοῖο σέλας προπάροιθεν ἰδόντες,
τό σφιν παρθενικὴ τέκμαρ μετιοῦσιν ἄειρεν,
Κολχίδος ἀγχόθι νηὸς ἑὴν παρὰ νῆα βάλοντο

485   ἥρωες· Κόλχον δ᾽ ὄλεκον στόλον, ἠύτε κίρκοι
φῦλα πελειάων ἠὲ μέγα πῶυ λέοντες
ἀγρότεροι κλονέουσιν ἐνὶ σταθμοῖσι θορόντες.
οὐδ᾽ ἄρα τις κείνων θάνατον φύγε, πάντα δ᾽ ὅμιλον
πῦρ ἅ τε δηιόωντες ἐπέδραμον. ὀψὲ δ᾽ Ἰήσων

490   ἤντησεν, μεμαὼς ἐπαμυνέμεν—οὐ μάλ᾽ ἀρωγῆς
δευομένοις, ἤδη δὲ καὶ ἀμφ᾽ αὐτοῖο μέλοντο.

        ἔνθα δὲ ναυτιλίης πυκινὴν περὶ μητιάασκον
ἑζόμενοι βουλήν, ἐπὶ δέ σφισιν ἤλυθε κούρη
φραζομένοις. Πηλεὺς δὲ παροίτατος ἔκφατο μῦθον·

---

53 For the expiatory rites of cutting off extremities (μασχα-
λισμός), cf. Aeschylus, *Choephori* 439 and Sophocles, *Electra*

site the island, had once built for Artemis. In its vestibule he fell to his knees, and in his final moments, as the hero breathed forth his spirit, he caught the dark blood flowing from his wound in both hands and stained red her silver-white veil and her robe as she pulled away. With her eye askance, the all-subduing, pitiless Fury clearly saw what sort of murderous deed they had done. The hero Jason cut off the extremities of the dead man, licked up some of his blood three times and three times spat out the pollution through his teeth, which is the proper way for killers to expiate treacherous murders.[53] He buried the limp[54] corpse in the ground, where to this day those bones lie among the Apsyrtian people.

As soon as the heroes saw in front of them the light of a torch, which the girl raised as a signal for them to come, they brought their own ship alongside the Colchian ship[55] and set about slaughtering the Colchian sailors, as hawks scatter flocks of doves, or wild lions scatter a great flock of sheep after leaping into the fold. Not one of them escaped death, for they overran them like fire and slew the entire crew. At last, Jason joined them, eager to lend a hand, but they needed no help; rather, by that time they were concerned about him.[56]

Then they sat down to devise a prudent plan for their voyage, and the girl came to join them as they deliberated. Peleus was the first to voice a proposal:

445. The scholiast says that the blood was spat into the mouth of the deceased.   [54] I.e. before rigor mortis could set in.

[55] I.e. the ship that had brought Apsyrtus.

[56] Jason was presumably occupied with burying Apsyrtus' corpse.

495 "ἤδη νῦν κέλομαι νύκτωρ ἔτι νηὶ ἐπιβάντας
εἰρεσίῃ περάαν πλόον ἀντίον, ᾧ ἐπέχουσιν
δήιοι. ἠῶθεν γὰρ ἐπαθρήσαντας ἕκαστα
ἔλπομαι οὐχ ἕνα μῦθον, ὅ τις προτέρωσε δίεσθαι
ἡμέας ὀτρυνέει, τοὺς πεισέμεν· οἷα δ' ἄνακτος
500 εὔνιδες, ἀργαλέῃσι διχοστασίῃς κεδόωνται.
ῥηιδίη δέ κεν ἄμμι, κεδασθέντων δίχα λαῶν,
ἤδ' εἴη μετέπειτα κατερχομένοισι κέλευθος."
ὣς ἔφατ'· ᾔνησαν δὲ νέοι ἔπος Αἰακίδαο.
ῥίμφα δὲ νηὶ ἐπιβάντες ἐπερρώοντ' ἐλάτῃσιν
505 νωλεμές, ὄφρ' ἱερὴν Ἠλεκτρίδα νῆσον ἵκοντό,
ἀλλάων ὑπάτην, ποταμοῦ σχεδὸν Ἠριδανοῖο.
    Κόλχοι δ' ὁππότ' ὄλεθρον ἐπεφράσθησαν
        ἄνακτος,
ἤτοι μὲν δίζεσθαι ἐπέχραον ἔνδοθι πάσης
Ἀργὼ καὶ Μινύας Κρονίης ἁλός, ἀλλ' ἀπέρυκεν
510 Ἥρη σμερδαλέῃσι κατ' αἰθέρος ἀστεροπῇσιν.
ὕστατον αὖ (δὴ γάρ τε Κυταιίδος ἤθεα γαίης
στύξαν, ἀτυζόμενοι χόλον ἄγριον Αἰήταο)
ἔμπεδον ἄλλυδις ἄλλοι ἀφορμηθέντες ἔνασθεν.
οἱ μὲν ἐπ' αὐτάων νήσων ἔβαν, ᾗσιν ἐπέσχον
515 ἥρωες, ναίουσι δ' ἐπώνυμοι Ἀψύρτοιο·
οἱ δ' ἄρ' ἐπ' Ἰλλυρικοῖο μελαμβαθέος ποταμοῖο,

511 αὖ δὴ γάρ τε Merkel: αὐτοὶ δ' αὖτε Ω
513 ἀφορμηθέντες L in ras. ASᵖᶜGD: ἐφορμηθέντες LᵃᶜSᵃᶜE

"Right now, while it is still nighttime, I recommend boarding our ship and rowing on a course opposite the one that our enemies are guarding. For at daybreak, once they see all that has happened, I do not expect that a single proposal—one urging further pursuit of us—will win them over, but like any people bereft of their king, they will be divided by bitter disagreements. And so with their forces divided in two, our route would be easier when we make our way back later on."[57]

Thus he spoke, and the young men approved the speech of Aeacus' son. They quickly boarded the ship and strained at the oars without stopping, until they reached the holy island of Electris, the farthest one of all, near the Eridanus river.[58]

When the Colchians became aware of their king's murder, they were determined to pursue the Argo and the Minyans over the entire sea of Cronus, but Hera held them back with terrifying lightning flashes from the sky. In the end, though, since they had come to loathe their dwellings in the Cytaean land in dread of Aeetes' savage anger, they went off in various directions and settled permanently. Some landed on the very islands the heroes had occupied and live there still, taking their name from Apsyrtus.[59] Others built a citadel by the dark and deep Illyrian river, where

[57] Since the Colchians guard the islands and the routes south to Greece, Peleus proposes sailing northwest as a diversion.

[58] Usually identified with the Po, but considered imaginary by Herodotus (3.115) and Strabo (5.1.9).

[59] For the Apsyrtians, see 4.481.

τύμβος ἵν᾽ Ἁρμονίης Κάδμοιό τε, πύργον ἔδειμαν,
ἀνδράσιν Ἐγχελέεσσιν ἐφέστιοι· οἱ δ᾽ ἐν ὄρεσσιν
ἐνναίουσιν, ἅ πέρ τε Κεραύνια κικλήσκονται
520 ἐκ τόθεν ἐξότε τούς γε Διὸς Κρονίδαο κεραυνοὶ
νῆσον ἐς ἀντιπέραιαν ἀπέτραπον ὁρμηθῆναι.
   ἥρωες δ᾽, ὅτε δή σφιν ἐείσατο νόστος ἀπήμων,
δή ῥα τότε προμολόντες ἐπὶ χθονὶ πείσματ᾽ ἔδησαν
Ὑλλήων· νῆσοι γὰρ ἐπιπρούχοντο θαμειαὶ
525 ἀργαλέην πλώουσιν ὁδὸν μεσσηγὺς ἔχουσαι.
οὐδέ σφιν, ὡς καὶ πρίν, ἀνάρσια μητιάασκον
Ὑλλῆες· πρὸς δ᾽ αὐτοὶ ἐμηχανόωντο κέλευθον,
μισθὸν ἀειρόμενοι τρίποδα μέγαν Ἀπόλλωνος.
δοιοὺς γὰρ τρίποδας τηλοῦ πόρε Φοῖβος ἄγεσθαι
530 Αἰσονίδῃ περόωντι κατὰ χρέος, ὁππότε Πυθὼ
ἱρὴν πευσόμενος μετεκίαθε τῆσδ᾽ ὑπὲρ αὐτῆς
ναυτιλίης· πέπρωτο δ᾽, ὅπῃ χθονὸς ἱδρυθεῖεν,
μή ποτε τὴν δήιοσιν ἀναστήσεσθαι ἰοῦσιν.
τούνεκεν εἰσέτι νῦν κείνη ὅδε κεύθεται αἴῃ
535 ἀμφὶ πόλιν ἀγανὴν Ὑλληίδα, πολλὸν ἔνερθεν
οὔδεος, ὥς κεν ἄφαντος ἀεὶ μερόπεσσι πέλοιτο.
οὐ μὲν ἔτι ζώοντα καταυτόθι τέτμον ἄνακτα
Ὕλλον, ὃν εὐειδὴς Μελίτη τέκεν Ἡρακλῆι
δήμῳ Φαιήκων. ὁ γὰρ οἰκία Ναυσιθόοιο
540 Μάκριν τ᾽ εἰσαφίκανε, Διωνύσοιο τιθήνην,
νιψόμενος παίδων ὀλοὸν φόνον· ἔνθ᾽ ὅ γε κούρην

the tomb of Harmonia and Cadmus is located,[60] and live among the Enchelean people. Still others dwell in the mountains called Ceraunian,[61] ever since the time when thunderbolts from Cronus' son Zeus stopped them from setting out to the island opposite.

And the heroes, once their return seemed safe for them, then fared on and fastened their cables to the land of the Hylleans, for a thick cluster of islands jutted out into the sea, thus making passage difficult for those sailing between them. The Hylleans no longer planned to do them harm as before,[62] but on the contrary showed them the way themselves, thereby earning the reward of a great tripod of Apollo. For Phoebus had given Jason two tripods[63] to take on the distant journey he was required to make, when he went to holy Pytho to inquire about this very voyage. It was fated that any land in which the tripod stood would never be ravaged by enemy invasions. Therefore, still today this tripod lies hidden in that land near the friendly city of Hyllus, deep underground, so that it might always remain unseen by mortals. But they did not find King Hyllus still alive there, he whom beautiful Melite bore to Heracles in the land of the Phaeacians. For Heracles had come to the palace of Nausithous and to Macris, the nurse of Dionysus, to cleanse himself of the murderous slaughter of his chil-

---

[60] After leaving Thebes, Cadmus and Harmonia settled in Illyria and were supposedly changed into snakes. The settlement is associated with Pola (Callimachus, *fr.* 11; Strabo 5.1.9) and the Encheleans are a tribe north of Epidamnus (Herodotus 5.61).

[61] "Thundering."

[62] When they were allied with Colchians (cf. 4.405–407).

[63] The other tripod will be given to Triton at 4.1547–1550.

Αἰγαίου ἐδάμασσεν ἐρασσάμενος ποταμοῖο,
543 νηιάδα Μελίτην, ἡ δὲ σθεναρὸν τέκεν Ὕλλον.
546 οὐδ᾽ ἄρ᾽ ὅ γ᾽ ἡβήσας αὐτῇ ἐνὶ ἔλδετο νήσῳ
    ναίειν κοιρανέοντος ὑπ᾽ ὀφρύσι Ναυσιθόοιο·
    βῆ δ᾽ ἅλαδε Κρονίην, αὐτόχθονα λαὸν ἀγείρας
    Φαιήκων, σὺν γάρ οἱ ἄναξ πόρσυνε κέλευθον
550 ἥρως Ναυσίθοος· τόθι δ᾽ εἵσατο· καί μιν ἔπεφνον
    Μέντορες, ἀγραύλοισιν ἀλεξόμενον περὶ βουσίν.
    ἀλλά, θεαί, πῶς τῆσδε παρὲξ ἁλός, ἀμφί τε
        γαῖαν
    Αὐσονίην νήσους τε Λιγυστίδας, αἳ καλέονται
    Στοιχάδες, Ἀργῴης περιώσια σήματα νηὸς
555 νημερτὲς πέφαται; τίς ἀπόπροθι τόσσον ἀνάγκη
    καὶ χρειὼ σφ᾽ ἐκόμισσε; τίνες σφέας ἤγαγον αὖραι;
        αὐτόν που μεγαλωστὶ δεδουπότος Ἀψύρτοιο
    Ζῆνα, θεῶν βασιλῆα, χόλος λάβεν, οἷον ἔρεξαν·
    Αἰαίης δ᾽ ὀλοὸν τεκμήρατο δήνεσι Κίρκης
560 αἷμ᾽ ἀπονιψαμένους πρό τε μυρία πημανθέντας
    νοστήσειν. τὸ μὲν οὔ τις ἀριστήων ἐνόησεν·
    ἀλλ᾽ ἔθεον γαίης Ὑλληίδος ἐξανιόντες

544–545 inseruit Brunck 539 (sed ὁ μὲν) et 539a: τυτθὸς ἐών
ποτ᾽ ἔναιεν· ἀτὰρ λίπε νῆσον ἔπειτα

64 Nausithous was king of Phaeacia (Alcinous' father according to Homer); Macris' story is told at 4.1131–1140. The fullest account of Heracles' madness and slaughter of his own children is in Euripides' *Heracles*.

65 Brunck added two verses, 539 (slightly adapted) and 539a,

dren.[64] There he fell in love with and subdued the daughter of the Aegaeus river, the water nymph Melite, who bore mighty Hyllus.[65] But when Hyllus grew up, he did not want to live on the same island under the haughty brow of Nausithous. He gathered a host of autochthonous Phaeacians (indeed, the hero, King Nausithous, helped him prepare his expedition)[66] and came to the sea of Cronus. There he settled, and the Mentores[67] slew him as he was defending his grazing cattle.

Come, goddesses,[68] how is it that beyond this sea,[69] around the Ausonian land[70] and the Ligystian islands (which are called the Stoechades),[71] countless traces of the Argo are clearly to be seen? What necessity and what need brought them so far? What winds conveyed them?

Apparently, when Apsyrtus was mightily cut down, anger seized Zeus himself, king of the gods, at what they had done, and he determined that they should cleanse themselves from the murderous blood through Aeaean Circe's instructions and suffer countless woes before returning home. None of the heroes, however, knew this, so they departed from the Hyllean land and sped far onward. They

---

found in some MSS, as verses 544–545: δήμῳ Φαιήκων. ὁ μὲν οἰκία Ναυσιθόοιο | τυτθὸς ἐὼν ποτ᾿ ἔναιεν· ἀτὰρ λίπε νῆσον ἔπειτα, "in the land of the Phaeacians. As a small child he once lived in the palace of Nausithous, but he left the island thereafter."

[66] Presumably to get rid of him.

[67] A Liburnian tribe north of Hyllus' city.

[68] The Muses.

[69] The Adriatic.

[70] I.e. Italy.

[71] The Ligystian (i.e. Ligurian) islands (Îles d'Hyères) are off the coast of southern France near Marseilles.

τηλόθι· τὰς δ᾽ ἀπέλειπον, ὅσαι Κόλχοισι πάροιθεν
ἑξείης πλήθοντο Λιβυρνίδες εἰν ἁλὶ νῆσοι,
565 Ἴσσα τε Δυσκέλαδός τε καὶ ἱμερτὴ Πιτύεια.
αὐτὰρ ἔπειτ᾽ ἐπὶ τῇσι παραὶ Κέρκυραν ἵκοντο,
ἔνθα Ποσειδάων Ἀσωπίδα νάσσατο κούρην,
ἠύκομον Κέρκυραν, ἑκὰς Φλειουντίδος αἴης,
ἁρπάξας ὑπ᾽ ἔρωτι· μελαινομένην δέ μιν ἄνδρες
570 ναυτίλοι ἐκ πόντοιο κελαινῇ πάντοθεν ὕλῃ
δερκόμενοι Κέρκυραν ἐπικλείουσι Μέλαιναν.
τῇ δ᾽ ἐπὶ καὶ Μελίτην, λιαρῷ περιγηθέες οὔρῳ,
αἰπεινήν τε Κερωσσόν, ὕπερθε δὲ πολλὸν ἐοῦσαν
Νυμφαίην παράμειβον, ἵνα κρείουσα Καλυψὼ
575 Ἀτλαντὶς ναίεσκε· τὰ δ᾽ ἠεροειδέα λεύσσειν
οὔρεα δοιάζοντο Κεραύνια. καὶ τότε βουλὰς
ἀμφ᾽ αὐτοῖς Ζηνός τε μέγαν χόλον ἐφράσαθ᾽ Ἥρη.
μηδομένη δ᾽ ἄνυσιν τοῖο πλόου, ὦρσεν ἀέλλας
ἀντικρύ, ταῖς αὖτις ἀναρπάγδην φορέοντο
580 νήσου ἔπι κραναῆς Ἠλεκτρίδος. αὐτίκα δ᾽ ἄφνω
ἴαχεν ἀνδρομέῃ ἐνοπῇ μεσσηγὺ θεόντων
αὐδῆεν γλαφυρῆς νηὸς δόρυ, τό ῥ᾽ ἀνὰ μέσσην
στεῖραν Ἀθηναίη Δωδωνίδος ἥρμοσε φηγοῦ.
τοὺς δ᾽ ὀλοὸν μεσσηγὺ δέος λάβεν εἰσαΐοντας
585 φθογγήν τε Ζηνός τε βαρὺν χόλον. οὐ γὰρ ἀλύξειν
ἔννεπεν οὔτε πόρους δολιχῆς ἁλὸς οὔτε θυέλλας
ἀργαλέας, ὅτε μὴ Κίρκη φόνον Ἀψύρτοιο

586 πόρους *wd*: πόνους *m*

374

left behind all the Liburnian islands, one after another in the sea, that had previously been filled with Colchians: Issa, Dysceladus, and lovely Pityeia. But then, after these, they passed by Corcyra, where Poseidon had settled the daughter of Asopus, fair-haired Corcyra, far from the land of Phlius,[72] having abducted her out of love. The sailors who see it from the sea, blackened by the dark woods all over it, call it Black Corcyra.[73] After this, delighting in a warm breeze, they sailed by Melite, steep Cerossus, and, lying far beyond them, Nymphaea,[74] where Queen Calypso, Atlas' daughter, lived; and they thought they could discern those mist-covered Ceraunian mountains.[75] And then Hera called to mind Zeus' plans for them and his mighty anger. Contriving to accomplish that voyage,[76] she stirred up storm-winds against them, in the grip of which they were being carried back to the rocky island of Electris. But all of a sudden, as they were rushing along, the hollow ship's speaking beam shouted out with a human voice, the beam that Athena had fashioned from Dodonian oak for the middle of the keel.[77] Deathly fear gripped them as they heard the voice telling of Zeus' grievous anger, for it said that they would not escape journeys[78] on the vast sea nor terrible tempests, unless Circe cleansed away the ruth-

[72] The Asopus river runs near Phlius in the area of Sicyon, west of Corinth; cf. 1.115–117. [73] A small island off Illyria, not the modern Corcyra (which A. calls Drepane).

[74] Homer calls it Ogygia; it is of unknown location.

[75] The southernmost region settled by the breakaway Colchians (cf. 4.518–521). [76] The one outlined at 4.552–555.

[77] It first spoke at 1.524–527.

[78] Or, reading πόνους, toils.

νηλέα νίψειεν· Πολυδεύκεα δ' εὐχετάασθαι
Κάστορά τ' ἀθανάτοισι θεοῖς ἤνωγε κελεύθους
590 Αὐσονίης ἔντοσθε πορεῖν ἁλός, ᾗ ἔνι Κίρκην
δήουσιν, Πέρσης τε καὶ Ἠελίοιο θύγατρα.
    ὣς Ἀργὼ ἰάχησεν ὑπὸ κνέφας. οἱ δ' ἀνόρουσαν
Τυνδαρίδαι, καὶ χεῖρας ἀνέσχεθον ἀθανάτοισιν
εὐχόμενοι τὰ ἕκαστα· κατηφείη δ' ἔχεν ἄλλους
595 ἥρωας Μινύας. ἡ δ' ἔσσυτο πολλὸν ἐπιπρὸ
λαίφεσιν, ἐς δ' ἔβαλον μύχατον ῥόον Ἠριδανοῖο,
ἔνθα ποτ' αἰθαλόεντι τυπεὶς πρὸς στέρνα κεραυνῷ
ἡμιδαὴς Φαέθων πέσεν ἅρματος Ἠελίοιο
λίμνης ἐς προχοὰς πολυβενθέος· ἡ δ' ἔτι νῦν περ
600 τραύματος αἰθομένοιο βαρὺν ἀνακηκίει ἀτμόν,
οὐδέ τις ὕδωρ κεῖνο διὰ πτερὰ κοῦφα τανύσσας
οἰωνὸς δύναται βαλέειν ὕπερ, ἀλλὰ μεσηγὺς
φλογμῷ ἐπιθρῴσκει πεποτημένος. ἀμφὶ δὲ κοῦραι
Ἡλιάδες ταναῇσιν ἐελμέναι αἰγείροισιν
605 μύρονται κινυρὸν μέλεαι γόον· ἐκ δὲ φαεινὰς
ἠλέκτρου λιβάδας βλεφάρων προχέουσιν ἔραζε·
αἱ μέν τ' ἠελίῳ ψαμάθοις ἔπι τερσαίνονται,
εὖτ' ἂν δὲ κλύζῃσι κελαινῆς ὕδατα λίμνης
ἠιόνας πνοιῇ πολυηχέος ἐξ ἀνέμοιο,
610 δὴ τότ' ἐς Ἠριδανὸν προκυλίνδεται ἀθρόα πάντα
κυμαίνοντι ῥόῳ. Κελτοὶ δ' ἐπὶ βάξιν ἔθεντο,
ὡς ἄρ' Ἀπόλλωνος τάδε δάκρυα Λητοΐδαο

590 ἔντοσθε w: ἔμπροσθε m   604 ἐελμέναι Gerhard:
ἀείμεναι L: ἀειμέναι AE: ἀήμεναι Livrea

less murder of Apsyrtus. It also commanded Polydeuces and Castor to pray to the immortal gods to give them passage into the Ausonian sea,[79] where they would find Circe, the daughter of Perse and Helius.

Thus the Argo shouted out in the darkness. The sons of Tyndareus stood up and raised their hands to the immortals and prayed for each of those things, while dejection gripped the rest of the Minyan heroes.[80] The ship sped on much further under sail, and they entered the innermost stream of the Eridanus, where once Phaethon was struck by a blazing lightning bolt on his chest and fell half-burned from Helius' chariot into the waters of that deep swamp, which to this day spews up noxious steam from his smoldering wound. No bird is able to spread its light wings and cross above that water, but it plummets in mid-flight into the flames. And round about, the maiden Heliades,[81] confined[82] in tall poplars, sadly wail a pitiful lament, while they shed forth from their eyes shining drops of amber to the ground. These are dried on the sand by the sun, and whenever the waters of the dark marsh wash over their shores from the blast of a howling wind, then all of them together are rolled into the Eridanus by the swelling flow. The Celts added the story that these are in fact the tears of Leto's

[79] The Italian (Tyrrhenian) sea west of Italy. Castor and Polydeuces (Pollux), the Tyndaridae, were guardians of mariners.

[80] Presumably at the prospect of the hardships predicted and because of their present helplessness.

[81] Daughters of Helius and hence Phaethon's sisters.

[82] Gerhard's emendation; the text is uncertain.

ἐμφέρεται δίναις, ἅ τε μυρία χεῦε πάροιθεν,
ἦμος Ὑπερβορέων ἱερὸν γένος εἰσαφίκανεν,
615 οὐρανὸν αἰγλήεντα λιπὼν ἐκ πατρὸς ἐνιπῆς,
χωόμενος περὶ παιδί, τὸν ἐν λιπαρῇ Λακερείῃ
δῖα Κορωνὶς ἔτικτεν ἐπὶ προχοῇς Ἀμύροιο.
καὶ τὰ μὲν ὣς κείνοισι μετ᾽ ἀνδράσι κεκλήισται.
τοὺς δ᾽ οὔτε βρώμης ᾕρει πόθος οὔτε ποτοῖο,
620 οὔτ᾽ ἐπὶ γηθοσύνας τράπετο νόος. ἀλλ᾽ ἄρα τοί γε
ἤματα μὲν στρεύγοντο περιβληχρὸν βαρύθοντες
ὀδμῇ λευγαλέῃ, τήν ῥ᾽ ἄσχετον ἐξανίεσκον
τυφομένου Φαέθοντος ἐπιρροαὶ Ἠριδανοῖο·
νύκτας δ᾽ αὖ γόον ὀξὺν ὀδυρομένων ἐσάκουον
625 Ἡλιάδων λιγέως· τὰ δὲ δάκρυα μυρομένῃσιν
οἷον ἐλαιηραὶ στάγες ὕδασιν ἐμφορέοντο.

ἐκ δὲ τόθεν Ῥοδανοῖο βαθὺν ῥόον εἰσεπέρησαν,
ὅς τ᾽ εἰς Ἠριδανὸν μετανίσσεται, ἄμμιγα δ᾽ ὕδωρ
ἐν ξυνοχῇ βέβρυχε κυκώμενον. αὐτὰρ ὁ γαίης
630 ἐκ μυχάτης, ἵνα τ᾽ εἰσὶ πύλαι καὶ ἐδέθλια Νυκτός,
ἔνθεν ἀπορνύμενος, τῇ μέν τ᾽ ἐπερεύγεται ἀκτὰς
Ὠκεανοῦ, τῇ δ᾽ αὖτε μετ᾽ Ἰονίην ἅλα βάλλει,
τῇ δ᾽ ἐπὶ Σαρδόνιον πέλαγος καὶ ἀπείρονα κόλπον

624 νύκτας Lw: νυκτὸς AE
627 εἰσεπέρησαν w: εἰσαπέβησαν m

[83] This digression is told very elliptically. Apollo's son by
Coronis is Asclepius, thunderbolted by Zeus for reviving a dead
man. In anger at his son's death, Apollo retaliated by killing the
Cyclopes who furnished Zeus' lightning. Zeus then banished

son Apollo, which are borne along by the swirling waters,
the innumerable tears he shed long before, when he went
to the holy race of the Hyperboreans, having left the bright
heaven at his father's rebuke, angry about his son whom
godlike Coronis had borne in bright Lacereia by the waters
of the Amyrus.[83] Such is the account told among those
people. But no desire for food or drink came over the
heroes, nor did their minds turn to joyous thoughts. But
instead, during the day they were sickened to exhaustion,
oppressed by the nauseous stench, which, unbearable, the
tributaries of the Eridanus exhaled from smoldering Phae-
thon, while at night they heard the piercing lament of the
loudly wailing Heliades, and, as they wept, their tears were
borne along the waters like drops of oil.

From there they entered the deep stream of the Rhone,
which flows into the Eridanus, and in the strait where they
meet the churning water roars. Now that river, rising from
the end of the earth, where the gates and precincts of
Night are located,[84] through one branch[85] disgorges onto
the shores of the Ocean, through another pours into the
Ionian sea,[86] and through a third pours its streams through

Apollo from Olympus. In this version he goes to the Hyper-
boreans; in other versions he is sent to Pherae as a servant of
Admetus (cf. Euripides, *Alcestis* 1–9). Lacereia is in Thessaly; for
some of these details, see Pindar, *Pythian* 3.1–53.

[84] In the far west.

[85] Presumably the Rhine, which flows into the North Sea. A.
imagines the Eridanus (Po), Rhine, and Rhone as connected.

[86] The Adriatic.

APOLLONIUS RHODIUS

ἑπτὰ διὰ στομάτων ἱεὶς ῥόον. ἐκ δ᾽ ἄρα τοῖο
635 λίμνας εἰσέλασαν δυσχείμονας, αἵ τ᾽ ἀνὰ Κελτῶν
ἤπειρον πέπτανται ἀθέσφατον. ἔνθα κεν οἵ γε
ἄτη ἀεικελίῃ πέλασαν· φέρε γάρ τις ἀπορρὼξ
κόλπον ἐς Ὠκεανοῖο, τὸν οὐ προδαέντες ἔμελλον
εἰσβαλέειν, τόθεν οὔ κεν ὑπότροποι ἐξεσάωθεν.
640 ἀλλ᾽ Ἥρη σκοπέλοιο καθ᾽ Ἑρκυνίου ἰάχησεν
οὐρανόθεν προθοροῦσα· φόβῳ δ᾽ ἐτίναχθεν αὐτῆς
πάντες ὁμῶς· δεινὸν γὰρ ἐπὶ μέγας ἔβραχεν αἰθήρ.
ἂψ δὲ παλιντροπόωντο θεᾶς ὕπο, καί ῥ᾽ ἐνόησαν
τὴν οἶμον, τῇ πέρ τε καὶ ἔπλετο νόστος ἰοῦσιν.
645 δηναιοὶ δ᾽ ἀκτὰς ἁλιμυρέας εἰσαφίκοντο,
Ἥρης ἐννεσίῃσι δι᾽ ἔθνεα μυρία Κελτῶν
καὶ Λιγύων περόωντες ἀδήιοι· ἀμφὶ γὰρ αἰνὴν
ἠέρα χεῦε θεὰ πάντ᾽ ἤματα νισσομένοισιν.
μεσσότατον δ᾽ ἄρα τοί γε διὰ στόμα νηὶ βαλόντες,
650 Στοιχάδας εἰσαπέβαν νήσους σόοι εἵνεκα κούρων
Ζηνός· ὃ δὴ βωμοί τε καὶ ἱερὰ τοῖσι τέτυκται
ἔμπεδον· οὐδ᾽ οἷον κείνης ἐπίουροι ἕποντο
ναυτιλίης, Ζεὺς δέ σφι καὶ ὀψιγόνων πόρε νῆας.
Στοιχάδας αὖτε λιπόντες ἐς Αἰθαλίην ἐπέρησαν

634 ἱεὶς Lᵃᶜw: ἵει L² in ras. AE   652 ἐπίουροι w:
ἐπίκουροι m

---

87 The actual Rhone flows into the Gulf of Lyons; the Sardin-
ian sea designates the Mediterranean Sea between Sardinia and
Spain.

380

seven mouths into the vast gulf of the Sardinian sea.[87] Then, from the Rhone, they entered the stormy lakes that spread throughout the vast territory of the Celts.[88] There they would have met with a wretched demise, for there was a certain branch leading to the gulf of Ocean, which they were about to enter inadvertently, and from which they would not have returned alive. But Hera leapt forth from heaven and shouted from the Hercynian peak.[89] All the men alike quaked with fear at her cry, for the great sky resounded terribly. They made their way back again with the goddess' help, and then recognized the route by which to travel and secure their return home. After a long time, they came to the shores washed by the sea, passing unassailed by Hera's devising through the countless tribes of Celts and Ligyans,[90] for the goddess shed a dense mist around them all the days they traveled. And then, by sailing their ship through the centermost mouth of the river, they disembarked on the Stoechades islands, safe and sound, thanks to the sons of Zeus.[91] For that reason altars and rites were established forever in their honor, for not only did they accompany that voyage as guardians, but Zeus entrusted them with ships of future sailors as well. Then, after leaving the Stoechades, they went on to the island of Aethalia,[92] where, wearied from their toil, they

---

[88] Presumably the lakes in Switzerland. Some take $\dot{a}\theta\acute{\epsilon}\sigma\phi a$-$\tau o\nu$ adverbially, *that spread for a vast distance*.

[89] Presumably in the Black Forest along the Rhine.

[90] I.e. Ligurians, inhabiting the coast along southern France and northern Italy.

[91] Castor and Polydeuces.

[92] Elba.

APOLLONIUS RHODIUS

655 νῆσον, ἵνα ψηφῖσιν ἀπωμόρξαντο καμόντες
ἱδρῶ ἅλις· χροιῇ δὲ κατ᾽ αἰγιαλοῖο κέχυνται
εὔκελαι· ἐν δὲ σόλοι καὶ τεύχεα θέσκελα κείνων,
ἔνθα λιμὴν Ἀργῷος ἐπωνυμίην πεφάτισται.
    καρπαλίμως δ᾽ ἐνθένδε διὲξ ἁλὸς οἶδμα νέοντο
660 Αὐσονίης, ἀκτὰς Τυρσηνίδας εἰσορόωντες·
ἷξον δ᾽ Αἰαίης λιμένα κλυτόν· ἐκ δ᾽ ἄρα νηὸς
πείσματ᾽ ἐπ᾽ ἠιόνων σχεδόθεν βάλον. ἔνθα δὲ
        Κίρκην
εὗρον ἁλὸς νοτίδεσσι κάρη ἐπιφαιδρύνουσαν·
τοῖον γὰρ νυχίοισιν ὀνείρασιν ἐπτοίητο.
665 αἵματί οἱ θάλαμοί τε καὶ ἔρκεα πάντα δόμοιο
μύρεσθαι δόκεον, φλὸξ δ᾽ ἀθρόα φάρμακ᾽ ἔδαπτεν,
οἷσι πάρος ξείνους θέλγ᾽ ἀνέρας, ὅς τις ἵκοιτο·
τὴν δ᾽ αὐτὴ φονίῳ σβέσεν αἵματι πορφύρουσαν,
χερσὶν ἀφυσσαμένη, λῆξεν δ᾽ ὀλοοῖο φόβοιο.
670 τῶ καὶ ἐπιπλομένης ἠοῦς νοτίδεσσι θαλάσσης
ἐγρομένη πλοκάμους τε καὶ εἵματα φαιδρύνεσκεν.
θῆρες δ᾽, οὐ θήρεσσιν ἐοικότες ὠμηστῆσιν
οὐδὲ μὲν οὐδ᾽ ἄνδρεσσιν ὁμὸν δέμας, ἄλλο δ᾽ ἀπ᾽
        ἄλλων
συμμιγέες μελέων, κίον ἀθρόοι, ἠύτε μῆλα
675 ἐκ σταθμῶν ἅλις εἶσιν ὀπηδεύοντα νομῆι.

657 εὔκελαι Brunck: ἴκ-(vel ἴκ-)ελοι Ω: εὔκελοι E | τεύχεα
mG: τρύχεα L²ˢˡS   Fränkel lacunam statuit inter εὔκελαι et ἐν
δὲ σόλοι
658 ἔνθα Beck, Hermann: ἐν δὲ Ω

382

wiped off their abundant sweat with pebbles, and these, like skin in color, are strewn along the beach. And there too are throwing-stones[93] and wondrous equipment of theirs,[94] where the place is named the harbor of Argo after them.[95]

From there they traveled swiftly across the waves of the Ausonian sea, keeping in view the Tyrrhenian shore. They came to the famous harbor of Aeaea and immediately cast the cables from the ship onto the beach. Here they found Circe washing her head with sea water, because she had been so frightened by dreams in the night. The rooms and all the walls of her palace seemed to her to trickle with blood, and a flame was consuming all the drugs with which until then she had bewitched any strangers who came, and she herself extinguished that raging flame with a victim's blood that she had scooped up in her hands, and then she ceased from deathly fear. That is why, when dawn came, she had arisen and was washing her hair and clothing in the waters of the sea. Beasts that resembled neither flesh-eating animals nor yet humans in any consistent form, but having a mixture of limbs from each, came forth in a throng, as when sheep in great numbers leave their pens and follow a shepherd. In the past as well, the earth itself

---

[93] The early discus was of stone (cf. Pindar, *Olympian* 10.72).

[94] Or, reading τρύχεα, *wondrous vestiges of them.*

[95] The text of lines 656–658 is unsound. Strabo (5.2.6) read one similar to 656–657: "because the scrapings, which the Argonauts formed when they used their strigils, became congealed, the pebbles on the shore remain variegated still to this day" (trans. H. L. Jones). Fränkel and Vian posit a lacuna in line 658.

τοίους καὶ προτέρους ἐξ ἰλύος ἐβλάστησεν
χθὼν αὐτὴ μικτοῖσιν ἀρηρεμένους μελέεσσιν,
οὔ πω διψαλέῳ μάλ᾽ ὑπ᾽ ἠέρι πιληθεῖσα,
οὐδέ πω ἀζαλέοιο βολαῖς τόσον ἠελίοιο
680   ἰκμάδας αἰνυμένη· τὰ δ᾽ ἐπὶ στίχας ἤγαγεν αἰὼν
συγκρίνας. τὼς οἵ γε φυὴν ἀίδηλοι ἕποντο,
ἥρωας δ᾽ ἕλε θάμβος ἀπείριτον. αἶψα δ᾽ ἕκαστος,
Κίρκης εἴς τε φυὴν εἴς τ᾽ ὄμματα παπταίνοντες,
ῥεῖα κασιγνήτην φάσαν ἔμμεναι Αἰήταο.
685   ἡ δ᾽ ὅτε δὴ νυχίων ἀπὸ δείματα πέμψεν ὀνείρων,
αὐτίκ᾽ ἔπειτ᾽ ἄψορρον ἀπέστιχε· τοὺς δ᾽ ἅμ᾽ ἕπεσθαι
χειρὶ καταρρέξασα δολοφροσύνῃσιν ἄνωγεν.
ἔνθ᾽ ἤτοι πληθὺς μὲν ἐφετμαῖς Αἰσονίδαο
μίμνεν ἀπηλεγέως, ὁ δ᾽ ἐρύσσατο Κολχίδα κούρην.
690   ἄμφω δ᾽ ἑσπέσθην αὐτὴν ὁδόν, ἔστ᾽ ἀφίκοντο
Κίρκης ἐς μέγαρον· τοὺς δ᾽ ἐν λιπαροῖσι κέλευεν
ἥ γε θρόνοις ἕζεσθαι, ἀμηχανέουσα κιόντων.
τὼ δ᾽ ἄνεῳ καὶ ἄναυδοι ἐφ᾽ ἑστίῃ ἀίξαντε
ἵζανον, ἥ τε δίκη λυγροῖς ἱκέτῃσι τέτυκται,
695   ἡ μὲν ἐπ᾽ ἀμφοτέραις θεμένη χείρεσσι μέτωπα,
αὐτὰρ ὁ κωπῆεν μέγα φάσγανον ἐν χθονὶ πήξας,
ᾧ πέρ τ᾽ Αἰήταο πάιν κτάνεν· οὐδέ ποτ᾽ ὄσσε
ἰθὺς ἐνὶ βλεφάροισιν ἀνέσχεθον. αὐτίκα δ᾽ ἔγνω
Κίρκη φύξιον οἶτον ἀλιτροσύνας τε φόνοιο.
700   τῶ καὶ ὀπιζομένη Ζηνὸς θέμιν Ἱκεσίοιο,
ὃς μέγα μὲν κοτέει, μέγα δ᾽ ἀνδροφόνοισιν ἀρήγει,

676 προτέρους L²ˢ|ω: προτέρης m

produced from mud[96] such creatures composed of various
limbs, when the earth was not yet solidified by the parch-
ing air, nor yet receiving sufficient moisture under the rays
of the scorching sun. But a long period of time put these
forms together and arranged them into species.[97] Thus did
those creatures of undefined form follow her, and bound-
less amazement seized the heroes. And at once, as each
one peered at the form and eyes of Circe, they easily af-
firmed that she was Aeetes' sister.[98]

Now when she had banished the fears caused by her
dreams in the night, she immediately retraced her steps,
and with a friendly gesture of her hand treacherously bade
them follow along. But the crew, on Jason's orders, stood
fast without reacting, whereas he took the Colchian girl
with him. The two of them followed in her path until they
entered Circe's hall, and she ordered them to sit on shining
chairs, perplexed at their coming. But in speechless si-
lence they rushed to the hearth and sat there, as is the cus-
tom for desperate suppliants, she having covered her face
·with both hands, and he having driven into the ground the
great hilted sword with which he had killed Aeetes' son;
nor did they ever raise their lowered eyes to look directly at
her. Circe immediately recognized the plight of a fugitive
and the sin of murder. Therefore, out of reverence for the
ordinance of Zeus, Protector of Suppliants—who mightily
hates murderers, but mightily protects them—she began

[96] The theory that life was generated from mud or slime goes
back at least to Anaximander (12A30 DK).
[97] This zoogonic digression draws heavily on the pre-Socra-
tics, especially Empedocles.   [98] Bright eyes are naturally
associated with the children of Helius.

ῥέζε θυηπολίην, οἵη τ᾽ ἀπολυμαίνονται
νηλειεῖς ἱκέται, ὅτ᾽ ἐφέστιοι ἀντιόωσιν.
πρῶτα μὲν ἀτρέπτοιο λυτήριον ἥ γε φόνοιο
705 τειναμένη καθύπερθε συὸς τέκος, ἧς ἔτι μαζοὶ
πλήμυρον λοχίης ἐκ νηδύος, αἵματι χεῖρας
τέγγεν, ἐπιμήγουσα δέρην· αὖτις δὲ καὶ ἄλλοις
μείλισσεν χύτλοισι Καθάρσιον ἀγκαλέουσα
Ζῆνα, παλαμναίων τιμήορον ἱκεσιάων.
710 καὶ τὰ μὲν ἀθρόα πάντα δόμων ἐκ λύματ᾽ ἔνεικαν
νηιάδες πρόπολοι, ταί οἱ πόρσυνον ἕκαστα·
ἡ δ᾽ εἴσω πελανοὺς μείλικτρά τε νηφαλίῃσιν
καῖεν ἐπ᾽ εὐχωλῇσι παρέστιος, ὄφρα χόλοιο
σμερδαλέας παύσειεν Ἐρινύας ἠδὲ καὶ αὐτὸς
715 εὐμειδής τε πέλοιτο καὶ ἤπιος ἀμφοτέροισιν,
εἴτ᾽ οὖν ὀθνείῳ μεμιασμένοι αἵματι χεῖρας
εἴτε καὶ ἐμφύλῳ προσκηδέες ἀντιόωσιν.

αὐτὰρ ἐπεὶ μάλα πάντα πονήσατο, δὴ τότ᾽ ἔπειτα
εἶσεν ἐπὶ ξεστοῖσιν ἀναστήσασα θρόνοισιν,
720 καὶ δ᾽ αὐτὴ πέλας ἷζεν ἐνωπαδίς. αἶψα δὲ μύθῳ
χρειὼ ναυτιλίην τε διακριδὸν ἐξερέεινεν,
ἠδ᾽ ὁπόθεν μετὰ γαῖαν ἑὴν καὶ δώματ᾽ ἰόντες
αὔτως ἱδρύθησαν ἐφέστιοι. ἦ γὰρ ὀνείρων
μνῆστις ἀεικελίη δῦνεν φρένας ὁρμαίνουσαν·

---

703 νηλειεῖς (vel νηληεῖς) Ω: νηλιτεῖς (vel νηλητεῖς)
Hölzlin, Wellauer, et al.

making the kind of sacrifice by which ruthless[99] suppliants are cleansed, when they supplicate at the hearth. First, to expiate murder, which cannot be undone, she stretched over them a piglet from a sow whose teats were still swollen from the birth of a litter, and wet their hands with its blood as she slit its throat. And again, with other libations she propitiated Zeus, invoking him as the Purifier, defender of supplications by murderers.[100] Her attendant Naiads, who ministered to her every need, carried all the defilements in a mass out of the house. But within by the hearth, she burned sacrificial cakes and propitiatory libations with wineless prayers,[101] that she might placate the anger of the terrible Furies, and that Zeus himself might be propitious and gentle to them both, whether with hands stained by the blood of a stranger or even of a relative, they were making supplication in their distress.

But when she had completed all of her tasks, she had them rise and sit on polished chairs, and she seated herself right in front of them. She immediately spoke and asked in detail about the purpose of their expedition and from where they had come to seek out her land and palace and sit as they had at her hearth. For indeed the horrible memory of her dreams entered her mind as she was pondering.

[99] I take "ruthless suppliants" as brachylogy for ruthless men who come as suppliants. Many edd. conjecture some form of νηλεῖτις with the unparalleled meaning of "very guilty" (first suggested by Aristarchus à propos of *Odyssey* 16.317).

[100] The text is uncertain. Vian reads Παλαμναῖον, Τιμήορον ἱκεσιάων, "Zeus of Murderers, Zeus Respecter of supplications."

[101] "Wineless" properly applies to the libations (of water, milk, and honey) poured on the flaming cakes. Offerings to the Furies contained no wine (cf. Aeschylus, *Eumenides* 106–109).

387

APOLLONIUS RHODIUS

725 ἵετο δ᾽ αὖ κούρης ἐμφύλιον ἴδμεναι ὀμφήν,
αὐτίχ᾽ ὅπως ἐνόησεν ἀπ᾽ οὔδεος ὄσσε βαλοῦσαν.
πᾶσα γὰρ Ἠελίου γενεὴ ἀρίδηλος ἰδέσθαι
ἦεν, ἐπεὶ βλεφάρων ἀποτηλόθι μαρμαρυγῇσιν
οἷόν τε χρυσέην ἀντώπιον ἵεσαν αἴγλην.
730 ἡ δ᾽ ἄρα τῇ τὰ ἕκαστα διειρομένη κατέλεξεν,
Κολχίδα γῆρυν ἱεῖσα, βαρύφρονος Αἰήταο
κούρη μειλιχίως, ἠμὲν στόλον ἠδὲ κελεύθους
ἡρώων, ὅσα τ᾽ ἀμφὶ θοοῖς ἐμόγησαν ἀέθλοις,
ὥς τε κασιγνήτης πολυκηδέος ἤλιτε βουλαῖς,
735 ὥς τ᾽ ἀπονόσφιν ἄλυξεν ὑπέρβια δείματα πατρὸς
σὺν παισὶν Φρίξοιο. φόνον δ᾽ ἀλέεινεν ἐνισπεῖν
Ἀψύρτου, τὴν δ᾽ οὔ τι νόῳ λάθεν· ἀλλὰ καὶ ἔμπης
μυρομένην ἐλέαιρεν, ἔπος δ᾽ ἐπὶ τοῖον ἔειπεν·
    "σχετλίη, ἦ ῥα κακὸν καὶ ἀεικέα μήσαο νόστον.
740 ἔλπομαι οὐκ ἐπὶ δὴν σε βαρὺν χόλον Αἰήταο
ἐκφυγέειν· τάχα δ᾽ εἶσι καὶ Ἑλλάδος ἤθεα γαίης
τισόμενος φόνον υἷος, ὅτ᾽ ἄσχετα ἔργα τέλεσσας.
ἀλλ᾽ ἐπεὶ οὖν ἱκέτις καὶ ὁμόγνιος ἔπλευ ἐμεῖο,
ἄλλο μὲν οὔ τι κακὸν μητίσομαι ἐνθάδ᾽ ἰούσῃ·
745 ἔρχεο δ᾽ ἐκ μεγάρων ξείνῳ συνοπηδὸς ἐοῦσα,
ὅν τινα τοῦτον ἄιστον ἀείραο πατρὸς ἄνευθεν,
μηδέ με γουνάσσηαι ἐφέστιος· οὐ γὰρ ἐγώ γε
αἰνήσω βουλάς τε σέθεν καὶ ἀεικέα φύξιν."
    ὣς φάτο· τὴν δ᾽ ἀμέγαρτον ἄχος λάβεν· ἀμφὶ δὲ πέπλον
750 ὀφθαλμοῖσι βαλοῦσα γόον χέεν, ὄφρα μιν ἥρως
χειρὸς ἐπισχόμενος μεγάρων ἐξῆγε θύραζε

388

Furthermore, she had longed to know the girl's native language from the moment she saw her raise her eyes from the ground. For all of Helius' offspring were clearly recognizable, because with the radiance from their eyes they cast far in front of them a gleam like that of gold. Then, in answer to each of her questions, the daughter of cruel-minded Aeetes, speaking in the Colchian language, gently told her about the expedition and the travels of the heroes, all their toils in the fierce contests, how she had gone astray on the advice of her distraught sister, and how she had fled far from the terrible threats of her father with the sons of Phrixus. She avoided mentioning the murder of Apsyrtus, but she did not at all fool Circe. But all the same, she pitied the weeping girl and responded with these words:

"Poor girl, truly you have contrived a wicked and shameful voyage. I do not think that you will escape Aeetes' heavy wrath for very long, for he will quickly go even to settlements in the land of Hellas to avenge the murder of his son, because you have carried out intolerable deeds. But since you are a suppliant and a blood relative of mine, I shall not devise any further harm for you, now that you have come here. But leave my palace in company with this stranger, whoever this unknown man is that you have taken for yourself without your father's approval, and do not supplicate me at my hearth, for I at least will not condone your designs or shameful flight."

Thus she spoke, and boundless sorrow seized the girl. She cast her robe over her eyes and poured forth tears of lament, until the hero took her by the hand and led her

APOLLONIUS RHODIUS

δείματι παλλομένην· λεῖπον δ' ἀπὸ δώματα Κίρκης.
οὐδ' ἄλοχον Κρονίδαο Διὸς λάθον, ἀλλά οἱ Ἶρις
πέφραδεν, εὖτ' ἐνόησεν ἀπὸ μεγάροιο κιόντας.
755 αὐτὴ γάρ μιν ἄνωγε δοκευέμεν, ὁππότε νῆα
στείχοιεν. τὸ καὶ αὖτις ἐποτρύνουσ' ἀγόρευεν·

"Ἶρι φίλη, νῦν, εἴ ποτ' ἐμὰς ἐτέλεσσας ἐφετμάς,
εἰ δ' ἄγε λαιψηρῇσι μετοιχομένη πτερύγεσσιν
δεῦρο Θέτιν μοι ἄνωχθι μολεῖν ἁλὸς ἐξανιοῦσαν·
760 κείνης γὰρ χρειώ με κιχάνεται. αὐτὰρ ἔπειτα
ἐλθεῖν εἰς ἀκτάς, ὅθι τ' ἄκμονες Ἡφαίστοιο
χάλκειοι στιβαρῇσιν ἀράσσονται τυπίδεσσιν·
εἰπὲ δὲ κοιμῆσαι φύσας πυρός, εἰσόκεν Ἀργὼ
τάς γε παρεξελάσῃσιν. ἀτὰρ καὶ ἐς Αἴολον ἐλθεῖν,
765 Αἴολον, ὅς τ' ἀνέμοις αἰθρηγενέεσσιν ἀνάσσει·
καὶ δὲ τῷ εἰπέμεναι τὸν ἐμὸν νόον, ὥς κεν ἀήτας
πάντας ἀπολλήξειεν ὑπ' ἠέρι, μηδέ τις αὔρη
τρηχύνοι πέλαγος· ζεφύρου γε μὲν οὖρος ἀήτω,
ὄφρ' οἵ γ' Ἀλκινόου Φαιηκίδα νῆσον ἵκωνται."
770 ὣς ἔφατ'· αὐτίκα δ' Ἶρις ἀπ' Οὐλύμποιο θοροῦσα
τέμνε, τανυσσαμένη κοῦφα πτερά. δῦ δ' ἐνὶ πόντῳ
Αἰγαίῳ, τόθι πέρ τε δόμοι Νηρῆος ἔασιν.
πρώτην δ' εἰσαφίκανε Θέτιν καὶ ἐπέφραδε μῦθον
Ἥρης ἐννεσίῃς, ὦρσέν τέ μιν εἰς ἓ νέεσθαι.
775 δεύτερα δ' εἰς Ἥφαιστον ἐβήσατο, παῦσε δὲ τόν γε
ῥίμφα σιδηρείων τυπίδων, ἔσχοντο δ' ἀυτμῆς
αἰθαλέοι πρηστῆρες. ἀτὰρ τρίτον εἰσαφίκανεν
Αἴολον Ἱππότεω παῖδα κλυτόν. ὄφρα δὲ καὶ τῷ
ἀγγελίην φαμένη θοὰ γούνατα παῦεν ὁδοῖο,

390

outside the palace trembling with fear, and they left the home of Circe.

Yet they did not go unnoticed by the wife of Cronian Zeus, but Iris alerted her when she saw them leave the palace, for Hera had instructed her to watch for when they would go to the ship. And so she ordered her again by saying:

"Dear Iris, come now, if ever before you carried out my orders, and set out on your swift wings and tell Thetis to come up out of the sea and join me here, because I have need of her. But then go to the shores where the bronze anvils of Hephaestus are struck with heavy hammers, and tell him to put to rest his fiery blasts until the Argo has passed them by. And go to Aeolus as well, Aeolus who rules the winds arising in the upper air, and tell him this wish of mine, that he calm all the winds under the sky, so that no breeze ruffles the sea, and yet let a favoring Zephyr blow until they reach the Phaeacian island of Alcinous."

Thus she spoke, and immediately Iris leapt from Olympus and cut through the air, having spread her light wings. She plunged into the Aegean sea at the place where the home of Nereus is. She approached Thetis first and issued the command in accord with Hera's instructions, and roused her to go to the goddess. Second, she went to Hephaestus and made him immediately stop using his iron hammers, and the sooty blasts of air ceased.[102] But thirdly, she approached Aeolus, the famous son of Hippotas. And while she conveyed her message to him as well and rested

---

[102] I.e. air from the bellows.

---

779 παῦεν Platt: παῦσεν Ω

780 τόφρα Θέτις Νηρῆα κασιγνήτας τε λιποῦσα
ἐξ ἁλὸς Οὔλυμπόνδε θεὰν μετεκίαθεν Ἥρην.
ἡ δέ μιν ἆσσον ἑοῖο παρεῖσέ τε, φαῖνέ τε μῦθον·
   "κέκλυθι νῦν, Θέτι δῖα, τά τοι ἐπιέλδομ' ἐνισπεῖν.
οἶσθα μέν, ὅσσον ἐμῇσιν ἐνὶ φρεσὶ τίεται ἥρως
785 Αἰσονίδης ἠδ' ἄλλοι ἀοσσητῆρες ἀέθλου,
οἵη τέ σφ' ἐσάωσα διὰ Πλαγκτὰς περόωντας
πέτρας, ἔνθα πυρὸς δειναὶ βρομέουσι θύελλαι,
κύματά τε σκληρῇσι περιβλύει σπιλάδεσσιν.
νῦν δὲ παρὰ Σκύλλης σκόπελον μέγαν ἠδὲ
        Χάρυβδιν
790 δεινὸν ἐρευγομένην δέχεται ὁδός. ἀλλά σε γὰρ δὴ
ἐξέτι νηπυτίης αὐτὴ τρέφον ἠδ' ἀγάπησα
ἔξοχον ἀλλάων, αἵ τ' εἰν ἁλὶ ναιετάουσιν,
οὕνεκεν οὐκ ἔτλης εὐνῇ Διὸς ἱεμένοιο
λέξασθαι (κείνῳ γὰρ ἀεὶ τάδε ἔργα μέμηλεν,
795 ἠὲ σὺν ἀθανάταις ἠὲ θνητῇσιν ἰαύειν),
ἀλλ' ἐμέ τ' αἰδομένη καὶ ἐνὶ φρεσὶ δειμαίνουσα
ἠλεύω· ὁ δ' ἔπειτα πελώριον ὅρκον ὄμοσσεν,
μή ποτέ σ' ἀθανάτοιο θεοῦ καλέεσθαι ἄκοιτιν.
ἔμπης δ' οὐ μεθίεσκεν ὀπιπεύων ἀέκουσαν,
800 εἰσότε οἱ πρέσβειρα Θέμις κατέλεξεν ἅπαντα,
ὡς δή τοι πέπρωται ἀμείνονα πατρὸς ἑοῖο
παῖδα τεκεῖν· τῷ καί σε λιλαιόμενος μεθέηκεν
δείματι, μή τις ἑοῦ ἀντάξιος ἄλλος ἀνάσσοι
ἀθανάτων, ἀλλ' αἰὲν ἐὸν κράτος εἰρύοιτο.

786 οἵη m: οἵως w

her swift knees from the journey, Thetis left Nereus and her sisters and went up from the sea to Olympus to the goddess Hera. She seated Thetis close by her side and revealed her injunction:

"Listen, now, divine Thetis, to what I want to tell you. You know how much the hero Jason is esteemed in my thoughts, along with the others who are aiding in his endeavor, and how I saved them when they passed through the Wandering rocks, where terrible tempests of fire roar and the waves seethe around the rugged reefs.[103] But now a journey awaits them past the great cliff of Scylla and Charybdis with its terrible spewing. But come! For ever since your infancy I raised you myself, and I have loved you more than all the other goddesses who live in the sea, because you did not deign to lie down in the bed of Zeus when he desired it (for he is always preoccupied with these acts, whether sleeping with immortals or with mortal women), but rather, respecting me and fearful in your thoughts, you shunned him. Then he swore a mighty oath that you would never be called the wife of an immortal god. But all the same, he did not stop eyeing you against your will, until venerable Themis told him everything—how in fact it was fated for you to bear a son greater than his father. Therefore, in spite of his desire, he gave you up out of fear, so that no one else might be his match and rule over the immortals, but he might retain his rule forever.

---

[103] The text is corrupt. The Wandering rocks, identified by A. as the Lipari islands off Sicily where Hephaestus has his forge, and through which they are about to pass, are here confused with the Clashing rocks at the entrance to the Black Sea. Perhaps there is a lacuna.

805 αὐτὰρ ἐγὼ τὸν ἄριστον ἐπιχθονίων πόσιν εἶναι
δῶκά τοι, ὄφρα γάμου θυμηδέος ἀντιάσειας
τέκνα τε φιτύσαιο· θεοὺς δ᾽ εἰς δαῖτα κάλεσσα
πάντας ὁμῶς· αὐτὴ δὲ σέλας χείρεσσιν ἀνέσχον
νυμφίδιον, κείνης ἀγανόφρονος εἵνεκα τιμῆς.
810 ἀλλ᾽ ἄγε καί τινά τοι νημερτέα μῦθον ἐνίψω.
εὖτ᾽ ἂν ἐς Ἠλύσιον πεδίον τεὸς υἱὸς ἵκηται,
ὃν δὴ νῦν Χείρωνος ἐν ἤθεσι Κενταύροιο
νηιάδες κομέουσι τεοῦ λίπτοντα γάλακτος,
χρειώ μιν κούρης πόσιν ἔμμεναι Αἰήταο
815 Μηδείης· σὺ δ᾽ ἄρηγε νυῷ ἑκυρή περ ἐοῦσα,
ἠδ᾽ αὐτῷ Πηλῆι. τί τοι χόλος ἐστήρικται;
ἀάσθη· καὶ γάρ τε θεοὺς ἐπινίσσεται ἄτη.
ναὶ μὲν ἐφημοσύνῃσιν ἐμαῖς Ἥφαιστον ὀίω
λωφήσειν πρήσσοντα πυρὸς μένος, Ἱπποτάδην δὲ
820 Αἴολον ὠκείας ἀνέμων ἄικας ἐρύξειν
νόσφιν ἐυσταθέος ζεφύρου, τείως κεν ἵκωνται
Φαιήκων λιμένας. σὺ δ᾽ ἀκηδέα μήδεο νόστον·
δεῖμα δέ τοι πέτραι καὶ ὑπέρβια κύματ᾽ ἔασιν
μοῦνον, ἅ κεν τρέψαιο κασιγνήτῃσι σὺν ἄλλαις.
825 μηδὲ σύ γ᾽ ἠὲ Χάρυβδιν ἀμηχανέοντας ἐάσῃς
ἐσβαλέειν, μὴ πάντας ἀναβρόξασα φέρῃσιν,
ἠὲ παρὰ Σκύλλης στυγερὸν κευθμῶνα νέεσθαι
(Σκύλλης Αὐσονίης ὀλοόφρονος, ἣν τέκε Φόρκῳ
νυκτιπόλος Ἑκάτη, τήν τε κλείουσι Κράταιιν),

---

[104] Peleus.
[105] Achilles.

And I gave you the best of the mortals to be your husband,[104] so that you might have a marriage dear to your heart and bear children. I invited all the gods together to the wedding feast and with my own hands raised the marriage torch, in return for that kindhearted respect of yours. But come, let me tell you an unerrring account: when your son[105] comes to the Elysian field—he whom the Naiads[106] are now tending in the dwelling of Cheiron the Centaur, though he longs for your milk—it is his fate to be the husband of Aeetes' daughter Medea.[107] So, as her mother-in-law, help your daughter-in-law, and Peleus himself as well. Why is your anger so firmly fixed? He made a mistake[108]— yes, but mistakes happen to gods as well. Truly I think that on my orders Hephaestus will cease stoking his raging fire and that Hippotas' son Aeolus will check the swift blasts of the winds, except for the steady Zephyr, until they reach the harbors of the Phaeacians. But you must devise their safe passage. The only dread is of the rocks and overbearing waves, which you can fend off with the help of your sisters.[109] And do not allow them to fall helplessly into Charybdis, lest she suck them down and carry them all off, nor to sail by the hideous den of Scylla—the deadly Ausonian Scylla, whom night-wandering Hecate, the one men call Crataïs,[110] bore to Phorcus—lest she swoop down

[106] Philyra and Chariclo; cf. 1.553–558.

[107] Ibycus, followed by Simonides, wrote that Achilles married Medea in the Elysian field (schol.).

[108] Explained below at 866–879.

[109] The Nereids.

[110] "Mighty One."

830 μή πως σμερδαλέῃσιν ἐπαΐξασα γένυσσιν
    λεκτοὺς ἡρώων δηλήσεται. ἀλλ᾽ ἔχε νῆα
    κεῖσ᾽, ὅθι περ τυτθή γε παραίβασις ἔσσετ᾽
            ὀλέθρου."
        ὣς φάτο· τὴν δὲ Θέτις τοίῳ προσελέξατο μύθῳ·
    "εἰ μὲν δὴ μαλεροῖο πυρὸς μένος ἠδὲ θύελλαι
835 ζαχρηεῖς λήξουσιν ἐτήτυμον, ἦ τ᾽ ἂν ἐγώ γε
    θαρσαλέη φαίην, καὶ κύματος ἀντιόωντος,
    νῆα σαωσέμεναι, ζεφύρου λίγα κινυμένοιο.
    ἀλλ᾽ ὥρη δολιχήν τε καὶ ἄσπετον οἶμον ὁδεύειν,
    ὄφρα κασιγνήτας μετελεύσομαι, αἵ μοι ἀρωγοὶ
840 ἔσσονται, καὶ νηὸς ὅθι πρυμνῆσι᾽ ἀνῆπται,
    ὥς κεν ὑπηῷοι μνησαίατο νόστον ἑλέσθαι."
        ἦ, καὶ ἀναΐξασα κατ᾽ αἰθέρος ἔμπεσε δίναις
    κυανέου πόντοιο· κάλει δ᾽ ἐπαμυνέμεν ἄλλας
    αὐτοκασιγνήτας Νηρηίδας· αἱ δ᾽ ἀίουσαι
845 ἤντεον ἀλλήλῃσι· Θέτις δ᾽ ἀγόρευεν ἐφετμὰς
    Ἥρης, αἶψα δ᾽ ἴαλλε μετ᾽ Αὐσονίην ἅλα πάσας.
    αὐτὴ δ᾽ ὠκυτέρη ἀμαρύγματος ἠὲ βολάων
    ἠελίου, ὅτ᾽ ἄνεισι περαίης ὑψόθι γαίης,
    σεύατ᾽ ἴμεν λαιψηρὰ δι᾽ ὕδατος, ἔστ᾽ ἀφίκανεν
850 ἀκτὴν Αἰαίην Τυρσηνίδος ἠπείροιο.
    τοὺς δ᾽ εὗρεν παρὰ νηὶ σόλῳ ῥιπῇσί τ᾽ ὀιστῶν
    τερπομένους· ἡ δ᾽ ἆσσον ὀρεξαμένη χερὸς ἄκρης
    Αἰακίδεω Πηλῆος· ὁ γάρ ῥά οἱ ἦεν ἀκοίτης·
    οὐδέ τις εἰσιδέειν δύνατ᾽ ἔμπεδον, ἀλλ᾽ ἄρα τῷ γε
855 οἴῳ ἐν ὀφθαλμοῖσιν ἐείσατο, φώνησέν τε·
        "μηκέτι νῦν ἀκταῖς Τυρσηνίσιν ἧσθε μένοντες,

on them with her horrible jaws and destroy the choicest heroes. But guide the ship to the place where there will be an escape, albeit narrow, from destruction."

Thus she spoke, and Thetis replied to her with these words:

"If indeed the force of the raging fire and the violent storm winds will truly cease, then I will confidently promise to save the ship, even if the waves oppose, so long as the Zephyr blows steadily. But now it is time to go on a long and immeasurable journey to find my sisters, who will help me, and to go to where the ships' stern cables are fastened, so that at dawn they may give thought to winning their voyage home."

She spoke, and, leaping down from the sky, plunged into the swirls of the dark blue sea. She called the rest of her sister Nereids to help. They heard her and gathered together. Thetis announced Hera's orders and quickly dispatched them all to the Ausonian sea. But she herself, more swiftly than a flash of light or rays of the sun when it rises above the distant horizon, sped rapidly through the water, until she reached the Aeaean shore of the Tyrrhenian mainland. She found them beside their ship, amusing themselves with stone-throwing and shooting arrows. She drew near and touched Aeacus' son Peleus on the hand, for he was, after all, her husband. And nobody could see her clearly, but she appeared before his eyes alone, and spoke:

"Now you must no longer linger on the Tyrrhenian

ἠῶθεν δὲ θοῆς πρυμνήσια λύετε νηός,
Ἥρῃ πειθόμενοι ἐπαρηγόνι· τῆς γὰρ ἐφετμῆς
πασσυδίῃ κοῦραι Νηρηίδες ἀντιόωσιν,
860 νῆα διὲκ πέτρας, αἵ τε Πλαγκταὶ καλέονται,
ῥυσόμεναι· κείνη γὰρ ἐναίσιμος ὕμμι κέλευθος.
ἀλλὰ σὺ μή τῳ ἐμὸν δείξῃς δέμας, εὖτ' ἂν ἴδηαι
ἀντομένην σὺν τῇσι, νόῳ δ' ἔχε, μή με χολώσῃς
πλεῖον ἔτ' ἢ τὸ πάροιθεν ἀπηλεγέως ἐχόλωσας."
865 ἦ, καὶ ἔπειτ' ἀίδηλος ἐδύσατο βένθεα πόντου·
τὸν δ' ἄχος αἰνὸν ἔτυψεν, ἐπεὶ πάρος οὐκέτ' ἰοῦσαν
ἔδρακεν, ἐξότε πρῶτα λίπεν θάλαμόν τε καὶ εὐνὴν
χωσαμένη Ἀχιλῆος ἀγαυοῦ νηπιάχοντος.
ἡ μὲν γὰρ βροτέας αἰεὶ περὶ σάρκας ἔδαιεν
870 νύκτα διὰ μέσσην φλογμῷ πυρός· ἤματα δ' αὖτε
ἀμβροσίῃ χρίεσκε τέρεν δέμας, ὄφρα πέλοιτο
ἀθάνατος καί οἱ στυγερὸν χροῒ γῆρας ἀλάλκοι.
αὐτὰρ ὅ γ' ἐξ εὐνῆς ἀναπάλμενος εἰσενόησεν
παῖδα φίλον σπαίροντα διὰ φλογός· ἧκε δ' ἀυτὴν
875 σμερδαλέην ἐσιδών, μέγα νήπιος· ἡ δ' ἀίουσα
τὸν μὲν ἄρ' ἁρπάγδην χαμάδις βάλε κεκληγῶτα,
αὐτὴ δὲ πνοιῇ ἰκέλη δέμας, ἠΰτ' ὄνειρος,
βῆ ῥ' ἴμεν ἐκ μεγάροιο θοῶς, καὶ ἐσήλατο πόντον
χωσαμένη· μετὰ δ' οὔ τι παλίσσυτος ἵκετ' ὀπίσσω.
880 τῶ μιν ἀμηχανίη δῆσεν φρένας· ἀλλὰ καὶ ἔμπης
πᾶσαν ἐφημοσύνην Θέτιδος μετέειπεν ἑταίροις.
οἱ δ' ἄρα μεσσηγὺς λῆξαν καὶ ἔπαυσαν ἀέθλους
ἐσσυμένως, δόρπον τε χαμεύνας τ' ἀμφεπένοντο,
τῆς ἔνι δαισάμενοι νύκτ' ἄεσαν, ὡς τὸ πάροιθεν.

shores, but at dawn loose the stern cables of your swift ship, in obedience to Hera, your helper, for on her orders the Nereid maidens are all coming to protect your ship on its way through the rocks called the Wanderers, because that is your destined route. But you must not point out my form to anyone when you see me coming with them, but keep it to yourself, lest you anger me even more than before, when you inconsiderately angered me."

She spoke and then plunged out of sight into the depths of the sea. Terrible sorrow struck him, because he had never again seen her come, since that time she first left his bed chamber, in anger because of noble Achilles, then a baby. For she would always singe his mortal flesh in the flames of a fire in the middle of the night, but then, during the day, would anoint his tender body with ambrosia, to make him immortal and to keep hateful old age from his body. But Peleus leapt from his bed and saw his dear son convulsing in the flames and let out a horrible yell at the sight, great fool that he was! When she heard it, she grabbed the baby and threw him screaming to the ground, and she herself, like a breeze in form, like a dream, went swiftly forth from the palace and leapt into the sea in anger, and thereafter never came back again. That is why helpless dismay fettered his mind. But all the same, he managed to relate all of Thetis' instructions to his comrades. They then dropped what they were doing and immediately ended their games; and they prepared supper and beds on the ground, in which, after eating, they slept through the night as usual.

885 ἦμος δ' ἄκρον ἔβαλλε φαεσφόρος οὐρανὸν Ἠώς,
δὴ τότε λαιψηροῖο κατηλυσίῃ ζεφύροιο
βαῖνον ἐπὶ κληῖδας ἀπὸ χθονός· ἐκ δὲ βυθοῖο
εὐναίας εἷλκον περιγηθέες, ἄλλα τε πάντα
ἄρμενα μηρύοντο κατὰ χρέος· ὕψι δὲ λαῖφος
890 εἴρυσσαν τανύσαντες ἐν ἱμάντεσσι κεραίης.
νῆα δ' εὐκραὴς ἄνεμος φέρεν· αἶψα δὲ νῆσον
καλὴν Ἀνθεμόεσσαν ἐσέδρακον, ἔνθα λίγειαι
Σειρῆνες σίνοντ' Ἀχελωίδες ἡδείῃσιν
θέλγουσαι μολπῇσιν, ὅ τις παρὰ πεῖσμα βάλοιτο.
895 τὰς μὲν ἄρ' εὐειδὴς Ἀχελωίῳ εὐνηθεῖσα
γείνατο Τερψιχόρη, Μουσέων μία· καί ποτε Δηοῦς
θυγατέρ' ἰφθίμην ἀδμῆτ' ἔτι πορσαίνεσκον
ἄμμιγα μελπόμεναι· τότε δ' ἄλλο μὲν οἰωνοῖσιν,
ἄλλο δὲ παρθενικῆς ἐναλίγκιαι ἔσκον ἰδέσθαι.
900 αἰεὶ δ' εὐόρμου δεδοκημέναι ἐκ περιωπῆς
ἦ θαμὰ δὴ πολέων μελιηδέα νόστον ἕλοντο,
τηκεδόνι φθινύθουσαι· ἀπηλεγέως δ' ἄρα καὶ τοῖς
ἵεσαν ἐκ στομάτων ὄπα λείριον. οἱ δ' ἀπὸ νηὸς
ἤδη πείσματ' ἔμελλον ἐπ' ἰόνεσσι βαλέσθαι,
905 εἰ μὴ ἄρ' Οἰάγροιο πάις Θρηίκιος Ὀρφεὺς
Βιστονίην ἐνὶ χερσὶν ἑαῖς φόρμιγγα τανύσσας
κραιπνὸν ἐυτροχάλοιο μέλος κανάχησεν ἀοιδῆς,
ὄφρ' ἄμυδις κλονέοντος ἐπιβρομέωνται ἀκουαὶ
κρεγμῷ· παρθενίην δ' ἐνοπὴν ἐβιήσατο φόρμιγξ.
910 νῆα δ' ὁμοῦ ζέφυρός τε καὶ ἠχῆεν φέρε κῦμα

When light-bringing Dawn was striking the edge of the sky, then, with the coming down[111] of a swift west wind, they left the land and went to their benches. Gladly they hauled the anchor-stones from the depths and wound up all the other lines[112] in due order; they hoisted the sail and pulled it tight on the sheets from the yard-arm. The brisk wind propelled the ship, and soon they spotted the beautiful island of Anthemoessa, where the clear-voiced Sirens, the daughters of Achelous, enchanted anyone who moored there with their sweet songs and destroyed him. Beautiful Terpsichore, one of the Muses, had slept with Achelous and bore them. At one time they looked after Demeter's mighty daughter[113] and played with her while she was still a virgin. By this time, though, they looked partly like birds and partly like maidens. Always on the lookout from their vantage point with its fine harbor, they often indeed robbed many men of their sweet homecoming, wasting them away through languor. And so with no hesitation, for these men as well, they were sending forth the delicate[114] voice from their mouths. Already they were about to cast the cables from their ship onto the beach, had not Thracian Orpheus, Oeagrus' son, strung his Bistonian lyre in his hands and rung out the rapid beat of a lively song, so that at the same time the men's ears might ring with the sound of his strumming, and the lyre overpowered their virgin voices. Both the Zephyr and the resounding waves rising astern bore the ship onward, as the maidens were

[111] I.e. from the upper air.

[112] The stern cables and the rest of the tackle.

[113] Persephone was abducted by Hades while playing with her friends.   [114] Lit. "lily-like."

401

APOLLONIUS RHODIUS

πρυμνόθεν ὀρνύμενον· ταὶ δ᾽ ἄκριτον ἴεσαν αὐδήν.
ἀλλὰ καὶ ὣς Τελέοντος ἐὺς πάις οἶος ἑταίρων
προφθάμενος ξεστοῖο κατὰ ζυγοῦ ἔνθορε πόντῳ
Βούτης, Σειρήνων λιγυρῇ ὀπὶ θυμὸν ἰανθείς·
915 νῆχε δὲ πορφυρέοιο δι᾽ οἴδματος, ὄφρ᾽ ἐπιβαίη,
σχέτλιος· ἦ τέ οἱ αἶψα καταυτόθι νόστον ἀπηύρων,
ἀλλά μιν οἰκτείρασα θεὰ Ἔρυκος μεδέουσα
Κύπρις ἔτ᾽ ἐν δίναις ἀνερέψατο, καί ῥ᾽ ἐσάωσεν
πρόφρων ἀντομένη Λιλυβηίδα ναιέμεν ἄκρην.
920   οἱ δ᾽ ἀχέι σχόμενοι τὰς μὲν λίπον, ἄλλα δ᾽
           ὄπαζον
κύντερα μιξοδίῃσιν ἁλὸς ῥαιστήρια νηῶν.
τῇ μὲν γὰρ Σκύλλης λισσὴ προυφαίνετο πέτρη,
τῇ δ᾽ ἄμοτον βοάασκεν ἀναβλύζουσα Χάρυβδις·
ἄλλοθι δὲ Πλαγκταὶ μεγάλῳ ὑπὸ κύματι πέτραι
925 ῥόχθεον, ἧχι πάροιθεν ἀπέπτυεν αἰθομένη φλὸξ
ἄκρων ἐκ σκοπέλων πυριθαλπέος ὑψόθι πέτρης,
καπνῷ δ᾽ ἀχλυόεις αἰθὴρ πέλεν, οὐδέ κεν αὐγὰς
ἔδρακες ἠελίοιο. τότ᾽ αὖ λήξαντος ἀπ᾽ ἔργων
Ἡφαίστου θερμὴν ἔτι κήκιε πόντος ἀυτμήν.
930 ἔνθα σφιν κοῦραι Νηρηίδες ἄλλοθεν ἄλλαι
ἤντεον· ἡ δ᾽ ὄπιθεν πτέρυγος θίγε πηδαλίοιο
δῖα Θέτις, Πλαγκτῇσιν ἐνὶ σπιλάδεσσιν ἔρυσθαι.
ὡς δ᾽ ὁπόταν δελφῖνες ὑπὲξ ἁλὸς εὐδιόωντες
σπερχομένην ἀγεληδὸν ἑλίσσωνται περὶ νῆα,

932 ἔρυσθαι Fränkel (cf. 1.401): ἐρύσσαι Ω

402

sending forth their indistinct[115] speech. But nevertheless, Butes, the noble son of Teleon, alone of the companions had leapt before this[116] from his polished bench into the sea, his heart melted by the clear voices of the Sirens, and he began swimming through the turbulent waves to go ashore, the poor man! And truly there and then they were about to take away his homecoming, but Cypris, the goddess who rules over Eryx, took pity on him and snatched him up while he was still in the swirling sea, and she graciously came and saved him to dwell on cape Lilybaeum.[117]

Seized by anguish, they left the Sirens, but other perils, worse ones destructive to ships, were facing them in the narrow confluences of the sea. For on one side the smooth rock of Scylla was coming into view, while on the other Charybdis was roaring incessantly as she gushed forth. Elsewhere the Wandering rocks were thundering under the mighty swell, where previously[118] blazing flame had spurted out from the peaks above the rock heated by the fire, and the air was clouded with smoke, nor could you have seen the rays of the sun. At this time, although Hephaestus had stopped working, the sea was still emitting hot steam. Here the daughters of Nereus were coming from every direction to meet them, and divine Thetis took hold of the rudder blade from behind to manage it among the Wandering rocks. And as when dolphins in calm weather leap up from the sea and circle a ship in schools as

---

[115] Or *ceaseless*.   [116] I.e. before Orpheus began playing.

[117] Mt. Eryx and cape Lilybaeum are on the western tip of Sicily, where there was a sanctuary of Aphrodite and Butes (Diodorus Siculus 4.83.1–2).

[118] I.e. before Iris got Hephaestus to stop working.

935 ἄλλοτε μὲν προπάροιθεν ὁρώμενοι, ἄλλοτ᾽ ὄπισθεν,
ἄλλοτε παρβολάδην, ναύτῃσι δὲ χάρμα τέτυκται·
ὡς αἱ ὑπεκπροθέουσαι ἐπήτριμοι εἱλίσσοντο
Ἀργῴῃ περὶ νηί, Θέτις δ᾽ ἴθυνε κέλευθον.
καί ῥ᾽ ὅτε δὴ Πλαγκτῇσιν ἐνιχρίμψεσθαι ἔμελλον,
940 αὐτίκ᾽ ἀνασχόμεναι λευκοῖς ἐπὶ γούνασι πέζας,
ὑψοῦ ἐπ᾽ αὐτάων σπιλάδων καὶ κύματος ἀγῆς
ῥώοντ᾽ ἔνθα καὶ ἔνθα διασταδὸν ἀλλήλῃσιν.
τὴν δὲ παρηορίην κόπτεν ῥόος· ἀμφὶ δὲ κῦμα
λάβρον ἀειρόμενον πέτραις ἐπικαχλάζεσκεν·
945 αἱ δ᾽ ὁτὲ μὲν κρημνοῖς ἐναλίγκιαι ἠέρι κῦρον,
ἄλλοτε δὲ βρύχιαι νεάτῳ ὑπὸ πυθμένι πόντου
ἠρήρειν, τὸ δὲ πολλὸν ὑπείρεχεν ἄγριον οἶδμα.
αἱ δ᾽, ὥς τ᾽ ἠμαθόεντος ἐπισχεδὸν αἰγιαλοῖο
παρθενικαὶ δίχα κόλπον ἐπ᾽ ἰξύας εἱλίξασαι
950 σφαίρῃ ἀθύρουσιν περιηγέι· αἱ μὲν ἔπειτα
ἄλλη ὑπ᾽ ἐξ ἄλλης δέχεται καὶ ἐς ἠέρα πέμπει
ὕψι μεταχρονίην, ἡ δ᾽ οὔ ποτε πίλναται οὔδει·
ὡς αἱ νῆα θέουσαν ἀμοιβαδὶς ἄλλοθεν ἄλλη
πέμπε διηερίην ἐπὶ κύμασιν, αἰὲν ἄπωθεν
955 πετράων· περὶ δέ σφιν ἐρευγόμενον ζέεν ὕδωρ.
τὰς δὲ καὶ αὐτὸς ἄναξ κορυφῆς ἔπι λισσάδος ἄκρης
ὀρθὸς ἐπὶ στελεῇ τυπίδος βαρὺν ὦμον ἐρείσας
Ἥφαιστος θηεῖτο, καὶ αἰγλήεντος ὕπερθεν
οὐρανοῦ ἑστηυῖα Διὸς δάμαρ, ἀμφὶ δ᾽ Ἀθήνῃ
960 βάλλε χέρας, τοῖόν μιν ἔχεν δέος εἰσορόωσαν.
ὅσση δ᾽ εἰαρινοῦ μηκύνεται ἤματος αἶσα,

it speeds along, sometimes showing up in front, sometimes behind, sometimes alongside, and joy comes to the sailors—thus the Nereids darted up in ranks before them and circled the Argo, while Thetis steered the course. And then, when they were about to collide with the Wandering rocks, the Nereids immediately lifted the hems of their garments above their white knees and rushed atop the very rocks and breaking surf, forming lines on either side. The current was rocking the ship from side to side, and all around the violent waves were rising and crashing against the rocks, which sometimes towered to the sky like cliffs, but at other times remained submerged in the deepest depths of the sea, and the raging swell covered them in floods.[119] And like girls by a sandy beach, who roll the folds of their garments to their waists and separate[120] to play with a round ball, and then one catches it from another and sends it high in the air, and it never touches the ground— thus the Nereids took turns sending the speeding ship from one to another through the air over the waves, always clear of the rocks, and all around them the water gushed and seethed. Lord Hephaestus himself, standing on the very top of a sheer rock as he leaned his broad shoulder on the handle of his hammer, watched them, and Zeus' wife, standing above the bright heaven, watched and kept throwing her arms around Athena, such was the fear that gripped her as she looked on. And as long as the portion of

---

[119] Unlike the Cyanean rocks that clash together, the Wandering rocks suddenly emerge from the depths so that ships crash into them.

[120] Some take δίχα with εἰλίξασαι, roll their garments out of their way.

τοσσάτιον μογέεσκον ἐπὶ χρόνον, ὀχλίζουσαι
νῆα διὲκ πέτρας πολυηχέας. οἱ δ᾽ ἀνέμοιο
αὖτις ἐπαυρόμενοι προτέρω θέον· ὦκα δ᾽ ἄμειβον
965 Θρινακίης λειμῶνα, βοῶν τροφὸν Ἠελίοιο.
ἔνθ᾽ αἱ μὲν κατὰ βένθος ἀλίγκιαι αἰθυίῃσιν
δῦνον, ἐπεί ῥ᾽ ἀλόχοιο Διὸς πόρσυνον ἐφετμάς·
τοὺς δ᾽ ἄμυδις βληχῇ τε δι᾽ ἠέρος ἵκετο μήλων,
μυκηθμός τε βοῶν αὐτοσχεδὸν οὔατ᾽ ἔβαλλεν.
970 καὶ τὰ μὲν ἑρσήεντα κατὰ δρία ποιμαίνεσκεν
ὁπλοτέρη Φαέθουσα θυγατρῶν Ἠελίοιο,
ἀργύρεον χαῖον παλάμῃ ἔνι πηχύνουσα·
Λαμπετίη δ᾽ ἐπὶ βουσὶν ὀρειχάλκοιο φαεινοῦ
πάλλεν ὀπηδεύουσα καλαύροπα. τὰς δὲ καὶ αὐτοὶ
975 βοσκομένας ποταμοῖο παρ᾽ ὕδασιν εἰσορόωντο
ἂμ πεδίον καὶ ἕλος λειμώνιον· οὐδέ τις ἦεν
κυανέη μετὰ τῇσι δέμας, πᾶσαι δὲ γάλακτι
εἰδόμεναι χρυσέοισι κεράεσσι κυδιάασκον.
καὶ μὲν τὰς παράμειβον ἐπ᾽ ἤματι· νυκτὶ δ᾽ ἰούσῃ
980 πεῖρον ἁλὸς μέγα λαῖτμα κεχαρμένοι, ὄφρα καὶ
    αὖτις
Ἠὼς ἠριγενὴς φέγγος βάλε νισσομένοισιν.

ἔστι δέ τις πορθμοῖο παροιτέρη Ἰονίοιο
ἀμφιλαφὴς πίειρα Κεραυνίη εἰν ἁλὶ νῆσος,
ᾗ ὕπο δὴ κεῖσθαι δρέπανον φάτις—ἵλατε Μοῦσαι,

---

121 Spring days were the longest (*Odyssey* 18.367). The jour-
ney through the rocks apparently lasted only as long as the added
hours of daylight in springtime, not the entire length of a spring

a spring day is lengthened,[121] for that long a time they toiled, heaving the ship out through the resounding rocks. Then the heroes, benefiting once again from the wind, sped onward and soon passed the meadow of Thrinacia, where Helius' cattle graze. Then the Nereids plunged into the depths like diving birds, for they had carried out the orders of Zeus' wife. But to the heroes came the bleating of sheep through the air, and simultaneously from nearby the lowing of cattle struck their ears. Phaethusa, the youngest of Helius' daughters, was shepherding the sheep in the dewy meadows, holding in her hand a silver crook, while Lampetia, in charge of the cattle, wielded a staff of shiny oreichalcum[122] as she followed behind them. The heroes could see for themselves the cows grazing by the waters of the river, throughout the plain and marshy meadow. Not one among them had a dark hide, but all were as white as milk and gloried in their golden horns. They passed by these cows during the day, and when night came they set out across the deep sea in high spirits, until early-rising Dawn once again cast her light on the travelers.

There is a fertile, expansive island[123] at the entrance of the Ionian strait in the Ceraunian sea, under which is said to lie the sickle—forgive me, Muses, not willingly do I

day (schol.), which would not fit the chronology of sunrise at 885 and night at 979.

[122] A fabulous metal or alloy like gold.

[123] Corcyra, modern Corfu, often identified with the land of the Phaeacians, which Homer calls Scheria. Its curved shape accounts for the alternate name Drepane ("sickle") and its association with Cronus' castration of Uranus (cf. Hesiod, *Theogony* 176–182).

985 οὐκ ἐθέλων ἐνέπω προτέρων ἔπος—ᾧ ἀπὸ πατρὸς
     μήδεα νηλειῶς ἔταμε Κρόνος· οἱ δέ ἑ Δηοῦς
     κλείουσι χθονίης καλαμητόμον ἔμμεναι ἅρπην·
     Δηὼ γὰρ κείνη ἐνὶ δή ποτε νάσσατο γαίῃ,
     Τιτῆνας δ᾽ ἔδαε στάχυν ὄμπνιον ἀμήσασθαι,
990 Μάκριδα φιλαμένη. Δρεπάνη τόθεν ἐκλήισται
     οὔνομα Φαιήκων ἱερὴ τροφός· ὡς δὲ καὶ αὐτοὶ
     αἵματος Οὐρανίοιο γένος Φαίηκες ἔασιν.
     τοὺς Ἀργὼ πολέεσσιν ἐνισχομένη καμάτοισιν
     Θρινακίης αὔρης ἵκετ᾽ ἐξ ἁλός. οἱ δ᾽ ἀγανῇσιν
995 Ἀλκίνοος λαοί τε θυηπολίῃσιν ἰόντας
     δειδέχατ᾽ ἀσπασίως, ἐπὶ δέ σφισι καγχαλάασκεν
     πᾶσα πόλις· φαίης κεν ἑοῖς ἐπὶ παισὶ γάνυσθαι.
     καὶ δ᾽ αὐτοὶ ἥρωες ἀνὰ πληθὺν κεχάροντο,
     τῷ ἴκελοι, οἷόν τε μεσαιτάτῃ ἐμβεβαῶτες
1000 Αἱμονίῃ. μέλλον δὲ βοῇ ἔπι θωρήξεσθαι·
     ὧδε μάλ᾽ ἀγχίμολον στρατὸς ἄσπετος ἐξεφαάνθη
     Κόλχων, οἳ Πόντοιο κατὰ στόμα καὶ διὰ πέτρας
     Κυανέας μαστῆρες ἀριστήων ἐπέρησαν.
     Μήδειαν δ᾽ ἔξαιτον ἑοῦ ἐς πατρὸς ἄγεσθαι
1005 ἵεντ᾽ ἀπροφάτως, ἠὲ στονόεσσαν αὐτὴν
     νωμήσειν χαλεπῇσιν ὁμόκλεον ἀτροπίῃσιν

1000 ἔπι Hölzlin: ἔνι Ω

---

124 The adjective χθόνιος can mean "of the underworld" (and
Demeter has strong underworld associations) or "indigenous, na-
tive, local."

repeat my predecessors' words—with which Cronus ruth-
lessly cut off his father's genitals. Others, however, say
it is the reaping scythe of indigenous[124] Demeter. For
Demeter once lived in that land and taught the Titans how
to harvest the bountiful grain, out of devotion to Macris.[125]
Since then the divine nurse[126] of the Phaeacians has been
called by the name Drepane, and thus the Phaeacians
themselves are descended from Uranus' blood.[127] To
them, after being held back by many hardships,[128] the Argo
came, aided by the winds, from the Thrinacian sea.
Alcinous and his people gladly welcomed the travelers
with sacrifices of thanksgiving, and the whole city was jubi-
lant over them—you would think they were exulting over
their own sons. And the heroes themselves rejoiced amidst
the throng, as if they had set foot in the very center of
Haemonia. But they were soon to arm themselves for com-
bat—so very close at hand appeared the immense army of
those Colchians who had passed through the mouth of the
Black Sea and between the Cyanean rocks in search of the
heroes.[129] They were determined to take Medea as their
own[130] to her father's home without discussion, or else they
were threatening to wage a devastating battle with severe

[125] Dionysus' nurse in Euboea, who fled to Drepane; cf. 4.540
and 1131–1140. The island was originally called Macris (schol.).

[126] I.e. the island.

[127] Which dripped onto the island when he was castrated
(schol.).

[128] A reference to the long detour which began at 4.552.

[129] This contingent was last mentioned at 4.303–304.

[130] The meaning of ἔξαιτον ("choice") is in doubt. Following
Vian, I take it as related to ἐξαιρέομαι, "claim as one's own."

αὖθί τε καὶ μετέπειτα σὺν Αἰήταο κελεύθῳ.
ἀλλά σφεας κατέρυκεν ἐπειγομένους πολέμοιο
κρείων Ἀλκίνοος· λελίητο γὰρ ἀμφοτέροισιν
1010 δηιοτῆτος ἄνευθεν ὑπέρβια νείκεα λῦσαι.
    κούρη δ᾽ οὐλομένῳ ὑπὸ δείματι πολλὰ μὲν
        αὐτοὺς
Αἰσονίδεω ἑτάρους μειλίσσετο, πολλὰ δὲ χερσὶν
Ἀρήτης γούνων ἀλόχου θίγεν Ἀλκινόοιο·
    "γουνοῦμαι, βασίλεια· σὺ δ᾽ ἵλαθι, μηδέ με
        Κόλχοις
1015 ἐκδώῃς ᾧ πατρὶ κομιζέμεν, εἴ νυ καὶ αὐτὴ
ἀνθρώπων γενεῆς μία φέρβεαι, οἷσιν ἐς ἄτην
ὠκύτατος κούφῃσι θέει νόος ἀμπλακίῃσιν,
ὡς ἐμοὶ ἐκ πυκιναὶ ἔπεσον φρένες, οὐ μὲν ἕκητι
μαργοσύνης. ἴστω ἱερὸν φάος Ἠελίοιο,
1020 ἴστω νυκτιπόλου Περσηίδος ὄργια κούρης,
μὴ μὲν ἐγὼν ἐθέλουσα σὺν ἀνδράσιν ἀλλοδαποῖσιν
κεῖθεν ἀφωρμήθην· στυγερὸν δέ με τάρβος ἔπεισεν
τῆσδε φυγῆς μνήσασθαι, ὅτ᾽ ἤλιτον, οὐδέ τις ἄλλη
μῆτις ἔην. ἔτι μοι μίτρη μένει, ὡς ἐνὶ πατρὸς
1025 δώμασιν, ἄχραντος καὶ ἀκήρατος. ἀλλ᾽ ἐλέαιρε,
πότνα, τεόν τε πόσιν μειλίσσεο· σοὶ δ᾽ ὀπάσειαν
ἀθάνατοι βίοτόν τε τελεσφόρον ἀγλαΐην τε
καὶ παῖδας καὶ κῦδος ἀπορθήτοιο πόληος."
    τοῖα μὲν Ἀρήτην γουνάζετο δάκρυ χέουσα·
1030 τοῖα δ᾽ ἀριστήων ἐναμοιβαδὶς ἄνδρα ἕκαστον·
    "ὑμέων, ὦ πέρι δὴ μέγα φέρτατοι, ἀμφί τ᾽
        ἀέθλοις

cruelty, both on the spot and later together with Aeetes' expedition.[131] But King Alcinous restrained them, in spite of their eagerness for war, because he was determined to resolve the violent quarrel for both parties without a battle.

But in a deathly panic, the girl pleaded again and again with Jason's very comrades; again and again she touched with her hands the knees of Arete, the wife of Alcinous:

"I implore you, O queen, be merciful and do not hand me over to the Colchians to take to my father, if indeed you yourself are also one of the race of mortals, whose minds rush headlong to disaster because of slight mistakes, just as my good judgment deserted me—but certainly not because of lust. Let my witness be the holy light of Helius, let my witness be the rites of Perses' night-wandering daughter,[132] not willingly did I leave that place[133] with foreign men, but horrible fear persuaded me to think of this escape, once I went wrong and had no other recourse. The belt of my virginity remains just as it was in my father's house, undefiled and untouched. Take pity on me, my lady, and win over your husband. May the immortals grant you a fulfilled life and fame and children and the glory of a city never sacked."

With those words, shedding tears, she implored Arete; and with these words she implored each man in turn among the heroes:

"It is on your account, O men of far greatest might, and

---

[131] It is not clear whether the Colchians believe that Aeetes will lead a further expedition or are referring to the failed one led by Apsyrtus.

[132] Hecate.

[133] Aea.

οὕνεκεν ὑμετέροισιν ἀτύζομαι· ἧς ἰότητι
ταύρους τ' ἐζεύξασθε, καὶ ἐκ θέρος οὐλοὸν ἀνδρῶν
κείρατε γηγενέων, ἧς εἵνεκεν Αἱμονίηνδε
1035 χρύσεον αὐτίκα κῶας ἀνάξετε νοστήσαντες.
ἥδ' ἐγώ, ἣ πάτρην τε καὶ οὓς ὤλεσσα τοκῆας,
ἣ δόμον, ἣ σύμπασαν ἐυφροσύνην βιότοιο,
ὕμμι δὲ καὶ πάτρην καὶ δώματα ναιέμεν αὖτις
ἤνυσα, καὶ γλυκεροῖσιν ἔτ' εἰσόψεσθε τοκῆας
1040 ὄμμασιν· αὐτὰρ ἐμοὶ ἀπὸ δὴ βαρὺς εἵλετο δαίμων
ἀγλαΐας, στυγερὴ δὲ σὺν ὀθνείοις ἀλάλημαι.
δείσατε συνθεσίας τε καὶ ὅρκια, δείσατ' Ἐρινὺν
Ἱκεσίην νέμεσίν τε θεῶν, εἰς χεῖρας ἰοῦσαν
Αἰήτεω λώβῃ πολυπήμονι δῃωθῆναι.
1045 οὐ νηούς, οὐ πύργον ἐπίρροθον, οὐκ ἀλεωρὴν
ἄλλην, οἰόθι δὲ προτιβάλλομαι ὑμέας αὐτούς.
σχέτλιοι ἀτροπίης καὶ ἀνηλέες, οὐδ' ἐνὶ θυμῷ
αἰδεῖσθε ξείνης μ' ἐπὶ γούνασι χεῖρας ἀνάσσης
δερκόμενοι τείνουσαν ἀμήχανον· ἀλλά κε πᾶσιν,
1050 κῶας ἑλεῖν μεμαῶτες, ἐμείξατε δούρατα Κόλχοις
αὐτῷ τ' Αἰήτῃ ὑπερήνορι· νῦν δὲ λάθεσθε
ἠνορέης, ὅτε μοῦνοι ἀποτμηγέντες ἔασιν."
    ὣς φάτο λισσομένη· τῶν δ' ὅν τινα γουνάζοιτο,
ὅς μιν θαρσύνεσκεν ἐρητύων ἀχέουσαν.
1055 σεῖον δ' ἐγχείας εὐήκεας ἐν παλάμῃσιν
φάσγανά τ' ἐκ κολεῶν, οὐδὲ σχήσεσθαι ἀρωγῆς
ἔννεπον, εἴ κε δίκης ἀλιτήμονος ἀντιάσειεν.

1057 ἀντιάσειεν ω: ἀντιάσειαν m

because of your trials that I am desperate—I, with whose help you yoked the oxen and reaped the deadly harvest of earthborn men; I, thanks to whom you will presently return to Haemonia and take back the golden fleece. And here am I, who lost my country and parents, my home, and all the joy of life, whereas I made it possible for you to live again in your country and homes, and you will yet behold your parents with joyful eyes. But a cruel fortune has indeed taken from me these delights, and I am detested as I wander with strangers. Beware your agreements and oaths, beware the Fury of suppliants and the resentment of the gods, if I fall into Aeetes' hands and am put to death with outrageous torment. I have for my defense no temples, no protective tower, no other refuge, but you alone. You are heartless in your cruelty and men without pity, and you have no shame in your hearts to see me stretching my hands to the knees of a foreign queen in helplessness. Yet, when you were eager to gain the fleece, you would have matched spears with all the Colchians and haughty Aeetes himself, but now you have forgotten your courage, although these men are but a single detachment."

Thus she spoke and pleaded, and every man whom she implored tried to reassure her and to assuage her grief. They brandished their sharp-pointed spears in their hands and their swords drawn from their sheaths, and declared that they would not withhold their assistance if she[134] should meet with an unrighteous judgment. And over the

[134] Or, reading ἀντιάσειαν, *they.*

στρευγομένοις δ' ἀν' ὅμιλον ἐπήλυθεν εὐνήτειρα
νὺξ ἔργων ἄνδρεσσι, κατευκήλησε δὲ πᾶσαν
1060 γαῖαν ὁμῶς. τὴν δ' οὔ τι μίννυνθά περ εὔνασεν
ὕπνος,
ἀλλά οἱ ἐν στέρνοις ἀχέων εἰλίσσετο θυμός,
οἷον ὅτε κλωστῆρα γυνὴ ταλαεργὸς ἑλίσσει
ἐννυχίη, τῇ δ' ἀμφὶ κινύρεται ὀρφανὰ τέκνα
χηροσύνῃ πόσιος· σταλάει δ' ὑπὸ δάκρυ παρειὰς
1065 μνωομένης, οἵη μιν ἐπισμυγερὴ λάβεν αἶσα·
ὣς τῆς ἰκμαίνοντο παρηίδες, ἐν δέ οἱ ἦτορ
ὀξείῃς εἰλεῖτο πεπαρμένον ἀμφ' ὀδύνῃσιν.
   τὼ δ' ἔντοσθε δόμοιο κατὰ πτόλιν, ὡς τὸ
      πάροιθεν,
κρείων Ἀλκίνοος πολυπότνιά τ' Ἀλκινόοιο
1070 Ἀρήτη ἄλοχος κούρης πέρι μητιάασκον
οἷσιν ἐνὶ λεχέεσσι διὰ κνέφας· οἷα δ' ἀκοίτην
κουρίδιον θαλεροῖσι δάμαρ προσπτύσσετο μύθοις·
   "ναὶ φίλος, εἰ δ' ἄγε μοι πολυκηδέα ῥύεο
      Κόλχων
παρθενικήν, Μινύαισι φέρων χάριν. ἐγγύθι δ'
      Ἄργος
1075 ἡμετέρης νήσοιο καὶ ἀνέρες Αἱμονιῆες·
Αἰήτης δ' οὔτ' ἄρ ναίει σχεδόν, οὐδέ τι ἴδμεν
Αἰήτην, ἀλλ' οἷον ἀκούομεν. ἥδε δὲ κούρη
αἰνοπαθὴς κατά μοι νόον ἔκλασεν ἀντιόωσα·
μή μιν, ἄναξ, Κόλχοισι πόροις ἐς πατρὸς ἄγεσθαι.
1080 ἀάσθη, ὅτε πρῶτα βοῶν θελκτήρια δῶκεν

weary men throughout the crew[135] came night, giver of rest from labors, and quieted all the earth alike. But as for her, sleep gave her not a moment of rest, but the heart in her breast whirled in anguish, as when a poor working woman whirls her spindle at night, and around her wail her orphaned children, for she is bereft of a husband, and tears drip down her cheeks, as she thinks of[136] what a sad lot has befallen her—similarly were Medea's cheeks wet, and her heart within her kept turning as it was pierced with sharp pains.

Now within the palace in the city, as before, King Alcinous and Alcinous' much-revered wife Arete were making plans about the girl in their bed during the night; and as a wife speaking to her wedded husband, she addressed him with affectionate words:

"Yes, my dear, come and please save this unfortunate girl from the Colchians and do the Minyans a favor. Argos[137] and the men of Haemonia are near our island, whereas Aeetes does not live nearby, nor do we know Aeetes at all, but only hear of him. This girl, though, who has suffered so terribly, has broken my heart[138] with her pleas. Do not, my lord, hand her over to the Colchians to take to her father's home. She made a blunder when she first gave the stranger the drugs to charm the oxen. Then

---

[135] Or, reading στρευγομένης, *as she remained in anguish among the crew.*   [136] Or, reading μυρομένης, *weeps over.*
[137] Here, as often in Homer, Greece proper.
[138] Lit. "mind."

1058 στρευγομένοις Ω: στρευγομένης Wifstrand
1065 μνωομένης w: μυρομένης m

φάρμακά οἱ· σχεδόθεν δὲ κακῷ κακόν, οἷά τε πολλὰ
ῥέζομεν ἀμπλακίῃσιν, ἀκειομένη, ὑπάλυξεν
πατρὸς ὑπερφιάλοιο βαρὺν χόλον. αὐτὰρ Ἰήσων,
ὡς ἄϊω, μεγάλοισιν ἐνίσχεται ἐξ ἕθεν ὅρκοις,
1085 κουριδίην θήσεσθαι ἐνὶ μεγάροισιν ἄκοιτιν.
τῶ, φίλε, μήτ᾽ οὖν αὐτὸν ἑκὼν ἐπίορκον ὀμόσσαι
θείῃς Αἰσονίδην, μήτ᾽ ἄσχετα σεῖο ἕκητι
παῖδα πατὴρ θυμῷ κεκοτηότι δηλήσαιτο.
λίην γὰρ δύσζηλοι ἑαῖς ἐπὶ παισὶ τοκῆες·
1090 οἷα μὲν Ἀντιόπην εὐώπιδα μήσατο Νυκτεύς,
οἷα δὲ καὶ Δανάη πόντῳ ἔνι πήματ᾽ ἀνέτλη
πατρὸς ἀτασθαλίῃσι· νέον γε μέν, οὐδ᾽ ἀποτηλοῦ,
ὑβριστὴς Ἔχετος γλήναις ἔνι χάλκεα κέντρα
πῆξε θυγατρὸς ἑῆς, στονόεντι δὲ κάρφεται οἴτῳ
1095 ὀρφναίῃ ἐνὶ χαλκὸν ἀλετρεύουσα καλιῇ."
ὣς ἔφατ᾽ ἀντομένη· τοῦ δὲ φρένες ἰαίνοντο
ἧς ἀλόχου μύθοισιν, ἔπος δ᾽ ἐπὶ τοῖον ἔειπεν·
"Ἀρήτη, καί κεν σὺν τεύχεσιν ἐξελάσαιμι
Κόλχους, ἡρώεσσι φέρων χάριν, εἵνεκα κούρης·
1100 ἀλλὰ Διὸς δείδοικα δίκην ἰθεῖαν ἀτίσσαι·
οὐδὲ μὲν Αἰήτην ἀθεριζέμεν, ὡς ἀγορεύεις,
λώιον· οὐ γάρ τις βασιλεύτερος Αἰήταο,
καί κ᾽ ἐθέλων, ἕκαθέν περ, ἐφ᾽ Ἑλλάδι νεῖκος
ἄγοιτο.

1086 αὐτὸν Ω: αὐτὸς Brunck
1103 ἄγοιτο Ω: ἄροιτο E

right away, seeking to cure one wrong with another, as we often do through our mistakes, she fled from her overbearing father's terrible wrath. But Jason, as I am told, has been bound ever since then with mighty oaths to make her his wedded wife in his palace. So, dear, do not then willingly make Jason himself go back on his oath, nor, because you allowed it, let a father in spiteful anger inflict intolerable harm on his daughter. For fathers are exceedingly jealous of their own daughters. Just consider what Nycteus devised for beautiful Antiope,[139] what tribulations Danae endured on the sea through her father's wickedness;[140] and recently, not far away, savage Echetus[141] stuck bronze pins in his daughter's eyeballs, and she wastes away from a lamentable fate as she grinds down bronze in a dark granary."[142]

Thus she spoke and pleaded, and his mind was softened by his wife's arguments, and he replied with these words:

"Arete, I could, by force of arms, drive off the Colchians and do the heroes a favor on the girl's behalf. But I am afraid of slighting the straight justice of Zeus, nor is it advisable to disregard Aeetes, as you propose. For no one is more kingly than Aeetes, and if he wished, even though he is far away, he might bring strife against Hellas. There-

[139] Pregnant by Zeus with the twins Zethus and Amphion, she fled her father's wrath. At 1.735 she is said to be Asopus' daughter.

[140] Acrisius sealed Danae and her infant Perseus in a chest and set them adrift on the open sea.

[141] A king of Epirus (on the mainland north of Corcyra), notorious in the *Odyssey* for mutilating strangers (*Odyssey* 18.84–87).

[142] I.e. he imposed on her the impossible task of grinding grains made of bronze. Her blindness makes the granary dark.

τῷ μ᾽ ἐπέοικε δίκην, ἥ τις μετὰ πᾶσιν ἀρίστη
1105 ἔσσεται ἀνθρώποισι, δικαζέμεν· οὐδέ σε κεύσω.
παρθενικὴν μὲν ἐοῦσαν ἑῷ ἀπὸ πατρὶ κομίσσαι
ἰθύνω· λέκτρον δὲ σὺν ἀνέρι πορσαίνουσαν
οὔ μιν ἑοῦ πόσιος νοσφίσσομαι, οὐδὲ γενέθλην,
εἴ τιν᾽ ὑπὸ σπλάγχνοισι φέρει, δηίοισιν ὀπάσσω."
1110   ὣς ἄρ᾽ ἔφη· καὶ τὸν μὲν ἐπισχεδὸν εὔνασεν
ὕπνος.
ἡ δ᾽ ἔπος ἐν θυμῷ πυκινὸν βάλετ᾽· αὐτίκα δ᾽ ὦρτο
ἐκ λεχέων ἀνὰ δῶμα· συνήιξαν δὲ γυναῖκες
ἀμφίπολοι, δέσποιναν ἑὴν μέτα ποιπνύουσαι.
σῖγα δ᾽ ἑὸν κήρυκα καλεσσαμένη προσέειπεν
1115 ᾗσιν ἐπιφροσύνῃσιν ἐποτρυνέουσα μιγῆναι
Αἰσονίδην κούρῃ, μηδ᾽ Ἀλκίνοον βασιλῆα
λίσσεσθαι· τὸ γὰρ αὐτὸς ἰὼν Κόλχοισι δικάσσει,
παρθενικὴν μὲν ἐοῦσαν ἑοῦ ποτὶ δώματα πατρὸς
ἐκδώσειν, λέκτρον δὲ σὺν ἀνέρι πορσαίνουσαν
1120 οὐκέτι κουριδίης μιν ἀποτμήξειν φιλότητος.
   ὣς ἄρ᾽ ἔφη· τὸν δ᾽ αἶψα πόδες φέρον ἐκ
μεγάροιο,
ὥς κεν Ἰήσονι μῦθον ἐναίσιμον ἀγγείλειεν
Ἀρήτης βουλάς τε θεουδέος Ἀλκινόοιο.
τοὺς δ᾽ εὗρεν παρὰ νηὶ σὺν ἔντεσιν ἐγρήσσοντας
1125 Ὑλλικῷ ἐν λιμένι σχεδὸν ἄστεος· ἐκ δ᾽ ἄρα πᾶσαν
πέφραδεν ἀγγελίην· γήθησε δὲ θυμὸς ἑκάστου
ἡρώων, μάλα γάρ σφιν ἑαδότα μῦθον ἔειπεν.
   αὐτίκα δὲ κρητῆρα κερασσάμενοι μακάρεσσιν,
ἡ θέμις, εὐαγέως τ᾽ ἐπιβώμια μῆλ᾽ ἐρύσαντες,

fore, it is proper for me to render a judgment that will be best in all men's eyes, and I will not hide it from you. If she is a virgin, I direct them to return her to her father, but if she is sharing a bed with a man, I will not separate her from her husband, nor will I hand over to enemies any offspring she bears in her womb."

Thus he spoke, and at once sleep put him to rest. But she put his wise words in her heart and immediately rose from the bed and went through the house. Her serving women gathered round, bustling after their mistress. She quietly summoned her herald and spoke to him, prudently urging Jason to have intercourse with the girl and not to petition King Alcinous. For, she said, he himself will go deliver his verdict to the Colchians, that if she is a virgin, he will hand her over to go back to her father's home, but that if she is sharing a bed with a man, he will not henceforth separate her from married love.

Thus she spoke, and his feet carried him at once from the palace, to report to Jason Arete's auspicious message and the intentions of god-fearing Alcinous. He found them keeping armed watch by the ship in the harbor of Hyllus near the city and announced the entire message. The heart of each hero rejoiced, because the words he spoke pleased them greatly.

Immediately they mixed a crater of wine for the blessed gods, as is proper, and after reverently leading sheep to the

---

1129 τ᾽ Π³⁰: om. Ω

1130 αὐτονυχὶ κούρη θαλαμήιον ἔντυον εὐνὴν
ἄντρῳ ἐν ἠγαθέῳ, τόθι δή ποτε Μάκρις ἔναιεν,
κούρη Ἀρισταίοιο περίφρονος, ὅς ῥα μελισσέων
ἔργα πολυκμήτοιό τ' ἀνεύρατο πῖαρ ἐλαίης.
κείνη δὴ πάμπρωτα Διὸς Νυσήιον υἷα
1135 Εὐβοίης ἔντοσθεν Ἀβαντίδος ᾧ ἐνὶ κόλπῳ
δέξατο, καὶ μέλιτι ξηρὸν περὶ χεῖλος ἔδευσεν,
εὖτέ μιν Ἑρμείης φέρεν ἐκ πυρός· ἔδρακε δ' Ἥρη,
καί ἑ χολωσαμένη πάσης ἐξήλασε νήσου·
ἡ δ' ἄρα Φαιήκων ἱερῷ ἐνὶ τηλόθεν ἄντρῳ
1140 νάσσατο, καὶ πόρεν ὄλβον ἀθέσφατον ἐνναέτῃσιν.
ἔνθα τότ' ἐστόρεσαν λέκτρον μέγα· τοῖο δ' ὕπερθεν
χρύσεον αἰγλῆεν κῶας βάλον, ὄφρα πέλοιτο
τιμήεις τε γάμος καὶ ἀοίδιμος. ἄνθεα δέ σφιν
νύμφαι ἀμεργόμεναι λευκοῖς ἐνὶ ποικίλα κόλποις
1145 ἐσφόρεον· πάσας δὲ πυρὸς ὣς ἄμφεπεν αἴγλη,
τοῖον ἀπὸ χρυσέων θυσάνων ἀμαρύσσετο φέγγος.
δαῖε δ' ἐν ὀφθαλμοῖς γλυκερὸν πόθον· ἴσχε δ'
        ἑκάστην
αἰδὼς ἱεμένην περ ὅμως ἐπὶ χεῖρα βαλέσθαι.
αἱ μέν τ' Αἰγαίου ποταμοῦ καλέοντο θύγατρες,
1150 αἱ δ' ὄρεος κορυφὰς Μελιτηίου ἀμφενέμοντο,
αἱ δ' ἔσαν ἐκ πεδίων ἀλσηίδες· ὦρσε γὰρ αὐτὴ
Ἥρη Ζηνὸς ἄκοιτις, Ἰήσονα κυδαίνουσα.
κεῖνο καὶ εἰσέτι νῦν ἱερὸν κληίζεται ἄντρον
Μηδείης, ὅθι τούς γε σὺν ἀλλήλοισιν ἔμειξαν

1132 πε[ρίφρονος Π30L: μελίφρονος L¹AωE

420

altar, on that very night they spread a bridal bed for the girl in the sacred cave where Macris once lived, the daughter of clever[143] Aristaeus, who discovered the keeping of bees and the oil of the olive, gained with much labor. She was the very first to take Zeus' Nysean son[144] to her bosom in Abantian Euboea, and moistened his parched lips with honey, when Hermes brought him out of the fire.[145] But Hera saw it and angrily drove her from the entire island. She then settled far away in the holy cave of the Phaeacians and bestowed immense prosperity on the inhabitants. Here, then, they spread the great bed and over it threw the gleaming golden fleece, so that the wedding might be honored and worthy of song. And for them the nymphs gathered many-colored flowers, which they brought in their white bosoms. Around them all flickered a radiance as of fire—such was the gleam that sparkled from the golden tufts of wool. The fleece kindled in their eyes a sweet longing, but reverence restrained each one, in spite of her desire, from putting her hand on it. Some were called daughters of the Aegaeus river, others haunted the peaks of mount Melite, and still others were woodland nymphs from the plains. For Hera herself, Zeus' wife, urged them to come in Jason's honor. To this day that holy cave is called Medea's cave, where the nymphs spread the

---

[143] Or, reading μελίφρονος, *Aristaeus, lord of honey*, or *sweet-tempered Aristaeus*.

[144] Dionysus.

[145] When pregnant with Dionysus, Semele was consumed by Zeus' lightning.

1155 τεινάμεναι ἑανοὺς εὐώδεας· οἱ δ᾽ ἐνὶ χερσὶν
δούρατα νωμήσαντες ἀρήια, μὴ πρὶν ἐς ἀλκὴν
δυσμενέων ἀίδηλος ἐπιβρίσειεν ὅμιλος,
κράατα δ᾽ εὐφύλλοις ἐστεμμένοι ἀκρεμόνεσσιν,
ἐμμελέως Ὀρφῆος ὑπαὶ λίγα φορμίζοντος
1160 νυμφιδίαις ὑμέναιον ἐπὶ προμολῆσιν ἄειδον.
οὐ μὲν ἐν Ἀλκινόοιο γάμον μενέαινε τελέσσαι
ἥρως Αἰσονίδης, μεγάροις δ᾽ ἐνὶ πατρὸς ἑοῖο
νοστήσας ἐς Ἰωλκὸν ὑπότροπος, ὣς δὲ καὶ αὐτὴ
Μήδεια φρονέεσκε· τότ᾽ αὖ χρεὼ ἦγε μιγῆναι.
1165 ἀλλὰ γὰρ οὔ ποτε φῦλα δυηπαθέων ἀνθρώπων
τερπωλῆς ἐπέβημεν ὅλῳ ποδί· σὺν δέ τις αἰεὶ
πικρὴ παρμέμβλωκεν ἐυφροσύνῃσιν ἀνίη.
τῶ καὶ τοὺς γλυκερῇ περ ἰαινομένους φιλότητι
δεῖμ᾽ ἔχεν, εἰ τελέοιτο διάκρισις Ἀλκινόοιο.
1170 Ἠὼς δ᾽ ἀμβροσίοισιν ἀνερχομένη φαέεσσιν
λῦε κελαινὴν νύκτα δι᾽ ἠέρος· αἱ δ᾽ ἐγέλασσαν
ἠιόνες νήσοιο καὶ ἐρσήεσσαι ἄπωθεν
ἀτραπιτοὶ πεδίων· ἐν δὲ θρόος ἔσκεν ἀγυιαῖς·
κίνυντ᾽ ἐνναέται μὲν ἀνὰ πτόλιν, οἱ δ᾽ ἀποτηλοῦ
1175 Κόλχοι Μακριδίης ἐπὶ πείρασι χερνήσοιο.
αὐτίκα δ᾽ Ἀλκίνοος μετεβήσετο συνθεσίῃσιν
ὃν νόον ἐξερέων κούρης ὕπερ· ἐν δ᾽ ὅ γε χειρὶ
σκῆπτρον ἔχεν χρυσοῖο δικασπόλον, ᾧ ὕπο λαοὶ
ἰθείας ἀνὰ ἄστυ διεκρίνοντο θέμιστας.
1180 τῷ δὲ καὶ ἑξείης πολεμήια τεύχεα δύντες
Φαιήκων οἱ ἄριστοι ὁμιλαδὸν ἐστιχόωντο.

422

fragrant linens[146] and joined the couple together. Meanwhile the crew, wielding their battle spears in their hands lest a band of enemies fall upon them with an unforeseen attack before they were ready, wreathed their heads with sprigs of leaves and then, to the bright accompaniment of Orpheus' lyre, tunefully sang the wedding song at the entrance of the bridal chamber. Yet it was not in Alcinous' domain that Jason, Aeson's heroic son, had wanted to celebrate his wedding, but in his father's halls after returning to Iolcus; and Medea herself also had the same intention, but necessity led them to make love at that time. But so it is: we tribes of woeful humans never enter upon enjoyment with a sure foot,[147] but always alongside our happiness marches some bitter pain. Thus, even though they melted in sweet love-making, fear gripped them both, as to whether Alcinous' decision would be carried out.

Rising Dawn was scattering dark night through the sky with her divine beams. The shores of the island smiled, as did the dewy paths far off in the plains, and there was noise in the streets. The citizens were stirring throughout the city, but so too were the Colchians far off on the tip of the peninsula of Macris.[148] Right away, as agreed, Alcinous came forth to announce his resolution concerning the girl. In his hand he held the golden scepter of law, under which the people throughout the city received straight judgments. And in his train, wearing their armor of war, marched the Phaeacian nobles in troops.

[146] Either as bed covers or as curtains.

[147] Lit. "a whole foot," i.e. "wholeheartedly, completely."

[148] Probably located on Corcyra, not on the mainland opposite as one scholium claims.

ἥρωας δὲ γυναῖκες ἀολλέες ἔκτοθι πύργων
βαῖνον ἐποψόμεναι· σὺν δ' ἀνέρες ἀγροιῶται
ἤντεον εἰσαΐοντες, ἐπεὶ νημερτέα βάξιν
1185 Ἥρη ἐπιπροέηκεν. ἄγεν δ' ὁ μὲν ἔκκριτον ἄλλων
ἀρνειὸν μήλων, ὁ δ' ἀεργηλὴν ἔτι πόρτιν·
ἄλλοι δ' ἀμφιφορῆας ἐπισχεδὸν ἵστασαν οἴνου
κίρνασθαι· θυέων δ' ἀποτηλόθι κήκιε λιγνύς.
αἱ δὲ πολυκμήτους ἑανοὺς φέρον, οἷα γυναῖκες,
1190 μείλιά τε χρυσοῖο καὶ ἀλλοίην ἐπὶ τοῖσιν
ἀγλαΐην, οἵην τε νεόζυγες ἐντύνονται.
θάμβευν δ' εἰσορόωσαι ἀριπρεπέων ἡρώων
εἴδεα καὶ μορφάς, ἐν δέ σφισιν Οἰάγροιο
υἱὸν ὑπαὶ φόρμιγγος ἐυκρέκτου καὶ ἀοιδῆς
1195 ταρφέα σιγαλόεντι πέδον κρούοντα πεδίλῳ.
νύμφαι δ' ἄμμιγα πᾶσαι, ὅτε μνήσαιντο γάμοιο,
ἱμερόενθ' ὑμέναιον ἀνήπυον· ἄλλοτε δ' αὖτε
οἰόθεν οἶαι ἄειδον ἑλισσόμεναι περὶ κύκλον,
Ἥρη, σεῖο ἕκητι· σὺ γὰρ καὶ ἐπὶ φρεσὶ θῆκας
1200 Ἀρήτῃ πυκινὸν φάσθαι ἔπος Ἀλκινόοιο.

αὐτὰρ ὅ γ', ὡς τὰ πρῶτα δίκης ἀνὰ πείρατ'
ἔειπεν
ἰθείης, ἤδη δὲ γάμου τέλος ἐκλήιστο,
ἔμπεδον ὣς ἀλέγυνε διαμπερές· οὐδέ ἑ τάρβος
οὐλοὸν οὐδὲ βαρεῖαι ἐπήλυθον Αἰήταο
1205 μήνιες· ἀρρήκτοισι δ' ἐνιζεύξας ἔχεν ὅρκοις.
τῷ καὶ ὅτ' ἠλεμάτως Κόλχοι μάθον ἀντιόωντες,
καί σφεας ἠὲ θέμιστας ἑὰς εἴρυσθαι ἄνωγεν

The women gathered outside the towers to watch the heroes, while men from the country joined them as they heard the news, for Hera had sent forth a true account. One man led a ram selected from all his sheep, and another a heifer not yet put to work. Others stood amphoras of wine nearby for mixing, while the smoke of the offerings billowed far away. The women brought garments made with great labor, as women will, and gifts of gold, and other kinds of adornment as well, of the sort that newly-weds are furnished with. The women marveled as they beheld the beauty and stature of the preeminent heroes, and they marveled at the son of Oeagrus[149] in their midst, as he beat the ground rapidly with his shining sandal to the accompaniment of his beautifully strummed lyre and song. And all the nymphs together, whenever the men sang of marriage, sounded forth the lovely wedding song. But at other times they sang by themselves and danced in a circle, in your honor, Hera, because it was you who put the thought in Arete's mind to communicate Alcinous' wise words.

Now, once he had proclaimed the terms of his straight judgment—and by that time the consummation of their marriage had become well known—he steadfastly kept to his word. Not even deadly fear or Aeetes' grievous rancor affected him, for he had bound both parties with unalterable oaths. Therefore, when the Colchians learned that their pleading was in vain, and when Alcinous ordered

[149] Orpheus.

1195 κρούοντα L^{ac}V^{ac}: κροτέοντα AωE
1196 μνήσαιντο Ω: μνήσαιτο Brunck

ἢ λιμένων γαίης τ᾽ ἀποτηλόθι νῆας ἐέργειν,
δὴ τότε μιν βασιλῆος ἑοῦ τρομέοντες ἐνιπὰς
1210 δέχθαι μειλίξαντο συνήμονας. αὖθι δὲ νήσῳ
δὴν μάλα Φαιήκεσσι μετ᾽ ἀνδράσι ναιετάασκον,
εἰσότε Βακχιάδαι, γενεὴν Ἐφύρηθεν ἐόντες,
ἀνέρες ἐννάσσαντο μετὰ χρόνον, οἱ δὲ περαίην
νῆσον ἔβαν· κεῖθεν δὲ Κεραύνια μέλλον Ἀμάντων
1215 οὔρεα Νεσταίους τε καὶ Ὤρικον εἰσαφικέσθαι.
ἀλλὰ τὰ μὲν στείχοντος ἄδην αἰῶνος ἐτύχθη·
Μοιράων δ᾽ ἔτι κεῖσε θύη ἐπέτεια δέχονται
καὶ Νυμφέων Νομίοιο καθ᾽ ἱερὸν Ἀπόλλωνος
βωμοί, τοὺς Μήδεια καθίσσατο. πολλὰ δ᾽ ἰοῦσιν
1220 Ἀλκίνοος Μινύαις ξεινήια, πολλὰ δ᾽ ὄπασσεν
Ἀρήτη, μετὰ δ᾽ αὖτε δυώδεκα δῶκεν ἕπεσθαι
Μηδείῃ δμωὰς Φαιηκίδας ἐκ μεγάροιο.
    ἤματι δ᾽ ἑβδομάτῳ Δρεπάνην λίπον· ἤλυθε δ᾽
        οὖρος
ἀκραὴς ἠῶθεν ὑπεύδιος· οἱ δ᾽ ἀνέμοιο
1225 πνοιῇ ἐπειγόμενοι προτέρω θέον. ἀλλὰ γὰρ οὔ πω
αἴσιμον ἦν ἐπιβῆναι Ἀχαιίδος ἡρώεσσιν,
ὄφρ᾽ ἔτι καὶ Λιβύης ἐπὶ πείρασιν ὀτλήσειαν.
ἤδη μὲν †ποτὶ† κόλπον ἐπώνυμον Ἀμβρακιήων,
ἤδη Κουρῆτιν ἔλιπον χθόνα πεπταμένοισιν

1214 νῆσον Ω: νήσου Pfeiffer | Ἀμάντων Et. Gen.:
Ἀβάντων Ω
    1224 ὑπεύδιος w: ὑπὲκ Διός m
    1228 ποτὶ Ω: ποθι Merkel: παρὰ Campbell

them to abide by his decrees or else keep their ships far from the harbors of his land, they then begged him to receive them as allies, because they were terrified of their own king's threats. So, for a very long time they lived there on the island with the Phaeacians, until the Bacchiadae, a tribe from Ephyra,[150] eventually settled there, and the Colchians went to an island opposite,[151] whence they would migrate to the Ceraunian mountains of the Amantes and to the Nestaeans and to Oricum. But all that took place after many an age had passed, and yet the altars that Medea set up there in the precinct of Apollo Nomius[152] still receive annual sacrifices to the Fates and the Nymphs.[153] When the Minyans departed, Alcinous gave them many guest-gifts, and Arete did the same; moreover, she gave Medea twelve Phaeacian serving women from her palace to attend her.

On the seventh day they left Drepane. A strong favoring breeze came in the morning under a clear sky,[154] and they were speeding onward, propelled by the gust of wind. But not yet was it destined for the heroes to set foot on Achaean land,[155] until they suffered still more in the far reaches of Libya. Already they had left behind the gulf named for the Ambracians, already with sails spread wide they had passed the land of the Curetes[156] and the line of

---

[150] An old name for Corinth.   [151] Or, reading νῆσον, *to the mainland opposite the island.*   [152] "Of Shepherds."

[153] The Fates were associated with births and marriages and the Nymphs took part in Medea's wedding.

[154] Or, reading ὑπὲκ Διός, *from Zeus.*

[155] A general designation of Greece south of Thessaly.

[156] Acarnania.

1230 λαίφεσι καὶ στεινὰς αὐταῖς σὺν Ἐχινάσι νήσους
ἐξείης, Πέλοπος δὲ νέον κατεφαίνετο γαῖα·
καὶ τότ᾽ ἀναρπάγδην ὀλοὴ βορέαο θύελλα
μεσσηγὺς πέλαγόσδε Λιβυστικὸν ἐννέα πάσας
νύκτας ὁμῶς καὶ τόσσα φέρ᾽ ἤματα, μέχρις ἵκοντο
1235 προπρὸ μάλ᾽ ἔνδοθι Σύρτιν, ἵν᾽ οὐκέτι νόστος
 ὀπίσσω
νηυσὶ πέλει, ὅτε τόν γε βιῷατο κόλπον ἱκέσθαι.
πάντη γὰρ τέναγος, πάντη μνιόεντα βυθοῖο
τάρφεα, κωφῇ δέ σφιν ἐπιβλύει ὕδατος ἄχνη·
ἠερίη δ᾽ ἄμαθος παρακέκλιται, οὐδέ τι κεῖσε
1240 ἑρπετὸν οὐδὲ ποτητὸν ἀείρεται. ἔνθ᾽ ἄρα τούς γε
πλημυρίς—καὶ γάρ τ᾽ ἀναχάζεται ἠπείροιο
ἢ θαμὰ δὴ τόδε χεῦμα, καὶ ἂψ ἐπερεύγεται ἀκτὰς
λάβρον ἐποιχόμενον—μυχάτῃ ἐνέωσε τάχιστα
ἠιόνι, τρόπιος δὲ μάλ᾽ ὕδασι παῦρον ἔλειπτο.
1245 οἱ δ᾽ ἀπὸ νηὸς ὄρουσαν, ἄχος δ᾽ ἕλεν εἰσορόωντας
ἠέρα καὶ μεγάλης νῶτα χθονὸς ἠέρι ἶσα
τηλοῦ ὑπερτείνοντα διηνεκές· οὐδέ τιν᾽ ἀρδμόν,
οὐ πάτον, οὐκ ἀπάνευθε κατηυγάσσαντο βοτήρων
αὔλιον, εὐκήλῳ δὲ κατείχετο πάντα γαλήνῃ.
1250 ἄλλος δ᾽ αὖτ᾽ ἄλλον τετιημένος ἐξερέεινεν·
 "τίς χθὼν εὔχεται ἥδε; πόθι ξυνέωσαν ἄελλαι
ἡμέας; αἴθ᾽ ἔτλημεν, ἀφειδέες οὐλομένοιο
δείματος, αὐτὰ κέλευθα διαμπερὲς ὁρμηθῆναι
πετράων· ἦ τ᾽ ἂν καὶ ὑπὲρ Διὸς αἶσαν ἰοῦσιν

narrow islands along with the Echinades themselves.[157]
The land of Pelops[158] was just coming into view, when at
that moment a deadly blast of the north wind seized them
in mid-course and carried them toward the Libyan sea for
nine whole nights and as many days, until they came far
into Syrtis,[159] where there is no getting back out again for
ships, once they are forced to enter that gulf. For ev-
erywhere are shallows, everywhere thickets of seaweed
from the depths, and over them silently washes the foam of
the water. Sand stretches along to the horizon, and no land
animal or bird travels there. Here it was that a flood tide—
for frequently indeed does this tide recede from the main-
land and then, rushing back again, violently disgorge itself
on the beach—suddenly drove them to the innermost part
of the shore, and very little of their keel was left in the
water. They leapt off the ship, and sorrow gripped them
when they looked at the sky and the expanse of vast land
stretching just like the sky into the distance without a
break. No watering place, no trail, no herdsmen's steading
did they see in the distance, but everything was wrapped in
a dead calm. And in despair one asked another:

"What is this land called? Where have the storm winds
cast us? Would that we had disregarded deadly fear and
dared to speed between the rocks the same way we came.
Truly it would have been better for us, even though going
beyond the decree of Zeus, to have perished in attempting

[157] The chain of small islands off the coast of southwestern
Acarnania.

[158] The Peloponnesus.

[159] The legendary shoals and desert coast of Libya where ships
became stranded.

1255 βέλτερον ἦν μέγα δή τι μενοινώοντας ὀλέσθαι.
νῦν δὲ τί κεν ῥέξαιμεν, ἐρυκόμενοι ἀνέμοισιν
αὖθι μένειν τυτθόν περ ἐπὶ χρόνον; οἷον ἐρήμη
πέζα διωλυγίης ἀναπέπταται ἠπείροιο."
ὣς ἄρ᾽ ἔφη· μετὰ δ᾽ αὐτὸς ἀμηχανίη κακότητος
1260 ἰθυντὴρ Ἀγκαῖος ἀκηχεμένοις ἀγόρευσεν·
"ὠλόμεθ᾽ αἰνότατον δῆθεν μόρον, οὐδ᾽ ὑπάλυξις
ἔστ᾽ ἄτης· πάρα δ᾽ ἄμμι τὰ κύντατα πημανθῆναι
τῇδ᾽ ὑπ᾽ ἐρημαίῃ πεπτηότας, εἰ καὶ ἀῆται
χερσόθεν ἀμπνεύσειαν· ἐπεὶ τεναγώδεα λεύσσω
1265 τῆλε περισκοπέων ἅλα πάντοθεν, ἤλιθα δ᾽ ὕδωρ
ξαινόμενον πολιῇσιν ἐπιτροχάει ψαμάθοισιν.
καί κεν ἐπισμυγερῶς διὰ. δὴ πάλαι ἥδε κεάσθη
νηῦς ἱερὴ χέρσου πολλὸν πρόσω· ἀλλά μιν αὐτὴ
πλημυρὶς ἐκ πόντοιο μεταχρονίην ἐκόμισσεν.
1270 νῦν δ᾽ ἡ μὲν πελαγόσδε μετέσσυται, οἷόθι δ᾽ ἅλμη
ἄπλοος εἰλεῖται, γαίης ὕπερ ὅσσον ἔχουσα.
τοὔνεκ᾽ ἐγὼ πᾶσαν μὲν ἀπ᾽ ἐλπίδα φημὶ κεκόφθαι
ναυτιλίης νόστου τε. δαημοσύνην δέ τις ἄλλος
φαίνοι ἑήν· πάρα γάρ οἱ ἐπ᾽ οἰήκεσσι θαάσσειν
1275 μαιομένῳ κομιδῆς· ἀλλ᾽ οὐ μάλα νόστιμον ἦμαρ
Ζεὺς ἐθέλει καμάτοισιν ἐφ᾽ ἡμετέροισι τελέσσαι."
ὣς φάτο δακρυόεις· σὺν δ᾽ ἔννεπον ἀσχαλόωντι,
ὅσσοι ἔσαν νηῶν δεδαημένοι. ἐν δ᾽ ἄρα πᾶσιν
παχνώθη κραδίη, χύτο δὲ χλόος ἀμφὶ παρειάς.
1280 οἷον δ᾽ ἀψύχοισιν ἐοικότες εἰδώλοισιν

1269 μεταχρονίην Ω: μεταχθονίην recc.

430

some great feat.[160] But now, what should we do, if we are
compelled by the winds to remain here even for a short
time? How desolate is the coast of this vast mainland that
stretches before us!"

Thus each spoke, and among them Ancaeus the helms-
man himself, in helplessness at their plight, addressed the
grieving men:

"We are surely doomed to a most horrible death, for
there is no escape from disaster, and facing us are the most
awful things to suffer, now that we have happened upon
this desert, even if winds should blow from the land. For
when I look into the distance, I see shallow seas every-
where, and the fretted water rolls endlessly over the gray
sand. And long before would this sacred ship have been
shattered miserably far from land, but the flood tide itself
brought it here aloft from the sea. But now the tide is rush-
ing back to the deep sea and only water too shallow for sail-
ing swirls around, barely covering the land. Consequently,
I affirm that all hope of returning home by sea is cut off.
Let someone else display his skill, for he can sit at the tiller
if he is eager to rescue us, but Zeus has no wish whatsoever
to bring about our day of homecoming after these toils
of ours."

Thus he spoke in tears, and all those experienced in
navigation agreed with the grief-stricken man. Then the
hearts within them all went chill, and pallor spread over
their cheeks. As when men roam like lifeless ghosts

---

[160] They are unaware that the Clashing rocks became immo-
bile after their passage.

1274 φαίνοι ἐήν Madvig: φαίνοιεν (vel φήνειεν) Ω

ἀνέρες εἰλίσσονται ἀνὰ πτόλιν, ἢ πολέμοιο
ἢ λοιμοῖο τέλος ποτιδέγμενοι ἠέ τιν' ὄμβρον
ἄσπετον, ὅς τε βοῶν κατὰ μυρία ἔκλυσεν ἔργα,
ἢ ὅταν αὐτόματα ξόανα ῥέῃ ἱδρώοντα
1285 αἵματι, καὶ μυκαὶ σηκοῖς ἔνι φαντάζωνται,
ἠὲ καὶ ἥλιος μέσῳ ἤματι νύκτ' ἐπάγῃσιν
οὐρανόθεν, τὰ δὲ λαμπρὰ δι' ἠέρος ἄστρα φαείνει·
ὡς τότ' ἀριστῆες δολιχοῦ πρόπαρ αἰγιαλοῖο
ἤλυον ἑρπύζοντες. ἐπήλυθε δ' αὐτίκ' ἐρεμνὴ
1290 ἕσπερος· οἱ δ' ἐλεεινὰ χεροῖν σφέας ἀμφιβαλόντες
δακρυόειν ἀγάπαζον, ἵν' ἄνδιχα δῆθεν ἕκαστος
θυμὸν ἀποφθίσειαν ἐνὶ ψαμάθοισι πεσόντες.
βὰν δ' ἴμεν ἄλλυδις ἄλλος ἑκαστέρω αὖλιν ἑλέσθαι·
ἐν δὲ κάρη πέπλοισι καλυψάμενοι σφετέροισιν
1295 ἄκμηνοι καὶ ἄπαστοι ἐκείατο νύκτ' ἔπι πᾶσαν
καὶ φάος, οἰκτίστῳ θανάτῳ ἔπι. νόσφι δὲ κοῦραι
ἀθρόαι Αἰήταο παρεστενάχοντο θυγατρί.
ὡς δ' ὅτ' ἐρημαῖοι πεπτηότες ἔκτοθι πέτρης
χηραμοῦ ἀπτῆνες λιγέα κλάζουσι νεοσσοί,
1300 ἢ ὅτε καλὰ νάοντος ἐπ' ὀφρύσι Πακτωλοῖο
κύκνοι κινήσουσιν ἐὸν μέλος, ἀμφὶ δὲ λειμὼν
ἑρσήεις βρέμεται ποταμοῖό τε καλὰ ῥέεθρα·
ὡς αἱ ἐπὶ ξανθὰς θέμεναι κονίησιν ἐθείρας
παννύχιαι ἐλεεινὸν ἰήλεμον ὠδύροντο.
1305   καί νύ κεν αὐτοῦ πάντες ἀπὸ ζωῆς ἐλίασθεν
νώνυμνοι καὶ ἄφαντοι ἐπιχθονίοισι δαῆναι
ἡρώων οἱ ἄριστοι ἀνηνύστῳ ἐπ' ἀέθλῳ·
ἀλλά σφεας ἐλέηραν ἀμηχανίῃ μινύθοντας

through a city, awaiting the outbreak of war or plague or an immense downpour of the kind that washes away the countless labors of oxen, either when statues sweat spontaneously and run with blood, and bellowings are heard in sacred precincts, or when at midday the sun brings on night from the sky[161] and the stars shine brightly through the air—so at that time did the heroes trudge aimlessly along the endless shore. Soon the evening darkness came on, and they piteously wrapped their arms around one another and said tearful farewells, so that each could then, apart from the rest, collapse on the sand and perish. They went off here and there, one further than the next, to choose a resting place, and, covering their heads with their cloaks, lay down without food or nourishment the entire night and next morning, in anticipation of an agonizing death. In a group by themselves, the maidens[162] were lamenting at the side of Aeetes' daughter. And as when, abandoned after falling from a cleft in the rock, unfledged chicks shrilly chirp, or as when, on the banks of the lovely-flowing Pactolus, swans raise their song, and all around them resound the dewy meadow and the river's lovely streams—thus did they let fall their golden hair in the dust and all night long wailed a piteous lament.

And so in that place all the best of the heroes would have departed from life, leaving no names and no traces for humans to know of them, with their mission unfulfilled, but as they languished in helplessness, heroines took pity

[161] I.e. a solar eclipse.
[162] The serving girls Arete had given Medea.

ἡρῶσσαι Λιβύης τιμήοροι, αἵ ποτ' Ἀθήνην,
1310 ἦμος ὅτ' ἐκ πατρὸς κεφαλῆς θόρε παμφαίνουσα,
ἀντόμεναι Τρίτωνος ἐφ' ὕδασι χυτλώσαντο.
ἔνδιον ἦμαρ ἔην, περὶ δ' ὀξύταται θέρον αὐγαὶ
ἠελίου Λιβύην· αἱ δὲ σχεδὸν Αἰσονίδαο
ἔσταν, ἕλον δ' ἀπὸ χερσὶ καρήατος ἠρέμα πέπλον.
1315 αὐτὰρ ὅ γ' εἰς ἑτέρωσε παλιμπετὲς ὄμματ' ἔνεικεν,
δαίμονας αἰδεσθείς· αὐτὸν δέ μιν ἀμφαδὸν οἶον
μειλιχίοις ἐπέεσσιν ἀτυζόμενον προσέειπον·
    "κάμμορε, τίπτ' ἐπὶ τόσσον ἀμηχανίῃ
        βεβόλησαι;
    ἴδμεν ἐποιχομένους χρύσεον δέρος· ἴδμεν ἕκαστα
1320 ὑμετέρων καμάτων, ὅσ' ἐπὶ χθονός, ὅσσα τ' ἐφ'
        ὑγρὴν
    πλαζόμενοι κατὰ πόντον ὑπέρβια ἔργα κάμεσθε.
    οἰοπόλοι δ' εἰμὲν χθόνιαι θεαὶ αὐδήεσσαι,
    ἡρῶσσαι Λιβύης τιμήοροι ἠδὲ θύγατρες.
    ἀλλ' ἄνα, μηδ' ἔτι τοῖον ὀιζύων ἀκάχησο·
1325 ἄνστησον δ' ἑτάρους· εὖτ' ἂν δέ τοι Ἀμφιτρίτη
    ἅρμα Ποσειδάωνος ἐύτροχον αὐτίκα λύσῃ,
    δή ῥα τότε σφετέρῃ ἀπὸ μητέρι τίνετ' ἀμοιβὴν
    ὧν ἔκαμεν δηρὸν κατὰ νηδύος ὕμμε φέρουσα·
    καί κεν ἔτ' ἠγαθέην ἐς Ἀχαιίδα νοστήσαιτε."
1330   ὣς ἄρ' ἔφαν, καὶ ἄφαντοι, ἵν' ἔσταθεν, ἔνθ' ἄρα
        ταί γε
    φθογγῇ ὁμοῦ ἐγένοντο παρασχεδόν. αὐτὰρ Ἰήσων
    παπτήνας ἀν' ἄρ' ἕζετ' ἐπὶ χθονός, ὧδέ τ' ἔειπεν·
    "ἵλατ', ἐρημονόμοι κυδραὶ θεαί. ἀμφὶ δὲ νόστῳ

on them, the guardians of Libya, who once upon a time met Athena, after she leapt gleaming from her father's head, by lake Triton's waters and bathed her.[163] It was midday, and all around the sun's most piercing rays were scorching Libya; they stood beside Jason and with their hands softly lifted his cloak from his head. But he turned his eyes away to the side out of reverence for the goddesses; and, visible to him alone, they spoke to the terrified man with gentle words.

"Unfortunate soul, why are you so stricken with helplessness? We know how you and your crew went on a quest for the golden fleece; we know every one of your trials—all the extraordinary deeds you accomplished on land and all those on water as you wandered over the sea. We are the solitary goddesses of this land, heroines endowed with human voices, Libya's guardians and daughters. Come, get up; no longer lament and grieve like this, but rouse your comrades. As soon as Amphitrite[164] unyokes for you Poseidon's well-wheeled chariot, then you and your companions must pay recompense to your mother for what she has suffered in carrying you for so long in her womb, and you may yet return to holy Achaea."

Thus they spoke and vanished at once from where they had stood, as their voices died away. But Jason looked around and sat up on the ground and spoke thus:

"Be gracious, noble goddesses of the wilderness! I have

[163] Athena's "birthplace," after she sprang fully armed (hence gleaming) from Zeus' head, was placed by lake Triton (cf. Aeschylus, *Eumenides* 292–293).
[164] Poseidon's wife.

435

οὔ τι μάλ' ἀντικρὺ νοέω φάτιν· ἦ μὲν ἑταίρους
1335 εἰς ἓν ἀγειράμενος μυθήσομαι, εἴ νύ τι τέκμωρ
δήωμεν κομιδῆς· πολέων δέ τε μῆτις ἀρείων."

ἦ, καὶ ἀναΐξας ἑτάρους ἐπὶ μακρὸν ἀυτει
αὐσταλέος κονίῃσι λέων ὥς, ὅς ῥά τ' ἀν' ὕλην
σύννομον ἦν μεθέπων ὠρύεται· αἱ δὲ βαρείῃ
1340 φθογγῇ ὑποτρομέουσιν ἀν' οὔρεα τηλόθι βῆσσαι·
δείματι δ' ἄγραυλοί τε βόες μέγα πεφρίκασιν
βουπελάται τε βοῶν. τοῖς δ' οὔ νύ τι γῆρυς ἐτύχθη
ῥιγεδανὴ ἑτάροιο φίλοις ἐπικεκλομένοιο·
ἀγχοῦ δ' ἠγερέθοντο κατηφέες. αὐτὰρ ὁ τούς γε
1345 ἀχνυμένους ὅρμοιο πέλας μίγα θηλυτέρῃσιν
ἱδρύσας, μυθεῖτο πιφαυσκόμενος τὰ ἕκαστα·

"κλῦτε, φίλοι· τρεῖς γάρ μοι ἀνιάζοντι θεάων,
στέρφεσιν αἰγείοις ἐζωσμέναι ἐξ ὑπάτοιο
αὐχένος ἀμφί τε νῶτα καὶ ἰξύας, ἠύτε κοῦραι,
1350 ἔσταν ὑπὲρ κεφαλῆς μάλ' ἐπισχεδόν· ἂν δ'
ἐκάλυψαν
πέπλον ἐρυσσάμεναι κούφῃ χερί, καί μ' ἐκέλοντο
αὐτόν τ' ἔγρεσθαι ἀνά θ' ὑμέας ὄρσαι ἰόντα·
μητέρι δὲ σφετέρῃ μενοεικέα τῖσαι ἀμοιβὴν
ὧν ἔκαμεν δηρὸν κατὰ νηδύος ἄμμε φέρουσα,
1355 ὁππότε κεν λύσῃσιν εὔτροχον Ἀμφιτρίτη
ἅρμα Ποσειδάωνος. ἐγὼ δ' οὐ πάγχυ νοῆσαι
τῆσδε θεοπροπίης ἴσχω πέρι. φάν γε μὲν εἶναι
ἡρῶσσαι Λιβύης τιμήοροι ἠδὲ θύγατρες·
καὶ δ' ὁπόσ' αὐτοὶ πρόσθεν ἐπὶ χθονὸς ἠδ' ὅσ' ἐφ'
ὑγρὴν

436

no clear understanding of your pronouncement concerning our return. Indeed, I shall call my comrades together and tell it to them, to see if we can find some indication of how to return, for the counsel of many is better."

He spoke, and leapt up, all filthy with dust, and shouted into the distance for his comrades, like a lion that roars as it seeks its mate through the forest, and the glens far off in the mountains tremble[165] at his deep voice, and the oxen in the fields and their herdsmen shudder with great fear. But to them his voice was not at all terrifying, for it was that of a comrade calling his friends. They gathered around him, hanging their heads. But he made them sit, in spite of their sorrow, together with the women near where the ship lay, and addressed them and told them everything:

"Listen, my friends. As I lay grieving, three goddesses, dressed in goat skins from the tops of their necks around their backs and waists, just like girls, stood right above my head. They uncovered me, pulling back my cloak with a light hand, and told me to get up myself and to go rouse you, and to pay generous recompense to our mother for what she has suffered in carrying us for so long in her womb, whenever Amphitrite unyokes Poseidon's well-wheeled chariot. But I am utterly unable to understand this prophecy. They said they were heroines, Libya's guardians and daughters, and moreover they claimed to

---

[165] Or, reading ὑποβρομέουσιν, *rumble.*

1340 ὑποτρομέουσιν Ω: ὑποβρομέουσιν Lac
1343 φίλοις *m*: φίλους L2pc*w*

437

1360   ἔτλημεν, τὰ ἔκαστα δίδμεναι εὐχετόωντο.
      οὐδ' ἔτι τάσδ' ἀνὰ χῶρον ἐσέδρακον, ἀλλά τις
         ἀχλὺς
      ἠὲ νέφος μεσσηγὺ φαεινομένας ἐκάλυψεν."
        ὡς ἔφαθ'· οἱ δ' ἄρα πάντες ἐθάμβεον εἰσαΐοντες.
      ἔνθα τὸ μήκιστον τεράων Μινύαισιν ἐτύχθη.
1365   ἐξ ἁλὸς ἤπειρόνδε πελώριος ἔκθορεν ἵππος,
      ἀμφιλαφής, χρυσέῃσι μετήορος αὐχένα χαίταις·
      ῥίμφα δὲ σεισάμενος γυίων ἄπο νήχυτον ἅλμην
      ὦρτο θέειν, πνοιῇ ἴκελος πόδας. αἶψα δὲ Πηλεὺς
      γηθήσας ἑτάροισιν ὁμηγερέεσσι μετηύδα·
1370   "ἅρματα μὲν δή φημι Ποσειδάωνος ἐγώ γε
      ἤδη νῦν ἀλόχοιο φίλης ὑπὸ χερσὶ λελύσθαι·
      μητέρα δ' οὐκ ἄλλην προτιόσσομαι ἠέ περ αὐτὴν
      νῆα πέλειν· ἦ γὰρ κατὰ νηδύος αἰὲν ἔχουσα
      ἡμέας ἀργαλέοισιν οἰζύει καμάτοισιν.
1375   ἀλλά μιν ἀστεμφεῖ τε βίῃ καὶ ἀτειρέσιν ὤμοις
      ὑψόθεν ἀνθέμενοι ψαμαθώδεος ἔνδοθι γαίης
      οἴσομεν, ᾗ προτέρωσε ταχὺς πόδας ἤλασεν ἵππος.
      οὐ γὰρ ὅ γε ξηρὴν ὑποδύσεται· ἴχνια δ' ἡμῖν
      σημανέειν τιν' ἔολπα μυχὸν καθύπερθε θαλάσσης."
1380   ὡς ηὔδα· πάντεσσι δ' ἐπίβολος ἥνδανε μῆτις.
      Μουσάων ὅδε μῦθος, ἐγὼ δ' ὑπακουὸς ἀείδω
      Πιερίδων, καὶ τήνδε πανατρεκὲς ἔκλυον ὀμφήν,
      ὑμέας, ὦ πέρι δὴ μέγα φέρτατοι υἷες ἀνάκτων,

        1373 αἰὲν ἔχουσα *w*: ἄμμε φέρουσα *m*
        1374 ἡμέας Ω: νωλεμὲς E

know full well everything that we ourselves had endured
up to now on land and on water. Then I saw them no longer
in their place, but some mist or cloud hid them in the midst
of appearing to me."

Thus he spoke, and all were astonished to hear it. Then
the most extraordinary portent appeared to the Minyans.
Out of the sea and onto the land leapt a prodigious horse of
enormous size, holding high its neck with golden mane. It
promptly shook the flowing sea water from its limbs and
set off at a gallop, its feet like the wind. At once Peleus re-
joiced and said to the gathering of comrades:

"I affirm that the chariot of Poseidon has just now been
unyoked by the hands of his dear wife, and I surmise that
our mother is none other than the ship itself, for truly, by
continually carrying us in her womb, she suffers with pain-
ful labors. Come, let us lift her up with steadfast strength
and untiring shoulders and carry her to the interior of this
sand-filled land, onwards where the swift horse has driven
his hoofs. For he will not plunge under the dry ground, and
I think that his tracks will show us some inland[166] recess of
the sea."

Thus he spoke, and his apt strategy pleased them all.
From the Muses comes this story, and I sing in obedience
to the Pierides; and this account I heard in all accuracy:
that you, O far mightiest sons of kings, by your strength

---

[166] The phrase κόλπον καθύπερθε θαλάσσης is unclear. I
have adopted Vian's interpretation. Other translations include
"bay above the sea" (Seaton), "bay of the sea to the north"
(Livrea), and "gulf which commands the sea" (Mooney).

APOLLONIUS RHODIUS

ᾗ βίῃ, ᾗ ἀρετῇ Λιβύης ἀνὰ θῖνας ἐρήμους
1385 νῆα μεταχρονίην, ὅσα τ' ἔνδοθι νηὸς ἄγεσθαι,
ἀνθεμένους ὤμοισι φέρειν δυοκαίδεκα πάντα
ἤμαθ' ὁμοῦ νύκτας τε. δύην γε μὲν ἢ καὶ ὀιζὺν
τίς κ' ἐνέποι, τὴν κεῖνοι ἀνέπλησαν μογέοντες;
ἔμπεδον ἀθανάτων ἔσαν αἵματος, οἷον ὑπέσταν
1390 ἔργον ἀναγκαίῃ βεβιημένοι. αὐτὰρ ἐπιπρὸ
τῆλε μάλ' ἀσπασίως Τριτωνίδος ὕδασι λίμνης
ὡς φέρον, ὡς εἰσβάντες ἀπὸ στιβαρῶν θέσαν ὤμων.

λυσσαλέοις δήπειτ' ἴκελοι κυσὶν ἀίσσοντες
πίδακα μαστεύεσκον· ἐπὶ ξηρῇ γὰρ ἔκειτο
1395 δίψα δυηπαθίῃ τε καὶ ἄλγεσιν. οὐδ' ἐμάτησαν
πλαζόμενοι· ἷξον δ' ἱερὸν πέδον, ᾧ ἔνι Λάδων
εἰσέτι που χθιζὸν παγχρύσεα ῥύετο μῆλα
χώρῳ ἐν Ἄτλαντος, χθόνιος ὄφις· ἀμφὶ δὲ νύμφαι
Ἑσπερίδες ποίπνυον ἐφίμερον ἀείδουσαι.
1400 δὴ τότε γ' ἤδη κεῖνος ὑφ' Ἡρακλῆι δαϊχθεὶς
μήλειον βέβλητο ποτὶ στύπος· οἰόθι δ' ἄκρη
οὐρὴ ἔτι σκαίρεσκεν, ἀπὸ κρατὸς δὲ κελαινὴν
ἄχρις ἐπ' ἄκνηστιν κεῖτ' ἄπνοος· ἐν δὲ λιπόντων
ὕδρης Λερναίης χόλον αἵματι πικρὸν ὀιστῶν
1405 μυῖαι πυθομένοισιν ἐφ' ἕλκεσι τερσαίνοντο.
ἀγχοῦ δ' Ἑσπερίδες κεφαλαῖς ἔπι χεῖρας ἔχουσαι
ἀργυφέας ξανθῇσι λίγ' ἔστενον. οἱ δ' ἐπέλασσαν

1384 ᾗ ἀρετῇ Ω: ᾗ τ' ἀρετῇ Brunck
1385 ἄγεσθαι Ω (cf. Smyth §2631): ἄγεσθε Flor.
1400 γ' ἤδη κεῖνος ω: δὴ τῆμος m

440

and your valor lifted high the ship and everything that you brought in the ship on your shoulders and carried it over the desolate dunes of Libya for twelve whole days and as many nights. And yet who could recount the pain and suffering those men endured in their toil? They were assuredly of the blood of the immortals, such was the task they undertook when forced by necessity. And as gladly as they had been carrying it far onward to the waters of lake Triton, so gladly did they wade in and set it down from their stout shoulders.[167]

Then, like raging dogs, they rushed in search of a spring,[168] for parching thirst oppressed them along with their suffering and pains. They did not wander in vain, but came to a sacred plain, where, until just the day before, Ladon, the serpent of the land, guarded the solid gold apples in the realm of Atlas,[169] while round about bustled nymphs, the Hesperides, singing a lovely song. But by this time it had been shot by Heracles and had fallen by the trunk of the apple tree, and only the tip of its tail was still twitching, while from its head down its dark spine it lay lifeless. Because the arrows had left the bitter venom of the Lernean Hydra[170] in its blood, flies were withering on the festering wounds. Nearby, the Hesperides were holding their silver-white hands on their golden heads and lamenting shrilly. The heroes approached all at once in a

---

[167] Vian takes ἀσπασίως ("gladly") only with θέσαν ("set it down"), but such a dislocation is extreme.

[168] Since it is an inland gulf of the sea, lake Triton is salty.

[169] In other traditions, the garden of the Hesperides was located in the far west.

[170] Slain by Heracles in a previous labor.

ἄφνω ὁμοῦ· ταὶ δ' αἶψα κόνις καὶ γαῖα, κιόντων
ἐσσυμένως, ἐγένοντο καταυτόθι. νώσατο δ' Ὀρφεὺς
1410 θεῖα τέρα, τὰς δέ σφι παρηγορέεσκε λιτῇσιν·
    "δαίμονες ὦ καλαὶ καὶ εὔφρονες, ἵλατ', ἄνασσαι,
εἴτ' οὖν οὐρανίαις ἐναρίθμιοί ἐστε θεῇσιν
εἴτε καταχθονίαις, εἴτ' οἰοπόλοι καλέεσθε
νύμφαι· ἴτ', ὦ νύμφαι, ἱερὸν γένος Ὠκεανοῖο,
1415 δείξατ' ἐελδομένοισιν ἐνωπαδὶς ἄμμι φανεῖσαι
ἤ τινα πετραίην χύσιν ὕδατος ἤ τινα γαίης
ἱερὸν ἐκβλύοντα, θεαί, ῥόον, ᾧ ἀπὸ δίψαν
αἰθομένην ἄμοτον λωφήσομεν. εἰ δέ κεν αὖτις
δή ποτ' Ἀχαιίδα γαῖαν ἱκώμεθα ναυτιλίῃσιν,
1420 δὴ τότε μυρία δῶρα μετὰ πρώτῃσι θεάων
λοιβάς τ' εἰλαπίνας τε παρέξομεν εὐμενέοντες."
    ὣς φάτο λισσόμενος ἀδινῇ ὀπί· ταὶ δ' ἐλέαιρον
ἐγγύθεν ἀχνυμένους· καὶ δὴ χθονὸς ἐξανέτειλαν
ποίην πάμπρωτον, ποίης γε μὲν ὑψόθι μακροὶ
1425 βλάστεον ὄρπηκες, μετὰ δ' ἔρνεα τηλεθάοντα
πολλὸν ὑπὲρ γαίης ὀρθοσταδὸν ἠέξοντο·
Ἑσπέρη αἴγειρος, πτελέη δ' Ἐρυθηὶς ἔγεντο,
Αἴγλη δ' ἰτέης ἱερὸν στύπος. ἐκ δέ νυ κείνων
δενδρέων, οἷαι ἔσαν, τοῖαι πάλιν ἔμπεδον αὔτως
1430 ἐξέφανεν, θάμβος περιώσιον. ἔκφατο δ' Αἴγλη
μειλιχίοις ἐπέεσσιν ἀμειβομένη χατέοντας·
    "ἦ ἄρα δὴ μέγα πάμπαν ἐφ' ὑμετέροισιν ὄνειαρ
δεῦρ' ἔμολεν καμάτοισιν ὁ κύντατος, ὅς τις ἀπούρας
φρουρὸν ὄφιν ζωῆς παγχρύσεα μῆλα θεάων

group, and at their sudden arrival the women instantly turned to dust and earth there on the spot. Orpheus recognized the divine portent and for his comrades' sake sought to comfort the nymphs with prayers:

"O goddesses beautiful and kind, be gracious, O queens, whether you are counted among the heavenly goddesses or those under the earth, or are called solitary nymphs,[171] come, O nymphs, holy offspring of Ocean, and appear before our longing eyes and show us either some flow of water from a rock or some sacred stream gushing from the ground, goddesses, with which we may relieve our endlessly burning thirst. And if ever again we return in our voyaging to the land of Achaea, at that time we will offer you, among the foremost goddesses, countless gifts, libations, and feasts in our goodwill."

Thus he spoke, beseeching them with a fervent voice, and from near at hand[172] they took pity on the suffering men. First of all, they made grass spring up from the earth; next, tall stalks sprouted from the grass into the air, and then flourishing saplings sprang straight up far above the ground. Hespere became a poplar, Erytheis an elm, and Aegle the sacred trunk of a willow. Then, changing from those trees, they appeared exactly as they were before—an extraordinary marvel! Aegle spoke with gentle words and answered them in their sore need:

"Truly, it seems, very great assistance in your time of troubles has come here—a most shameless man, whoever he was who robbed our guardian serpent of his life and

---

[171] Like Libya's guardians at 4.1322.

[172] Although they have vanished, they remain nearby. Some take ἐγγύθεν as temporal, "soon."

APOLLONIUS RHODIUS

1435 οἴχετ᾽ ἀειράμενος· στυγερὸν δ᾽ ἄχος ἄμμι λέλειπται.
ἤλυθε γὰρ χθιζός τις ἀνὴρ ὀλοώτατος ὕβριν
καὶ δέμας, ὄσσε δέ οἱ βλοσυρῷ ὑπέλαμπε μετώπῳ,
νηλής· ἀμφὶ δὲ δέρμα πελωρίου ἔστο λέοντος
ὠμόν, ἀδέψητον· στιβαρὸν δ᾽ ἔχεν ὄζον ἐλαίης
1440 τόξα τε, τοῖσι πέλωρ τόδ᾽ ἀπέφθισεν ἰοβολήσας.
ἤλυθε δ᾽ οὖν κἀκεῖνος, ἅ τε χθόνα πεζὸς ὀδεύων,
δίψῃ καρχαλέος· παίφασσε δὲ τόνδ᾽ ἀνὰ χῶρον,
ὕδωρ ἐξερέων, τὸ μὲν οὔ ποθι μέλλεν ἰδέσθαι.
ἥδε δέ τις πέτρη Τριτωνίδος ἐγγύθι λίμνης,
1445 τὴν ὅ γ᾽ ἐπιφρασθείς, ἢ καὶ θεοῦ ἐννεσίῃσιν,
λὰξ ποδὶ τύψεν ἔνερθε· τὸ δ᾽ ἀθρόον ἔβλυσεν ὕδωρ.
αὐτὰρ ὅ γ᾽ ἄμφω χεῖρε πέδῳ καὶ στέρνον ἐρείσας
ῥωγάδος ἐκ πέτρης πίεν ἄσπετον, ὄφρα βαθεῖαν
νηδύν, φορβάδι ἶσος ἐπιπροπεσών, ἐκορέσθη."
1450   ὣς φάτο· τοὶ δ᾽ ἀσπαστὸν ἵνα σφίσι πέφραδεν
             Αἴγλη
πίδακα, τῇ θέον αἶψα κεχαρμένοι, ὄφρ᾽ ἐπέκυρσαν.
ὡς δ᾽ ὁπότε στεινὴν περὶ χηραμὸν εἱλίσσονται
γειομόροι μύρμηκες ὁμιλαδόν, ἢ ὅτε μυῖαι
ἀμφ᾽ ὀλίγην μέλιτος γλυκεροῦ λίβα πεπτηυῖαι
1455 ἄπληστον μεμάασιν ἐπήτριμοι· ὣς τότ᾽ ἀολλεῖς
πετραίῃ Μινύαι περὶ πίδακι δινεύεσκον.
καί πού τις διεροῖς ἐπὶ χείλεσιν εἶπεν ἰανθείς·
   "ὦ πόποι, ἦ καὶ νόσφιν ἐὼν ἐσάωσεν ἑταίρους
Ἡρακλέης δίψῃ κεκμηότας. ἀλλά μιν εἴ πως
1460 δήοιμεν στείχοντα δι᾽ ἠπείροιο κιόντες."
   ἦ, καὶ ἀμειβομένων, οἵ τ᾽ ἄρμενοι ἐς τόδε ἔργον,

444

took the solid gold apples of the goddesses and went off, while horrible grief remains for us. For a man came yesterday, utterly destructive in his violence and bodily strength, and his eyes glared from under his fearsome brow, a man with no pity! Around his body he wore the raw, untanned skin of an enormous lion, and he carried a stout branch of olive and a bow, with which he shot arrows and killed this beast. At all events, he too came here, like anyone traversing this land on foot, with a savage thirst, and rushed throughout this area in search of water, which indeed he was not likely to see anywhere. But here near lake Triton is a certain rock, which—by his own devising or else through a god's prompting—he kicked at the base with his foot, and the water gushed out in a flood. Leaning both of his hands and chest on the ground, he drank a huge quantity from the cleft rock, until, stooped forward like a grazing animal, he satisfied his enormous belly."

Thus she spoke, and they immediately rejoiced and ran gladly toward the place where Aegle had pointed out the spring to them, until they reached it. And as when earth-burrowing ants swarm in multitudes around a narrow crack, or when flies light in throngs around a tiny drop of sweet honey in insatiable eagerness—thus did all the Minyans then cluster around the spring from the rock. And undoubtedly one of them, his lips still moist, said joyfully:

"How astonishing! Even though he is far away, Heracles has saved his comrades who were dying of thirst. If only we might find him on his way as we cross the mainland."

Thus he spoke, and responding to his words, those fit

APOLLONIUS RHODIUS

ἔκριθεν ἄλλυδις ἄλλος ἐπαΐξας ἐρεείνειν·
ἴχνια γὰρ νυχίοισιν ἐπηλίνδητ' ἀνέμοισιν
κινυμένης ἀμάθου. Βορέαο μὲν ὡρμήθησαν
1465 υἷε δύω πτερύγεσσι πεποιθότε, ποσσὶ δὲ κούφοις
Εὔφημος πίσυνος, Λυγκεύς γε μὲν ὀξέα τηλοῦ
ὄσσε βαλεῖν, πέμπτος δὲ μετὰ σφίσιν ἔσσυτο
      Κάνθος.
τὸν μὲν ἄρ' αἶσα θεῶν κείνην ὁδὸν ἠνορέη τε
ὦρσεν, ἵν' Ἡρακλῆος ἀπηλεγέως πεπύθοιτο,
1470 Εἰλατίδην Πολύφημον ὄπῃ λίπε· μέμβλετο γάρ οἱ
οὗ ἔθεν ἀμφ' ἑτάροιο μεταλλῆσαι τὰ ἕκαστα.
ἀλλ' ὁ μὲν οὖν Μυσοῖσιν ἐπικλεὲς ἄστυ πολίσσας
νόστου κηδοσύνῃσιν ἔβη διζήμενος Ἀργὼ
τῆλε δι' ἠπείροιο· τέως δ' ἐξίκετο γαῖαν
1475 ἀγχιάλων Χαλύβων· τόθι μιν καὶ μοῖρ' ἐδάμασσεν,
καί οἱ ὑπὸ βλωθρὴν ἀχερωίδα σῆμα τέτυκται
τυτθὸν ἁλὸς προπάροιθεν. ἀτὰρ τότε γ' Ἡρακλῆα
μοῦνον ἀπειρεσίης τηλοῦ χθονὸς εἴσατο Λυγκεὺς
τὼς ἰδέειν, ὥς τίς τε νέῳ ἐνὶ ἤματι μήνην
1480 ἢ ἴδεν ἢ ἐδόκησεν ἐπαχλύουσαν ἰδέσθαι.
ἐς δ' ἑτάρους ἀνιὼν μυθήσατο, μή μιν ἔτ' ἄλλον
μαστῆρα στείχοντα κιχησέμεν. οἱ δὲ καὶ αὐτοὶ
ἤλυθον Εὔφημός τε πόδας ταχὺς υἷέ τε δοιὼ
Θρηικίου Βορέω, μεταμώνια μοχθήσαντες.
1485   Κάνθε, σὲ δ' οὐλόμεναι Λιβύῃ ἔνι Κῆρες ἕλοντο.
πώεσι φερβομένοισι συνήντεες, εἵπετο δ' ἀνὴρ

1478 μοῦνον Ω: μοῦνος Ε²

446

for this task separated and set off in different directions
to search, because his tracks had been effaced when the
sand was shifted by the nighttime winds. The twin sons
of Boreas set out, relying on their wings; so too did Eu-
phemus, trusting in his nimble feet; next was Lynceus, able
to cast his sharp eyes afar; and fifth to speed off with them
was Canthus. Now in his case, the destiny of the gods and
his own valor urged him on that quest, so that he could
learn for certain from Heracles where he had left Eilatus'
son Polyphemus,[173] for he was determined to ask him ev-
erything about his comrade. But Polyphemus, after found-
ing a famous city among the Mysians, out of yearning for
the expedition went far across the mainland in search of
the Argo. But in the meantime, he came to the land of the
Chalybes who dwell by the sea, and it was there that fate
overcame him, and a tomb was erected for him under a tall
white poplar, a short distance from the sea. But on that day,
at least, Lynceus thought he had seen Heracles all alone,
far away in that endless land, as a man on the first day of the
month[174] sees (or thinks he sees) the moon through the
clouds. He went back to his comrades and reported that no
longer could any other searcher overtake him on his way.
And the others too returned, swift-footed Euphemus and
the twin sons of Thracian Boreas, after laboring in vain.

But you, Canthus, the Fates of Death seized in Libya.
You happened upon pasturing flocks, and a shepherd was

[173] Polyphemus was left behind with Heracles in Mysia as they
searched for Hylas (cf. 1.1240–1283).
[174] When the new moon begins.

447

αὐλίτης, ὅ σ’ ἐὼν μήλων πέρι, τόφρ’ ἑτάροισιν
δευομένοις κομίσειας, ἀλεξόμενος κατέπεφνεν
λᾶι βαλών· ἐπεὶ οὐ μὲν ἀφαυρότερός γ’ ἐτέτυκτο,
1490 υἱωνὸς Φοίβοιο Λυκωρείοιο Κάφαυρος
κούρης τ’ αἰδοίης Ἀκακαλλίδος, ἥν ποτε Μίνως
ἐς Λιβύην ἀπένασσε θεοῦ βαρὺ κῦμα φέρουσαν,
θυγατέρα σφετέρην· ἡ δ’ ἀγλαὸν υἷέα Φοίβῳ
τίκτεν, ὃν Ἀμφίθεμιν Γαράμαντά τε κικλήσκουσιν·
1495 Ἀμφίθεμις δ’ ἄρ’ ἔπειτα μίγη Τριτωνίδι νύμφῃ·
ἡ δ’ ἄρα οἱ Νασάμωνα τέκεν κρατερόν τε
    Κάφαυρον,
ὃς τότε Κάνθον ἔπεφνεν ἐπὶ ῥήνεσσιν ἑοῖσιν.
οὐδ’ ὅ γ’ ἀριστήων χαλεπὰς ἠλεύατο χεῖρας,
ὡς μάθον οἷον ἔρεξε. νέκυν δ’ ἀνάειραν ὀπίσσω
1500 πευθόμενοι Μινύαι, γαίῃ δ’ ἐνὶ ταρχύσαντο
μυρόμενοι· τὰ δὲ μῆλα μετὰ σφέας οἵ γ’ ἐκόμισσαν.
    ἔνθα καὶ Ἀμπυκίδην αὐτῷ ἐνὶ ἤματι Μόψον
νηλειὴς ἕλε πότμος· ἀδευκέα δ’ οὐ φύγεν αἶσαν
μαντοσύναις· οὐ γάρ τις ἀποτροπίη θανάτοιο.
1505 κεῖτο δ’ ἐπὶ ψαμάθοισι μεσημβρινὸν ἦμαρ ἀλύσκων
δεινὸς ὄφις· νωθὴς μὲν ἑκὼν ἀέκοντα χαλέψαι,
οὐδ’ ἂν ὑποτρέσσαντος ἐνωπαδὶς ἀίξειεν·
ἀλλ’ ᾧ κεν τὰ πρῶτα μελάγχιμον ἰὸν ἐνείη

1500 πευθόμενοι E: πυθόμενοι Ω: πυθόμενον Wifstrand
1508 ἀλλ’ ᾧ κεν Merkel: ἀλλά κεν ᾧ Ω

448

tending them, who, fighting in defense of his own sheep
while you wanted to take them to your famished comrades,
struck you with a stone and killed you. For indeed he was
no lesser man, this Caphaurus, the grandson of Lycoreian
Phoebus and the chaste maiden Acacallis, whom Minos
once sent off to live in Libya, although she was his own
daughter, because she was pregnant with the heavy off-
spring of the god. And to Phoebus she bore a splendid son,
whom they call Amphithemis as well as Garamas.[175] And
Amphithemis thereafter lay with a Tritonian nymph, who
then bore him Nasamon and mighty Caphaurus, who on
that day slew Canthus in defense of his own lambs. But he
did not elude the harsh hands of the heroes, once they
learned what he had done. And when the Minyans were
aware,[176] they took up his corpse and carried it back, and
buried it in the earth as they mourned him. And as for the
sheep, they carried them off for themselves.

Then, on that same day, ruthless fate also seized
Ampycus' son Mopsus. He could not escape cruel destiny
through his prophetic arts, for there is no averting death.
Lying in the sand, avoiding the noonday heat, was a fear-
some snake. Too sluggish on its own to strike an unwilling
foe, it would not even spring up to face anything that re-
treated. But once it injects its black venom into any of the

---

[175] The Garamantes, a pastoral tribe in Libya, were named for
him (cf. Herodotus 4.174). They bordered on the Nasamones.

[176] Most manuscripts have πυθόμενοι ("having learned"),
which is metrically impossible. The only viable reading is
πευθόμενοι ("learning," "being aware"). Wifstrand's πυθόμενον
("rotting") with "corpse" is not convincing. With any reading, the
sentence is very elliptical.

ζωόντων, ὅσα γαῖα φερέσβιος ἔμπνοα βόσκει,
1510 οὐδ' ὁπόσον πήχυιον ἐς Ἄιδα γίγνεται οἶμος,
οὐδ' εἰ Παιήων, εἴ μοι θέμις ἀμφαδὸν εἰπεῖν,
φαρμάσσοι, ὅτε μοῦνον ἐνιχρίμψῃσιν ὀδοῦσιν.
εὖτε γὰρ ἰσόθεος Λιβύην ὑπερέπτατο Περσεὺς
Εὐρυμέδων—καὶ γὰρ τὸ κάλεσκέ μιν οὔνομα
    μήτηρ—
1515 Γοργόνος ἀρτίτομον κεφαλὴν βασιλῆι κομίζων,
ὅσσαι κυανέου στάγες αἵματος οὖδας ἵκοντο,
αἱ πᾶσαι κείνων ὀφίων γένος ἐβλάστησαν.
τῷ δ' ἄκρην ἐπ' ἄκανθαν ἐνεστηρίξατο Μόψος
λαιὸν ἐπιπροφέρων ταρσὸν ποδός· αὐτὰρ ὁ μέσσην
1520 κερκίδα καὶ μυῶνα πέριξ ὀδύνῃσιν ἑλιχθείς,
σάρκα δακὼν ἐχάραξεν. ἀτὰρ Μήδεια καὶ ἄλλαι
ἔτρεσαν ἀμφίπολοι· ὁ δὲ φοίνιον ἕλκος ἄφασσεν
θαρσαλέως, ἔνεκ' οὔ μιν ὑπέρβιον ἕλκος ἔτειρεν,
σχέτλιος· ἦ τέ οἱ ἤδη ὑπὸ χροῒ δύετο κῶμα
1525 λυσιμελές, πολλὴ δὲ κατ' ὀφθαλμῶν χέετ' ἀχλύς.
αὐτίκα δὲ κλίνας δαπέδῳ βεβαρηότα γυῖα
ψύχετ' ἀμηχανίῃ· ἕταροι δέ μιν ἀμφαγέροντο
ἥρως τ' Αἰσονίδης ἀδινῇ περιθαμβέες ἄτῃ.
οὐδὲ μὲν οὐδ' ἐπὶ τυτθὸν ἀποφθίμενός περ ἔμελλεν
1530 κεῖσθαι ὑπ' ἠελίῳ· πύθεσκε γὰρ ἔνδοθι σάρκας
ἰὸς ἄφαρ, μυδόωσα δ' ἀπὸ χροὸς ἔρρεε λάχνη.
αἶψα δὲ χαλκείῃσι βαθὺν τάφον ἐξελάχαινον
ἐσσυμένως μακέλῃσιν· ἐμοιρήσαντο δὲ χαίτας
αὐτοὶ ὁμῶς κοῦραί τε νέκυν ἐλεεινὰ παθόντα
1535 μυρόμενοι· τρὶς δ' ἀμφὶ σὺν ἔντεσι δινηθέντες

450

living and breathing creatures which the life-giving earth
sustains, the way to Hades for it is no more than a cubit,
even if Paean[177] (if it is right for me to say this openly)
should apply antidotes, once it bites with its fangs. For
when godlike Perseus Eurymedon (for his mother called
him by that name) flew over Libya bringing the newly-
severed head of the Gorgon to his king,[178] all the drops of
dark blood that fell on the ground produced a brood of
those snakes. Mopsus stepped on the tip of its tail, when he
planted the sole of his left foot. And coiling in pain around
the middle of his shin and calf, it bit and tore the skin.
Medea and her handmaids fled in terror, but he bravely
stroked the bloody wound, because that wound did not
pain him terribly, the poor man! For indeed already under
his skin was spreading a numbness that paralyzes the body,
and a thick darkness was pouring over his eyes. Right away
he laid his heavy limbs on the ground in helplessness and
grew cold. His comrades and the hero Jason gathered
around him, astonished beyond measure at his sad demise.
And not even for short time after he died could he lie
under the sun, because the poison began at once rotting
the flesh within, while the hair on his body liquified and ran
off his skin. Quickly they hastened to dig a deep grave with
bronze mattocks, and the men and women alike tore their
hair as they lamented the dead man's pitiful suffering.
After marching in arms three times around the corpse as it

[177] Apollo the Healer.
[178] Polydectes, king of Seriphus, forced Perseus' mother
Danae to marry him. Perseus brought back Medusa's head and
turned him to stone.

εὖ κτερέων ἴσχοντα, χυτὴν ἐπὶ γαῖαν ἔθεντο.
ἀλλ᾽ ὅτε δή ῥ᾽ ἐπὶ νηὸς ἔβαν, πρήσσοντος ἀήτεω
ἂμ πέλαγος νοτίοιο, πόρους τ᾽ ἀπετεκμαίροντο
λίμνης ἐκπρομολεῖν Τριτωνίδος, οὔ τινα μῆτιν
1540 δὴν ἔχον, ἀφραδέως δὲ πανημέριοι φορέοντο.
ὡς δὲ δράκων σκολιὴν εἰλιγμένος ἔρχεται οἶμον,
εὖτέ μιν ὀξύτατον θάλπει σέλας ἠελίοιο,
ῥοίζῳ δ᾽ ἔνθα καὶ ἔνθα κάρη στρέφει, ἐν δέ οἱ ὄσσε
σπινθαρύγεσσι πυρὸς ἐναλίγκια μαιμώοντι
1545 λάμπεται, ὄφρα μυχόνδε διὰ ῥωχμοῖο δύηται·
ὣς Ἀργὼ λίμνης στόμα ναύπορον ἐξερέουσα
ἀμφεπόλει δηναιὸν ἐπὶ χρόνον. αὐτίκα δ᾽ Ὀρφεὺς
κέκλετ᾽ Ἀπόλλωνος τρίποδα μέγαν ἔκτοθι νηὸς
δαίμοσιν ἐγγενέταις νόστῳ ἔπι μείλια θέσθαι.
1550 καὶ τοὶ μὲν Φοίβου κτέρας ἵδρυον ἐν χθονὶ βάντες·
τοῖσιν δ᾽ αἰζηῷ ἐναλίγκιος ἀντεβόλησεν
Τρίτων εὐρυβίης, γαίης δ᾽ ἀνὰ βῶλον ἀείρας
ξείνι᾽ ἀριστήεσσι προΐσχετο, φώνησέν τε·
"δέχθε, φίλοι, ἐπεὶ οὐ περιώσιον ἐγγυαλίξαι
1555 ἐνθάδε νῦν πάρ᾽ ἐμοὶ ξεινήιον ἀντομένοισιν.
εἰ δέ τι τῆσδε πόρους μαίεσθ᾽ ἁλός, οἷά τε πολλὰ
ἄνθρωποι χατέουσιν ἐπ᾽ ἀλλοδαπῇ περόωντες,
ἐξερέω· δὴ γάρ με πατὴρ ἐπίστορα πόντου
θῆκε Ποσειδάων τοῦδ᾽ ἔμμεναι· αὐτὰρ ἀνάσσω
1560 παρραλίης, εἰ δή τιν᾽ ἀκούετε νόσφιν ἐόντες
Εὐρύπυλον Λιβύῃ θηροτρόφῳ ἐγγεγαῶτα."

received full burial honors, they heaped a mound of earth on top.

But when they had boarded their ship and, with a south wind blowing over the sea, began searching for passages to leave lake Triton, for a long time they had no plan and spent all day drifting aimlessly. And as a snake goes wriggling on its crooked way when the hottest light of the sun is scorching it, and with a hiss turns its head this way and that, and its eyes shine like sparks of fire in its agitation, until it enters its hole through a crevice—thus the Argo, in search of a navigable outlet from the lake, wandered about for a long time. And suddenly Orpheus advised taking Apollo's great tripod from the ship and placing it as a propitiatory offering to the indigenous divinities to secure their return. So they disembarked and were setting up Phoebus' gift on the shore, and wide-ruling Triton met them in the guise of a young man. He picked up a clod of earth and offered it as a guest-gift to the heroes, and said:

"Take this, friends, since I do not now have here with me any magnificent guest-gift to give to suppliants.[179] But if in any way you are seeking the passageways of this sea, as men often need to do when traveling in a foreign land, I will tell you. For my father Poseidon made me well acquainted with this sea, and I rule over the shore— if perhaps, though living far away, you have heard tell of a certain Eurypylus, born in Libya, the home of wild animals."

---

[179] Or *to visitors*. The verb ἄντομαι can mean "meet" or "supplicate."

ὣς ηὔδα· πρόφρων δ᾽ ὑποέσχεθε βώλακι χεῖρας
Εὔφημος, καὶ τοῖα παραβλήδην προσέειπεν·
"Ἀπίδα καὶ πέλαγος Μινώιον εἴ νύ που, ἥρως,
1565 ἐξεδάης, νημερτὲς ἀνειρομένοισιν ἔνισπε.
δεῦρο γὰρ οὐκ ἐθέλοντες ἱκάνομεν, ἀλλὰ βορείαις
χρίμψαντες γαίης ἐνὶ πείρασι τῆσδε θυέλλαις
νῆα μεταχρονίην ἐκομίσσαμεν ἐς τόδε λίμνης
χεῦμα δι᾽ ἠπείρου βεβαρημένοι· οὐδέ τι ἴδμεν,
1570 πῇ πλόος ἐξανέχει Πελοπηίδα γαῖαν ἱκέσθαι."
    ὣς ἄρ᾽ ἔφη· ὁ δὲ χεῖρα τανύσσατο, δεῖξε δ᾽
        ἄπωθεν
φωνήσας πόντον τε καὶ ἀγχιβαθὲς στόμα λίμνης·
    "κείνη μὲν πόντοιο διήλυσις, ἔνθα μάλιστα
βένθος ἀκίνητον μελανεῖ· ἑκάτερθε δὲ λευκαὶ
1575 ῥηγμῖνες φρίσσουσι διαυγέες· ἡ δὲ μεσηγὺ
ῥηγμίνων στεινὴ τελέθει ὁδὸς ἐκτὸς ἐλάσσαι.
κεῖνο δ᾽ ὑπηέριον θείην Πελοπηίδα γαῖαν
εἰσανέχει πέλαγος Κρήτης ὕπερ. ἀλλ᾽ ἐπὶ χειρὸς
δεξιτερῆς, λίμνηθεν ὅτ᾽ εἰς ἁλὸς οἶδμα βάλητε,
1580 τόφρ᾽ αὐτὴν παρὰ χέρσον ἐεργμένοι ἰθύνεσθε,
ἔστ᾽ ἂν ἄνω τείνησι· περιρρήδην δ᾽ ἑτέρωσε
κλινομένης χέρσοιο, τότε πλόος ὕμμιν ἀπήμων
ἀγκῶνος τετάνυσται ἀπὸ προύχοντος ἰοῦσιν.
ἀλλ᾽ ἴτε γηθόσυνοι, καμάτοιο δὲ μή τις ἀνίη
1585 γιγνέσθω, νεότητι κεκασμένα γυῖα μογῆσαι."

1562 ὑποέσχεθε Madvig: ὑπερέσχεθε Ω
1564 Ἀπίδα S: Ἀτθίδα Ω S^mg

Thus he spoke, and Euphemus gladly held out his hands for the clod and said the following in reply:

"If by chance, hero, you are familiar with Apis[180] and the sea of Minos, answer our questions truthfully. For we have not come here willingly, but, brought to the borders of this land by northern storm winds, we carried the ship above ground across the mainland to the waters of this lake, bearing its heavy weight. And we have no idea where a passage extends[181] to get to the land of Pelops."

Thus he spoke, and Triton stretched out his hand and said as he pointed far off to the sea and the deep mouth of the lake:

"That is the outlet to the sea, where the deep water is most calm and dark. On either side seethe white breakers clearly in view, and there is a narrow passage between the breakers to make your way out. That misty sea extends to the divine land of Pelops beyond Crete. But steer to the right when you enter the swell of the sea from the lake, and hug the coastline so long as it stretches northward, but when the coast turns and slopes in the other direction, then a safe voyage lies before you, if you go away from the projecting cape. Go in joy, and as for exertion, let there be no distress when limbs endowed with youth must toil."

[180] An ancient name for the Peloponnesus.
[181] Or, reading ἐξανάγει, *leads out*.

1566 βορείαις *w*: βαρείαις *m*
1570 ἐξανέχει Ω: ἐξανάγει *d*
1583 τετάννυσται ἀπὸ Brunck: τετάννυσται ἰθὺς ἀπὸ Ω

ἴσκεν εὐφρονέων· οἱ δ᾽ αἶψ᾽ ἐπὶ νηὸς ἔβησαν
λίμνης ἐκπρομολεῖν λελιημένοι εἰρεσίῃσιν.
καὶ δὴ ἐπιπρονέοντο μεμαότες· αὐτὰρ ὁ τείως
Τρίτων ἀνθέμενος τρίποδα μέγαν εἴσατο λίμνην
1590 εἰσβαίνειν· μετὰ δ᾽ οὔ τις ἐσέδρακεν, οἷον ἄφαντος
αὐτῷ σὺν τρίποδι σχεδὸν ἔπλετο. τοῖσι δ᾽ ἰάνθη
θυμός, ὃ δὴ μακάρων τις ἐναίσιμος ἀντεβόλησεν·
καί ῥά οἱ Αἰσονίδην μήλων ὅ τι φέρτατον ἄλλων
ἤνωγον ῥέξαι καὶ ἐπευφημῆσαι ἑλόντα.
1595 αἶψα δ᾽ ὅ γ᾽ ἐσσυμένως ἐκρίνατο, καί μιν ἀείρας
σφάξε κατὰ πρύμνης, ἐπὶ δ᾽ ἔννεπεν εὐχωλῇσιν·
  "δαῖμον, ὅ τις λίμνης ἐπὶ πείρασι τῆσδε
      φαάνθης,
εἴτε σύ γε Τρίτων, ἅλιον τέρας, εἴτε σε Φόρκυν
ἢ Νηρῆα θύγατρες ἐπικλείουσ᾽ ἁλοσύδναι,
1600 ἵλαθι, καὶ νόστοιο τέλος θυμηδὲς ὄπαζε."
  ἦ ῥ᾽, ἅμα δ᾽ εὐχωλῇσιν ἐς ὕδατα λαιμοτομήσας
ἧκε κατὰ πρύμνης. ὁ δὲ βένθεος ἐξεφαάνθη
τοῖος ἐών, οἷός περ ἐτήτυμος ἦεν ἰδέσθαι.
ὡς δ᾽ ὅτ᾽ ἀνὴρ θοὸν ἵππον ἐς εὐρέα κύκλον ἀγῶνος
1605 στέλλῃ ὀρεξάμενος λασίης εὐπειθέα χαίτης,
εἶθαρ ἐπιτροχάων, ὁ δ᾽ ἐπ᾽ αὐχένι γαῦρος ἀερθεὶς
ἕσπεται, ἀργινόεντα δ᾽ ἐπὶ στομάτεσσι χαλινὰ
ἀμφὶς ὀδακτάζοντι παραβλήδην κροτέονται·
ὣς ὅ γ᾽ ἐπισχόμενος γλαφυρῆς ὁλκήιον Ἀργοῦς
1610 ἧγ᾽ ἅλαδε προτέρωσε. δέμας δέ οἱ ἐξ ὑπάτοιο
κράατος ἀμφί τε νῶτα καὶ ἰξύας ἔστ᾽ ἐπὶ νηδὺν
ἀντικρὺ μακάρεσσι φυὴν ἔκπαγλον ἔικτο·

Thus he spoke with kind intent, and they immediately boarded the ship in their zeal to row out of the lake. And they were eagerly speeding onward, but in the meantime Triton picked up the great tripod and appeared to enter the lake, after which no one saw him, so suddenly did he disappear along with the tripod. Their hearts were cheered that one of the blessed gods had auspiciously met them, and they urged Jason to select the finest of all the sheep and to sacrifice it and propitiate the god. Without delay he quickly selected one and, raising it up, slew it over the stern and spoke in prayer:

"O god, whoever you are who appeared on the borders of this lake, whether you are Triton, the portent of the sea, or whether the sea-dwelling daughters call you Phorcys or Nereus, be gracious and grant a heart-warming completion of our return home."

He spoke, and with these prayers slit the sheep's throat and threw it over the stern into the waters. The god rose from the depths and appeared in his true form. And as when a man conducts a swift horse into the wide circle of a racecourse, and, having grasped the obedient horse by its bushy mane, immediately runs alongside, and the horse proudly keeps pace with its neck lifted high, and the gleaming bit clanks about its mouth as it champs it from side to side—thus did the god take hold of the hollow Argo's keel and lead her forward to the sea. His body, from the top of his head and all around his back and waist to his belly, was exactly like the awesome form of the blessed

---

1598 σύ γε w: σε m: σέ γε Merkel | Τρίτων LᵖᶜwE: Τρί-
των' L ante ras.

1607 ἐπὶ m: ἐνὶ w

αὐτὰρ ὑπαὶ λαγόνων δίκραιρά οἱ ἔνθα καὶ ἔνθα
κήτεος ἀλκαίη μηκύνετο· κόπτε δ᾽ ἀκάνθαις
1615 ἄκρον ὕδωρ, αἵ τε σκολιοῖς ἐπινειόθι κέντροις
μήνης ὡς κεράεσσιν ἐειδόμεναι διχόωντο.
τόφρα δ᾽ ἄγεν, τείως μιν ἐπιπροέηκε θαλάσσῃ
νισσομένην· δῦ δ᾽ αἶψα μέγαν βυθόν· οἱ δ᾽
        ὁμάδησαν
ἥρωες, τέρας αἰνὸν ἐν ὀφθαλμοῖσιν ἰδόντες.
1620   ἔνθα μὲν Ἀργῷός τε λιμὴν καὶ σήματα νηὸς
ἠδὲ Ποσειδάωνος ἰδὲ Τρίτωνος ἔασιν
βωμοί, ἐπεὶ κεῖν᾽ ἦμαρ ἐπέσχεθον. αὐτὰρ ἐς ἠῶ
λαίφεσι πεπταμένοις, αὐτὴν ἐπὶ δεξί᾽ ἔχοντες
γαῖαν ἐρημαίην, πνοιῇ ζεφύροιο θέεσκον.
1625 ἦρι δ᾽ ἔπειτ᾽ ἀγκῶνά θ᾽ ὁμοῦ μυχάτην τε θάλασσαν
κεκλιμένην ἀγκῶνος ὕπερ προύχοντος ἴδοντο.
αὐτίκα δὲ ζέφυρος μὲν ἐλώφεεν, ἤλυθε δ᾽ αὔρη
ἀργεστᾶο νότου· χήραντο δὲ θυμὸν ἰωῇ.
ἦμος δ᾽ ἠέλιος μὲν ἔδυ, ἀνὰ δ᾽ ἤλυθεν ἀστὴρ
1630 αὔλιος, ὅς τ᾽ ἀνέπαυσεν ὀιζυροὺς ἀροτῆρας,
δὴ τότ᾽ ἔπειτ᾽ ἀνέμοιο κελαινῇ νυκτὶ λιπόντος
ἱστία λυσάμενοι περιμήκεά τε κλίναντες
ἱστόν, ἐυξέστῃσιν ἐπερρώοντ᾽ ἐλάτῃσιν
παννύχιοι καὶ ἐπ᾽ ἦμαρ, ἐπ᾽ ἤματι δ᾽ αὖτις ἰοῦσαν
1635 νύχθ᾽ ἑτέρην. ὑπέδεκτο δ᾽ ἀπόπροθι παιπαλόεσσα
Κάρπαθος· ἔνθεν δ᾽ οἵ γε περαιώσεσθαι ἔμελλον
Κρήτην, ἥ τ᾽ ἄλλων ὑπερέπλετο εἰν ἁλὶ νήσων·
τοὺς δὲ Τάλως χάλκειος, ἀπὸ στιβαροῦ σκοπέλοιο

gods, but below his hips stretched the tail of a sea creature that forked this way and that. He beat the surface of the water with spines, which below divided into curved points like the horns of the moon. He guided the ship until he propelled her on her way in the open sea, and then suddenly plunged into the great abyss. The heroes let out a cry when they beheld this strange miracle with their very eyes.

In that place is the harbor of Argo, and there are traces[182] of the ship and altars to Poseidon and Triton, for they stayed there that day. But at dawn, with sails spread wide, they kept the same desert shore on their right and ran with the blowing Zephyr. The following morning they saw both the cape and the gulf of the sea lying beyond the jutting cape. Suddenly the Zephyr ceased, and a clearing south wind came; and their hearts rejoiced at its sound. But when the sun had set and the herdsmen's star[183] had risen, the one that brings rest to weary plowmen, then, because the wind had died in the dark of night, they furled the sails, lowered the tall mast, and labored at the polished oars all night and through the day, and yet again when the following night came on. The distant island of rugged Carpathus welcomed them, and from there they were going to cross over to Crete, which surpasses[184] all the other islands in the sea, but Talos, the man of bronze, by break-

[182] It is not known what these might be.

[183] Hesperus, the evening star, brings animals and people home (cf. Sappho, *fr.* 104a).   [184] There is disagreement as to the nature of Crete's superiority: size, elevation, or location.

1614 ἀλκαίη Flor.: ὁλκαίη Ω
1628 χήραντο LE: κεχάροντο w

ῥηγνύμενος πέτρας, εἶργε χθονὶ πείσματ' ἀνάψαι
1640 Δικταίην ὅρμοιο κατερχομένους ἐπιωγήν.
τὸν μὲν χαλκείης μελιηγενέων ἀνθρώπων
ῥίζης λοιπὸν ἐόντα μετ' ἀνδράσιν ἡμιθέοισιν
Εὐρώπη Κρονίδης νήσου πόρεν ἔμμεναι οὖρον,
τρὶς περὶ χαλκείοις Κρήτην ποσὶ δινεύοντα.
1645 ἀλλ' ἤτοι τὸ μὲν ἄλλο δέμας καὶ γυῖα τέτυκτο
χάλκεος ἠδ' ἄρρηκτος, ὑπαὶ δέ οἱ ἔσκε τένοντος
σύριγξ αἱματόεσσα κατὰ σφυρόν· αὐτὰρ ὁ τήν γε
λεπτὸς ὑμὴν ζωῆς ἔχε πείρατα καὶ θανάτοιο.
οἱ δέ, δύῃ μάλα περ δεδμημένοι, αἶψ' ἀπὸ χέρσου
1650 νῆα περιδδείσαντες ἀνακρούεσκον ἐρετμοῖς.
καί νύ κ' ἐπισμυγερῶς Κρήτης ἕκας ἤερθησαν,
ἀμφότερον δίψῃ τε καὶ ἄλγεσι μοχθίζοντες,
εἰ μή σφιν Μήδεια λιαζομένοις ἀγόρευσεν·
   "κέκλυτέ μευ, μούνη γὰρ ὀίομαι ὔμμι δαμάσσειν
1655 ἄνδρα τόν, ὅς τις ὅδ' ἐστί, καὶ εἰ παγχάλκεον ἴσχει
ὃν δέμας, ὁππότε μή οἱ ἐπ' ἀκάματος πέλοι αἰών.
ἀλλ' ἔχετ' αὐτοῦ νῆα θελήμονες ἐκτὸς ἐρωῆς
πετράων, εἵως κεν ἐμοὶ εἴξειε δαμῆναι."
   ὣς ἄρ' ἔφη· καὶ τοὶ μὲν ὑπὲκ βελέων ἐρύσαντο
1660 νῆ' ἐπ' ἐρετμοῖσιν, δεδοκημένοι ἥν τινα ῥέξει
μῆτιν ἀνωίστως· ἡ δὲ πτύχα πορφυρέοιο
προσχομένη πέπλοιο παρειάων ἑκάτερθεν
βήσατ' ἐπ' ἰκριόφιν· χειρὸς δέ ἑ χειρὶ μεμαρπὼς
Αἰσονίδης ἐκόμιζε διὰ κληῖδας ἰοῦσαν.

ing off boulders from the rocky cliff, prevented them from fastening their cables on land when they reached Dicte's haven for mooring.[185] Being the last of the bronze race of men born from ash trees still living in the time of the demigods,[186] he had been given to Europa by Cronus' son to be the island's guardian, and he made three tours[187] of Crete on his bronze feet. Although all the rest of his body and limbs were of bronze and invulnerable, beneath the tendon by his ankle was a vein carrying blood, and the thin membrane that covered that vein determined the outcome of life or death. And so the heroes, even though overwhelmed by fatigue, immediately rowed their ship away from the shore in terror. And then they would have fled far from Crete in misery, oppressed both by thirst and pain, had not Medea spoken to them as they were pulling away:

"Listen to me. I think that by myself I can defeat that man for you, whoever he is, even if he has a body wholly of bronze, so long as he does not also have untiring life force. Come then, hold the ship here at ease beyond the range of his stones, until he yields to me in defeat."

Thus she spoke, and they held the ship steady with their oars away from the missiles, waiting to see what sort of scheme she would unexpectedly carry out. She drew a fold of her purple robe over both cheeks and mounted the upper deck, and Jason took her hand in his and guided her

---

[185] This Dicte is probably located in the northeastern corner of Crete (Vian).

[186] For the bronze race sprung from ash trees that preceded the race of demigods (i.e. the epic heroes), see Hesiod, *Works and Days* 143–160.

[187] I.e. each day (schol.).

1665 ἔνθα δ' ἀοιδῇσιν μειλίσσετο, μέλπε δὲ Κῆρας
θυμοβόρους, Ἀίδαο θοὰς κύνας, αἳ περὶ πᾶσαν
ἠέρα δινεύουσαι ἐπὶ ζωοῖσιν ἄγονται.
τὰς γουναζομένη τρὶς μὲν παρακέκλετ' ἀοιδαῖς,
τρὶς δὲ λιταῖς· θεμένη δὲ κακὸν νόον ἐχθοδοποῖσιν
1670 ὄμμασι χαλκείοιο Τάλω ἐμέγηρεν ὀπωπάς·
λευγαλέον δ' ἐπὶ οἷ πρῖεν χόλον, ἐκ δ' ἀίδηλα
δείκηλα προΐαλλεν ἐπιζάφελον κοτέουσα.
    Ζεῦ πάτερ, ἦ μέγα δή μοι ἐνὶ φρεσὶ θάμβος
        ἄηται,
εἰ δὴ μὴ νούσοισι τυπῇσί τε μοῦνον ὄλεθρος
1675 ἀντιάει, καὶ δή τις ἀπόπροθεν ἄμμε χαλέπτει,
ὡς ὅ γε χάλκειός περ ἐὼν ὑπόειξε δαμῆναι
Μηδείης βρίμῃ πολυφαρμάκου. ἂν δὲ βαρείας
ὀχλίζων λάιγγας ἐρυκέμεν ὅρμον ἱκέσθαι,
πετραίῳ στόνυχι χρίμψε σφυρόν· ἐκ δέ οἱ ἰχὼρ
1680 τηκομένῳ ἴκελος μολίβῳ ῥέεν. οὐδ' ἔτι δηρὸν
εἱστήκει προβλῆτος ἐπεμβεβαὼς σκοπέλοιο·
ἀλλ' ὡς τίς τ' ἐν ὄρεσσι πελωρίη ὑψόθι πεύκη,
τήν τε θοοῖς πελέκεσσιν ἔθ' ἡμιπλῆγα λιπόντες
ὑλοτόμοι δρυμοῖο κατήλυθον, ἡ δ' ὑπὸ νυκτὶ
1685 ῥιπῇσιν μὲν πρῶτα τινάσσεται, ὕστερον αὖτε
πρυμνόθεν ἐξεαγεῖσα κατήριπεν· ὣς ὅ γε ποσσὶν
ἀκαμάτοις τείως μὲν ἐπισταδὸν ᾐωρεῖτο,
ὕστερον αὖτ' ἀμενηνὸς ἀπείρονι κάππεσε δούπῳ.
    κεῖνο μὲν οὖν Κρήτῃ ἐνὶ δὴ κνέφας ηὐλίζοντο
1690 ἥρωες· μετὰ δ' οἵ γε νέον φαέθουσαν ἐς ἠῶ

as she went between the benches. Once there, she propitiated with songs and chanted the praises of the heart-devouring Fates of Death, the swift hounds of Hades, who roam throughout the air and hunt down the living. In her supplications she summoned them three times with songs, three times with prayers. And adopting a mind bent on harm, she bewitched bronze Talos' eyes with her hate-filled stares. She gnashed her teeth in bitter anger against him and sent forth destructive phantoms with vehement hatred.

Truly, Father Zeus, great astonishment confounds my mind, if in fact death comes not only through disease and wounds, but even from afar someone can harm us, just as he, though made of bronze, yielded in defeat to the power of Medea the sorceress. So, as he was hefting heavy stones to prevent them from reaching anchorage, he grazed his ankle on a sharp-pointed rock, and his ichor[188] flowed out like molten lead. Not for long did he stand astride the jutting cliff, but like some enormous pine tree high in the mountains, which woodsmen had left half hewn with their sharp axes when they came back down from the forest; and during the night it is at first shaken by breezes, but then at last breaks off at the base and crashes down—so did Talos totter for awhile from side to side on his tireless feet, but then at last, in his weakened state, fell with a tremendous crash.

So in fact the heroes spent that night in Crete. Then, just as dawn was shining, they built a shrine to Minoan

---

[188] It serves as blood for the immortal gods.

1665 μέλπε m: θέλγε w   •

ἱρὸν Ἀθηναίης Μινωίδος ἱδρύσαντο,
ὕδωρ τ᾿ εἰσαφύσαντο, καὶ εἰσέβαν, ὥς κεν ἐρετμοῖς
παμπρώτιστα βάλοιεν ὑπὲρ Σαλμωνίδος ἄκρης.
αὐτίκα δὲ Κρηταῖον ὑπὲρ μέγα λαῖτμα θέοντας
1695 νὺξ ἐφόβει, τήν πέρ τε κατουλάδα κικλήσκουσιν·
νύκτ᾿ ὀλοὴν οὐκ ἄστρα διέσχανεν, οὐκ ἀμαρυγαὶ
μήνης· οὐρανόθεν δὲ μέλαν χάος ἠέ τις ἄλλη
ὠρώρει σκοτίη μυχάτων ἀνιοῦσα βερέθρων.
αὐτοὶ δ᾿ εἴτ᾿ Ἀίδῃ εἴθ᾿ ὕδασιν ἐμφορέοντο
1700 ἠείδειν οὐδ᾿ ὅσσον· ἐπέτρεψαν δὲ θαλάσσῃ
νόστον ἀμηχανέοντες, ὅπῃ φέροι. αὐτὰρ Ἰήσων
χεῖρας ἀνασχόμενος μεγάλῃ ὀπὶ Φοῖβον ἀύτει,
ῥύσασθαι καλέων· κατὰ δ᾿ ἔρρεεν ἀσχαλόωντι
δάκρυα· πολλὰ δὲ Πυθοῖ ὑπέσχετο, πολλὰ δ᾿
            Ἀμύκλαις,
1705 πολλὰ δ᾿ ἐς Ὀρτυγίην ἀπερείσια δῶρα κομίσσειν.
Λητοΐδη, τύνη δὲ κατ᾿ οὐρανοῦ ἵκεο πέτρας
ῥίμφα Μελαντείους ἀριήκοος, αἵ τ᾿ ἐνὶ πόντῳ
ἧνται· δοιάων δὲ μιῆς ἐφύπερθεν ὀρούσας,
δεξιτερῇ χρύσειον ἀνέσχεθες ὑψόθι τόξον·
1710 μαρμαρέην δ᾿ ἀπέλαμψε βιὸς περὶ πάντοθεν αἴγλην.
τοῖσι δέ τις Σποράδων βαιὴ ἀνὰ τόφρ᾿ ἐφαάνθη
νῆσος ἰδεῖν, ὀλίγης Ἱππουρίδος ἀγχόθι νήσου·
ἔνθ᾿ εὐνὰς ἐβάλοντο καὶ ἔσχεθον. αὐτίκα δ᾿ ἠὼς
φέγγεν ἀνερχομένη· τοὶ δ᾿ ἀγλαὸν Ἀπόλλωνι
1715 ἄλσει ἐνὶ σκιερῷ τέμενος σκιόεντά τε βωμὸν
ποίεον, Αἰγλήτην μὲν εὐσκόπου εἵνεκεν αἴγλης

Athena, drew water, and went on board, in order to row
past the Salmonian headland[189] as soon as possible. But
suddenly, as they were hastening over the wide Cretan sea,
the kind of night men call "the shroud" held them in terror.
No stars penetrated that deadly night, nor beams of the
moon, but from the sky came black chaos or some other
kind of darkness arising from the deepest depths. They
themselves had not the slightest idea whether they were
drifting in Hades or on the waters. So, they entrusted their
voyage to the sea, helplessly unaware as to where it was
taking them. And Jason raised his hands and in a loud voice
cried out to Phoebus, calling on him to save them, and
the tears poured down in his distress. Many gifts he prom-
ised to bring to Pytho, many to Amyclae, and many to
Ortygia—countless gifts.[190] And you, Son of Leto, a ready
listener, came swiftly down from the sky to the Melanteian
rocks, which lie in the sea. And alighting on one of the twin
peaks, you raised aloft in your right hand your golden bow,
and that bow sent out a dazzling gleam in all directions.
Then appeared a tiny island for them to see, one of the
Sporades near the small island of Hippuris, and there they
cast anchors and stayed. Soon dawn rose and was shining
its light. They built a glorious precinct for Apollo and a
shaded altar in a shady grove, invoking Phoebus as Aegle-
tes[191] because of his far-seen gleam, and they called the

---

[189] Cape Sidero at the eastern tip of Crete.   [190] These
were the main Greek sanctuaries of Apollo at Delphi (Pytho),
Sparta (Amyclae), and Delos (Ortygia).   [191] "Gleamer."

1711 ἀνὰ Lᵃᶜ: ἀπὸ L² in ras. AwE
1712 ἀγχόθι w: ἀντία m

Φοῖβον κεκλόμενοι· Ἀνάφην δέ τε λισσάδα νῆσον
ἴσκον, ὃ δὴ Φοῖβός μιν ἀτυζομένοις ἀνέφηνεν.
ῥέζον δ᾽ οἷά κεν ἄνδρες ἐρημαίῃ ἐνὶ ῥέζειν
1720 ἀκτῇ ἐφοπλίσσειαν· ὃ δή σφεας ὁππότε δαλοῖς
ὕδωρ αἰθομένοισιν ἐπιλλείβοντας ἴδοντο
Μηδείης δμωαὶ Φαιηκίδες, οὐκέτ᾽ ἔπειτα
ἴσχειν ἐν στήθεσσι γέλω σθένος, οἷα θαμειὰς
αἰὲν ἐν Ἀλκινόοιο βοοκτασίας ὁρόωσαι.
1725 τὰς δ᾽ αἰσχροῖς ἥρωες ἐπεστοβέεσκον ἔπεσσιν
χλεύῃ γηθόσυνοι· γλυκερὴ δ᾽ ἀνεδαίετο τοῖσιν
κερτομίη καὶ νεῖκος ἐπεσβόλον. ἐκ δέ νυ κείνης
μολπῆς ἡρώων νήσῳ ἔνι τοῖα γυναῖκες
ἀνδράσι δηριόωνται, ὅτ᾽ Ἀπόλλωνα θυηλαῖς
1730 Αἰγλήτην Ἀνάφης τιμήορον ἱλάσκωνται.
    ἀλλ᾽ ὅτε δὴ κἀκεῖθεν ὑπεύδια πείσματ᾽ ἔλυσαν,
μνήσατ᾽ ἔπειτ᾽ Εὔφημος ὀνείρατος ἐννυχίοιο
ἁζόμενος Μαίης υἷα κλυτόν. εἴσατο γάρ οἱ
δαιμονίη βῶλαξ ἐπιμάστιος ᾧ ἐν ἀγοστῷ
1735 ἄρδεσθαι λευκῇσιν ὑπὸ λιβάδεσσι γάλακτος,
ἐκ δὲ γυνὴ βώλοιο πέλειν ὀλίγης περ ἐούσης
παρθενικῇ ἰκέλη· μίχθη δέ οἱ ἐν φιλότητι
ἄσχετον ἱμερθείς· ὀλοφύρετο δ᾽ ἠύτε κούρην
ζευξάμενος, τὴν αὐτὸς ἑῷ ἀτίταλλε γάλακτι·
1740 ἡ δέ ἑ μειλιχίοισι παρηγορέεσκεν ἔπεσσιν·
    "Τρίτωνος γένος εἰμί, τεῶν τροφός, ὦ φίλε,
        παίδων,

    1719 οἷά κεν w: ὅσσα περ m

466

barren[192] island Anaphe,[193] because Phoebus made it appear to them when they were distraught with terror. They sacrificed such things as men on a deserted shore could provide to sacrifice, so that when Medea's Phaeacian handmaids saw them pouring libations of water on the blazing brands, they could no longer contain the laughter in their breasts, for they had always seen lavish sacrifices of oxen in Alcinous' palace. The heroes enjoyed their jesting and scoffed at them with obscene language, and pleasant insults and scurrilous taunts were kindled among them. And so, from that jesting of the heroes, the women on the island hurl similar taunts at the men, whenever in their sacrifices they propitiate Apollo Aegletes, guardian of Anaphe.

But when, from that place too, they had loosed their cables in good weather, then Euphemus remembered that night's dream out of respect for Maia's famous son.[194] For he had dreamed that the divine clod,[195] which he held in his palm against his breast, was being moistened with white drops of milk, and that from the clod, small as it was, came a woman resembling a virgin. Overcome with insatiable desire, he made love to her, but then lamented as if he had had intercourse with his daughter, whom he had been nourishing with his own milk. But she comforted him with gentle words:

"I am Triton's child, my friend, the nurse of your chil-

[192] Or *rugged*.
[193] "Apparition."
[194] Hermes, god of dreams.
[195] Which Triton had given him (cf. 4.1551–1555).

οὐ κούρη· Τρίτων γὰρ ἐμοὶ Λιβύη τε τοκῆες.
ἀλλά με Νηρῆος παρακάτθεο παρθενικῆσιν
ἂμ πέλαγος ναίειν Ἀνάφης σχεδόν· εἶμι δ᾽ ἐς αὐγὰς
1745 ἠελίου μετόπισθε, τεοῖς νεπόδεσσιν ἑτοίμη.”
    τῶν ἄρ᾽ ἐπὶ μνῆστιν κραδίη βάλεν, ἔκ τ᾽
        ὀνόμηνεν
Αἰσονίδη· ὁ δ᾽ ἔπειτα θεοπροπίας Ἑκάτοιο
θυμῷ πεμπάζων ἀνενείκατο, φώνησέν τε·
    “ὦ πέπον, ἦ μέγα δή σε καὶ ἀγλαὸν ἔμμορε
        κῦδος.
1750 βώλακα γὰρ τεύξουσι θεοὶ πόντονδε βαλόντι
νῆσον, ἵν᾽ ὁπλότεροι παίδων σέθεν ἐννάσσονται
παῖδες, ἐπεὶ Τρίτων ξεινήιον ἐγγυάλιξεν
τήνδε τοι ἠπείροιο Λιβυστίδος· οὔ νύ τις ἄλλος
ἀθανάτων ἢ κεῖνος, ὅ μιν πόρεν ἀντιβολήσας.”
1755   ὣς ἔφατ᾽· οὐδ᾽ ἁλίωσεν ὑπόκρισιν Αἰσονίδαο
Εὔφημος, βῶλον δὲ θεοπροπίησιν ἰανθεὶς
ἧκεν ὑποβρυχίην. τῆς δ᾽ ἔκτοθι νῆσος ἀέρθη
Καλλίστη, παίδων ἱερὴ τροφὸς Εὐφήμοιο·
οἳ πρὶν μέν ποτε δὴ Σιντηίδα Λῆμνον ἔναιον,
1760 Λήμνου τ᾽ ἐξελαθέντες ὑπ᾽ ἀνδράσι Τυρσηνοῖσιν
Σπάρτην εἰσαφίκανον ἐφέστιοι· ἐκ δὲ λιπόντας
Σπάρτην Αὐτεσίωνος ἐὺς πάις ἤγαγε Θήρας
Καλλίστην ἐπὶ νῆσον, ἀμείψατο δ᾽ οὔνομα Θήρης
ἐξ ἕθεν. ἀλλὰ τὰ μὲν μετόπιν γένετ᾽ Εὐφήμοιο.

    1746 τῶν Merkel: τῷ δ᾽ Ω | κραδίη m: κραδίη wD
    1749 πέπον w: πόποι m   1763 Θήρης m (om. w): Θήρα
Fränkel e Σ   1764 ἐξ ἕθεν Ω: ἐκ σέθεν Wendel e Σ

dren, not your daughter, for Triton and Libya are my parents. Entrust me to the daughters of Nereus to live in the sea near Anaphe, and I shall later emerge into the sunlight, on hand for your descendants."

He had stored the memory of these things in his heart, and recounted them to Jason. Then, after poring over the prophecies of the Far-Shooter[196] in his spirit, Jason lifted his voice and said:

"Truly, my dear friend, great and glorious fame has been allotted to you, for after you cast the clod into the sea, the gods will turn it into an island, where later generations of your children will dwell,[197] because Triton gave you this piece of the Libyan mainland as a guest-gift. It was he and no other of the immortals, who met us and gave it to us."

Thus he spoke, and Euphemus did not render invalid Jason's response, but in joy at his prophecies threw the clod into the depths. From it arose the island of Calliste,[198] divine nurse of Euphemus' descendants, who in former times lived on Sintian Lemnos,[199] but, driven from Lemnos by Tyrrhenians, went as residents to Sparta. When they left Sparta, Theras, the noble son of Autesion, led them to the island of Calliste, and he changed the name to Thera after his own name.[200] But these things happened long after Euphemus.[201]

---

[196] Apollo.   [197] Seventeen generations later, according to Pindar, *Pythian* 4.10.   [198] "Most Beautiful" island, later called Thera.   [199] The Sintes were early inhabitants of Lemnos (cf. 1.608).   [200] Or, reading Θήρα . . . ἐκ σέθεν, it *took its name from yours, Theras*.   [201] A. traces the migrations and colonizations from Lemnos to Sparta to Thera. Eventually the Thereans will colonize Cyrene in North Africa. Cf. Pindar, *Pythian* 4.1–63 and Callimachus, *Hymn* 2.71–79.

1765   κεῖθεν δ᾽ ἀπτερέως διὰ μυρίον οἶδμα λιπόντες
Αἰγίνης ἀκτῆσιν ἐπέσχεθον. αἶψα δὲ τοί γε
ὑδρείης πέρι δῆριν ἀμεμφέα δηρίσαντο,
ὅς κεν ἀφυσσάμενος φθαίη μετὰ νῆάδ᾽ ἱκέσθαι·
ἄμφω γὰρ χρειώ τε καὶ ἄσπετος οὖρος ἔπειγεν.
1770   ἔνθ᾽ ἔτι νῦν πλήθοντας ἐπωμαδὸν ἀμφιφορῆας
ἀνθέμενοι κούφοισιν ἄφαρ κατ᾽ ἀγῶνα πόδεσσιν
κοῦροι Μυρμιδόνων νίκης πέρι δηριόωνται.

    ἵλατ᾽ ἀριστήων μακάρων γένος· αἵδε δ᾽ ἀοιδαὶ
εἰς ἔτος ἐξ ἔτεος γλυκερώτεραι εἶεν ἀείδειν
1775   ἀνθρώποις. ἤδη γὰρ ἐπὶ κλυτὰ πείραθ᾽ ἱκάνω
ὑμετέρων καμάτων, ἐπεὶ οὔ νύ τις ὕμμιν ἄεθλος
αὖτις ἀπ᾽ Αἰγίνηθεν ἀνερχομένοισιν ἐτύχθη,
οὔτ᾽ ἀνέμων ἐριῶλαι ἐνέσταθεν, ἀλλὰ ἕκηλοι
γαῖαν Κεκροπίην παρά τ᾽ Αὐλίδα μετρήσαντες
1780   Εὐβοίης ἔντοσθεν Ὀπούντιά τ᾽ ἄστεα Λοκρῶν,
ἀσπασίως ἀκτὰς Παγασηίδας εἰσαπέβητε.

1773 ἀριστήων Ω: ἀριστῆες Fränkel, Vian

From there they swiftly left behind a great expanse of sea and stopped on the shores of Aegina. At once they contended in a friendly competition over fetching water, to see who could draw it and return first to the ship, since both need and a steady breeze hurried them on. There to this day, the sons of the Myrmidons[202] put full amphoras on their shoulders and with their very nimble feet contend for victory in a race.

Be gracious, you race of blessed heroes,[203] and may these songs year after year be sweeter for men to sing.[204] For now I have come to the glorious conclusion of your toils, since no further trial befell you as you returned home from Aegina, nor did any storm winds block your way, but after calmly passing by the Cecropian land[205] and Aulis within Euboea[206] and the Opuntian towns of the Locrians,[207] you gladly set foot on the shores of Pagasae.

---

[202] I.e. Aeginetans, who traced their ancestry from the Myrmidons, Achaeans originally from Thessaly.

[203] Or, reading ἀριστῆες, Be gracious, heroes, offspring of the blessed gods.

[204] Or to sing to men.

[205] Attica.

[206] Aulis actually lies in Boeotia across the Euripus strait from Euboea.

[207] Locri, north of Boeotia, was called Opuntian after Opus, a legendary king (cf. Pindar, Olympian 9.57–66).

FRAGMENTS

The exiguous remains of Apollonius' other poems, if genuine, attest to a number of elements also found in the *Argonautica*: city-founding, the aetiology of animals, places, and customs, and the pathos of love and untimely death.

Fragments 1–2 cite three lines from Apollonius' *Canobus*, a poem of uncertain length in choliambics that told of the death by snakebite of Canobus, Menelaus' helmsman, for whom the Egyptian port of Canopus was named. Fragment 3 contains no direct quotation, but alludes to Apollonius' treatment of the death of Canobus in Egypt.

Fragment 4 from a scholium to Nicander's *Theriaca* alludes to Apollonius' poem on the founding of Alexandria, which contained an aetiology of poisonous snakes from drops of the Gorgon's blood.

Fragment 5, cited without authorship in Cramer, *Anecdota Graeca*, is attributed to Apollonius because Tzetzes quotes the fourth verse and says it comes from Apollonius. There has been, however, disagreement about whether to assign it to the founding of Caunus or of Cnidus, and the logical progression of the first three lines is unclear. That

472

Apollonius treated the stories of Lyrcus and Byblis in his *Founding of Caunus* is claimed in the titles to Parthenius, *Love Stories* 1 and 11.

Fragment 6 states that Apollonius' *Founding of Cnidus* included an aetiology of the name of a Thracian place called Psykterios.

Fragments 7–9 from Athenaeus concern the love of Apollo for Ocyroe of Samos and the metamorphosis of Pompilus, a fisherman who tries to help Ocyroe escape abduction by the god, into a fish of the same name.

Fragment 10 from Stephanus of Byzantium cites an incomplete sentence from Apollonius' *Founding of Rhodes* to illustrate his use of the feminine form of Dotium, and Fragment 11 from a scholium to Pindar's *Olympian* 7 alludes to Apollonius' aetiology of the Rhodian practice of fireless sacrifices that differs from Pindar's account.

Fragment 12, by far the most extensive and interesting, is cited by Parthenius without author. It has been attributed to Apollonius' *Founding of Lesbos* on the basis of content (Peisidice is from Methymna on Lesbos), vocabulary, and style, but it could also be the work of an imitator.

Fragment 13, an epigram attributed in the *Palatine Anthology* to Apollonius the Grammarian, is probably not by Apollonius Rhodius.

The numbering and text of the fragments are based on J. U. Powell, *Collectanea Alexandrina* (Oxford 1925) 4–8.

1 Κάνωβος. Steph. Byz. s.v. Κόρινθος

. . . καὶ σύνθετον Κορινθιουργής ὡς Ἀττικουργής. Ἀπολ-
λώνιος ὁ Ῥόδιος Κανώβῳ·[1]

Κορινθιουργές ἐστι κιόνων σχῆμα

  [1] Κανώβῳ Meineke: Κανώπῳ [δευτέρῳ] codd.

2 Κάνωβος. Steph. Byz. s.v. χώρα

. . . Ἀπολλώνιος ἐν τῷ Κανώβῳ·

τέρψει δὲ νηῶν ὁ γλυκύς σε χωρίτης
πλόος κομίζων δῶρα πλουσίου Νείλου.

  1 τέρψει δὲ νηῶν Pinedo: τρέψει δὲ νηὸν AV: στρέψει δὲ
νηὸν R | χωρίτης Meineke: χωρίτης codd.

3 Κάνωβος. Schol. ad Nicand. *Ther.* 305

καὶ Ἀπολλώνιος δέ φησι τῶν πληγέντων ὑπὸ αἱμορ-
ροΐδος ῥήγνυσθαι καὶ τὰς οὐλάς.[1] Schol. ad Nicand. *Ther.*
312: ἡ αἱμορροῒς ἔδακε Κάνωβον, τὸν κυβερνήτην τοῦ
Μενελάου, καθεύδοντα ἐν τῷ πρὸς Αἴγυπτον αἰγιαλῷ, καὶ
ἐνῆκεν αὐτῷ ἰόν.

  [1] v.l. ὠτειλάς

1 *Canobus*. Stephanus of Byzantium, entry for
"Corinth"

and the compound "of Corinthian-workmanship" is like "of
Attic-workmanship." Apollonius Rhodius says in his *Canobus*:

of Corinthian workmanship is the form of the columns

2 *Canobus*. Stephanus of Byzantium, entry for
"country"

Apollonius says in his *Canobus*:

And the sweet voyage of ships will delight you, the one
bringing your countrymen the gifts of the rich Nile.

3 *Canobus*. Scholium to Nicander, *Theriaca* 305

And Apollonius says that when people are bitten by the
"blood-letter" even their scars burst.

Scholium to Nicander, *Theriaca* 312:

the "blood-letter" bit Canobus, the helmsman of Menelaus,
while he was sleeping on the beach that faces Egypt, and in-
jected its poison into him.

4 Ἀλεξανδρείας Κτίσις. Schol. ad Nicand. *Ther.* 11

περὶ γοῦν τῆς τῶν δακνόντων θηρίων γενέσεως, ὅτι ἐστὶν
ἐκ τῶν Τιτάνων τοῦ αἵματος, παρὰ μὲν τῷ Ἡσιόδῳ οὐκ
ἔστιν εὑρεῖν. Ἀκουσίλαος δέ φησιν ἐκ τοῦ αἵματος τοῦ
Τυφῶνος πάντα τὰ δάκνοντα γενέσθαι. Ἀπολλώνιος δὲ ὁ
Ῥόδιος ἐν τῇ τῆς Ἀλεξανδρείας κτίσει ἀπὸ τῶν σταγό-
νων τοῦ τῆς Γοργόνος αἵματος.

5 Καύνου Κτίσις. Parth. Ἐρ. Παθ. 1

περὶ Λύρκου· ἡ ἱστορία παρὰ Νικαινέτῳ ἐν τῷ Λύρκῳ καὶ
Ἀπολλωνίῳ Ῥοδίῳ Καύνῳ. Parth. Ἐρ. Παθ. 11: περὶ
Βυβλίδος· ἱστορεῖ Ἀριστόκριτος περὶ Μιλήτου καὶ
Ἀπολλώνιος ὁ Ῥόδιος Καύνου κτίσει. Cramer, *Anecd. Par.*
4.16:

  οὐδ᾽ ἵπποι ὀρθρινὰ κατὰ κλισίας χρεμέθεσκον,
  ἀλλὰ βόες πλείῃσι παρηυνάζοντο κάπῃσιν,
  νηυσὶ δὲ πρηκτὰ κέλευθα Χελιδονίης ἀπὸ πέτρης
  Πληγάδας ἀξείνους καὶ ὅπου Φινήϊα δόρπα
5 Ἅρπυιαι ἄτλητον ἐπὶ ψώαν πνείεσκον.

    1 ὀρθρινὰ Meineke: ὀρθριναὶ codd.
    2 ἀλλὰ codd.: οὐδὲ Meineke

6 Κνίδου Κτίσις. Steph. Byz. s.v. Ψυκτήριος

τόπος ἐν Θρᾴκῃ, ἀπὸ Ἡρακλέους ἀναψύξαντος τὸν ἱδρῶ-
τα ἐν τῷ καταπαλαῖσαι τὸν Ἀδραμύλην, καθώς φησιν
Ἀπολλώνιος ἐν Κνίδου κτίσει.

4 *The Founding of Alexandria.* Scholium to Nicander,
  Theriaca 11

Concerning the origin of biting animals, that they come from
the blood of the Titans, this is not to be found in Hesiod. But
Acusilaos says that all biting creatures came from the blood of
Typhon. And Apollonius Rhodius says in his *Founding of Alexandria* that they came from the drops of the Gorgon's blood.

5 *The Founding of Caunus.* Parthenius, *Love Stories* 1
  (on Lyrcus)

The story is found in Nicaenetus in his *Lyrcus* and in Apollonius Rhodius in his *Caunus*.

Parthenius, *Love Stories* 11 (on Byblis):

Aristocritus tells this story in his *On Miletus* and Apollonius
Rhodius in his *Founding of Caunus*.

Cramer, *Anecdota Parisina* 4.16 (cited without author):

Nor were horses neighing in the early morning by the huts,
but the cattle were lying beside the full mangers, and the
ways had been traversed by ships from the Chelidonian
Rock[1] to the inhospitable Plegades and where the Harpies
used to breathe an intolerable stench on Phineus' meals.

[1] Promontory at the southern tip of Lycia.

6 *The Founding of Cnidus.* Stephanus of Byzantium,
  entry for Psykterios ("Cooling")

a place in Thrace, taking its name from Heracles, who cooled
off his sweat when he threw Adramyles in wrestling, as Apollonius says in his *Founding of Cnidus*.

477

7 Ναυκράτεως Κτίσις. Athen. 7.283de

Ἀπολλώνιος δ᾽ ὁ Ῥόδιος ἢ Ναυκρατίτης ἐν Ναυκράτεως
κτίσει τὸν Πομπίλον φησὶν ἄνθρωπον πρότερον ὄντα
μεταβαλεῖν εἰς ἰχθὺν διά τινα Ἀπόλλωνος ἔρωτα· τὴν
γὰρ Σαμίων πόλιν παραρρεῖν ποταμὸν Ἴμβρασον,

τῷ ῥά ποτ᾽ Ὠκυρόην νύμφην, περικαλλέα κούρην,
Χησιὰς εὐπατέρεια τέκεν φιλότητι μιγεῖσα,
Ὠκυρόην, ᾗ κάλλος ἀπείριτον ὤπασαν Ὧραι.

8 Ναυκράτεως Κτίσις. Athen. 7.283f

ταύτης οὖν ἐρασθέντα Ἀπόλλωνα ἐπιχειρῆσαι ἁρπάσαι.
διαπεραιωθεῖσαν δ᾽ εἰς Μίλητον κατά τινα Ἀρτέμιδος
ἑορτὴν καὶ μέλλουσαν ἁρπάζεσθαι εὐλαβηθεῖσαν Πομ-
πίλον τινὰ θαλασσουργὸν ἄνθρωπον καθικετεῦσαι ὄντα
πατρῷον φίλον, ὅπως αὐτὴν εἰς τὴν πατρίδα διασώσῃ,
λέγουσαν τάδε·

πατρὸς ἐμεῖο φίλου συμφράδμονα θυμὸν ἀέξων,
Πομπίλε, δυσκελάδου δεδαὼς θοὰ βένθεα πόντου,
σῷζέ με.

9 Ναυκράτεως Κτίσις. Athen. 7.284a

καὶ τὸν εἰς τὴν ἀκτὴν διαγαγόντα αὐτὴν διαπεραιοῦν.
ἐπιφανέντα δὲ τὸν Ἀπόλλωνα τήν τε κόρην ἁρπάσαι καὶ

7 The *Founding of Naucratis*. Athenaeus, *Deipno-sophistae* 7.283de

Apollonius of Rhodes or of Naucratis, in his *Founding of Naucratis*, says that Pompilus, formerly a man, was changed into a fish because of an erotic passion[1] of Apollo. For along-side the city of the Samians flowed the river Imbrasus,

to whom Chesias, daughter of a noble father, once bore the nymph Ocyroe, a beautiful girl, after making love with him—Ocyroe, upon whom the Horae bestowed boundless beauty.

[1] For Ocyroe of Samos.

8 The *Founding of Naucratis*. Athenaeus, *Deipno-sophistae* 7.283f

Then Apollo, having fallen in love with her,[1] tried to abduct her. But she crossed over to Miletus during a festival of Arte-mis, and when about to be abducted took the precaution of en-treating Pompilus ("Escort"), a fisherman who was a friend of her father's, to convey her safely to her native land, by saying this:

cheering the like-minded heart of my father, your friend, Pompilus—you who know the swift depths of the horrid-sounding sea—save me.

[1] Ocyroe.

9 The *Founding of Naucratis*. Athenaeus, *Deipno-sophistae* 7.284a

And he led her to the shore and ferried her across. But Apollo appeared and abducted the girl and turned the ship to stone,

479

τὴν ναῦν ἀπολιθώσαντα, τὸν Πομπίλον εἰς τὸν ὁμώνυμον
ἰχθὺν μεταμορφῶσαι, ποιῆσαί τε τὸν

πομπίλον ὠκυάλων νηῶν παιήονα δούρων

1 παιήονα δούρων G. Murray: αιηονονα δουρον A

10 Ῥόδου Κτίσις. Steph. Byz. s.v. Δώτιον

πόλις Θεσσαλίας . . . τὸ θηλυκὸν Δωτηίς . . . καὶ Δωτιάς
. . . Ἀπολλώνιος ὁ Ῥόδιος ἐν Ῥόδου κτίσει·

                                        ὅσσα τε γαίης
†ἔργα τε Δωτιάδος πρότεροι κάμον Αἱμονιῆες

11 Ῥόδου Κτίσις. Schol. Pind. Ol. 7.86b

καὶ Ἀπολλώνιος ὁ ποιητής φησιν ἄπυρα τοὺς Ῥοδίους
ἱερὰ θύειν διὰ τὴν πρὸς Ἥφαιστον ἕνεκα τῶν γάμων
ἔχθραν, ὅτι ἐπεδίωξε τὴν Ἀθηνᾶν βουλόμενος συμμι-
γῆναι.

12 Λέσβου Κτίσις. Parth. Ἐρ. Παθ. 21.2

μέμνηται τοῦ πάθους τοῦδε καὶ ὁ τὴν Λέσβου κτίσιν
ποιήσας ἐν τοῖσδε·

ἔνθα δὲ Πηλεΐδης κατὰ μὲν κτάνε Λάμπετον ἥρω,
κὰδ δ' Ἱκετάονα πέφνεν ἰθαιγενέος Λεπετύμνου

1 ἥρω P: Ἴρου Gale e Steph. Byz. s.v. Λαμπέτειον . . . ἀπὸ
Λαμπέτου τοῦ Ἴρου
2 κὰδ Gale: ἐκ P

and changed Pompilus into a fish of the same name,[1] and made him

the pompilus, savior of the planks of sea-swift ships

[1] For various accounts of the pompilus, see Athenaeus, *Deipnosophistae* 7.282e–284d.

10 *The Founding of Rhodes*. Stephanus of Byzantium, entry for "Dotion"

a Thessalian city . . . its feminine form is Doteïs . . . and Dotias, which Apollonius Rhodius uses in his *Founding of Rhodes:*

. . . and all the things of the land and the works(?) of Dotias the former Haemonians constructed

11 *The Founding of Rhodes*. Scholium to Pindar, *Olympian* 7.48

And Apollonius the poet says that the Rhodians make fireless sacrifices because of their hatred for Hephaestus on account of his amorous designs, since he pursued Athena, wishing to have intercourse with her.

12 *The Founding of Lesbos*. Parthenius, *Love Stories* 21.2 (on Peisidice)

the poet of *The Founding of Lesbos* also relates this sad affair in these words:

Then Peleus' son[1] killed the hero Lampetus, and he slew Hicetaon, son of indigenous Lepetymnus[2] and of

[1] Achilles.
[2] Eponym of a mountain near Methymna, the second-largest city of Lesbos.

481

νίέα Μηθύμνης τε, καὶ ἀλκηέστατον ἄλλων
αὐτοκασίγνητον Ἑλικάονος ἔνδοθι πάτρης
5 †τηλίκον Ὑψίπυλον· θαλερὴ δέ μιν ἄασε Κύπρις·
ἡ γὰρ ἐπ᾽ Αἰακίδῃ κούρης φρένας ἐπτοίησεν
Πεισιδίκης, ὅτε τόν γε μετὰ προμάχοισιν Ἀχαιῶν
χάρμῃ ἀγαλλόμενον θηέσκετο, πολλὰ δ᾽ ἐς ὑγρὴν
ἠέρα χεῖρας ἔτεινεν ἐελδομένη φιλότητος.

εἶτα μικρὸν ὑποβάς

10 δέκτο μὲν αὐτίκα λαὸν Ἀχαϊκὸν ἔνδοθι πάτρης
παρθενικὴ κληῖδας ὑποχλίσσασα πυλάων,
ἔτλη δ᾽ οἷσιν ἰδέσθαι ἐν ὀφθαλμοῖσι τοκῆας
χαλκῷ ἐληλαμένους καὶ δούλια δεσμὰ γυναικῶν
ἑλκομένων ἐπὶ νῆας ὑποσχεσίης Ἀχιλῆος,
15 ὄφρα νυὸς γλαυκῆς Θέτιδος πέλοι, ὄφρα οἱ εἶεν
πενθεροὶ Αἰακίδαι, Φθίῃ δ᾽ ἔνι δώματα ναίοι
ἀνδρὸς ἀρίστηος πινυτὴ δάμαρ (οὐδ᾽ ὅ γ᾽ ἔμελλεν
τὰ ῥέξειν), ὀλοῷ δ᾽ ἐπαγάσσατο πατρίδος οὕτω·
ἔνθ᾽ ἥ γ᾽ αἰνότατον γάμον εἴσιδε Πηλείδαο
20 Ἀργείων ὑπὸ χερσὶ δυσάμμορος, οἵ μιν ἔπεφνον
πανσυδίῃ θαμινῇσιν ἀράσσοντες λιθάδεσσιν.

5 lacunam post Ὑψίπυλον statuit Knaack
6–7 κούρης . . . Πεισιδίκης Heyne: κούρης . . . Πεισιδίκῃ P
8 θηέσκετο Gale: θυέσκετο P
10 μὲν Legrande: μὰν P
16 ἔνι (immo ἐνὶ) Meineke: ἐν P

Methymna, and the most valiant of all others, the brother of Helicaon, in his fatherland, young(?) Hypsipylus. And blooming Cypris led her[3] astray, for she confounded the mind of the girl Peisidice with love for the Aeacid,[4] when she watched him among the front ranks of the Achaeans, delighting in battle; and often did she raise her hands into the liquid air, wishing for his love.

then, a bit further on, he continues

And immediately the maiden received the Achaean host into her fatherland by prying up the bars of the gates, and she dared to behold with her own eyes her parents struck by bronze and the chains of slavery on the women being dragged to the ships, on account of Achilles' promises, that she might be gray-eyed Thetis' daughter-in-law, that her in-laws might be the Aeacidae, and that she might dwell in Phthia in the home of the foremost hero as his prudent wife—but he was not going to do those things—and she exulted in the disastrous fate of her fatherland. Then she beheld a most grievous marriage to Peleus' son, poor girl, at the hands of the Argives, who slew her, one and all, by striking her with a shower of stones.

[3] Peisidice.
[4] Achilles.

APOLLONIUS RHODIUS

13 Epigramma. *A.P.* 11.275 (Ἀπολλωνίου Γραμματι-
κοῦ)

Καλλίμαχος τὸ κάθαρμα, τὸ παίγνιον, ὁ ξύλινος νοῦς·
αἴτιος ὁ γράψας Αἴτια Καλλίμαχος.

13 Epigram. *Palatine Anthology* 11.275, attributed to
    Apollonius the Grammarian

Callimachus: that piece of rubbish, that joke, that blockhead.
The cause of this is the author of *The Causes*, Callimachus.

INDEX

Abantes. *See* Amantes

Abantian, epithet of the island of Euboea, 4.1135

Abarnis, a city of the Troad, 1.932

Abas: (1) of Euboea, father of Canethus and grandfather of Canthus, an Argonaut, 1.78; (2) of Argos, reputed father of Idmon, an Argonaut, 1.142; 2.815, 824, 857

Abydos, a city of the Troad, 1.931

Acacallis, a daughter of Minos, 4.1491

Acastus, from Thessaly, son of Pelias, an Argonaut, 1.224, 321, 1041, 1082

Achaean, of a region in the northern Peloponnesus, 1.177; of Greece in general, 1.284; 3.601, 639, 775, 1081; 4.195, 1226, 1329, 1419; fr. 12.10: Achaeans, fr. 12.7. *See also* Hellas; Panachaea

Achelous, a river of Aetolia, 4.293, 893, 895

Acheron: (1) a river of Hades, 1.644; (2) a river in Bithynia, 2.355, 743, 901

Acherusian headland, in Bithynia, 2.354, 728, 750, 806, 844

Achilles, of Phthia, son of Peleus and Thetis, 1.558; 4.868

Acmonian forest, near the Thermodon river, 2.992

Actor: (1) of Opus, father of Menoetius, an Argonaut, 1.69; (2) of Opus, father of Irus and grandfather of Eurytion, an Argonaut, 1.72; (3) father of Sthenelus, 2.911, 916

Admetus, from Thessalian Pherae, an Argonaut, 1.49

Adrasteia: (1) a city and plain of the Propontis, 1.1116; (2) a nymph, the nurse of Zeus, 3.133

Aea, the main city of Colchis, 2.417, 422(2x), 1094, 1141, 1185, 1267; 3.306, 1061; 4.131, 255, 277, 278; Aeaean, 3.1136; 4.234

Aeacus, a son of Zeus, 3.364: sons of Aeacus (Aeacidae), (1) Peleus, 2.869, 886; 3.515; 4.503, 853; (2) Telamon,

1643; sea of Cronus, 4.327, 509, 548

Ctimene, a city of Thessaly, 1.68

Ctimenus, of Thessaly, father of Eurydamas, an Argonaut, 1.67

Curetes: (1) divinities of Crete, 2.1234; (2) inhabitants of Aetolia, 4.1229

Cyanean rocks, clashing rocks at the entrance to the Bosporus, 1.3; 2.318, 770; 4.304, 1003. See also Clashing rocks

Cyclopes, workers in Hephaestus' forge, 1.510, 730

Cyllenus, one of the Idaean Dactyls, 1.1126

Cypris, a name of Aphrodite, 1.615, 803, 850, 860, 1233; 2.424; 3.3, 25, 37, 76, 80, 90, 127, 549, 559, 936, 942; 4.918; fr. 12.5. See also Cytherea

Cyrene, mother of Aristaeus, 2.500

Cytaean, i.e. Colchian, 2.399, 403, 1094, 1267; 3.228; 4.511

Cytherea, a name of Aphrodite, 1.742; 3.108, 553. See also Cypris

Cytissorus, a son of Phrixus, 2.1155

Cytorus, a city of Paphlagonia, 2.942

Cyzicus: (1) king of the Doliones, 1.949, 962, 1056,

1076; (2) a city on a peninsula in the Propontis, 2.765

Dactyls, mythical figures associated with Mount Ida, in Crete, 1.1129

Daira, a name of Hecate, 3.847

Danae, mother of Perseus, 4.1091

Danaans, epic name for Greeks, 4.262

Danaus, father of Amymone 1.133, 137

Dardania, a city of the Troad, 1.931

Dascylus: (1) king of the Mariandynians and father of Lycus, 2.776; (2) son of Lycus, 2.803

Dawn (Eos, Erigenes), 1.519, 1280, 1360; 2.450, 1285; 3.824, 828, 1224; 4.885, 981, 1170

Deileon, of Tricca, a son of Deimachus, 2.956

Deimachus, of Tricca, father of Deileon, Autolycus, and Phlogius, 2.955

Delos, island sacred to Apollo and Artemis, 1.308. See also Ortygia

Delphyne, a snake at Delphi, 2.706

Demeter (Deo), 3.413; 4.896, 986, 988

Deucalion, son of Prometheus,

INDEX

3.1087; sons of Deucalion, rulers in Thessaly, 4.266

Dia, an island in the Aegean, perhaps Naxos, where Ariadne was abandoned, 4.425, 434

Dictaean, of Mount Dicte in Crete, 1.509, 1130; 2.434

Dicte, a port of Crete, 4.1640

Dindymum, a mountain on Cyzicus, 1.985, 1093, 1125, 1147

Dionysus, son of Zeus and Semele, 1.116; 4.424, 540. *See also* Nysean

Dipsacus, son of the Phyllis river, gave Phrixus hospitality, 2.653

Dodonian, of Dodona in Epirus, 1.527; 4.583

Doeas, a plain inhabited by Amazons, 2.373, 988

Dog Star. *See* Sirius

Doliones, inhabitants of Cyzicus, 1.947, 952, 961, 1018, 1022, 1058; Dolionian, 1.1029, 1070; 2.765

Dolops, Thessalian hero with a tomb on the shore of Magnesia, 1.585; Dolopian, Thessalian, 1.68

Dotias, a city of Thessaly, fr. 10.2

Drepane, island of the Phaeacians, later Corcyra, 4.990, 1223

Dryopians, people of north central Greece punished by Heracles, 1.1213, 1218

Dysceladus, one of the Liburnian islands in the Adriatic, 4.565

Earth (Gaea), 1.762; 2.39, 1209, 1273; 3.699, 716

Echetus, a wicked king of Epirus, 4.1093

Echinades, islands at the mouth of the Achelous, 4.1230

Echion, from Thessaly, an Argonaut, 1.52

Eërie, ancient name for Egypt, 4.267, 270

Egypt, 4.268

Eidyia, wife of Aeetes and mother of Medea and Chalciope, 3.243, 269

Eilatus, of Larisa, father of Polyphemus, an Argonaut, 1.41, 1241, 1248, 1347; 4.1470

Eileithyia, the goddess of childbirth, 1.289

Elare, mother of Tityos, 1.762

Eleans, of Elis in the western Peloponnesus, 1.173

Electra, daughter of Atlas, 1.916 (island of Samothrace belongs to her)

Electris, an island in the northern Adriatic, 4.505, 580

Electryon, Mycenaean hero, 1.748

Elysian field, where in the afterlife Achilles will be married to Medea, 4.811

Encheleans, a people of Illyria, 4.518

INDEX

Fair harbor, on western side of Cyzicus, 1.954

Fair mouth, southern entrance to the Ister, 4.306, 313

Far-Shooter (Apollo), 1.958; 2.518; 4.1747

Fates (Moirae), 4.1217

Fates of Death (Ker, Keres), 1.690; 2.258; 4.1485, 1665

Floating islands, 2.285, 297

Fury (Erinys), 2.220; 3.704, 776; 4.476, 1042; plural, 3.712; 4.386, 714

Gaea. *See* Earth

Ganymede, favorite of Zeus, playmate of Eros, 3.115

Garamas, son of Apollo, also called Amphithemis, 4.1494

Genetaean headland, on the Black Sea, 2.378, 1009

Gephyrus, one of the Doliones, 1.1042

Geraestus, a promontory of Euboea, 3.1244

Glaucus, sea divinity, Nereus' interpreter, 1.1310; 2.767

Gorgon, Medusa, 4.1515

Graucenii (v.l. Traucenii), a people near the Ister, 4.321

Gyrton, a city of Thessaly, 1.67

Hades: (1) god of the underworld, 2.353, 4.1666; (2) the underworld, 2.609, 642, 735; 3.61, 704, 810; 4.1510, 1699

Haemonia, a name for Thessaly, 2.504, 690; 3.1090, 1244; 4.1000, 1034; Haemonians, 2.507; 4.1075; fr. 10.2

Hagnias, of Siphae, father of Tiphys, an Argonaut, 1.105, 560, 1296; 2.557, 854

Halys, a river of Paphlagonia, 2.366, 953, 963; 4.245

Harmonia: (1) a nymph, mother of the Amazons, 2.990; (2) wife of Cadmus, 4.517

Harpies, tormentors of Phineus, 2.188, 223, 252, 264, 289, 298, 461; fr. 5.5

Hecate, daughter of Perses, 3.251, 478, 529, 738, 842, 915, 985, 1035, 1211; 4.247, 829. *See also* Brimo; Crataïs; Daira; Perses

Heliades, daughters of Helios, 4.604, 625

Helicaon, of Methymna, brother of Hypsipylus, fr. 12.4

Helice, the great Bear, 2.360; 3.745, 1195

Helius, god of the sun, 1.172; 2.1204; 3.233, 309, 362, 698, 999; 4.221, 229, 591, 698, 727, 965, 971, 1019

Hellas, properly Thessaly, generally of Greece, 1.336, 416, 904, 1292; 2.414, 459, 637, 891, 1141, 1164, 1192; 3.13, 29, 262, 339, 356, 375, 391, 406, 993, 1060, 1105, 1122, 1134; 4.98, 204, 349, 369, 741, 1103. *See also* Achaea; Panachaea; Panhellenes

Helle, daughter of Athamas, sis-

498

INDEX

Iapetus, a Titan, father of Pro-
metheus, 3.866, 1087
Ida, mountain in the Troad,
1.930
Idaean, of Mount Ida in Crete,
1.1128, 1129; 2.1234; 3.134
Idas, from Arene, son of
Aphareus, an Argonaut,
1.151, 462, 470, 485, 1044;
2.830; 3.516, 556, 1170, 1252
Idmon, from Argos, son of Abas
(but really of Apollo), an
Argonaut, 1.139, 436, 449,
475; 2.816, 850
Ilissus, a river of Attica, 1.215
Illyrian river, the Rhizon, 4.516
Imbrasian, an epithet of Hera,
1.187; of the Imbrasus river
on Samos, 2.866
Imbros, an island in the
Aegean, 1.924
Indians, whom Dionysus left to
come to Thebes, 2.906
Iolcus, a city of Thessaly, 1.572,
906; 3.2, 89, 1091, 1109,
1114, 1135; 4.1163
Ionian, 4.289, 308, 632, 982;
Ionians, 1.959, 1076
Iphias, a priestess of Artemis at
Iolcus, 1.312
Iphiclus: (1) maternal uncle of
Jason, an Argonaut, 1.45, 121;
(2) from Aetolia, son of
Thestius, an Argonaut, 1.201
Iphinoe, a woman of Lemnos,
1.702, 703, 709, 788
Iphitus: (1) from Boetian
Oechalia, son of Eurytus, an
Argonaut, 1.86; 2.115; (2)

from Phocis, son of
Naubolus, an Argonaut, 1.207
Iris: (1) a goddess, messenger of
Hera, 2.286, 298, 432; 4.753,
757, 770; (2) a river of the
Black Sea, 2.367, 963
Irus, of Opus, father of Eurytion,
an Argonaut, 1.72, 74
Ismenus, a river of Boeotia,
1.537
Issa, one of the Liburnian is-
lands in the Adriatic, 4.565
Ister, a river of Thrace, the
Danube, 4.284, 302, 309,
325
Isthmian, of the Isthmus of
Corinth, 3.1240
Itonian, epithet of Athena,
1.551
Itymoneus: (1) one of the
Doliones, 1.1046; (2) a
Bebrycian, 2.105
Ixion, tried to rape Hera, chained
in the underworld, 3.62

Jason, son of Aeson and
Alcimede, 1.8, 206, 232, 349,
409, 534, 1330; 2.122, 211,
491, 871, 1158, 1281; 3.2, 28,
66, 143, 357, 439, 474, 566,
922, 1147, 1194, 1246, 1363;
4.63, 79, 107, 165, 170, 352,
393, 454, 489, 1083, 1122,
1152, 1331, 1701; Jason's
helper (Athena), 1.960; Ja-
son's spring, on Cyzicus,
1.1148; Jason's way, on
Cyzicus, 1.988. See also
Aeson, son of Aeson

500